A GREATESEVIL STIRS IN TH

You couldn't understand the sacrifices I have made in order to ensure my continued survival with that ineffectual mind you possess, the man said. *Even now, wasted as I am, I am the most powerful being you have ever been in the presence of. You will spend your life that I spare so generously that you may serve me, and then only as long as you serve me well. I will have back that which was stolen from me. You will give me succor, or I will see you sacrificed toward that end anyway.* His single eye bored into her mesmerizing and horribly vacant at the same time.

The malenti fought, trying to break free of his grip. Her fingers and talons only scraped across the hard flesh, unable to break the skin.

ONE WHO SWIMS WITH SEKOLAH.

THE TAKER. IAKHOVAS.

He plucked an eyelash from his single eye, then said words unlike any Laaqueel had ever heard. The tattoos covering his body glowed with a dim unearthly light. When it stopped he held a black quill in his free hand instead of an eyelash. His hand darted forward and he buried the quill in the tender flesh below her left breast.

Laaqueel felt the quill penetrate her flesh, hot and cold at the same time. All resistance faded from her as her body went lax. None of her limbs were her own anymore.

The man took his hand back from her flesh and gestured at the sliver's entry point. The malenti felt it move again, sliding more deeply into her body, coiling and nestling next to her heart like a poisonous worm. She stared at the man holding her so effortlessly with one hand.

TURN BACK WHILE YOU STILL CAN.

I am Iakhovas, he told her in his deep whispering voice. *You will call me master*

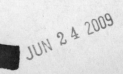

More books by Mel Odom

Wrath of the Blue Lady
(December 2009)

Hunters of the Dark Sea

Quest for the Trilogy
Boneslicer
Seaspray
Deathwhisper

Hellgate London
Exodus
Goetia
Covenant

Left Behind: Apocalypse
Apocalypse Dawn
Crucible
Apocalypse Burning
Apocalypse Unleashed

NCIS
Paid in Blood
Blood Evidence
Bloodlines

FORGOTTEN REALMS

THREAT FROM THE SEA

MELODOM

RISING TIDE

UNDER FALLEN STARS

THE SEA DEVIL'S EYE

Wizards
OF THE COAST®

The Threat From the Sea Omnibus

Published by Wizards of the Coast LLC

Printed in the U.S.A.

Cover art by Raymond Swanland
Interior Art and Map by Sam Wood

Rising Tide originally published January 1999
Under Fallen Stars originally published October 1999
The Sea Devil's Eye originally published May 2000

First Printing:

9 8 7 6 5 4 3 2 1

ISBN: 978-0-7869-5055-3
620-21978740-001-EN

U.S., CANADA,
ASIA, PACIFIC, & LATIN AMERICA
Wizards of the Coast LLC
P.O. Box 707
Renton, WA 98057-0707
+1-800-324-6496

EUROPEAN HEADQUARTERS
Hasbro UK Ltd
Caswell Way
Newport, Gwent NP9 0YH
GREAT BRITAIN
Save this address for your records.

Visit our web site at www.wizards.com

RISING TIDE

Dear Chandler Lewis Odom,

I'm dedicating this book to you, my child, on the eve of your first birthday. In this last year, I've seen you change so much, from the little Burrito Baby we brought home all wrapped in swaddling—to the pint-sized tornado that blazes through our house on two short legs with incredible speed.

And through it all, be it jam-smeared or glinting with irrepressible mischief, I love that smile of yours. Blond hair and blue eyes, face of an angel and the occasional soul of a scamp, you're the perfect combination to be you.

With this book, I offer you my wishes in your life. That it be long and filled with wonderment, that you reach up and touch stars if you've a mind, that you never know loneliness or pain that can't be shared with friends. And that you never in a day of your life have cause to doubt your father's love for you.

UNDER FALLEN STARS

This here tale of seafaring adventure and skullduggery in the seas of Faerûn is dedicated to them what brung it to ya, matie!

To our brave Cap'n, Philip Athans, who guided the story clear of unforgiving shoals and hostile waters filled with crafty and carnivorous beasties.

To First Mate and stellar Navigator, Steven Schend, who mapped out the "under" Realms and them what live there to give us here this fine whopper of a story.

To Admiral Mary Kirchoff, arrr, pretty lady though she is, she done give us this here fine vessel and kept a weathered eye peeled that we kept her afloat.

As for your well-meaning scribe here, I'm the wind what fills the sails.

THE SEA DEVIL'S EYE

This book is dedicated to Ethan Ellenberg

My friend and agent, who has stood with me during the darkest hours, given me his belief in me when my own flagged, and has helped me reach for dreams that I might have once thought out of my grasp.

Thank you.

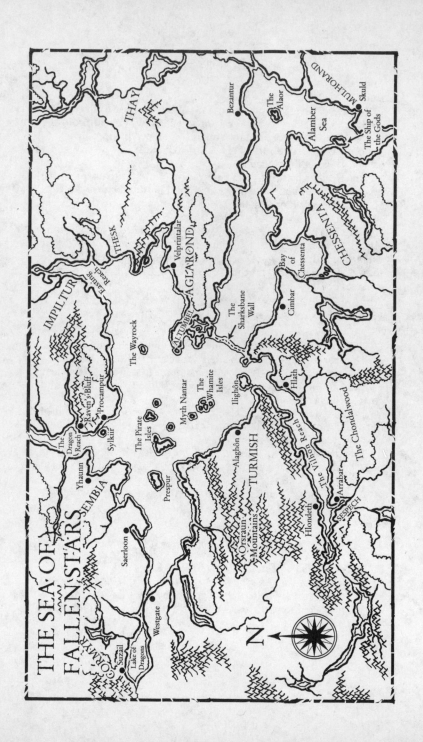

RISING TIDE

PROLOGUE

"You have followed a lie all these months, Priestess Laaqueel, or a figment dreamed up by your deformed malenti mind. We have had enough. We go no further."

The harsh words challenged Laaqueel's self-control as she stood in the mud covering the ocean floor. *Malenti*, uttered like a curse, still cut through her. Her heritage was all sahuagin despite her appearance. As fierce and hard inside as any of her people, her body and face came from the unfathomable tie between the sahuagin race and the sea elves. Only her unique mutation had further deformed her. Instead of the greenish-silver or blue skin of the aquatic elves, her skin took on the pinkish hue of surface dwellers, setting her even more apart and making her a target among her own people.

Little light from the surface world penetrated the murky depths around her and all that it touched held a bluish cast deepening toward indigo. Reds seldom penetrated the gloom at that depth. She stared at the abyssal hills surrounding the party, created from the line of volcanoes that still racked the savage land of Chult a hundred miles and more to the west.

Crustaceans roamed those hills, moving slowly under the great pressure of the depths. Every now and again one disappeared, seized and dragged into burrows dug into the mud by hidden predators. Manta rays and eels glided through the water, staying well away from the sahuagin party.

Somewhere out there, Laaqueel felt certain, lay the prize she'd come so far to claim. She took a deep breath through her mouth, flushing fresh saltwater into her system and the excess through her gills, and turned to the three sahuagin priestesses assigned to her quest.

"I am senior among you, Thuur," Laaqueel announced. "As long as I remain such, no one may speak to me the way you have."

At a few inches under six feet in height, the malenti was the shortest of the group. She wore her long dark hair tied back in a single braid. Besides her breasts, the long hair was the biggest difference between herself and her tribal sisters. She was cursed with the ugly body of a sea elf as well; all rounded and soft looking, wrapped in that pale complexion. If she spent too long under the sea without spending time in the sun, that color paled to the color of a frog's stomach. On this journey she'd chosen to wear only the traditional sahuagin harness to carry her gear. The decision further flaunted the differences between her and her kin, but she had learned over her long life that those differences couldn't be hidden. She had used them to make herself stronger in her faith and her convictions.

"Senior you may be," Thuur replied, "but you are no longer fit to command us."

Laaqueel felt the sahuagin priestess move through the water behind her. Even though she resembled a sea elf, much of her senses remained those of her own people. The lateral lines that ran from her neck to her hips picked up the motion, and she was already gliding into a defensive position.

"Beware what you say," Laaqueel warned harshly as she turned to face the other priestess. She tightened her grip on the metal trident she carried. "You've already said enough that your words might be construed as a blood challenge between us."

Thuur stood tallest among them. Her anterior fins lay back against her head, and her huge mouth was partially open to reveal her ferocious fangs. Her black eyes gleamed with cruel light. She wore the true colors of the sahuagin race, the nearly black green on her back that turned a truer green on her flat stomach. The fins on her shoulders, arms, and legs were black. Her tail was deep yellow, telling any sahuagin male that she was past the age for mating. As a female now, her worth lay in whatever office she laid claim to. For the last ten years or more Thuur hungered for the senior priestess position Laaqueel now held within the tribe.

Saanaa and Viiklee, the other two priestesses, held their own council, but they didn't stand with Laaqueel as they should have.

"I know what I say," Thuur said. Her broad, finned feet slid through the greasy black mud, assuming an attack stance. "I think we should turn back now." She touched the loaded crossbow hanging from her waist.

The lateral lines in Laaqueel's body turned more sensitive, reading every flicker of movement Thuur made. "We won't turn back until we've found what we've come for," she said steadily.

"You're dooming us to wander these forsaken hills forever."

"Has your faith been shaken, Sister?" Laaqueel made her voice harsh and challenging. With Thuur, she knew there was no way to speak of reason. "Sekolah guides this quest. You should trust that."

"I trust Sekolah, not some diseased abomination who has been given status by Baron Huaanton purely by accident of her birth."

"That status was earned," Laaqueel said, "not given as freely as you say. As a malenti, I was trained to be an assassin from the moment I was born. I've lived among the surface dwellers as a spy and helped our village grow. I've slain our enemies, and I've stolen their secrets. If High Priestess Ghaataag had not seen the promise in me to better serve Sekolah, I would still be among the hated elves as Haaunton's dagger."

In truth, the spy training was somewhat wasted. Laaqueel's deception among the surface dwellers had been limited to brief excursions. With her pale skin, she'd been forced to adopt disguises and pass herself off as a surface dwelling elf among the sea elves, or a sea elf among the surface dwellers. She'd been the least effectual of all the malenti in her tribe. Had Priestess Ghaataag not sensed Sekolah's blessed fin moving in her as a hatchling, she'd have been put to death the moment she'd been discovered among the newborn.

Thuur continued moving, turning Laaqueel to put the malenti's back to Saanaa and Viiklee. "You worked a glamour over the high priestess," Thuur accused. "She would never have granted you the position otherwise."

"Sekolah granted my position," Laaqueel argued. "High Priestess Ghaataag only followed his direction."

"You lie!" Thuur declared, sneering and throwing an accusatory clawed hand toward her. "Long have we known Sekolah as an uncaring god. He gave us courage and fierceness in battle, and fertility to make sure that our numbers would always be strong in our wars. How dare you even suggest Sekolah would care enough to intercede on behalf of an ill-bred malenti over his true children. It's sacrilege."

Laaqueel continued moving. The insult cut through to her heart, touching all the insecurities she'd carried for the long years of her life. If not for the calling of the priesthood and her belief in Sekolah, there would have been no place in all the world for her. "We can settle this when we return to our village."

Thuur laughed derisively, the effort causing her to expel bubbles into the surrounding ocean that quickly floated toward the surface. "If we continue on this insane quest, you know we'll never return home." She shook her great head, her black eyes steady on Laaqueel's emerald ones. "No, we'll settle this now."

"There can be only one way between us, then." Laaqueel crouched, her senses flaring. She brought her trident up, the three tines facing the other priestess.

"To the death, malenti," Thuur agreed, issuing the blood challenge. "I say that you are weak and unable to fulfill the duties of your office. Further, I charge that you have no business living among true sahuagin." She kicked free of the mud, taking to the water where her battle skills were most effective. "If you wish, I'll spare your life and you may live it among those elves you say you despise so much."

The offer was a further insult. Laaqueel expected no less. When Ghaataag had assigned Thuur, who was her bitterest rival, the high priestess had explained that the problem would take care of itself during the quest—one way or another.

Laaqueel expanded her trachea and air bladder to increase her buoyancy. Though her legs weren't jointed in two places as well as her ankle like a true sahuagin and she had no tail, her training and experience in underwater combat were extensive. She'd faced more combatants than Thuur and had slain a greater variety of them.

Opposite Thuur in the sea's cold embrace, she held her trident in one hand. "Let Sekolah take the weakest among us that the tribe may grow ever stronger."

Thuur reached for the crossbow dangling from her waist and brought it up. She snapped off her shot as soon as she had it level.

Laaqueel focused on the quarrel as it erupted from the crossbow. She reached into the water with her free hand, spreading her fingers so the webbing between them could be more effective. Her toes spread as well as she kicked her legs. Her body turned, allowing the barbed quarrel to flash past her, missing her by only inches.

Thuur dropped the crossbow as soon as she fired it, seizing her trident and swimming to the attack. Laaqueel met her, choosing not to use any of the spells she had available to her as priestess. There were greater things to fear in the ocean than a jealous rival.

Thuur shoved her trident viciously at Laaqueel's midsection, intending to impale her. The malenti shoved her own trident at her opponent's weapon, interlocking the tines. Using the momentum of Thuur's greater weight and strength in the water, Laaqueel bent her body and flipped over the junior priestess.

The malenti kept hold of her trident with one hand as Thuur managed to disengage the weapons. Before the other priestess could turn, Laaqueel slipped a broad-bladed knife free of her shin sheath. Coming down behind Thuur, she hacked at the priestess, slashing her across the back and cutting deeply into her dorsal fin. Blood filmed the water in a dark and murky haze.

Thuur screamed in pain and rage. She kicked the water, churning hard, and flipped around. Getting the trident in front of her again, she swam at Laaqueel.

The malenti used her trident to batter the other weapon away, and allowed Thuur to come close. When the priestess was within range, Laaqueel buried the broad-bladed knife between her opponent's ribs. She tried to draw it out, but the ribs and tough muscle trapped the blade.

Laaqueel released the weapon and swam away as Thuur turned on her again. Before she could get completely clear, Thuur landed a backhanded blow against the side of her face. Pain wracked the malenti, but she remained in control of herself.

"You'll die for that, malenti!" Thuur screeched. She tore the knife from her body, then flipped gracefully in the water and threw it at Laaqueel.

The knife sped through the water at the malenti's throat. She lifted the bracer that covered her left arm from wrist to elbow and deflected the knife. The impact still sent a shock wave that partially numbed her arm. She forced herself into motion, drawing the trident back as she flipped. When she came forward again Thuur had moved, but Laaqueel's lateral lines had already picked up the priestess's new position. The malenti hurled the trident with all her strength.

The three-tined weapon sped true, impaling Thuur through the heart. She jerked spasmodically as the blow sent death thundering through her system. Her eyes widened in disbelief as she stared at the trident that claimed her life. She wrapped both hands around it but lacked the strength to pull it free. Her mouth opened, gulping down water, and fresh blood streamed from the gills on the sides of her neck.

"Finish it," Thuur croaked as she held onto the trident's haft. "I deserve that much from you. Don't let me suffer."

"Your heresies condemn you," Laaqueel said as she closed on the priestess. "I am merely your judgment." She popped the retractable claws from her fingers, another physical difference that separated her from the hated sea elves. She stared into Thuur's black gaze.

"Your quest is true, honored one," Thuur gasped as she settled gently onto the ocean's mud floor, no longer able to stand or swim. Silt dusted around her in a small cloud. "May Sekolah grant that you find it."

"And may the Great Shark take you with him into the Wild Hunt that you may forever taste the fresh flesh of our enemies," Laaqueel answered.

"Meat is meat," Thuur said. "Let me make you stronger."

With great speed and care, she raked her claws across Thuur's throat. "Meat is meat. You will never leave us."

Blood misted out at once, spreading through the ocean. Laaqueel smelled and tasted it even in the saltwater. Hunger pains vibrated in her stomach. She took the dead priestess's knife and began slicing.

"Come, my sisters," she invited. "Meat is meat."

The other two joined her, wolfing down the gobbets of flesh as she sliced them free. More blood stained the water, spreading outward. Even a drop of it in thousands of gallons of water, Laaqueel knew, would draw predators, and they came. Some crawled on multi-jointed legs while others slithered through the water and still more finned their way to the death site.

All stayed back from the sahuagin, acknowledging them as the strongest of predators.

Vibrations through her lateral lines told Laaqueel when the sharks arrived. She glanced up, watching five of the great creatures swim in a circle overhead. She reached out to the predators with her mind, sending out a danger message that would hold them at bay.

The sharks continued to circle until the sahuagin finished eating what they could of Thuur. Meat was meat, and a fallen sahuagin comrade became a meal for the others. That way, the essence of the individual never left the community.

When they were gorged, Laaqueel ordered her party away, allowing the sharks to descend to finish what was left of the corpse. They divided Thuur's possessions and the meager provisions they'd managed to put together three days ago between them. The dead sahuagin was the most they'd had to eat in weeks.

She swam, leading them further south, drawn by the promise of the story she'd discovered almost two years ago. With no other options open to her, the research she'd done offered her the only chance she had at a true and productive future among her tribe.

She had no choice but to believe.

Hours later, Laaqueel stopped the group for the night, camping in the lee of a sunken Calishite sohar. The three-masted merchant ship showed signs of the battle that had sent it to the ocean floor. Blackened timbers thrust up from the dark mud, canting hard to starboard. Wisps of ivory-colored sailcloth still clung to the rigging of the two surviving masts.

Judging from the condition of the wreck and the way the skeletons were picked clean to the bone, the malenti guessed that the ship had been underwater for little more than ten years. Barnacles clung to the broken timbers and sea anemones clustered in small groups. Schools of fish hid inside the broken hold, taking cover from predators.

True dark filled the ocean when the sun sank around the curve of the world. The inky blackness restricted even Laaqueel's sensitive vision until she could see only a few feet in front of her. She sat with her back to the broken ship, her arms wrapped around her knees in a posture the true sahuagin could never manage. In the elf communities she'd infiltrated over the years, she'd learned that such body language in the surface cultures signaled a wish to be alone.

Saanaa and Viiklee maintained their own counsel, sitting apart from her. They'd not spoken to her since she'd slain Thuur.

Finally it was Saanaa, the youngest, who crossed the distance first. Only a few yellow spots showed in her tail. "Favored one," she said, "forgive our uncertainty."

"There is no forgiveness for weakness," Laaqueel told her coldly. "Uncertainty can be viewed as weakness."

Saanaa's gills flared in anger. "Make no mistake about my strength, favored one. Just as Thuur died for her convictions, I stand ready to follow you wherever you lead."

"Good." As sahuagin, she knew she didn't have to worry about the other two surviving priestesses joining together to kill her. Their culture provided for one-on-one fighting among the community, and no challenges could be made to one who was wounded.

"Neither of us have heard how you came to find the record of the one you seek."

"I don't need to explain myself to you," Laaqueel said. "It's enough that Senior Priestess Ghaataag saw fit to send you with me. You should have taken that as a compliment."

"I do, but I wish to know more for myself, that I may be stronger," Saanaa said. She crouched, folding her arms in on herself, fitting her fins in tight against her body.

Laaqueel thought briefly of ignoring the other priestess. Though Saanaa's argument had merit, the malenti still had that privilege. The months had worn on Laaqueel, too, though it didn't touch her resolve. After being raised as a malenti, trained to be a spy, and moving among the hated sea elves and surface dwellers the few times she was able to mask her true nature, she welcomed the hunt she was on. No matter how long it took her, where she had to go, or what she had to do to accomplish it, she'd never felt more like a sahuagin than during this quest.

"I found a record regarding Sekolah," she said, talking only because she wanted to hear it aloud again, to strengthen her own resolve, "that was older than anything I'd ever seen before."

"A sahuagin book?"

Laaqueel shook her head and brushed her hair back. It was an all too elven gesture she hated picking up, but the long hair often drifted into her face. If she'd had her way, she'd have hacked the hair from her head, but it was a necessary part of her permanent disguise.

"No," she answered. "I found it during a stay with the sea elves almost five years ago."

The sahuagin books were created of strung bits of stone and shell on knotted thongs, each tied to a ring of bone or sinew. The way the shells, knots, and stones hung together represented sounds in the sahuagin tongue. Just shaking the sahuagin book created a series of sounds that gave the title. That was why many referred to them as "singing bundles."

"An elven book, favored one?" Saanaa asked.

"It was written by a human."

"About the sahuagin?" Disbelief sounded in the younger priestess's voice.

"Yes."

"It had to have been filled with lies."

"Incredibly," Laaqueel said, listening to her own words to further her resolve, "it held many truths."

"The sahuagin who gave our history to whomever wrote this book must have been enspelled." Saanaa shuddered. All sahuagin had an innate fear of anything magical.

Laaqueel shared that legacy. Even her time among the sea elves, who had no magic of their own either, hadn't prepared her to see the things she'd seen in her roving. Humans bent the very elements to their will and threw fireballs through the air when they wished. She'd seen it done. Power granted by Sekolah, however, was never in question. The Great Shark wielded magic and gave it to his most favored and most faithful of priestesses.

"I think so too," the malenti stated. "There was much in there about our communities as they were thousands of years ago." Actually, the community life described in the book hadn't changed much even now, though the places that were described were no longer on any sahuagin maps Laaqueel had ever seen. "I found among the myths of Sekolah a story that captured my eye and my heart."

"It was not about Sekolah?" Viiklee asked. She sat watching, her black eyes gleaming with interest. She had crept much closer to share in the tale.

"No. The book was written by a man named Ronassic of Sigil. He'd already documented other ocean life and marine cultures. He carried forth a treatise concerning the origins of the malenti as being a bridge between the sahuagin race and the cursed sea elves. He held that one evolved from the other, suggesting that sahuagin were created from the time the first sea elves took to the oceans. I find that heretical. I believe that the malenti are Sekolah's chosen sacrifices, the claws to lay bare the throats of the enemies of the sahuagin."

Neither of the other priestesses saw fit to disagree.

"In his book," Laaqueel went on, "he gets a great number of things wrong, but in the creation myths concerning the Great Shark and how the sahuagin were given to the seas, he mentioned another being of power."

"Daganisoraan?" Saanaa asked.

"No," Laaqueel answered, pitching her voice low to fully hold the attention of her audience. Daganisoraan was a common figure in sahuagin tales, featured as both hero and villain depending on the myth. "This was before even Daganisoraan's time, and though I searched the book, the only name I ever found given to him was One Who Swims With Sekolah."

"Maybe," Viiklee said, "One Who Swims With Sekolah was the first sahuagin."

"No." Laaqueel shook her head. "He was someone . . . some*thing* . . . very powerful."

"Why haven't we heard more about him?" Saanaa asked.

"I don't know. Perhaps he was there in the beginning but gone before Sekolah saw fit to put the first sahuagin into the oceans. Only the thinnest of whispers managed to survive concerning him."

"What happened to him?"

Laaqueel took the small whalebone container from between her breasts. The container was hollowed out, carved in the shape of a shark. She unstoppered it and poured out six red and black stones into her palm. The red was so true, so inviolate, that it was visible even at this depth and in the gathering darkness. All of stones had holes drilled through them. "I don't know. The book mentioned that he was locked away from the rest of the world to be taught a lesson."

"By Sekolah?" Viiklee demanded.

"No. By another of the gods or goddesses that walked this plane of existence during that time. One Who Swims With Sekolah was imprisoned. He's never been seen since."

"Yet this book mentioned him?" Saanaa asked. "No sahuagin records remember him?"

"Our records," Laaqueel reminded, "don't tell of him. I have read them all and consulted with the other priestesses regarding this matter. None remember One Who Swims With Sekolah, but we don't have access to all sahuagin records."

"What makes you think you can find this being?" Viiklee asked.

Laaqueel ran a forefinger through the six red and black stones in her palm, revealing the runes inscribed on them. "I've given the last five years of my life to the search for the truth in this matter. Only a few months ago, I discovered these in a loremaster's keep at Baldur's Gate."

"Where the humans live." Viiklee spat a curse, roiling the water around her angular face.

"Yes. Magic surrounds these stones."

Saanaa and Viiklee drew back, making protective wards against the hated magic. "You should have destroyed them," Saanaa hissed. "To even carry them around with you is sacrilege." The sahuagin coiled restlessly, edging away.

"There is nothing foul about these stones," Laaqueel said, turning them in her palm. She deftly plucked a short length of worked sinew from her trident hilt and with practiced ease threaded it through the stones, making sure they were in the proper order and tying the correct number of knots between them as she'd learned.

"The runes mean nothing, a false trail laid for the surface dwellers," she continued. "Someone tried to discover the secret of the stones and assigned names to the runes, and some have even used magic to try to read them. Humans and elves don't understand the nature of the sahuagin written language, and none who tried ever learned the truth of the stones."

Finished, she held the ring of knots and stones out, then shook them. They clattered against each other.

The message, to a sahuagin's internal ear and lateral lines, was clear: "Seek out One Who Swims With Sekolah."

"You see?" Laaqueel asked. "Above water where a sahuagin's hearing doesn't operate properly even should one be there, the song of the stones wouldn't be clear. If the book I found hadn't mentioned the existence of the stones, I wouldn't have known. Even then, tracking down the stones was not an easy matter. They were part of a collection assembled by a historian from Skuld, a human city in the land of Mulhorand."

"I've never heard of this place, honored one," Saanaa stated.

Laaqueel knew she had them gripped by the story. If anything, the sahuagin definitely knew the value of a story. There were many concepts new to them, and the stones—with their curse of magic—lay before them.

"Mulhorand is believed to be the oldest continually inhabited human country," she said. "It's located in the ocean the surface dwellers call the Sea of Fallen Stars."

"I know of our home sea, the Claarteeros Sea, the one the humans call the Trackless Sea and the Sea of Swords," Viiklee stated. "I know of the Veemeeros Sea, which they've named the Shining Sea, but I have never heard of the sea you speak of."

"It's an inland sea." Laaqueel watched their eyes widen. As young priestesses, their view of the world was kept deliberately small to encourage strength in their beliefs. Trained as a malenti spy to go into the cities of elves, Laaqueel had been taught early about the geography of the world even beyond what the humans termed the Sword Coast. She remembered how she'd felt when she'd first been told of the Sea of Fallen Stars. The idea of a land-locked sea was frightening.

"How can such a thing be?" Saanaa asked.

Laaqueel turned her hands outward, exposing the webbing between her fingers to show even they were empty. It was a purely sahuagin gesture, not the spasmodic shrug she'd learned of the humans and elves.

"It must be Sekolah's will," Viiklee stated.

"Perhaps."

"Are there sahuagin there?" Saanaa asked.

"I don't know. I've heard stories, but nothing I was able to confirm. The sea elves living along the Sword Coast take very little interest in anything outside their own villages and trading needs. The humans I've had chance to meet were more interested in filling their pockets with gold and silver than in answering questions I might advance, and I was trained not to draw too much attention to myself."

"Living in such a fashion must have been hard," Saanaa said.

"I hated it," Laaqueel admitted. "Elven and human ways are not meant for sahuagin. They are too soft, too greedy. I welcome the day that we are able to push them from the sea and from the coastal lands and take back our world in the waters." She paused. "Still, Sekolah gave each sahuagin the currents of his or her life . . ."

". . . and it is up to each to swim with them," the other two priestesses finished the familiar phrase.

"As we swim with this one now," Laaqueel added.

"Did the book you read mention that Sekolah was within this Sea of Falling Stars?" Viiklee asked.

"As far as I know," the malenti answered, "Sekolah was never there, nor was One Who Swims With Sekolah."

"How did the stones get there?" Saanaa asked.

Laaqueel shook them again, causing them to repeat their message. "It's a mystery, one of many I hope to find answers for."

"How do you know One Who Swims With Sekolah is here?" Viiklee asked. "Why aren't we looking for him in the Sea of Falling Stars?"

"Because the book mentioned that One Who Swims With Sekolah's final resting place was in the Veemeeros Sea. It wasn't called that in the book, but from the description of the land with terrible giant reptiles nearby, it could only be this place."

"If only the sea weren't so large," Saanaa sighed.

Uncoiling, filled instantly with anger, Laaqueel backhanded the younger priestess. An explosion of bubbles erupted from her gills. "Sacrilege! The sea is our life!"

Saanaa cried out in pain, covering her face. "I didn't mean it!" she cried. "Forgive me, favored one. I meant only that our task would be easier—"

"Sekolah never meant for sahuagin life to be easy," Laaqueel snapped, "else he would never have given the sahuagin so many enemies." She was going to add more, a sermon already on her tongue.

Before she could begin, the stones pulled gently from her hand, drifting into a current. Laaqueel watched them, feeling the old fear of magic twisting her stomach into knots around her last meal. Her abilities as priestess, she knew, rivaled those of some mages, but those abilities were given by the Great Shark, awarded to those whose prayers were truest, loudest, and strongest.

Viiklee and Saanaa drew back quickly, raising a murky cloud from the mud floor. They raised their tridents in defense.

The ring of stones rose just out of Laaqueel's arm's reach. They whirled through the water, clicking and resonating their message over and over. A pale scarlet glow gleamed from each of the stones, then grew stronger as the stones spun faster. The message became louder, and the lights turned into a blurred circle of luminescence.

Laaqueel steeled herself, then took a step toward the stones. Immediately, the stones retreated from her, moving the exact distance she did. The message was clear.

"Come," Laaqueel commanded, picking up her trident and adjusting her harness.

The sahuagin priestesses didn't bother to disagree.

Silently, the malenti guided them through the darkness, her eyes focused on the scarlet whirl of the stones. She gave herself over to the current, following her destiny.

Two days later, the whirling stones stopped and hovered over a mound of abyssal hills that radiated heat. Somewhere below the surface, Laaqueel knew, volcanoes rumbled in uneasy slumber.

Over the last two days, none of them had slept. Their guide had never stopped, pulling them on with the allure of one of Sekolah's savants during a Wild Hunt. Thankfully, the stones had gone relatively slowly, considering how fast sahuagin could swim, allowing them to take turns darting out for prawn, fish, and oysters to provide for the others. A sahuagin's diet required heavy meals anyway to provide the necessary energy to maintain body heat and muscle tone, but the demands of the last two days had drained all their reserves. Even eating along the way, they'd all lost weight during the chase.

Laaqueel watched the wheel of spinning stones slow and glide into position less than a foot above the ocean floor. She knifed through the water, dropping to the mud within easy reach of the stones. Her bare feet slid through the loose silt and she felt the underlying rock strata. She also felt the heat of the volcanoes beneath the surface, warmer than the water around her.

The stones continued repeating their message. In the two days that the priestesses had followed it, the words had never stopped. Now, though, an echoing resonance came from the rock bed beneath the inches of loose silt.

"Nothing grows here, honored one," Saanaa stated quietly, "nor does anything linger."

The malenti gazed in all directions, moving slowly. Her muscles quivered from the continued strain of the last two days spent swimming. What Saanaa said was true: nothing grew within a hundred paces in any direction. Nor did any sea creature make a home or swim within the circumference. The water above her remained clear for the same distance as well.

An uncomfortable feeling, just below the threshold of fear, filled her. It manifested as a vibration that raced through her bones, chilling her to the marrow. Even the water she gulped through her mouth and washed through her gills felt tainted and heavy.

The stones clicked and repeated the message. She felt the words in her lateral lines, then felt them through her webbed toes as the rock beneath her picked up the resonance even more strongly.

Seek Out One Who Swims With Sekolah

SEEK OUT ONE WHO SWIMS WITH SEKOLAH

SeekOutOneWhoSwimsWithSekolah

SEEKOUTONEWHOSWIMSWITHSEKOLAH

The words drummed into her mind, demanding action.

"Favored one," Viiklee called. "The stones—"

"I hear them," Laaqueel replied. She knelt, dropping to her knees in the heated mud, finding it near scalding.

"Look." Saanaa pointed at the ribs of a giant lizard sticking up through the rock and mud.

Laaqueel was familiar with the creature from her studies and from her time among the sea elves and surface dwellers, knowing it had come from the nearby land of Chult. The creature's huge skull gleamed bright white against the dark water. A man's bones, crushed and twisted, hung in the huge mouth between the teeth. Whatever had killed the giant lizard had been quick.

Laaqueel listened to the savage beat of the command initiated by the whirling stones. She knelt in the mud, ignoring the heat, and bowed her head. She prayed with all her heart to Sekolah, knowing that the Great Shark seldom involved himself even in the affairs of the sahuagin, his children. He was a demanding and ungenerous god.

Saanaa and Viiklee knelt and added their prayers with hers.

SEEK OUT ONE WHO SWIMS WITH SEKOLAH!

Though involved in her prayers, Laaqueel also heard the hollow echo of the sound played in the rock strata beneath her. Her lateral lines echoed with it as well. Despite the sea above and around her, she knew that an empty chamber lay below her, a pocket created by the cooled magma from a volcano. Her knowledge of Chult, the primordial land to the southwest of her current position was slim, but she knew about the massive quakes and volcanoes that had shaped and reshaped the land. It was possible that the bones of the great lizard in the mud nearby had gone down with a piece of what had been Chult at one time. Possibly it was from a small island that had existed in a chain around the major continent.

The great lizard's death had been quick, too quick for it to even finish the meal it had caught. An erupting volcano could cause such a death, the malenti knew. The fires and heat created by some volcanoes could strip the meat from a body, even sour and poison the water.

The abyssal hills themselves were formed from volcanoes that had cooled. These dead volcanoes often left chambers and empty pockets located within them.

Laaqueel rose to her feet and walked away from the spot where the stones whirled. The reflected cadence coming from the rock strata lessened with each step she took. Twenty paces away, she couldn't feel it anymore.

She returned to the stones, feeling the cadence grow again. She experimented in the other directions as well, finding it to be the same with all three. The stones had marked the spot.

"Something lies below, honored one," Saanaa whispered.

"I know." Laaqueel knelt in prayer again, taking the circlet of shark's teeth from a tie to her harness at her waist. Like the singing bundles of her people, and the spinning ring of stones, the shark's teeth had been knotted and tied to reproduce sounds that were a prayer in the sahuagin language.

The shark's teeth rattled as she shook them, crying out Sekolah's name. She listened to the chant, pacing the words of her prayer with the cadence, growing faster as she summoned the power the Great Shark had given her. Feeling it reach its peak within her, she shoved her hand forward.

The power surged through the water from her hand, leaving a wake of brightly colored bubbles. When it struck the rock, a hollow booming gong sounded deep inside the cavern below. In seconds, the rock changed, softening, turning to loose mud. When the power had drained her, leaving her weak and gasping water in big gulps, Laaqueel swam to the site below the stones. She shoved her trident deep into what had once been rock, raking aside what was now mud.

It only took a minute to breach the outer shell of the chamber. Saanaa and Viiklee helped her widen the hole. Darkness gaped up at them, but the echoed resonance of the rattling stones sounded louder, echoing still more as the first chamber funneled the noise into another chamber further on.

When the hole was wide enough, Laaqueel waved the other priest-esses back. Even their sahuagin vision couldn't penetrate the gloom trapped inside. She spotted a school of luminous fish out beyond the one hundred pace mark from the open chamber. They glowed pale blue-green. Gathering her trident in both hands, she swam toward the fish, bursting in among them too quickly for them to save themselves. The trident flicked out rapidly, impaling five of the fish.

She adjusted her air bladder and hung motionless in the water. For the first time she noticed that not even the perpetual ocean currents moved through the dead zone. She popped her retractable claws from her fingers and quickly gutted the fish. Saanaa and Viiklee swam close and snapped up the floating strings of intestines.

"Meat is meat," Saanaa said in appreciation. Still, she saved several choice bits of the fish for Laaqueel.

Reaching the light-producing organs of the fish, the malenti care-fully freed them. When she had all five, she took a glow lamp from the bag of holding tied to her harness. Carefully, she nicked each of the organs with a claw to open them, then squeezed the liquid contents up into the neck of the translucent bladder of the glow lamp. All five fish barely gave up a handful of the luminous gel. Keeping the bladder tight, she brought it to her mouth and breathed in, further inflating the glow lamp and giving it some buoyancy. At that depth, it was hard breathing enough air into the bladder to inflate it.

Sealing the bladder, Laaqueel swirled the gel around, causing it to glow more brightly. It wasn't enough to hurt her sensitive eyes, but it would serve to illuminate the chambers below the ocean floor. She used a seaweed cord to tie the glow lamp to her trident.

"Here, favored one," Saanaa said, offering the fish pieces she'd saved.

"Meat is meat," Laaqueel acknowledged. She ate the repast quickly, then swam back to the rough-edged opening. She entered without pause, summoning her belief and her courage. There was nothing she wouldn't do to improve her standing among her people. Her findings, she felt certain, would empower the sahuagin race as it had never been before. The surface dwellers would live in fear even on land and never darken the sea with their ships again. That hope gave her more reason to go on than any.

The glow lamp illuminated the chamber, showing the rough, uneven walls created by the cooling lava. The interior looked like a patchwork of blacks and grays even with the light. A narrow fissure in the floor of the first chamber led down into the second. As Laaqueel surveyed it, pushing the glow lamp down inside with the trident, the glowing stones went into motion again. They whirled and clacked, and dropped through the fissure.

Seek Out One Who Swims With Sekolah
SEEK OUT ONE WHO SWIMS WITH SEKOLAH
SEEKOUTONEWHOSWIMSWITHSEKOLAH

After only a brief hesitation, Laaqueel ventured through the fissure, a prayer on her lips. The light from the glow lamp reflected from the tiny bubbles streaming from her mouth as she prayed.

The next chamber was bigger, and the chant given off by the stones was echoed in basso booms. A tunnel that had been created by an explosion of trapped gases opened the wall to the malenti's right. She stayed alert for anything moving around her, but nothing lived in the chambers.

Eight more chambers came and went, each of varying size. Laaqueel was no longer sure of what direction she was headed in—save down, always down. The water warmed around her, conducting the heat from the trapped volcano around her.

She swam through the next chamber, arriving in an oblong cave that was larger than anything she'd been in so far. The illumination from the glow lamp wasn't strong enough to reach from side to side. She released air from her bladder, losing enough buoyancy to drop herself and the inflated glow lamp through the murk, straining her vision to spot the floor below.

Only a few feet up, she spotted the mosaic in the floor. Squares as long as her arm, reduced only to light and dark by the pale blue glow of the lamp, connected with each other. Even then, the squares were only a remnant of the floor as it had been.

Laaqueel held the glow lamp aloft and paced as she measured the section. Irregularly shaped, and twenty strokes by thirty, the floor section canted across the bottom of the volcanic chamber. Black charring scored the surface. Broken furnishings, furniture as well as crafted coral pieces, piled amid the broken clutter gathered at the lowest end of the floor section.

The malenti sorted through the debris, using the long knife from her shin sheath to shift the broken pieces in case anything dangerous lived in it. However, whatever enchantment kept living things from intruding above also kept them from below. She took four beautiful coral pieces that captured her eye, watching as Saanaa and Viiklee found treasures of their own.

"Beware," she told the other priestesses. "It may be that these are Sekolah's possessions and we'll have to give them back."

"Until then," Viiklee agreed covetously, "but only until that time."

The debris left no doubt that it had come from a civilized place, but whether it was carried a long distance or still more of it lay under the rubble of the chambers, Laaqueel didn't know. She glanced upward, remembering the whirling stones. The constant chanted command had faded into the background of her hearing, but still throbbed inside her mind.

The stones circled above and to her right, waiting. "Come," she told the others, "we'll explore further later." She increased her buoyancy again and swam to the stones. She held the glow lamp before her, the trident still at the ready.

When she neared, the stones fluttered and took off again. They whirled through the water and through a long, narrow shaft. It lead to a small room still and cold as a tomb despite the heat coming from the volcano trapped below. Primitive fear of the unknown prickled the malenti's skin as she neared the mouth of the shaft.

In the light given off by the glow lamp, a shadowy figure took shape out of the darkness. Instead of being illuminated, it seemed to take the darkness into itself, turning darker even than black pearl.

"What is it, favored one?" Saanaa called from behind.

"A man," Laaqueel answered.

"Not a sahuagin?"

"No." The malenti let the disappointment sound in her voice. She knew she'd spoken the truth, yet that didn't explain the fear that cut through her.

"Maybe we should look for another chamber," Viiklee said. "There must be others."

Laaqueel stared at the stones hovering over the top of the still figure of the man.

Seek Out One Who Swims With Sekolah

SEEK OUT ONE WHO SWIMS WITH SEKOLAH

They came to an abrupt stop, and the silence struck as forcibly as a whale sounding.

"No," she replied. "This is where we were led."

She forced herself to go forward. Once inside the room, the chill grew stronger, became an arctic cold. She couldn't fathom how the water wasn't frozen solid by whatever glamour possessed the room. She had no doubt that the room was enchanted.

She lifted the glow lamp and played it over the figure. Resembling a surface dweller, he stood a full head taller than the malenti, and inches above the other priestesses. His hair was pulled back in a cluster of tangles secured by carved bones with intricate runes. Harshness tightened his face, narrowed his single eye and turned it down at the corners. The other eye was a hollow socket surrounded skin puckered by the scar of a long-healed burn. He wore a mustache that ran down to his chin, then flared back up his jawline to join his sideburns, leaving his dimpled chin clean-shaven. Hollow-cheeked, he looked wasted and emaciated, that fact showing even more starkly since he was totally naked, starved yet wiry. In the pale light of the glow lamp, his skin tone was as pale as a bled corpse. Dark tattoos scribed in broad strokes covered his body, creating a mosaic of color and sharp lines on every square inch of skin.

His solitary eye stared through her.

Fearful but needing to know, Laaqueel reached out and touched him with her knife point. The sharp edge grated on the man's petrified skin, not even leaving a mark in its passage.

"He's dead, favored one," Saanaa said. "He's not the one we came for."

"Let's leave this tomb," Viiklee pleaded.

Laaqueel stepped closer to the petrified man who looked so unlike anything she had expected. "No," she commanded, "this is the one we came for."

"This can't be One Who Swims With Sekolah," Viiklee argued. "He looks like a—a surface dweller. A human, not even an elf."

She glanced up at them as they hovered over the petrified man, then back at the statue's hard face. " 'There in his cold grave' " Laaqueel quoted from the text she'd read, " 'barren of life and bereft of the powers he'd once commanded, lost to the luxuries he'd once had, lies One Who Swims With Sekolah. Dead—yet undead, too, turned as hard and as cold as his heart that left love forsaken.' " The common tongue she'd learned as part of her training was sometimes less precise than the sahuagin tongue, so there was a margin for error, but the stones didn't lie.

"What love?" Saanaa asked.

"I don't know," Laaqueel admitted.

"Humans only know to love another human," Viiklee stated. "Their understanding of that emotion is pathetic. Wisdom dictates loving your race, not an individual. The race is what will persevere."

That was the sahuagin view, Laaqueel knew, and one seldom shared by the humans or elves. Those races tended to think individuals first and race second.

"If this is One Who Swims With Sekolah, who did this to him?" Saanaa asked.

"The book didn't say."

"What are we supposed to do with a dead human?" Viiklee demanded.

"He isn't dead," Laaqueel answered.

"The story said he lay in his tomb," Viiklee pointed out.

"It also said he was dead, yet undead. Maybe he can't be killed."

"He's dead," the younger priestess argued. "Even a hatchling would know that." Sahuagin knew about death; the weak died early, eaten by its fellow hatchlings.

"We'll see," Laaqueel said as she opened the whalebone container around her neck again and removed a ring. Cast in gold, the ring was a simple band studded with diamond chips that reflected the pale blue-green luminescence of the glow lamp.

"What's that?" Saanaa asked.

"A ring."

"I can see that, honored one."

"A very special ring." Laaqueel slid the ring onto the petrified man's forefinger. The magic in the ring caused it to adjust to the man's finger with an unsettling fluid grace. It slid into place, then began to glow. "This ring was mentioned in the book," she continued. "It took a year and a half to find. It's supposed to return One Who Swims With Sekolah to life."

"More magic," Viiklee spat in disgust. "Only the magic bestowed by Sekolah is trustworthy."

"I have prayed," Laaqueel said, "that these things be blessed in Sekolah's hungry gaze. We've been brought here without harm."

"Thuur died," Viiklee reminded.

"By choosing to thwart Sekolah's plan for us," the malenti reminded her companion. As Laaqueel watched, the petrified man took on a different pallor, adding color to the bone-hue he wore. She touched him, finding his skin slightly pliable now. "It's working."

"How long will it take, honored one?" Saanaa asked.

"However long it takes, we'll be here," Laaqueel said. "We're not leaving."

Sudden movement sensed through her lateral lines woke Laaqueel, letting her know something had moved in front of her. She blinked her eyes open and searched for the glow lamp. Hours after the discovery of the petrified man, she'd assigned shifts, taking the first one herself. Saanaa and Viiklee had protested, not wanting to stay in the cold tomb. Laaqueel had ignored them. The cold might be uncomfortable, but it wasn't harmful. Still, she'd surprised herself by being able to sleep.

"Saanaa," the malenti called out.

There was no answer, and she couldn't see either of the two priestesses in the illumination given off by the glow lamp.

Laaqueel pushed herself to her feet and leaned toward the glow lamp attached to her trident. Earlier, the luminescence had almost filled the room. Now it covered less than half of it. The gel hadn't lost its ability to illuminate so quickly.

The preternatural chill vibrated through Laaqueel again. Her lateral lines registered more movement, but it didn't feel like either of the two priestesses. She was attuned to their physical motions and would know them even in the dark.

This was different.

She pushed the glow lamp toward the area where the petrified man had been. He was gone, but the light played over the twisted corpses of the two junior priestesses. They lay in pieces across the cavern floor, shredded by a large predator.

Disbelief paralyzed Laaqueel. They'd been killed while she slept—without her waking. She had no clue why she'd been spared. Sensing the movement again, she turned quickly to face it, bringing her hands up to defend herself.

A hand, hard as stone and cold as ice, battered through her defenses and locked around her throat. Hooked fingers painfully invaded her gill slits to further choke her.

The man's face illuminated gradually at the other end of that impossibly thin arm, like he'd allowed the light to finally touch him. He smiled, and it was the cruelest expression Laaqueel had ever seen.

His words touched her mind without being spoken. They were cold and hard, singing like gong notes inside her head, but came across as a whisper. *You thought to sneak quietly in here and steal from me, didn't you, little thief,* he accused. His words were heavily accented, lilting and almost musical.

Overpowered by the invasion in her mind, Laaqueel couldn't answer.

You couldn't understand the sacrifices I have made in order to ensure my continued survival with that ineffectual mind you possess, the man said. *Even now, wasted as I am, I am the most powerful being you have ever been in the presence of. Now, by my grace, you will spend your life that I spare so generously that you may serve me, and then only as long as you serve me well, little thief. Long have I been gone from this world, for thousands of years, and I will have back that which was stolen from me. You will give me succor, or I will see you sacrificed toward that end anyway.* His single eye bored into hers, mesmerizing and horribly vacant at the same time.

Struggling against the glamour the man projected, the malenti fought, trying to break free of his grip. Her fingers and talons only scraped across the hard flesh, unable to break the skin. Her toe claws raked his chest but skittered harmlessly across.

He plucked an eyelash from his single eye, then said words unlike any Laaqueel had ever heard. The tattoos covering his body glowed with a dim, unearthly light. When it stopped, he held a thin sliver of a black quill in his free hand instead of an eyelash. He let her see it for just a moment, then his hand darted forward and he buried the quill in the tender flesh below her left breast.

Laaqueel felt the quill penetrate her flesh, hot and cold at the same time. All resistance faded from her as her body went lax. None of her limbs were her own anymore.

The man took his hand back from her flesh and gestured at the sliver's entry point. The malenti felt it move again, sliding more deeply into her body, coiling and nestling next to her heart like a poisonous worm. She stared at the man holding her so effortlessly with one hand.

I am Iakhovas, he told her in his deep, whispering voice. *You will call me master.*

The Sea of Swords
9 Mirtul, the Year of the Gauntlet (1369 DR)

1

"How much for a few hours of your time, boy?"

Jherek stopped coiling the thin rope he was going to use to repair the ship's rigging and looked at the young Amnian woman who'd stopped in front of him. His heart seemed to hang in his throat. He'd watched her during the voyage, never dreaming such a wealthy and pretty woman would ever notice him, much less speak to him.

Barely over nineteen, he stood nearly six feet tall and his lean frame was corded with muscle from the hard work he'd done since he'd been a boy. His light brown hair was threaded through with sun-bleached highlights from constant exposure to the salt and sun. He wore only an abbreviated leather ship's apron that hung to his mid-thighs and held numerous pockets for the tools he needed and a short-sleeved shirt. The sun had burned his skin a dark bronze and made the pale gray ice of his eyes stand out even more. He went shaven, not liking the facial hair worn by most of the other sailors. Gold hoop earrings hung from both ears.

"Lady," he said formally, after giving careful consideration to his words, "if there is anything you need, Captain Finaren and his first mate will see that you have it. You and your party have hired the best—"

"We've hired the best sea captain in all of the Duchy of Cape Velen. Yes, we've all been told that." The woman waved his words away, rolling her dark eyes skyward as if bored.

Jherek felt embarrassed and awkward, partly that she'd turned his words and made them sound small in that Amnian accent of hers, and because she was so incredibly beautiful.

He figured she wasn't much older than he was, surely no more than five years his senior. She wore a turban as was the custom of the Amnian wealthy, festooned with gold and silver coins and small jewels to further show her ranking even among the merchant class. Her hair was pulled up under the turban, leaving her delicate face uncovered. Her eyes were big dark moons of liquid fire and she had a nose that some might consider too short but that Jherek found attractive. Her red silk cape fluttered around her, caught by the soft southerly breeze coming across the Sea of Swords. Bracelets sewn into the cape kept it around her, but it didn't conceal her slender, womanly figure. Even that was barely restrained in a beaded bodice and gauze pantaloons over a matching girdle. Delicate slippers encased her feet.

"If I'd thought your precious Captain Finaren could have given me what I needed," the Amnian woman said, "I'd have gone straight to him."

She took a step closer to him and traced a line with her forefinger down from his lower lip, across his chin, and down to his chest, toying briefly with the ceramic teardrop as big as her thumb that hung from a leather thong around his neck. Her hand continued dropping to the flat planes of his stomach.

Jherek stepped back before she could go any further. He was suddenly acutely aware of the other ship's mates halting their work to watch. Even the other Amnians aboard paused in their endless conversations of money and exchange rates to watch him.

"Instead," the Amnian woman said, "I came to you. You should be flattered."

"Lady," Jherek said helplessly. He felt certain that he was the brunt of some joke he didn't understand, but he had no idea what to do about it.

"I am called Yeill," she said. "I am the favorite daughter of Merchant Lelayn." She raised an arched eyebrow. "You are familiar with Merchant Lelayn, aren't you?"

"Aye," Jherek replied. "Of course." Merchant Lelayn had hired *Finaren's Butterfly* to take the Amnian party to Baldur's Gate for trading, then bring their cargo back home to Athkatla, also known as the City of Coin, in Amn. He wished he'd been quicker with the ropes and had gone back up into the rigging before the woman had caught him, but he had no one to blame but himself. Over the last few days of the trip she must have seen him gazing at her.

"Good," Yeill stated. "I thought there might be some brains inside that pretty head of yours, though they aren't all that necessary for what I have in mind." She placed a hand on his bicep, squeezing the muscles there. "You are in very good shape."

Jherek flushed red, feeling the burn across his cheeks, like he'd faced the wind for an entire shift at the tiller. He gazed past her, noting a small group of white heggrims flying low around the cog. The birds kept pace with the ship, waiting for any garbage that might be thrown overboard.

Finaren's Butterfly skimmed smoothly across the water, rocking back and forth across the swells. The ship's colorful sails gave her her name and the few remaining that weren't damaged from the recent storm belled out, catching the wind. Other hands hung in the rigging, repairing the storm damage.

"So how much for a few hours of your time, boy?" she asked again. "I'm willing to pay you, though after the way I've seen you mooning after me, I know I wouldn't have to."

It *was* his fault. Jherek dropped his eyes from hers, no longer able to look at her even out of politeness. She had caught him gazing at her. It was his ill luck that had followed him all of his life showing itself again. There was never a day that he wasn't forced to remember that it dogged his every step. His tongue felt thick, and no words came to it.

"I have heard you called Jherek," she said. "Is that your name?"

"Aye, lady." Jherek struggled to get the words through his tight throat. "If I've offered you any affront, I apologize. The captain would have the skin from my back for such a thing."

She smiled. "I've no doubt that he would. Your Captain Finaren seems a man the Amnian can easily understand. His life revolves around his bottom line, and how well he can line his pockets, but you've offered me no affront."

Jherek felt relieved, only wanting to scurry up the rigging and get away from the woman's gaze. He'd fought pirates and sea creatures for the future of *Finaren's Butterfly*, but he felt naked and outmatched talking to the woman.

"Thank you, lady."

"Yet," she added, lifting both brows again. Curious lights, like embers, flew through her dark eyes. "Would you deny me the pleasure of your company then, young Jherek?"

"Lady, I have no way with social graces, and I lack in my education," Jherek said honestly. He knew he was lying, though. Madame Iitaar and Malorrie had seen to his education since he was twelve, and they had both been demanding taskmasters.

"I'm not looking for a gifted conversationalist, Jherek." Yeill swirled her cape around herself, revealing the lean body cloaked beneath. "My father has done well with his trading in Baldur's Gate. I can afford to be generous."

"There are many other crewmen," Jherek said.

"You are by far the most handsome."

Jherek flushed again. Never had a woman been so shameless in her pursuit. Even the scullery maids of the Figureheadless Tavern along the eastern dock walk in Velen were not so forceful.

"Perhaps you've not seen me in good light, lady," he said.

"Can it be?" she asked with obvious delight. "Handsome *and* modest?" She wrinkled her brow, then a smile dawned on her crimson lips. "Or is there more to it?"

Jherek shouldered the rope. "I have to get back to work, otherwise

22

it will be the barnacle detail for a month for me if the captain finds me dallying."

Yeill's voice sharpened. "You'll stay here till I say you can go, boy."

Part of the old resentment at being unfairly commanded and ordered welled up in Jherek, and it almost loosened his tongue before he seized control of it. "Aye, lady."

"My father hired this ship and all the men aboard it to see to our needs during our voyage," the Amnian woman stated. "That work won't be shirked."

Jherek bowed his head, using the motion to break the eye contact. "Aye, lady."

"How old are you, boy?"

"Nineteen."

"Yet you are only a deckhand, not a mate."

"I've not had the promise of potential."

"Then your captain lacks ability in picking his men. When the storm wracked this ship yesterday morn, you were the first to climb up into the rigging and cut the ropes to save at least some of the sails."

"I don't think I was the first." Jherek knew that he was, though. The rigging held no fears for him, even in the worst of storms.

She ran her eyes over him again, lingering on the apron across his narrow hips. "Tell me, boy, have you never been with a woman before?"

Jherek steeled himself and faced her. His answers had to be his own and truthful, and she was demanding them. "No."

She stroked his face with the back of her hand. "With your looks, that has to be by choice."

Jherek reached up and captured her hand in his, then slowly removed it from his face. "Aye."

"You *do* like women?"

"Not all of those I've met," Jherek told her, skating the thin line of insubordination, "but in the way you mean, aye."

"Do you find me unattractive then?"

"I think you're a very beautiful woman."

"So you're content to merely look at me?" Her gaze mocked him.

"I don't know you," Jherek said, "nor do you know me."

"I'm willing to get to know you," Yeill stated forcefully, "and pay you for the opportunity."

"I'm not for sale. Not that way." Jherek released her hand and took a step back, just out of her reach. Nausea touched his stomach in response to her offer.

"Ridiculous," the Amnian woman snapped. "Everyone is for sale."

"Not me," Jherek said.

She raked him with her fiery eyes. "You tread in dangerous waters, boy. Maybe you don't remember who you're dealing with."

"I remember."

"Do you realize the insult you offer me, boy?"

"There's no insult intended. You asked for something that I'm not prepared to sell."

"You think so much of it, then?"

Jherek wished he could have said more. She would have understood had she been where he'd been, had lived on as little as he'd been given in his early life. There was so little left that was truly his.

"What you ask for can't be bought, lady, only given."

"You speak of hearts, boy."

"I speak of love."

She laughed at him derisively and asked, "You believe such a thing exists?"

"I want to believe," Jherek said. In truth, he didn't know, but he wasn't prepared to settle for anything less than the true love Malorrie's tales had told of.

"A fool believes in love."

He let some of the anger out then, in his own defense. "You would trouble yourself over a fool, lady?"

She smiled at him, prettily, but her eyes were hard and cutting as barnacles. "If he had a handsome face and a soft touch," she answered, "and I had the price. Trust me, boy, I do have your price."

Jherek settled the ropes more securely about his shoulder. "Lady, I mean no offense, but I must get to work." Behind her, he saw Captain Finaren step onto the main deck, leaning on the railing and looking down at him.

"You're a foolish boy," Yeill stated. "You'll regret this." Without warning, she slapped him.

Jherek saw the blow coming and chose not to dodge it entirely. Malorrie's martial training included close-in fighting as well as the blade. Her open hand collided with his cheek and he felt one of her rings cut his face. Blood trickled down his cheek and he tasted it inside his mouth as well. She'd hit harder than he'd expected.

"Tell your fellow sailors that you made an improper advance toward me," the Amnian woman whispered roughly. "If you don't, trust me when I say that you'll regret it."

He met her gaze. "If you think that I would choose to dishonor you," he told her in an equally low voice, "you still show your ignorance of the kind of man I choose to be."

"You're no man," she said. "A man would have come to me himself, days ago." She turned sharply and walked away from him.

Jherek stood there, his face burning crimson, and listened to the jeering catcalls of the other sailors. Shaking a little with the anger and fear that nearly consumed him, he walked to the nearest rigging and leaped up into the ropes. He climbed swiftly, edging out to the area that he'd been assigned to repair.

When he showed no sign of responding to the catcalls and off-color comments, the other sailors gave up baiting him. High above the deck, feeling the morning sun soak into him, he let go of the emotions, pushing them out of his body. Madame Iitaar had been the first to get him past the fear that had become his birthright. She had taught him to trust himself, and gradually a handful of others, but he was at his best when he was alone.

His fingers worked cleverly, almost without him thinking about it. He braided the new rope in with the old rigging, then cut away the frayed pieces. The cries of the heggrims, following after *Finaran's Butterfly* for the garbage that was dumped every morning and after every meal, soothed him. He chose a new piece of rope and paused long enough to gaze out across the water.

The ocean spread rolling and green. He loved the sea, loved the sailor's life, loved the autonomy of living aboard ship. Those things took him away from large groups of people. Interacting with others, especially when they didn't make sense, drained him and often left him dispirited.

He breathed in the salt air and felt invigorated. The Amnians would be gone soon, and they'd be home in Velen for a few days. He found he was looking forward to it more than usual.

"What happened betwixt you and that girl, lad?"

Jherek sat in the rigging, tied in now as he worked the more narrow and more tricky spots on the mast. The storm yesterday morning had been unforgiving, ripping across the cog's decks and doing exterior damage that would be repaired at a later time.

"What's she saying?" Jherek asked carefully.

Captain Virne Finaren stood on the nearby mast arm, a short burly man of sixty and more years who hadn't given up any aspect of his duties to his ship. The captain still hand-trained the more capable of his crew. He'd taught Jherek the few things the boy hadn't known about ships.

"She's saying that you made improper advances toward her," Finaren said.

He wore a full beard the yellow color of Calim Desert sand, spotted now with winter silver. The sun had tightened his eyes, making them slits across copper pupils. His face was seamed from exposure to the elements and a dagger thrust had left a harsh scar above his right eyebrow. He wore a doublet, breeches, and boots. A red kerchief kept his long hair from his eyes.

Jherek didn't say anything, keeping his hands busy.

"I'm caught in a bit of a muddle," the captain admitted as he went on.

"Why?" Jherek asked.

"A crewman of mine making advances against a woman on my ship, he's a crewman going to get a taste of the cat."

Jherek knew Finaren was referring to the cat-o'-nine-tails he kept for ship's discipline. "Very well," he said.

"Very well?" Finaren repeated after a moment.

"Aye," Jherek said.

"You'd let me take the hide from your back, and we both knowing that pretty little tramp is lying like a rug?"

"I didn't say she was lying," Jherek pointed out.

"Lad," Finaren said, "we both know she's lying. You've never offered any man or woman—or beast, that I know of—anything in the way of an insult. Even them that you've killed in a fight you've never slurred before, during, or after."

Jherek said nothing, feeling bad that his ill luck was affecting Finaren as well. "I was looking at her," he admitted. "Maybe if I hadn't been doing that, she wouldn't have embarrassed herself."

"Valkur's brass buttons, boy!" Finaren exploded. "You're a seaman. You spend a netful of your life away from kith and kin, and the sight of a good woman. Even a sailor clinging to a sinking spar would gaze on Umberlee with favor, and her the cold bitch goddess she is that spares no man venturing out on the ocean. When we go out on the salt as a way of life, we know what we're giving up."

"I'm sorry," Jherek said.

A lump swelled in his throat as the confusion touched him. In every situation he truly believed there was a right thing to do, a fair thing. But for the life of him, he couldn't see what it was in this instance.

"Every manjack on this ship has been looking at them women," Finaren growled, "including meself. A fiery little wench like that, she gets a man's blood up. Trouble is, she knows it, too, the little tart. She could've had any man on this cog, yet she went out of her way to reach for you."

"Captain, I didn't mean for any of this to happen," Jherek said. "I've tried to stay away from the Amnians as you suggested."

It had been easy, in fact, since the merchants had partied constantly since being aboard ship and Jherek had never liked being around loud, raucous people. Drinking seemed to blur the lines of polite society, and take away even the rules a lot of good people stood by when they were sober.

"I know, lad. We've just got a wicket of trouble to deal with. The girl's father is demanding some kind of recompense."

"I could offer him an apology."

"That's good of you, but he's looking for something more along the monetary lines. I'm loath to give it to him. I can be a tight-fisted old miser meself, and I believe he knows what really happened betwixt you and that little tramp. He also knows I daren't tell him off without proof of it." He looked away, turning his attention back to the ship he'd spent so much of his life on.

Below, two members of the ship's crew sat in chairs mounted on the aft deck. Most of *Butterfly*'s supply of fresh fish was taken up in nets, but swordfish had been spotted running on the salt earlier. The meat was a delicacy, but the swordfish had a habit of tearing up nets. The sailors sat in the chairs and fished with hooks. It was a lot of work, but it saved the nets. The fishing had also become something of a pastime aboard ship, and men gambled over who would be the first to land a catch.

"Well, lad," Finaren said after a short time, "it's my problem to think on. I just wanted to get the right of it from you."

Jherek nodded, understanding full well the predicament the captain was in. "If there's anything I can do, let me know. I'll gladly do it."

Finaren looked at him with fondness, then dropped a heavy hand on Jherek's shoulder. "Aye, lad, I know that you would. You've been more honest with me than any man I've ever sailed with." He shook his head. "You've enough weight to bear, young Jherek, without dealing with the bilge offered by a selfish and conceited twit of a girl. No, I'll stand up and take care of this. Nobody's going to ramrod this ship but me. You just steer clear of any further encounters with those Amnians. I'll not have you spilling some young fop's guts and garters across my deck because he's trying to show out for Merchant Lelayn."

"Aye, captain."

"Have you had anything to eat, lad?"

"Not since morningfeast."

"The mid-day meal was an hour ago, lad."

"I didn't want to come down."

Finaren nodded. "I know. You stand steady up here. I know you like the solitude anyway. I'll have Cook put together a kit and have it sent up."

"Thank you."

"Faugh. It's nothing, lad. Not many men would have let that girl slap them and walk off the way you did. Nor would they have kept a civil tongue in their heads."

Jherek also knew of no other sailors who carried the dark secret he did. If that secret were to get out, it would see him clear of sailing—if it didn't get him killed outright. Captain Finaren had hired him on in spite of knowing the truth.

Yeill was wrong, Jherek knew, love did exist. He knew that because he loved the old sea captain for the way he accepted him in spite of the birthright that marked him. He watched Finaren nimbly descend to the lower decks, bellowing out orders to the ship's crew at once.

Some of the tense knot gripping Jherek's stomach released. He took a moment to himself and said a small prayer to Ilmater, the Crying God, asking for the strength to go on, then he returned to his work on the rigging.

By late afternoon, only an hour or so short of eveningfeast, the winds deserted *Finaran's Butterfly*. She slowed to the point of becalming, which was bad enough, but then the Amnians started drinking and partying again, deciding they were bored.

Jherek sat in the crow's nest, curled up with a novel of chivalric romance Malorrie had suggested. He'd also brought a treatise on civil disobedience that he fully intended to discuss with Malorrie when he reached Velen. The whole thought of civil disobedience, for the right reasons and under auspicious circumstances, was confusing. Jherek had read it twice during the voyage, and it still didn't set any easier on his mind. Right was right, and to suggest that it might not be right at times was too much for him to think on.

Taking a pause in the book, holding his place with a finger, he leaned over the edge of the crow's nest and looked down at the cheering and screaming Amnians thronging the ship's stern. His reading was getting increasingly harder as the roil of dark clouds coming in from the west took away his light. He wondered if they were in for another storm.

"Umberlee take the lot of them," Hagagne grumbled, climbing up the rigging to reach Jherek.

Hagagne was in his late thirties, a sallow man with loose skin that never seemed to quite brown enough and left him constantly reddened and peeling. He was bald on top and had an unruly fringe of hair around his head.

"What's going on?" Jherek asked the sailor.

"They've decided to fish," Hagagne answered, perching on the edge of the crow's nest as Jherek made room.

Jherek watched as deckhands brought the two fishing chairs out and set them up. Yeill and one of the Amnian young men sat in the chairs and belted themselves in with the leather restraint straps.

"They saw Marcle and Dawdré fishing earlier," Hagagne said, "and decided it would be great sport."

Jherek knew Marcle and Dawdré had done all right for themselves, bringing in ulauf and whitefish on the long poles as well as the swordfish. A lot of meat had been salted and put back in the ship's larder.

"They've even got a wager going on," Hagagne said with a harsh laugh.

Jherek looked the question at him.

"If the young bitch—"

"Please don't call her that," Jherek said, but his voice carried sheathed steel.

Hagagne shrugged, taking no offense. "If the young *lady*," the older sailor amended, "wins, she gets one of the dandy's breeding stallions, something he seems to be particularly proud of. If he wins, he gets to spend the night in her silks."

A cold depression settled over Jherek's shoulders.

"You liked her, didn't you lad?" Hagagne asked. "Even after that bit she done for you?"

"I don't even know her." Jherek watched the young woman with a heavy heart, knowing his words were more true than he'd thought earlier.

"You've a tender heart, Jherek. All you young brooding ones do." Hagagne pulled a pouch from his work apron and took out a pipe carved in the likeness of a sea horse. The sea horse's curled tail created the bowl. He filled it with pipeweed, lit up, and said, "Lucky for you it'll pass, and glad you'll be of it."

Once Yeill and her competitor were lashed in, the long fishing poles were attached to the chairs and locked in. As the hooks were baited, the gathered Amnians cheered again and passed around several bottles of the wine they'd been drinking since they boarded in Athkatla.

"Her father knows of the wager?" Jherek asked.

"Aye, and he was one of the first to encourage the competition. To hear him tell it, his daughter's luck is phenomenal." Hagagne grinned evilly. "Only we know about the one that got away, don't we, lad?"

Seeing no humor in the remark, Jherek refrained from responding.

Deckhands threw the baited hooks into the slight wake behind the cog. Yeill and her competitor worked the reels at once, letting more fishing line out. Another deckhand poured out a bucket of chum from the big barrel kept in the stern.

"What about the situation with the Amnians?" Jherek asked.

"You mean about the girl's da breathing down the cap'n's neck?"

"Aye."

"They reached an agreement."

Jherek felt even lower, wondering how much profit Finaren had lost because of him. Even volunteering to give up his wages for the trip wouldn't cover the loss, he was sure. "Do you know what it was?"

"Aye." Hagagne relit his pipe and smiled broadly. "The cap'n said he thought that Merchant Lelayn would hate to try to make a raft of his precious cargo and float it back to Athkatla from the Sea of Swords. The Amnian merchant, why, he agreed that was truly so."

"Why did he do that?"

"I got this story only secondhand, you understand," Hagagne said, "so I might not have the right of it, but I do know what was basically said."

Jherek waited impatiently. Hagagne was one to draw on his stories.

"Cap'n told Merchant Lelayn that he had him a crewman willing to take lashes from the cat over what that little bit—that daughter of his had done," Hagagne said. "Cap'n told him that he couldn't do no less than stand by his crewman, and he'd be damned if anybody was going to skipper this ship other than him. Also told Merchant Lelayn that he couldn't do any less than pay for ship's passage ahead of time now, what with all the confusion his daughter had caused."

"The fee was paid?" Jherek asked in disbelief.

Hagagne nodded, puffing on his pipe contentedly. "In gold. Neghram seen it himself."

Before Jherek knew it, a smile lifted his lips. Maybe his luck was finally changing.

"Not many cap'ns would have done what the cap'n done," Hagagne stated. His head was wreathed in pipeweed smoke. "I might not have believed it myself if I hadn't been on the ship that done it."

"Still," Jherek said, not able to fully shake the doubt that had lived within him all his life, "standing up for me might not have been the best thing to do. The Amnians will get word of what Captain Finaren has done and *Butterfly* will be on their black lists."

"Kind of thought the same thing, lad. Seems Merchant Lelayn mentioned that to the cap'n. Said he didn't care to do business with a man who didn't keep his mind on business. Then the cap'n, he told the Amnian that an honest man was worth his weight in gold to a man in business for himself, and the passage to and from Baldur's Gate aboard this ship didn't come close to that amount. Said him not standing up for you might mean losing you, and that was his bottom line."

Jherek knew that wasn't true. Getting a berth on a ship's crew had been hard, even in Velen. If it hadn't been for Madame Iitaar and his experience working in Shipwright Makim's yard, Captain Finaren wouldn't have given him a second glance. If not for *Butterfly*, he didn't know what ship he would have crewed aboard. There were too many experienced sailors in the Duchy of Cape Velen, and none of those bore his sins.

"In the end," Hagagne went on, "Merchant Lelayn agreed that the cap'n standing up for you *was* good business. Said when he got back to Athkatla, he'd put another cargo together and ship with *Butterfly* again."

"That is good news," Jherek said.

"Aye. With the cap'n and *Butterfly*, we'll do all right. Not many got the rep of either of those."

It was something to take pride in and Jherek did, even though the edicts of Ilmater preached against such feelings. He glanced back at the Amnians below. "I'll wish them good luck in their fishing."

"From up here," Hagagne suggested.

"Aye."

Hagagne gave him a side-long glance. "And hope that the lady wins so that she doesn't have to live up to her end of the wager?"

Jherek's face burned. Thoughts of the young woman sharing her bed silks with anyone didn't set easy with him even though she wasn't what he'd thought she was.

"Don't be so embarrassed, lad. Your heart's full of love at your age, and there's nothing wrong with it, but you could do with a little seasoning, if you'd allow yourself. I know some of the tavern wenches who wouldn't mind a tumble if you'd only ask."

Ignoring the comment, Jherek gazed up at the darkening clouds.

The storm seemed more threatening than ever. The shadows had chased the green from the Sea of Swords, turning even the water dark. Off in the distance, pale flickering lightning knifed through the sky.

"You reading again?" Hagagne asked, picking up the book.

"Aye."

"Never found a knack for reading meself," the crewman said, "but I like being read to well enough. What's this book about?"

"A liege's man," Jherek said. "He joined the king's army to fight against the goblin hordes threatening the kingdom, only to find that he's falling in love with his liege's lady."

"Does she know?"

Jherek nodded. "The lady's marriage was an arranged one. She doesn't love her liege. She loves the warrior."

"Perhaps when you have time, you'd read this one to me." Hagagne picked up the thick volume. "I'd predict a short, unhappy ending, but I tell by the heft of this book that's not the case."

"No." Jherek loved the intricacies of the plot, loved the way the liege's man was at war with his own feelings and the rules he'd laid down for himself. He still didn't know how the story would end. "Aye, I'll read it to you if you'd like."

Hagagne clapped him on the back. "Now there's a good lad. I shall look forward to it."

Jherek replaced the volume in his kit, brought to him earlier by a crewman the captain had sent up. His eye wandered back to the cog's wake to study the fishing lines. He and Hagagne watched in silence for a few moments, then watched Yeill's line suddenly draw taut.

A cheer rose from the throats of the Amnians, showing the effects of the wine they'd been drinking. It died away when the shark's dorsal fin broke the water.

The triangle of cartilaginous flesh looked impossibly large. The brute's gray mottled head broke water next, the fishing line trapped in its snarl of teeth.

The cheers turned to a panicked chorus of fear.

Jherek rose to his feet, yelling down from the crow's nest. "Cut the line! Cut the line!"

The line was stout, unbreakable. *Butterfly* had a large crew and she had to feed them. The Sea of Swords held big fish, and the captain wanted none of them to get away once they were hooked. The enchantment on the lines he'd paid for kept them from breaking, though they could be cut. Still, two men had been pulled from *Butterfly*'s deck before.

Captain Finaren himself moved first, shoving his way through the ring of Amnian wealthy. He drew his cutlass and pulled it back to swing.

Timbers groaned and screeched as Yeill's fishing chair yanked free of the deck and tore through the railing. She was gone in an instant, pulled under by the big shark she'd hooked.

Jherek stood in the crow's nest and drew his seaman's knife from his leg sheath. The knife blade was a foot long, thick and heavy, with a saw-toothed back for cutting through bone. The small handle barely filled his fist.

"Sea devils!" someone shouted.

Glancing to his left, Jherek saw a sahuagin manta surface on *Butterfly*'s port side. The oblong barge used by the sahuagin to travel above or below water was much smaller than most of its kind that the young sailor had heard described. Like all of its kind that he'd heard about, the manta had been cobbled together from ships wrecked at sea or scavenged from shorelines. The boards were stained green with undersea scud from being submerged for so long, but fitted neatly into a wedge shape that made it very maneuverable. It rode low in the water, but the finned shapes of the sahuagin could be seen hunkered down on the benches. They paddled furiously, moving in response to a measured cadence, totally focused on their prey.

Jherek had heard stories about mantas that crewed as many as six hundred sahuagin, but firsthand stories were few and far between. Most men who saw them perished in the sea devils' attack. From his initial estimate, he guessed that there were forty or fifty sahuagin aboard, easily twice the number of crew aboard *Butterfly*.

Captain Finaren bawled out orders at once, calling his crew into action.

Jherek looked at the water where Yeill had gone under. He couldn't see her.

"Lad," Hagagne called from the ship's rigging, already moving down to the deck himself. He stopped when he realized what Jherek was about to attempt. "Leave her. She's probably already in that shark's belly by now and not worth your life even if she isn't."

"I can't."

Hagagne reached back for the young sailor, but Jherek avoided the other man's grasp. Without another word, he dived from the crow's nest, plummeting toward the dark water.

2

Jherek hit the ocean cleanly, holding his hands before him to break the surface tension and lessen the chance of injury from impact. Still, the force of hitting the water nearly drove the breath from his lungs. The cold bit into him with jagged, angry teeth. The sahuagin manta was ahead and on the port side of *Finaren's Butterfly* so he knew he wouldn't immediately be seen by the sea devils aboard their barge.

He also knew that the shark that had taken Yeill's hook hadn't bitten by chance. The sahuagin ran with the sharks. He didn't doubt the danger that more sharks would be around as he attempted to save the Amnian woman.

The darkened sky above the ocean cut down on the visibility beneath the water as well. Pale colored sand covered the rolling ocean floor, and brain coral stood up in bunches, like tumors. A coral reef that housed dozens of multicolored fish hiding from the sharks ran in an irregular line to his right. As always, being below the ocean line filled Jherek with a sense of ease. Everything moved more slowly here, and it seemed more open to him than even the sky. He could feel the water, feel the pressure of it against his body, feel the current that mixed warm and cold water in layers. He felt at home there.

Jherek swam hard, the knife still clenched in his fist. The pressure on his ears told him he'd gone down thirty feet or more. He searched the water and spotted Yeill still in the fishing chair less than fifty feet from his position, sinking slowly. He turned toward her and swam hard.

Two sharks glided in sinuous circles around her, close but not closing in. One of them still had the fishing line in its mouth. Beyond the

33

sharks, three sahuagin clutching spears kept watch. They spotted him and did nothing but spread out, assuming he was fool enough to swim to his own death.

Jherek looked at them, matching all the stories he'd heard with the sight of the monsters before him. The sahuagin were huge in build, their bodies massive with muscle across the shoulders. Their legs with the extra joint looked grotesque. Broad faces with flaring fins sticking out into the water on either side of its head held dozens of narrow teeth, the black lips curled back to expose them in a threatening grimace. Their bite, Jherek had been told, could rip gobbets of flesh from a man, and the sea devils literally feasted on their victims, often before they died. Their tails whipped back and forth to help them maintain their position. The webbing between their long fingers and toes made their hands and feet look impossibly large.

Fear filled Jherek as he closed on the circling sharks, yet he was drawn to the act of attempting to save the young woman's life as surely as a compass needle was drawn north. He couldn't leave the young woman to her fate. Despite the water around him, his mouth was dry. He estimated that Yeill was less than twenty feet below the ocean's surface.

One of the sharks pulled away from the other and sped at Jherek, mouth gaping to reveal its teeth.

Without hesitation, Jherek dodged, kicking out hard and twisting in the water like a porpoise. All his life the water had been his element, and even though he moved well in a ship's rigging and on the ground, it was nothing like the way he moved in the water. He'd won every swimming meet he'd ever entered at Velen as a boy, and he'd dived deeper and better than anyone in the town, including seasoned sailors.

Madame Iitaar had suggested that it was because Jherek was linked to the sea, but even her powers of divination couldn't tell her how. Jherek only knew that there was no place he'd ever felt more at home. The years as a shipwright's apprentice on land watching ships he'd repaired and help build put out to sea had been hard, and he could never imagine living in a landlocked city.

Stroking furiously, he glided under the shark, missing it by inches. He decided not to use the knife. There was too much of a chance it would get stuck in the shark's body and he'd lose it. He didn't want the sharks in a blood frenzy.

His move caught the sahuagin by surprise as well. Evidently they'd felt confident of their shark's kill. Their finned heads turned to him as he swam to Yeill's side, their black eyes glinting with malicious light. The woman struggled with the seat restraints, trapped in the chair.

Jherek's blade freed her at once, slicing easily through the leather straps. He grabbed the Amnian woman, pulling her from the chair and shoving her toward the surface.

An explosion of bubbles came from the mouth of one of the sahuagin. Immediately, both sharks turned their attention to Jherek.

His lungs burned as he watched the sharks and sea devils. He knew from his studies that the sahuagin controlled sharks and used them for war as well as security, though that control was a tenuous thing at times. He gripped the ceramic teardrop Madame Iitaar had given him when he set to sea.

Back in Velen, Madame Iitaar was known as a diviner and alchemist. She couldn't easily craft healing potions or some of the more exotic potions, but most things that related to the sea she could make without problem. She'd given him a shark repellent potion in the ceramic teardrop.

With the teardrop in his hand, he waited till the sharks were within ten feet, silent gliding death. He crushed the ceramic teardrop in his hand, releasing the strong potion inside. A yellow glowing cloud filled the water around him, swelling out to envelope the sharks even before they were on him. He reached out with his free hand, catching the lead shark's blunt snout. The rough, sandpaper hide pressed against his flesh, but he used the shark's momentum with his own to slide above it.

By the time the shark slid under him, the potion took effect. Both sharks jerked spasmodically, reacting to the potion's unique alchemy. Madame Iitaar had told Jherek the potion would create deep fear in the sharks, causing them to flee for their lives, and she was as good as her word. The sharks spun around and began to accelerate gracefully away. The sea devils tried to command them back into the cloud of repellent, but the sharks were more afraid of Madam Iitaar's concoction than their sahuagin masters. As a result, the sharks turned on their controllers, recognizing them instead of the now fading yellow cloud as the source of the threat that filled their simplistic nervous systems. The sahuagin broke ranks at once.

One of the sharks succeeded in seizing a sahuagin in its jaws. A bloody cloud darkened the water, spreading outward. The second shark pursued one of the other sahuagin, leaving the third one free.

Lungs near to bursting from the time he'd been underwater and the effort he'd expended, Jherek stroked for the surface. He sensed the last sahuagin coming after him, cutting the distance in heartbeats, feeling the hate and excitement that it radiated, imagining he could almost read its thoughts.

He surfaced twenty feet from the young Amnian woman and drew in a deep lungful of breath. "Swim to the ship!" he ordered, gasping. "Now!"

He glanced ahead, seeing that *Butterfly* was coming about. Captain Finaren hadn't given up on them. Even though the cog turned hard about, filling the sails with the almost listless straight wind rather than the cross-breeze she'd been making do with all day, she kept her port side to the marauding sahuagin aboard the manta.

The young Amnian woman screamed and cried, and Jherek knew she was in real danger of causing herself to drown before she reached *Butterfly*.

He turned from her regretfully, aware now too that the sounds of combat came from the cog. He took a final breath, judging the sahuagin had to be almost on him, and dived beneath the water again. He blinked, trying desperately to clear his vision while the blood from the sahuagin and sharks clouded the water.

The third sahuagin swim-flipped and thrust its trident as Jherek sank into the water. It was less than fifteen feet out. Reacting quickly, knowing he had no chance to escape the wicked tines completely by attempting to dodge, he shoved his knife hand up. The blade connected with the trident, slipping unerringly between the tines and jarring against the base. The force of the blow vibrated Jherek's shoulder and elbow painfully. The scrape of metal on metal rang in his ears, though blunted by the water.

The sahuagin was on him, lashing out with talons from both hands and feet. Moving swiftly, faster than the wide-webbed foot that ripped up toward his midsection, Jherek grabbed the sahuagin's scaled ankle in his free hand while keeping the trident turned from him with the other. He used the foot's downward ripping action to shove himself down, gliding under the sea devil, then twisting to come up behind it. The unexpected move caught the sahuagin by surprise, but it moved to defend itself.

The creature slapped at Jherek with its tail, the gristled tip of it slashing a cut across his chest. Jherek ignored the pain of the wound and kicked hard, driving himself into position to reach out and capture the sahuagin's head in his free arm before it could move away.

The sea devil bucked and twisted, swimming in fear now instead of being so confident. Instinctively, the creature dived, heading for the depths that protected it from so much of the human race.

Struggling to maintain his grip against the pull of the ocean and his opponent's slick, scaled body, Jherek felt the pressure increase against his ear drums. Much past sixty feet, he knew, and he risked a case of the rapture of the deeps even if he survived to reach the surface. He'd seen men who'd survived the rapture, though their bodies had been bent and twisted forever by it.

Desperate, he located the sahuagin's sound chamber in back of its wide mouth by touch, then drove his blade through the thin membrane, up into its inner ear, and into the brain beyond. He didn't stop pushing until the hilt stopped against his opponent's jawline.

The sahuagin convulsed at once as death claimed it.

Spots spiraled in Jherek's gaze when he released the dead sea devil. Still jerking as its nervous system gave out, the sahuagin sank, disappearing into the lower reaches of the sea. The young sailor swam for the surface. He spotted the second shark, already floating belly-up, a silent testament to the deadly skills of the sahuagin. The sea devil that had slain it moved only feebly nearby, offering no threat.

After surfacing, Jherek allowed himself only two quick breaths to recharge his aching lungs, then struck out for *Butterfly*. He watched deckhands hang oil lamps along the starboard side of the cog, their first line of defense against the sea devils. The sahuagin fear of fire held them back at first, and the brightness of the light hurt their eyes.

He overtook Yeill while she was still seventy yards from the cog. The young Amnian woman struggled, barely keeping her face above the water. When he came up on her from behind, she screamed in fear and turned around to swat at him with her hands. As a result, she went down at once.

Jherek grabbed her, wrapping an arm under her jaw as they both sank. He returned the knife to his shin sheath, secured his grip on her, and pulled them both back up. "Stop fighting," he commanded in a rough voice, hoping to get through her fear.

"Jherek?" she gasped, looking up at him.

"Hang on," he told her.

She spat water and snuffled as she cried, "There are fish men attacking the ship."

He felt sorry for her then, in spite of everything else she'd done to him that day. For all her posing and wealth, she remained yet a child. "They haven't taken her," he replied, "and they won't."

"Jherek!" a voice called from above as *Butterfly* bore down on them. She was coming fast enough that white caps rolled along her bow.

"Here!" he shouted back, blinking his eyes to clear them of the saltwater.

"Valkur's brass buttons, boy," the sailor yelled down. "Jumping in shark-infested waters like that, you must figure you got some kind of charmed life. I tell anybody that back home, they're going to chase me out of the tavern for telling tall tales. I hadn't seen it myself, I'd have called the man who told me about it a liar."

Jherek kept swimming. He'd never fully understood the things that moved him, but he knew what he couldn't do, and he couldn't have left the woman to die.

"Skiff's coming down, but we're keeping it tied up. Watch 'er as she comes down."

"Come ahead," Jherek said, treading water and watching *Butterfly*'s approach, knowing it was going to be a near thing.

The skiff dropped down the side of the cog, the lines whirring through the pulleys. The little boat landed on the water with a flat *smack* that threw a wave of cold water over Jherek. Thinking she was going under again triggered another panic attack on Yeill's part. Jherek held her, speaking calmly to her as soon as their heads were above water again.

He reached out and grabbed the skiff's edge, feeling his bruised shoulder muscles writhe in agony as they took the sudden drag.

"I've got her, lad." Old Covvey, the sailor with the most seniority on *Butterfly*, took Yeill's wrist in his gnarled, scarred hand. He pulled her aboard the leaping skiff, dragged along through the cog's wake.

Jherek let the woman go, then caught the skiff's edge with his other hand and pulled himself aboard. He stepped over Yeill, who lay scared and shivering in the bottom of the skiff.

"Haul away," Jherek yelled up to the men manning the skiff's lines.

They started pulling at once, bringing the small craft up. They alternately railed against him and congratulated him on his success in saving the girl. The general consensus seemed to be that he'd gone insane, and everyone knew the gods favored those too stupid to save themselves.

Jherek didn't wait for them to tie the skiff off, knowing Covvey would take care of his charge. The young sailor leaped up and caught the hauling ropes and climbed. Level with the cog's railing, he swung his body out and landed lithely on the deck.

He scanned the opposite railing, seeing Finaren and the ship's crew hard pressed to defend against boarders. Despite the difference in height between the cog and the manta, the sahuagin attacked viciously.

"C'mon, you sea dogs!" Finaren bellowed at the rigging crew. "*Butterfly*'s no pig to be wallowing in the trough! Make her fly or I'll have the hide off your backs when we get to Velen!"

The ship's crew reacted to their master's voice. Wind cracked in *Butterfly*'s sails, creating distance from the sahuagin manta. The Amnian passengers stood balled up in the ship's prow, protective of their own circle.

Jherek raced across the pitching deck, pausing only long enough to take the cutlass and hook Hagagne offered. He had no special weapons, comfortable with any that found their way into his hands. Malorrie had seen to it that he was trained in a cross section of them.

"Glad to see you made it, lad," Hagagne stated with relief as he fell in behind. "Thought I'd never see you again after you diving into them sharks like that. You do it again, though, you better hope them sharks have at you. I'll chomp on you myself if they don't."

Jherek ran the cutlass and hook through his work apron strap, then took the short bow and quiver of arrows Hagagne offered. He was one of the better archers among the crew.

"Hawlyng!" Finaren yelled.

"Aye, Cap'n," Hawlyng responded.

"I'll want to be using that fire projector today, Hawlyng!"

"Aye, sir. I've got 'er up and ready. Just you say when."

"Now!" Finaren howled. "I'm up to my arse in these damned deep devils!"

Jherek stepped to the railing as the crew made room for him. He notched an arrow to the string as he surveyed the manta coming around. The sahuagin clung to the sides as well as manning the oars. Their scaled bodies writhed in the effort of propelling their craft along with the oars. With the darkening sky full of storm clouds, they were crouched in shadow, but Jherek could easily spot the silvery eyes that haunted many sailors' dreams.

A sahuagin drummer stood in the prow, croaking out a rhythm. Jherek recognized it as serving the same purpose as a drum beater on a trireme. Flaming arrows from *Butterfly*'s crew fell into the water and occasionally sunk home in the manta, creating bright spots of yellow flame against the darkness as they flew. When they hit the sahuagin craft, the oarsmen pulled back from the fires, but one of them would always fin a wave of water over it and put it out.

"You get that girl back?" Finaren asked.

"Aye." Jherek smoothed his wet hair back from his face, getting the measure of *Butterfly*'s lunges across the uneven ocean. They were rising and falling little over fifty paces opposite each other, but at the distance, that fifty paces stretched out even further, making shots difficult.

"Good," the captain growled, "but that was a damn fool thing you did."

"I couldn't let her drown or get eaten by a shark."

"You ever stop and think you ain't got much choice in some of those matters, lad?" Finaren sounded angry, hotter than Jherek had ever heard him.

Irritation and insecurity stung the young sailor at the same time. "You mean you think it's possible the sahuagin out there are going to take *Butterfly* this evening?" He meant it to come out harder, but he really wasn't sure. There were a lot of sahuagin out there.

"Not my ship," Finaren answered. "Leastways, not while I'm able to draw a breath. Now be a good lad and put a shaft through that croaking monstrosity in the prow. They have us on speed, but they're a brute while *Butterfly*'s a lady who knows how to dance. Still, they're going to run us down if we let them. Even this puny wind won't always be in our favor as we move around."

Jherek concentrated on his shot and loosed the fletchings. The arrow caught the sahuagin in the thigh, causing it to bark in pain. Still, it snapped the arrow off and went back to croaking cadence. The young sailor drew another shaft, watching the manta draw nearer. When the craft was less than thirty paces away, he released the second arrow.

The fletching suddenly appeared in the sahuagin's thickly muscled neck and the croaking halted immediately. It toppled over the side, clawing at its neck as it tried to dislodge the arrow.

"Hard to starboard!" Finaren shouted.

The boatswain yelled the order back and the ship's crew and helmsman made the adjustment. *Butterfly* came about regretfully, losing the wind and slowing immediately.

Jherek fired four more arrows, hitting targets scattered across the manta. The thick sahuagin hide turned two of his arrows as surely as chain mail when they didn't hit flush. At the distance, it was almost impossible to avoid hitting something.

Finaren held onto the railing as the ship crested a wave that slammed into her side. Quarrels from the sahuagin crossbows stuttered into *Butterfly*'s side and ripped through her sails. A man screamed only a few feet from Jherek, clutching the quarrel that suddenly appeared in his chest.

"It burns!" he screamed, falling to his knees. "Selûne watch over me." He lasted only a moment, praying fervently to his goddess before he passed out.

"Poison," Finaren noted. "Umberlee take them deep what use such things."

Jherek fired another pair of arrows before the manta closed on *Butterfly*. For a moment, he thought the sahuagin craft was going to strike the cog, then the manta cleared *Butterfly*'s stern by inches, charging past. The sahuagin hurled spears and tridents as they went by, croaking angrily.

The cog's crew started to cross over to the port side.

"Stay, you dogs," Finaran shouted. "Helmsman, bring us around harder to starboard. I want a hundred and eighty degree turn."

"Aye, cap'n," the helmsman called back.

Butterfly came about. Sailcloth cracked overhead as the crew flipped the booms around. She caught the full breeze again in heartbeats. The spinnaker blossomed like a night rose in full passion and pulled the ship forward.

"Crafty though them creatures may be," Finaren said, "they still don't understand the wind and what a kind mistress she might be."

Jherek watched as the sahuagin struggled to bring their craft under control. Finaran was right about the speed the sea devils had, and they would have outrun *Butterfly* had the attack led into a race.

"Bring her around, helmsman, toward them sea devils," Finaran commanded. "I want to shear her oars off on the port side. In another minute we're going to wake them up to what a war at sea is all about."

The manta almost stalled in the water as the sahuagin struggled to regain control of their craft. They floundered, struggling to turn the manta around.

"They got no draw on that boat," Finaren said. "It sits flat on the water, and once they get it started in a direction, they can make it go fast, but maneuverability becomes an issue. Hawlyng . . ."

"Aye, cap'n?"

"That fire projector, Hawlyng, are you ready with it?"

"Aye, sir."

Jherek glanced over his shoulder and saw the fire projector mounted on pivots come around to point at the stalled manta. The projector's maximum range was forty yards. At the moment, the manta was out of range, but the young sailor didn't doubt that it would come in again.

"Helmsman," the captain called out, "shear them oars. The rest of you dogs hold onto to whatever you got, and Umberlee take them beasties what's come upon us!"

3

Butterfly bore down on the manta, speeding closer. The sahuagin stared at her, their silvery eyes picking up light from the oil lamps swinging crazily from the railing. A renewed flurry of spears and quarrels thudded against the cog, finding few targets. A sailor went down with a trident through his guts, squalling in fear and pain.

Jherek held himself steady, an arrow pulled back. When *Butterfly* came down again, her prow nosing toward the manta, he fired arrows as quickly as he could draw the string. Even under Malorrie's tutelage, he didn't come close to the skills of an elf bowman in terms of speed, but he was deadly accurate at this range. He aimed at the sahuagin on the port side of the manta, driving them back into their shipmates when they fell.

A string of sharp thundering cracks followed *Butterfly* as she sheared through the sahuagin oars on the manta's port side, her prow cracking the paddles like kindling. When they finished the pass, Jherek saw that nearly every oar on that side of the sea devils' craft had been splintered and rendered useless.

A ragged cheer ripped free of the throats of *Butterfly*'s crew.

"Hawlyng," Finaren bawled.

"Aye, Cap'n."

"Have you got that thrice-damned craft of fishy blackhearts in your sights?"

"Aye, Cap'n."

"Fire away and send 'em back to Umberlee's caresses."

The fire projector belched a thin stream of flaming, explosive liquid that served immediately to drown the cheers of the cog's crew. Most sailors didn't like the weapons. They sat like waiting death on a ship's deck, as able to work against a crew as for one. Jherek had seen them explode on ships' decks during battle before, ruptured by a catapult shot. Twice, damaged fire projectors had sent both ships to the ocean floor before any real salvage could be made.

Against the sahuagin, it was the most frightful weapon for the sea devils outside of magic.

The launched flames showered down over the manta, catching even the wet wood and the sahuagin unlucky enough to be standing there on fire. Sahuagin worked immediately to put the fire out, but oil-based as it was, they only spread it for the moment and made it burn hotter.

In the stern, Hawlyng shouted curses at the sahuagin from beside the fire projector. He didn't see the first of the sea devils climbing over the railing of the cog's squared stern castle. Before anyone could shout a warning, the sahuagin threw a spear that caught the mate in the side, pinning him to the stern castle walls.

"Clear that stern, you flea-bitten rum dogs, and Umberlee take any that lags behind!" Finaren shouted.

Jherek tossed the bow aside and slid the cutlass and hook free. He ran for the stern, charging up the starboard side steps that led into the stern castle with the other sailors. The lead sahuagin thrust out with its trident, intending to impale Hawlyng again.

Swinging the hook, Jherek caught the tines of the trident and yanked them aside. They buried in the wooden deck. Before the sahuagin could recover, the young sailor thrust the point of his cutlass between the creature's open jaws. Fangs snapped off at the impact, and the sword slid through the back of the sahuagin's neck. Jherek twisted the blade savagely, making sure to cut the sea devil's spine. Even if it didn't die right away, it was paralyzed.

Butterfly's crew crowded onto the stern castle, and the sounds of battle swamped over Jherek. The young sailor pulled his cutlass free with effort, then kicked the sahuagin backward as Malorrie had taught him. The creature's dead weight slammed into two of his fellows and drove them all backward into the ocean again.

"Die hu-*maan*!" a sahuagin snarled in the common tongue as it stabbed at Jherek with a trident. Its voice out of the water, wrapping around unaccustomed words, sounded flat and out of breath, a nightmarish gasp of rage and hate.

The young sailor turned the trident with the cutlass, losing the sword's use for a moment while it was trapped in the tines. The sahuagin swiped at him with its free hand, the talons black and sharp as razors.

Unflinching, Jherek took the attack to the sahuagin rather than retreating. All the fear inside him was concentrated on survival, and Malorrie's training made sure each move he made was smooth as Dalelands spider silk. He swept the hook up, catching the sahuagin's hand and driving the curved point through the creature's palm, stopping it only inches from his face. Before the sahuagin could react either to the counterblow or the pain, Jherek headbutted it in the face.

Off-balance, the sahuagin stumbled backward. Still holding the impaled hand on the hook, Jherek slid back and freed the cutlass with a slither of metal on metal that threw off sparks. He swung with all his might at the sahuagin's corded neck. The heavy blade bit deeply into his opponent's flesh, almost cutting through. It dropped with a harsh gargling croak, then died.

Jherek freed his weapons, watching as Finaren swung an oil lantern into the face of another boarding sahuagin. The lantern shattered and oil covered the creature's head, wreathing it in flames. It screamed horribly, clawing at its face, then toppled back into the dark water. The scent of burned flesh clung to the stern castle, overwhelming even the fishy musk from the sahuagin.

"Hold us steady, helmsman," Finaren commanded. "Keep us into the wind and let's put this place behind us."

Jherek fought on, slashing at his opponents. Two sailors went down around him, both with grievous wounds. He kept himself poised, riding out the pitch and yaw of *Butterfly* as she sailed across the ocean. He cut and thrust, blocking a dagger thrust with the cutlass, then ripping a sahuagin's throat out with the hook.

One of the passengers at the top of the port stairs threw out his hands, thumbs touching. Jherek caught the movement from the corner of his eye. Flames shot from the passenger's fingers, arcing across the stern castle and splashing across three sahuagin. All three sea devils released their holds on the stern railing and dropped into the ocean.

Catching a trident thrust by another sahuagin with the hook, Jherek turned it aside and kicked the sea devil in the face. He followed with a thrust through the creature's heart. Thrusting the hook through the sahuagin's harness, he dragged the body to the railing to clear it from the stern deck. He sheathed the cutlass and grabbed one of the corpse's legs and levered the body over the railing.

A sahuagin net spun up at him from a sea devil clinging to the ship's stern. It settled over the young sailor before he had a chance to move. Cruel fish hooks woven into the net bit into his flesh. Blood flowed from a dozen small injuries as the net drew tight.

Jherek screamed in pain, instinctively pulling back against the net in an attempt to escape. The effort only drove the hooks more deeply into his flesh. Luckily, there was no burn of sahuagin poison, but the weight and the strength of the sahuagin at the other end pulled him forward. He caught the edge of the railing in one hand and with the hook, watching as the hooked bits of his skin stood out. The pain ripped another scream from his throat.

A cold voice entered his mind. *Live, that you may serve.*

Fire leaped from one of the burning sahuagin still on deck onto the net. The strands parted like hairs over an open flame.

Jherek stumbled back onto the deck. The pain from the hooks was sharp and tearing, almost blinding in its intensity, but he saw that the sailors had successfully broken the sahuagin attack. The manta still burned in the distance, looking like a single torch in the night. Sea devil corpses littered *Butterfly*'s wake, catching the pallor of the lightning flashing through the wine-dark clouds overhead.

Claustrophobia tightened over Jherek more tightly than the net. He didn't like closed in places. Hooking his fingers in the net, he started pulling, hoping to dislodge some of the hooks.

"Stand easy, lad," Finaren ordered, striding close. "Damned nets are hard to get away from. Lucky that this one got burned the way it did."

Jherek took a deep breath and relaxed the way Malorrie had taught him. He distanced the fear, giving himself over to the peaceful pitch and yaw of *Butterfly*'s rolling deck. Finaren hadn't seen the way the net had parted.

"Carthos, Himtap," Finaren called out, "get some snips and get the lad free of that net." The captain regarded Jherek. "You stay here, lad. I got the rest of me crew to look in on, and some of them need burying. I got to save them what I can."

"Aye, sir." Jherek started to nod, then stopped when the hooks pulled at his flesh. One of them had embedded in the back of his head.

Finaren walked away.

Jherek crouched and slid his knife free of the shin sheath. Hagagne joined him, working gently to cut away the strands of the net. The first thing to do was cut sections of it away, then go after the individual hooks.

Malorrie's training allowed him to ignore the majority of the pain, but it was still difficult. Cutting the strands became automatic, and he turned his thoughts to the cold voice that had whispered to him.

Live, that you may serve.

He'd heard the command before. The first time had been when he was a child, fallen from his father's ship during a battle and nearly drowned. The voice had been more gentle, then, but perhaps he only remembered it that way. At that time, a dolphin had swum close to him and nosed him to the surface. His life had been spared then, as it had probably been spared this night, and there was no clue why, or by whom.

It had been three years since he'd last heard the voice. He'd thought it might be gone for good, with no explanation of why it had involved itself with him. Even Madame Iitaar with all her magic, and Malorrie with his insight, could offer no illumination concerning the voice. All of them, however, did what they had to, drawn together by whatever mystery linked them. Both his mentors had offered only the consolation that when the time came to know, he would.

Live, that you may serve.

But serve what? And why hadn't he been given more direction?

"You saved my daughter's life, and for that I owe you."

Jherek shivered as Hagagne poured whiskey from Captain Finaren's private stock onto the small wounds made by the fish hooks. Twenty-three of them had been removed from the young sailor's flesh. The process had been demanding and painful. Once free of the sahuagin net, the ends of the hooks had been snipped, then the barbs twisted around and pressed back out the flesh at a different spot than the entry point. The wounds had doubled in number. He stood in the stern castle, stripped to the leather work apron that had been proof against the net hooks.

"You don't owe me anything," Jherek replied, returning Merchant Lelayn's gaze full measure. "Captain Finaren takes care of his passengers."

"Take *something*," Hagagne whispered hoarsely as he sloshed the whiskey over the wounds in the young sailor's back. "By Umberlee's eyes, you jumped into a sea of sharks to save the bi—girl."

Jherek knew he couldn't. Anything he took would only tie him to the memory of the young Amnian woman and what had gone between them, and he didn't want that. He'd been wrong about her and that confused him. His passion toward her, toward what he thought she was, had seemed true. Even if he'd chosen not to act on it, the memory of her face would have filled some of the empty nights he experienced these days. Now he would remember only her harsh words and the slap. The price was too high. He shook his head.

"I can be very generous, boy."

"I'm sure that you can, sir," Jherek said, "but there's nothing I need."

"You're a deckhand, for Lliira's sake," the Amnian merchant blustered. "Surely there's something you could use."

A turban covered his head and a fiercely forked beard thrust out from the bottom of his chin. He was a fat man dressed in silks, and Jherek smelled the perfumes and spices he wore on his body.

"No," he said softly. "I thank you for the offer."

Finished with Hagagne's ministrations and wanting to get away from Yeill's hostile gaze, not really understanding how she could be angry with him, Jherek picked up his cutlass and the hook. Both weapons badly needed cleaning.

Yeill and her father talked behind him, a frenzy of conversation that he chose to ignore. Four men had died in the sahuagin attack. The ship's crew had packed their bodies in the hold, to take back to their families in Velen. Wet sand covered the scorched places in the deck where the fire projector and the mage's spell had started brief fires. Finaren already had his ship's mage out assessing the damage, which appeared minimal to Jherek.

Hagagne followed Jherek. "You're a hero, lad, you should take something."

Jherek made his voice hard. "No."

"They'll view it as disrespectful."

Turning to the man, the young sailor said, "I can't take anything from them. Don't you understand?"

Hagagne looked back into Jherek's eyes, then gave a heartfelt sigh. "Aye, lad, I guess that maybe I'm not so old that I've forgotten how harsh that first bloom of youth can be. I've an alternative, though, if you're willing to hear it."

Jherek listened.

"Take something for the crew," Hagagne urged. "Saving Ulnay and Morrin used up the last of the healing potions the cap'n had on hand. He wouldn't admit it and doesn't know that I know that, but I do. Them Amnians, they took on a shipment of healing potions in Baldur's Gate. They can spare some to replace what we used defending them."

The option made sense, but Jherek still didn't like it. He wanted nothing more to do with the Amnians. He took a deep breath to collect himself, then turned back to Merchant Lelayn and Yeill and said, "There is something."

"Name it," the Amnian merchant stated.

Jherek noticed the reluctance in the man's demeanor, though. Merchant Lelayn didn't mind offering to give, but the giving left him cold. "Healing potion, sir."

"A smart lad could do all right by himself reselling it." The Amnian merchant nodded in grudging approval and said, "How much do you want for saving my favorite daughter's life?"

"Whatever you think you can spare, sir," Jherek replied. "I won't haggle with you."

The answer seemed to surprise the merchant. He snapped his fingers and one of his men came forward. "Take ten healing potions from our stores and see that the boy gets them."

Jherek bowed his head in thanks. At the price the potions could command, Merchant Lelayn was being quite generous.

Captain Finaren joined them, his blouse stained with burn holes from the fire that had splattered from the lantern he'd smashed. Soot and blood stained his beard and face.

Merchant Lelayn turned to the captain. "Do you know how the sahuagin came to attack this vessel out of those upon the sea today?"

Finaren's eyes narrowed. "Anybody who travels the Sword Coast knows that the sahuagin are a danger. A man making his living at sea, he's taking risks. I've never encountered them before today, and maybe I was well overdue."

"You profess it to be merely bad luck, Captain?" Lelayn challenged.

Jherek chose to walk away, not believing the Amnian merchant could waver between being so generous, then turning so petty. His wounds stung. In truth, some of them hurt badly and a couple needed stitches that Finaren had put in himself. Once he got back to Velen, he knew Madame Iitaar would finish healing him properly.

He stood by the mast, watching Yeill. Even in her wet clothes, the merchant's daughter was beautiful. His wounds and the fatigue that always settled in after a battle dulled his senses. He was grabbed roughly from behind before he knew it, and someone slid a knife up under his chin.

"Don't you try anything," a gruff voice commanded. "Or I'll slit you from wind to water."

Jherek froze, the knife biting lightly into his flesh. He smelled the spice and perfume that covered the man holding him, knowing at once that he was one of the Amnian party. His guess that the man was one of the sellswords employed by the Amnians was proven correct when he saw the man's bracer with the house crest on it.

Finaren turned toward them, his bearded face brimming with anger. "What in the nine hells do you think you're doing?" His voice cracked with authority, and every sailor within hearing distance turned at once, their hands upon their swords and daggers.

"Our being attacked was no mere bad luck," the Amnian sellsword stated angrily. "We were set up, Merchant Lelayn, and here's the evidence of it."

Jherek realized for the first time that he'd been walking around without his shirt. That fact was brought home to him even more when another Amnian sellsword grabbed his left arm and twisted it viciously. The sellsword held a torch close to reveal the colorful tattoo inside Jherek's left bicep.

The tattoo featured a flaming skull wearing a mask of chains leaving only the eyes and fanged mouth unbound. It didn't look like anything human. It wasn't supposed to. It was part of the legacy left him by his father.

"Do you recognize this mark, Merchant Lelayn?" the sellsword asked.

"Falkane's claiming mark," the merchant spat. "There's a price on the head of any pirate from Falkane's ship." He turned back to Finaren. "Maybe you'd like to explain how you came to get one of the bloodiest pirates of the Sea of Swords aboard your ship . . . as part of your crew."

Jherek's breath tightened in his throat. He glanced around at *Butterfly*'s crew, seeing the surprised looks on their faces. None of them had known. It had been his secret, his and Finaren's. Now the secret was out and very likely to get him killed. His bad luck still claimed him, leaving him no one to turn to.

The knife at his throat didn't waver.

4

Laaqueel glided through the dark waters outside Waterdeep Harbor, staying in the shadow of the pentekonter on the surface above her and mentally preparing herself for the coming battle. She swam just under the ship, between the oars that swept the water on either side of it. Her pale skin made her stand out in the darkness, not blending in like her fellow sahuagin did or even a sea elf would. Below her, the ocean floor looked dark and was kept clean of debris. She knew the mermen who lived in the waters around Waterdeep helped keep the area orderly. They were also one of the major threats to the subterfuge they were attempting.

The unaccustomed cold of the northern waters chilled her. This early in the year, chunks of ice still floated whole through the Sea of Swords, frozen islands reminding her of how far from home she'd swam.

The cold numbed her body, but her mind ran unfettered by discomfort. Her thoughts were filled with grim doubts and she murmured a constant prayer to Sekolah that they might be granted success.

The pentekonter was sixty feet long and stood tall in the water. It had a rounded prow that made it look sluggish, but whether pushed by wind or pulled by oars, it moved quickly for a surface dweller's craft. Two banks of oars, one of them below the raised deck, allowed even greater speed when necessary. Hollow outriggers helped the ship maintain stability, and promoted the use of the second bank of oars.

Big as it was, the ship provided plenty of cover for the malenti and the dozen or so sahuagin that had needed to immerse themselves in the life-giving sea again for a short time during their voyage. Less than two hundred yards away, her sensitive vision picked up the underwater torches marking the boundaries of Deepwater Isle. Along with the warships that patrolled the nearby waters, it was Waterdeep's first line of defense.

In all of her life, she'd never been this close to the city. Waterdeep was called the City of Splendors, and from her vigil aboard the pentekonter, she knew the name was well deserved.

Some of the tall buildings in the different wards were impressive. They jutted up from the cityscape, possessing color and character that were unique. Those in the Castle Ward, especially Waterdeep Castle, were works of art even to her eyes. The daring plunge from the cliffs to the sea in the North Ward had taken her breath away even seeing the area from afar. Sahuagin villages were built close to the ocean floor, depending on tunnels to link them. In the water, heights only gave an enemy more area to attack. Gravity wasn't as forceful in the ocean as it was in the air.

At another time she thought she might have liked to walk along the winding and hilly streets of the city just to see what was there. It was a city worth exploring—after the surface dwellers had been driven from it.

That was what Iakhovas intended to do this very night.

She was certain that Iakhovas wasn't telling all he knew, or revealing all that he wanted in tonight's raid. He never did. Waterdeep had over one hundred thousand people in the city, more than four times the forces Iakhovas had gathered for the attack.

Thanks to the humans Iakhovas and his other malenti spies had paid off over the last three years in preparing for tonight, they had good maps of the city. Iakhovas had made certain of that. Even now thinking of him and knowing how he schemed and sacrificed her people made the obsidian quill lodged next to her heart grow too hot to be comfortable. Over the years of their relationship, she'd learned the quill allowed him to control her through pain and kept him informed on when she told truth or falsehood. Never a day had gone by that she didn't know it was there.

She breathed in through her mouth, taking the water and pushing it through her gills, flushing her system. For fifteen years, since that night in the underground tomb in the Shining Sea, she'd served him, watching him grow and take the power she'd wanted and was prevented from having by an accident of birth.

Still, there had been changes that benefited her. She was now High Priestess in her village. Iakhovas had made himself one of the nine princes, and that was only during the times he deigned to stay with the sahuagin. There were plenty of absences he had that were never explained. Nor was she in a position to demand answers, though at times she sorely wanted to.

"Most favored one," a nearby sahuagin called to her.

"Yes," she asked.

The sahuagin male bowed his head in deference and said, "Prince Iakhovas requests that you join him."

She dismissed him with a wave of her hand then swam toward the opening in the bottom of the ship above her. The sahuagin had captured the vessel in the Moonshae Isles almost two years ago then quietly sunk it so the repairs Iakhovas wanted could be done. One of those changes had been the construction of a water well amidships that allowed sahuagin entry to the ocean. They could stay out of water for four hours at a time, but immersion for an equal amount of time was required before they were back at full strength.

Swimming through the well, Laaqueel continued on through the submerged lower compartment where sahuagin rowers worked the massive oars to propel the craft. They all looked at her, respect in their silvery eyes. The pentekonter's outriggers were attached to the hull and had been specially modified to compensate for the hole in the ship's hull, letting the ship ride lower in the water.

Grabbing the ladder leading up to the ship's second level, Laaqueel pulled herself from the water, automatically feeling the dryness in the air even at sea level, and the extra weight from sheer gravity. She hated being out of the water, resonating with the fear that never quite left her no matter how much experience she had with being on the surface.

Her breath tightened as it ran through her gills. Breathing air was hard work, and she always remained conscious of having to inhale and exhale. In addition, her movements were no longer as fluid as they were in the water. She felt heavier on the surface. She was always acutely aware that her lateral lines no longer sent information to her. Water dripped from her as she walked, draining from her hair and body, and the sahuagin harness she wore.

Thirty men occupied the ship's upper hold. Short and thin, dressed in common clothing and carrying short swords, they didn't look threatening, but the sewer stench that clung to them made everyone give them a wide berth. All of them furtively stared after her with lust because of her near-nudity.

She ignored their interest. Choosing to dress as a sahuagin had been her choice, and she wasn't going to be bothered by them. They knew their place in the forces of Prince Iakhovas, and they knew their place around her after she'd killed the first one who'd touched her.

Iakhovas had assembled these men even as he had the four ships that made up their invasion force. All of them suffered from the curse of lycanthropy, changing forms between human and rat as easily as a sahuagin might strap on another harness.

Laaqueel would rather have taken the whole shipload of wererats to the bottom of the Sea of Swords and drowned them. She went up the stairs leading out of the hold onto the deck. Giving her sight a moment to adjust to the surface conditions, she turned and found Iakhovas standing in the prow.

"Laaqueel," he called out to her in that strong, whispering voice. He stood with his arms folded over his chest, staring out over the port city. He sensed her without facing her.

"I'm here, exalted one," she said.

"Of course you are." Iakhovas turned to her, a smile on his hard face.

He'd grown since she'd found him those years ago. In fifteen years, he'd grown stronger as he found those things that had been lost to him. She accompanied him on some of those forays, following him to hidden places in the sea where they found objects that still remained mysterious to her.

One of the first had been a circlet that gave him control of some sea creatures, giving him the power to communicate and order them about. He'd taken that from some of the mermen who'd relocated to Waterdeep and now lived in underwater caves off Waterdeep Isle. Another had been the bloodstone globe that allowed him to control weather that Laaqueel had to assassinate a Calishite gem merchant for when he raised his price to something more than she could afford. She'd narrowly escaped with her life during that mission.

Iakhovas had never taken her into his confidence, though, never explained himself to her. Nor did he tell her much of the objects he had collected. Later, he'd employed groups that went out to retrieve the objects for him, using any who could be bought or bribed, including the morkoth who were lifelong enemies of the sahuagin. He still did.

One group of pirates worked in the Sea of Fallen Stars for him, gathering objects as well as information. When they had an object, they sent it through a dimensional door that connected the pirate's ship to the sahuagin palace. With those objects in his possession, Iakhovas had grown more powerful, and he'd grown physically. At first, Laaqueel hadn't been certain of the correlation, but she was certain now. Though she'd tried to spy on him, she couldn't. She even thought he'd been leading her on at times, letting her almost see, tantalizing her with his secrets only to take them away at the last moment.

At present he was head and shoulders taller than Laaqueel, and he no longer looked emaciated. His body had filled out, becoming broad and supple. The runic tattoos spread out to fill the extra skin, but still hadn't become any more legible to her. He wore a black silk blouse and black breeches with silver buckles and chains over black boots. A sea-green cloak hung from his shoulders to his ankles, more an affectation than any real comfort from the cool breezes swirling through the port city.

Laaqueel stopped in front of him and waited.

Only running lanterns glowed on board the pentekonter, enough to obey the Waterdhavian harbor rules. Little of the deck was occupied, but the sailors were more of the wererats Iakhovas had involved in the raid.

The weak light traced patterns across Iakhovas's face. He would have been handsome by human standards, Laaqueel knew, even with the scars that tracked his features. No matter what magic he'd worked over the past fifteen years to rebuild himself, he hadn't been able to remove those scars. He'd grown a short beard and mustache that covered some of them. A sea-green patch that matched his cloak covered his empty eye socket. Even his hair had grown, filling in the patchy areas and dropping past his shoulders now, turned coal black.

"How may I aid you, exalted one?" she asked.

"Why, little malenti, I merely wanted you to join me at the beginning of our triumph over the surface dwellers," he stated. He shifted, lithe as a dancer on his feet in spite of the moving deck. "You have your own desires for power, though it's remained somewhat elusive for you in spite of the fact I've raised your station in life and among your own people. I've recognized you for your worth though they didn't. For all of your years of support, you deserve that." He waved a hand at the port city, then clasped it into a fist. "I would offer you a kingdom, little malenti, if I ever cared enough to share."

Laaqueel knew him well enough to know that was the real reason. Iakhovas wanted an audience for his conquest—an audience who knew all of the truths, or at least knew more of the truths than the sahuagin tribes who'd listened to him did. He loved the complexities of his own plotting, and the layers of subterfuge he manipulated seemingly so easily, loved the way his whispering voice seemed to have a hypnotic effect on those who listened. He had the power to advance his ideas and make others believe they'd thought of them.

"Gaze upon Waterdeep, little malenti, which the surface dwellers descry and proclaim as the crown jewel of all Faerûn," Iakhovas said. "I have been told that people journey to this place, expecting to enjoy pleasures they don't have at home, and feel safe and secure in their rented beds." He smiled, and the expression was filled with evil. "Ah, but tonight, tonight we strip that from them, never more to return, as we shatter the spine of her navy."

The Waterdhavian Naval Harbor lay farther to the north, managing two water gates of its own. The navy was one of the chief concerns the malenti had about the night's raid. The Waterdhavian Navy had always defended the shores of the city well, and of course there were the mermen.

"We've not gotten the bulk of our forces past the harbor gate yet," she reminded.

Despite the power he held over her and the potential he offered, she couldn't always simply agree with him. He was no true sahuagin, even though the others believed he was. In the intervening years, she'd come to understand why the sahuagin of her own tribe hadn't readily accepted her even after Baron Huaanton had named her as a protected ward after her birth. Her own exterior was an accident of birth. Iakhovas only masqueraded as a sahuagin. In her heart, she was sahuagin.

She'd helped him manage that masquerade only through coercion, and even now it didn't set well with her. After she'd found him, he'd made her spend two years with him in the Veemeeros where she'd found him, teaching him about Faerûn. Everything seemed new to him, but he was careful not to reveal anything about his own origins. Even Laaqueel's spy training hadn't helped her gather information about him.

Once they'd returned to her village, he'd used his powers to turn himself into a sahuagin hatchling, and she'd introduced him into a hatchling area. He'd maintained his own development in the village, but had kept contact with Laaqueel. She had named him in the brief ceremony after the surviving hatchlings were introduced into the tribe, giving him his own name at his request, though it wasn't a sahuagin name. Everyone in the village had believed it was because she was malenti, wanting to flaunt her difference, but Baron Huaanton had allowed the name to stand.

Now, though, Baron Huaanton was King Huaanton and Iakhovas, though only age thirteen in the sahuagin years, was a prince. Normally it took almost three hundred years to attain such a rank by serving the community and taking advantage of events that transpired, but he had used his magic and curried favor with Huaanton by maneuvering a duel with Huaanton's senior and killing the last prince in battle. Unable to take the position himself because of the sahuagin code regarding such advances, Huaanton had become prince. Huaanton had also realized how dangerous Iakhovas was for the first time and had stood behind Iakhovas's bid for the baronial vacancy. None of the other chieftains had tried to challenge his right to do that. When Huaanton had slain the last king and taken over the position, he'd promoted Iakhovas again. Laaqueel had never discovered if it was because Huaanton feared Iakhovas, or if the sorcerer had helped place Huaanton on the throne.

"Oh, little malenti, do you have such a small faith?" he asked.

"No," she admitted, choosing not to react to the insult. Her faith resided where it always had: with Sekolah. She had received no sign that she wasn't doing exactly as the Great Shark wanted her to, "but the forces arrayed against us are formidable."

He turned and gazed again out across the harbor. "Those forces are only formidable when pitted against a lesser opponent. Make no mistake, little malenti, I'm not that and never have been." He smiled, oozing confidence. "No one these days has ever seen anything like me. Even in my own day, no one was like me."

"But to take Waterdeep . . ." Laaqueel said.

"Stand corrected, little malenti, we're not *taking* Waterdeep," Iakhovas said. "We're presenting the surface world their options, throwing down the gauntlet so to speak. The surface dwellers need to be put on notice that they're living near these waters only on my sufferance. I will take back that which is rightfully mine no matter how many of them have to perish." He touched the patch covering his empty socket unconsciously. "I will be made whole again, and I will reclaim my proper station as the oceans' master."

"If we can't take the city, why send all these sahuagin to their deaths?" she asked.

"More humans will die this night than sahuagin," he told her. "You have my promise on that."

The way that he always referred to the humans as their species, and a despised one at that, let Laaqueel know he didn't consider himself one of them. For awhile she'd thought he might be of elven blood, but he had the gills and webbed hands and feet of a sea elf and used magic as easily as a sahuagin spilled blood. The accursed sea elves knew no magic except for that granted to their priests and priestesses.

He offered no clue as to what he truly was.

His power of illusion was incredible, steeping him in layers of deceit and trickery. She wasn't certain if she'd ever seen the true being she knew as Iakhovas. The sahuagin recognized him as a fellow being, and the wererats and other humanoids saw him as one of their own, even when they were all standing in the same place, and no one questioned it.

"Why should any sahuagin die if it's not necessary?" she asked.

"Because, little malenti, I have need of their deaths, and they must prove their fealty to me if I'm to champion their cause in this world." Iakhovas surveyed the nearing warning lights of Waterdeep Harbor. Anchored buoys clanged in the distance near Deepwater Isle, warning of the shallows there. "Sacrifices must be made. As I've learned, this is the last day in Ches, a time of holidays in Deepwater."

Laaqueel had learned that even as Iakhovas had. The Waterdhavians called the festival Fleetswake. During that time the mariners and the city gave homage to Umberlee, the dread sea goddess. Umberlee's Cache lay in the belly of the sloping bowl of Deepwater Harbor on the other side of Darkwater Isle. In years past, offerings to Umberlee had been dropped on the harbor floor, then mermaid shamans had broken that floor open to the great cavern system below that no one had ever mapped out. Every now and again, the malenti spotted the magical beam of the lighthouse near Umberlee's Cache skate below the dark waters ahead of them. It was used to guide the merfolk that were part of Waterdeep's defense hierarchy.

"The promise and bounty of Fleetswake convokes ships from over all Faerûn, giving the surface dwellers a dream of shared peace and prosperity," Iakhovas went on. "Traders, warriors, craftsmen, bards, and thieves, all will be represented on those cobblestone streets. There will be many in Waterdeep to tell the tale of the battle this night. They will spread that tale to the corners of all Toril, their wagging tongues making the story larger and more intense as it is passed along."

"The surface dwellers could be incited to hunt the sahuagin down."

Iakhovas laughed loudly. "Little malenti, let them come. Let them rise above their cowardice, strap their weapons about their loins, and sail out into these seas that I have marked as mine. If they sail out into the sea after us, they sail only to their deaths. In fact, it will only help my cause if part of this war is played out in our element. We can bare our teeth and our claws, and show them the foolishness of any sort of resistance. It will also serve to threaten the other sahuagin tribes who haven't seen fit to join our effort."

"The surface dwellers could unite."

Iakhovas shook his head. "Not according to everything I've studied about these jealous cultures," he told her. "These nations of surface dwellers have long histories of bitter feuds and rivalry over trade agreements, religion, and politics. What countries can hope to survive if they follow a path laden with those traps and snares? No, even should they endeavor to agree on a common enemy, we shall own the seas. In their limited intelligence and greed, the surface dwellers may have learned to cross the oceans, but they'll never master them, never the way I have."

Laaqueel had other doubts that she almost voiced. She didn't, though, since she knew Iakhovas would counter each of them with an argument of his own.

"Ready yourself, little malenti," Iakhovas ordered, pointing at the approaching small lateen-sailed galley bearing Waterdhavian colors. The galleys supported the navy rakers that provided protection for the harbor.

The malenti moved forward, standing at her master's side and holding her trident at the ready. She carried a sword belted at her waist. She didn't much care for the weapon, but she'd been trained to use it.

"Ahoy, *Drifting Eel*," a mariner wearing the uniform of the Waterdeep Guard called out. A dozen other men stood in the galley's prow, armed with heavy crossbows and swords. The crew aboard her matched speeds with the pentekonter easily, pulling alongside and remaining only a few yards out from the bigger ship's oars.

"Ahoy," Iakhovas called back.

"State your name, home port, and business within Waterdeep Harbor," the guard ordered, waving men into action who shined bullseye lanterns over the pentekonter.

"I stand before you, birth-named Iakhovas, captain of *Drifting Eel*. As for a home port, we hail from Snowdown, in the Moonshaes. Why we're here? Why, man, it's Fleetswake, a time of revel and a time of profit for a man who's got coin to be spent and a cargo worth buying. I'd not forsake Waterdeep's hospitality at this time for anything."

The guard smiled and looked tired. "You're getting here late," he said.

"Aye," Iakhovas replied, "and had the parsimonious storm we had the ill-favor to encounter and embrace two days ago had been more inclined than I, I'd not be here at all."

"How much damage did you take on?" the guard asked. A frown creased his face. "I don't want any lagging ships standing in the way of the shipping lanes. If you're not all together, you can moor up outside the harbor and pay passage on some of the service boats to get inside the city."

"Trust me," Iakhovas answered. "Should anything go wrong with this vessel, you'll be the first to know. I've seen to the repairs, and now I'm ready to make back the losses I've incurred."

The harbor guard shined his lantern at the pentekonter's water line. "You're riding low, Cap'n Iakhovas."

Even the modified outriggers hadn't been able to compensate for the ship's increased draw made necessary to keep the sahuagin rowers aboard underwater. Laaqueel had hoped it wouldn't be as apparent when they arrived at night, but the surface dwellers knew their vessels.

"My dear fellow, the sheer amount of cargo we're carrying is justification enough to force us to sit low in the water," Iakhovas replied.

"You must have brought a lot."

"Everything we found we were able to pack into the hold."

"I'm Civilar Nöth of the Waterdeep Guard," the man said. "Prepare to be boarded and present your manifests."

Iakhovas called out the order to lower the rope ladder. One of the wererats kicked it and sent the rope ladder bundle spilling down the side of the pentekonter. The bottom several rungs landed in the water with a flat splat.

The civilar and two of his people swarmed up the ladder with practiced ease. Laaqueel noted that they kept their hands on the hilts of their short swords, and something magical clung to one or more of them. Her priestess training had made her sensitive to magic auras. She considered invoking the gifts given to her from Sekolah but didn't. The spells the Shark God had given her needed to be held for a later time.

Iakhovas's magic seemed to know no bounds, though. The malenti remembered in the beginning, after she'd found him, that his powers had been so scarce she'd nearly escaped him half a dozen times. Now he commanded large amounts of magic easily, and that seemed to grow with each item he recovered.

The glamour Iakhovas had cast over the pentekonter held, making *Drifting Eel* look like a normal ship with a normal crew.

The civilar crossed the deck and took out the blank sheet of paper Iakhovas handed him. "Everything here's satisfactory," he declared after a moment. "I'd like to take a look at the hold."

"Of course." Iakhovas raised his one-eyed gaze to Laaqueel. "My associate will show you the way, if you please."

Laaqueel nodded, but remained silent. She didn't know if Iakhovas's spell rendered her as a male or female and she didn't want her voice to betray it, if that was possible. The sorcerer's abilities had never failed. She led the Waterdhavian Guardsmen down into the hold, readying her own spells if she needed them.

If the civilar and his entourage noticed her duck away from the lantern's bright light when they brought it close, they didn't give any indication. She paused at the bottom of the hold, looking out over the sahuagin still working at the oars. They kept up the cadence, seated in the murky water that lapped over their heads.

The civilar and his companions halted on the steps, held back by the illusion Iakhovas maintained over the pentekonter. "You people worked hard to get all these things in here," he said appreciatively.

Laaqueel only gave him a slight nod, not having a clue what the man thought he saw.

"May Tymora smile on you and bless you with her favors," the civilar said. He turned and went back up the steps.

"I presume all below decks was found to be in good standing?" Iakhovas asked when they walked back on deck.

"It was fine," the civilar said. "I'll get you clear of the East Torch Tower gate."

Iakhovas glanced at the man, fixing his single eye upon him and making a gesture with two fingers. "You mean the Stormhaven Island gate."

"Of course I do," the civilar responded.

"Passage for all four ships," Iakhovas went on.

"Aye. Passage for all four ships."

"And you'll stay with us to make sure we get through."

"I'll stay with you," the civilar said. "In the last few hours our orders were to take everyone through the East Torch Tower gate except under special circumstances."

"Good," Iakhovas said in a quiet, low voice. "Signal your men and secure passage for us."

The civilar took two torches from a waterproof pouch on his back. They reeked of oil. He struck a flint and the sparks leaped onto the first torch, catching immediately. He lit the second torch with the first.

Laaqueel took an involuntary step back when the combined torches blazed up. The acrid smoke dried the back of her throat and irritated her gills. Smoke made breathing in the open air even less tolerable.

Waving the torches in a brief pattern, the civilar stepped back. "You can proceed, my lord."

Laaqueel didn't miss the address. She could tell from Iakhovas's cruel smile that she wasn't supposed to.

None of the other members of the Guard said anything, just stood at military attention.

"Puppets," Iakhovas stated. "They say what I want and hear only what I want them to, and never a thought enters their heads unless I place it there myself."

The wererat crew milled on the deck as *Drifting Eel*'s pilot brought them around to the Stormhaven Island gate. The gate was strategically located for Iakhovas's plan. The Waterdhavian Naval Harbor lay immediately to the northwest of the outer gate. Once the outer gate was taken down, the full thrust of the waiting attack would begin. By that time the sahuagin warrior groups circling Waterdeep by way of the mud flats to the north would attack the West Gate and split the city's forces.

North of the naval harbor, the great, bald craggy mountain where

Waterdeep Castle had been built stood overlooking the entire city. Lights burned in various places along Piergeiron's Palace, announcing only some of the City Watch secured areas. Closer to the shore along the Dock Ward, the Watching Tower, the Harborwatch Tower, and Smuggler's Bane Tower all looked out over the Great Harbor. A grim fortification occupied the right side of Stormhaven Island gate.

Despite the iron control she'd developed as a sahuagin, a spy, a priestess, and as the only one who knew more of Iakhovas's secrets than anyone else, Laaqueel's stomach fluttered as she watched the huge metal nets that served as gates lower out of their way to the sea bed below. When they were up, getting a ship through was almost impossible.

Surface dwellers occupied the fortifications and towers above the harbor waters. Mermen, mermaids, and sea elves kept patrol in the depths. The proof of the attack, Laaqueel knew, would be learned in the next handful of minutes.

"It's time, little malenti," Iakhovas said, "assume command of your forces and insure that these gates remain open so that the rest of our *navy* will be able to join us. Do not fail me."

She nodded, her eyes meeting his solitary gaze. "I won't."

The Waterdhavian Guard members gave no notice of having overheard the conversation.

Laaqueel left the deck and went down the stairs. The sahuagin warriors gathered in the hold looked up at her expectantly. "It's time. No one lives. Only our enemies are around us."

"We are ready to slay in the name of Great Sekolah, most favored one," a four-armed chieftain roared. "Meat is meat. Our enemies will regret meeting We Who Eat."

The malenti remembered his name as Bouundaar, an aggressive male who'd worked his way up in rank quickly. The overly aggressive ones always did under Iakhovas's watchful eye. "Three teams, Chieftain Bouundaar, quickly."

"It has already been done, most favored one."

"Then come. You and your team are with me. The others go to attack the defenses at the bottom of the harbor and the fortification to the east."

"It shall be as you say, most favored one."

Laaqueel dived into the cold water without another word, and the battle for Waterdeep Harbor began.

5

The dream overtook Jherek while he lay in *Butterfly*'s brig, filling him with the same cold dread that all memories of his father did when they haunted his sleep.

He swam in the blue-green of a sea. He didn't know which sea it was, nor did he care. He was free. He'd spent days in the brig at the insistence of the Amnian merchant.

He took joy in the feel of the warmth of the sea against his skin, at the currents that brushed against him. He knew at once it was a dream because he could breathe underwater. Looking up, he couldn't see the surface, and looking down he found a sea bed scattered with coral and fish.

He swam for a time, racing fish and finding that he was faster than them. Exuberant, he flashed through the water, diving and twisting and rolling through the ocean in great loops.

Only a short time later, he spotted the largest clam he'd ever seen. It was ten feet across, nearly that deep, and possessed a ridged alabaster shell. Curiosity gripped him and he was drawn to it. As he watched, it started to slowly open.

Jherek floated in the water, mesmerized by what was happening. Even before the clam was halfway open, he spotted the woman inside.

She was beautiful, close to his age, and had platinum blond hair that framed a nut-brown complexion. Since she wasn't dressed, he could see all her generous curves and womanly gifts.

Jherek was embarrassed, but somehow he felt it was right to simply gaze at her.

She smiled at him and waved. "Jherek," she cooed.

He heard his name plainly. Even his unconscious mind knew it was a dream, but he couldn't ignore that siren call. He swam down to her, realizing that she was a mermaid, her lower body that of a fish, all sheathed in iridescent green scales.

Instead of being appalled, he found her nature made her even more attractive to him. He stopped just short of her, gazing in wonder as she sat on the pink bed of the clam.

She reached out to him, laying her palm along the side of his face. Her touch was warm, soft. A string of shaped fire coral figurines lay between her breasts.

"Lady," he said in a thick voice.

"*Shhhh*," she admonished him, "I'm here to talk to you, to warn you."

"Warn me of what?" Jherek asked. "I've already been locked in *Butterfly*'s brig. When I get back home, I'll probably be hanged in the dockyards."

"No," she told him. "That's not going to happen. You've made friends, Jherek, and they'll stand you in good stead. You must not lose heart or hope. Things have been given to you, but you must seek out the key that opens the understanding you need."

He shook his head. "No. This is only a dream. Something my mind has culled from one of Malorrie's romantic stories."

"Dear, sweet Jherek," she rebuked softly, "so much doubt."

He felt guilty at her tone. "Aye," he agreed, "but I've got reasons."

"You'll understand in time," she assured him. "You've been given the burdens you carry only so that you may become who you should be. Running water shapes stone but it doesn't do so overnight."

"I don't understand."

"You will. You must trust that."

The look she gave him drew the promise, "I'll try."

Her face took on a more somber look. "Know, too, that there are those who would stop you in your journey," she said. "They fear you, fear what you will become, and with good cause because your life will touch the lives of many. I came to you in this dream so that you may take heart in this time of despair. There is a darkness out there, greater than any darkness you've known. It has already moved against part of the world you know, and it will be your crucible. Should you live, understanding and more will be yours."

"And should I die, lady?"

She looked at him, gave him a small smile, and said simply, "Don't."

Jherek wanted to talk to her further, to explain things as he saw them and to tell her of the ill fortune that had been his birthright, but she looked away from him. Cold horror now shaped her features.

He looked up instinctively, his attention drawn to whatever she saw.

At first, it was only a dim shape lost in the horizonless vast of the sea, then it came closer with astonishing speed. He realized it was a shark when it was still a distance away, recognizing the dorsal fins. He'd dreamed of sahuagin and sharks a lot since the recent attack on *Butterfly*. Reaching down to where he normally carried his shin knife, he found only bare skin. He had no weapons.

He reached for the girl. "Come, lady," he said, "while there is yet time."

She resisted, pulling against him, and said, "No, Jherek. This is not a thing that can be fled from. This is something that you must face."

He grabbed her wrist, desperately wanting to pull her to the sea bed below. The great shark was bigger than he'd thought, swelling into sight. Fear took him then when he saw that it was thirty, forty, or more feet in length.

Its skin was a stained gray, like ivory that had been rubbed with charcoal, the black coloring worked into the veins and scratches. When it came closer, he saw that the veins and scratches were tattooed runes and old scars. One eye was liquid black, malignant, magnetic. The other was only a puckered hole, dark with the hollow and the scarring around it.

Without warning, the girl slipped through Jherek's fingers. The clam closed over her again, a fort protecting her from the approaching dreadnought.

Before Jherek could move, the shark was on him. It opened its fanged mouth and swallowed him whole. Trapped in the shark's teeth, he discovered whatever ability had let him breathe underwater was now gone.

Death came for him.

Jherek fingered the scabbed and itching cut along his throat, remembering the Amnian sellsword's blade from three days ago. Nightmares had continued to plague him the previous nights, and he knew there'd be no relief tonight either. They'd put in at Athkatla two nights before, then made the journey on into Velen.

He sat at a back table in the Figureheadless Tavern and looked out the dirty window at the eastern dock walk over the waves lapping up onto the beaches of Velen. His stomach knotted and clenched repeatedly as he considered all his ill luck of the past few days.

It would have been better, he thought dismally, if Captain Finaren had let the sellsword slit his throat that day. *Butterfly*'s captain had talked with the Amnian merchants, explaining that Jherek had never been a true part of Falkane's crew aboard *Bunyip*, only a captured youth pressed into service on the pirate vessel who'd managed to escape with his life.

Lelayn had reluctantly accepted the story. There was no proof to the reports that Captain Falkane was in league with the sahuagin, but the

Amnian merchant had demanded that Jherek be held in the ship's brig. Though Finaren hadn't been happy about complying with the order, the brig was where the young sailor had found himself.

Jherek had lain on the hard bed with no light to read his books and no company. The ship's crew had been busy with repairs, and probably no one wanted to speak with him now anyway. With nothing to occupy his hands or mind, the darkness that always waited to consume his soul had riven him, tearing at him with the gale fury of a summer squall and as persistent as the seasonal rains. His grip on the world around him had come loose, freeing many of the old demons that he'd walled away with Madame Iitaar's and Malorrie's help and guidance. He hadn't forgotten the old fears that lived with him, but he had been surprised at how fierce they seemed now. Where the nightmares had come from was no mystery, but the one with the shark continued to gnaw at him.

Even Captain Finaren hadn't come to see him. The Amnian sellswords had rotated at guard duty over the brig as well on Lelayn's orders, insuring that Jherek hadn't been working with anyone else aboard *Butterfly*.

He hadn't seen Yeill again either, and he'd had mixed feelings about that, which surprised him. Both father and daughter had conveniently forgotten that he'd risked his life to save her's and he couldn't bring himself to remind them of it. That kind of chest-thumping behavior didn't sit well with him.

After the Amnian trading party had been unloaded in Athkatla, Finaren had released him from the ship's brig. The captain had apologized, saying he'd had no choice in the matter. Jherek had accepted the declaration stoically, with not a word said other than thanks for releasing him. Finaren had also ordered the crew not to be asking a lot of questions. He went on to tell them that all of them had stories and secrets they'd rather not have out in public without a couple drafts of mead to cushion the experience.

Finaren went on again to tell them that Jherek had never been a pirate, only someone captured by Falkane's vicious crew. That had been a bald-faced lie, though, and Jherek knew they both were aware of it.

Rather than face the crew, the young sailor had retreated to the crow's nest, pulling extra duty there, and spending the rest of his time mending nets and sleeping out on the deck in a hammock. No one talked to anyone mending nets. Finaren had a standing rule aboard *Butterfly* that men who could talk to someone mending nets could join in. A wagging tongue didn't stop fingers from working.

Jherek had wanted things to heal aboard *Butterfly*. He also knew that he'd have to take steps to make sure that happened, but he couldn't. That tattoo upon his arm marked him as different from those men in these waters. Falkane and his men had reputations as being the fiercest, blood-thirstiest pirates in the Sea of Swords, and they had some of the largest bounties offered for them. Rumor had it that even other pirates of the Nelanther feared Falkane and *Bunyip*'s crew.

After Athkatla was behind them and the wind filled *Butterfly*'s sails again, Jherek had hoped that things would return to normal aboard the cog. When they didn't, he was saddened but not surprised. Bad luck ran in his blood, showing in that flaming skull tattoo. Just before they'd docked at Velen, Finaren had told him not to help with the loading and with the rigging and to meet him at the Figureheadless Tavern later.

Finaren's choice of meeting places fit Jherek's mood. The tavern was a dive, queen among the cheap diversions that took the coppers and silvers from a working sailor's purse. He knew that Finaren had been aware of the tension among the crew. Even Hagagne had been quieter than normal, and he'd mentioned nothing more about having Jherek read to him.

The young sailor sat at a back table and nursed a mug of hot tea. He didn't really favor the tea, but he didn't drink mead or the liquors the tavern served. The barkeep kept watch on him. The Figureheadless was a place where pirates met, and where honest work on the sea was discussed at a table where a murder might have been plotted only moments ago.

The walls held no decor except stains from drink, oily hair, and blood. Sawdust covered the heavy walkways and looked like it should have been changed days ago. The tavern's three serving girls had already been by and offered themselves—for a price. He'd politely declined, and his thoughts had wandered inadvertently back to Yeill, wondering how someone so beautiful could look at life the way she did. For the tavern girls, it was just another means to make a couple silvers, and though he couldn't condone it, he at least did understand.

How was it that having wealth and not having wealth so often put the people who had and didn't have it in the same camp? he wondered. He realized it wasn't so much like a camp as it was like the table in front of him. People had to fill the seats on both sides, one giving and the other taking, each in turn, to fulfill the business between them.

In its basest terms, he supposed it was business, like Finaren sitting across from merchants who needed goods shipped to and fro.

It was still no way to live life. Coins were a means, not tools of war and not some counting system in a game. What mattered about life was the way a man lived it.

There were those, he knew, who would never get the chance to live a decent life at all no matter what was in their hearts. He felt immediately guilty at that, thinking of the time Madame Iitaar and Malorrie had spent with him these past years. Closing his eyes, he lowered his head and folded his hands, praying to Ilmater that he have the strength not to find fault with others for his own troubles and that he wouldn't slight what he had been given.

When he blinked his eyes open, he found Finaren standing there. The captain had his hat in his hands as he waited quietly.

"I didn't mean to intrude on your prayers, lad," the older man said in his deep voice.

Jherek pushed himself from his chair and turned up a hand to offer the seat across from him. "You're not intruding, sir."

"I'm not one to get between a man and his god," Finaren said, easing himself into the chair.

Jherek gave him a small smile and took his own seat. "Did you get the repairs set up for *Butterfly*?"

"Aye, and rogues that they are, they're going to charge a man an arm and a leg to have them done." Finaren waved to one of the serving girls and called, "Wench, you've got a restless man here dying of thirst. Bring me a bottle of your harshest who-hit-Nate and be damned quick about it."

Jherek was surprised at how demanding the captain was. As rough and prickly as he was at sea, he remained the epitome of good manners around children and women.

Finaren looked at him, then sighed. His shoulders slumped. "Being hard on the lass, aren't I?"

The young sailor shrugged, feeling even more nervous than he had when Finaren first sat down. The captain could bluster and yell louder than any man Jherek had ever known, but only in its proper time and place.

"I am and I know it, lad," the captain added. "There's no excuse. Rest assured that she'll see a healthy stipend for any troubles I might offer."

The serving girl brought a bottle and thick glass and put them before Finaren.

The captain thanked her and pulled the cork from the bottle. "Care for a libation, lad? Trust me, I think we're both going to need it."

Jherek's stomach flip-flopped, and he had to force the words out. He'd often seen Finaren take a drink and knew the man kept a ship's keg tapped, but he'd never seen the captain in a drunken stupor. He noticed for the first time the stink of liquor already on Finaren's breath and said, "No, thank you."

Finaren filled the glass in front of him and put the bottle away unstoppered. "Me, I'm going to get royally pissed back at *Butterfly*, lad." He drained off half the contents of the glass, then had a coughing fit that ended with, "I've damn sure earned it."

Jherek said nothing, already not liking the turn the conversation was taking.

"Valkur's brass buttons, lad, would that you were not who you are." Finaren met his level gaze, and Jherek saw the pain in the older man's eyes.

"But I am," Jherek whispered, barely able to get the words out.

"It's one thing for me to tell my crew a white lie for a good reason," Finaren said.

"I never asked that," Jherek said.

"I know that, lad. Hell, I'm not blaming you for me putting me own head in a noose on that one. You came to me and told me about that tattoo, same as you told Shipwright Makim who you were, and it was my choice not to tell the crew about it."

Jherek remembered that decision. Even though Finaren had made the choice, he'd hated living that lie around men who on occasion trusted him with their lives.

"They wouldn't have stood for it," Finaren said. "Me, I don't know how I'd agreed to let you ship with me."

Jherek opened his mouth to speak, not sure what he was going to say.

"You just shush, lad," the captain cautioned. "I'm here to make my peace, and I'll not have you taking blame on yourself where there's none. I could have done it another way, but I knew there'd be some of them men wouldn't stand for having you aboard. Selûne grant me some good fortune here that they never find out who you *truly* are."

Shards of hot tears stung the backs of Jherek's eyes but he wouldn't let them fall. He grew angry at himself, knowing how the conversation was going to end, and frustrated with himself that he could have believed even for a moment that it was going to go any other way.

There was no way to escape his heritage. The flaming skull tattoo marking him as one of Falkane's pirate crew had been magically administered, put on by Falkane himself. Falkane hand picked his crew, taking the hardest men a reaver's life could turn out, and he tied them to him for the rest of their lives by the tattoo. Nothing could erase that tattoo once it had been inscribed. Jherek had tried everything. Even before Madame Iitaar had attempted to remove it with her magic, he'd even tried to cut it from his flesh, leaving the scars that marked it.

"Lad, one of the most unfair things in life is the fact that a man can't pick the man who fathered him." Finaren's voice took on an unaccustomed thickness. "That day you came to me, why that's as clear in my mind as if it were yesterday. You were only a lad. Hell, you still are, but then you didn't have all the muscle and height you've picked up these past few years. You were just a spindly boy, not even shaving."

Jherek remembered, too. He'd thought Madame Iitaar was punishing him for wanting to go to sea and had set his interview up with the crustiest captain that operated out of Velen to discourage him. Finaren's demeanor had been hard to take.

"I thought I'd have you out away from the city a half day's journey and you'd be crying for your ma," Finaren went on. Even though he knew Madame Iitaar wasn't Jherek's natural mother, he'd always referred to her that way, "but I saw that look in your eyes when you talked about the sea, and I knew it came from the fire in your belly a man always has when he's fallen in love with the briny blue."

"There's no other place I'd rather be," Jherek said.

"I know, lad, and a man with that kind of passion, he's going to find the way of it. That's why, even after you told me who you are, and showed me the tattoo when I doubted, that I let you sail old *Butterfly*. I turned down growed-up men to put you on her deck."

Jherek knew it was true. Malorrie maintained contacts among the docks and had relayed the stories to him.

"Damn your father's eyes, lad," Finaren said, "I can't be taking you with me any more. We've had a good run of luck these past few years. I tell you now, I've never had a finer man crewing aboard *Butterfly*. Umberlee take me now if I'm lying."

"No one said anything to me these last couple of days," Jherek protested, knowing that was just as damning as anything. He just wasn't ready to let go.

"I know, lad, but plenty's been said to me since then. Your birthright has almost split my crew. Some are for you and some are against you. Almost had guts spilling out on ship's decks tonight when the matter was brought up, and I can't have that. I've got to have a crew like the fingers on a hand, always together and always working to stay that way. Otherwise I'm out of business and someone else'll be owning *Butterfly*. That's a thought that makes the blood run cold." Finaren shook his head sorrowfully and finished his glass. "What if they learned the *real* truth of the matter?"

"I don't know," Jherek whispered. Even then, it hurt to get the words out.

"You aren't just a boy who escaped impressment," Finaren stated. "You're Bloody Falkane the Wolf's *son*!" He paused and made a brief luck sign in Selûne's name. "There are those who'd kill you hoping to get back at that man."

Jherek leaned back in his chair, defeated. He looked at the table, suddenly realizing what it meant: one man giving and one man taking. Only there were no deals he could make and he knew it.

"You hate me, don't you, lad?" Finaren asked gruffly.

"No," Jherek answered honestly.

Finaren looked away for a time, then gradually met his eyes again. "I hope you mean that, lad. It'd break me heart if you did."

Jherek tried to get around the hurt and loss that filled him. During the last few years, other captains had offered him employment after learning how good he was aboard ship and how skilled he was with marine craft as well as weapons. He'd turned them all down, even the offers that came with more wages attached. For a moment he resented the fact that he hadn't accepted them, hadn't left Finaren and gone his own way, but he knew if another captain had discovered the truth about his birth, he'd have been hung from a yardarm if he hadn't had his throat slit first.

"Maybe I can get a ship somewhere else," he said.

Finaren nodded. "Aye, there's a thought, but try somewhere far from the Sword Coast where the flaming skull tattoo won't be as heatedly remembered."

"Could you give me a letter of recommendation?"

"Aye, that I could, lad, but are you sure you want to ask me for one? Someone asks around down here, they're going to find out about this. By morning, this whole town will know and tongues will still be wagging."

Jherek knew he was right.

"Maybe the Sea of Fallen Stars," Finaren suggested. "You find a captain, tell him your da was a fisherman, that you learned the trade from him. They see what you can do, you'll move up smart enough."

Shaking his head, Jherek said, "I can't lie. I didn't lie to you, and I'm not going to lie to someone else. There'll be another captain out there willing to take a chance on me."

Finaren hesitated for a moment, then shook his head sorrowfully. "I hope you're right, lad, but you're going to be looking for one few and far between. You're no stripling boy now. You're almost a man full-grown. Most men will look on you as more of a threat. Valkur's brass buttons, Jherek, how many of them sahuagin did you kill in that battle? How many pirates and other creatures before that?"

"I couldn't tell you."

"Look for a way to get rid of that tattoo," the captain advised. "That'd be the first thing to work on."

"Madame Iitaar couldn't get rid of it."

"Meaning no disrespect whatsoever, lad, but your ma don't know everything that's under the sun. Mayhap you'll find a mage in one of them countries around the Inner Sea who'll know just what to do."

Jherek nodded, not knowing what he was going to do. The only true home he'd ever known was here in Velen. Leaving it while on a ship, knowing he was going to return, was one thing. Moving was an entirely different matter.

"I do know one thing, though, lad," Finaren stated. "Traveling around and hiring mages, that's going to cost some money."

Jherek nodded. That was another problem that he was going to have to think on.

"There," Finaren said with a small smile, "I *can* help." He took a leather bag from under his blouse and pushed it across the table.

Jherek hefted it, surprised at how heavy it was.

"Go on," Finaren said, "take a look."

Untying the strings, Jherek peered in surprised to see a collection of gold pieces and gems. He looked up at the captain. "What's this? If this is charity—"

Finaren held up an authoritative hand and interrupted, "Hold your water, lad. Charitable I may be, foolish I am not. What you've got there you've rightly earned. When I hire a man onto my ship, I set aside a bit of the wages I pay him that he don't know about. Bonuses, you might call them, for every voyage we take together. I know men living on ships don't always put back for them rainy days. So when I got a man laid up by illness or injury, or I got a man don't come back to his family, I can see to it he don't go hungry or homeless. Or unburied if it comes to that.

That there's the coin I've been putting aside for you, and I managed to scrape together a little over two thousand gold pieces worth of gems to pay for them healing potions you got from the Amnians. Unless you'd rather have the draughts and try to sell them yourself."

"No. I know you've been generous." Jherek also recalled that the ship didn't have any healing potions aboard, and for every one he tried to sell, he'd be forced to think about Yeill again. He didn't want that either.

"You might be able to double your money on those potions," Finaren pointed out.

"One of the things you always taught me was to take the money up front if I wasn't sure where I'd be the next day."

"Good lad," the old captain congratulated. "I kept the crew aboard *Butterfly* till just before I came to meet you here, but they'll be telling tales up and down the docks tonight. You might warn your ma that some angry people could show up at her house."

For the first time, the cold realization that he might not have a choice about staying in Velen struck Jherek. The town had been Madame Iitaar's home for dozens of years. She'd buried a husband there, and other family as well. Malorrie had been buried there himself. Neither of them might be willing to move.

Finaren read the look on his face. "You hadn't thought about that, had you, lad? About the fact that once this is out in this town, you might be forced to move?"

"No," Jherek replied honestly. He looked out the dirty window and tried to imagine living anywhere else. He couldn't. The only life he'd known before Velen was his father's ship.

"Even if someone here don't try to kill you," Finaren warned, "didn't you say Falkane might come looking if he knew where you were?"

The possibility seemed small now, but Jherek remembered how much it had frightened him when he was younger. "I don't know."

"Get out of town, lad," Finaren said. "That's my advice. For what it's worth."

"I'll think about it." The stubborn streak that had helped Jherek survive the hardships he'd experienced up to now surfaced.

Finaren started to argue. Jherek could tell by the way the captain's lips jerked and his eyes narrow. Then the older man shrugged. "As you think, lad." He stoppered his bottle. "As for me, I've got to go so you can be going."

Jherek nodded, not wanting the man to walk away from him, but knowing there was no way to hold him.

"You put that purse away and keep it safe," Finaren ordered as he rose from his chair.

"Thank you."

"Know something else, Jherek: if there's ever a time I can be of help to you—in any way—you don't hesitate to come to me. Right now, I've done all I can."

"I know."

"Come here, lad, that I can say a proper good-bye."

Jherek stood, hugging the old man back as fiercely as Finaren hugged him. He didn't know if it was Finaren's tight hold or his throat swelling with emotion that shut off his wind.

Finaren cuffed him on the back of the head and stepped back. Tears gleamed in the old man's eyes and ran down unashamedly into the rough crags of his weathered face. "I want you to know something else, lad," he said in a thick, hoarse voice. "If me wee boy that Umberlee had taken from me so long ago had turned out to be anything like the kind of man you are, there wouldn't have been a prouder da in all of Faerûn."

"Thank you," Jherek said with difficulty. His heart felt like lead in his chest, stillborn and heavy. He hadn't even known Finaren had lost a son or even been married. He watched helplessly as the captain grabbed his bottle from the table and turned around. He walked away, his legs still bent from all the days at sea.

Jherek tucked the purse inside his shirt and left a couple silvers on the table for the serving girl. He wiped his face and walked outside. The smell of the sea hit him more strongly when he walked outside. Full dark had descended on Velen while he'd been waiting in the tavern. Several ships occupied the small port, their rigging beating rhythmically against the masts in the strong breeze.

His steps turned automatically toward the alleys he'd often traveled to the docks from Madame Iitaar's house. When he'd worked for Shipwright Makim, he'd spent most of his evenings watching the ships put out to sea. When he'd gone to Madame Iitaar's to live after being hired to repair her roof, he'd often stolen away when she wasn't looking to spend time at the docks. When he'd put together enough money to buy a small skiff, he'd sailed it every evening and every free day he had.

He paused on a familiar promontory on a hillock in back of Hient's Glass Shop. The breeze cut across from the east, coming in over the Drake Gate that lead overland out of the city. He thought about traveling through the forest, knowing he might not be safe on any ship. He disliked the idea immediately. The sea was his life. It had birthed him and held an attraction he couldn't shake.

A woman's scream cut through the night from the east. He turned at once, tracking the scream as the echoes died around him. With all the noise coming from the docks, he doubted anyone else heard. He moved through the alleys, unable to ignore the plea for help, dreading the place he was sure it was taking him to.

6

Laaqueel felt grateful as the salty sea closed over her when she dived into the ocean through the hole in bottom of *Drifting Eel*. She didn't even mind the terrific cold. She took a deep draught in through her mouth and blew the excess out through her gills, soaking them. Sahuagin warriors filled the water around her.

She swam toward Smuggler's Bane Tower quickly, following the retreating line of chain nets. The nets left streamers of bubbles in the water that helped mask her approach. She took what cover she could, knowing the glamour Iakhovas had over the ship wouldn't extend much past the hull of the pentekonter.

The next few minutes would tell the success of the invasion or the death of thousands of sahuagin. The malenti thought it would be worth it if Iakhovas's own death could be guaranteed. The ebony quill near her heart quivered, as if the sorcerer was letting her know he could sense her traitorous intentions. She regretted the thought immediately. Sekolah had never indicated that Iakhovas's quest in any way went against the desires of the Great Shark.

When she reached the sandy beach on the inside of the great harbor, she unfurled one of the hook-filled nets from her side and shook it out. She raced up onto the beach without breaking stride. The harsh clanking of the steel nets filled the air.

Five men wearing the uniform of the Waterdhavian Guard lounged at an open area talking and filling pipes. A small lantern hung from a pole overhead, providing them a small light to congregate by. One of them spotted the malenti as she ran up onto the beach. He started to yell a warning to his companions.

Still in motion, Laaqueel moved smoothly, drawing her trident back and letting fly. She was as skilled with the weapon above water as she was below. Her weapons masters had seen to that.

A heartbeat after leaving her hand, the trident slammed into the guard's chest and drove him backward against the stone wall.

Trained and efficient, the guard members went into action at once. Having both hands free, Laaqueel whirled her net over her head and threw it. The net splayed out, the lantern light reflecting from the dozens of sharp barbs tied in the mesh. It hit the man in front, then the weighted ends swung around the man nearest him, trapping them together. Both men went down screaming as the other's struggles only set the hooks more deeply.

A sahuagin spear took a fourth man high in the chest, entering from the side and ripping through his lungs. He didn't have enough breath left to scream in pain.

The fifth man made it up the short flight of steps carved into the stone at the base of the Smuggler's Bane Tower. A quarrel fletched his back as he dashed through the doorway at the top of the steps. His yells for help were audible even above the clanking retreat of the nets.

The door slammed shut as Laaqueel freed her short sword and started up the stone steps. She turned to Bounndaar, raising her voice so she could be clearly heard. "Get crossbowmen along the shoreline. Those men in the tower are going to know about us in a moment."

"At once, most favored one." Bounndaar turned and yelled orders to his men.

Laaqueel faced the door, standing on the small porch area before it. The windlass controls to raise and lower the nets occupied the lower section of the tower. Two narrow, winding staircases led to the floors above. Saying a quick prayer and calling on Sekolah to allow her power to be strong, she threw her open hand against the iron-bound wooden door blocking entrance to the tower.

She felt the magical wards protecting the door resist her spell, then felt them collapse on themselves. Immediately, the door warped, sprung out of its hinges by her magic. She said another prayer when she took up a small hammer from her harness, using up another of her spells. Concentrating hard, not as familiar with this spell because she seldom used it, ignoring the bustle of activity on the other side of the door, she imagined the glowing force around the hammer, making herself see it in her mind.

Bracing herself, she swung the hammer wrapped in magical force against the warped door. The door tore free of its moorings at once, exploding back into the foyer beyond and striking down half a dozen human guardsmen.

Laaqueel, her strike force gathering behind her, stepped through the door, her sword naked in her fist. "Bouundaar," she croaked in a dry voice. The effort necessitated by maintaining the hammer of magical force gave her a headache, knotting muscles through her shoulders and back. The headache was made worse by the lanterns clinging to the walls. She slitted her eyes against the brightness as she sought targets for the hammer.

She struck without mercy, knowing the Great Shark would approve. Every time the hammer landed, guards died and their blood spattered over her. She spared none of them. Bouundaar, seeing that she was weakened by her efforts, placed himself directly in front of her and ordered two sahuagin warriors into place on either side of her. They kept the humans back with tridents and spears.

Feeling the hammer fading from her, slipping through her mental grip, she flung it one last time, knocking a surface dweller from the circular staircase. He flew backward, then smashed against the torch and the wall behind him and dropped lifeless to the floor. The torch sconce dropped from the wall, showering him with sparks and filling the foyer with the stink of burned hair.

Laaqueel regretfully let go of the hammer of force, feeling it disappear from the physical plane. She started another prayer and pushed her way through Bouundaar. She pointed at the staircase, telling the chieftain to put sahuagin on guard there. By the time she reached the flight of stairs leading down into the area where the windlass that controlled the nets was, she had her next spell ready.

The windlass room was large, forty feet by forty feet, she estimated. The device was in the center of the room, constructed of several ratcheting gears that clanked hurriedly as the three men operating it tried to raise the nets again. The nets held wards that normally repelled most fish from the harbor, allowing no sharks or other predatory marine creatures, but they wouldn't stop the sahuagin forces.

"Damned fish-heads!" one of the men bawled in warning.

Laaqueel heard the *thrum* of crossbows behind her and watched as the short quarrels buried their vicious barbs in flesh and wood. She thrust out a hand and the magic spewed from her palm, plunging the room into total blackness. With their greater night vision, the sahuagin weren't totally blinded. The light spilling in the door leading down to the windlass area was enough.

The crossbow quarrels put another man down at the windlass. Laaqueel vaulted to the floor, silent as her own shadow, and swung her sword. The keen edge hamstrung the man trying desperately to turn the ten-foot tall wheel. He screamed and reached for his injured feet. The malenti ended the screaming by slashing his throat.

Without remorse, she grabbed one of the Waterdhavian Guardsmen on the floor, locating him by the string of curses and pained cries that came from him. She levered the man up in one hand, then unerringly shoved him into the grind of gears operating the nets.

The man screamed anew as the big gears bit into him, but the sounds quickly went away as the gears drew him in. Bone crunched and the metallic strain of the gears trying to mesh filled the basement.

The gears stopped.

Bouundaar's men worked efficiently in the darkness, talking to each other in their own tongue as they covered the floor and tracked down the last of the surface dwellers. All of them were dead by the time Laaqueel reached the top of the stairs.

More sahuagin held the bottom of the dual stairwells. Nets stretched above them, blocking entrance into the room.

Laaqueel ran back out onto the sandy beach in front of Smuggler's Bane Tower. Her gaze raked across Waterdeep Harbor and spied *Drifting Eel* at once. Mermen attacked the vessel, some of them riding the giant sea horses they used as mounts. Thankfully there weren't as many of them as Laaqueel had feared. The advance party group had struck the mermen hard, as Iakhovas had planned.

The one-eyed prince remained standing in the prow of the pentekonter, his massive cloak billowing in the breeze behind him. The other three ships followed sedately behind, disgorging more sahuagin into the great harbor.

Suddenly the malenti's vision cleared even more and she saw the sorcerer plainly. *Ah, there you are, little malenti*, her master's voice sounded in her mind. *You've endeavored so fiercely these past years to always keep me in your sight, do not give up the race now.*

She knew he mocked her. Even diligent as she'd been about her spying on him, he had managed to hide so many things from her.

Iakhovas stretched a hand out at her before she could move.

Nausea twisted through Laaqueel, and it felt like her air bladder had burst. Her vision blanked for a moment and she took a step back even though she knew what was going on. When her foot touched down again, it wasn't on sandy beach, but on *Drifting Eel*'s wooden deck. The quill implanted so close to her heart gave the sorcerer such power over her.

Civilar Nöth and his Waterdhavian Guardsmen stood at attention behind the sorcerer.

"Now," Iakhovas said, a malevolent spark in his single dark eye, "now I will educate the surface dwellers in the poignancy of true horror, a skill at which I am a unparalleled. I've forgotten much more than they've ever had the misfortune to experience."

He reached into the folds of his cloak and brought out an ornate headband chipped from a single black sapphire. Long labor had gone into the creation of the circlet. Not only did it have a perfect circumference, but tiny sharks had been chipped into it in bas relief, creating a twisting serpentine of figures.

Laaqueel recognized the headband as the one he'd forcibly taken from the mermen fourteen years ago, bringing total destruction to their village and sending the few survivors fleeing for their lives. Laaqueel had traveled with him then, knowing that Iakhovas had somehow managed a magical link with the headband and with the other items he searched for so diligently.

The malenti's attention was drawn to the mermen trying to encircle *Drifting Eel*. A crossbow shaft leaped from one of them, speeding toward her face. She turned slightly, letting it go past, not caring that it struck one of the wererats. The creatures could only be harmed by silver or magical weapons. The quarrel that buried itself in the creature's back was only a momentary inconvenience that drew a squeal of pained rage.

Twisting again and moving across the deck, Laaqueel continued praying, putting her skills to use. Taking a pinch of sulfur from one of the waterproof pouches on her harness, she directed the spell at the merman who'd shot at her. A luminescent column formed in the air before her, not even as bright as a glow lamp. It leaped at its target.

Hit by the magical stream of scalding heat, the merman cried out, his skin drying out and blackening. His corpse tumbled through the water, disappearing.

Casting again, knowing how much danger the mermen represented, Laaqueel touched the shark talisman that represented her faith to Sekolah and cast her next spell. She threw a hand outward and a pale lavender stingray burst into being. It sailed through the air and took to the water, attacking the mermen at once. Most of those it touched succumbed to the magic, freezing up in fear and disappearing beneath the water. The remaining mermen were routed, chased off by the crossbows in the hands of the wererats.

Iakhovas put the circlet on and turned to face the open Smuggler's Bane Tower. Laaqueel wasn't sure of the extent of the power the headband gave the sorcerer over those he chose to influence, but she'd seen that the effect could be all-consuming, uniting those with intelligence as well as animals who normally didn't get along well.

"Come," he crooned, "obey my words and destroy my enemies. Unite with We Who Eat in our labors."

Laaqueel knew he was projecting his voice, making sure it reached the hearing of the army he'd amassed for the night's raid. Even Huaanton and the other sahuagin didn't know the extent of the destruction Iakhovas planned. They knew only about the joined sahuagin tribes. They knew nothing of the aboleths, giant turtles and dragon turtles, eyes of the deep, giant crabs, and dozens of sharks, more than any sahuagin could ever hope to control. She was sure there were others even she didn't know about.

With the presence of all those creatures she knew the sahuagin would assume Sekolah was aiding in their attack. Iakhovas would become even more favored among her people for being aided by the Great Shark, while she was only tolerated while he looked upon her with generosity. Part of the small hope she'd nurtured inside herself for the last fifteen years, that her own position among her tribe would improve, died then. Every advance she got was at Iakhovas's behest. She would forever be his puppet. As long as Sekolah willed it, so she would remain alive.

Fatigued from the spellcasting, she gazed out through the open gates, aware of the Waterdhavian Watch galleys and rakers converging on the area. In the dark distance beyond the reach of the harbor lights, Iakhovas's navy moved in. She saw the flat shapes of the sahuagin mantas break water near the naval harbor, followed by the sleek heads of giant creatures that broke the surface behind them. Even more creatures, Laaqueel knew, swam beneath the harbor's waves.

Conch horns echoed across the harbor, sounding a general alarm. A Waterdhavian raker plunged across the harbor, aiming itself at the sahuagin flagship. Slender and top-armored, the battle vessel carried fire-pot catapults and large deck-mounted crossbows. Less than a hundred yards away, the raker crew opened fire with one ballista.

The six foot shaft sped through the air and ripped into the pentekonter's side. Vibrations shuddered through the vessel as it penetrated just above the waterline. From the location of the damage, Laaqueel was sure some of the sahuagin rowers below had been injured or killed.

Iakhovas threw out an arm and said something that arcane language of his that Laaqueel had never understood. His tattoos glowed and his arm changed, becoming a hard-ridged fin almost four feet in length. Her feminine intuition told Laaqueel this shape was closer in truth to the real nature of the sorcerer than any she'd seen him use.

He slashed the jointed fin at the three Waterdhavian Guardsmen, slicing their heads from their bodies. The fin changed back to his arm as he turned to the malenti.

"Do not forget yourself here, my little malenti," he said, "I've a battle to win. Hie you below and inspire those rowers to work harder. We're found out now and time works against me. I want to make the shoreline before this vessel is seized."

She ran to the hold and got the drum beater's attention.

"Yes, most favored one?" the warrior inquired.

"As fast as you are able," she ordered. She saw the damage the giant crossbow bolt had done, impaling the two sahuagin who'd shared an oar. Their bodies still twisted on the shaft as they continued dying.

"Yes, most favored one."

She returned to the deck, following Iakhovas as he ran back to the stern. The wererats scattered before the sorcerer, snarling in their high-pitched voices. Iakhovas held onto the railing as the pilot brought *Drifting Eel* around.

"We're leaving the harbor," Laaqueel said.

"Good. You are not as blind as I sometimes feared." Iakhovas seemed distracted, concentrating on the small bloodstone globe nestled in his palm.

Wererat archers stood at the railing and exchanged fire with the crew aboard the Waterdhavian raker.

"But leaving the harbor means leaving our forces here," Laaqueel protested.

Iakhovas gave her a harsh look. "Little malenti, you fear for your warriors when in truth Sekolah bred them and birthed them to die," he told her. "They are not alone in this struggle; it's my war and I've found them shield mates and comrades. I've done what I can do. There are matters that demand my attention. You're welcome to remain here if you so choose."

She looked at him, knowing he was certain she wouldn't stay. She would lose her chance to see what he was up to. "No," she said.

"So be it," he replied, "but you will allow me the necessary time to work the spells I've set up. I'll not suffer any interruptions. Even from you, my little malenti."

Iakhovas placed his other hand on top of the small bloodstone gem, then drew it slowly back. The gem enlarged like a bubble, the surface becoming even less stable.

One of the wererat archers staggered back from the railing, transfixed by one of the giant crossbow bolts that had crashed through his thin chest. Bone shards glinted in the moonlight.

Iakhovas tossed the bloodstone bubble into the air and it promptly disappeared. Laaqueel noticed the harbor breezes died suddenly. A moment more and a sudden wave erupted from under the harbor's surface and drank down the Waterdhavian raker. There were no survivors.

The spell was subtle in other respects, spreading out across the harbor without giving away where it had started. Laaqueel knew none of the magic-fearing sahuagin would attribute it to Iakhovas, only to Sekolah.

Storm winds and crashing waves continued striking the Waterdhavian crafts as *Drifting Eel* pushed toward the Dock Ward shoreline. The battle in the harbor had reached the docks. Mariners bolted from taverns and from the Helmstar Warehouse, the Mermaid's Arms festhall, and Arnagus the Shipwright's building. Lights blossomed up and down Dock Street. The streets started to fill, and sahuagin were filling them as well.

Some of the Fleetswake revelers had pitched tents along the docks and others had even gone so far as to place tents across their boat decks. Lanterns blazed at some of them, throwing shadows across the tents as the drunken sailors and merchants tried to rally against the invading sahuagin forces.

Drifting Eel raced for an empty loading berth among the docks as lantern lights from ships at anchorage played over the deck. Iakhovas called down the hailing tube himself, ordering the sahuagin rowers to reverse direction. The sorcerer dropped the anchor himself with a wave of his hand that sent the man-sized weight spinning through the air, stopping the play of chain as soon as the anchor touched the harbor bottom. *Drifting Eel* halted too late, slamming into the dock pilings and knocking them loose from their moorings.

Laaqueel fell but rolled to her feet while the wererat deckhands went sprawling. She brandished her sword as she pursued Iakhovas, who hadn't lost his footing at all, standing as surely as an outcropping of coral.

The sorcerer bolted over *Drifting Eel's* side and dropped four feet to the splintered dock. He reached inside his cloak and drew out a rapier with an ornate handle fashioned from an impossibly large shark's tooth.

The malenti hesitated only a moment before following the sorcerer. She dropped to the dock, trailed immediately by two dozen wererats. Iakhovas was already in motion, leaving her no doubt that he was already moving on whatever hidden agenda he'd planned for the night.

She turned and glanced back out into the harbor in time to see the first fiery catapult launches from Waterdeep Castle high overhead. The flaming loads arced across the black sky like comets, then crashed down amid the three sahuagin ships with uncanny accuracy. Two of the ships broke under the onslaught and started sinking as Waterdhavian rakers closed in.

The storm created by Iakhovas's spell continued growing, gathering force. Four foot waves rippled up on the harbor water, then cascaded over the side of Dock Street in spite of the ramparts. The sea wall around the harbor also served as a breakwater against storms that traveled inland from the Sea of Swords. Against a storm that started within the harbor itself, there was no protection.

A raker bore down on the surviving sahuagin ship. Before it could reach its opponent, a dragon turtle rose up from the depths and capsized the raker. The creature was over fifty feet long from its snout to its tail. The shell alone was thirty feet around and was dark green in color with sections that came to sharp points. The huge clawed feet spread over two yards with the webbing between the toes. Horned ridges stood out on its wattled neck. Fierce orange eyes glowed in the dark, and its mouth was a curved, cruel sword slash. Its attention drawn to the Waterdhavian sailors, the monster turtle's head darted out and it gulped down three in quick succession.

Men shouted around Laaqueel, but none tried to attack her as they manned posts along the harbor. She assumed that the illusory glamour Iakhovas was using remained in place. Turning, she sprinted to catch up to him, making it easily since he wasn't traveling fast.

"What are we here for?" she demanded when she drew even.

"Fear not, my little malenti, my reasons for being here coincide with your own," he answered. "To properly fight a war, weapons require careful choosing. In my studies, I have unearthed the fact that one is here, one that I desire greatly."

"You staged this invasion, sacrificed my people, to get something that belonged to you?" Laaqueel, even after the fifteen years she'd seen him in action, couldn't believe it.

He turned his dark eye on her, glaring. "Don't ever presume to question my methods or my reasons, little malenti, otherwise you'll never grow to be the sahuagin you want to be so badly. I no longer require your services these days as much as would benefit you. Do not be foolish enough to disregard that. It is a true fact." He continued walking, turning onto an alley off Dock Street and heading east.

She fell into step at his side and slightly behind him, following in silent protest. It wasn't the first time he'd intimated that he could change her into a sahuagin. Judging from his power, she assumed it was possible.

Possible, but only if he didn't get them all killed while foraging through Waterdeep. She tightened her grip on her sword and trailed him into the waiting darkness of the alley.

7

Jherek's heart hammered as he poised on the balls of his feet, the cutlass naked in his fist. The heavy humidity from the sea left a sheen of sweat across his body from his run. No one else had responded to the woman's shrill screams for help, but it was possible no one else had heard her over the noise from the docks.

Seven Cuts Court occupied a wide space in the street leading to Drake Gate and to the wooded coastal trails to Murann and Tordraken. Sandwiched between a building that had once housed a bakery but now stood vacant since a string of unsolved murders had begun there and a leather goods shop specializing in used overland travel gear, Jherek gazed out at the court. The only sound now was the gurgle of the fountain, fed by the artesian well, in the court's center.

Shadows draped the area. No lights burned there after the sun went down. Every mayor to hold office in Velen since the murders started tried to find a means of lighting the court and ending the curse there, but none had ever been successful. Torches and lanterns were lit, but mysteriously extinguished as soon as full dark had claimed the city.

The curse began when a severed foot was found in the court. Most in Velen believed the foot was placed there as a warning to someone, but the stories varied as to who the warning was for. Some said it concerned a Shadow Thief who'd failed in his assignment. Some said it was a warning to Hieydl, the old baker whose son had moved the family business, over an affair of the heart. The foot, over the years, ended up belonging to hundreds of people in the stories that circulated.

There was one truth about Seven Cuts Court in all of Velen: no one went there alone at night. Since the morning the foot had been discovered in the court, people who foolishly ventured into the court at night alone ended up dead—all of them from seven similar deadly slashes—and the victim's right foot was always taken.

Most believed it was the work of a vengeful ghost. For all its acceptance of its ghosts, Velen also housed a number of poltergeists that had to be banished from time to time. None of the clergy or professional ghost-chasers had been able to exorcise whatever haunted the court after dark.

Jherek didn't know what he believed, but he'd always stayed away from the place. Now he had no choice. He took a fresh grip on the cutlass and moved into the shadows of the court.

The attack came without warning and faster than Jherek thought possible. Only his keen hearing saved him when he heard the rustle of leather armor to his left. Instinctively, he went down and to the right. At sea a sailor had to stay low. Losing contact with the deck or the rigging during a storm or an attack often meant death.

He rolled on his shoulder and pushed up on his knees. The cutlass came on line in front of him, and he squared himself up behind it as Malorrie had always taught him.

The leather-clad attacker bolted from the shadows, following up his immediate strike confidently, expecting to overpower his victim before he could get to his feet. A sword's steel splintered the weak moonlight, sweeping toward Jherek's head.

The young sailor turned the sword blow with the hook, feeling the impact shiver down along his arm. His attacker's strength pushed the hook across, making Jherek use the cutlass to block as well. Even then, the sword stopped scarce inches from his throat.

The man roared a curse, his dark face hidden by a scarf wrapped around his face. His breath smelled like he'd spent the night in a tavern.

As the man yanked his sword back, Jherek put his weight on one knee and lashed out with his other leg. He hooked his foot behind the man's ankle, tripping him.

Jherek got to his feet as the man fell backward. Even big as he was, the attacker shoved himself to his feet with surprising speed.

"Tricky whelp, eh," the big man said. "Won't be enough." He charged forward, swinging his blade with all his might.

Jherek met the blow with his cutlass. Sparks leaped from the roughened metal and rained down over the young sailor's clothing. Driven back by the impact, Jherek stumbled for his footing, his boot soles sliding across the cobblestones. He barely got the sword up in time to defend himself again.

Though fear filled him, coiling through his guts like a rabid mouse, Jherek focused his mind and skills. He kept his arm hard and relaxed at the same time, parrying the big man's raw attack with skill and strength, forced to give ground before it. Twice he got the cutlass in for blows to the body, but the edge wasn't able to bite through the leather armor. Metal clanged, filling the court with unaccustomed noise. The young sailor couldn't help wondering how many ghosts they were attracting as an audience, and he knew not all of them were benign.

"Gonna die this night, whelp," the big man promised. "Gonna spill me some cursed pirate's blood in the bargain, maybe lay claim to that bounty on that tattoo you're sporting so high and mighty on your arm." The big sword came down again.

Hearing the man's words stung Jherek, touching off the unforgiving anger that lay inside him. Malorrie had always taught him that the anger he felt was his greatest weapon, and his greatest weakness. The difference lay in control, and in whether that anger was directed inward or outward.

Jherek parried the sword blow with his cutlass, ducking down and to the side to turn it away from him and to the right. Before the big man could move, the young sailor whipped in with the hook and buried it behind the man's knee. He yanked, setting it deep.

The big man roared in pain, trying desperately to get away. He bent down to grab for the hook.

Jherek straightened, unable to bring the cutlass's blade into play. Instead, he slammed the hard metal of the basket hilt into his attacker's face, breaking his nose and sending blood in all directions. Close as he was, he felt the warmth of the man's blood splash across his own face.

The big man squalled in renewed agony, and fear was in there now as well. He put out a big hand and gouged at Jherek's eyes with hard-taloned fingers.

The young sailor went backward automatically, protecting his vision. He let go of the hook, twisting as he did so. If the man didn't have access to a healing potion or a cleric, he'd have a permanent limp. Breathing hard, Jherek moved backward two more steps, getting the distance he needed to finish the fight.

The big man stood with effort, hobbled by his injured leg. He worked at rubbing the blood from his eyes with his free hand. He kept hold of the long sword, pushing it out in Jherek's general direction.

Jherek hesitated. It was one thing to take a man's blood in the heat of battle, but another to take it when the man was so obviously helpless.

"Vyane!" the big man called.

Realizing the man wasn't alone, Jherek whirled. He brought the cutlass up to a ready position as his eyes scanned the shadows around the court. He saw the woman standing in the darkness gathered at the opposite end of the court, below the hand-lettered sign that advertised Blackthorn's Brew, the most popular festhall in all of Velen.

She was slim-hipped and long-haired, as small as the man was large. Her face looked elven, but Jherek wasn't sure. She wore dark clothing, a rider's outfit, one used to rough handling. A light breeze lifted her hair from her shoulders in a fluttering halo, and wiggled the fletchings of the quarrel nestled in the groove of the crossbow she held.

Jherek saw her hand clench, letting him know she'd fired. With Malorrie's training, he knew there was a chance of avoiding the bolt as it leaped from the bow. A speeding quarrel couldn't change course in mid-air unless it was magical in nature. All he had to do was move, but when he did, it was already too late.

The woman's beauty surprised him, making him wonder how anyone so pretty could cold-bloodedly feather someone she didn't even know.

The heavy bolt crashed into his chest, burying deep just below his left shoulder. His arm went numb at once even as his chest seemed to catch on fire. The impact knocked him backward and he stumbled as he tried to regain his balance. The numbness spread down his spine, stilling his legs. He fell.

"Vyane!" the big man yelled again.

"Silence, Croess," the woman said with an accent that Jherek couldn't place.

"The little bastard nearly killed me. Look what he's done to my leg."

Jherek lay on his back and tried to breathe. He couldn't. It was like the crossbow bolt had nailed his chest closed. He lay still, staring up into the sky, at the stars he'd gotten so accustomed to while on watch in *Butterfly*'s crow's nest. He couldn't even blink or move his eyes as he watched the woman approach.

"Your own fault," she told the big man without sympathy. "You moved on him from out of the shadows. He should have been dead before he even knew you were there."

"You saw how quick he was," Croess protested. "Fanged demons take me if I'm lying, but he's hardly more than a boy and he fights like a damned whirlwind."

"You knew he would be something different. We were told that." She stared down at Jherek with empty eyes and said, "A crossbow bolt did for him just fine." She glanced across Jherek and added, to someone, "You said there was gold?"

"Aye," a man said.

Jherek strained to hear better, but the numbness filling his body seemed to affect his ears as well. He was certain he knew the voice.

"Old Finaren, he's soft on his people. Always puts something aside for them. Knew he'd give it to this boy even with him being what he is."

The elf woman knelt and went through Jherek's clothing. Her practiced fingers found the leather pouch Finaren had given him. She tossed it, seeming to weigh its worth in that single motion. "So young," she said, standing. "Pity."

"We should take his head," Croess said. "Prove to that damned wizard that we did what we set out to do."

"No," the woman replied. "He'll take our word."

"His foot, then," the big man said. "We'll make it look like the ghost that's supposed to haunt this place was responsible for killing him."

"After you've gone and bled all over the place?" the woman taunted. She shook her head. "No, I'll not have him mutilated. The old woman who raised him will be allowed to bury all of him."

"Maybe that's not your choice," the big man grated. "It was me that got hurt. I'll do as I damn well please."

"Try, and he won't be the only one who dies here tonight," the woman promised.

Silence filled the court for a moment, then Jherek heard the big man limp away. His hearing dwindled, making it impossible for him to hear anything else that might have been said. His vision blurred, then finally turned dark. He felt stilled, buried in the icy core of his own shadow, wearing it like a shroud.

Through it all, even though the fear and anger burned through him, he wondered where the voice was. Why wasn't it commanding him again, telling him to live so that he could serve?

The darkness crept in and stole even his thoughts away.

8

Laaqueel paused at the top of the wooden steps leading up to Fishgut Court. The battle taking place out in the harbor was drawing all of Waterdeep's attention. More sailors and shopkeepers ran toward the harbor. Several of them brushed past Iakhovas and his wererat group, letting her know his spell still masked them. She studied the harbor, amazed that the attack had made it this far. Even when Iakhovas had made his plans, she'd had her doubts.

Another fiery salvo came from Waterdeep Castle's catapults, painting flaming lines through the dark sky for a moment, then splashing down in the water in a violent flash of sparks and hisses that overrode even the screaming fear and rage and disbelief coming from the surface dwellers. Fingers of oily fire splayed out over the waves stirred up by Iakhovas's wizard's storm. The waves crashed ten feet high now, slopping over the sides of many vessels at anchor and shoving them into each other.

A Waterdhavian Watch wizard rode a flying carpet out over the harbor toward a floundering raker besieged by sahuagin boarding from the water. The malenti watched the wizard start his gestures to unleash a spell. Her instinctive fear was of fire, knowing how quickly her people perished when fought with that element. She said a quick prayer to Sekolah to spare the sahuagin warriors because the dead could not fight and she knew the Great Shark would understand that. The sahuagin didn't see him, and she wished she could call out a warning.

Despite the howling winds being stirred up by the storm, the flying carpet held steady. It even held steady when the brine dragon's head erupted from the uneven water. The dragon was nearly thirty feet in length and had a triangular, wedge-shaped head filled with sharp teeth.

Covered with ridged and craggy scales that didn't fit well together, the creature was a virulent green. Yellow tufts ridged its head, running from between its eyes and becoming standing scales as they went on down its back. It had flippers instead of claws. Snapping its wide mouth open, it clamped down over the wizard, swallowing him and the carpet whole. The dragon disappeared below the surface again just as quickly.

"Laaqueel," Iakhovas called in a harsh voice.

She turned to face him.

"We're not here to *win*, little malenti," the wizard told her. Lightning suddenly savaged the skies, a forked white-hot sword that sheathed itself in purple umber, then winked out. In the brief, eye-stinging flash of light, Iakhovas's tattoos stood out harshly against his skin. "But neither then shall your people lose more than the surface dwellers."

Knowing it was the best she was going to get, she nodded. As she turned to take another look at the action in the harbor, a dragon turtle surfaced. It stretched his ponderous head out, unveiling the scaled armor protecting its neck, and breathed a cloud of scalding steam over sailors manning a nearby cargo ship. The men died instantly, their corpses throwing off gray smoke as they cooled in the night. Maybe the sahuagin wouldn't win this battle, but the malenti knew that this night would never be forgotten in the history of the City of Splendors.

"Haste, little malenti," Iakhovas told her. "Even now, with all the strength I've gathered, I'm not without limits. Should I not get what I've come for this night, the sahuagin sacrifices will indeed be for naught. I am their savior whether you wish it so or not."

Laaqueel tightened her grip on her sword. Was he lying, or was he telling the truth about his limitation? She didn't know. She gazed into his black eye, knowing the patch over his other eye was a silent promise that he wasn't infallible, unless it was a sacrifice he'd willingly made at some time in exchange for something he wanted more.

She also knew that he wouldn't tolerate her questioning him. She hurried up the steps after him, moving around the sign at the top of the stairs that advertised Fishgut Court's attractions and businesses.

Iakhovas moved with confidence, working his way through the maze of streets that had Laaqueel lost almost immediately. In the sea, she'd always been able to get a perspective on the sahuagin communities by simply swimming above them. Here on land she was locked in with only two dimensions open to her. Despite her limited familiarity with coastal towns, she didn't feel comfortable straying out of sight of the sea.

They left sight of the harbor almost immediately, though, and she tried to remember the streets as she saw the signs. Adder Lane came first, clearly marked. Ahead and on the left, a number of lanterns with different colored glass illuminated the full-sized carved creature out in front of an inn called the Rearing Hippocampus. Bouncers stood watch over the doors, their hands never far from their swords.

As Laaqueel passed them, a small group of sailors ran toward the inn, bellowing about the attack in the harbor. Iakhovas led his group down Adder Lane onto Gut Alley, cutting across to Snail Street, then turning left there. When they reached an intersection with Shesstra's Street, Iakhovas turned right onto Book Street.

An older man with two young women stepped from a small shop. The painted letters across the boarded over bay window declared the place to be an herbalist's. The business looked like it had fallen on hard times. The man and women were dressed in ill-fitting clothes that had seen better times.

Without warning, one of the young women screamed and grabbed the older man's arm, pointing at Iakhovas and the wererat group.

Iakhovas's attention swiveled onto her at once. "Execute the woman!" he ordered. "Damn her and the rudimentary skill she has for the true seeing. Humans should never have been allowed magic!"

His words hammered into Laaqueel. For the woman to have seen through the illusion Iakhovas wove with his magic, she had to have used magic of her own, but what magic was that?

What did she see when she saw Iakhovas as he really was?

The wererats broke ranks quickly, giving chase at once. Laaqueel pushed herself, feeling incredibly sluggish on the surface, but letting her desire to know more about her master push her to greater speed.

Obviously knowing that they weren't going to be able to outrun their pursuers, the man barked orders to the screaming women to keep running, then turned to face the first of the wererats. He slipped a long, slim club from his belt and called out in a harsh voice.

The lead wererat grinned in anticipation. As he moved to the attack, Laaqueel watched the creature's human features drop away, becoming increasingly ratlike.

The shopkeeper swung his club with precision and skill, slipping past the wererat's sword. When the club reached the wererat's skull, it crashed through bone and brain, killing the creature at once.

From her studies, Laaqueel knew the wererats could only be harmed in any form other than their human ones by silver or enchanted weapons. The club represented a definite threat. She pulled up a step, allowing the pack of wererats to overtake her.

"Afraid?" one snarled at her as it changed into a rat man.

Laaqueel ignored the creature, feeling no disgrace at allowing it to attack the shopkeeper. Three wererats leaped at the man, driving him backward as they swung their short swords and snapped their vicious teeth.

A cold shiver prickled through Laaqueel as she took up the chase again. The young woman's own abilities for magic had been revealed when she saw through Iakhovas's illusion and the man's by his club. The malenti knew it probably didn't end there, but she gave chase, skirting around the snarling bodies of the wererats taking the shopkeeper to the ground by force. Still the man fought them, even knowing he was going to die. Every time the hand-carved club landed, wererat bones broke.

The extra effort required simply to breathe above the surface drained Laaqueel. Her gills flared open in an effort to compensate. The two women ahead of her grew closer, though, and none of the residences around them threw open their doors to help. Book Street remained deserted.

The women rushed into an alley to the left.

Laaqueel caught the corner of the building with her free hand and whipped her body around. The alley surprisingly turned sharply, almost switching back on itself to the right.

The woman who'd seen through Iakhovas's illusion reached for a perilously stacked pile of refuse at the side of a fishmonger's shop. Standing taller than a man, packed with fish tripe and bones from a few days' business as well as rotting vegetables and other garbage, the pile came down in a wet rush.

Battered by the garbage coming down on top of her and swarming underfoot, Laaqueel nearly fell. She caught herself on one hand and kept going forward. Huge rats came down in the refuse as well. One of them whipped through her hair in its fright, and two others clung to her body. She swept the one from her hair, then hurled herself up against the side of the building to knock the ones off her back.

The women continued to scream fearfully.

Hoarse voices shouted overhead, and a few lights came on. No one came to investigate and no one peered too closely from the windows above ground level.

The malenti caught up with the second woman first. She swung her sword, bringing the flat of the blade down hard. The woman stopped running at once, dropping to the ground and laying stunned.

Still in full stride, Laaqueel grabbed the other woman by her hair and yanked her from her feet. The woman came down hard on the muddy cobblestones. The breath left her lungs in a rush.

Breathing hard, her gills not quite able to meet the demands being made on them, the malenti held her sword under the woman's throat. She looked into the surface dweller's eyes, seeing the fear there and relishing it. Fear meant power.

"Tell me—" Laaqueel gasped. "—tell me—what you saw!"

The young woman cried, tears flowing freely from her eyes as she shook her head and panted, "I can't."

Knowing the wererats were going to be on them within minutes, Laaqueel yanked the woman up and dragged her back to where she'd left the first woman. The malenti laid her sword on the ground and held the woman with one hand. She laid her other hand on the unconscious woman's face. She prayed in her tongue, the sahuagin clicks echoing in the alley even over the continued shouts by the people inside the houses.

In answer to her prayers to Sekolah and to the power she wielded in the Great Shark's name, the unconscious woman's face writhed with sudden infection-filled weals. As she finished the prayer, the weals erupted in bloody pus. The woman moaned with the pain even though she was unconscious, barely clinging to her life.

Laaqueel fixed her hot gaze on the woman and shook her. "Tell me!" she roared. "Tell me what you saw or she'll die in agony!"

It took two attempts for the woman to get any words out. "I can't!" she cried finally. "Tymora help me, what I'm telling you is the truth. I was doing a true seeing, looking at an object brought to us by a sailor who wanted to know if it had any magic about it. When we heard the screams coming from the harbor, I went outside. I didn't mean to see you."

"What did you see?"

She shook her head. "The rat men," she said. "You, and—"

"What about the other man?"

She struggled to make her mouth work.

"Better you welcome Umberlee's dark caresses than leave yourself in my hands, child," Laaqueel promised.

"I can't tell you," the woman said, "because I've never seen anything like it."

"What?" the malenti demanded. She heard the slap of feet on the cobblestones, coming closer. Whether they were wererats or Waterdhavian Watch, she was almost out of time.

"It was huge. Fearsome. All fins and teeth and—*evil* of the darkest sort. It *hungers*!"

Before Laaqueel could ask anything further, a green glow surrounded the woman. In the next instant her body came apart in thousands of flying sparks.

The malenti leaped back, startled and fearful of getting burned. The green sparks held neither fire nor heat, though, swirling into the air and winking out in a matter of heartbeats. Nothing remained of the woman. Laaqueel forced herself to her feet, seeing Iakhovas at the alley's mouth.

He gave her a baleful glare with his single eye.

The creaking wheels of a wagon drew Laaqueel's attention. She shifted to face the alley, spotting the black plague wagon rolling toward her at once. Ebony sheets fluttered in the wind.

No driver held the reins, and no draft animals pulled the wagon. It rolled slowly at Laaqueel, and the malenti knew she was looking at more of the hated surface dweller magic.

9

"Wake up, boy!"

The stern voice scratched Jherek from the comfortable womb of darkness that had settled over him like a shroud. He wanted to tell Malorrie that he was dead, but he knew it wasn't true. The quarrel still burned deeply in his chest.

"Who did this to you?" Malorrie demanded.

Jherek ignored the question as he opened his eyes. "What are you doing here?" His voice carried a whistle with it, and he knew it was caused by his left lung filling up with blood from the puncture wound. It already felt like rocks had been shoved into his chest, making it harder to breathe.

"You were late home to sup, boy," Malorrie said. "Madame Iitaar sent me to bring you home. She knew when *Butterfly* put into port and how long she takes to off-load." He made a sour face. "From the looks of things, she's going to be properly vexed that she didn't send me sooner."

"It's been kind of inconvenient for me as well," Jherek told him honestly.

"You'll not die."

Jherek didn't disagree. If anyone knew death, it was Malorrie. The old phantom had never admitted when he'd died, nor given any details on the how of it.

He knelt over the young sailor, concern etched in his translucent eyes, his gaze as always made somewhat confusing because he could be seen through. He was dressed as he always was in warrior's chain mail with a deep scarlet tabard that hung to his ankles. It carried no coat of arms, no insignia of any kind. He carried a broadsword sheathed at his hip, stripped of any ornamental designs that might have offered a clue as to the phantom's background. His face belonged to that of a man in his middle years, and his nature made it hard to tell the color of his skin or hair or the thin mustache that stained his upper lip, but Jherek always felt the phantom's eyes in life had been the blue of the seas.

"Mayhap you should lay here, boy, until I get some help."

"No," Jherek croaked. "This is Seven Cuts Court, remember? It's a wonder I'm not dead already."

"That arrow sticking out of your chest . . . it's possible the ghost that haunts this place thought you were already dead." The statement was Malorrie's attempt at a joke, but he spoke truth as well.

The likelihood traced cold fingertips along Jherek's spine. He had no idea how long he'd lain there after he'd passed out. It was still night, and his lung hadn't completely filled up, so he knew it couldn't have happened long ago. There was no sign of the elven woman or her partner.

The young sailor rolled over, then used his hands and knees to push himself up into a crawling position. It was awkward with the quarrel sticking out of his chest. Still it was short. If he'd been pierced with a cloth yard shaft, he might not have been able to get to his feet at all.

Standing, he swayed dizzily. He felt Malorrie clamp a hand on his elbow, helping steady him. He also knew the cost the old phantom had to endure himself with the contact. Where a true ghost had no problems touching a living being and doing harm, the geas that had been laid on Malorrie to prevent his rest in the afterlife also kept him from making contact with many of those still living. If he did lay hands upon them, the whisper of life-force that maintained him was drained by the living.

When Jherek had first come to Velen seven years ago, he'd fallen and broken a leg. Malorrie had been the first to find him. The phantom, ever considerate, tried to care for Jherek only to find to the consternation of both that touching a wounded person drained his life-force even more rapidly. Malorrie had never told Jherek how he'd happened to be in Velen, or why he'd decided to befriend him as a young boy, but Jherek had learned then that the price the old knight had paid had been high. In all his years, both alive and while dead, Malorrie said he'd never met or heard of another like him.

At times, even conversation with other flesh and blood people outside of Madame Iitaar and Jherek left Malorrie weakened. It was a hardship for the phantom, the young sailor knew, because Malorrie was one of the most sociable people he'd ever met. Over the years, Malorrie had always been there with a story, a comment, or simply a kind word.

"Easy does it, boy. Walk before you run," Malorrie advised.

Jherek wrapped his hand around the quarrel and steeled himself.

"What are you planning to do?" Malorrie asked.

"I'm going to pull the bolt out," Jherek said in a hoarse, weak voice. Truthfully, the thought of yanking the quarrel out of his chest unnerved him.

"No," Malorrie said, placing a hand over Jherek's. "Leave it in."

"It hurts," Jherek protested. He tried to take a deep breath and couldn't. The tightness in his chest almost panicked him. "It's hard to breathe."

"The wound's making it hard to breathe, boy," Malorrie said, "not the quarrel. Most likely it's helping block some of the bleeding. Leave it for Madame Iitaar to handle."

Jherek was only too willing to leave the quarrel in place.

"Feel ready to try a few steps?"

He nodded, noticing the black spots on Malorrie's arm. As he watched, another formed, wrapping itself around the phantom warrior's wrist. "Let me go," he rasped, realizing the contact was rapidly draining Malorrie's afterlife.

"Why?"

"I won't have your second death on my hands," Jherek gasped. He pulled weakly, trying to escape the phantom's grip. With the appearance of the black spots, he knew Malorrie had to be in pain as well. Yet the old warrior said nothing about it.

"You can hardly stand, and Madame Iitaar's is further up Widow's Hill."

Jherek pulled his hand from the phantom's weaker grip. Fever gripped him, causing perspiration to coat his face. "*My* death if I can't make it, Malorrie, not yours. I've cost too many people too much in this life already."

Malorrie drew himself up to his full height, standing inches over the young sailor. "Damn you for that pigheadedness, boy. Accept help when it's offered."

"Not when it costs so much."

"That's my choice to make."

"Aye," Jherek agreed as he gathered his cutlass and hook, then took his first step toward home, "and mine. Can you tell me that you'd make it up that hill while helping me?"

"I can."

Jherek took another trembling breath, getting even less air this time than the last. The left side of his chest had gone completely numb, and a coldness spread across his shoulders. "Swear it to me, and remember that we've never had any lies between us."

"I can't."

Jherek nodded, moving slowly. "Don't be so quick to speak against my pigheadedness either. It's going to get me to the top of that hill." He looked up before him, seeing the incline swell dramatically upward. He'd never thought about how high Widow's Hill was in years. Even as a youth he'd flown up and down the trails to the harbor like a bird. He focused on the two-story house at the top of the hill, feeling its pull. That was home, the only home he'd ever known.

"Just you see that it does," Malorrie commanded, "because the first time you falter and fall, I'm going to drag you by the hair to that house if it kills us both."

Jherek didn't doubt for a moment that the phantom would do exactly that. Malorrie's word was his bond. As he walked, the young sailor tried not to think of the wages that had been stolen from him. It was gone, as was his job aboard *Butterfly*. He didn't dwell on those things, though, but on Madame Iitaar, who'd raised him for the last handful of years and more, who'd shown him the only mother's love he'd ever known.

In his eyes he was a failure, but he knew she wouldn't see it that way. Madame Iitaar had always shown hope for him even though he was sure he would only break her heart.

10

". . . and salty diamonds stained the maiden's cheeks,
as she laid the sod o'er her gallant knight.
Though the battle claimed her man,
Her heart stayed forever true."

His eyes closed, Pacys listened to his voice echo in the large room and knew that he'd fully claimed his audience. His fingers dwelled upon the strings of his yarting for a few beats more, mourning the loss of the lady for the man. Except for his song and the last fading chords of the yarting, silence filled the room.

Taking a deep breath, the old bard opened his eyes. Men wept openly, their voices hushed so they wouldn't reveal their pain and out of deference to his voice. The candles illuminating the room showed the emotions on the faces of the priests and the other faithful of Oghma. Shadows and candle smoke clung to the large beams showing through the ceiling.

Even large as it was, the room was near to overfilled. Fifty men and more sat around the plain pine board tables or stood along the unadorned walls of the meeting hall. Plates and cups scattered over the table were the only remnants of the fine meal they'd enjoyed before he'd started singing.

"I stand corrected, old man," a young priest said, rising to his feet. "Your voice has seasoned like fine whiskey." Tears mixed freely in with his beard. "I'll gladly stand the price of a tune such as that." He picked up an unused bowl and dropped a silver piece onto it. He passed it to the man on his left, who added more coins.

"There's no need for the bowl," Pacys said with a smile. "Tonight, in a much honored tradition for those in my trade, I sing for my supper," He hoisted a tankard of ale that had warmed during the ballad, "and for the drink afterward." He sipped the ale and found it warm, but he'd gotten used to drinking it just like that over the years of his long travels.

The bard was old, had seen seventy-six winters in his time, and showed his hard life in wrinkles and the stringy meat that clung stubbornly to his bones. He shaved his head these days, giving in to the baldness that had claimed him in his fifties. The sun had darkened his skin to the tone of old leather and turned his eyebrows silvery. He went clean-shaven and wore the newest breeches and doublet he'd had left in his kit. His clothing was serviceable, not gaudy as some in his calling preferred. His voice and his tales kept him employed, not a costume. He sat easily on one of the round dinner tables that filled the room, his legs crossed despite his years. Thick beeswax candles burned on either side of him, placed by him so that their light fell across his face.

"Another song," a man at one of the nearer tables pleaded.

Pacys smiled, loving the sound of the passion in the man's voice. His fingers carelessly caressed the yarting's strings, plucking melodious notes that haunted the large room. "Another song, gentle sir? And what would you have? A ballad of great daring in which fair Kettlerin reversed the schemes of Thauntcir Black-Eyed to gain back the heart of her lover? An epic poem of grand adventure of Derckin and Dodj and how they found the lost treasure of Gyschill, the Topaz Dragon of the Far North? Or a seafaring lyric of ghost ships that plunder the Sword Coast still?"

"Enough, good Pacys," Hroman said, standing at a table to the bard's left. He was a short man like his father, Pacys knew, but broad shouldered and good-natured. It was strange to see him as he was now, well into his forties when the bard wanted only to remember the boy as he recalled him. "You've entertained these layabout priests of Oghma well for the past three hours."

"And only whetted our appetites for more," another priest lamented. He was an older man among those around him, but Pacys felt he was still ten years his junior. Looking around the crowd, the bard knew he was probably the oldest man there.

Hroman laughed, and he sounded a great deal like his father, Pacys discovered. He was also full of the same fire of command. Sandrew the Wise, the high priest of the Font of Knowledge in Waterdeep, had proven his name by lifting Hroman to a place of command within the temple.

"Yes, and he'll be here tomorrow night as well," Hroman said, "unless you strip the voice from him tonight with your demands."

"Will you be here tomorrow, Pacys?" a priest roared.

The bard's fingers still moved across the yarting's strings, instinctively plucking out a soft tune that underscored Hroman's words and lent them even more weight. Part of his magic was in lending his music to words and making them more commanding. "Yes. I plan on being in Waterdeep for a tenday or more this trip."

"We want to hear all your songs and your tales," one of the younger priests said.

Pacys only grinned in appreciation, then reached down and snuffed the candlewicks between his fingertips. The hard calluses from playing the yarting for sixty years didn't let the heat through. "As many that we are able to share," he promised.

Hroman chased them out of the big room.

Pacys unfolded his legs, feeling the knee joints pop back into place and creak in protest. The legs were always the first to go, from too many miles spent walking, too many hours spent on a table or in a chair. He took a moment to place the yarting in its leather and brass case, then hooked his boots up by their tops in his free hand.

"Oghma has truly blessed you, old friend," Hroman said.

"I fear I played for a captive audience tonight," Pacys said. "With all the building that is still going on here, I suspect they've seldom seen much in the way of entertainment."

"More than you think," Hroman said. "Tallir, the lad who first started the singing tonight, had thought of becoming a bard before Oghma touched him and brought him into our fold."

"Pity," Pacys said, meaning it, "the boy has a rare and golden voice."

Hroman smiled. "I'll tell him you said so. It took a lot of nerve for him to get up in front of the group tonight, knowing you were going to perform."

"I hope I did not offend him."

Pacys took his travel kit from under the table where they'd eaten. It was tattered and scuffed, showing signs where he'd repaired it himself, serviceable but with no art about the stitching. Shouldering the kit and the yarting case, he gathered the iron-shod staff that lay under the bench.

"You didn't," Hroman said. "I saw young Tallir with a quill and parchment, writing furiously in that bastardized symbology he's developed for himself to take notes. He's skillful with it. I'd dare say he's written down every word you uttered tonight and will add it to his own repertoire."

"Those songs and tales aren't mine," Pacys said. "They've been given to me on the road, things that anyone can pick up. Though, in truth, I should give him the names of the bards who first arranged them." It was the only way a bard achieved fame and a certain kind of immortality, the old bard knew. It was something that had escaped Pacys for all his years.

"You'll have time to set him right tomorrow." Hroman grabbed their plates and headed for the kitchen. "Let me drop these off with the cook staff and I'll show you to your room."

"I'd planned on supper," Pacys admitted, "but I hadn't intended to beg a room as well."

"Pacys," Hroman said, "it's by High Priest Sandrew's will that you will always be a guest within this temple."

"He's a generous man," Pacys said.

"I'll send word to him in the morning that you are here. I know he'll want to come, and it would do him good to be away from his projects for a time."

"You mean the building of the Great Library?" Pacys asked.

Hroman handed the stack of dishes to a priest in a stained white apron in the kitchen. Hroman took a candle from a box on one of the tables and lit it from the stove. He guided Pacys back to the large room and out into the hallway leading back to the personal quarters. The rumble of voices and bits of song, good-natured teasing and prayer filled the hallway as the bard walked by the doors.

"You know about the library?" Hroman asked.

"Of course," Pacys said. "Besides songs and tales and physical comedy a bard claims as his bag of tricks, there is always the news."

Hroman nodded and said, "Of course . . ."

He said something more, but Pacys couldn't hear him, lost in the aching melody of the music that had been drifting through his brain for the last few months. The strains and chords were clearer now than they had been in years. He paused, listening for more, but the music was taken from him, leaving only what he'd learned this time. He looked up at Hroman, who gazed at him with concern.

". . . you all right?" the priest asked.

"I'm fine."

"Perhaps the wine," Hroman suggested, "or the lateness of the hour. I didn't even think to ask how many days you'd been traveling to reach Waterdeep."

"It's not that," Pacys replied. He hesitated, not wanting to say too much. Hroman was the son of one of his best and truest friends, though. "Come. Show me to my room and we'll talk."

Hroman looked indecisive for a moment, then walked further down the hallway. "We've not got an extra room at the moment. With the building of the new temple and the additional clergy Sandrew has put on, we're packed into these rooms like tuna in a fisherman's hold."

The current Font of Knowledge was located in a row house on Swords Street. They hoped to have the new temple finished this year. "I can take a room at an inn, or sleep outside."

"No," Hroman said with some force. "Even if I could be so cold-hearted, Sandrew would give me a tongue-lashing that would shame me for weeks. I'll give you my room."

He pushed open a door on the right. Weak candlelight flickered over the room, revealing the narrow bed under the only window, a small bookshelf against one wall next to a small fireplace, a wardrobe, and a compact desk.

"Where will you sleep?" Pacys asked.

"We've a common room."

"I could stay there," the bard protested.

"As could I," Hroman said. "Please take this room. As a priest, there's not much I have to offer in the way of tangible assets, but I can make a gift of this. I have earned it with my work, and it's mine to give."

Pacys saw the earnestness in the younger man's gaze and nodded. "As you say," he said humbly as he laid the yarting gently on the bed and sat. "Take up a chair and we'll talk."

Hroman pulled the chair out from the desk, then took a wine bottle from the book shelves. He smiled as he sat. "I've been saving this for something special, if you've a stomach for it."

"For wine, I'll always have the stomach," Pacys said, smiling, "though not always the head."

"Isn't that the way of it?" Hroman said. "This is from our own press. One of our best vintages."

"Maybe we should save it for another time."

"When you're leaving?"

"That would seem a more appropriate time."

Hroman's face darkened. "I'd rather say hello over a bottle of wine than good-bye. I've said enough good-byes of late." He unstoppered the bottle and handed it to the bard.

Pacys took it. "I heard about your father," he said. "I'm sorry. If I'd known, I'd have been here."

"I know." Hroman took a deep breath and looked away for a moment. His eyes gleamed and he said, "He left a letter for you. It took him a long time to write it. Lucid moments were very few . . . very hard for him at the end."

A chill touched Pacys. Last year when he'd died, Hroman's father had been five years Pacys's junior. Death didn't scare the bard, but old age, infirmity, and mental loss did. It was hard not to grow more terrified with each passing year.

"Then I shall read it with pleasure," Pacys said.

"I've not read it," Hroman said, "so I don't know what he had to say, or if any of it makes sense."

"Your father was a good man," Pacys told him. "He'd not leave anything behind that didn't reflect that. I need only look at you to know that."

"Kind words," Hroman acknowledged.

"And truly meant." The bard held up the wine bottle. "To your father. One of the best men I ever knew. Fearless in heart and strong in his faith." He drank deeply from the bottle, then passed it back to the priest. The wine was sweet and dry.

Hroman drank deeply too. "What brings you to Waterdeep, old friend? A simple longing to see the Sword Coast again?"

"Compulsion," Pacys admitted. "My end time lies not too far before me now, and I'm not fool enough to believe any other way."

Hroman started to object and Pacys shushed him with a raised hand.

"Kind words lie out of kindness, young Hroman, that's why numbers were invented."

Hroman passed the wine bottle back across.

"I come on a quest," Pacys said. "Of sorts."

"Of sorts?"

"I can't say that it's a true quest," the old bard admitted. "I can only hope for divine intervention." He drank again, passed the bottle back, then pulled the yarting from the bed and opened the case. He took it across his knee and strummed the strings. Even though it was in perfect pitch, he twisted the tuning pegs, gradually returning them to the positions they were in. "Listen." His hands glided across the strings, fingertips massaging the frets.

Music, beautiful and as true as rainwater, filled the room.

"Dear Oghma, but I've never heard the like," Hroman said when Pacys stopped playing.

"Neither have I," the old bard said. "Not outside of my head."

"What is it?"

"I don't know." Pacys's hands worked the yarting, underscoring their conversation with the lyrical sound. "Fourteen years ago, when last I saw you and your father here in Waterdeep, I was given that piece of a song. It came to me in a dream. That was the same night the mermen first came to live in Waterdeep Harbor."

"The ones who claimed that a great horror had risen in the seas to the south and destroyed their village," Hroman said. "I remember. Piergeiron kept the City Watch on double shifts for a time afterward."

Pacys nodded and asked, "Do you think I am a good bard?"

Hroman seemed surprised by the question. "Of course. Any time you showed up in Waterdeep, taverns requested you. Lords and ladies. You had a hearth and a home anywhere you wanted. Why you chose to spend so much time with a poor priest of Oghma used to astound my father."

"Your father and I were kindred spirits," Pacys said. "A slight tilting of the past of either one of us, and it might have been us filling the other's shoes. Your father had an excellent voice, but he chose to serve Oghma more directly than I, though I felt the pull of the priest's robes as well. Felt it most strongly."

"I didn't know."

"Now you do, and now you'll know why I see that I am not the bard everyone believes me to be." Pacys kept strumming the yarting, playing the melody over and over, wishing more might come to him. "Any bard might sing the songs of another, or tell the tales once he has heard them. It's a bard's gift to tell any tale, sing any song that he's heard. Most can even offer their own rendition of that tale or song, but none may approach the original singer's or teller's power for that song or story." He plucked the strings, gathering the crescendo that lurked in the backbeat of the tune he played. "To know true power as a bard, there must be a tale or a song that is always and forever acknowledged to belong to the composer."

Hroman nodded. "It's like that with treatises written by those inspired by Oghma."

"Yes." Pacys turned his melody to bittersweet memory. "I've covered the lands of Faerûn, sang and orated in castles and palaces, relayed bawdy tales in the crassest of coast dives among the harshest of men, and given voice to some of the most spiritually uplifting music in temples scattered across those lands. I've traveled and seen things that most men only dream of, had adventures that fire a young boy's heart as he listens to the tales his fathers and kin tell around a campfire at night, or by the safety of the home hearth, but never—*never*—in that time have I crafted a song that will be remembered as mine."

Hroman remained silent.

"What about you?" Pacys asked. "Are there treatises in Sandrew's Great Library that you have authored? New ways of thinking about old things? Or old ways of thinking about new things?"

"Yes."

"Then you have been gifted," Pacys said in a dry voice, "and you should never forget to give thanks for that. In some distant time, a young priest will open a scroll you have written and know your thinking."

"That doesn't mean he'll agree with it."

In spite of the darkness that threatened to quench his spirit in the night of the city and after all the miles he'd walked that day, Pacys smiled. "Whether they lay accolades at your feet or descry everything you've put on paper, they'll remember and know you. That's immortality of a kind."

"You feel that's what you're missing?"

Pacys broke the bittersweet melody and went back to the haunting one again. They were part of the same thing, he knew that in his heart and in his talent, but how to bind them? What words went with the music, he had no clue.

"How much did your father write, Hroman," he asked, "that's going into Sandrew's Great Library?"

"Tomes."

"Exactly. Your father was a man of letters, a man who thought well and deep, a man I treasured as a friend. I could lay my soul bare on several levels and trust him to have a care with it." Pacys paused a moment, listening to the music he made. "I wanted to talk with him again and see if he could offer any direction for this melody that haunts me so."

Hroman waited in silence a moment before saying, "Would you mind talking of it with me?"

"Over a bottle of the temple's finest vintage?" Pacys asked. He shook his head. "I'd not mind at all. I couldn't imagine better company."

"When you played tonight, during a couple of the old songs I remembered from times past when you were here, I could almost see my father sitting in the shadows. Your music always soothed him."

"I worked very hard for it to."

99

"Then why isn't it enough that you brought so much happiness to people?"

"Because," Pacys said, his voice thickening in spite of his skill, "I want a part of me to live forever. I want bards years from now to say that they have this song, whatever it is, by way of Pacys the Bard. I want it to be a song of such magnitude that it brings tears to the strongest of men and brings strength to the weakest of men. I want a story of love so pure and unfulfilled that it will truly hurt all who hear it. I want to fill the listeners with fear when they hear of the villain."

"That's a difficult request."

Pacys smiled gently. "I could settle for no less."

"You've written songs before, written tunes."

"Nothing like that," the bard said wistfully.

"You said a quest drew you back to Waterdeep."

Pacys drank from the bottle again, wetting his throat with the wine. "Fourteen years ago, I felt the touch of Oghma on me. When I watched those mermen swim into the harbor, I knew. The first notes came to me then and wouldn't leave my thoughts. Your father was at a table with me down on Dock Street."

"And nothing has happened since?"

Shrugging, Pacys said, "A chord here, a note there. In the early years, I followed my heart, desperate to find out why I'd been given that much of the song but nothing else. I traveled more than ever, going into places I'd never thought I'd go, and into countries I'd never even heard of at all. I increased my repertoire considerably."

"Never finding the song?"

"No. A tenday ago, I was in Neverwinter as a guest of Lord Nasher. I was talking to him, strumming my yarting as I am doing with you now, and a large section of one of the bridging sequences was given to me." Pacys turned his attention back to his instrument and played it. He knew the power of the piece when he saw Hroman sit back in slack-jawed amazement.

"I have never," the priest whispered, "heard *anything* so beautiful."

"Nor have I." Stating the truth almost broke Pacys's heart because the music was unfinished.

"Can't you finish it?"

Pacys shook his head. "I've tried. Everything I've tried to graft onto it sounds false."

"Why come here if you were given that piece in Neverwinter?"

"Lord Nasher's interested in magic," Pacys said. "That's no secret. Of late, he's been counseling with a young woman who's caught his eye and claims some clairvoyance through a deck of cards she uses to tell fortunes. She laid out a pattern for me and told me I'd find the next piece of the secret of the song back where it first began for me."

"Waterdeep?"

Pacys nodded. "There can be no other place."

Hroman was silent for a time. "The music you played, it was beautiful, but it spoke of war to me. Of violence and anger, and men dying by the handfuls."

"Yes," Pacys agreed reluctantly.

"That can't happen here. This is the safest place along the Sword Coast."

"That's what I thought too, Hroman, but this music is like no other I've ever encountered. It's mine, crafted by the gods and given to me."

The priest hesitated. "Which gods, my friend? Have you stopped to ask yourself this?"

"I've prayed," Pacys said. "Since I first heard that music fourteen years ago, I've prayed every day to Oghma to reveal the secrets of it. The pattern the girl laid out for me in Neverwinter showed Oghma's hand in what was going on. There's no evil working here. Not in my part of things."

"Then I will pray for you as well, and for this city should such a thing ever touch her shores." Hroman drank from the wine bottle and passed it back.

A hurried knock sounded on the door as Pacys drank down the dregs of the bottle.

"What is it?" Hroman asked.

"The city's under attack," a young, bearded priest announced as he stuck his head around the door, "out in the harbor. Sahuagin and sea monsters have been called in from the deeps. A storm the like of which no one has ever seen before. They're saying . . . I'm told the guard are all but decimated out in the harbor. There's a fear that the sahuagin will push on into Waterdeep herself."

Pacys pushed himself from the bed. "Do you have horses?" he asked Hroman.

"Yes." Hroman gave orders at once, striding out into the hall. His voice crackled like thunder through the hallway, waking priests and clergy from their beds.

The old bard trailed after the priest, his heart beating with excitement. He took only his yarting at first, then reached back for the staff that had been his constant companion almost as long as the instrument had been. The fragments of the song filled his mind, pushing out the fear and wonderment of the attack. For the moment, nothing else mattered but the song.

11

"Can you make it?" Malorrie asked.

"Aye." Jherek took another shuddering breath, straining against the blood-bloat in his injured lung. Crimson spilled over his chin now as well and stained the back of his hand where he wiped it away. "Just need—a moment—get my second wind."

Widow's Hill, like Captain's Cliff, separated the affluent from the common in Velen. The houses in the area ranged in all sizes and architecture. Madame Iitaar's home, and Jherek always thought of it as such even though it was also his home, stood two stories tall, with a widow's walk stretching out from the top floor to overlook the harbor. A high-peaked roof with a handful of different surface slants jutted up toward the dark skies. Lights burned behind the multi-paned glass windows but the house remained dark. The shutters still hung on the house because of the seasonal storms.

He stumbled along the partially overgrown trail made by children sneaking back and forth to the harbor without knowledge of their parents. At times the grade grew so steep he had to lean into it with his hands and force his way up. His blood-filled lung weighed him heavily.

Malorrie followed along at his side. As usual, the phantom's feet never even stirred the grass. He didn't try to help. "Gods, but you're an obstinate boy."

Jherek ignored him and grabbed a sapling. He pulled himself up further, then seized branches and used them to make his way. Spots swam in his vision by the time he reached the crest.

A four foot high wooden fence painted a pristine white surrounded Madame Iitaar's front yard. Upkeep of that fence had been one of

Jherek's first chores after he'd gone to live with the woman. Over the years, he'd painted and mended it several times, taking pride in what he'd been able to accomplish. Rose bushes and flowers filled crushed clamshell beds, and a small pond occupied the northeastern corner. Tall steps led up to the front porch where handmade rocking chairs looked out to sea.

Jherek staggered across the narrow and rutted wagon road that wove up through Widow's Hill. He paused at the gate, unable to focus enough to work the simple lock that held it closed.

"Allow me." Malorrie flicked it open, then shoved the gate aside.

As Jherek walked past the small pond, a watery coil slithered up from the mossy depths and thrust itself in his direction. Instantly the cold chill he always got when the water weird's full attention settled on him cut through him like a knife. He'd never liked the creature, but Madame Iitaar maintained it as a guardian against footpads. He kept his eyes on the creature's wedge-shaped head as it stared at him while he went up the steps to the porch.

Perspiration filmed his face by the time he reached the top step. His vision was so blurred that he thought he was seeing things at first. In the shadows laying across the expansive porch, the table and chairs weren't immediately noticeable.

His travel kit sat on the table, neatly packed and squared away. The backpack beside it bulged. Over the years, he hadn't bothered to collect many personal things because anything that didn't fit in a pack couldn't go with him if he had to leave. He didn't doubt that all of his possessions had been gathered on the table.

Seeing them there took away the last of his flagging strength and he sat numbly on the porch. His breath rasped hollowly in his ears.

He'd always thought of his stay with Madame Iitaar as transitory at best. He supposed he should have been surprised that his stay had lasted as long as it had. Obviously, now it was over.

Word from Finaren's crew had already climbed Widow's Hill.

12

Laaqueel stared at the approaching black plague wagon, her heart hammering in her chest. She clenched the short sword in her fist as she said a prayer and prepared one of the spells that had been given her by Sekolah.

"Do not waste your fears or spells on that thing, my little malenti," Iakhovas growled behind her. "What you see before you in all its gaudy trappings is an apparition, a bad dream without substance. This alley was named for that worthless abuse of power."

Laaqueel drew back uncertainly. The wagon unnerved her, but so did Iakhovas's knowledge of it. She'd helped prepare him regarding Waterdeep and she'd never heard of it.

"My time is wasting away," the wizard told her. He waved an arm, drawing his wererats to him. "You've already stepped over the line this night by questioning that damned woman, little malenti; have a care not make another such mistake. Tolerance is a virtue and I am not a champion of virtues. I judge you on your worth, and it's only outweighed by your frivolity or incompetence."

Ducking her head to avoid the cold gaze of his eye, Laaqueel remained still as the plague wagon passed her. She thought she saw the bones of the dead littering the wagon bed, but it might only have been a trick of the moonlight. When the wagon reached the end of the alley, it shimmered once and disappeared, taking with it the mournful creak of the wheels.

Iakhovas took the lead again without hesitation. He passed the first building across the alley on the left and stopped in front of the door to the second.

Laaqueel stopped behind him. She felt the dryness of her eyes as the lids dragged across them. Her skin felt tight as the harsh winds from the storm out in the harbor whistled up through the narrow streets and alleys leading up the inclines. She glanced back at the harbor. From her position, she could barely see the harbor, but it spread out from the Dock Ward, the flatness of the water contrasting sharply with the rolling pitch of the hills the city had been built on.

Several griffons from Waterdeep's air corps filled the air over the harbor. Their distinctive eagle wings and heads on their lions' bodies made them stand out against the smoke-filled night sky. Catapults still threw flaming missiles into the water inside the harbor and further out to sea where more sea creatures had gathered. Fire spread along the Dock Ward, burning buildings as well as ships at anchor. Laaqueel knew Iakhovas had spoken the truth when he said Waterdeep would bear the scars of the night's attack for years to come. It would become a symbol to her people that the hated surface dwellers could be driven from their own territory.

It would strike fear into the hearts of the humans.

She didn't delude herself, though. She knew she wasn't sure that Iakhovas was there because of Sekolah. The wizard had never denied knowing the Great Shark, but neither had he spoken of what relationship might exist between them.

The glyphs on the doors and wall surrounding them suddenly blazed with lambent emerald light. Laaqueel turned, raising her free hand in her defense with a spell at the ready.

"Be still, little malenti," Iakhovas commanded.

He centered himself in front of the door and spoke in that language Laaqueel had never been able to identify. Tattoos on his cheek, neck, and left forearm glowed with a matching green light, then shot out in beams no wider than a forefinger. The tattoos' beams touched the guardian glyphs built into the door and calmed them to dim glows.

Intrigued, Laaqueel glanced up at the battered sign hanging overhead: Serpentil Books & Folios. Constructed of sandstone, the shop's exterior showed signs of suffering through harsh weather conditions and dozens of years. The wares window where goods were normally displayed to attract passersby was crudely boarded over, leaving her with the impression that the business had been closed for a long time.

Iakhovas gestured at the door. In response, it opened with a creak and a flash of hot, bright light. The stench of burned clams swirled through the air for an instant. Without hesitation, the wizard strode into the building. He waved the wererats into position at the doorway.

"Come," he ordered Laaqueel.

The malenti followed him carefully, aware of the warning prickles running through her nervous system. The room was filled with books. Deep-hued bookshelves lined the wood-paneled walls and stood in stacks across the floor. Laaqueel had never seen so many books in her life. Only a few of the titles were visible to her, formed of raised gilt letters in gold, silver, and brightly colored thread. All of them seemed to concentrate on the hated field of magic.

A soft glow of blue light intensified in the back of the long room.

"You dare enter my sanctum unannounced?" a raspy voice challenged.

Turning, bringing her short sword up into the ready position, Laaqueel stared through the weak blue light.

A man sat at the other end of the long room. Piles of books occupied the shelves staggered all around him and stood in stacks across the rectangular table in front of him. The light came from glowing globes that floated behind him, leaving him only a featureless silhouette. Two empty chairs sat across the table from him.

"You know me, Serpentil," Iakhovas offered, "and it will be your mistake if you do not. I scheduled this meeting with you at this time." He walked closer to the table.

The silhouette sat silent and dark for a moment. Laaqueel noted the thin-fingered hand that rested lightly on a slim black volume closest to the man, then the man pointed at the glowing globes behind him. Obediently, the globes floated higher and forward, shedding more light over the table and the man sitting there.

He was dark complexioned and long faced like a sea horse. Hooded eyes halfway concealed a burning gaze. His long black hair hung to his shoulders and his chin sported an aggressive tuft of beard. His clothing was simple and unadorned. He indicated the chairs across from him.

"You may sit."

Iakhovas ignored the chairs and remained standing. "I've not time to be taken liberties with. If you're Jannaxil Serpentil then we should conclude our business with haste."

"I'm Jannaxil," the man said. He kept the slim black volume in his hand, stoking it absently. "What business is that?"

"I've never found coyness becoming," Iakhovas warned.

"And I've never found admitting guilt to someone who could be with the Waterdhavian Watch to be especially profitable," Jannaxil stated. His eyes narrowed. "I don't know you."

Iakhovas reached into his magical cloak and brought out two heavy books. "Then let your greed recognize these and provide me all the introduction I require for this transaction." He laid them on the table. Jannaxil immediately reached for them, larceny in his darting eyes.

Laaqueel recognized the books. She had been wondering about them for the last month. Three months ago, she'd succeeded in attacking a surface dweller cargo ship and taking the ship's scribe prisoner. It had been at Iakhovas's request. Back in the sahuagin village where Iakhovas ruled as a prince, the wizard had put the scribe to work copying two of the ancient texts they had found in different places over the years at his direction. The malenti hadn't seen the use in any of them because she couldn't read them, much less in duplicating their contents. A month ago, Iakhovas had killed the scribe and fed him to the sharks that had been charmed into watching over the village.

Jannaxil flipped through the texts with a practiced eye. "These are not the originals."

"No," Iakhovas agreed. "You don't have the price for the originals."

"If these copies exist, there could be others," the book dealer replied shrewdly.

"After I deliver these to you," Iakhovas agreed, "even more copies could be made, each of which you could sell. Do not make the mistake of trifling with me."

Jannaxil closed the books and leaned back in his chair. His eyes flicked to Laaqueel and she felt him evaluating her. She was aware of the way he held his right hand protectively, and of the old knife scar that showed there. He cut his gaze back to Iakhovas. "Tell me something of the nature of the thing I'm trading you for these."

"The nature?" Iakhovas repeated. "What you have is mine. I've come to claim it. Be glad that I'm willing to give you anything for it instead of just taking it and your life."

"Perhaps taking it wouldn't be as easy as you believe," Jannaxil said. "It may look like I'm here alone, but trust me when I say this place is safeguarded."

"Not against me," Iakhovas whispered in his cold, malevolent voice, getting closer, threatening the other man by his sheer size. "Never against me and all that I could bring to bear on you, human. The war that's going on in the harbor I delivered it unto Waterdeep's door. I control forces and powers that you've yet to see in your shallow life. Give me the talisman while you still have a bargain laid before you."

The book dealer looked ready to argue more, then grew deathly quiet as he stared at Iakhovas.

Though Laaqueel didn't see the wizard change, she noticed that Iakhovas's shadows on the wall of shelves behind them suddenly swelled to gigantic proportions. There was a symmetry to the new shadow, but it possessed harsh angles as well. The overall shape seemed familiar, but it was gone again before the malenti could figure out the pattern.

"I'll not trouble myself to ask for it again," Iakhovas warned.

Pale and contrite, Jannaxil said, "Of course." The book dealer tapped a section of his desk three times with a forefinger. In response, a drawer opened up in the table top, looking much deeper than the table was thick. The book dealer called out a name. "Wonvorl." A triangular talisman of diamond and pink coral floated up from the magical drawer. He took it from the air and tossed it to Iakhovas.

The wizard caught the talisman easily. He rolled his left sleeve back, revealing a gold-worked band that encircled his arm above his biceps. In the weak light of the floating globes, Laaqueel couldn't make out the details of the scrollwork cut into the band. There appeared to be a number of slots cut for different items. Some of them had been filled, but nearly all were empty. The triangular talisman fit into its appointed slot easily. A bright spark flashed against Iakhovas's palm, then quickly died away. He rolled his sleeve back down.

"What is that?" Jannaxil asked hoarsely. "That talisman was without a doubt one of the oldest things I've ever seen. And that band, I've never seen workmanship like that."

"Nor will you ever see its like again," Iakhovas stated. He turned and walked from the book shop. Laaqueel fell into step behind him.

Outside, Iakhovas headed back down Book Street, retracing their path to the docks. The wererats formed a loose perimeter around them. The streets were filled with Waterdhavian citizens with weapons, all running frantically in the direction of the harbor.

"We came here for that?" Laaqueel asked after a short time.

"Yes." The wizard glanced at her, a cruel smile on his face mocking her. "Don't be mislead by the talisman's size, my little malenti. Even small keys are known to open big doors."

Laaqueel's anger ignited within her. "What is it?"

"Perhaps, someday, I'll let you know, if it amuses me to do so."

She spoke again without pausing to think. "My people have fought and died this night for that thing. We should at least know—"

Iakhovas wheeled on her, using his size to tower above her. "You think perhaps you should at least be allowed to know what they've fought and died for? Is that what you're trying to say?"

Laaqueel felt her face tighten even further under the rampant emotions that surged through her. She tried to speak but couldn't.

"You have to learn your place, little malenti," Iakhovas grated in his harsh whisper. "I am giving you and your people the means to wipe the surface dwellers from the seas of Toril, and even drive them back into the interior that the sahuagin can claim the coastal lands as well. I'll even protect you from whatever enemies would try to take this empire from you."

"For what?" Laaqueel demanded.

He shook his head. "Once, my little malenti, I ruled the seas of this world, and I choose to do so again."

"Sacrilege!" Laaqueel said. "Sekolah—"

"—Has more pressing matters than paying attention to one puny world out of all those open to him," Iakhovas finished for her. "Why else have the sahuagin had to rely more on themselves than on their god?"

"Sekolah teaches us to be unmerciful, trains us to be strong through hardship. Self-sufficiency is valued above all things."

"If your people were truly self-sufficient," Iakhovas said, "they wouldn't need me now, would they? They would have already dealt with the hated surface dwellers, but they haven't. The success we've had here tonight will only lead to more successes in the future."

Laaqueel searched for a reply, but none came readily. Her attention shifted to a Waterdhavian Watch group that raced down the walk across the street. Two of the men wore wizard's robes showing the watch's colors of black, gold and green that were apparent even in the moonlight. She watched their heads turn as they came across from Iakhovas.

"Hold there!" one of the watch wizards ordered. He pulled a red glowing wand from his robes. The other guardsmen came around like a school of fish, turning as one.

Laaqueel appreciated their training but knew it made them dangerous if they saw through the illusion Iakhovas had cast.

"Who are you people?" the watch wizard demanded. Citizens trapped between the two groups on the street quickly thinned around them, leaving them facing each other.

"We have a ship out in the harbor," Laaqueel replied after realizing Iakhovas wasn't going to answer.

"I want to see your papers," the wizard said, gesturing to one of the men around him. Several of the other watch members had drawn heavy crossbows.

"They have the sense that something is wrong," Iakhovas said. "They smell the sewer scent of the wererats. Even I couldn't disguise that from those who are magically adept. Stand ready."

Laaqueel wished they were closer to the harbor. There she would be at least *near* her element.

"Slay the man who approaches us," Iakhovas commanded quietly, "as soon as he's near enough to make sure of the kill."

Laaqueel stretched her empty hand down, hiding it behind her leg. She flipped her retractable claws out and waited. When the man stood across from her and reached out for her papers, she struck. Her claws flashed across his throat, opening his jugular in a crimson rush. He fell to the street clutching at his torn throat.

The watch wizard pointed his wand. A bright flare shot from the end of it, wriggling like an eel and the color of fire coral. The mystic bolt streaked at Laaqueel's face. Before it could reach her, Iakhovas stretched out a hand. Tattoos along his arm glowed. In the next instant, the bright flare disintegrated into a shower of purple sparks, like a candle that had been snuffed out.

"Attack!" Iakhovas ordered. He dropped a hand in front of Laaqueel. "Not you, little malenti. The wererats possess a resistance to any weapons that aren't silver or have magical properties. You will remain with me."

The wererats shrugged forward, chittering in a semi-human language mixed with high, piercing squeaks. They brandished their swords, shapeshifting into their hybrid forms. The watch members held their ground, immediately moving shield men forward while the heavy crossbowmen fired at Laaqueel and Iakhovas. All of the arrows struck an invisible barrier and shattered, the pieces dropping into the street.

Iakhovas gestured at the wizard in an intricate pattern and spoke only a few words.

The human screamed in fear and pain as the spell took him. His arm holding the wand changed into limestone and the transformation kept moving, petrifying the whole man in seconds. He lost his voice in mid-yell.

The crossbow quarrels pierced the flesh of the wererats but didn't slow them in any way. They hacked into the guards, killing a few at first, then barely held their ground as the superior swordsmanship of the watch members ground them to a standstill.

The second watch wizard flung an arm forward. When it was out in front of him, a roiling mass of flames leaped from his hand and streaked toward Iakhovas and Laaqueel.

Instinctively, the malenti cowered away from the fireball. The basic fear of fire ingrained in her people proved too strong to resist. Iakhovas turned his hand out again and the tattoos glowed once more. Before the fireball could gather power and explode, it was snuffed out.

Wind rose around her, gathering strength quickly, then pressed outward across the street, picking up dust and loose debris and hurling it into the tangled knot of wererats and Waterdhavian Watch members. Small stones gathered up and flung by the wind broke the windows of the buildings behind the combatants.

Iakhovas stepped forward, drawing an imaginary bow as he spoke a lyrical incantation. When he released the make-believe string, a gossamer arrow that looked like glazed white pearl with a foul reddish undercast streaked across the street and pierced the second wizard's stomach.

The watch wizard shrieked in pain and fell to his knees. His hands gripped the shaft protruding from his belly, and smoke curled up from his flesh. Just as the other watch members started to beat the wererats back, dozens of black and gray furry bodies charged from nearby alleys. The rat horde responding to the calls of the wererats swarmed over the watch members, penetrating the weak spots in their armor, getting underfoot, and dropping from the eaves overhead.

Threatening yells grew louder from the surrounding citizens, and Laaqueel recognized that the danger their party was in was far from over. A man came at her. She beat his sword aside, then ripped the side of his face open and kicked him back into the street.

"Let us take our leave," Iakhovas said. "They will attempt to shut the harbor down soon, and I've no wish to be here when they do. We've little time left to effect our escape." He turned and fled into the shadows of the nearest alley.

Panic vibrated in Laaqueel as she realized if she lost sight of Iakhovas she wouldn't be able to find her way back to the harbor. She ran after him, followed by the wererats.

After a moment, the surface dwellers took up the pursuit, staying well back of the party of invaders. Still, Laaqueel knew their courage would grow as their numbers did.

13

"This is going to hurt."

Jherek looked up into Madame Iitaar's watery brown gaze and wanted to tell her that nothing could hurt more than finding his belongings packed when he returned home. He said nothing, though why he should respect her feelings at the moment was something he didn't understand. What was really confusing was the way Madame Iitaar seemed so concerned about him now, after she'd packed him out of her house.

"I know," he said instead. He had trouble speaking around the tightness in his chest, caused from the blood-filled lung and his own inner turmoil.

"You're going to be all right, though, Jherek," the old woman promised.

Once, Jherek had been told, Madame Iitaar had been the most beautiful woman in all of Velen. Vestiges of that beauty still showed in the square lines of her face, in the broad forehead revealed by the way she wore her gray hair pulled back in a long braid. Her half-elven heritage showed in her pointed ears and the lines of her face. She didn't wear any of her accustomed jewelry due to the lateness of the hour. The cerulean blue bodice and long leather skirt she had on looked fresh, as if she'd dressed only a short time ago. She was usually early to bed, but tonight she'd been up waiting.

The young sailor sat on the porch as she'd directed, his legs splayed straight ahead of him. She'd cut his shirt from him in order not to jostle the quarrel embedded in his chest any further. Dried blood smeared his chest and stomach and stained his breeches. Streaks of it turned the hardwood floor of the porch brown in places. He regretted that; he knew how Madame Iitaar treasured a clean porch for her guests.

"Aye, ma'am," he gasped.

The pain in his chest had died away to a dull throb, but the increased pressure in his wounded lung was frightening. Even when everything around him had been out of his control, he'd always been able to control himself, his body. Now, not even that existed.

"Before I can give you a healing potion to cure your wounds," Madame Iitaar said, "I've got to get that quarrel out of you."

"Aye, ma'am."

She touched the feathered shaft carefully. Despite her advanced years, her hands remained steady. "I can't pull that quarrel out."

Jherek tried to talk, but his voice seemed caught for a moment. "I know."

She held his face in her work-roughened hands. "I could give you a sleep draught, Jherek, but I wouldn't be able to rouse you before dawn." She hesitated. "There's a ship you must catch tonight."

Jherek stared into her eyes, not knowing what to say. Madame Iitaar wasn't just kicking him out of her house, she was banishing him from the city.

"She's called *Breezerunner*," Madame Iitaar said. "Do you know her?"

"Aye, ma'am. She runs north, along Sword Coast." Jherek broke into a coughing fit and fresh blood bubbled up from his injured lung.

"She leaves port in only a few hours," the woman said. "I've paid for passage for you under another name. They won't know you. Do you understand?"

"Aye, ma'am."

Questions filled Jherek's mind, pricking at the hurt her words caused him. Before he could utter any of them, Madame Iitaar shoved an open hand at the quarrel, stopping less than an inch short of actually touching it. The young sailor thought he saw blue sparks flare from her fingertips, but he couldn't be sure because in the next moment pain ripped through his chest. He tried to scream but couldn't.

The arrow jerked inside him as if it had been shot yet again. He felt it pierce his back and come out the other side, propelled by Madame Iitaar's magic. He jerked, trying to escape the agony, but Madame Iitaar wrapped her arms around his shoulders and held him to her until it passed. He made himself be still, not wanting to accidentally hurt her. Shudders quivered through his body like he was a tuning fork. Perspiration broke out along his brow and upper lip. Fresh blood spilled down his chest and back.

He tried to speak, but blood gurgled up from the wounded lung, a new torrent unleashed. He started drowning then as the other lung filled as well and couldn't find the heart to break free of Madame Iitaar's grip. He'd always feared he'd be alone when he died, and no one would care. At least here, in her arms, he could hold onto the illusion of family.

14

"Oghma grant us mercy."

Pacys hung onto the wagon seat as Hroman prayed and steered the pulling team along Dock Street beside him. The intersection to Ship Street lay just ahead, but the bard knew there'd be no passing along it. The sahuagin had risen from the waters of the harbor and taken their battle into the Mermaid's Arms festhall and to the shipbuilding shed of Arnagus the Shipwright, filling the streets there. Men ran with torches, but the light from the fires spreading uncontrolled across the harbor lit the area up. The storm out on the water lashed high waves over the docks, well above the normal waterline.

Looking further out into the harbor, Pacys looked across the burning husks of ships in the docks. Sailors ran the decks with buckets of wet sand and water, but Pacys knew it would never be enough to save them all. Mystical lightning lit up the savage sky, streaking down from on high to targets in the water below. The electrical display looked at home in the whirling storm.

"Oghma damn all sahuagin for their black hearts and insatiable, hellish appetites," Hroman cursed. He pulled his team up short, causing them to whinny in protest. They reared and bucked in their traces, eyes rolling white.

"It isn't only the sahuagin," Pacys said in disbelief. He watched the heads of huge creatures breaking the water of the harbor and identified only a few of them. Never had he seen so many of them gathered in one place. "There's something very wrong here. The sahuagin alone could never bring all these creatures together."

A flaming catapult load from Castle Waterdeep flared through the night sky and burst against a giant turtle's shell. The huge carapace shattered and the dying creature sank beneath the water. The giant turtle had pushed its way through the temporary structures that had been built over the waters of Smuggler's Dock to celebrate Fair Seas Festival, leaving only carnage in its wake.

Griffon riders patrolled the sky armed with bows and arrows. Only a few had thought to arm themselves with pitch-pots to fire their arrows. The Waterdhavian air corps proved merciless in their attack, swooping out over the harbor as well as the dock area to track down their quarry. When a flaming arrow embedded in a sahuagin, the sea devil dropped at once, torn by painful convulsions.

A cog with its prow burned nearly to the waterline finally gave up its struggle to remain afloat. The ship went down with several hands aboard. None of them had a chance to make it back to shore. A savagery of sharks lay in wait below the water. The storm-tossed waters roiled even more when the marine predators attacked the men.

Hroman bellowed at his priests, urging them into the battle. He was as quick thinking as his father, Pacys noted, listening to how the younger man broke the priests off into groups, charging each with taking control of the other wagon loads of priests arriving from the Font of Knowledge. Some were told to aid in fighting, while others were commanded to set up communication lines and medical treatment centers.

A cold chill ran through the bard as he watched the priests. Pacys knew it would be too little too late. Corpses of the Waterdhavian Watch and Guard members littered Dock Street as far as the eye could see. Mixed in with them were sahuagin, aboleths, mermen, sea horses, men who were trapped in near-rat bodies or near-wolf bodies with flippers instead of hands, marine trolls, and even the twenty foot mottled green body of a giant bloodworm stretched halfway out of the harbor water. Pacys didn't know if the heaving waves had thrown the worm ashore or if it had followed its prey there.

He left Hroman's side as the priest led his people into battle. The bard took his own path through the world as he'd always done, even though doing that had taken him so far from the lands he'd known and the people he'd loved.

Waterdeep was a favorite place, filled with precious memories and merchants who'd had deep pockets for a bard who could sing or tell a tale properly. He grew more afraid that even should the city withstand the current aggression, it would never be the same again.

The yarting hung down over his back, and he carried the staff in his right hand. Pacys made for the pilings lining the docking berths. Fleetswake had drawn ships from all over Faerûn. With the light given off by the burning ships, he spotted the different flags easily. From the way it looked in the harbor at the moment, they'd all come to lose their ships and cargo, maybe even their very lives.

Another wave crashed over the pilings, throwing water across the old bard's robes. Half a body came with it, thudding heavily onto the wet cobblestone street. The upper torso of a man rolled drunkenly on the street with the water splashed out away from it. The dead man lay facedown, his left arm ending in splintered bone where his hand and forearm had been.

Despite the roaring wind that followed the lashing waves in, Pacys heard another sound. Music echoed in his head, harsh, unforgiving notes that spoke of pain and confusion, of an evil darkness that wanted only to consume. It was the most hurtful and fearful thing he'd ever heard.

Drenched as he was, standing at the edge of the harbor where so many still fought for their lives, the old bard opened himself up to the music, memorizing it note by note. Even though he kept his eyes open, his vision blanked out before him and the slap of running feet against wet cobblestones around him muted to silence. Acrid wood smoke from the burning ships still singed his nose and burned his lungs. He ignored the irritation, marking the notes, choosing the pitch of the voice that would accompany it.

The words, Oghma help him, the words came so easily to his lips.

> *"O City of Splendors who stands so steep,*
> *Taken by a black-hearted horde from the deep.*
> *Sahuagin fangs, sahuagin jaws,*
> *Shark-kin,*
> *Wedded to darkest evil with power so old.*
> *Black storm-tossed waters, yellow fire that gnaws,*
> *Thought lost to the world of men,*
> *Tempered to anger that burns so cold.*
> *He comes, riding on a black wave,*
> *Looking for a world to enslave."*

Moonlight splintered through Pacys's vision, drawing him away from the intoxicating music. He wanted to scream in frustration, knowing he'd been so close to the song, then he spotted the marine scrag crawling over the pilings in front of him.

The trollkin snarled its rage as its dark eyes locked with the bard's. It heaved itself from the splash of the waves overtaking Dock Street and landed on its wide, webbed feet. Seaweed colored hair hung limply to the broad, sloping shoulders. Green scales made up the thick skin that covered it, and the smell it exuded almost made Pacys gag. It hurled itself at the bard in a rush, without warning. A handful of claws cut the air toward the old man's face.

15

"Open your mouth and drink," Madame Iitaar commanded. "Drink if you would live."

Jherek opened his mouth automatically, obeying the woman. He wanted to tell her there was no way he could drink; he couldn't breathe. He wanted to tell her that he didn't want to live. She was kicking him out of her home. Why would she care?

He tasted the minty flavor of the special healing potion that she brewed in her home roll across his tongue. She'd used it before, to cure a fever that had nearly claimed his life after he'd moved in with her six years ago, and again to heal his broken leg. Some of the pain filling his head vanished as the potion worked its magic, spreading out through him in warm vibrations.

"Swallow," Madame Iitaar instructed.

Jherek held the potion in his mouth. Even as it cleared his thoughts and took the pain from his head, he knew it wouldn't remove the ache in his heart. It was better to be dead, he decided. Still, he was surprised how much of him wanted to live. It took every bit of control he could muster not to swallow the healing potion even with the rising blood gorging his throat.

"Jherek," Madame Iitaar said, sounding more concerned, "I'm no priest to work a heal spell with nothing but my hands. You have to swallow if I'm to save you." She stroked his throat, the way she'd done when he was twelve, lying abed so sick and scared.

He wanted to tell her there was no fear of death for him now. Leaving was the best thing, and it would be so easy. His vision dimmed.

She shook him. "Jherek."

Then the voice thundered in his head. *Live, that you may serve! The time is near!*

Stunned by the proclamation, Jherek swallowed the potion. He tried to speak, to ask more, but couldn't. The elixir ran down into his stomach, gathering speed like the falling wave of an incoming tide until it crashed inside him, then spread throughout his body like water coming down off a snowcap, filling in every crack and crevice. He felt like his body was on fire, burning to a cinder. His muscles writhed against each other, and the torn ones in his chest knitted, leaving only a curious itch.

He drew in a hoarse breath, filling his mended lungs. As he breathed, shamed by what he'd thought and what he'd wanted to do in spite of Madame Iitaar's efforts, he opened his eyes.

She stood in front of him, her face as angry as he'd ever seen. "What did you think you were doing?" she asked.

Jherek couldn't have answered if he'd wanted to. He couldn't even meet her eye. He looked out across the yard beyond the porch.

"Answer me, Jherek," she ordered, "and look at me when you do."

Reluctantly, he swiveled his gaze toward her. "I was thinking," he said in a halting voice choked with his pain, "that perhaps it would be easier if I died. I didn't think that it mattered, as long as I left this house."

"Is that what you think? That I'm chasing you from this house?" Madame Iitaar lifted her gaze to meet Malorrie's. "Didn't you talk to him?"

"Lady," the phantom said, "when I found the boy, he already had the quarrel in him and he was bleeding to death. There was no time to explain things."

Her face softened further. "So the first thing you saw when you reached this house," she said, "*your* house, were your things packed on that table?"

Jherek didn't answer. He didn't know what to say. The shock of the voice speaking to him twice over such a short time, losing his employment on *Butterfly*, finding his things packed, and being so close to death had left him empty-headed.

"Come inside," she said more gently. She took him by the arm, guiding him with the surprising strength she'd always had. "I've got a kettle of stew on. We need to talk, and you need to catch *Breezerunner* before she sets sail. There's not much time and you must hurry."

16

Pacys ducked beneath the marine scrag's open-taloned blow, scuttling out of the way with a quickness learned over decades fighting for his life. His muscles and bones were no longer those of a young man, but he knew how to use what he had, and it didn't take much to kill, not if a man knew where to strike.

His feet moved across the soaked cobblestones as surely as an acrobat's or a dancer's. He stood again as the scrag's talons whisked by his head. Folding his staff under his arm and taking a fresh grip on it, he lifted the iron-shod pole and swept the opposite end into the scrag's head with all his strength.

The iron cap at the end of the staff rang against the scrag's head. Mottled green skin split and ichor oozed out, streaking the creature's face.

The scrag grunted in pain, staggered only a little by the blow. It turned quickly, ripping the other hand across at Pacys's stomach.

The old bard reversed his staff and speared it down toward the cobblestones at his feet. He had it braced by the time the scrag's blow came and used it to block the talons away from his body. The end of the staff braced against the cobblestones skidded only a little from the impact, but the blow missed him. Then he was in motion again, stepping back and to the scrag's left. The creature snarled in frustration and anger. It reached for the bard, trying to get hold of him.

As his attacker stepped forward, Pacys lifted his staff between the scrag's legs, tangling them. The creature fell, yowling in surprise, and landed on the cobblestones three yards away. It recovered quickly, pushing itself to its feet. The blood that had splattered its face made it look even more menacing.

Breathing faster than he knew he would have been in his younger years, Pacys twisted the middle of the staff. Foot-long steel blades suddenly flared from the ends of the bard's weapon and locked into place.

The scrag saw the blade too late. Before it had taken three steps, it impaled itself on the staff.

Knowing that trolls in general were hard to kill without fire or acid, Pacys used the leverage afforded by the staff. He planted the other staff blade against the cobblestones and prayed the steel was tempered strong enough to hold. Using the power of the scrag's charge and his own strength, the bard flipped the ten foot tall creature over, throwing it onto one of the nearby burning boats still tied up at the dock.

When the scrag hit the blazing ship, its skin popped and crackled, turning black immediately and splitting open to reveal the red meat below. The creature died before it could scramble off the ship into the water.

Breathing hard, Pacys scanned the nearby water again, looking for further enemies. He twisted the staff once more and withdrew the hidden blades. Mist whipped in from the storm brewing out in the harbor, making him narrow his eyes. He reached for the song, hoping that more of it was there for him.

Some words came to mind as he attempted to describe what was happening, but they were disjointed fragments of the song he'd been weaving together. The battle for the harbor continued. Savvy sea captains mustered their crews and managed to repel some of the boarders. A dragon turtle breathed out steam and burned a griffon and its rider from the sky. The blackened corpses tumbled into the dark water, then the turtle in turn was attacked by a group of mermen mounted on sea horses. The mermen darted at the huge creature, throwing javelins into it. When the turtle had enough, it dived underwater, but the mermen didn't give up the chase and dived on their mounts as well.

A woman's shriek drew the bard's attention. He whipped his head back to look toward the Mermaid's Arms. The festhall had become a bloodbath as sahuagin fought with the patrons. A mass of other fights still filled the street and intersection in front of the festhall. Pacys couldn't help wondering about how many would die before morning.

He drank in all the sights, feeling guilty at being so greedy to see all the carnage. He knew there were other bards in the city, and he knew they'd all have their tales to tell of the battle for Waterdeep Harbor. Realization of that made a small kernel of doubt grow inside him. A wave of heat washed over him from the burning ships at the nearby docks, pushed by the howling winds blowing across the harbor from the Sea of Swords. The stench of brine, tainted with smoke, interspersed with blood, filled the air.

Knowing he could go no further down Dock Street, Pacys turned and went back the other way, back toward Asteril's Way. He saw the guild hall of the Order of Master Shipwrights and noticed the large group of

Waterdhavian Guard that had gathered there. Evidently someone had decided to use the two-story guild hall as a staging area.

Pacys ran hard, feeling the familiar aches and twinges start in his knees, and the shortness of breath that plagued him these days. He didn't give in to the infirmity.

Another wave broke over the top of the pilings to his left and cut his feet out from under him. He got to his feet with effort, hacking and coughing as he tried to clear the brine from his lungs.

A loud smack sounded behind him, too loud to be anything human sized. Remembering the dead giant worm he'd seen, the bard turned and stared behind him, raising the staff to defend himself. He thought he had a momentary glimpse of a twenty foot long fish that started pulling itself along by four tentacles, but he saw instantly that his mind must have been playing tricks on him.

Ardynn stood before him, her brunette hair falling past her shoulders in a wavy mass of curls. She stood as tall as him, but had the full glow of a womanly body scarcely concealed by the white gossamer pantaloons she wore over a crimson body suit that left her arms and legs bare. Gold bracelets adorned her wrists and ankles, and the small ruby he'd given her all those years ago dangled from the fine gold chains wrapping her forehead. Her teeth were clean, white, and even. The barest trace of cinnamon scent clung to her as she came closer.

"Have you forgotten me so soon, young minstrel?" she asked in that mocking way she had.

"No." Pacys answered. There was no way he could forget her. The memory of when the bard had arrived at Maskyr's Eye had inspired a number of songs he'd written in his youth and later disguised for presentation in his travels. He'd been seventeen at the time, already tired of the life of farmer and horse breeder, and she'd awakened in him the wanderlust that followed him throughout his life.

Ardynn had been then as she was now, just as beauteous, and her voice sounding like elf-made honey. She'd sung at the Wizard's Hand, one of the finest inns in all the Vast. At the time, she'd been four years older than he was. She'd come to see the village because she'd heard of it and had never been there. When she'd left three days later, Pacys had gone with her despite his father's wishes. He could count on the fingers of one hand how many times he'd returned to the village in the decades since.

"Come kiss me, fool," she said. She lifted her arms out to him.

More than anything, Pacys wanted to go to her, but he didn't. He'd traveled with Ardynn for two years, learning the craft of the bard first, then learning of love, from her. At the end of two years, she'd left him. Ardynn had never been one to be tied down or responsible for too long. For Pacys, there'd been other teachers, other lovers, as he knew there had been with her. His heart, however, refused to feel the pull of any other as much as it did Ardynn.

The bard steeled himself, gathering his wits. The clamor of battle still echoed around him, but it sounded far away, in another place. It was hard to think, and somewhere in the back of his mind he knew there was a reason for that. "Where—" His voice locked up on him. "Do you love me?" He knew that hadn't been the question he'd meant to ask.

She laughed at him and the sound reminded him of sunlit waters trembling through a pebble bed on a distant and early morn. "Of course I love you," she answered. "I could love no other. If you won't come to me, I'll come to you." She walked toward him.

He felt the staff in his hands, but his hands were curiously numb, the familiar grain of the wood hard to touch. He concentrated against the thickness in his mind as the roaring wind pushed against him.

"Where—where was the last place you saw me?"

"Tell me," she entreated.

"It was in Thar," Pacys said. "We'd both heard through our respective sources of the archeological dig going on there by Fannt Golsway. He'd been hired by Thusk Tharmuil to investigate stories of the ogre empire that had been there before Beldoran killed the creatures out a hundred years before."

"I remember," Ardynn said.

"In those days, Golsway was at his apex," Pacys went on, warming to the bones of the story. "He actively pursued knowledge and legend, finding out where the two met and where they parted."

"Yes." Her hand was only inches from his face.

"We both went there, hoping for a song or a tale, thriving on the same adventure that drove Golsway. He was a tight-mouthed man, but when he was ready to tell you of things, he held nothing back and had much to give. I've got a dozen and more songs and tales that I've woven from his experiences."

"I remember." She smiled more broadly.

"Golsway found his legend to be half true," Pacys said. "I got the song of his discoveries, and you, dear sweet Ardynn, you *died*."

He knocked her hand away with the staff, certain that he'd just saved his own life. The thing that called itself Ardynn drew back, her eyes narrowing in hatred and anger.

Pacys marshaled his strength against the thickness trying to fill his mind. Gradually, he pushed it away, allowing him to remember other things. He found the spell he sought and got himself ready to use it.

"You died when we were attacked by an orc horde drawn by Golsway's success, as were we. I tried to save you, but I couldn't. I prepared your grave myself, carrying you to the top of the coldest mountain I could find . . . where predators wouldn't find you, and I buried you."

"It was a bad dream," Ardynn said.

"No, you're only a memory, stolen from my mind," Pacys said in a harsh voice. "I buried the real Ardynn high on that mountain with my own hands. It took me eight days to leave her side, to find the strength inside myself to go. I'd been three days without water. It was winter and all the streams at the top of the mountain were frozen and snow-covered. I was the only one to come down from that mountain."

Ardynn lashed at him with her arm.

Pacys blocked with the staff and unleashed the magical energy pent up inside him. Over the years, he'd developed an ability toward things magical in nature and had added to his cache of skills.

Ardynn's image melted away, leaving the bulk of an aboleth. Twenty feet long and resembling an overfed trout with its bulbous head and fluked tail, the creature was blue-green with gray splotches. Four ten foot tentacles grew from its head. One of them was coiled up in pain, but the other three flicked out toward the bard.

Fool, the aboleth called out in its mind speech. *Your reflexes have only afforded you a small respite. I will have you, and once having you, I'll add your thoughts and memories to those I've already ingested.*

Pacys blocked the stabbing tentacles as they whipped toward him. Water slopped over the pilings again, almost toppling him from his feet. He completed his spell and felt the tingle run through his body as it took effect. Once he was certain the spell had worked, he stepped to the side, noticing the way his feet still splashed through the pools of water spread across Dock Street.

The aboleth used its tentacles to turn itself. The slitted purple-red eyes stacked one atop the other on its big head slid in their orbits as they searched for him. The tentacles flailed out for him, missing by inches.

Being able to turn himself invisible over the years had proven both entertaining and a good defensive strategy. The old bard twisted the staff again, baring the hidden blades. He breathed like a blacksmith's bellows pump, and the brine stung the back of his throat. As always, anything that bothered his throat concerned him. If his voice was damaged in any way, his career was over.

Pacys the bard, the aboleth called out, *I know you're still here. I can feel you, feel your thoughts in my mind.*

What good does it do you, O rancid beast? Pacys asked without speaking. He moved quietly and quickly, circling around behind the large fish. Carefully, he avoided any pools of water. His foe was intelligent enough to pick up the signs of an invisible person's passage even if it couldn't see him.

I'll find you, the aboleth threatened. *I'm much smarter than you.*

Who's brought you here? Pacys continued circling, gaining ground on the large creature as it pulled itself about with its tentacles.

The promise of a feast.

The sahuagin?

No. Another. The aboleth made a contented belch with its gills. *I've already eaten three humans this night. By morning I'll know what they were, who they were, and in the days that follow, I'll assimilate all.*

The thought chilled Pacys. The fact that aboleth were capable of absorbing the knowledge of those they'd eaten was known to him. Not all of that knowledge was useful to the aboleth. They lived beneath the water and couldn't do the manual labor of a human. Tentacles didn't replace hands. The old bard knew that the creatures maintained humans as slaves as well. He'd heard the stories of those few who had escaped.

You, old bard, would be a pearl to cherish, to be shown and to be coveted among my people. Even from the brief mind touch I made with you, I know you've lived a long time and know much. The aboleth continued turning. *I also know what you're afraid of. You're old, Pacys, and you haven't many years left. The song you're searching for will never happen, unless, after I eat your brain, I compose it myself. I could offer you that immortality you seek so desperately.*

Cold, hard laughter hammered Pacys's mind. He took a fresh grip on his staff, prepared his spell, and leaped to the creature's back.

The aboleth bucked at once when it felt him land on its side. Slime and muck covered its scaly skin. Pacys worked hard to pull himself up into position. Thankfully, the four tentacles streaking toward him all at the same time behind the creature's head got in each other's way. He raised the staff and plunged it down into the aboleth's topmost eye, planting it deep.

Immediately, the aboleth mind screamed in pain. It flopped, pushing itself up on two of its tentacles while two more flailed for the embedded staff. One of them seized it and pulled.

Holding tight and staying low, Pacys hung onto the wooden shaft of the staff and got to his feet. He leaped from the aboleth and readied himself for the coming fall, keeping his body loose. He pointed a forefinger at the embedded staff and unleashed the mystical energy he'd summoned.

A jagged lightning bolt jetted only a few inches from his fingertips and lanced into the staff. Drawn by the metal under the staff's outer wooden surface, the electrical charge ripped down into the aboleth's brain, sundering it in a fiery explosion of sparks. It died screaming.

Even prepared and skilled as he was, Pacys hit Dock Street's cobblestones hard. The impact knocked the wind from his lungs and, from experience, he thought he felt a rib crack. He rolled as best he could and pushed himself to his feet, saying a quick prayer to Oghma with his thanks. He recovered his staff from the torn and charred aboleth's corpse, breathing shallowly through the stench of it.

Gazing out into the harbor, he noticed that some of the surviving ships and Waterdhavian Guard rakers had managed to gather in a small flotilla. Flaming arrows sped from the ships' decks but the distance was too great for Pacys to know if they were hitting their targets. Still, it was a good sign they were able to assemble.

Though the ships out in the harbor numbered perhaps a third of what they had in the beginning, the number of griffon riders continued to grow as more of the aerial garrisons flew in. More of the air corps seemed to be wizards or joined by wizards. Spells flew through the air, sizzling, sparkling, and flaming, seeking down through the storm-tossed waves to their targets.

Hurting and unable to draw a full breath with the damaged rib, Pacys trotted toward the gathering of watch and guard at the Order of Shipwrights' guild hall. Many of the men carried torches, and the bard guessed it was because the sahuagin's natural fear of that element. As he saw them standing there, though, the song returned to his head. He sought for the words, putting the pain out of his mind, shelving it with the fatigue he'd feel later.

"Halt!" a guard warned, stepping out from the crowd in front of the guild hall. He raised a crossbow to his shoulder and peered over it. "Who goes there?"

Pacys raised his hands high over his head, holding onto the staff. He scanned the young soldier's face with a poet's eye, noting the fear and the disbelief, the pain and the courage that fired the soldier's eyes. They were the untroubled blue of a calm sea, the color of true sapphire, and Pacys knew they would never again view the world the same way. Soot stained the young man's tanned face, and dark blood from a cut along his temple wept down his cheek.

"I am Pacys, a bard."

A grizzled sergeant stepped from the pack of Waterdhavian defenders, pressing his hand gently against the young man's crossbow. "Take that thing off him, Carthir. That man's no enemy. Did you see what he did to that damned aboleth?"

"No sir," the young man replied. "Things haven't looked the way they were supposed to at all tonight." He lagged a little in removing the crossbow's threat.

"Stay back," the sergeant told Pacys. He was a short, blocky man with gray in his hair and beard. From the markings on his uniform and the scars that showed on his hands, arms, and face, the bard knew the sergeant was a career soldier. He'd already seen his share of hard times, but the night's battle was leaving its mark on him as well. His left hand was swathed in blood-stained bandages. "Only the Watch and Guard are allowed past this point."

"I understand," Pacys said. "How bad are things around the rest of the city?"

"Damned sea devils have attacked all along the coastline of the city," a junior civilar said, brushing burned hair from his shoulders. His right eye had swelled shut, or maybe it was gone entirely and he was standing there by a miracle of will. "Not as much as they have the harbor—everything here is more at sea level—but they've been there all the same."

"Will the city stand?" Pacys asked.

A crowd that had gathered along the sidewalks and streets just past the line the watch and guard had made pulled closer, and several men took up the same question the bard had asked. In seconds, the question became a cry that swelled until it echoed over the crash of the incoming waves and the storm.

The sergeant growled out an affirmative. Pacys saw rather than heard the man reply. He'd learned to read lips a long time ago. None of the crowd heard the answer, and the bard didn't know if the man felt comfortable enough to make the announcement in a louder voice.

The crowd came forward, no longer held back by the authority the uniforms brought with them. "Tell us!" a spokesman cried out. "Will Waterdeep stand?"

"Get back! Get back!" a senior civilar ordered, pushing at his own men to clear a circle ten feet across. Almost immediately, an azure star dawned in the circle five feet above the cobblestones in front of the guild hall.

Pacys turned and stared at the star, captivated by the color and the way it appeared out of nowhere. The azure star exploded suddenly, blossoming out to fill the ragged ten foot circle. The powerful flash temporarily blinded all who were watching, and the booming crackle of thunder that followed it quieted the fearful cries and questions of the townspeople.

When the azure starlight died back, a silhouette of a man on horseback took shape in the circle. As Pacys's vision returned, he recognized the man on the huge white horse.

Even ahorse, the man looked tall and heavily muscled in his upper body and legs. Full plate armor covered him, primarily a silver that gleamed in the moonlight and reflected the burning fires and torches around him, but the black and gold colors of the watch and guard striped it as well. A white tabard with his family crest covered his chest and he carried his helm under one arm. His face was strong and square and solemn. Gray touched his temples but his youth and vigor were evident. A shield covered his left arm as he reined in the stamping war-horse.

After a moment, he raked his fierce gaze over the enlisted men and civilians. "I am Piergeiron!" he roared in a loud voice that echoed from the buildings and over the water. "Called Paladinson and Known Lord of Waterdeep." He drew his great sword Halcyon and held it aloft so it gleamed. "As long as I can fight, this city will remain standing and be free!" He lifted the sword, and as if in answer, a salvo of flaming rock seared across the sky from Castle Waterdeep's catapults. They splashed down in the harbor around the bloodworms and dragon turtles, the biggest targets immediately available.

A frenzy ripped through the crowd of soldiers and townspeople alike. Pacys wasn't immune to it himself, feeling lifted immediately by the presence of the Waterdhavian lord.

The war-horse Dreadnought stamped restlessly, causing its full plate barding to ring. Piergeiron kept the animal under control. "I came here tonight to take the battle to those who dare raise arms against this, *our* city, our *home*! Now who stands with me?"

A triumphant cheer sounded around the guild hall and must have carried down Dock Street. In seconds, men down at Ship Street picked up the rallying cheer as well. Piergeiron Paladinson's name quickly became a battle cry.

The big man clamped his helm on his head and put spurs to his horse as his men cleared the way to Dock Street. Dreadnought reared as lightning split the sky asunder, casting livid purple light over the silver armor of man and horse. Then he was off, and the crowd of soldiers and townspeople followed in his wake, an army raised where only fearful men had stood before.

Gasping and in pain, Pacys followed. His nimble mind pushed and pulled at words, jerking them into the order and cadence he wanted, smithing them into his song, polishing the ones that felt right. He knew Piergeiron had chosen his means of appearance, and the salvo of catapult loads that had followed. If they lived, if Waterdeep survived, Oghma be merciful and just, but what a song the bard would have to leave as his legacy.

12 Mirtul, the Year of the Gauntlet

17

"Live, that you may serve," Jherek said in frustration. "Madame Iitaar, I don't understand."

He sat at her table, finishing up the meal she'd prepared. As she'd promised, the venison stew was thick and hearty, filled with vegetables cut up fresh from the garden she and the household cook maintained.

Located in the front of the house, the dining room looked seaward. The ships in the harbor were visible from the height up Widow's Hill. Jherek knew which one was *Butterfly* even from this distance, and he caught himself looking wistfully at the ship more than he was comfortable with.

As with the rest of the house, the dining room kept mementos of its mistress's long and involved life. Jherek only knew a few of the stories behind the many objects that lined the shelves or occupied wall space. Madame Iitaar rarely talked about them, and he wasn't ill-mannered enough to ask. The table was round, hand-carved by her late husband from a great tree he'd felled. That same tree had also given him the lumber he'd needed to build the eight chairs for the table, her bed, and her bedroom suite. All of those, Jherek knew, had been wedding gifts he'd made for her before they married.

Madame Iitaar looked at him from where she sat at the head of the table. "Jherek, there's a reason for you being here."

"In your house?" the young sailor asked bitterly, thinking of his traveling kit packed outside. He felt good again, thanks to the healing potion and the hot meal. "That seems to have come to an end tonight."

She shook her head. "No. We've been through a lot together these past years. This will not break us. As long as I have a home, you'll have a home. That I swear to you on my husband's grave."

127

That, Jherek knew, was her firmest promise, and there was no arguing with it. "What am I supposed to do?"

"Live," she answered simply, "which is why I've arranged to send you on *Breezerunner* tonight. You must take it to Baldur's Gate. The vision I've had recently indicates that you'll find more of your destiny there. That ship is new to these waters, so no one aboard her will know you. Possibly they've heard of you while they've been in port, but they don't know you by sight."

"Running off in the middle of the night isn't being the kind of man I want to be," Jherek said stubbornly.

"You go so that you may see more clearly," the woman said. "That's something about you I've seen in my dreams of late. In order to grow, you must first leave Velen."

Her words struck a chord within the young sailor, and he remembered the dream of the mermaid in the clam. She had said something along the same lines, but with that memory came the image of the great shark, and that left him feeling cold.

"How many challengers do you think you'll find in Velen when the cock crows on the morrow?" Malorrie demanded. As usual, the phantom leaned against the window overlooking the harbor, his arms crossed over his chest.

Jherek paused, knowing Malorrie was right. "I don't know." He used a knife to cut a hunk off the bread loaf on the wooden platter in the middle of the table, then used the bread to sop up the soup from his bowl. He guessed the incredible hunger he felt was one of the side-effects of the potion.

"Well, boy, there'll be plenty of them, I can assure you."

"I could fight."

"And be killed, perhaps," the phantom agreed. He looked at Jherek sternly. "I know that's unfair to say, but who's to say you'll only face one foe, or that they'll come at you where you can see them?" He shook his head. "Perhaps you'll kill one of those boys you've grown up with since you've been here. Would that be better?"

"No," he admitted, "but I don't want to be driven from home."

"I'm glad you feel that way," Madame Iitaar said with a small smile. "I guessed that was the way you felt, but you've never said so, not in so many words."

"This is *your* home," Jherek said, hastening because he felt like he'd overstepped his bounds, "but I've enjoyed the time I've spent here."

"Good, but you need to realize this isn't the only home you'll know," the woman said. "Your home was also *Butterfly* and the sea. That will always be your true home, Jherek. I've seen it in the castings I've done concerning you. In the future, you're never far from the oceans."

"Everything now seems destined to keep me from the sea," Jherek said. "I couldn't sail with—" His voice faltered. He couldn't bring himself to say the word "father." "—with the crew of *Bunyip*."

"The river always finds its way out to sea eventually," Madame

Iitaar stated. "The ties that bind you to the sea are as strong as any of those in nature."

" 'Live, that you may serve.' But serve who?" he asked. "For what reason?"

She looked at him and shook her head. "I don't know, but I know I've had a part in this. In all the years I've lived here, my home has never been harmed by the weather. Some thought it was because of the location, and others thought I managed a weather control spell. The same year the wind ripped the shingles from my roof, I'd also learned about a young boy who worked for Shipwright Makim who was good with wood and his hands. As you know, I went to Shipwright Makim and made a bid for your time since all the other roofers in Velen were busy, too busy even for me. It wasn't long after that I found out you were renting space in a stable for a bed and asked you to move in here. That's not behavior I'm accustomed to."

"Then why did you do it?" Jherek demanded.

"After I saw you, I was given a dream that you would be the one to repair the roof on my house. As you know, I never ignore my dreams. They all come true."

Jherek put sweet butter on another piece of bread. He didn't really feel like eating, but his survival instinct made him eat. When he'd first come to Velen as a homeless boy, before he'd gotten the job with Shipwright Makim, there'd been several hungry nights. He'd learned to eat his fill whenever he could since he didn't know when the next opportunity would occur. Thinking of leaving Velen inspired the same kind of fear in him, especially when he remembered how the wages Finaren had given him had been taken.

"Whoever—whatever—I am to serve, is it good or evil?" he asked.

Madame Iitaar shook her head. "I can't say. As you know, those things don't touch me the same way they do others. I look at the person and how I relate to him or her. Even the best person is capable of an unkind word or thought, and even those who're considered evil by others are capable of gentleness and mercy. I judge them by their dealings with me and with what I see."

The answer didn't sit well with Jherek. It never had. Growing up as he had in the wild and lawless abandon of pirates, unnourished by a mother's hand or gentle kiss, he'd known no security. When he'd arrived in Velen, fleeing for his life, he'd lived in absolute fear that had left him paralyzed for days before his meager store of stolen rations had given out and he'd had to find a way to eat. Even then, he knew he'd never steal. He'd made rules for himself, starting out with the things he knew he would never do. Working hard at the jobs he'd found, especially on *Butterfly*, he was just starting to figure out what he *could* do.

"You have a choice," Malorrie put in, turning to better face Jherek. "When the time comes, you'll have a choice whether or not you serve whatever has marked you."

"How do you know?"

"Because I know you," the phantom said. "I've trained you, boy, and so has the lady. We know what's in your heart. No one will lead you where you don't want to go."

"How can you be so sure I'll have a choice?"

"Because I did." Malorrie paused, reflecting. The window behind him showed through him. "I'd been dead a long time, boy, when I was asked to seek you out and train you."

Jherek was too stunned to speak.

Malorrie smiled in that wry way of his, drawing himself up to his full height. "You thought your meeting me was simply a chance encounter?"

"Velen is filled with ghosts."

"Not mine. I was summoned here from somewhere else."

That was news to Jherek, who'd always assumed the phantom had been a native. He knew Malorrie's body was buried on Widow's Hill. "Summoned by who?"

"A man I once knew and trusted. A man who'd died for me when the time came. When he asked me to look after you and train you in the ways of thinking and swordsmanship, I agreed."

"Did he know me?"

Malorrie shook his head. "This man died long before you were born, boy. He couldn't have known you. He was asked to contact me by someone else."

"Why you?"

"I don't know. There was a chance I wouldn't have been able to train you, I suppose. Phantoms and ghosts, even here in Velen, are usually not taken up with."

Jherek paused, trying to take it all in. "Why haven't you ever told me all this before?"

Malorrie shrugged. "I'd always assumed there'd be a right time to go into all of it, boy. Now, there's no more time. You're leaving and you'll be given your choice soon enough."

Jherek finished mopping up the last of the soup with the bit of bread he had left. "What if I'm not given a choice about whether I serve this—this thing?"

Malorrie gave him a dark glance and said, "Trust me, boy. With life, there's always a choice."

"Come, Jherek," Madame Iitaar said. "If you're going to be at that ship on time tonight, you have to be going."

"Thank you for the meal," he said as he always did when she cooked for him. He cleared the dishes from the table and took them into the kitchen.

After a few unbelievably fast moments, he stood again on the porch, ready to leave everything he'd ever truly known and ever trusted. The brine in the air from the harbor filled his nostrils.

"I've put aside a few silvers for your trip," Madame Iitaar said, folding a coin pouch into his hand. "Be careful. Should you need anything, the captains along the Sword Coast trade routes will be able to get a message to me."

"Thank you, lady," Jherek said graciously, "for all that you have done for me these last years."

The old woman's eyes brimmed with tears and she reached for Jherek with strong arms, pulling him close and holding him tight for a moment. "It was my pleasure, Jherek, and it will be again. This I know to be truth." She pushed him back, holding him at arm's length to take a final look at his face. She touched his cheek lightly. "By Azuth, how you have grown and yet how young you yet remain in spite of everything. Come back home as soon as you can, son."

Tears streaked Jherek's cheeks as well, and for once, he didn't feel shamed by them. "I will," he promised.

Malorrie cleared his throat, and said, "I'll do my leave-taking here as well, boy. If I followed you to the dock and someone aboard *Breeze-runner* spotted me, it might draw unwelcome attention to you." He extended a hand.

Jherek took the phantom's hand, feeling the strength in the grip. "Thank you, too," he said. "I would never have survived at sea without your training, nor would I have completed myself as much as I have without your guidance in reading."

"Just you remember," Malorrie said, "love is more powerful than any magics. It'll make a strong man weak and a weak man strong. Don't be afraid to give of yourself when you're asked and you believe in the cause."

"I won't."

"There's my boy," the phantom said, tousling Jherek's hair.

Jherek shouldered his travel kit and turned his steps toward the docks. His mind was numb with all the changes he'd been through, all the things he'd lost, but the smell of the brine in the air reminded him he still lived. He paused only once in his journey, stopping in the tree line to gaze back at the house that had offered him the only security he'd ever known.

Live, that you may serve.

The words nestled coldly in his thinking, like a serpent coiled in the early dawn. He went down the hill, losing sight of the house as he entered the lower reaches of the city.

18

Pacys joined the battle in front of the Mermaid's Arms festhall as soon as he caught up with the group Piergeiron Paladinson led. The guard and watch members spearheaded the charge after their commander. The great war-horse showed no hesitation about rushing into the sahuagin ranks, breaking them down with his weight and ferocity. Dreadnought reared and brought iron-shod hooves down on the heads of the sea devils within reach, crushing them. Piergeiron swung his sword and chopped into the sea devils.

It was bloody work, and the bard followed the carnage. His feet, legs, and arms grew slippery with the coppery blood of men and sahuagin. He swung the staff with skill, avoiding the tridents of the invaders, and slashed them with the concealed blades.

Piergeiron wheeled his mount around in a half circle that knocked a small group of sahuagin in all directions. "Put fire in front of the building," he roared. "Use the lanterns!"

Watch members grabbed the lighted lanterns from the festhall's entrance and broke them on the ground in front of the building. The lanterns' reservoirs carried over a gallon of oil each, enough to burn through most of the night. More decorative lanterns had been added for Fleetswake, and those were taken as well. In seconds, a line of oil was laid before the festhall then fired. Black smoke coiled up from it, making it hard to breathe. The sahuagin cowered at once, though, breaking from their assault on the festhall.

Pacys whirled with more skill than speed, using his hands and wrists to deflect the trident shoved at his face instead of jerking his body out of the way. In a continuous motion, he whipped the staff back and slit the throat of the sahuagin standing in front of him.

"Stand back!" a man nearby warned.

Turning, Pacys spotted a broad shouldered dwarf running from the festhall's interior only half dressed. The dwarf carried a flaming sahuagin high over his head. He threw the burning sea devil into a small group of its fellows and all the sahuagin when down, struggling to get away from the flames.

The dwarf's face radiated hatred. "Try and interrupt Ol' Waggitt's night of fun after all them days at sea, will ya?" he shouted. "Scare them girls what smell so nice and be so willing? Gonna give you a taste of Bloodrazor for your trouble, you damn beasties!" He reached back over his shoulder and freed a double-bitted broadaxe. With a harsh cry of challenge, he hurled himself into the group of sahuagin.

Pacys recognized the dwarf's name. He was a fierce pirate from the north, but now his axe was turned in the service of defending the city. All surface dwellers, upstanding citizens as well as rakehells, depended on Waterdeep.

The sahuagin broke and retreated back to the pilings, trying to hold their position amid crates and barrels that were in the process of being off-loaded from the docked ships.

Piergeiron wheeled his mount again, yanking his sword from the skull of the sahuagin he'd just killed. He got his horse steadied under him and the light from the line of fire defending the Mermaid's Arms festhall gleamed across his broad face when he lifted his visor.

Pacys painted the man's look in his mind's eye, knowing he'd forever have that image. Strong pictures stayed with him. He looked past Piergeiron and saw that Arnagus the Shipwright's building still stood. Men fought from the warehouse doors, holding their own. The half-finished ship that had stood in dry dock was now wreathed in flames.

The Waterdhavian lord rallied his troops around him, then spurred his horse, calling out for archers to strike. Arrows feathered the cargo and the sahuagin, killing some while driving the rest to cover. Pacys joined the charge, following the watch and guard members.

Before they reached the sahuagin, a monstrous head lifted from the ocean still lapping over the pilings. Piergeiron held the charge up, but Pacys knew it would be too late.

The giant sea snake towered twenty feet out of the water, well within striking range of Dock Street. The wedge-shaped black and green head split suddenly, revealing large fangs and a forked tongue. The snake lashed out at once, and Piergeiron spurred his horse again, raising his shield high to intercept the strike.

Less than a yard's length from the Waterdhavian lord, the sea snake was seized by a giant disembodied hand that reached down from the sky. The thumb and fingers wrapped around the neck. The hand stopped the snake's strike just short of Piergeiron's shield. In a show of incredible strength, the hand yanked the sea snake from the harbor and held it high overhead amid the circling griffon riders.

Pacys judged the snake close to seventy feet long, the biggest of its kind he'd ever seen. As he watched it coil and try to constrict the hand holding it, he didn't doubt that the snake would keep some would-be sailors from ever going to sea again. The snake's presence reminded every watcher of how unknown the depths were and how much of them covered Toril.

The giant disembodied hand squeezed more tightly, holding the snake high overhead with ease despite the creature's struggles to escape. All of the fighting nearby that Pacys could see came to a halt as combatants stared at the strangling snake.

Piergeiron turned in his saddle and lifted his helm. A small smile twisted his lips and his eyes lighted with fire. "Maskar Wands," he said, "hail and well met."

Pacys turned quickly. In all his wanderings through Waterdeep and the rest of Faerûn, he'd never met the man, one of the Sword Coast's greatest wizards. He moved away from the men around him, seeking a clearer view.

Maskar Wands stood in a flying chariot drawn by a pair of red fire-drakes whose claws struck sparks from the sky as they ran. Though not six feet tall, Maskar appeared regal and grave. The wizard's hairline had receded over the years to reveal his broad forehead, but silver hair still flowed in the wind. He wore the robes of a wizard, with a family crest—three gold stars on a field of purple with a black sleeve—was worked into the chest of the garment.

"Hail and well met, Lord Piergeiron," Maskar called back. His dark gaze never left the strangling snake in the sky above the harbor. "I came as quickly as I was able."

Excited murmuring drifted through the crowd Piergeiron had led into battle. Maskar Wands, though one of Waterdeep's most famous residents, didn't put in many public appearances, but when he did, it was to let everyone know his opinion on the ways magic was being abused. He and Khelben Arunsun had argued extensively on the subject, and bards scattered across Toril waited lustfully for the war everyone was certain would inevitably take place between the two wizards.

Piergeiron turned back to his command. "I want this street secured," he ordered. "Take your men down to East Torch Tower, find those who yet survive there, and get them organized. I want whatever ships are there to be appropriated and used to retake this harbor."

One of the watch captains nodded, then led his command across the intersection of Dock and Ship Streets, through the tangle of corpses.

Maskar gestured at the chariot and firedrakes and they disappeared. From all the legends Pacys had heard about the man, he knew Maskar Wands disapproved of any abuse of magic. The wizard gazed blackly at the snake hanging from the huge hand he'd conjured.

"Now," he said sternly, "now we show these invaders that Waterdeep will *never* bend, much less break."

He gestured at the fire consuming the building beside the Mermaid's Arms and the flames stopped reaching across the building, bending to the mage's will. Pacys watched as the fire gathered itself, then shot skyward in a whirling mass of colorful pyrotechnics that spread across the dark heavens around the sea snake constricting around the giant, disembodied hand. The pyrotechnics limned the struggle, making it visible for miles, drawing all eyes.

The bard saw Maskar speaking, but his voice seemed to come from high overhead, a thunder of threat. "You've made a mistake in attacking the City of Splendors this night," the mage roared. "Retreat while you can. There will be no mercy."

Even before the echoes of his voice died away, the disembodied hand closed more tightly. The *crack* of the giant sea snake's vertebrae snapping echoed over the harbor. Still, the great creature struggled, its body refusing to admit defeat or death.

The hand disappeared at a spoken word from the archmage. As the writhing mass of coils plummeted toward the water, the wizard pointed again. A fireball scored a direct hit on the snake, wreathing it in flames that burned with white-hot intensity. Only ashes drifted down to hit the storm-tossed water.

"*No mercy!*" Maskar repeated in that booming voice.

Pacys glanced around him, looking at the smoke-stained, bruised and battered faces, and saw renewed hope glow in the eyes of the Waterdhavians around him. They tightened their grip on their chosen or confiscated weapons. The battle for the city wasn't lost, but it was yet to be won.

Laaqueel stood in the mouth of a sewer drain, the vile water trickling through a channel to her left. After the confrontation with the watch group and citizens had begun filling the city's streets, Iakhovas had guided them into the maze of sewers beneath Waterdeep. The wizard showed an unsettling familiarity with them and brought them quickly to one overlooking the harbor from Coin Alley.

She watched the charred ash from the burned sea snake cascade onto the roiling water of the harbor. Her eyes still ached from the explosion of light only a moment ago.

"Ah, little malenti, that man," Iakhovas declared, "could possibly prove a worthy opponent should the opportunity present itself. There are so few humans who are." He smiled rakishly. "Another time, perhaps."

"When we try to get back across that harbor," Laaqueel said coldly, "you'll get your opportunity then."

Iakhovas shook his head. "See, this is why I've planned everything, why I am the master and you serve me. We're not adventuring out into the harbor any more this night."

"How do you propose to leave?"

In reply, Iakhovas handed her a thin medallion from his cloak. "I've taken care to make my own doors and egresses, little malenti. I give you this and an escape route that goes with it. Accept this, a token of my appreciation for your efforts thus far, and a down payment on those you'll provide again in the future. Say your name when you close your fist on it and you'll be transported back to my castle."

Laaqueel took the medallion and looked at it. About the size of a silver piece and constructed of cut crystal, it bore a compass rose on both sides. "Magic?" she asked derisively.

"Yes."

She let her look of displeasure let him know how she felt about magic.

"Of course, you can always choose to stay here and die," Iakhovas suggested, "but I don't think that will serve Sekolah."

"How do I know this will work?"

"Because I crafted it, little malenti."

One of the wererats strode forward out of the shadows. They'd assumed their hybrid forms while in the sewers to enhance their vision. Laaqueel recognized him as Manistas, the leader of the pack Iakhovas had made his deal with.

"What's going on here?"

Iakhovas faced the wererat leader. "I'm taking my leave," he said. "Your services are no longer needed and your people can go."

"Go where?" The wererat's pink and gray tongue slithered out of its mouth nervously. "There's no place for us to go in this city. Two of us were recognized by members of the Watch. They know we were with you."

"Then I suggest you take your departure of Waterdeep at your earliest convenience," Iakhovas said without sympathy, "or slay the two among you who were recognized. Either way, I've delivered you your gold for tonight's bit of business."

Manistas unsheathed his sword, fell back into a defensive posture, and said, "You're not going to just leave us here."

"Attacking me will be your last mistake," Iakhovas assured him in a low voice, "should you choose to act so unwisely."

Reluctantly, the wererat backed away, but kept his sword out.

"What you do here won't be forgotten," Manistas promised.

"You hired on for mere gold with nothing of yourselves at stake except that which you were willing to risk in your greed," Iakhovas said. "Your loyalty was fleeting at best. You and your people live off the surface dwellers, Manistas, as did your ancestors. You have no love of the sea for what it is. As the humans do, you live in spite of the sea, taking from it what you will with no thought to the needs of the deep. If I have need of you or your people again, I'm sure your greed will let you forget this transgression, or mayhap someone else's will."

The wererat leader tightened his grip on his short sword and said, "If you do contact me again, know now that the price will be higher . . . much higher."

Iakhovas laughed, and the sound of it trapped in the sewer chilled Laaqueel's blood. Looking at her, he said, "Do not tarry long, little malenti. I do fear I shall leave you in unkind company."

He broke the medallion and spoke a word of command. Blue vapor coiled from the two halves of the medallion and wreathed him. A sharp crack of thunder filled the sewer and he disappeared. The broken medallion pieces hit the ground where he'd been standing.

Laaqueel felt the smooth edges of the medallion in her fingers and thought about the magic power inherent in it. Her stomach rolled in nervous fear. What she'd been through with Iakhovas had been terrifying enough, but to trust herself to the spell locked in the medallion was the most fearful consideration she'd ever been forced to make. It would have been better to face an enemy in combat.

Even the deep shadows trapped in the sewer weren't enough to blind her to the small hand gestures Manistas made. In response, the wererats slowly fanned out before her, blocking her way back into the sewer channel. Dozens of red glints from true rats covered the underground tunnel behind them

"We know you don't like magic, priestess," the wererat leader stated. "He used you as he used us. Perhaps together we might be able to turn the tables on him." He took a step forward, the short sword dropping to his side.

"So you would offer me a partnership?" Laaqueel demanded.

Manistas nodded, his rat's eyes never leaving her face. "Yes. It's more than he offers you."

Laaqueel considered unleashing one of her spells on him, to show him the true error of his ways and his poor judgment, but she was already tired, needing the embrace of the sea around her to return her strength. The other wererats closed in, getting well within springing distance.

"Maybe I'd even offer you more," the wererat leader said. "You're a very beautiful woman, and I can afford to be generous."

Hollow booms sounded outside the barred sewer shaft, and the stench of lightning filled the air, prickling Laaqueel's skin. She didn't respond and tried to break the medallion, only her fingers wouldn't obey her will.

The wererat to her right sprang, a short blade glinting in his paw-like hand.

Afraid then, knowing the wererats would pull her down with their sheer numbers, Laaqueel hurled the crystal medallion at her feet. It shattered against the stone and the blue smoke curled up around her, bringing the strong salty scent of purple seaweed with it. She screamed her name and she was gone, ripped away by Iakhovas's magic.

"There!" a man in a guard's uniform yelled, pointing.

Pacys turned, watching as the sahuagin manta bobbed only inches below the surface. The silvery black eyes of the sahuagin hanging onto their underwater craft gazed up at the humans aboard the great galley the Waterdhavian Guard had appropriated as a staging platform for the battle.

"I see them, I see them!" a sailor yelled. He grabbed a lantern from a peg on the railing and quickly started up into the rigging. "I'll signal the warning!"

In response to the first man's yell, the senior civilar in charge of the group aboard the galley called his men into position. They lined the railing alongside the bard.

Glancing at their faces, knowing the past hour since the battle had begun hadn't been easy, Pacys saw the pride and the dedication on the faces of the men. He'd heard prayers as they worked, from men calling on their gods to protect not only their families and them, but for protection to be offered to friends and neighbors as well.

A steel fishing net stretched between the galley Pacys was on and the one a hundred feet away. Though the storm had finally started dying down, the waves hammered unmercifully against the ship's hull. The deck shuffled erratically beneath Pacys's feet.

The cable supporting the top part of the net remained slack, creating a big U-shape into the harbor. The man in the rigging waved his lantern. A lantern on the other ship waved back in response.

"They see us!" the captain yelled up at his mate. "They have the wind working for them. Tell them to circle around and come into us. We'll scoop these damned sea devils up before they can run!"

Pacys hung onto the railing, not believing the sahuagin would run. They'd attacked the harbor with the intention of destroying all they could, but there appeared to be no real objective other than destruction. Thinking that way bothered the bard. No military exercise was conducted without some kind of end in mind, and the sahuagin had to have known they couldn't completely destroy Waterdeep.

The sea creatures had quickly lost interest in the attack during the last several minutes. They'd deserted in earnest, hurried on their way by the Waterdhavian Guard and the wizards and sailors who'd joined their ranks. The huge corpses of dragon turtles, sea snakes, eyes of the deep, sharks, and even a giant jellyfish floated in the harbor and required negotiation by ships. A dead giant squid had even washed up onto Dock Street, taking the defensive line that had been set up there out of the battle until a sufficient number of sturdy draft animals could be used to haul it away.

The other galley's sails filled with wind and it sped up, cutting a half circle through the water as it surrounded the manta. The huge net slithered into place around the sahuagin craft.

"Pull 'em up, boys!" the captain bawled. "Kelthar!"

"Aye, sir!" the first mate called back.

"Prepare that oil and heave it when I tell you."

"Aye, sir."

Pacys watched the silvery shimmer of the steel net as it rose up under the sahuagin manta. The craft was one of the large ones, fully seventy-five feet wide and two hundred feet long. The net couldn't get around all of it, but it settled around two-thirds of it.

The net seized the manta and brought it the rest of the way to the surface. Sahuagin clung to it, looking like crayfish babies that clung to the mother's tail, so thick on it they were crowded in on each other. There were more than he expected.

"Tymora stay with us," one of the sailors cried out. "There must be four, five hundred sahuagin on that craft!"

The galleys each normally carried a crew of a hundred and fifty, but almost twice that number were on them now as the fighting men of Waterdeep took the battle to their enemy. The numbers between sahuagin and Waterdhavian forces were roughly equal, Pacys guessed, but the sea devils pound for pound were the fiercest fighters.

Knowing their craft was tied up in the net, the sahuagin started swarming up the net toward the crews. Tridents flashed in their hands, and several of them loosened the throwing nets they carried. They navigated the steel net easily, their wide feet allowing them to climb with no threat of slipping through.

One of them stopped, hands raised in a beseeching posture. Pacys studied the shells and skulls the sahuagin wore on chains around her body and knew from stories that she must be a priestess. The bard turned to the captain.

"She's preparing a spell," he warned.

"Nonsense," the old man yelled back gruffly. "Damned sea devils don't believe in—"

"She's a priestess," Pacys said. "That kind of magic they understand just fine."

"Galm," the captain called, looking troubled.

One of the guardsmen turned.

"Put a shaft through that one," the captain instructed. "Man here says she could be calling something nasty up our way."

The guard nodded and pulled his bow back. Before he could fire, light around the ship suddenly extinguished, and the night's full darkness descended again, no longer held back by the galley's lanterns. The captain cursed loudly and ordered his men to the railing.

Pacys stared hard into the gloom, unable to detect more than a slither of occasional movement. The vibration of the sahuagin warriors clambering along the steel net lashed through the galley. A slaughter was coming, the bard knew, and the defenders aboard the ship would be fighting among themselves before it ended.

"Hold them back, boys!" the captain bellowed. "You may not be able to see them, but you can by the gods smell them when they come aboard."

Pacys steadied his staff, leaving the hidden blades in place so he couldn't offer too much threat to his companions. His stomach heaved in fear and his hands slid on the staff.

Without warning, the lights of the ship became visible again while the sahuagin were only yards away, scrambling up the net as quickly as they could. Glancing skyward, Pacys spotted a flying carpet above them.

"Maskar Wands," the captain called up, "thank you for your help. Hail and well met."

"Hail and well met," the wizard called down, then he gestured again and a great font of flames speared from his fingers and rained down over the sahuagin on the net. Most of them died in that instant, but a wave crawled up over the galley's railing.

Like the other men, Pacys was forced back by the desperate sahuagin. He wielded the staff with grim certainty, breaking open heads and tangling the sahuagins' legs where he could. A trident laid his arm open during the battle, but he kept fighting. Men died around him, but sahuagin died in greater numbers.

Incredibly, the sahuagin faltered in their charge and were driven back. Only a few escaped back into the harbor.

Breathing hard, his limbs shaking with effort, Pacys gazed out at the harbor. Only a few skirmishes remained within the breakwater walls, and the guard was making short work of them. He drew in the air deeply, smelling the salt and not knowing if it was from the sea or from the blood, his or someone else's, that covered him.

The torches at the guard stations along the breakwater blazed more brightly, probably magically enhanced. They threw light over the harbor, driving back the darkness that had tried to consume the city.

The bard turned and looked back at Waterdeep, listening to the splashes made as the galley's crew threw the dead sahuagin over the side. Mount Waterdeep soared above the harbor, standing tall and majestically proud.

The melody that had haunted Pacys for the last fourteen years rose inside his head again. He listened to it, not surprised to find that it was still incomplete. If this battle were to be granted to him as his song, his legacy to leave the world, none of the other bards would have been witness to it. He believed now, more strongly than he'd ever believed, that he was meant to make an enduring song with his craft, a song that would fire the hearts and stir the souls of men. It was his destiny, and his life had been spared tonight because of it.

This was only the opening movement, though. There had to be much more to come. Somewhere, the malign being that had put the invasion together was planning and plotting. Oghma granted Pacys the intelligence to know that, just as he was sure the rest of Waterdeep's leaders must be thinking the same thing: what had been gained here tonight? The city had stood.

He shook his head, knowing he wasn't going to understand everything yet. He trusted that he'd be guided further.

Looking around, he saw the faces of the men as they gave aid to the wounded, gave comfort to the dying, and made peace with the dead.

It was hard, harsh work, and would leave more scars than physical wounds ever would.

Pacys wished he had his yarting, but it was back at the Font of Knowledge. Still, he didn't let the lack of an instrument stop him. He sang a cappella, his voice sweet and true as it flowed over the galley's deck and out into the harbor. The song was an original of his that he called "Bind My Wounds and Fill My Heart." It had been written on a battlefield, conceived in the heat of war, and nurtured to fruition that same night as so many fought their final battle with death and lost.

As he sang he found that the song gave him strength and relief as well. A few of the men even knew the song and joined him on the chorus.

There was nothing, he knew, that would ever take away the losses that Waterdeep had suffered tonight.

19

"You don't have to do that."

Jherek looked up and spotted *Breezerunner*'s ship's mage looking down at him. He hung down the side of the ship from two ropes, trussed up in a leather harness, using a barnacle spade to work on the ship's hull. "I like working with my hands," he told her.

"I couldn't think of much harder work." She waved at the hot sun blazing down over the becalmed water and added, "Or much harsher conditions."

She wore her copper colored hair short, hardly any longer than his. Her skin was browned from the sea and sun, but freckles stippled the bridge of her short nose. Her eyes were reddish brown, wide and full. She seemed friendly and liked to smile. Her mouth was generous and full-lipped, and he'd yet to see a displeased look on her face. From her position in the crew, he guessed that she was a few years older than he was. In the three days he'd been aboard *Breezerunner*, he'd never talked to her.

Jherek nodded. He couldn't think of much harder work either, which was why he'd chosen it. Perspiration covered him and the leather straps chaffed at him. He'd stripped down to knee-length breeches and a short-sleeved blouse. Both were drenched from the slight sea spray and sweat. Neither improved the way he smelled. "I'm not used to being a passenger."

"You're a sailor?" she asked.

"Aye." He took time to inspect the barnacle spade's edge again. He'd found that he liked looking at the ship's mage, but after the experience with the Amnians aboard *Butterfly* he'd taken pains not to allow himself too many glances in her direction. Still, staying in his cabin hadn't been an answer he could live with. When he'd seen the ship's crew ordered to scrape barnacles from the hull that morning he'd gone to the ship's mate, volunteered, and been grudgingly allowed. The mate had thought him deranged for even asking, even more so when he'd actually shown up for the work detail.

"Where's your ship?" she asked.

He glanced up at her, shading his eyes with his free hand as the sun came over the bow when *Breezerunner* dipped into the water, and said, "In Umberlee's arms." He hated telling the lie, but there was nothing else to do.

"You crewed aboard *Silver Dassel*?"

"Aye." The lie went against Jherek's nature. It felt like a wedge between them. He'd never forget he'd lied to her. Telling her the truth, though, was out of the question. *Silver Dassel* had gone down nearly a tenday ago, pulled down by a sahuagin raiding party not far from where *Butterfly* had been attacked.

"I'm sorry," she said. "It must have been hard."

Jherek let his silence be his only answer. Most of *Silver Dassel's* crew, including her captain, old Vinagir, hadn't come back. Many of the rest had scattered, trying to find new ships that would take them.

"I didn't know you were working on the hull till this afternoon when I did my inspection," she told him. "When Creil told me you'd volunteered for this and had booked a passage, I had to come see for myself."

Jherek smiled at her and shrugged. "I'm sure you've seen barnacles scraped off a hull before, lady." He studied the clean wood he'd left behind and said, "Unless I'm doing something wrong."

"Call me Sabyna. I'm no high-born to be flattered with titles."

"All right," he agreed, but the familiarity didn't feel comfortable to Jherek.

"The job you're doing," Sabyna said, "is probably better than any of the crew that Creil put together." She passed down a capped jar full of water at the end of a net pole.

"Thank you, lady." He drank the water, tasting the cool clean of it, then sent the jar back up.

She leaned her elbows on the railing and gazed down at him. She wore a long-sleeved dark green blouse tucked into loose-legged white breeches that showed off her womanly figure, and knee-high black leather boots that matched the wide black leather belt that supported a small bag and a brace of throwing knives.

"There's more work to be done about this ship if you've a mind," she said.

"Aye. I'd like that very much."

"Captain Tynnel says you're bound for Baldur's Gate."

"Aye."

"Hoping to find another ship there?"

"If I can."

She raised an eyebrow. "Impress the captain during the rest of the journey as you already have, maybe you'll find a berth here by the time you reach Baldur's Gate."

Jherek nodded. He didn't think a berth on *Breezerunner* had been what Madame Iitaar had had in mind, but he felt stubborn about what he was supposed to do. *Live, that you may serve.* Perhaps he could do that best aboard *Breezerunner*. It felt good to think about.

"I've been ship's mage aboard *Breezerunner* for five years," she told him. "I've got some influence of my own."

Jherek didn't know how to respond to that, so he didn't.

"I've also taken the liberty to talk to the captain on your behalf regarding the work you're doing on *Breezerunner*. Keep working and you'll be compensated. It won't be a full hand's pay—our budget won't allow it—but you should see a good return on your booking passage."

"You don't have to do that, lady."

"Sabyna."

She remained quiet, waiting till he looked her in the eye.

"Sabyna," he repeated.

"I've also noticed that you usually take a meal to your cabin and eat by yourself."

"Aye. You seem to be quite observant, la—Sabyna." Jherek felt a little irritated with her attention. He hadn't noticed that she'd been observing him, and it unnerved him to think that she might be watching him so closely.

"I'm ship's mage," she stated simply. "It's my responsibility to keep *Breezerunner* seaworthy and in good repair. I also log our charts for navigational purposes, check up on our pilot, and keep track of where everything is on this ship. I've developed a good eye for detail and I'm not easily distracted."

"You sound like you're very good at what you do."

"Thank you. I am."

Despite the unease he felt, Jherek had to smile at the confidence the woman projected.

"You're laughing at me?" she asked.

"No, lady."

"Sabyna."

"Aye."

"You *are* laughing."

Amazed at the lightness in his heart in spite of the depression that had clung to him over the past three days, Jherek looked up at her again. "Maybe a little."

Her thin brows arched over her eyes. "Over these next few days if you stay interested in helping out with ship's chores, you'll find out exactly how good I am."

"I look forward to the challenge."

"That's good, but for the moment, I'd be interested in knowing whether you'd look forward to having eveningfeast with me tonight, as part of your repayment for the work you're doing."

The offer took Jherek totally by surprise. He swung along at *Breeze-runner*'s side as she cut through the nearly flat waves, feeling more at home hanging from the ropes than in dealing with the ship's mage's question.

"Is there a problem?" she asked.

"No."

"I don't think you're in a position to tell me that you've got a previous engagement," Sabyna said. "I'm not one to tolerate lying."

Her words stung Jherek, knowing he'd lied to her already and there was no way to take it back.

"So if you tell me anything other than yes, or that you'd rather *not* dine with me, I'd be inclined to cut these ropes and see how long you can float." She sounded gruffly threatening, but merriment lighted her eyes.

Jherek felt the pressure close in around him. The recent experience with the Amnians burned in his mind. Yiell's selfish and temporary interest in him had changed his whole life. He didn't want to think something else bad was going to happen, but it wouldn't have surprised him. A polite refusal was on his tongue when it betrayed him. He glanced up at the ship's mage and said, "Aye."

"Good," she exclaimed. "I'll come around to your cabin this eve and collect you."

He nodded, feeling like a boulder had lodged at the back of his throat and he just couldn't swallow it. His stomach turned flips.

"What's your name?" she asked.

"Malorrie," he replied, choosing the phantom's name because it was seldom heard and he knew he'd always react to it, but it was another lie between them. It seemed he couldn't stop telling them.

"I've got a further warning then, Malorrie."

He shaded his eyes as he looked up at her, wondering if she'd be able to see the lie in his gaze.

"I cook my own meals, and I like exotic, spicy dishes. We may find out how strong your stomach is."

She smiled at him, then she was gone and Jherek found himself even more drenched in sweat than he'd been before. He forced himself to concentrate on the job at hand and not dwell on the things that might go wrong that evening.

Back on deck with the sun setting out in the Sea of Swords, looking like a molten gold ball settling into the flat azure of the ocean, Jherek waited his turn in line at the community water barrel bolted into the railing. The man in front of him took out a large dipperful of fresh water and poured it over his own head, washing away some of the accumulated dried salt that had come from the sea breeze.

The men in line behind Jherek complained, some of them loudly.

Jherek didn't blame them. Fresh water when a ship got becalmed was worth its weight in gold. It wasn't meant to be wasted on a voyage.

The man took another dipperful and splashed it over his head again, ignoring the complaints. He was a big man, broad shouldered and heavy bellied, easily weighing a hundred pounds more than Jherek. He had shaggy black hair that fell below his shoulders, a full beard that reached to his chest, and enough body hair to make him look even more like an ape. Small daggers as long as a finger hung from earrings in both ears. He wore a cutlass in a sash and had two fingers missing from his left hand.

"Damn it it, Aysel," someone growled, "back away from the water and stop wasting it."

Aysel muttered a curse and tossed the dipper back into the barrel. He ran his thick fingers through his wet hair and walked to the side.

Jherek took the small cloth from his kit, wet it in the barrel, then wrung it out and stepped away. Working carefully to conserve the water in the cloth, he washed the salt from his face, then worked on the rest of his body that had been exposed to the spray.

"You pay attention, Aysel," a harsh voice used to command barked.

Drawn to the voice, Jherek looked up to the forecastle. Captain Tynnel stood there, arms crossed over his chest. He was a short man of small stature, but Jherek had heard nothing but good of the man while he'd been aboard. His hair was the bleached blond of old bone and he had a hatchet head for a face beneath his plumed, tri-corner hat. His piercing blue eyes belonged on a falcon. He pointed at Jherek and said, "There's a man knows how to treasure water. I don't see you having some of that same respect, you're going to be a long time between ships when we reach Baldur's Gate. Understand my drift, sailor?"

"Aye, sir," Aysel responded with a clenched jaw. He shot Jherek a murderous glare then stomped off. Several of the sailors called out jeers behind his back.

"You," the captain said, pointing his bony chin at Jherek, "boy."

"Aye, sir."

"Come up. I'd have a word with you if I might."

"Aye, sir." Nervous, Jherek ascended the narrow stairs leading up to the forecastle.

"There's nothing to be worried about, boy," the captain said when Jherek stood before him. "Just wanted a word with you."

"Aye, sir."

"Sabyna's mentioned you to me today, the work you'd done, and the fact that she'd like to give you more of it till we reach Baldur's Gate. That would be acceptable to you?"

"Aye, sir."

"I'll return some of the money you paid for your passage, but I won't be able to return it all. I've got a profit to make, investors to keep happy."

"I understand, sir."

"I thought you might. Did she mention you might be able to find a berth on *Breezerunner* when we got to Baldur's Gate?"

"Aye, sir."

"I guessed that she might. I told her I wanted to tell you myself. She's always been headstrong." Tynnel narrowed his eyes. "Where're you having eveningfeast tonight, boy?"

"With the lady, sir."

"Lady?"

"Ship's Mage Sabyna, sir."

"I must admit, that doesn't entirely surprise me either. That girl's got a good head on her shoulders, but she's impulsive too. Makes her damn good at her job. Most of the time."

Jherek remained quiet, not knowing where the conversation was headed. A captain had the right to question his crew's behavior aboard ship.

"She comes from good stock," the captain said. "Her father's a ship's mage, and one of her brothers. Another's a ranger in the Moonshaes, all of them good people." He took out a pipe and filled it with pipeweed, then lit it with considerable effort. "She's been crewing aboard *Breezerunner* for a few years. When her da let her come take this post, I gave him my word I'd see nothing come to harm her. I stand by my word." He looked up at Jherek through the haze of smoke. "In all those years, she's had only a few other men to eveningfeast. She shows a lot of discretion."

The revelation didn't surprise Jherek, but it did turn him a little cold wondering what the statement implied.

"Those men I knew," the captain went on. "I can't say that I always approved, but I did know them. I don't know you at all."

"I can cancel on her invitation," Jherek offered.

In fact, he thought it would take some pressure off if he was told not to go. He hadn't been able to turn the invitation down on his own. It wouldn't have been the right thing to do, especially to a lady.

The captain looked at him in disbelief. "You'd cancel eveningfeast with Sabyna on my say so?"

"Aye, sir. I'm just looking for passage to Baldur's Gate. I wouldn't want to cause any trouble."

Shaking his head, the captain laughed slightly. "Every manjack aboard this ship has tried to get close to her and she won't have any of them, and you were asked by her."

Jherek didn't see what that had to do with anything so he kept quiet.

"No," the captain said. "You go on to eveningfeast and have a good time, but I won't suffer to see that young woman hurt in any way."

"No, sir. Not by me."

"Prepare yourself for a treat. Sabyna is a good cook."

Dismissed, Jherek walked away, but he couldn't help wondering how the captain knew.

"Can I get you something to drink?"

"Water, please," Jherek replied, fidgeting.

"I've got a meager selection of wines," Sabyna offered.

"Water will be fine."

He stood just inside her doorway and gazed around at the tiny room that was her personal quarters. A small bookshelf covered one wall, filled with tomes and knickknacks that he felt were more personal items than magical ones. A miniature fold-out desk was built into another wall and pigeonholes held correspondence, files, and paper. At the moment, the desk doubled as a dining table. The chair was on one side of it instead of in front of it, and the bed was within reach of the desk on the other.

"Water it is. Have a seat," Sabyna invited.

She worked over a large food tray sitting on the floor. Dressed in breeches and a sleeveless yellow blouse, she looked more feminine than ever, and she smelled of lilacs.

Jherek took one look at the neatly made bed and felt as out of place as he'd ever felt before. He wore a long sleeved shirt to hide the tattoo, and his best breeches.

"Thanks," he said, and took the chair.

"Do you like spicy food?" she asked, removing covers from dishes on a tray she'd brought from the galley.

"Aye," he answered politely.

Food was food, and it got a man from one meal to the next. Madame Iitaar's dishes, made from the vegetables and fruits from her garden, had always been particularly pleasant, though.

"I got some of these recipes from another ship's mage who'd traveled to Maztica. Spices are part of the prime ingredients to any meal prepared there, she told me."

"It smells good."

"Thank you." Sabyna served out, putting portions of the different dishes onto plates and placing the plates on the desk. "Have you ever had Maztican food?"

"No."

"Then be careful."

Tense because of the closeness forced by the size of the room, Jherek followed her lead, taking a flat, thin piece of bread and mixing some of the vegetables she'd prepared with a cheese concoction. He wrapped it all in the bread then ate. He was surprised at how hot it was, but after the curry Hagagne and some of the others used aboard *Butterfly* he found it wasn't anything he couldn't handle. A sailor's palate wasn't a cultured thing, but it was sturdy enough.

"I saw the captain speaking to you."

"Aye."

"Did he warn you about me?"

Jherek worked at building another bread sandwich out of the ingredients, adding the spiced chicken chunks as well, and said, "Aye."

"There's not much I miss on this ship," Sabyna said. "I can't afford to and do a good job." She picked at her food. "So what did he tell you?"

"To watch my manners around you," Jherek said honestly. "To keep in mind that you're a lady and to treat you as such."

"As if I would allow myself to be treated any other way." Her voice carried a strain of sarcasm and anger. "If he hadn't sailed with my father, I'd not put up with his interference. Overly long noses are never welcome."

"He cares about you," Jherek pointed out. "That's not necessarily a bad thing."

She regarded him in silence for a moment. "I can look out for myself."

"Aye. I understand. I think the captain just wanted to remind me that others were looking on as well." Jherek continued eating slowly, matching her pace and her movements. Thankfully, his hunger overpowered his feeling of ill ease and she proved to have as big an appetite as he did.

Her conversation drifted, and she skillfully probed his background. He replied to her questions and to the broad statements she made, but kept his answers brief without seeming to be secretive. For the most part, he told her the truth, just not all of it.

His concerns never went away, but he found himself enchanted with her company. Loquacious as she was and as taciturn as he remained, she told a number of stories. After dinner was finished and he'd helped her put the utensils away, she took a flask of spring water she said came from Icewind Dale and guided him back up to the main deck.

Jherek thought briefly of claiming to be tired, but he knew it would have been another lie to add to those he'd already told. He'd also found he enjoyed the ship's mage's company. The last three days of being alone in a group of strangers with his future so uncertain had been hard. When he was with her, he found he didn't worry about the future quite so much.

Sabyna, daughter of Siann Truesail, sat on the prow of *Breezerunner* only a little later, within easy speaking distance of the young sailor who'd so caught her attention. She watched him as he sat cross-legged and gazed out at the sea, surprised at how comfortable she felt with him.

Still, he remained an enigma, and her wizard's mind constantly pried at the why and how of things, not tolerating mysteries of any kind. Exactly what the young sailor who called himself Malorrie represented, she wasn't sure, but she knew he'd lied at least about his name.

She'd used a light spell to read his surface thoughts when she'd talked to him earlier in the day and had gleaned that. The spell wasn't something she was especially proud of, but as ship's mage, information meant profit and often survival for the ship and crew. However, there was no indication that he meant *Breezerunner* or her crew any harm.

He watched the star-spattered sky overhead, rocking easily with the ship's motion. The prow lifted and descended across the rolling waves, and the rigging creaked as it was pushed along by the prevailing winds.

"You love the sea, don't you?" she asked, knowing it was true even before her spell confirmed it.

"Aye," he answered without hesitation. "I can't imagine having a life without it."

From his tone and from what she was able to pick up from his thoughts with her magic, she got the impression he was feeling pressure to make some kind of decision. "How long have you been at sea?"

"All my life, lady. I was born at sea."

That was unusual in these days, Sabyna knew. A good midwife could tell when a babe had dropped into position to be born, and women didn't take to sea at that time unless the need was great.

As if realizing he'd told too much, the young sailor said, "I was born almost a month premature, on a long voyage in harsh seas. Luckily, I survived it."

"What about your mother?"

He shook his head, his eyes picking up pale fire from the gibbous moon. "I lost her."

"I'm sorry."

"Aye."

"I was raised on a ship myself. My father's a ship's mage."

"So the captain said."

That irked Sabyna. Her business was her own. As she thought that, she felt a twinge of guilt for trying to pursue the young sailor's secrets herself.

"Tynnel was being awfully generous with his information," she said. "That's not like him."

The young sailor shrugged. Sabyna noted the dark circles under his eyes and felt bad for keeping him up so late when he'd obviously been worn out by his previous journey. She knew that wasn't right. He looked healthy, not worn down, so whatever strain he was under was mental, not physical.

Still, she wasn't ready to part company with him yet. "My mother kept after my three brothers and me to study our lessons," she told him. "When we were young, we looked on ship's chores as great fun. It wasn't until we were older that we learned we were supposed to resent work like that."

He laughed and she decided she liked the sound of it. His laugh was low and gentle, like it was something he wasn't used to doing.

"In ports where we traded, some folk made comment that a ship was a small place for children to grow up—dangerous even—but we had the sea, wide and deep and beautiful, filled with wondrous things, and no reason to fear it or anything in it till my brother Dannin was killed in a pirate raid fourteen years ago."

He nodded, suddenly somber for no reason that she could explain. "I'm sorry for your loss," he said.

Despite all the years that had passed, Dannin's death still hurt. Tears brimmed in her eyes, feeling hot against the cool breeze drifting in from the sea. She got angry at herself momentarily for the loss of control, but there was something about the young sailor that reminded her of her lost brother. Dannin had barely been sixteen, younger than either of them now. She remembered and missed her brother's smile most of all. Dannin was always the most easygoing of her siblings.

The look in Jherek's pale eyes suggested that he wanted to say more but he didn't.

Sabyna sensed that whatever stilled his tongue was wrapped up in one of the secrets he kept to himself. "Besides scraping barnacles," she asked him, "what else can you do?"

"I've worked for a shipwright and built ships from the ground up, from dry dock to harbor."

"I've got a list of repairs I'd like made over the next few days," she told him. If he accepted, she knew she'd be seeing more of him, and maybe she'd get a solution to the enigma he presented. At the very least, he made enjoyable company. "Most of them are only cosmetic, but I'd like them completed. We've only got a couple men who're decent carpenters. If you've got skill, maybe I can get Tynnel to pay some extra wages."

"I'd be happy to look at the repairs, and whatever you can pay would be fine."

He looked like he was about to say something else, but his eyes cut away from hers.

"It could be Tynnel's offered purse would be so small that I'll have to supplement your pay with meals." Part of Sabyna cringed when she was so bold as to say that. She knew her mother wouldn't have approved at all.

"I'd enjoy that."

She gazed out at the horizon, where the wine-dark sky descended and touched the flat surface of the Sea of Swords. "So what is it that draws you to the sea?"

"I don't know, lady," he answered politely, "but I do know that I've felt the pull of it every day of my life."

"Would you like me to foretell your future?" she asked.

He paused, as if weighing the risk, then said simply, "Aye."

"Give me your hand."

Hesitantly, he offered it.

She took his hand in hers and studied it in the pale moonlight. It felt rough and hard, a working man's hand. A few scars from fish knives, nets, and other sharp instruments crisscrossed the natural lines in his palm, making it confusing in the shadows.

"Wait here. I'll need more light."

"If this is going to be trouble for you, I'd rather not."

"It's no trouble," Sabyna said.

He gave her a short nod, but clearly didn't look happy about the extra effort.

She pushed herself up and walked to the railing to get one of the spare lanterns tucked away there. She lit it from the one already burning a few feet away, and returned. She concentrated on his palm, trying to divine what she could of him and the possible futures that waited on him. The divination she attempted wasn't part of a spell, but was based on simple teaching about the lines on the palm. At least it was an excuse to speculate and talk about those speculations.

"You have a long life line," she said, reading the automatic signs, "but there are breaks in it, indicating a change in location or your view of the world." She felt him try to pull the hand away, but maintained her hold. "The breaks in your heart line show that you've had disappointments in your life."

Without warning, a jolt of electricity sizzled through her mind. Her vision glazed over, suddenly filled with the sight of a great sea battle involving dozens of ships. She stood on a deck, and the vision was so strong that she felt the movement of the ocean. She smelled blood and the salt of the sea, different in some regard from the Sea of Swords.

She looked around in the vision, knowing she was seeing it from the young sailor's eyes, but not knowing how it came to be since none of her magic would enable her to do this. Whatever the source, it came from outside her and forced her to see. The ship rocked suddenly and she turned in the direction the force had come from in time to see a boarding party swinging aboard the ship.

A tall man with wild black hair and fiery brown eyes dropped onto the deck before her. A short, thrusting goatee and mustache covered his cruelly handsome face. He was dressed in black, tight breeches tucked into buccaneer's boots and a black shirt with belled sleeves left open to reveal the tattoo of the flaming skull wearing a chain mask that left only the eyes and fanged mouth uncovered. Another tattoo on his left cheek showed a shark-like creature with a black haired mane twisted in mid-strike.

Selûne help her, she recognized the man at once, and she prayed him dead in the same instant.

The man attacked at once, and she wielded her sword to parry the heavy-bladed falchion he swung. Afternoon sunlight glinted from the blades. He drew back immediately, setting himself to swing again.

The vision was rudely interrupted and Sabyna's senses returned to her own body, to her own time. The young sailor held her, steadying her as another shudder passed through *Breezerunner*, shaking the whole ship as the dulled *thud* of impact echoed up through the hold.

"We've run aground," the young sailor said, helping her to her feet in spite of the way the ship jerked and tossed. "We'll be lucky if we haven't torn the bottom out of her!"

20

"Impossible," Sabyna said, pushing her way free of the young sailor. "We're miles from land." She had trouble standing as *Breezerunner* continued rocking while its length cleared the obstruction. Rushing to the railing, she peered down into the dark water, knowing the obstruction had to be underwater or the pilot and lookouts would have seen it.

Jaxx in the crow's nest sounded general quarters on the conch shell kept there for that purpose. The mournful wail filled the night. Men erupted out onto the ship. Many of them were half-dressed, and the night shift carried lanterns that threw dizzying ellipses across the deck.

"What in the three by three hells's going on here?" Tynnel yelled. He stood in the open doorway of his cabin under the stern castle, a cutlass naked in his fist.

"Hit something, cap'n!" Jaxx called down.

"What?"

"Don't know, cap'n. Didn't see anything then, and don't see anything now."

"Mornis," Tynnel shouted.

"Sir," the first mate called back.

"Get down into that hold and let me know what kind of shape we're in." The captain strode across the deck, glancing in all directions suspiciously. He closed on Sabyna. "I thought you kept a spell on this vessel that would warn us in the event of a possible collision."

"I do," the ship's mage said. "I renewed it this afternoon." She faced the captain with certainty. "Whatever we hit, it's less than thirty feet in length and underwater." The spell she'd managed to put on *Breezerunner* would notify them of anything bigger than that, or any stationary object above the water line. "Probably it's drifting as well."

Mornis reappeared at the top of the hold, gasping. He was a man in his middle years, his head shaved bald though he wore a forked gray beard. "We appear to be whole, cap'n, not taking on any water that I could find."

Tynnel waved him off, glancing briefly at the young sailor standing beside Sabyna, then back at the ship's mage. "I want to know what kind of shape my ship's in," he told her in a harsh voice.

Sabyna felt a momentary flicker of fire at the tone in his voice, but she pushed it out of her mind, clearing her thoughts so she could work her spells. She wasn't going to forget the treatment, and they *would* talk about it later. Just because she was occupying herself with company didn't mean she was letting down on the job.

She also didn't blame Tynnel for his gruffness; his ship was his life and his freedom. Without it, he'd be land-bound or working for someone else. Even independent ship owners relied on investors to a degree, and bringing a cargo in late or not at all risked financial disaster.

Pushing out her breath to further relax, she headed for the hold. The spell came easily to her lips and she took a one inch unflawed steel disk from her belt pouch that she kept with her. She rubbed it between thumb and forefinger as she descended into the hold.

"May I accompany you?" Jherek asked.

Glancing to her side, Sabyna saw the young sailor stepping in to match her pace. She looked past him, further down the stairs leading into the hold and saw Tynnel's face lit by the lantern he carried. The captain didn't look happy about what he saw there.

"Yes," she said. "That'll be fine."

A little bit of score settling now wouldn't hurt, she thought. She'd been doing her job and Tynnel would have to admit that. She seized the lantern one of Mornis's men held, then walked the prow through the narrow corridor formed between the crates and huge wine flasks they intended to trade and sell along their route.

The air inside the hold was damp and fetid. It always was this time of year and so near the Shining Sea. Moisture clung to the oaken beams in places, gleaming under the lantern light.

At the prow she passed the young sailor her lantern, then spoke her spell. At the end of it, she tossed the steel disk into the air. Instantly, it burst into bright, hot flame and charred to nothing. Even before it finished burning away, her mage's senses had increased. She could feel the striations and pressures within the ship's structure like it was a second skin over her own bones. Even the cool of the sea lapped at her, and the wind sweeping *Breezerunner*'s deck prickled along her skin.

She walked the length of the ship. When she reached the other end, her spell-enhanced senses died away. Perspiration trickled down her cheeks and her head hurt from the stress and strain. "The ship's fine," she announced.

Tynnel didn't look any happier. "What did we hit?"

"We could go back and look," Sabyna suggested. She was curious herself, and she hated not at least making the effort to find out.

The captain led the way back to the main deck and shouted out the order to change the sails and bring *Breezerunner* around. "Can you pinpoint the area?" he asked her.

"I can give you my best guess," Sabyna answered.

Slowly, the ship came around, working with the wind. After only twenty minutes' searching, one of the sailors called out, "Found it, cap'n! Sunken ship by the looks of it!"

Sabyna felt a chill shoot through her stomach. A ship sunk this far out from Amn, there'd be no chance for any survivors that hadn't made the lifeboats or a rescue ship. It was too far to swim and the ocean was filled with savage creatures. She followed Tynnel to the starboard side and gazed out at the water as *Breezerunner* slowed from a crawl to a gentle bob fully stopped on the ocean's surface.

Three men handled lanterns in the prow, lowering them over the side by ropes. As clear and as clean as the sea was, even the lantern light at full night was enough to reveal the outlines of the small cog listing nearly upside down in the water. The stern area wasn't visible at all.

Tynnel gave orders to lower a rowboat with Mornis in charge. Shrill squeals whined around the deck as the block and tackles were used. The first mate quickly picked his people.

"Probably a damned waste of time," the captain said angrily as he peered at the stricken ship, "but we've got to investigate and see if there's any potential salvage value."

"She's not resting on the bottom," Sabyna said. "She's drifting. That's why we passed over her instead of her ripping our bottom out. There won't be any salvage. I've never seen a cog less than thirty feet long, and if it was longer than that, my alarm would have sounded. What we're seeing out there is *part* of a ship. Something broke it in half."

"We'll see."

"I'd like to go with the rowboat crew," she said.

He glanced at her with a sour expression. "I'd feel better if you stayed aboard *Breezerunner.*"

"My magic will allow me more salvaging time and ability than anyone else you could send," she pointed out. "In these currents, that ship could be gone in moments, taken completely to the bottom."

Tynnel gave a short nod. "First sign of trouble, I want you back here."

Sabyna joined the rowboat crew, scrambling down the rope ladder that had been thrown over *Breezerunner*'s side. Her feet reached the rowboat and Mornis guided her to secure footing.

"Lady."

She looked up at the young sailor who lied about his true name. "What?"

He held a lantern and the illumination turned the bronze of his face to smooth butter. "I've some experience in salvage work," Jherek said. "If I could be of assistance?"

"We don't need some wetnose along on something that could be a dangerous bit of business," Mornis stated gruffly. "Assuming there's nothing nasty waiting in that ship's carcass, if it goes down, there could be a hell of an undertow."

"He's worked as a shipwright," Sabyna said. "He could be of help." She glanced to the right and saw Tynnel standing there. "Captain?"

"Let him go," Tynnel said. "It's Sabyna's call."

Sabyna knew he was giving her back some of the authority and respect he'd stripped from her earlier. She kept the smile from her face and nodded to the young sailor.

Jherek joined them in the rowboat, hardly causing any rocking. Seating himself, he took up an oar and shoved it into an oarlock, then awaited commands.

Sabyna deliberately distanced herself from him and watched him as she sat in the middle of the rowboat. The slat felt hard and unyielding.

Mornis bawled out orders, getting the rowing groups into action. The rowboat came about smartly in the water, cutting through the gentle waves to the area marked from above by the lanterns.

Reaching into the bag of holding at her waist, Sabyna seized the hunk of ivory and off-white cloth inside and unfurled it into the air before her. All of the rowboat's crew except the young sailor drew back.

The cloth resembled a patchwork quilt without the stitching. When Sabyna released the cloth, the scraps fluttered and flew, twisting as if caught in a gentle hurricane. Then they bunched into a serpentine figure that wafted gently in the breeze six feet above the boat and the cowering sailors.

"Guard," Sabyna ordered.

The serpentine shape stretched out and flattened, riding the winds just above and in front of the rowboat.

"What is that?" Jherek asked.

Sabyna looked at him, searching for any reproach in his gaze. She didn't find it and guessed that he'd never heard of the creature. "That's a raggamoffyn," she told him. "My familiar."

"Some say those are creatures of evil," Jherek said, and several of the sailors quietly agreed with him.

Sabyna watched the raggamoffyn change its shape as if luxuriating in the freedom. Since it wasn't well received aboard *Breezerunner*, she didn't often let it out of the bag of holding except in her cabin.

"Some are evil, I suppose," she agreed. "Some are only pranksters and don't know anything of accountability. Pretty much, they're whatever they want to be. The raggamoffyns known as shrapnel are evil to the core. There are those who say that they're a race of creatures unto themselves, and still others who say they are the minions of a faceless wizard with a black heart. I don't know what to believe about all that, but this raggamoffyn does what I ask it to."

"I see."

The rhythmic sweep of the oars through the water provided an undercurrent to their conversation. Sabyna held her lantern aloft, searching the water ahead of the rowboat. The raggamoffyn involuntarily flinched away from the flame, creating a momentary bow in its present linear shape. "Its name is Skeins. I created it when it came time for me to take a familiar. The cloth it's made of is the shroud that covered my brother Dannin for his funeral service. I was ten when he died and I saved it, knowing exactly what I was going to do with it. When it was time, I sought out another raggamoffyn and made it perform the rites necessary to give life to Skeins."

"Ship the oars," Mornis ordered. "Get ready to pull away."

Sabyna stood in the rowboat's prow, gazing down into the water where the cog lay. The ship twisted and turned a little, rocking with the currents that held it. The wreckage appeared lifeless, white wood showing where some of the hull had been splintered and cracked under pressure.

Something thumped the inside of the ship, the hollow gonging noise echoing through the water was barely heard above the creak of the rowboat.

Jherek listened to the thumping coming from inside the wrecked cog. It sounded across the flat sea, and stopped after less than a minute.

"All right," Mornis said, "I need two volunteers to investigate the wreck."

None of the sailors raised their hands.

"I'll go," Jherek said.

"An' you're a damn fool if you do," Aysel said from further back in the stern.

Jherek had seen the big man come aboard when the rowboat had been loaded, but had ignored him. He ignored him again and rose easily to his feet. He pulled off his boots and shucked his cutlass, keeping only the hook and a knife in a scabbard on his shin.

"Anyone else?" Mornis asked.

No one volunteered.

Jherek didn't blame them. If someone else had volunteered to go, he'd have let them. The water was dark, the illumination wouldn't travel very far into it, and there was no telling what lay below. He walked to the rowboat's edge and started taking deep breaths to completely fill his lungs for the dive.

"Brave bunch, aren't you?" Mornis challenged. He pulled off his own boots, then his shirt. He kept a long saw-toothed knife. He flicked his gaze to Jherek. "You might want to take that shirt off too, lad."

"I'll be all right," Jherek replied, not wanting to chance the tattoo being seen. "The water will be cold."

The first mate chuckled. "About to dive into something like that," he gestured at the sunken cog, "and you're worried about a little chill." He shook his head. "You ready to do this?"

"Aye." Jherek marshaled his control, pushing away the fear that filled him. He didn't know any of these people, much less whoever might be in the sunken cog. He had no business jumping into that water, but he couldn't pass it up either.

"I've got a candle here that's got a bit of magic in it," the first mate said, rummaging in the pouch he kept at his waist. "Once it's lit, it'll burn underwater as well. Mage who sold it to me called it a candle of everburning. Cost me a lot, but a man at sea in the dark, light gets to be a most precious thing, you know?"

"Aye," Jherek said. He knew from experience how hopeful lights, even along an unknown coastline, could make a crew feel.

Mornis lit the candle and it caught with no problem even in the breeze blowing over the rowboat. He stepped to the rowboat's edge and dropped into the water.

Jherek followed the man, cleaving the water cleanly, not leaving the rush of bubbles behind the way *Breezerunner*'s first mate did. He focused on the candle in the first mate's hand. The soft yellow glow belled out almost ten feet in all directions before the darkness of the water absorbed it.

The dulled splash of another body diving into the water sounded behind Jherek. He turned and looked up, watching as Sabyna swam toward him. The raggamoffyn took to the water as well, eeling through the ocean with more grace than the young sailor would have credited the creature with. He paused and waved the ship's mage back. She shook her head at him and kept swimming.

Turning his attention back to the cog now that he was near enough to see it, Jherek knew from the way it had broken in half that the ship had been sheared by its enemy. Arrows jutted out along the hull above where he believed the waterline would have been. A man's body, bloated and swollen from its time at sea and showing signs of having been attacked by small marine predators, twisted in the ship's rigging that dangled down from the broken deck.

With the way the cog was tilted, Jherek knew nothing survived in the cargo hold. It had been broken open to the sea and all compartments filled. That left only the stern cabin.

Evidently Mornis had the same thought because the first mate swam for the cabin at once. The cabin's door was tucked away under the ladder leading to the stern castle. On its side as the ship was, the cabin door faced down.

The thumping echoed through the sea, sounding eerily displaced and more immediate in the water. The first mate put his shoulder to the door and pushed but couldn't budge it.

The thumping repeated, suddenly showing more vigor, and Jherek knew someone was still alive on the ship. He swam to the first mate's side. Mornis moved the candle, showing the gaps between door and frame had been pressed together by the structural damage done to the cog and the depth's pressing in at it. The lock inside held it closed.

Desperate, his time to stay underwater with the oxygen in his lungs already growing short, Jherek used his knife to pry out the hinge bolts, letting them drop to the ocean bed hundreds of feet below. He sunk his hook into the wood beside the door to give himself more leverage, then flipped around so he could slam his feet into the door.

When he kicked out the third time, already going light-headed from lack of oxygen and from the effort he was expending, the door turned sideways in its frame.

Mornis reached up and yanked it away, then swam inside with the candle leading the way.

Jherek went after him, trusting that some kind of air existed inside the cabin if someone was still alive. If there wasn't, he felt he could still make the surface before he passed out.

Books and other debris swirled around in the murky water, lit up by the candle. Even as he neared the surface inside the cabin, he glimpsed the boy standing there against one wall, immersed up to his chest.

The boy couldn't have been over nine years old, Jherek knew as he surfaced. Small framed and lean, the boy clung to the sconce mounted on the wall with fading strength. He held onto a brass candlestick with the other, using it as a weapon. His black hair was plastered against his head, and his eyes and nose were reddened from crying.

Jherek took a deep, shuddering breath and waited, giving the boy space. Mornis knew the boy was panic-stricken and stayed back as well.

"Easy, lad," the first mate said softly. "We're here to help you. Heard you knocking. You look like you're about all done in."

"They're all dead!" the boy screeched, fresh tears wetting his face. He held the candlestick threateningly.

"I know, lad. We seen 'em." Mornis swam forward, offering his hand. "I need you to come with me. We've got to be getting you out of here."

"Stay away!"

"Lad, you've been trying to save yourself for a long time from the looks of things," Mornis said, "but you can't hold on much longer. This old ship, she ain't going to last much longer neither."

"I don't know you," the boy shrilled. "I want my father!"

Jherek felt helpless, watching the boy trapped between grief and fear. It was a bad place to be. He knew from personal experience. His father's voice haunted him. *So, are you gonna be a pirate and take your place proper on* Bunyip, *or ain't you? Live or die, boy. The choice is simple.* He forced the words away, tucking them back into that piece of his mind where the nightmares hid.

"What's your name?" Jherek asked softly and calmly.

The boy refused to answer, drawing big gulps of air as he frantically looked from one face to another.

"My name's Jherek." Too late, he remembered that he was supposed to keep his identity secret. If Sabyna or Mornis noticed, though, they kept it to themselves. He didn't think he'd even been introduced to the first mate. "Tell me your name."

"Wyls," the boy said. "My father put me in here and told me to stay. Where is he?"

Jherek shook his head and kicked with his feet to take some of the distance away between them. "I don't know, but we can try to find out."

"He should be coming for me," the boy cried. "He told me he'd be back."

Jherek took another deep breath, maintaining eye contact with the boy. He willed both of them to be calm. His heart hammered in his chest, though, and he knew his lungs were struggling with the trapped air in the cabin. The ship must have been underwater for hours. Maybe there'd been more air trapped in the pocket earlier, but what was left was fouled from being breathed again and again.

"Let me take you to him."

"Will you help me find him?"

Jherek looked at the hungry, desperate gaze. "I'll help you if I can." He lifted his hand from the water, offering it to the boy. Water dripped from his fingers, making concentric circles across the ocean surface trapped in the room with them.

"Liar!" The boy struck out with the candlestick.

Jherek barely had time to draw his hand back before the instrument smacked into the water. From the corner of his eye, he saw Sabyna wave her hand.

In response, her raggamoffyn familiar shot up from the water in his serpent's shape. Before anyone could react, the raggamoffyn exploded into hundreds of wet fabric pieces that flew through the air. They hovered around the boy like a bee swarm, twisting and turning like gulls gliding through storm weather. The fabric pieces covered every inch of the boy's body, including his eyes, nose and mouth, slamming into place with wet splashes. When the raggamoffyn finished, the boy looked like a mummy. He screamed, his voice thin and hollow, echoing in the limited space. The raggamoffyn held fast, following every movement with its shape. The boy clawed at the fabric pieces, trying to rip them free.

"Foul beast," Mornis exclaimed, drawing back fast enough to make even the magic candle gutter for an instant.

Jherek started forward, his knife already in hand.

"Leave him alone," Sabyna said.

Torn by what was going on, feeling guilty for even being a part of it, he glanced back at her. The boy's screams continued unabated. "This isn't right. He's going to be more scared than ever."

She looked at him and didn't flinch from the accusation in his eyes or the whimpers the boy had been reduced to. "This way he'll live," she said. "We all will. Can't you feel the currents changing?"

Now that she'd mentioned it, Jherek did feel it, and he knew what it meant. "It's getting colder," he said. "We're sinking again."

"Aye," she said. "If we'd waited for the boy to get calm enough on his own. . . ."

"She's right," Mornis said. "I don't like that thing either, but it's saved us some time." He took a deep breath and disappeared under the water until only a faint glow from the magic candle was visible.

The boy fell silent suddenly, then lurched free of the sconce and waded into the water after Mornis.

As the light left the cabin, Jherek looked at the ship's mage. Her face remained calm, but there were unshed tears in her eyes.

"It was the only way," she told him in a shaky voice. "Skeins will keep him safe enough till we reach the surface. The raggamoffyn is controlling his body now."

"Aye," Jherek replied. "You did what you could."

"You don't think I should have done this."

"Lady," Jherek said, "I only know what I should do. I wouldn't dare to presume to tell another what to do."

"You're so young," she said. "How'd you get to be so judgmental?"

"I'm not."

"You are," she said. "Maybe you don't realize it yet. You're going to have a hard, narrow path ahead of you." Without another word, she dived beneath the rising water that claimed the interior of the cabin.

Jherek followed her, feeling the whole cog slide deeper into the ocean. He felt confused about her, about what she'd said. He didn't know what he was going to do about that, or why he felt he had to do anything at all.

21

The boy sat inside Mornis's cabin less than an hour later, wrapped tightly in a blanket now instead of the raggamoffyn. He ate warmed-over chowder greedily from a beaten metal bowl, pausing only to chew the chunks of fish.

"Do you know who the pirates were that attacked your ship?" Captain Tynnel asked.

The boy shook his head, still chewing. "No, sir."

One of the few *Breezerunner*'s captain had allowed into the room, Jherek stood near the doorway, watching the boy. Wyls was educated and mannered, the son of a merchant who'd hired the cog as transport. He'd had a good life ahead of him, the young sailor reflected. Now all that had been lost, unless there was family he could get home to.

Wyls stared into the chowder bowl. "They came out of nowhere and attacked our ship," he said. "The captain tried to run, but they had a faster ship. My father locked me in the cabin before they got on our ship, but I heard the fighting." His breath seized up in his throat.

"Easy, lad," Tynnel said, dropping a hand to the boy's head. "You just take your time. I only need to know a few more things, then you can sup till you've a full belly and cover up in those blankets."

The boy nodded and continued holding the bowl in both hands. After a moment, he asked in a broken voice, "What else do you need to know?"

"When did the pirates attack the ship?"

"It was early, soon after morningfeast. I remember because I'd only been out on deck a short time before my father locked me away."

"When did they break the ship up?"

"After the fighting stopped and they looted the cargo hold. I remember hearing the winch creaking. I unlocked the door and lay under the bed. When the room was searched, they were hurrying so much they didn't find me. I locked the door again after they left."

"Then they broke the ship?" Tynnel asked.

"Yes. I was looking out the window when they sailed their ship over ours." Wyls looked up at the captain and asked, "Will you help me find my father?"

"Aye, we'll search, lad. Maybe they were put off in a lifeboat."

The boy nodded.

Even though he knew why Tynnel had said what he did, it sickened Jherek to hear the lie. If the boy's father yet lived, he'd have demanded sanctuary for his son as well. Jherek left the cabin, satisfied the boy was going to be taken care of.

Back on the main deck, he stopped at the railing and breathed deeply. He still carried a chill from swimming even though he'd changed clothes. Glancing at the prow, he spotted Sabyna sitting there alone. She was swaddled in a heavy woolen blanket.

Uncomfortable with how things had been left between them after the encounter over the raggamoffyn, Jherek went to the ship's galley and got two bowls of chowder from the cook. A pot was generally kept going for the men taking the night shift.

He carried the bowls of chowder to the prow. "I thought maybe you'd like some soup," he said quietly, extending one of the bowls.

She looked up at him, then took it graciously. "Thank you." She put the bowl in her lap, gray tendrils wafting around her as *Breezerunner* sailed in ever-widening circles in the attempt to find other survivors of the pirate attack.

"May I join you, lady?" he asked, feeling uncomfortable and afraid that she'd tell him no.

"You'd want to sit with me after what I did to that boy?"

"Aye."

She shook her head. "Then sit."

He did, folding his legs. The wind had a chill bite to it now. He ate the chowder in the silence that stretched between them.

"Are you cold?" she asked, setting her bowl aside.

"I'm fine."

"You're shivering."

"Only a little."

"Here," Sabyna said, stretching the blanket out, offering him part of it.

Hesitantly, Jherek took the blanket and wrapped himself in it. Immediately, he became overly conscious of her body heat saturating the blanket, and of the way she smelled of lilacs in spite of the swim.

"Is the boy all right?" she asked.

"He's eating, and from the look of him, he'll be sleeping soon. He told the captain that Skeins scared him, but he understands why it had to be done."

"Good." Sabyna pushed wet hair from her brow. "He'll start to feel the real pain in the next couple of days, when he realizes he's survived and his father hasn't."

Jherek knew that was true, and that there was nothing he could do to spare the boy that pain. Living hurt was a fact he'd learned early, and one that had stayed with him the longest. "What will Tynnel do with him?"

"The best he can," Sabyna answered. "He'll post for the boy's family and leave him with a temple in Athkatla when we reach the port for care. He'll check on him, but that boy could well end up being an orphan. It happens. This is a hard world."

"Aye." Jherek hunkered in the blanket for a time, wishing he felt more like sleeping. He felt drawn to the woman. In the three days aboard ship, he'd watched her and liked what he saw. Rescuing the boy the way she had, though, had shown him some of the differences that lay between them. He wished it would have made him like her less. The attraction, however, remained.

"I heard the boy tell Tynnel that pirates took the ship," Sabyna said.

Jherek nodded.

"Pirates killed my brother," she went on in a voice so quiet it was almost a whisper, "but I told you that, didn't I? My father was ship's mage on *Glass Princess* back then."

The ship's name struck a chord in Jherek's memory. Something moved restlessly in his mind and he instinctively shied away from it. Anything that far back couldn't be good.

"We were attacked by Falkane's ship, *Bunyip*."

Jherek's heart skipped a beat.

"I remember it well," Sabyna continued. "My mother and I had just put away the remains of morningfeast, and a fog swelled up from the south as it sometimes will during this time of year. Only on that day, *Bunyip* was following it in. We ran a race for a time, our sails filled with the wind."

Jherek remembered the ship then, and the chase. He'd been five, clinging to the ship's rigging as his father had commanded. It was his job to put out any fires that might start on the deck when the boarding began. Merchant ships who knew they were going to be taken often retaliated by trying their hardest to make taking them dangerous to the pirates. He always stayed near the wet sand barrels that he used to put out any fire arrows that struck *Bunyip*. The pirate vessel's namesake, a creature of the seas half seal, half shark, was known for the characteristic roar it unleashed before it took its prey. Falkane had ordered a specially made klaxon created to make the same roar, only much louder. Jherek remembered it ringing in his ears that day.

"In the end," Sabyna went on, "*Bunyip* closed on us. The boarding crew was more merciful in those days than they are now."

"I know," Jherek said hoarsely.

"Falkane ordered the captain and most of the crew killed. It was butchery, but he spared my father and a few other men, my other two brothers who were still yet children themselves. He also spared my mother and the women on the ship."

Images flickered through Jherek's mind of that day, more details available than he'd ever been able to remember in the past. He'd clung to the railing, scared and crying as he always did when he saw the vicious bloodletting that happened on a ship *Bunyip* had grappled onto.

"My brother Dennin was sixteen, still a boy, but with a man's growth. His magic could have been strong, but he denied it, called to the blade. Before my father could stop him, he challenged Falkane to a duel." Sabyna shook her head. "It was no duel. It was an execution."

Jherek didn't remember that. At the time he'd been standing by the railing, sure even as a child that he could no longer endure the fear and the sheer evil that radiated from his father and the pirate crew. Men and women had been murdered—and worse—on *Bunyip*'s deck, and his father had made him witness most of the atrocities.

During the boarding then the two ships had gotten off tandem on a wave and knocked forcibly together. He'd fallen over the railing and into the ocean between the two ships. Though he was a good swimmer, he couldn't overcome the undertow created by the ships and the sea. In the end, he'd given up, accepting death as a respite from the harsh and unloved life he'd been forced to live.

He remembered floating downward, looking up at the keels of the two ships over him, watching as the turquoise world around him slowly faded to black. On the brink of drowning, he'd heard the voice for the first time.

Live, that you may serve. Nothing more, but the voice had left him feeling enraptured, stronger.

A pair of dolphins had swam under him, nosing under his arms and swimming with him back to the surface. One of his father's pirates had spotted him and leaped in to save him. Afterward, he'd been more hopeful for a time, but that had faded as the days of waiting for more direction had turned into months and years. Now with the way events had gone in Velen, Jherek felt it had only been to prolong the agony of his life.

"After he finished with the ship," Sabyna went on, "Falkane burned it to the waterline. He gave my father Dennin's body, as a token of respect he'd said, because my brother had died well."

"I'm sorry," Jherek said, the cold touching him again, but coming from inside this time. Still, his mind whirled. Perhaps Madame Iitaar's divination was correct. It wasn't just mere chance that had placed him on the same ship as a woman who'd been there at the time the dolphins had rescued him. Or was it? He wished that he was more certain.

Live, that you may serve.

But serve who?

"I'm not telling you this because of the boy," Sabyna said. "I did what

I had to down there even if it did frighten him more than he should have been, and we both have to live with that. Nor am I telling you this because I want you to understand how I feel about pirates. I'm telling you these things because I want you to know me."

Jherek remained silent, knowing part of her talk was from the aftermath of the risk they'd taken. Talking at such times, Malorrie had assured him, was a natural thing, a way of putting things behind a person.

"If I could," she continued, "I'd kill every pirate on every sea, on all of Toril, and stretch their bodies out for the gulls to feed on."

The tattoo on the inside of Jherek's arm seemed to catch fire. It marked him indelibly for her, made him a part of what she most hated. There was no denying his heritage, and his bloodline only made it worse.

"Tynnel's stand on pirates is the chief reason I signed on with *Breezerunner*," she said. "He's got a reputation for taking the fight to pirates, and he keeps the extra men on board to handle any encounter with them that may come along." She turned to him. "I've a harsh side to me, one that surprises a lot of people. Is that too much for you to handle?"

He hesitated, trying to figure it out for himself. His head rebelled from what she was saying, thinking that her logic was skewed. It was one thing to stand against an evil, but another to stalk it as much like a predator as the evil itself. In the end, he went with his heart.

"No, it's not too much for me to handle."

She looked at him, her eyes searching his. "Good, because I find myself liking you—maybe more than I should—and if I'm too honest for you too quickly, I can only offer my apologies."

Her revelation shocked Jherek and he didn't know what to say.

"Surprised?" she asked.

"Aye," he croaked.

"Surprised that I'd be so forward?"

He shrugged.

"I live on a ship, as you have. It's a small world. Things will pass you by if you don't reach out for them. Do you understand?"

Jherek nodded, realizing that her talk was there to bolster her courage in revealing so much of herself.

"There's not much time to get to know someone you feel—*drawn* to," she continued. "I've learned that I have to deal with my feelings quickly to make sure of where I stand. I can't afford distractions in my job, and I've found you've become very distracting. If I don't deal with it now, I fear it's only going to get worse. I don't want that, but neither do I want to confuse you, and I know from other times that I'm capable of that. I'm trying to be fair to both of us. It would be easier if I felt you weren't interested."

Jherek understood. Finaren had kept *Butterfly* operating in the same fashion. If men didn't get along, they admitted and confronted each other, and truces were worked out. If talking didn't settle it, they fought, though no killing was permitted. If the one fight didn't settle matters, Finaren picked one of the men and helped the other, if he was a good worker, find another ship.

He tried to think of something to say, but no words came readily to his lips. Luckily, she continued, making a effort to fill the uncomfortable silence that had threatened to come between them.

"When you put a woman on a ship," Sabyna said, "you affect ship's morale. I can't afford to get close to any man on this ship. Such a thing has a tendency to split the crew. Yet, I'm a woman still, with womanly desires. It's one thing to entertain myself on shore leave, but those are transitory things. *Breezerunner* is my home, and it makes me feel good about myself to invite someone into my home and fix a meal for them, share a conversation. Do you understand?"

"Aye, I think that I do," Jherek answered, looking into her impassioned gaze, knowing what she felt in part. He'd never had what he considered a home to himself, except maybe the loft over the barn he'd rented before Madame Iitaar had taken him into her home. He'd never allowed himself to get close to others, not even *Butterfly*'s crew, because of his secret.

"I'm no common woman to be treated in a casual manner." She looked away. "Should you get a berth on this ship when you get to Baldur's Gate, things between us would change. I don't fraternize with crew, and you need to know that as well."

He nodded. Her honesty felt much different from the Amnian woman's from three days ago. There were no demands being put on him, only an interest evidenced. Strangely, he found that it frightened him more than the Amnian woman's bald advances.

"What's on your mind?" Sabyna asked.

He looked away from her, not knowing what to say.

"Tell me if I've completely embarrassed myself," she said in a contrite voice, "but I know no other way to let someone know what I'm thinking other than to tell them."

Hearing the uncertainty in her voice, Jherek turned back to face her. "No, lady, you've not embarrassed yourself. I think you show great sense and have courage to speak your mind."

"Then what?"

"I—"

She waited, which made it even harder to speak.

"I thought eveningfeast tonight was just in appreciation for the work I'd been doing," he stated finally.

"You accepted because you liked the idea of a meal cooked only for you, or being seen with the only female on the ship's crew? If that's the case, then I was wrong about you." She wrapped up more tightly in her part of the blanket.

"No, lady, that's not it. I took your eveningfeast invitation because I wanted to get to know you more."

"You didn't think I'd invited you for the same reason?"

"No, I didn't."

Sabyna laughed softly. "In some ways, for a sailor, you're very naive," she said. "Why wouldn't you think I'd be interested in you?"

"I'm very common, lady."

"You work hard, yet you keep to yourself. You're opinionated, but you keep those opinions to yourself. You're brave and caring. Tonight has shown me that. Those are all traits a woman could be interested in." She paused. "You said you'd wanted to get to know me better. What about me made you feel that way?"

Surprisingly, Jherek found the answer to that easy, if somewhat disconcerting to admit. "I liked your smile," he told her, "and I liked the way you handle yourself. You walk this deck confidently, lady."

"My beauty didn't turn your head?"

Jherek faced her, not believing he hadn't thought to comment on her beauty. In all the stories he'd read, the heroes always talked of their lady love's beauty. She wasn't his lady love, he reminded himself, and life didn't always have a happy ending the way it did in the romances.

"Lady, as you've said, I'm naive about some things, but one thing I have learned is that beauty can be deceptive."

"Touché," she replied, looking into his eyes. She smiled at him.

Jherek became even more aware of the way the blanket enfolded the two of them, and of the scent of lilacs. The moonlight ignited copper flame highlights in her damp hair. She *was* beautiful.

"You lie as well," she replied calmly, without accusation. "I don't know if your name is Malorrie or Jherek."

"Lady—" Her words tore at Jherek's heart. He'd never wanted to lie to anyone.

She placed her fingers against his lips. "Shush. I feel I know you. I think you believe you have reasons for lying about the things you lie about. I won't have you lying any further to me, not if I'm going to get to know you, and I won't push you to tell me anything you're not ready to say."

He waited, smelling the lilac softness of her fingers.

"Do you understand?"

"Aye, lady," he said softly.

She stared at him in silence for a moment, then broke the eye contact. "You need to get some sleep," she said, "as do I. Tynnel will keep a crew out searching for any more possible survivors, but I don't think there'll be any. We can talk more tomorrow."

"As you wish."

She smiled at him. " 'As you wish,' " she repeated. "I like the sound of that."

Jherek flushed. At the moment, looking into her eyes, the response had seemed so appropriate, culled from the pages of books he'd read, of the romances in the stories, but aloud like that, with Sabyna drawing attention to it, it seemed to strike a false note. "I only meant—"

"It's all right. I meant what I said, I do like the sound of it. I've grown up around the sea and seafaring men all my life. Men's lips often move before their brains have full sails up. I'll warn you now, if you start coming across as a dandy, I'll have none of it. The man I had dinner with, the one who was polite and kind and thoughtful, and maybe a bit flustered, that's the one I enjoy. If he turns out to be a bit of drama or a flummery, I warn you now I'll be greatly disappointed." She took her blanket back and stood.

Jherek stood as well, and he was surprised how chill the wind felt now after being wrapped in her blanket. He took the empty bowls, intending to drop them in the galley after they parted.

"Are you still interested in helping out with the work *Breezerunner* needs?"

"Of course."

She started to go, then turned back to him. "There's one other thing I want to mention to you."

"Aye."

Her manner turned even more darkly serious. "When I read your palm earlier, I had a vision. I've never had one before, but I know that's what it was. It was interrupted by the collision."

Jherek felt his stomach turn small and cold, wondering what she'd seen. After living with Madame Iitaar as she gave divinations all those years, he believed in such magic.

"I don't know how far in the future, but at some point, you're going to cross swords with Falkane the Salt Wolf. It will be at sea, but it's a sea I've not seen."

Suddenly dizzy, feeling like the deck itself had dropped out from beneath him, Jherek made himself remain standing.

"That surprises you?" she asked.

"Aye."

"Why?"

"I'm just a sailor, no king's man or corsair to pursue the pirates of the Nelanther."

Her eyes examined his face. "It might not come true," she said finally. "The vision felt like it was sometime in the future, but the events aren't set. If you stay on your present course, I feel it will happen, but visions aren't written in stone. Good night. I'll see you in the morning."

Jherek watched her walk away, reveling in the sight of her while at the same time feeling more wary than ever. After leaving the dishes with the cook, he took himself amidships and hung out a hammock. He'd stayed in the cabin below decks for the last three nights, sharing the space with other travelers and some of the ship's crew. Tonight, though, he wanted to sleep out under the stars, hoping it would clear his head.

He laid on the hammock and draped the heavy blanket Madame Iitaar had made and he'd gotten from his traveler's kit over him. The wind slipped across his face. He wondered about the ship's mage, wishing he had Malorrie there to talk to him about the way she made him feel and the confusing things she said and did.

He thought about the vision of his father she'd said she had. He didn't doubt that she'd had the vision, but he did question whether it was going to come true. There was no reason his path would cross his father's ever again. If it did, he had no doubt that blood would be spilled and one of them might die.

The last thought he had, though, was of what might be waiting for him at Baldur's Gate.

22

Seated atop the royal flier, skimming through the depths at top speed, Laaqueel looked out over King Huaanton's village. It was spread across the rocky seabed three hundred feet and more below the surface, located between the Nelanthers and the Moonshaes, as the surface dwellers termed the ground above water. By Huaanton's reckoning, those areas were still part of his domain, just held by invaders. Iakhovas, Laaqueel knew, had promised to bring those regions under Huaanton's control soon.

The terrain was broken, peaking and gliding in mismatched sections that left troughs and valleys scattered over it. The deepest section of it was the canyon that ran through the ocean bed. Perpetual murk hung over the area, masking the pale blue light that actually made it to that depth. Surface dwellers, even with their magic potions and items that allowed them to breathe underwater and withstand the crushing depths, wouldn't see the village with their weak eyes unless they were on top of it. By that time, sharks, sahuagin guards, and traps all stood ready to kill them.

The village was huge, lining both sides of the immense canyon. Buildings crafted of great blocks of stone sat barnacle-covered on both sides. Despite all the killing that had gone on by each sahuagin king who'd held court at the site, there still existed the rumor that the buildings had once been on the surface, and that immense changes had shaken all of Toril in the past.

The flier, propelled by sahuagin swimmers gripping the t-bars underneath, changed its glide approach to a steeper angle and slid down into the canyon. Dozens of sahuagin dwellings, looking like bumps and abnormalities, clung to the canyon walls. Sharks and sahuagin guards lounged in the cracks and crevices leading into tunneled labyrinths that honeycombed the village. More tunnels, likewise filled with traps and guards, twisted and threaded through the canyon walls and beyond on both sides. Over seven thousand sahuagin lived there.

The sahuagin tiller guided his craft down to the bottom of the canyon, then cut sharply into a defile that looked like a shadow against the uneven floor. They burst through into the darkness. Even with her vision, Laaqueel was hard-pressed to see through the gloom. It would take a little time for her eyes to fully acclimate to the new darkness. Even attacking sahuagin would be at a disadvantage to the palace guards inside.

The flier leveled out and slowed, easing into the tunnel the manta almost filled from side to side. The tunnel walls were slick from usage. Dozens of guards filled the receiving chamber, and Laaqueel knew traps covered every inch of the area. The water felt colder inside the passage. In all her life, she'd only been to the king's village once before, and never through the tunnels that led to the main palace.

Iakhovas sat beside Laaqueel in the flier, concentrating on another of the artifacts that his search parties had brought to him of late. The wizard didn't appear to be impressed by being invited to the royal village at all. The attack on Waterdeep was six days in the past, and Iakhovas was already planning his next steps.

The malenti was aware of how much the surface world was talking about the attack because Iakhovas had assigned her to gather information. She'd resented being taken from the village. From so far away she couldn't watch the wizard as closely as she want to. She was getting the feeling that Iakhovas was spending more time away, too, maybe on the surface. His casual disregard for all the history surrounding them now made her angry.

"You should be more respectful," she said.

He lifted his head from the object he was studying, fixing her with his one-eyed gaze. "I bid you to take care in what you choose to say, little malenti. It doesn't take much effort to detect a note of insubordination in your voice."

She swallowed her anger but didn't break eye contact. "A true sahuagin would feel reverent about this place. It was the first home of the sahuagin."

"How came you to this belief?"

"It's what I've been told."

"Then it would probably shatter your certitude to know that everything you've heard about that is a fabrication."

The announcement was like a sudden, unexpected slap across the face. Before Laaqueel could figure out how she wanted to reply and still ensure her own survival, the tunnel took a sudden turn to the left and up. At the end of the new tunnel, the largest clam Laaqueel had ever seen opened at their approach.

Fifty or more sahuagin guards, dressed in harnesses bearing the royal seal, a white shark set against the dark blue of the ocean, filled the area. Their tridents were black, cut from the shafts of obsidian that were mined from the veins created by underwater volcanic eruptions in the area hundreds of years ago. Serviceable and distinct, the weapon of each sahuagin guard of the Royal Black Tridents was never out of the bearer's hand from the time he was given it to the time he died. Even then, it passed from the guard to his hand-picked successor. They were ruled only by the king and the nine official Royal Tridents.

The sahuagin guards bristled, flanking the flier as Iakhovas gave the command for it to stop. In a heartbeat, the flier pulled to a full halt and hung suspended in the air, the fins of the sahuagin below maintaining the distance above the cavern floor.

One of the guards moved forward and set his trident deliberately on the front of the flier. He was one of the most fearsome sahuagin Laaqueel had ever seen. Scars lined his powerful torso and one of his ears had been bitten off in battle. Bite marks from another sahuagin pinched up his right cheek, giving him a mocking, cruel smile that revealed a few fangs. The flesh had turned dead white from the injury.

"I am Soothraak, First Honored among the Royal Black Tridents. No one goes any further without my leave," the sahuagin challenged.

Iakhovas stood and stretched to his full height, answering the challenge with his own. Due to his glamour, Laaqueel knew the sahuagin viewed him as one of their own. "I am Iakhovas, a prince of We Who Eat, and you will address me as your superior or there will be a promotion within your ranks, First of the Nine." His voice rolled over the assembled guard.

For a moment Laaqueel believed the guard leader's pride was going to be too much for him and he would attack. Iakhovas didn't back down, almost leaning toward the other in anticipation.

The guard took his trident from the flier and backed away, spreading his arms out away from his body, baring his vulnerable stomach and throat to attack. "In the Exalted One's name, I bid you welcome, Most Honored One."

"Meat is meat," Iakhovas responded. "I come with the preparations of a feast."

Soothraak stood at attention again. "So we have heard. Many of our people died in the attack on the surface dwellers."

"They were inadequate and Sekolah found them wanting, ever reaving the weak from our blood," Iakhovas responded. "I bid you make certain to tell the other side of that tale. There were also a number of We Who Eat who successfully completed their mission, proving their worth. We have bared our fangs and claws, and we have tasted the surface dwellers' blood. A new fear has been installed in them, and they will pass that fear onto their children and their children's children."

The guard started to say something else, but Laaqueel interrupted him, putting the teeth of the office of priestess into her words. She'd come too far with Iakhovas to allow him to be brought down. Her future was directly tied to his, and there was no denying that, as well as Sekolah's guidance. "Do you think the Most Exalted One would like to know you wasted the time of one who waits to eat with him?"

"No, More Honored One," the guard said.

"Do not dare be insubordinate at this moment," Iakhovas commanded. "Address this female as Most Honored One and show her the respect she is due as my high priestess. Know that not only is she my high priestess, but she is One Most Favored by Sekolah. She speaks his wishes, and to stand in their way is to bare your throat to the Great Shark himself."

When Laaqueel saw the chastised look appear on Soothraak's face, pride flared through her. After all her long years of devotion, Sekolah was seeing to it that she was properly honored. Iakhovas's demands that she be so honored offered proof that the Great Shark had put the currents before her. She felt ashamed that she'd had doubts. Even the attack on Waterdeep had gone exactly as Iakhovas had promised. Shipping from that city had all but stopped.

"Meat is meat, Most Honored One," the Black Trident said. "My address from this moment on shall be more adequate."

Soothraak lifted his hand and the Royal Black Tridents broke ranks around the flier. Iakhovas sat and ordered the craft forward again. The giant clam waited, open-mouthed, then the pealing tone of a great bell echoed through the chamber. Slowly, the clam closed, revealing the tunnel mouth above it that the open shell had hidden.

The flier barely fit through the tunnel, and the way became even darker. The dim blue glow of lichens stained the walls, allowing an ease in navigation. Twice, the flier nudged up too close to a wall, and the sound of the wood scraping against the rock echoed painfully in Laaqueel's ears. She felt the increased pressure of the current that overtook them before she realized what it was.

In the current's grip, the flier twisted through the tunnel, having no real choice about what direction it traveled or how fast it was going to get there. The flier came out of the tunnel in a rush, emptying into a great basin lined with white limestone rock. The rock along the bottom had merely been dropped into place, the rocks in the walls and ceiling of the enclosed space had been affixed.

Laaqueel knew the purpose behind the rock. Purely defensive in its design, the white limestone backlit anyone who entered the chamber, stripping away shadows that invaders could normally hide in. The next line of defense was the huge net that spanned the mouth of the other tunnel leading from the basin. Metal glinted, mixed with the dulled brightness of old bone, letting her know that hundreds of barbed hooks had been woven into the net.

More members of the Royal Black Tridents stood on the rock shelf protruding from the other tunnel. Most of them carried crossbows, bone shafts tipped with fish fins lay in the grooves.

Sudden motion touched Laaqueel through her lateral lines. Whatever had moved was huge, immediately threatening. She turned, pushing herself up from the flier's seat to find the source.

A white cloud seemed to lift and separate from the limestone wall on her left. Even with her vision, she found it hard to discern what the motion belonged to.

The drifting white cloud shifted again and a red eye flared into focus, fully ten feet across. Once she had the eye, Laaqueel recognized the rest of the creature as an albino kraken.

Laaqueel stood, immediately frightened. The kraken was the largest of its kind she'd ever seen. From the tip of its triangular head to the ends of its two longest tentacles, it had to be over one hundred fifty feet in length. All eight tentacles wavered in the water around it, floating on the constant current that eddied through the chamber. Still, they moved with frightening speed, slithering around the flier.

Besides the power the gigantic creature wielded with its tentacles, Laaqueel knew from experience that it squirted a poisonous ink cloud. There were other abilities as well, and the creature possessed a superior intellect. She'd only seen two before. Both those had ruled the regions they'd been in, allowing no habitation by aquatic elves or anything near human.

She eased into position, bringing her trident up in line with the creature. It wouldn't do much good against the kraken, she was sure, but having the weapon there made her feel a little more secure.

The kraken glided into position above the flier, dangling over it. The tentacles whipped languidly through the water, curling and almost brushing against the craft. The sahuagin bristled with weapons as they faced the creature.

"Ah, little malenti, this is truly a fascinating specimen."

Laaqueel glanced at Iakhovas, surprised to see the look of absolute joy that crossed the wizard's scarred face.

"I knew not if they yet lived, hadn't dared to dream that it would be so."

"Yes," she said, "and they also kill."

"This creature will not harm me," he told her confidently. "Once, when I was young and the world was too, I knew them all."

"Even so, this won't be one of those."

"Given the life spans the creatures have, there's no chance," he agreed, shaking his head, "but I guarantee you, little malenti, this creature will know me."

She looked at him, wondering if he told the truth. Kraken didn't stay anywhere near each other, much less near any creature that they didn't rule. She knew this one had to have been kept captive, forced to serve the sahuagin king. It was one of the secrets of the sahuagin royalty she was now privy to.

The sahuagin guard at the other tunnel hailed them.

Iakhovas gave the flier pilot orders to take the craft closer. The sahuagin swimming beneath surged forward, wanting to put as much distance as possible between themselves and the kraken, but the kraken drifted effortlessly in their wake, spreading out wide and resembling a net not quite closing around them.

King Huaanton stood at the forefront of the Royal Black Tridents. Almost nine feet tall and still growing slowly these days, the sahuagin monarch carried a body sculpted in wide and hard planes of muscle. He was old enough that his scale coloration was almost black, a natural camouflage at the deepest levels of the sea. His combat harness bore the shark seal of Sekolah and was festooned in shells and shark's teeth. He carried the ornate shark bone trident with inlaid gold that had been handed down for centuries from king to king. That trident, Laaqueel knew, was a guarantee that the sahuagin holding it would fight to the death to hold his station. Huaanton had stripped it from his dead predecessor after a challenge battle not far from the sahuagin city.

"Iakhovas," Huaanton called out.

The wizard turned at last, drawing his gaze from the kraken, but Laaqueel knew the observance of the command had been too slow. Huaanton wouldn't let that go.

"Exalted One," Iakhovas called back. "At your behest, I have returned to your august presence that I might serve you."

Laaqueel grew more afraid as the kraken continued closing the distance. Iakhovas didn't seem to care. The net stretched tight before them, the kelp laced with bone shards to prevent anyone from easily cutting through. Until it was lowered or removed, it trapped them with the kraken.

"You find yourself on the wrong side of the net," Huaanton stated with the hint of a threat. "One of my predecessors found that creature and captured it while it was young, then it was walled in here until it grew too large to escape. Now the beast is deliberately kept hungry. Only the fact that it knows we'd starve it to death if it attacked you unbidden keeps it from eating you now."

"Perhaps, Exalted One," Iakhovas said, "and perhaps there is more to this creature's behavior than you know."

He sprang from the flier, cleaving the water and streaking upward. He moved like a born swimmer, instinctively knowing how best to move his body.

The kraken's tentacles rippled in response to Iakhovas swimming closer. For a moment, it looked like the gargantuan creature was actually going on the defensive.

Laaqueel watched, hypnotized by the sight of the man looking so diminutive against the kraken's huge mass. She forced herself to stand in the flier, but she had a spell at the ready, willing to strike the creature with a scalding jet of heated water. If Iakhovas died, her ambitions and privileges died with him, and so did her ability to better serve Sekolah.

The kraken floated upside down, its arrowhead-shaped body pointed down toward the cavern floor so its tentacles splayed out around it.

Iakhovas floated near one of the eyes, looking like he was locked in some kind of conversation with the giant squid.

Without warning, the kraken started glowing, outlined by a soft purple-blue light that shifted and moved like fiery flames. Iakhovas reached out and placed a hand next to the kraken's huge eye. The wizard grinned as he turned to face Huaanton.

"Just as I perceived," Iakhovas said confidently. "I, and my mission, have been given Sekolah's blessings. Laaqueel has brought me the message and kept me in line with the Great Shark's desires."

Laaqueel believed the wizard was magically controlling the kraken. She didn't want to believe that he had some kind of bond with them that had existed before he'd been turned into stone and left for dead, or that Sekolah had offered the wizard protection. She wished she didn't have her doubts.

With a lightning quick flick, the kraken reached out a tentacle and stripped one of the sahuagin warriors from the flier. The warrior never had a chance, although he succeeded in burying his trident in the creature's flesh. While the warrior still struggled, the kraken brought him to its mouth and bit down, shredding the sahuagin's legs. Blood clouded the water, running in black swirls against the white limestone background.

The royal guard surged forward, hooking their webbed hands in the net separating them from the kraken and the dying sahuagin. They shouted out at the giant squid in anger and fear while the men in the back instantly surrounded Huaanton, urging him back into the tunnel.

The king shook them off, chasing them back from him with warnings. The guards pulled back reluctantly, caught between the need to do their job and their responsibility to obey the king.

The kraken chomped again, biting the dying sahuagin in two at the waist. Hunks of meat and entrails spilled out into the water. Slowly, the kraken raised Iakhovas toward its mouth.

Laaqueel shifted, getting ready to loose the magic she had awaiting her command.

As you were, little malenti. Do not try to take any part in this upon pain of death. Iakhovas's voice spoke into her mind. *Huaanton has grown over bold these past few years and must be reminded of his true place in the events that are unfolding. I will not suffer him threatening me and undermining my authority while I go off to fight his wars.*

Laaqueel forced water through her gills, flushing her body. She didn't act, but her spine became as tight as a bowstring. The wizard's insubordination was going to be the death of them both.

The kraken stopped moving the tentacle holding Iakhovas within a few feet of its maw. The wizard slashed out with a hand that resembled a hard ridge of bone for a moment. The bone ridge sliced through one of the chunks of meat from the sahuagin warrior.

Laaqueel knew the illusion of being a sahuagin that Iakhovas maintained on himself probably translated to using his claws.

Iakhovas opened his mouth wide and ate the gobbet of flesh he'd hacked off. "Meat is meat," he declared.

The royal guard stared at him in awe. The story, the malenti knew, would spread throughout the kingdom, then into the other villages. In the telling, as with all stories, it would grow, making the wizard a creature of myth. The truth itself was incredible, a tale that sahuagin everywhere would enjoy: a warrior prince of their own, held in the embrace of a half-starved kraken, and eating choice bits of a meal almost out of its mouth. She glanced at Huaanton.

The sahuagin king's features gave nothing away even to her practiced eye, but Huaanton had to have known the position the showdown had pushed Iakhovas into.

Iakhovas grabbed an arm that had been torn free of the dead sahuagin's torso and was floating nearby. He offered it to the kraken, feeding it the arm out of his hand. Carefully, the kraken took the gift of food, not even grazing the wizard's skin with its fangs. Once the rest of the sahuagin had been eaten, the kraken brought Iakhovas down to eye level again. A brief communication took place, then the kraken stretched forth its tentacle and replaced Iakhovas on the flier.

Laaqueel stepped back from the white tentacle, barely able to control the fight or flight instinct that filled her. She prayed to Sekolah to grant her the strength she needed and to not let any of her emotions show.

The kraken withdrew its tentacle but remained close, rippling in the currents that filled the huge chamber. Iakhovas turned to face Huaanton, and Laaqueel recognized the challenge the wizard had engineered. Huaanton had used the threat of the kraken against Iakhovas, hoping to show the power he had over him. Instead, Iakhovas had stripped that threat away and converted it into a threat of his own. Everyone in the chamber knew he was protected by Sekolah's blessing, and they knew he had some degree of control over the kraken.

Now it remained to be seen if Huaanton had the courage to drop the net that held the kraken back.

Facing Iakhovas, Huaanton lifted an arm and gave the order. Immediately, the net separated down the middle, drawn in two opposing directions by pulley systems that looked like they'd been salvaged from the ships of surface dwellers. The shrill of the support lines being taken up on the pulley drums echoed through the water with piercing harshness.

Iakhovas deliberately waited until the opening was larger than he needed. Although the royal guard shifted nervously around him, their tails twisting through the water, Huaanton let the net be drawn back even further. He stood, solid as stone, a sahuagin who exemplified the core of all that his people were taught to revere. There was a ferocity that clung to him in defiance of his own mortality.

Another moment passed, then Iakhovas gave the order to the flier's tiller. The flier surged forward and joined Huaanton and his group on the rocky ledge. Even the flier's crew quickly spread out, some of them swimming up to fill in the space in the water above the ledge. All of them held their weapons tightly and faced the kraken.

Swimming from the flier, Iakhovas never glanced back. The shrill of the pulleys sounded again as the net crews drew it closed.

Reacting a little slowly, her own attention divided in three different directions, Laaqueel swam to join Iakhovas. She dropped into place beside him only a heartbeat behind the wizard's own landing. She felt the hard stone of the ledge beneath her feet, worn smooth by centuries of usage.

"We'll talk," Huaanton said.

"Of course, Exalted One," Iakhovas agreed. "I'd have this no other way."

Turning, the sahuagin king launched himself upward, his webbed hands and feet catching the water at once. He swam for one of five sahuagin-sized tunnels above him. Iakhovas followed.

Laaqueel joined them, swimming behind three of the royal guard who trailed Iakhovas. Only one of the tunnels would lead to the royal palace, and even it would only provide an entry to the maze of tunnels that eventually took a knowing swimmer there. The sahuagin mind loved mazes, and learning complicated ones was a challenge. The other tunnels led to other places, and some of them would lead only to certain death by traps or creatures. Underwater races knew to fear sahuagin mazes.

She followed their lead, marking each turn in her mind, knowing that she was swimming even deeper into Iakhovas's own maze of treacheries. Those, she felt certain, she'd never learn completely.

23

"Waterdeep was all but destroyed, the way I hear it."

Jherek's attention was riveted to the speaker in spite of the press of people crowding the marketplace around him. He carried a bag of packages over his shoulder, items Sabyna had purchased for the ship or for her own personal use.

"I hear all her ships went down, and all those gathered for Fleet-swake," another man said.

Jherek couldn't believe it. A cold tendril of fear arced out from his spine across his shoulders despite the sweltering heat of Ath-katla's Waukeen's Promenade. Though not overly far from the Sea of Swords, the fifty foot walls of the marketplace enclosed the stadium and trapped the heat from the noonday sun inside despite the entry arches at ground level.

"What's wrong?" Sabyna asked, looking up at him from the table covered with spices, baking goods, and cooking utensils. She'd wanted to try a new dish that evening while they were in port. Cooking for two had seemed to make her even more adventurous.

Jherek craned his head toward the two seamen standing near one of the supports that held the next level above. The terraced levels were seventy-five feet across and packed with merchants hawking wares of all kinds at tables and booths. Uniformed guards occupied the mar-ketplace in impressive numbers, which helped drive up the cost of the goods being offered.

"Did you hear that?" he asked her.

"What?"

"Those two sailors . . . they're talking about ships sinking at Waterdeep."

Jherek nodded at the two sailors. Both men were dressed down, looking like they'd just stepped from their ships. Already other sailors were starting to collect around them, eager to hear more.

Quickly, Sabyna made her selections and didn't bother haggling with the merchant, paying his price when she could have easily talked him down. Today the market had belonged to the buyer. Now Jherek knew why. Waterdeep did a lot of trading with the Amnians, and if ships had been destroyed, usual markets could no longer be counted on.

Sabyna placed her hand on the inside of his arm and guided him toward the sailors, covering the pirate's tattoo that he desperately kept hidden from her beneath his shirt. Despite the haze of vegetable and fruit scents, the strong smell of cured meats, and the herbalist burning incense only a few tables down, Jherek could still smell the lilac scent that clung to her. Her fingers gripped his arm tightly and she stayed at his side, doubling their size against the ebb and flow of the crowd.

He'd dined with her every night for the last three nights since the boy had been recovered from the sunken wreck, but she'd never come this close to him in all that time. Their conversations had been good, of experiences and humor, but she'd never asked him what his real name was or why he was in hiding. Each night, after each meal, it became harder not to tell her, harder not to remove the lic that existed between them, but the tattoo branded him as a pirate. He felt certain she'd never be able to accept that, especially since it had been his father who'd killed her brother. For the moment, he enjoyed the warmth of her fingers against his arm even with the sweltering heat that assailed them.

The sailors looked up at her approach.

"Hail and well met," she addressed them.

"Hail and well met, lady," a white-haired sailor in Amnian dress responded. He touched the tips of his fingers to the triangle of copper coins attached to his blue turban. His beard was white like his hair, and so was the fierce mustache that flared straight out at the sides.

"You've news of Waterdeep?" Sabyna said.

"Aye," the sailor replied, "but only bad news, I'm afraid. You're from there?"

"No. I'm Sabyna, ship's mage of *Breezerunner*, helmed by Captain Tynnel. We've traded there and I have a few friends who live there."

One of the other sailors glanced at the old one. "*Breezerunner*'s a good ship, Narik. Heard of her. And her captain's a good man."

Narik nodded. His rheumy eyes regarded Sabyna, then flicked over Jherek. "Are you bound, then, to Waterdeep, lady?"

"Not on this trip," Sabyna said. "We're only going as far north as Baldur's Gate."

"Tell your captain what I tell you. There'll be plenty of gold for a man willing to take his ship into Waterdeep for the next few months. If he's willing to chance the risk to his life and ship."

"He'll probably already know," she said, "but tell me why."

"You've heard nothing?" Narik asked.

Sabyna shook her head. "We only got into the harbor this morning. We were becalmed for a time since leaving Velen."

"Waterdeep was invaded," Narik said.

"By who?" Jherek asked.

He remembered the City of Splendors from the trips he'd taken there with Finaren. During his visits he'd never been daring enough to go very deeply into the city. Most of *Butterfly's* crew had their usual haunts along the Dock Ward, rarely venturing out of the festhalls and taverns, places where Jherek had never felt overly comfortable. He'd spent mornings in *Butterfly's* rigging just watching the sun come up behind the towering mountain where Castle Waterdeep stood. As tall as the mountain was, the shadow of the heights hung over the harbor long after the sun rose in the morning. Sunlight came into the coast from the water as the sun climbed, making it look like the morning light came in on the tide.

"The sahuagin. There were thousands of them, over a month ago at the end of Fleetswake, and they got into Waterdeep Harbor before the guard knew it. Her navy proved no defense against the invaders' forces."

"What forces? Ships?" Jherek asked. He'd watched the Waterdhavian Guard on maneuvers. Very few crews could hold a candle to what they could do with their rakers, and that wasn't even taking into account the other defenses that lined the city's shores.

"Oh, the sea devils had no few of those," Narik confirmed.

"From the stories I've heard, the sahuagin had captured fifteen or twenty vessels, then sailed them right into the harbor slick as the snot from a dung-eating camel," another man stated.

"The guard would have caught that," Jherek objected.

"They didn't, boy," the man said testily, one hard knuckled hand fisting on the curved dagger in his waist sash.

"Sorcery was involved," Narik said, soothing his comrade's temper. "We know that for sure. Besides the guard missing those ships full of sahuagin, a storm summoned by some sorcerous intent whipped over the Dock Ward and tore down a number of buildings."

"Aye," a black sailor interrupted. "I heard Arnagus the Shipwright even lost a vessel that he was building in dry dock when the water lifted it out to the harbor. I've been told the waves were twenty and thirty feet tall."

"The sahuagin don't have anything to do with sorcery," Sabyna pointed out.

"Well, they did this night," Narik told her. "In addition to the thousands of sahuagin and the storm, there were all manner of sea creatures who fought side by side with the sea devils."

"How was that possible?" Jherek asked.

"That's what the mages in Waterdeep are asking right now," the sailor answered. "The city's properly defended and warded, but that attack, even with the extra manpower in port, was disastrous."

"Does Waterdeep still stand?" Sabyna asked.

"Aye," Narik replied. "By the grace of the gods and the strength of Lord Piergeiron's arm, and Maskar Wands's and Khelben Arunsun's magic. Many lives were lost, but the sahuagin were turned. In the meantime, shipping's all but stopped coming out of Waterdeep. Merchants are sitting in the ruins of the Dock Ward offering princely sums for any ship that would take their goods out. The only news we've got out of there has been from caravans traveling overland."

"In part, most cargo captains fear the return of the sahuagin," a skinny sailor with a wandering eye said, "and they have been responsible for bringing a few ships down. They sail those cursed mantas and attack any ship alone at sea."

Jherek remembered the sahuagin attack on *Butterfly*, feeling a chill rattle through him now that he knew that assault had been part of a larger agenda.

"Most cargo ships don't carry a crew big enough to repel a manta complement of sahuagin," the sailor with the wandering eye went on. "I've heard they've taken twenty ships over the last five days, and mayhap more than that since these stories were given only by survivors of attacks."

"The sahuagin haven't ever meant to leave survivors," Narik said, "not unless they were planning on torturing them later."

Jherek couldn't believe the numbers of ships the sailors were talking about, or the fact that the sahuagin were acting together so well. For the moment, he forgot his own problems, forgot even that Sabyna had not taken her hand from his arm. His mind wandered, wrestling with the problem of how the attack had taken place and what it must have been like to be there. He wished Malorrie was there to talk to. Though Madame Iitaar was familiar with history and battles and even politics, Malorrie relished in such discussions. He silently wished he'd been there, able to lend his blade to Waterdeep's defense.

"What the sea devils haven't claimed," Narik went on, "the pirates have. They seem to have gathered in the Nelanther and decided that Waterdeep's ill luck was their good fortune. They've taken a dozen and more ships that we know of that's been bound in either direction in the Sea of Swords."

"That's why there are so many fighting men gathered in Athkatla today," the black sailor said. "The festhalls and taverns are filled with mercenaries and sellswords waiting to be picked up by captains who're courageous enough to brave the waters north of here."

"Lady," Narik said, "if you're bound to Baldur's Gate, talk to your captain if he hasn't already heard. Those are dangerous waters these times. There are some tongues wagging that during Fleetswake in Waterdeep that someone tried to rob Umberlee's Cache and all of this is part of a curse the Bitch Queen has put on Waterdeep."

"They blame the actions of the sahuagin as well on her?" Sabyna asked.

Narik shrugged and said, "Lady, who else could summon up storms and cause the sea creatures that were seen in the invasion of Waterdeep to align themselves with the sea devils? Many sailors have seen Umberlee's hand in this. There's no other explanation."

Sabyna thanked them for the news, then headed out of the marketplace, threading through the large crowds.

"We've got to find Tynnel," she said to Jherek. "I'm sure he already knows, but if he doesn't, he needs to know now, and we need to make plans for the trip to Baldur's Gate. If we're going to make it at all."

"Aye," Jherek replied.

An eagerness moved through him, though, along with the fear. Memory of the pirate-stricken vessel they'd found the boy in filled his mind. He wasn't afraid for himself, but for the pretty ship's mage.

"You try the festhalls and taverns," she went on as they exited the marketplace and walked out onto the street beyond, "while I try the mercantile houses where we normally do business. We'll meet back on *Breezerunner.*"

"As you wish," he told her.

She turned and gave him a fleeting smile, but it didn't quite touch the worry he saw in her eyes. "Be safe," she said, "until I see you again." She gave his arm a final squeeze, letting him know she'd been aware of the prolonged contact as well, then hurried across the busy street.

Jherek stood and watched her, admiring the smooth roll of muscle shown by her breeches and the easy way that she moved, not showing much of a sailor's rolling gait when on land. Apprehension flared through him, though, when she disappeared from sight down an alley leading deeper into the Amnian city. It was like a small, cold voice had whispered that he'd never see her again.

He almost went after her then, but he stopped himself. He'd given his word he'd try to find the captain. He turned and went down the street toward the docks where the festhalls and taverns thrived.

24

"We need to make another attack."

Huaanton regarded Iakhovas silently after the statement. The sahuagin king's stance made it clear to Laaqueel that that wasn't something he wanted to hear.

The malenti waited tensely, knowing Iakhovas should have reacted to the king's unspoken displeasure. For the last twelve years he'd lived among them as one of their own and the wizard knew enough to recognize the body language. By rights, he should have avoided eye contact at any cost and perhaps even swum up over Huaanton's head, baring his midriff to possible attack as a rebuke and a show of his loyalty.

Iakhovas merely stood there, his back to one of the four thick crystal windows that peered out over the sahuagin city in the chasm. In fact, he not only appeared unrepentant but mutinous, and Laaqueel was certain that attitude ran over into the illusion he wore for the king.

Huaanton's throne room and audience chamber was huge. Thousands of years had gone into the planning and construction of it. Made of limestone blocks each over an arm span wide and more than that tall, the sahuagin castle looked like another bump on the canyon wall from the outside. It was seven stories tall inside, the lower three sunk into the ledge of outthrust rock spurring from the chasm side, and the other four looking like a natural rock projection.

The throne room was on the second floor down, below Huaanton's personal quarters and treasury. A massive throne carved from whale bone in the shape of a shark leaping from the water with its jaws distended occupied one end of the room. The open mouth contained the seat, large enough even for Huaanton's massive girth.

Images of sharks and sahuagin were cut in bas-relief on the limestone blocks of the walls. The largest stones depicted battles from sahuagin history, myth interwoven with truth until it was all memory. The largest piece, on the opposite end of the room from the throne, showed the meeting of the sahuagin and Sekolah, whom they chose as their god.

The carving of Sekolah, the Great Shark, held a shell in his teeth, shaking it. Tiny sahuagin finned away from him in all directions, coming from the shell. According to history, Sekolah had been victorious in chosen battle against a behemoth of the deep. The Great Shark had gone forth, singing his song of joy and been pleasantly surprised to hear other voices singing back to him. The shell containing the sahuagin had floated up to him on a spray of bubbles, drawn by the joy coming from Sekolah. Once the Great Shark had spread them across the sea, the sahuagin had prospered and multiplied even further.

"More than two thousand sahuagin died in the attack on Waterdeep," Huaanton stated.

"Easily twice that many surface dwellers perished," Iakhovas said. "The sahuagin who died served their purpose in killing the enemy, but they were weak. The strong members of our people came back from that war, and our race will be the stronger for it. The next hatchlings will all be of true warriors' blood, a legacy wrought by the testing of our mettle in battle."

Huaanton's magnetic black gaze pinned Iakhovas, but the wizard didn't flinch from the eye contact.

Laaqueel silently prayed that Iakhovas wouldn't overstep his bounds. If he did, he'd bring swift and certain death down on them both. Twenty sahuagin guards ranged around them, their faces impassive, but the malenti knew they'd act at once if their king rightfully called them into action.

"They died," Huaanton agreed, "and by that proved they were inadequate to survive, but another strike against the surface dwellers right now might not be the wisest thing we could do."

"Would you have them think they've broken the sahuagin spirit?" Iakhovas asked.

Laaqueel respected the wizard's ability to choose his words well. They were borderline on accusing Huaanton of cowardice, but they were presented so that the perception was on the part of the surface dwellers, not Iakhovas.

"We still take their ships," the sahuagin king pointed out.

"Only because they foolishly continue to believe they maintain control over the seas," Iakhovas replied. "In this we need to be thankful for their own egotistical designs. We do not have to take the fight to them; they bring it into our home territory with every ship they sail. Still, they must be broken of this inflated view of themselves."

"But the ships appear in less numbers than before."

"In what they call the Sea of Swords," Iakhovas said, "your summation is true. However, even that is too much. All that is needed is for a few ships, or perhaps only one, to brave the sea successfully and they will forget the message that has been delivered to them. A human's memory isn't as long or as gifted as that of a sahuagin's. A human will forget and believe again that they can venture out onto the sea. We need to raid their shores, raze their communities, and see them run broken and splintered before us." He paused. "Sekolah demands no less of his children if they are truly to be his children."

"You claim the ear of Sekolah," Huaanton said, "when none of my priestesses claim any such contact."

"Not his ear," Iakhovas responded, "his voice. He speaks to me through my priestess. I seek only to obey, as should any true sahuagin."

The sahuagin king turned slowly toward Laaqueel, his tail flipping through the water in annoyance. That slight gesture was enough to emphasize the difference between him and her.

Huaanton spoke slowly, giving his words weight. "Why speak through such a . . . flawed vessel?"

Laaqueel instantly dropped her eyes as was the sahuagin custom. She let her arms drift away from her body at her sides, leaving herself defenseless. "I don't know, Exalted One," she replied, and that was partially the truth. As Iakhovas had pointed out, how could she have found him without Sekolah's intervention? Why hadn't another found the story of One Who Swims With Sekolah? What had made him choose her over the two true sahuagin priestesses who had been with her?

"Have you heard the Great Shark?" Huaanton demanded.

"No," Laaqueel answered, "though I have been given visions."

Those visions of combat and strife, of the sahuagin killing surface dwellers at the sides of massive beasts, had been constant for the last year. It could have been nightmares, brought on by listening to Iakhovas's plans for the sahuagin, but they could have been visions as well.

"Do you believe in these visions?"

Next to her heart, the black quill Iakhovas had inserted under her breast stirred in warning. A chill ran down her spine and her face went numb. "Yes," she replied. She knew to answer in any other fashion would have meant sudden death. She believed in Sekolah and she believed in her place in the Great Shark's plans. Wherever Iakhovas led, she believed it would only strengthen the sahuagin. He was a harsh taskmaster, and his chosen war would only strengthen her people.

She felt Huaanton's eyes on her, but she knew he could go no further without opening the way to a challenge from either herself or Iakhovas.

"I live only to serve the will of Sekolah," Iakhovas stated. "Should anything try to stand in the way of that, I would be honor bound to see that thing—that person—destroyed as one of the Great Shark's enemies."

When her lateral lines signaled that Huaanton had turned from her, Laaqueel glanced back up and saw Iakhovas squarely meeting the sahuagin king's gaze.

"Since you've been among us," Huaanton said, "you've been overly ambitious."

"You lay that ambition so easily at my fins," Iakhovas replied slowly, "but I claim no part of it. The ambition, as you incorrectly call it, is merely the doctrine I've been given by my god to obey. I will not turn away from it."

"Twelve years of age," Huaanton said, "and you're already a prince."

"I've taken on the challenges Sekolah has laid before me, and they led me into those positions as the currents dictated," Iakhovas replied. "I rose from warrior to lieutenant, to baronial guard, to chieftain, and then baron because there was a need and because the Great Shark expected no less of the tool he would shape me into."

"You challenged and killed everyone who stood in your way."

"Fairly," Iakhovas said, "and obviously with Sekolah's blessing or I would not have survived. Three years ago, when Slaartiig came to your village where you then ruled as baron and laid claim to the crystal ball your warriors salvaged from a surface vessel they'd sunk, I challenged him for you because his claim to your property was unjust, as fits the rules that Sekolah has handed down to our people. No one expected me to live against such odds as that. Yet I did."

That wasn't all the story, Laaqueel knew. Iakhovas had actually targeted the surface vessel for the sahuagin raiders, then helped them take it. They'd later used the ship in the raid against Waterdeep, but it also had something on board that he'd laid claim to without the warriors seeing. Only she'd known, and then only because he'd told her, relishing his victory.

The crystal ball had been an additional find, one that Iakhovas hadn't been overly interested in. It allowed the viewer to see many places, but they lacked the magic phrases to unlock all its secrets to make it into the weapon Huaanton had hoped it would be. If Iakhovas knew the secret of the crystal ball, he never told.

"You killed Slaartiig," Huaanton said.

"And my actions justified my reasons for defending you in the eyes of the Great Shark and our people," Iakhovas pointed out. No matter what the illusion his spellwork painted for the sahuagin, Laaqueel saw the anger in his scarred face. "You challenged the old king over a matter of cowardice, and you yourself ripped free the trident that you now hold as a sign of your office from his dead hand, proclaiming yourself king. None of the other princes challenged for your position. They recognized your right to be king, read in the currents of everything that had happened that it was what you were destined for."

The other eight sahuagin princes also, Laaqueel remembered, recognized that Iakhovas had been the first to lay his trident at Huaanton's feet, swearing to defend him against all enemies. They already knew what kind of fighter the wizard was.

"You yourself appointed me prince," Iakhovas said, "with every confidence that I'd carry out the demands of that position and support you in every way, which, if you'll review my actions since that time, I have done. Why hesitate to believe in me now, when another victory is within our reach?"

"We fight our battles to win," Huaanton stated. "The one you seek to set before us is unwinnable."

"We fight to sharpen our claws and prove our worth to Sekolah," Iakhovas said, and his words rang true in Laaqueel's ears. "Waterdeep was only the first step. There need to be many more."

"What would you suggest?" the sahuagin king asked.

"Again you confuse the issue before you, Exalted One. These are the wishes—nay, the commands—of Sekolah himself. He speaks through my high priestess."

Huaanton turned to Laaqueel and asked, "How does he instruct you?"

"He doesn't say anything, Exalted One," the malenti said, hating her part in the present subterfuge. "He gave me a vision of a human city called Baldur's Gate."

"Where is this city?"

"Along what the surface dwellers call the Sword Coast," Laaqueel answered. "It's south of Waterdeep."

"This place is important to the surface dwellers?"

"Yes."

Huaanton shifted, his tail lashing out restlessly. "How so?"

"Between Waterdeep and the country they call Amn, Baldur's Gate is the last city of any size that the surface dwellers can use as a stronghold," Iakhovas stated. "It lies almost sixty miles inland, on a flow of moving freshwater they call Chionthar."

"We can't go into fresh water," Huaanton argued.

"The priestess has had the vision," Iakhovas said. "We cannot deny Sekolah's wishes. When we put an army there, we have to trust that a way will be made."

"That army would also be exposed to the surface dwellers. Waters trapped by land don't run as deeply as the sea."

"We shall strike at night, at a time when their defenses will be most relaxed. The surface dwellers won't see us clearly but we will see them easily. Also, Baldur's Gate lacks the size and protection that Waterdeep possessed. They are as a hatchling to a full-grown warrior. It will not be a battle, it will be a ruination."

Huaanton appeared to consider Iakhovas's words, but Laaqueel knew enough about the sahuagin king to know that he wasn't overjoyed at them either. A lot was at stake.

"You're asking too much," the king said finally.

Iakhovas grimaced. Laaqueel felt certain that the illusion he was projecting to the rest of those in the room didn't show the anger. "Exalted One," he said carefully and quietly, "I need to remind you I'm not the one doing the asking. It is more along the lines of a command than any conjecture requiring sufferance on your behalf."

Kicking across the room, Huaanton sat in the open shark's mouth throne. He kept the inlaid gold and shark bone trident upright beside him.

"I want a sign that this is what Sekolah wants," he demanded.

"*Sacrilege*!" Laaqueel exploded, moving toward the sahuagin king with enough fire in her voice and menace in her approach that the royal guards moved quickly to intercept her.

Her emotion came out of the conviction of her office. Born a malenti, an automatic outcast from her own people, she'd been given nothing but the Great Shark to believe in, and she did believe. Even with the involvement of Iakhovas, she believed that there had been some reason she'd been allowed to glimpse the truth of the legend and find the ancient wizard, though she couldn't recognize that reason at the time.

"Sekolah freed the sahuagin into these waters and gave them the strength and the ferocity to go forth and take what they needed," she said. "*That* is the only sign a true believer should ever need!"

Huaanton swiveled his great head to her. The guards' tridents stopped within inches of the high priestess.

She raised her hand in warning, the sound of her praying voice loud enough to carry on the currents that filled the room. Their instinctive fear of even her magic made them drop into nervous defensive positions, but they readied to charge, obviously wanting to deal with her quickly.

"Stop!" Huaanton ordered.

Reluctantly yet relieved, the royal guard stepped back, but they didn't put their weapons away.

"You run the risk of insult, priestess." The sahuagin king glowered at her.

Laaqueel thought quickly. "I run that risk only to keep you from blaspheming, Exalted One. Our two positions—the warrior's to lead the sahuagin race, and the priestess's to guide the sahuagin in their beliefs—are both necessary. A warrior keeps the sahuagin alive in the now, and a priestess keeps the sahuagin alive forever. Our two paths must never work at cross purposes."

"I agree," Huaanton said. "That's why I want Sekolah to give some sign to my priestesses before this next battle takes place."

"Sekolah is not a god you can put demands on."

Laaqueel assumed a level stance, no longer subservient to the sahuagin king. Her eyes met his. The Great Shark would demand no less. In the past, the warrior's way and the priestess's way often conflicted. Both drew on the same resource of followers, but during most of those times compromises could be worked out.

"He doesn't want parasites as his worshipers; he wants warriors."

"I agree," Huaanton said, "but I see before me a malenti, a birth defect, claiming to be a conduit for a god. Wouldn't *you* question that?"

The insult hit Laaqueel like a physical blow. She didn't trust herself to speak until she'd dealt with the anger that filled her.

"Then, at your own peril, you'll have your sign," Iakhovas said.

Huaanton looked at the wizard as if wanting to question whether the statement had been a threat. Instead, he asked, "When?"

Laaqueel didn't dare look at Iakhovas, afraid that her doubt and fear would be apparent to everyone. How could Iakhovas promise something like that?

"A tenday from now," Iakhovas went on. "It will be here, in your city, for all sahuagin to see." He paused, his eyes rebelliously focused on Huaanton's. "When that sign is delivered, there will be no doubt about what is to be done."

"I will look for you here," the sahuagin king said. "You'll be guests at the palace."

For Laaqueel the offer translated simply that they'd be *prisoners* of the palace. She watched numbly as Iakhovas excused them from the sahuagin king's audience chamber. They were accompanied by the royal guard through the maze of tunnels, swimming back to where the flier was tied up.

I perceive my error now, little malenti, Iakhovas said in her mind.

By promising a sign from Sekolah? she asked. *If we don't come here in a tenday, Huaanton will rightly have us hunted down and brought to him. We'll be thrown into the gladiatorial amphitheater and used as sport. Should we show up and there's no sign, we'll end up in the same place.*

Little malenti, Iakhovas mocked, *you concern yourself overmuch with matters that are entirely trivial. I have cared for you fifteen years, elevated you into the position of high priestess for a prince from being a junior priestess and spy for a baron. Miracles are easy to accomplish if you have those who wish to believe in them.*

Laaqueel resented the words, but knew they carried the strength of truth.

No, he said confidently, *there will be a sign. My chief oversight lay in reasoning that I could accomplish everything I need to as anything less than king.*

She stared at him through the darkness filling the maze tunnel. He smiled, and his single eye blazed with conviction.

25

Jherek pushed in through the double doors of the Copper Coronet in the row of festhalls fronting Athkatla's docks and opened his eyes to their fullest against the darkness that clung to the tavern's interior. Raucous voices in a dozen and more languages spilled over into the street beyond the doors, beaten back only by the street vendors hawking their wares to wandering ships' crews.

He waited a moment, letting his eyes adjust to the gloom. Even at midday, the tavern's darkness appeared to be an inviting cool, a place where secrets and guilt could be shared. Pipeweed smoke, dimly lit from candles on the scarred tables and wall sconces, curled toward the stained ceiling. Sea-roughened men reached for waitresses, cracking off-color jokes or making half serious offers given the benefit of graphic gestures. The waitresses for their part flirted with the men, working for the small tips that came their way.

The Copper Coronet was one of Athkatla's many dives. Pirates and smugglers met there to arrange business, and journeymen cutpurses gathered there to find victims. Sawdust covered the floor, sopping up spilled ale or blood as the need arose.

Jherek breathed shallowly through his nose. He'd never felt at home in such a place. Even the taverns in Velen had never become overly familiar or comfortable. He'd gone because Finaren had often concluded ship's business there, and sometimes to briefly share in celebrations he'd been invited to.

Men stood at the sturdy bar that lined the other side of the room, hoisting tankards of ale and laughing at witticisms or stories told by others. The bartender was a short, broad man with a bald head and flaring mustache. He regarded Jherek with a flat, uninviting gaze as he wiped an ale tankard out with a frayed and stained towel. A copper crown, evidently the item the tavern took its name from, rested haphazardly on the yellowed ivory skull of a crocodile jutting from the wall behind the bartender. A handful of teeth were broken in the reptilian grin.

A slim waitress approached Jherek, balancing a tray on one bony hip. Her skirt was cut short enough to embarrass the young sailor, and he kept his eyes on hers. She smiled at him, showing a missing front tooth. Dark sandy hair flared out across her shoulders.

"Can I get something for you, sailor?"

"No," Jherek replied. "I'm looking for the crew of *Breezerunner*."

"I think I noticed them earlier," she admitted, moving close enough that Jherek could feel the heat from her body.

Involuntarily, he took a step back. Dropping his eyes from hers, he couldn't help glancing at the long legs revealed by the short skirt. They were white from not having seen enough sun but still held the roundness of youth. He glanced up at her again and saw she was smiling even more broadly.

"I need to find them," he told her.

Beyond the waitress, other men in the tavern were starting to look at him, evidently noticing his distress at handling her and her attentions. One old sailor with a peg leg slapped his leg with glee, watching intently.

"I'll give you a hand," the waitress replied. She reached forward, dragging her fingers across his stomach.

He felt the heat of her touch through his shirt. Taking another step back, he broke the contact.

"I thought you wanted my help," she challenged. Above her smile, he noticed her eyes had taken on cold, calculating lights.

"Aye," Jherek answered nervously. "Could you point me in the right direction?"

"Yes. I can get you pointed in the right direction."

Her hand dropped to the front of his breeches, seizing his belt and pulling him forward till their bodies met. Before Jherek could decide how he could easily break out of her grip without hurting her or appearing too rude, she leaned in and kissed him, biting gently at his lips.

"Enough!" he said with iron in his voice.

He took her wrist in his hand and broke her grip, lifting her arm between them to use as a lever to keep her away.

"Are you sure?" she taunted. Her smile seemed brighter and colder than ever.

Blood pounded in Jherek's temples. He was embarrassed and angry, not understanding what he'd done to deserve such treatment at the serving girl's hands. Over the roar of anger that filled his ears, he also heard the rollicking laughter of the sailors.

"Unhand the woman," the bartender growled.

Jherek glanced at the big man and saw the oaken club he rested easily across the bar top. Reluctantly, the young sailor complied, stepping back again out of the woman's easy reach.

She closed on him at once and a fresh wave of braying laughter filled the bar.

Nimbly, Jherek pulled out a nearby chair and placed it between them, creating a momentary barrier against the woman's unwelcome attention.

Without hesitation, she stepped up into the chair. The tavern patrons hooted and shouted their support. She flung her arms wide, preparing to throw herself at Jherek, sensing that the young sailor wouldn't let her hit the floor.

"Essme!" the bartender called in his thunderous voice.

The waitress hesitated.

"It's enough," the bartender told her. "You've had your fun. Get back to work."

Reluctantly, the serving girl stepped down, away from Jherek. "Another time," she promised throatily, and blew Jherek a kiss.

Face flaming with humiliation, Jherek almost turned and fled the tavern. Only a recognized voice stilled him.

"What's wrong with you, boy?" a man gruffly demanded.

Jherek turned toward the man stepping out of the shadows behind him. He recognized Aysel from *Breezerunner*'s crew, and the three men that stood behind him as the sailor's cronies.

"You too good for women a regular sailor has to bed down with if he's to know something warm and willing?"

The small daggers hanging from Aysel's ears glinted in the dim light. His thick mane of black hair was held back in a rawhide thong, but his beard was unkempt, frosted with ale foam. His open shirt revealed the pelt of dark hair that coiled on his massive chest and covered his big belly.

Jherek guessed at once that Aysel and his companions had put the waitress up to her performance. He felt shamed that he'd reacted as he had, letting the deceit get to him. He should have thought more clearly and found a way to stop the serving girl without obviously rebuffing her. Malorrie, he knew, wouldn't have reacted in the same fashion, but the woman's advances had been too bold, too blatant, and somehow Aysel had sensed what effect they would have on him.

"You stand in a tavern filled with seafaring men who know how to appreciate a real woman's charms," Aysel stated. "Every manjack here probably feels insulted at the way you disrespected that woman." He glanced around and got the support, halfhearted as it was, of the rest of the sailors in the tavern.

"No disrespect was meant," Jherek replied. His voice sounded tighter and higher than he'd intended. He glanced at the serving wench, watching her move easily through the tables, back to business as usual. "Nor do I think any was taken."

Aysel raised his voice. "How about that, Essme? Do you wish to let bygones be bygones? I stand ready to take up arms in your defense."

He shifted, revealing the battle-axe at his side. The haft was four feet long, and the double-bitted head rested on the spur jutting from the top on the sawdust strewn floor, in a position to be easily swept up into action.

Jherek altered his stance, taking in air as Malorrie had instructed. He wasn't sure what was going on, but he knew that Aysel had borne him enmity since their first meeting on *Breezerunner* at the water barrel when Tynnel had called the man down for his behavior.

"I'm here on business," the young sailor stated easily.

"What business is that?" Aysel demanded.

"I need to speak with the captain."

"Cap'n's not here," Aysel said. His eyes remained flinty hard with challenge and anger. He raised his voice even louder. "Essme!"

The serving girl looked back at the broad sailor, and every head in the tavern snapped around to watch what was going on.

"What?" she asked.

"I asked if you wanted me to stand up for you in this matter of ill charity. A man should not be so cavalier as to spurn a woman's offered charms."

The serving girl appeared hesitant, then finally waved the offer away. Jherek got the impression she wasn't sure how much of the action was still play.

"It's no bother," she replied. "I claim no foul. After all, he's just a boy, not like one of the real men that fill this room."

The tavern goers shouted in glee, banging their empty and not-so-empty tankards down on their tables. A number of jests and curses filled the air at Jherek's expense.

Clamping his jaw tight, Jherek struggled to rein in his anger. Since being driven from Velen, having his identity and home stripped from him by circumstance, he'd been aware of the dark anger that had filled him, but it had been mixed in equal parts with the sense that he'd somehow deserved every bad thing that had happened to him. Evil clung to blood. That was believed by most people, and even Jherek admitted there was some truth to it.

Maybe he didn't deserve a home as other people did, and maybe one of the most feared and hated pirates of Faerûn was all the family he'd ever had, but he didn't deserve Aysel's treatment. The man was more on his level. Jherek rested his hand on the worn hilt of his cutlass.

"Is Captain Tynnel here?" Jherek asked, pushing himself above the anger that swirled within him.

"Why?" Aysel demanded.

"I was sent to get a message to him."

"By who?" the big man asked. "Sabyna? She seems to be the only one you talk to these days. Always running after her with your nose up her skirts."

A tremor filled Jherek's arm and he barely stilled himself from drawing steel against the man. "Have a care," he said softly. "I'll not have her honor trampled while I'm standing nearby."

"Her *honor*?" Aysel guffawed, seeming genuinely amused. "She's a damned ship's mage, boy. She's used to men of the sea, *and* their ways. You jump on deck with your manners and your baby face and think she's just as virginal as you?"

Thunder crackled ominously in the back of Jherek's mind. He felt the precious control Malorrie had trained into him coming unhinged. His fingers felt like wire meshed around the cutlass's hilt. He tried to ignore Aysel's coarse words.

"If you see the captain, let him know I was looking for him."

He took three steps back, out of reach of the big man's battle-axe, stepping around a table to put between them as well, then turned and walked away. He made himself release the cutlass.

"She's known men before, boy," Aysel called after him, "better men than you."

Every word cut into Jherek. He tried to force them from his mind.

"These past few days," Aysel continued, "I've tried to understand what it was she sees in you besides that courtly manner and those smooth features, but damn me if I've been able."

Jherek walked, breathing deeply, searching desperately for the control that Malorrie's training had given him.

"One thing I want to know, boy," Aysel roared.

Jherek was almost to the door, but not out of earshot.

"I want to know if she's as good looking naked as I've thought she was," Aysel said.

Anger took Jherek then, snapping to life the way a candle wick took to flame. He made himself reach for the door as his breath tightened and turned cool in his throat.

"I look at her," Aysel said, "sometimes with the sun behind her and you can just about see through some of those clothes she wears. I see enough, then I go back to my hammock and think about her."

The tavern crowd urged him on, asking rude questions and making ribald statements.

"I imagine how she looks," Aysel croaked, "all sweaty from being used hard, and the way she smells. Like a woman instead of those fragrances she wears. And then I—"

The sailor got no further.

Jherek turned, slipping through the distance separating him from Aysel like a barracuda. He left the cutlass sheathed because he didn't think the big sailor would have time to bring the battle-axe up to defend himself. In fact, Aysel seemed stunned, barely beginning to react as Jherek vaulted to the tabletop and threw himself at the man. He flung his arms wide, taking in all of Aysel's broad frame. The bigger man wrapped his meaty arms around the young sailor as they slammed backward.

Aysel's breath whooshed out of him when he hit the floor, and his grip on Jherek broke. The young sailor pushed himself up and drew back a fist. Raw emotion burned through him. He seized Aysel by the hair with his free hand, knotting his fingers securely.

"Poke your fun at me, Aysel, and talk of me without respect, but not the lady. A lady's honor is her own, and I won't stand by while you defile it with your words." He hammered the man in the face, putting all his strength into the blow.

Aysel's head snapped to the side and blood gushed from his split lip. He roared with inarticulate rage, shoving against the floor with his hands and feet in an effort to dislodge Jherek.

Drawing his arm back, Jherek set himself to strike again. Before he could, rough hands wrapped around his arms and face, pulling him off Aysel. Jherek struggled against the three men that held him, tearing free of their grip. He turned to face Aysel again.

Aysel recovered quickly, pushing himself to his feet and fisting the haft of the battle-axe. Blood dripped down his swelling lips, turning his smile crimson. He wiped them with the back of his free hand and looked at the bloody smear.

"By the gods, you little bastard," the big man declared, "now *that* you're going to die for!"

26

"Your song is beautiful."

Turning from the westering sea spreading out from Waterdeep, Pacys looked down at the speaker.

The priest Hroman looked up at him. A sling held his right arm, broken in the raid on the city. A healing potion would have quickly righted it, but even Waterdeep's vast stores had been hard pressed trying to save lives. Even Hroman's own abilities to heal himself through prayer had been given to the makeshift hospitals scattered throughout the city.

"Thank you for your kindness," the bard replied. His fingers caressed the yarting's strings, making bridges and notes soundlessly, though his ear could hear every one through the touch of his fingers. "It's only one of the many songs that will be sung about the battle for Waterdeep . . . nothing unique." He felt bad about sounding so bitter. "Forgive me, my friend. I must sound very selfish in light of all that these people have been through."

The streets around the Dock Ward teamed with a number of extra wagons pressed into service on behalf of the Dungsweepers' Guild. Debris filled several of the big carts, and their drivers headed them toward the Rat Hills while others came back for more. Their wheels clattered across the cobblestones, a constant undercurrent to all of the other activity filling the dock.

Out in the harbor, fishing vessels plied the waters with nets, sieving in the dead and the wreckage left from broken and burned ships. Not as many of the ships as had at first been feared had been lost during the attack. Even the damage to the waterfront along Dock Ward was reparable once new wood was brought in.

Most of the city's dead had been reclaimed, but a large knot of people still gathered at Arnagus the Shipwright's where the watch brought any corpses they recovered. So many were still missing, and many more than that were gone.

Hroman shook his head. "After something like this, it's only natural to start acting human again. It makes the world small again, and you only have to think about your own troubles—which don't seem too large for a time."

Pacys nodded. "You've grown wise, like your father. He'd be proud."

"I hope so."

The bard sat at the edge of a badly listing dock. Over half of it had broken off during the attack and rough splinters shoved out from the end. He noticed the dark circles under the priest's eyes. "Have you eaten?"

"Not yet. I've been working the night shift at the hospital, giving aid where I could, and last rites for those that needed them." Tears of frustration and near-exhaustion glittered in Hroman's haunted gaze. "We seem to lose so many more of the weak ones during the night."

"Yes," Pacys replied. "I think it's because the night is more tender, more accepting. A dying man doesn't seem to fight quite so hard when death is disguised as sleep."

"It's still death."

"Each man has his own race to run, Hroman. Even you can't stop that."

"No, but Oghma willing, I'll interfere with it whenever possible."

"Come," Pacys said gently, gesturing to the dock beside him. "Sit and share morningfeast with me. Several of the festhalls and taverns have remained opened night and day since they were able. Piergeiron, Khelben, Maskar, and several others of the city's officials and wealthy have opened their own larders to stock the kitchens of every establishment willing to serve a meal to those who are helping clear the city."

"I suspect a lot of graft is going on through the city while such generosity is being shown," Hroman said sourly. Still, he sat beside the old bard, stretching out awkwardly as he struggled to find comfort.

"The guard is policing the streets with a heavy hand, and even the most arrogant of nobles and merchants are rumored to be helping keep the distribution paths open and safe," Pacys said, removing the cloth that covered the basket he'd been given a few minutes ago. He'd played the yarting, trying to soften all the destruction and sadness that he'd toiled in for the last few days.

On the first day he'd helped remove most of the debris that clogged Ship Street and the nearby streets fronting the harbor. On the second day, since he was one of the eldest and suffered wounds of his own from the battle, he'd helped wash the corpses that had been recovered, getting them ready for burial. Most funerals were small things handled in the other wards. In the days since, the tasks had alternated between clearing away and recovering the dead.

"And how are you?" Hroman asked. "I'm forgetting my manners."

"Well."

"What about the wound in your side?"

Pacys stretched gingerly. A sahuagin trident had gouged his side, requiring a number of stitches, and there was the wound in his arm. Still, he appeared to be mending, though slowly.

"Troubling," the old bard admitted, "but not disabling."

Hroman glanced around at the battered and broken shops and taverns. "So many people lost everything they had."

"At least they live," Pacys pointed out, "that those material losses may be grieved over. They'll rebuild."

"In time," Hroman agreed. He scratched at a dried blood stain on his shirt. "So is this the song that you believed you were called for to sing?"

Pacys hesitated, searching his feelings again for the answer himself, finding mostly a brittle, hollow ache left over from the raid. He shook his head. "I don't know."

"I listened for a time just now," Hroman admitted, "before you knew I was there."

Pacys didn't refute the statement. He'd known the priest was there. A man living on the road, singing for his meals and lodging, such a man learned more than just pretty words and a lively tune.

"Your song truly is beautiful, old friend," Hroman said honestly. "I felt the pain of this city and the people who live here, and I felt the fear that still hangs about in the shadows."

"There are too many songs like it already, and more coming."

Pacys drew a knife from his boot and cut slices from the small half loaf of bread he'd been given in the food basket. He covered the slices with ham spread made fresh that morning, then passed a sandwich to the priest.

Hroman accepted it with thanks.

"On every street corner," Pacys said, "you'll find a bard. They're all composing songs about the raid, even those who weren't in Waterdeep that night. They've come from far and wide, trailing word of the story back."

"This is what you believed you were called for?"

"Yes," Pacys said, "and I still believe that, but there is something missing."

"What do you mean?"

"I've worked on the song about the raid for days," the old bard replied, "and have it shaped much as I want it, but there's more."

"More? You're sure of that?"

"Yes. Even as much work as I've done on it, the song yet remains unfinished."

"How do you know?"

Pacys smiled at the younger man. "How do you know a prayer is left unfinished?"

"Every priest is trained on the elements of a prayer," Hroman replied.

"There's the invitational, the declaration, the body of the message, and the closing."

"Sadly," Pacys said, "many bards believe it's the same with a song or a tale. Jokes, however, may be so mechanically inclined, but even within that art there are a number of allowances. In your vocation, my friend, the mind trains the ear, but in mine it's the ear that trains the mind."

"You remain hopeful, then."

Pacys smiled. "I yet live, and my song is undone. I've been following it for fourteen years. I can't allow myself to believe that I've been led this far and there will be no crescendo."

Quietly and efficiently, Hroman bowed his head and asked a blessing on the meal. Pacys joined him, finding his spirits even further lifted by the sincere belief in Hroman's words as he asked for peace and healing to descend on the city.

When the priest finished, the bard glanced up and out at the harbor. The morning sun was nearer to noon now, and the water glinted with diamond-bright highlights. He watched as a small group of mermen surfaced beside a large fishing boat with a boom arm hanging out over the water. Ropes led down into the harbor, letting the bard know they were going to attempt another underwater salvage.

"We're missing so many things," Pacys mused.

"They'll be replaced," Hroman stated. "Oghma willing, and if the need for whatever's been lost is strong enough."

"I'm not talking about city things." The old bard offered the small cup of cherry tomatoes that had been packed in the basket. They were exotic, grown in Maztica, and proof that the most exclusive of larders had opened to feed the people who worked in the city. Hroman took a couple with a nod of thanks. "I'm talking about the song. We don't know who arranged the attack on Waterdeep, or why."

"It was the sahuagin," Hroman pointed out. "We all saw them. As to why, the sahuagin have never gotten along with people living on the surface."

"The sahuagin don't use magic," Pacys pointed out. "They don't like it, and they don't trust it. That night, of all things that can be said about it, was filled with magic. It's more than the sahuagin. There's an enemy out there who has aligned himself against Waterdeep . . . maybe more than just Waterdeep."

"I can only pray that you're wrong," the priest said.

Pacys nodded. "I pray that as well, but in my heart I know I'm right. This song is far bigger than any I've ever done. When I finish, we'll have to know who has commanded this thing and why."

"Not all songs are as neatly sewn," Hroman objected. "In 'Pemdarc's Folly' the hero is kept constantly in the dark as to who's controlling the events in his life, as is the audience. Likewise with 'Lillinin' and 'The Calling of Three Shadows.' There are dozens of songs that don't fit the criteria you're saying exists."

"Not epic songs," Pacys objected in a soft voice. He popped one of the cherry tomatoes into his mouth and chewed. The fruit was pulpy and delicious. "Those all have the same ingredients."

Hroman was silent for a moment, as if hesitant. "Not all of those songs are finished, old friend. 'Cask of Torguein' remains incomplete to this day because the bard who wrote it—"

"Tweul Silverstrings," Pacys said automatically. A bard was trained to give every master his due. Otherwise, how would a true bard worthy of the mantle gain fame?

"—had his heart ripped out by a peryton up in the Cloud Peaks. 'Onyx Eyes' is unfinished because the bard—"

"Lohyis Tautsham," Pacys supplied.

"—was found drained of blood in a spider's web in Undermountain. 'Sandcastle Kings In Flight' is only a fragment left by the composer—"

"Harbier Funnelmouth."

"—who hasn't been seen in one hundred and twenty years." Hroman frowned. "I could go on."

"Because your father, Oghma rest his soul," Pacys said, "saw to it you had a good education without being cloistered away in priest's vestments."

Hroman took another bite of his sandwich. "All I'm saying is that we were fortunate to live through the bloodletting the other night, and there are enough people jumping at shadows in this city."

Pacys knew that was true. In response to the attack, all the land-based entrances into Waterdeep had been battened down with a siege mentality. The guard's rakers patrolled well past the harbor. There would be no more surprises.

Yet with all the might and ferocity that earmarked the attack, Pacys knew that whatever enemy the city faced didn't have to depend on surprise. The sahuagin could only come from the sea, but there were no guarantees that the sea devils hadn't aligned themselves with the orcs or goblin hordes that occupied the hill country and forests beyond Waterdeep.

Carefully, Pacys steered the conversation onto safer ground, discussing the events and people of the last few days that weighed heavily on Hroman. Several of the junior priests leaned on him for guidance. Few had experienced such a vicious attack before and it left many with their faith shaken.

During the talk, the bard sliced up the small loaf of sweetbread he'd been given in the basket and added grapes and chunks of apple to the repast. His wineskin, thankfully, was plentiful. When the meal and the conversation was completed, Hroman excused himself, nearly asleep as he sat there.

Pacys bade his friend good-bye and took up the yarting again. He decided to allow himself only the small luxury of a few more minutes of playing before he returned to the work he'd volunteered for.

As he walked out to the splintered end of the dock, he noticed a small skiff putting in at Arnagus's. The crowd awaiting news of their loved ones hurried down to meet the skiff's crew, and the wailing and weeping of the grief stricken ones who learned the final fate of family members and friends rolled over the bard. Their sadness and despondency struck a chord in him. Effortlessly, his fingers plucked the strings, finding the resonance in himself that matched their grief. He wasn't surprised when new notes and chords emerged, tying in with those that had already come to him.

He sat on the end of the dock and gave himself over to the music, building what he'd already figured out to the new sections. Words came to tongue quickly, and he sang of the trouble Waterdeep faced, of the fears and the uncertainties that lie ahead.

His mind searched ahead as his eyes roved over the harbor. He'd been speaking truly to Hroman: things were missing. The song was epic in scope, but it wouldn't be complete without all the ingredients. To be epic, the song had to have the touch of darkness, the schemer who'd designed the raid and marshaled the magic against Waterdeep had to be known. But where did this darkness lie?

There had to be a hero, someone who took the fight to that encroaching darkness. Waterdeep, he knew, was filled with heroes of every stripe; adventurers and warriors who dared and risked their lives countless times. It was those people who were even now rebuilding all that had been lost, promising that the city would flourish again. Still, as his fingers massaged the yarting's strings, none of their names rang true. He felt certain it would be someone no one had heard of, but where was this person?

His shook his head in an effort to clear it. His heart felt leaden. He'd spent fourteen years of his life chasing this song, yet it seemed destined to remain just out of his touch.

"Tale-spinner."

The voice was so soft that Pacys at first didn't realize it had been spoken. He quieted the yarting with a palm pressed against the strings, then approached the dock's edge.

A merman swam in the water in the shallows. His upper body was well developed, broad from swimming beneath the waters and from the hard life such a being lived, but his waist and below belonged to a fish. Faded pink scars striped his torso, cutting through the tan skin of his upper body and leading down to the silver scales that covered his lower half. He flicked his tail casually, keeping his head and shoulders above the waterline. Dark brown hair trailed wetly down his back, matched by a full beard. A necklace of coral and shells matched the ones wrapping his wrists, each piece carefully selected to match elegantly. He carried a trident in one hand.

"You know me," the merman said, sweeping his tail with just enough energy to remain atop the water, "from a night fourteen years gone."

"Yes," Pacys replied. It wasn't hard to remember the merman. Pacys had helped save his life when the mermen came into the harbor fleeing some great evil that had pursued them from the Sea of Swords. "I'd thought you were going to die back then."

The merman nodded, a grim smile on his face. "I almost did, and I had the chance again only a few nights ago."

"All of us did."

"I recognized you from your song," the merman said.

The old bard knew the mermen treasured songs as part of their culture. He'd borrowed some of their music and tales for his own over the years and was no stranger to their race.

"You played some of that song the night we arrived," the merman said.

Pacys was genuinely surprised the merman remembered. He'd sat quietly on the shore those many years ago, watching as the injured mermen were pulled from the water for treatment, asking for asylum from whatever had pursued them. He'd discovered the first of the song then.

"Yes," the old bard said. "You've a good ear for music."

"You are part of this," the merman said.

Pacys didn't deny the charge.

"I am shaman to my people," the merman said. "I'm called Narros."

Pacys gave his own name, then sat at the edge of the dock so they could be closer. None of the sailors around them paid any special attention to their conversation, but they remained wary. Over the last few days, the sailors in the harbor had accidentally attacked the mermen and other underwater denizens living in the shallows, fearing them to be returning sahuagin. So far there'd been no deaths on either side, but tensions and suspicions were running high.

"It won't end with the attack of a few days ago," Narros said.

"I know," the old bard replied. "Many of these people think it will. The rest all hope so."

The merman shook his head, flicking water from his hair. "It's already escalating. My people have been foraging along the Sea of Swords, seeking out information as Lord Piergeiron requested. More and more ships are being taken at sea."

"By the sahuagin?"

"And other things," Narros answered. He hesitated for a moment. "There are few survivors."

Pacys waited impatiently, wondering what had brought the merman to him. Usually they didn't have much to do with humans or other surface dwellers past whatever trade they needed to do.

"The evil reaching out now," Narros said, "was prophesied by my people. We knew when it rose against us fourteen years ago, despite the warding we created, that it had arrived. Now it has grown even stronger."

Intrigued, Pacys focused on the man. "Could I hear that prophecy?"

"Yes," Narros replied. "You have to. In my prayers of late I've discovered that you are part of it."

27

Jherek watched Aysel draw the double-bitted battle-axe back with both hands. Blood still poured down the sailor's chin from his split lips.

The floor around the fight cleared immediately. Even Aysel's cronies must not have trusted their companion's anger or aim. They released Jherek even as he worked one of his hands free.

He pushed himself back, narrowly avoiding the battle-axe slashing horizontally across his chest. The spiked tip of the axe head cut through his shirt and striped him with sudden, burning pain. Warm blood spilled down his chest. His anger melted somewhat then as he gave himself over to survival.

Still off-balance from his release from the men who'd been holding him, and from the effort at escaping the first axe blow, Jherek couldn't move quickly enough to attempt closing with Aysel. The big sailor moved at him immediately, drawing the axe back again.

Grasping a wooden chair, Jherek heaved it up in time to intercept the axe coming down at his head. The axe blow shattered the chair to splinters in the young sailor's hands, but it gave him time to spin away. The axe thudded home in the tavern's wooden floor, sending up a spray of sawdust.

"Get him!" Aysel bawled, yanking the axe from the floor. "Hold him and I'll have the head from his shoulders!"

A man leaped on Jherek from behind, forcing him forward over a nearby table. The side of the young sailor's head slammed against the tabletop and scattered tankards in all directions.

"Get him now!" the man shrilled in Jherek's ear.

By the time Jherek got his legs under him properly, the axe was already whistling toward his head. He pulled back with all his strength, slipping under the man's weight.

The axe thudded into the table only inches in front of Jherek's eyes. There was enough power in the blow to split the tabletop, and splinters dug into the young sailor's cheek.

Hooking a foot behind the leg of the man holding him, Jherek pulled and lunged back at the same time. He went down backward on top of the man in a tangle of arms and legs. Already in motion, he came to his feet in a smooth roll. One of Aysel's companions reached for him, whipping a dagger forward.

Jherek raised an arm and blocked the dagger thrust, catching the man's wrist on his forearm with enough force to crack the small wrist bones. Even as the man cried out in pain, the young sailor grabbed a metal serving pitcher from another table and slammed it against his attacker's head with a deep *bong*. The man's knees buckled and he went down screaming.

"Are you still willing to die for Sabyna's honor now, boy?" Aysel didn't waste any time stepping across the man's unconscious body and unloading with the axe again.

Jherek shifted, shuffling to the side, feeling the wall behind him come into contact with him unexpectedly. He dropped into a crouch with his back to the wall. The axe thudded into the hard wood, wedging in tight.

Aysel tugged on the haft, struggling to free his weapon. It came loose, ripping wood from the wall in long splinters.

"Not die," Jherek replied hotly, "but I'll stand for her."

"Because she's shared her body with you?" Aysel taunted. "Is that anything to die for?"

Jherek felt the anger in him turn to ice, and he knew that emotion peaked higher in him than he'd ever thought it could. Even with everything that had happened to him in his life, he'd never felt that way, not at his father, nor at fate, both of which had conspired against him since he'd been born. He ripped the cutlass free of his waist sash, pushing himself up and away from the bigger man.

With a final yank, Aysel pulled the axe from the wall. He saw the cutlass in Jherek's hand, then spread his own hands along the four foot haft of the battle-axe. He grinned wolfishly, full of confidence.

"I've chopped up bigger men than you, boy, and them better armed and armored."

A small movement at Jherek's side alerted him to the man slipping up on him. He whirled and kicked, blocking the man's sword swing with a booted foot and whipping the cutlass's pommel into the man's forehead, stunning him. Even as the man fell away from him, Jherek continued his spin, raising the cutlass blade to block Aysel's axe blow, sliding it over him, then past.

Sweat, blood, and sawdust covered him as he set himself more properly behind his sword. His lungs labored from his exertion and the emotion that filled him.

Aysel drew back, setting himself with his weapon as well. The axe danced in his hands. The fact that he was missing two fingers on his left hand didn't seem to bother him at all. The battle-axe twirled end over end, creating what seemed to be a constant barrier in front of the big sailor.

"I wasn't always a sailor, boy. I've been fighting men longer than I've been at sea."

"I'm not surprised," Jherek said. "Only two things draw a man to the sea and a sailor's life. The love for the sea itself, or crimes committed on dry land so bad that staying there is no longer an option."

Without warning, the battle-axe twisted in Aysel's hands, the blade licking out at Jherek's throat.

Jherek batted the axe head aside with the flat of his cutlass. Metal rang out in the tavern. Seeking to enlarge on the opening he thought he'd created, Jherek stepped forward. In the close confines, the four foot axe haft could be unwieldy in the hands of most.

Aysel was fully aware of his weapon's strengths and weaknesses, though, and the big sailor didn't try to strike with the axe head again. Instead, he hammered the haft into Jherek's face.

Jherek had only enough time to turn his head and pull his chin down. The heavy wooden haft, sheathed in steel, connected with his forehead and the ridge of bone over his right eye instead of his nose. Pain thundered into his head, and his vision went white for a moment. His jaw snapped shut.

"Foolish move, boy, trying to take a seasoned axe man like that," Aysel crowed with sadistic delight. The axe spun in his hands again as he readied himself to take advantage of his success.

Jherek stepped back, quickly and automatically raising the cutlass to cover his retreat, and stepping so that his good eye was turned more toward his opponent. However, the stance also left him with a shorter sword reach. He blinked hurriedly, guarding against the pain that assailed him and trying to clear his vision. Doubled images of Aysel drawing the axe back for another swing moved before him.

Jherek moved the way Malorrie had taught him, reading the big man's body movements rather than trying to keep track of the axe. He leaped up, pulling his legs high to avoid the sweeping axe blow aimed to cut his ankles from under him. When he landed on the floor again, he launched a back-handed slash with the cutlass, aiming it at Aysel's face, guessing the man would step backward to avoid it.

Instead, Aysel lifted the end of the axe haft and blocked the cutlass. Sparks flew from the steel sheath, and the hard wooden shaft held. The big man flicked the sword away, then stepped in and buried the axe haft in Jherek's stomach.

Bright comets of pain ignited in the young sailor's skull as his breath fled his lungs. He was certain the blow broke ribs, and he remained on his feet out of sheer defiance. Aysel closed again, stumbling, surprised maybe that Jherek hadn't fallen. His breath burned hotly on the young sailor's neck.

"Had enough, boy?" Aysel snarled.

Twisting, keeping his body contact against the bigger man to keep him off-balance so he couldn't bring either end of the battle-axe back into play, Jherek balled up his left fist and smashed it into Aysel's throat.

The big sailor stumbled backward, grabbing for his injured throat with one hand. His breath came in harsh gasps.

"No," Jherek grated out. "You're still standing."

He wiped at his injured eye with his free hand, finding some of the blurred vision was caused by blood. He wiped his eye clear on a shirt sleeve, aware that the swelling had already half closed it. Still, he could see better. He lifted the cutlass and slashed.

Aysel grabbed the axe with both hands again and blocked the blow.

Warming to the task, pushing the pain away, Jherek moved the cutlass confidently. He remained on the attack, deliberately aiming blows that he knew Aysel could block and had no choice but to do so, beating back any opportunity for offense. The big man held his ground for a moment, wavering, but in the end he was forced back.

Despite Aysel's claim to the tavern crowd at the beginning of the fight, Jherek's courage and skill in the face of greater numbers arrayed against him won over the watchers. They howled at him, supporting him, demanding Aysel's blood.

Jherek didn't intend to kill the man if he could help it. Aysel's lack of manners didn't mean he should be killed. Senses alert, and the combat skills Malorrie had drilled into him functioning at their peak with the adrenaline rushing through his body, Jherek swept the cutlass forward too fast for Aysel to dodge. At the last minute, he turned the sword so the flat of the blade thumped solidly into the big man's jawline.

Stunned, Aysel stumbled back, working hard to keep the battle-axe up.

Before Jherek could take advantage of his success, a chair crashed into him, breaking across his back and shoulders. The young sailor went down to his knees, doubling over on his fiery ribs. He tried to catch his breath and couldn't as he turned to face Aysel's cohort.

The sailor tossed the shattered remains of the chair away, then stepped in and kicked Jherek in the face.

The man's foot caught Jherek on the chin, snapping his head back. The young sailor didn't try to fight the force, working to roll with it as much as possible. He gripped the cutlass, stubbornly hanging onto it. The man came at Jherek again, stamping his feet down at him viciously, snarling curses.

Avoiding the kicks when he could, blocking them with his arms when he couldn't, Jherek rolled across the sawdust covered floor under a table. The man reached for the table and ripped it away, spilling tankards and platters over the side.

Jherek tasted blood in his mouth, realizing his lips had been split by the kick to his chin. He surged up with the overturned table, setting himself. His opponent hadn't expected him to attack and was caught unprepared. Jherek swung the cutlass, thudding the sword's heavy-cast knuckle bow into the man's forehead. The shock of the impact shuddered all along Jherek's arm.

The sailor's eyes glazed and his knees buckled. He let out a long breath and crumpled to the floor, unconscious.

Spotting the movement of the tavern crowd shifting around him, Jherek turned as Aysel came toward him. Growling in rage, the big sailor swept the battle-axe at Jherek.

The young sailor lifted the cutlass to his defense, managing to catch the broad axe on his blade for an instant before it slid off. The axe's keen edge razored across his left arm, slicing his bicep open and sending fresh blood cascading down his arm. It went partially numb at once, and a burning fear raced through him that the axe blow had permanently damaged his arm.

Aysel's power and weight knocked him from his feet. Unable to use his wounded arm well, Jherek fell awkwardly, slamming down on his back across the remnants of a chair. Aysel gave him no respite, closing his hands together at the end of the battle-axe and swinging hard.

Forcing his wounded arm to work, Jherek grabbed the cutlass's broad blade and blocked the descending axe. The impact felt like it tore his shoulders free, and he couldn't hold the axe back. Instead, he turned it aside. The move also cost him the cutlass, tearing it from his hands. Desperate, every move agony, Jherek kicked the big man in the crotch as he tried to pull the axe back. Aysel screamed in pain.

Pressing his slight advantage for all it was worth, Jherek slipped his fishing knife from his boot. He twisted, holding the knife tightly, then plunged it through Aysel's foot. Sharp and driven forcefully, the keen knife cut through the boot leather and slipped between the bones of the big man's foot. It thudded home solidly in the hardwood floor.

"Umberlee take you for your dark cowardice, you little bastard!" Aysel shouted. He pulled at his axe, bringing it up.

Ignoring the burning pain that filled his body and the salty taste of blood filling his mouth, Jherek forced himself to his feet. He stepped into Aysel, seizing the man's left arm in a hold Malorrie had taught him. Moving in close to the bigger man, holding the arm in a controlling position, Jherek pulled with his upper body and twisted at the same time.

Aysel left the floor, his foot tearing free of the floor with the knife still in it.

Jherek brought the big sailor down hard on the floor. Aysel reached for him, but Jherek slid away. As the big man hobbled to a standing position, grabbing dazedly at the knife impaling his foot, Jherek grabbed a broken chair leg from the floor and swung it from his shoulder.

The chair leg crashed into Aysel's temple with a dulled *smack*, turning his head.

Incredibly, the man remained standing for a moment.

Jherek watched uncertainly, fighting to sip his breath past the broken feeling in his ribs. If Aysel continued fighting, he wasn't sure he had anything left. Still, he kept his grip on the chair leg, then Aysel fell, pitching face forward onto the floor. Sawdust gusted up when he hit.

Kneeling with difficulty, Jherek felt the man's neck, relieved when he found a pulse. He'd never killed a man in anger before, and after the close call today, he knew he never would. Challenging Aysel's affront to Sabyna's honor had been a natural thing for him, something he knew he'd never be able to walk away from, but next time, he promised himself, he'd have a clearer head.

Hurting all over, his breath coming in short, painful gasps, Jherek stood. He surveyed the tavern, surprised at the destruction that had been wrought. Aysel's companions were unconscious as well, laying tumbled in the wreckage.

"Now, by Tyr," a grizzled old man at the front of the tavern crowd shouted, "that was a damn *fight!*"

Several of the other tavern goers loudly agreed. They came around Jherek and pounded him on the back.

Jherek's knees buckled from the impact and he almost went down. The man caught him, wrapping an arm around his shoulders and laughing at how expended the young sailor was.

"Gave 'em all you had, didn't you, boy?" the old man asked.

"Aye," Jherek croaked, "maybe more." His vision still swam and his injured eye had swollen totally closed. Despite the pain that filled him, he felt proud. His cause had been just, and he'd won. At the same time, he realized how prideful and arrogant that thought was. He didn't think Malorrie would have approved. Madame Iitaar would have given him one of those reproachful looks that Jherek had always felt could have peeled paint.

The old man took part of Jherek's weight and hauled him to the bar. "A man willing to fight like that against such odds, I'll stand him to a drink. Even if I have hold him up at the bar!" The rough men around them broke into laughter.

The bartender thumped a tankard of ale in front of Jherek, then pointed at the serving wenches. "Go through their pockets," he told them, "and take enough gold to pay for the damages." He looked at Jherek. "House rules: loser always pays the damages . . . one way or another."

Jherek struggled to cling to his senses, but he didn't reach for the ale. Still, it felt good to be standing among the rough crowd, momentarily accepted as one of their own. He felt guilty too. The fight wasn't something to be proud of.

"Drink up, boy," the old man said, slapping Jherek on the back. "It'll wash the blood out of your mouth and prevent infection. Hell, you drink enough, you won't even feel the pain."

The crowd laughed, yelling enthusiastically.

Jherek shook his head politely, then regretted it instantly when a new wave of pain fired through his skull. It felt like pieces of it were missing. "Don't drink," he said.

"What?" the old man asked.

"I said I don't drink," Jherek replied.

The old man passed the knowledge on to his comrades flocked together at the bar. "A fighting man always drinks," the man said, turning back to Jherek.

"Can't," Jherek said, thinking quickly, not wanting to offend his newfound friends. "It's my belief."

The old man drew back in wry surprise. "Now there's a piss-poor god for you—one that doesn't allow a man an honest drink now and again." He suddenly slammed his sword arm across his chest in benediction. "May Tyr protect a warrior who speaks his own mind so carelessly."

"No offense taken," Jherek said.

"What will you drink?" the man asked.

"Water, please."

Hrumphing in displeasure, the bartender said, "I've got some I keep around here for cutting drinks I sell to the young Amnian fops who come around wanting to talk it up later that they've been to this place." He rummaged under the counter and brought up a bottle. "Here it is." He poured a quick tankard and sat it before Jherek.

"Thank you." Jherek took up the tankard and drank, tasting the coppery salt of the blood in his mouth. His wounded arm throbbed dully. Glancing at it, he pulled the sliced cloth away.

"You're going to need a few gathers in that one, boy," the old man said. "I know a cleric who does such work out of his temple. He'll expect a few silver pieces to be donated to his god in return, and a couple gold if you want him to bless it."

Jherek nodded and sipped his water again. Nausea swamped his stomach and he fought to keep its contents in place. He'd never felt that way when he'd fought the sahuagin, nor when he'd fought pirates out on the open seas, but Aysel wasn't as bluntly evil in his ways as they'd been. The big sailor had only been a man with an undisciplined tongue and low manner.

Standing there, swaying slightly, Jherek knew the fight could have easily ended with any one of them dead, and it would have been his fault.

Malorrie had always taught him never to strike in anger, and to fight only when fighting would save a life.

Jherek knew he could have walked out of the tavern, but he'd chosen not to. At the same time, though, he knew he couldn't allow Sabyna's honor to be bandied about so lightly. It would have offended him to stand there and let the comments be aired.

"Get out of my way!"

Recognizing the voice at once, Jherek turned and watched as Captain Tynnel strode through the tavern's double doors. He watched Tynnel survey the makeshift battlefield and felt even more uncomfortable about what he'd done. The serving wenches ceased looting the pockets of the unconscious men and backed hurriedly away, hiding the coins they'd taken in the pockets of their skirts.

"Who did this?" the captain roared. His fist knotted around the sword he wore. His gaze challenged every man in the tavern. A dozen *Breezerunner* crewmen stood behind him. All of them looked ready to fight.

The tavern crowd separated, revealing Jherek. The young sailor stepped forward on trembling legs. "I did," he answered.

8 Tarsakh, the Year of the Gauntlet

28

"The story was given to my people generations ago," Narros said, "at the same time we were given custody of the headband that was to be kept under our protection."

"Headband? From whom?" Pacys asked. He sat on a pile of moss on the floor across from a low table made of gathered stones in the middle of the small underwater cave out in Waterdeep Harbor that the merman shaman made his home.

The cave was ten feet tall and only slightly wider than that. Mosaics of shells, stones, and bits of colored glass gleaned from trading with the merchants in Waterdeep and crafted into pictures of mermen fishing the depths occupied prominent places on the walls. Out of deference to the bard's weaker surface vision, a small glow lamp gleamed on the table.

Pacys was able to survive underwater due to the emerald bracelet he wore. The merman shaman had given it to him at the dock. The magical powers of the bracelet let him breathe the water as air, turned away most of the cold, and removed the pressure from the depths. If it hadn't been for the flotsam and jetsam that occasionally floated through his view and the inquisitive fish that came up to him, the bard would have noticed the difference between the submerged cave and the surface world even less.

"Our stories say that the first of our group was given the prophecy and the headband by Eadro the Deliverer, Lord of the Sunlit Shadows."

The bard easily recognized the name of the mermen god. Eadro was also worshiped by the locathah, though the means of worshiping the god differed wildly among the races as well as the regions.

"There was a time," Narros went on in his deep voice, "generations and generations ago, when a great evil was inadvertently loosed upon the world."

Unconsciously, Pacys's hands strayed to his yarting. The magic of the bracelet, he'd discovered, had extended to his clothing and his instrument. Delicately, his fingers plucked at the strings, sorting out the rhythm that came into his mind as the merman spoke. "What was the nature of this great evil?"

Narros shook his head and his beard and hair floated through the currents that swept around him. The motion was disconcerting to Pacys even though he'd experienced the deep before.

All of the adult merfolk were engaged in helping with the salvaging efforts going on in Waterdeep Harbor and beyond. On their way down from the docks Narros had encountered half a dozen or more of his kin and sent each one away in turn with different orders. Some were asked to help with salvage, others to patrol for the many stray sharks still trapped in the harbor and feasting on Waterdeep's dead. One, an impressive merman warrior named Thraxos, had come to Narros to tell the shaman he'd received his orders and was ready to go.

"Be off with you then, Thrax," Narros had said, respect evident in his tone and expression. "It's a long swim, my friend, and I fear we'll never see each other again."

Thraxos had only nodded and turned, swimming away. It seemed that the City of Splendors was still sacrificing her finest in the war that had come upon them so suddenly.

Quick movement darted at one of the doors carved into this part of Waterdeep Isle. Narros had two small children in the house with him that he'd chased to rooms in the back of the dwelling. One of them was a little girl, scarcely longer than three feet from the top of her head to the bottom of her fins. The other was a boy old enough to wear an adult's knife strapped to his upper arm.

"I'm sorry for the interruption," Narros said. "Alyyx has her mother's curiosity."

"It's quite all right," Pacys said and gave the merchild a smile. "I've always loved children. I don't mind them being here."

"Well enough." Narros spoke in his own tongue, then slapped his powerful tail fin gently on the floor.

The little merchild arced through the water, fast as a dolphin. In the blink of an eye she twisted and managed to come to a thumping rest tucked safely inside her father's arms. Contented, she thrust a thumb into her mouth and watched Pacys with wild-eyed innocence.

"I apologize," Narros said. "She's never seen a human this close before."

"Don't apologize," Pacys replied. "I've made most of my living by my own curiosity, or teasing it out of others."

The young merboy entered the room more cautiously, maintaining his distance from the bard.

Pacys continued plucking the yarting, listening to the refrain that had popped into his head. The melody fit so completely with the part of the song he'd figured out regarding Waterdeep he knew that he was on the right path. The confirmation excited him, making him forget some of the aches and pains he suffered from over his last few days of hard labor.

Narros picked up the thread of his tale effortlessly, a born storyteller himself. "The evil is a creature," he said, "the like of which has never been seen. Our legends have it that once he swam with gods in the world of the seas, though not a god himself. Once, he was a predator, with not much more in his life than his nature. At that time he swam with Sekolah."

"The sahuagin shark god?" Pacys asked.

"Yes. Our tales hold it that this creature was one of the first in the waters of this world. Mermen had not filled the seas, nor had Sekolah shaken the sahuagin from their shell as yet. This abomination curried the favor of the gods, lusting after more power for himself. It's said that Umberlee herself evidenced an interest in him for a time, then took him as a consort."

"Of all the tales I've learned in my life," Pacys said, "I've never heard any about this."

"Listen to the stories of the sea people again," Narros said. "Sometimes he's referred to as a being or force called the Taker. In others he's confused with the Trickster. I believe Umberlee removed herself from the tales, though a sorceress is sometimes referred to in her stead. He fell out of favor with her hundreds of generations ago, and she sentenced him to death. Her rage was so great that she moved oceans in her effort to kill him, only he didn't die. He's been lying dormant, like anemones that are caught in a tidal pool that evaporates, waiting to be revived. Now he lives again."

Pacys continued listening, his mind whirling with the possibilities. More than anything he remained cognizant of the music he strummed on the yarting. The tune was cold and distant, threatening, and when played properly he knew it would be commanding in the piece he was writing. The sheer force of the tune left goosebumps pebbling his flesh. It belonged to the evil that had attacked Waterdeep, stronger even than the notes he'd picked out for the sahuagin.

"As Umberlee's pet," Narros said, "he gained an image of himself as increasingly powerful, as he was. The Bitch Goddess saw to that. She gave him powers, trained him in sorcery, and gave him magical instruments that he used to build an empire in what your people call the Shining Sea. He's not yet what he was, but our prophecies say he will be again."

As Pacys continued playing involuntarily, an image of a vast labyrinth rising above the sea floor appeared in his mind's eye. It wasn't the first time that such a thing had happened. He'd experienced other clairvoyant times when the music surged strongly in him. He closed his eyes for a moment, trying to fix the structure more clearly.

"Alabaster walls, blued by depths and age,
Hugged to the sea floor with Umberlee's blessing,
Lighted only by darkest evil,
Fired by jealous rage."

The words resonated in his head, and he stopped himself short of giving voice to them. He opened his eyes again, focusing on the shaman. "Do you have a name for him?" he asked.

Narros shook his head. His little girl reached out unexpectedly, floating free of her father's arms. Her soft, webbed hand reached out and caught Pacys by the chin. Going with the child's gentle but insistent push, Pacys twisted his head and bared his neck.

"Alyyx has noticed you don't have gills," Narros said. Gently, he captured his daughter and pulled her back into his arms.

Reaching into his pocket, the bard took out the small leather bag that contained the colorful marbles he used to exercise his fingers and keep them limber for the musical instruments he played. The merchild took them with obvious delight and began inspecting them.

"We were given no name for him," Narros said, "and we were bade never to speak of him except as the Taker or the Trickster. He was to be given no real identity. We've always believed that once his name was known, his power would grow again and he would be called forth from his deep slumber."

"What about the circlet?" Pacys asked. "What did it do?"

"I don't know, but he came for it fourteen years ago and wiped out over half our village taking it." A somber look filled Narros's face. "Our dead were scattered around us, torn limb from limb as if in the jaws of some great sea creature."

"Did you see him?"

"Only as a shadow," the merman shaman answered, pain filling his gray eyes, "the greatest, largest shadow anyone had ever seen, and like nothing we'd ever seen before."

The hurt distraction in the merman's eyes testified vividly to how well he remembered the night.

"Were the sahuagin with him?" Pacys asked after a moment.

"No. The Taker came alone, in the dead of night when even the sea is dark. I lost two of my sons in that battle."

"I'm sorry," Pacys said.

Narros gave his daughter a brief hug.

"Eadro willing," the small merboy stated in a serious, quiet voice, "one day I'll be strong enough to avenge my brothers."

Pacys glanced at the boy, suddenly realizing he wasn't old enough to have known his deceased brothers. The family's loss and hurt had already spanned a generation in the merman's own family.

"The prophecy," Narros went on, "told us that we might fail in protecting the circlet from the Taker, but it never mentioned at what cost. After it was over, we cared for our dead, then we swam for Waterdeep."

"Why Waterdeep?" Pacys asked.

"Because the prophecy told us the Taker would arise again, soon after his first appearance, and the place he would first strike terror into the hearts of the surface dwellers would be in their greatest city."

"Waterdeep," Pacys breathed. He was aware of the tune changing on the yarting.

"There could be no other," the shaman agreed. "Great detail was given in the prophecy of the city that would be attacked. Its towers and great heights, the fact that it was wrapped in magic and was home to champions."

"So you came here," Pacys said, "seeking asylum from Lord Piergeiron and the others."

"Yes."

"You never mentioned that Waterdeep would be attacked."

Narros eyed the bard honestly. "Do you think any would have believed us? And that was fourteen years ago. There was no guarantee that it wouldn't have been a hundred and fourteen years after we lost the circlet. It could have been the next day." He paused. "We just wanted to be here, to give an accounting of ourselves and to get a chance to avenge our sunken. We'd hoped to make a difference during the battle."

"I'm sure you did." Pacys had already heard stories of the mermen's valor during the battle for Waterdeep, and of the extra effort even the wounded had gone to while trying to save the men in the harbor.

"Even if we'd told the lords of Waterdeep about the attack, they wouldn't have been prepared. They wouldn't have given much credence to our fears."

"No," Pacys agreed. "They might not have believed you, and even the ones who did wouldn't have been any more prepared than they were after fourteen years. But why did he want to attack Waterdeep?" Unconsciously, he drifted over into the piece he'd written for Waterdeep, the music gentle to his ear.

"The prophecy is vague about that," Narros admitted. "Part of it is a warning to the surface dwellers and to bind the sahuagin further to his cause. A few lines suggest that he went into the city itself to reclaim one of his lost weapons to use in his conquest of the surface world."

"Was there any hint about what this weapon was supposed to do?"

Narros patted his daughter on the head. "With it, he's going to sunder a land, fill an ocean with fire and fury, and free a trapped people who live for evil as he does. Waterdeep was only the first of the cities that are going to learn to live in fear of the ocean. He is going to come to power in the outer sea, then in the inner one, and when it is revealed, all are going to fear his name."

Pacys absorbed the story, amazed by the depth and complexity that it offered. Prophecies were powerful things; not just for the people who believed in them, but the world itself was forced to deal with them.

"How are we supposed to stop him?" the old bard asked.

"I don't know," the shaman answered. "Our own prophecy hints that the prophecies of other undersea races are linked to the reappearance of this creature, and each will have other pieces to the story. One man will weave all of those stories together, spin them into a tale that will live forever in the history of this world." He locked his gaze on Pacys. "That man is you."

Hope fired through Pacys's heart, but he reached for it and held it down. "You can't know that," he whispered hoarsely.

" 'A human tale spinner,' " Narros quoted, " 'old enough to be at the end of his life, yet still living on the edge, seeking to fill the emptiness that his own self-imposed quest has laid upon his soul, all his days given to the perfection of his craft. The music of his great song will replenish him till he is near bursting, like a deep water fish that streaks unwisely toward the shallows. Once he has gathered the song and given it to the worlds above and below, he'll be forever remembered as Taleweaver, he who sang of sand and sea and united the history of all peoples who have the sea in their blood.' " He pointed at the yarting, the strings still ringing in the old bard's hands. "I heard the song you played that night when my people arrived in this harbor. You couldn't know it, it is a sacred song, given only to my people at the time Eadro gave us the circlet. He told my ancestors then that the song would be given to the Taleweaver, and that was how we'd know him."

"If you knew then," Pacys protested, "why didn't you say something?"

Narros shook his head. "We were bound to silence. Remember? No one could speak of the Taker . . . not until after he reappeared."

"How can you be so sure I'm the one?"

"Since we've been here, your hands have ever been busy, made slave to the music that now holds you in thrall. Truly, you are the one. I was guided to you this morning because you still have your part to play."

"What part?" Pacys's heart hammered inside his chest. The song was one thing; he could commit to that, but what else remained before him?

"There is a man—hardly more than a boy by your counting of years, one who has always lived with the sea in his heart despite being abandoned to land—who will find a way to confront the Taker," Narros said. "He will find the weapon and he will find the way, but it will be only after he finds himself, discovers what he truly is. To do that, you'll have to seek him out and touch his heart. He's been shattered by his experiences, and others have worked to make him whole, given him much of what he needs, but he'll never be able to become what he needs to be without you. If you're not there for him, it could be that our very world will fall." The merman smiled comfortingly. "Take pride in the fact that he will be one of the very best of your kind."

"What do I need to do?" Pacys asked.

"Find him," Narros answered, "and help him find himself."

The sheer enormity of the situation put a righteous fear in Pacys.

How to find one man in all of Faerûn when not even a name existed was beyond him.

"But where do I start looking?"

Narros shook his head. "Our prophesy says it will be in a city on a great river that stands as a door to the above and below worlds."

Pacys's mind raced and only one city came to mind though he knew of dozens. "Baldur's Gate," he said.

"I have thought so too."

"I'll find him there?"

"You'll see him there," the merman answered. "As to what takes place, I can't say. You'll have to find a way and trust the bond that exists between you."

Suddenly, Pacys noticed his wandering hands had moved on to a new piece, one that he'd never played before, one that he'd never heard played before. It was uplifting, a light in the darkness, a fragile mixture of bravery and fear, and he recognized it at once.

Alyyx slapped her tail against her father's torso happily. The smacking sounds somehow intermingled with the piece Pacys played, bringing hope.

"That's the hero's song," she cried out enthusiastically, turning to her brother. "Don't you hear him coming, Shyl?"

The merboy nodded, a small grin turning his lips.

Despite his own doubts and fears about everything the merman shaman had told him, Pacys couldn't help smiling. It *was* a hero's song. His fingers moved across the strings with growing confidence, seeking out the melody.

Narros reached out and clapped him on the shoulder. "You'll find him, Taleweaver," he said. "Wherever he is, it's your destiny to find him. Go first to Baldur's Gate and seek him there."

29

Tynnel's eyes narrowed as he walked toward Jherek. He gestured at Aysel and his fallen comrades. "Get them on their feet."

Crewmen split up and helped the fallen men to stand. Aysel remained hard to rouse. One of the serving wenches approached and spilled a tankard of ale into his face. Aysel woke, spluttering and cursing, instantly flailing around for his weapon. Three crewmen restrained him. When Aysel realized Tynnel was there, he quieted immediately.

"Why did you fight them?" Tynnel asked.

Jherek had no ready answer.

"Because of that damned woman," one of Aysel's comrades called out. "Having women aboard a ship, Cap'n, that's always been—"

Tynnel quieted the man with a steely glance, then shifted his attention back to Jherek. "You fought them over Sabyna?"

"Aye," Jherek admitted, but he was reluctant to repeat the terrible things Aysel had said.

"Was she here?"

"No, sir. She's been looking for you."

"I know that," Tynnel said in a clipped voice. "I just came from her when I heard one of my crewmen had been involved in a brawl here. I don't allow fighting in the ports we ship in, not if you're a part of my crew. I could have lost three crewmen in this debacle that I can presently ill afford to lose."

"He started it, Cap'n," Aysel shouted. "Raised his hand against me, and I had every right to defend myself. My mates were there to make sure he didn't slit my gullet before I had a chance to defend myself."

Surprise lighted the captain's eyes. "Is that true?" Tynnel demanded of Jherek. "Did you strike the first blow?"

Before Jherek could answer, the old man spoke up. "It wasn't the boy, Cap'n," he said. "The big man there had a foul mouth on him, goaded the boy into the fight."

Tynnel's eyes never left Jherek's. "Thank you for your comments, sir, but I live in a world where fights are fought with words or with swords. If you find yourself outclassed in either, that's fine, but they are to remain separate on my ship, and swords are not allowed." His words carried an edge.

"It was the big man," the old warrior said, "who threw the first blow. I saw him, and so did most of those in the tavern."

Confirmation of the old man's statement echoed in the tavern as the others took up the young sailor's defense. Jherek looked around them, totally surprised.

"Don't you worry none, boy," the old man whispered. "A scrapper like you with his heart in the right place, even rogues such as these will come around and stand up for him. Your cap'n's a tough but fair man, but his rules are his own and he sticks by 'em."

"Is that what happened, Malorrie?" Tynnel demanded.

The captain's use of the alias Jherek had borrowed for the voyage underscored the liberties he'd taken with the truth already. He didn't hesitate about his answer. "No, sir. It was I who made the argument physical."

Tynnel's harsh gaze softened a bit then, and his voice as well. "That's too bad. When I hired Sabyna on as ship's mage, we were both aware of the complications a woman brought to a ship of men. There's a rule about—"

"I'm not a crewman," Jherek interrupted, "nor was this fight over her."

"If nothing had been said about Sabyna, would you have fought these men?"

Jherek took a deep breath in through his nose. Even with only one eye, he saw there was no arguing with Tynnel's position. The fear that rode him clawed its way through his stomach, tightening his muscles so his ribs pained him even more. "No, sir."

"I say that the argument was over her," Tynnel stated. He reached into his coin purse and took out coins. "I'm returning your ship's passage, and I'm adding what I think is a fair price for the work you did aboard."

Jherek listened to the captain's words, not believing he'd just been thrown off the ship. It wasn't right, but the sinking feeling in the pit of his stomach told him Tynnel wouldn't entertain any arguments about the matter. Despite everything, his ill luck held true, the most constant companion he'd ever had.

"Keep the coins," Jherek said in defeat. What silver he had wouldn't leave him much to buy another berth on a ship bound for Baldur's Gate, but it was only fair.

"I can't keep it," Tynnel said.

"You didn't have a hand in this fight," Jherek said. "You earned your pay."

"I won't keep the passage fare," Tynnel stated, "and you earned the extra."

Jherek saw the determination in the captain's eyes and respected it. "Then keep it for the boy we rescued from the shipwreck. Even the orphanage here in Athkatla can use a donation while they try to find his family." It was as close as he could figure to balancing the score between them.

Tynnel stared at him a moment longer, then put the coins away. "I'll do as you ask." Tynnel lowered his voice then, speaking so he could be heard only by Jherek. "I'm sorry this has to happen," he said, "but I have rules for a reason."

"I know," Jherek said. "I understand."

Rules were a big part of Jherek's life as well. They'd offered security for him that his upbringing and early years hadn't allowed. From time to time, they'd even held his bad luck away, and he knew no one rule could be broken without sacrificing all the others.

"I'll have your things sent here," Tynnel said, "you can't come back to the ship."

Jherek nodded, grimly accepting the judgment, and asked, "You know about the dangers along the Sword Coast? The sahuagin attack on Waterdeep?"

"And the other ships as well," Tynnel said. "We've sailed dangerous waters before."

An image from the dreams he'd had about the great shark surfaced in Jherek's mind, sending a cold shiver down his spine when he thought of Sabyna out on the Sea of Swords. "Perhaps not as dangerous as these," he said. "Sail safely."

"And you." Tilting his head, Tynnel nodded. "I'll tell her you're here, and I won't stop her from coming to see you if she wishes." He turned and walked away.

Aysel brushed free of the crewmen herding him out the door. "This ain't over, boy!" the big man roared, pointing at Jherek. "Me and you and her, this little jig ain't heard the final tunes yet."

Jherek almost said something, but he refrained. Tynnel wouldn't allow anything to happen to the ship's mage. Still, he could warn her if she came to see him before she set sail. The possibility that she wouldn't left him feeling empty. He also had no clue what he was supposed to do next.

Live, that you may serve.

The words haunted him, taunted him, and—by turn—tormented him. If some greater power had taken an interest in his life, why wasn't it making its desire more clear? Why make every step increasingly difficult? Had whatever destiny that had been laid before him somehow gotten tangled up with the bastardized birthright that was his? The gods weren't infallible. Perhaps he'd been chosen wrongly. Even a small mistake made by a god might stretch across mortal lifetimes before it was caught.

"C'mon, boy," the old warrior said, taking Jherek gently by the arm. "Best have that wound tended to. The longer it stays open, the greater chance for infection to settle in."

Reluctantly, Jherek went with the man. He had no answers to any of the questions or problems that plagued him. He drew the attention of the serving wench who'd taken part in Aysel's scheme.

"If a woman should come searching for me. . . ." he said.

The serving wench bobbed her head. "I'll tell her straight away where to find you." Moisture glinted in her eyes. "I'm sorry for the way things turned out. I thought it would only be a joke. You deserved to be treated better than this."

"It's not your fault, lady," Jherek said softly. "The ill luck was mine. It always has been." He touched her shoulder gently and managed a small smile, then he stepped out into the harsh Amnian sunlight, smelling the sea so near, yet so far away.

He considered the ships out in the harbor, his eyes drawn to one in particular.

30

Laaqueel surveyed her image in the mirror with growing distaste. Iakhovas's magic had woven an illusion over her that even she couldn't pierce. She held her hand up to her reflection. Looking at her hand, she saw the webbing between her fingers, but the mirror image didn't have it. Her fingers looked clean and smooth, grotesquely human, without any means of real defense. The hated tan color that marked her as different from the aquatic elves she was supposed to resemble most took on a hue that was more brown in the reflection. Cosmetics adorned the totally elven face she spied in the mirror, emphasizing her eyes and making them suddenly seem too large, her lips too full. Rose blush touched her pronounced cheekbones.

Thankfully, she wore the combat leathers Iakhovas had bade her wear while they were in the city. After they'd arrived, he'd ushered her into the suite, telling her there was not much time. The garments were of dark brown leather that was creased and worn, supple in its age. They covered her trunk and legs, leaving her breasts partially bared. Knee-high boots with flaring sides encased her feet too tightly. A long sword hung at her hip, almost touching the hardwood floor. A russet-colored cloak hung to her ankles, heavy with all the throwing knives, caltrops, and garrotes that she'd stored in the secret pockets she'd discovered.

"Despite what you yourself might think, little malenti, you look ravishing."

Keeping her expression neutral, not wanting to show the anger she felt or the unrest caused by the fact she hadn't heard him enter, Laaqueel turned to face her master and said, "I only hope to look satisfactory."

Iakhovas nearly filled the door opening into the large suite. He

225

looked like himself to her, and she wondered if he was covered by an illusion as well. He was taller than most men, taller even than the occasional Northman she'd encountered in her spying efforts along the Sword Coast.

"Wearing a true human's guise is hard," he said, "especially when you know you are so much more."

His garments were azure and black, the colors bold and striking. His two-toned cape held the color scheme, black on the outside and azure on the inside. For once, he looked as though he had two eyes, and she knew the intensity of his illusion was deeply layered but built on the way she was normally allowed to see him. It reminded her again that she might not have ever truly seen his real face.

"Trust me when I say you look more than satisfactory." Iakhovas walked to one of the room's many windows and pulled the curtain back. Beyond the glass a cityscape spread out, the streets and alleys seen below their position stringing out to reach the sea. Wagons and dray horses lined those streets as the dockhands and sailors went about their business.

"Where are we?" she asked.

He kept his back to her and lifted one of the windows. The salty ocean breeze wafted into the room, washing out the stench of incense that had made it hard for Laaqueel to breathe. She hadn't been able to lift the window herself and guessed that he'd used his magic to ward them closed. Wherever they were, the increased power of his illusion and the security he was maintaining told her he didn't entirely feel safe there.

Nearly a tenday had passed since the confrontation with Huaanton. Iakhovas had not spoken of the sahuagin king any more, but he'd been absent from her much, not telling her where he'd traveled, and acting even more driven than she'd ever seen him. Every day he'd been gone had been agony for Laaqueel, not knowing what he was doing but knowing how tightly her fate was woven with his. The time when he was supposed to deliver the "miracle" to the sahuagin king was only five days away.

Laaqueel had seen no miracles on the horizon.

Then, this morning, he'd stepped back through one of the dimensional doors he kept in his sahuagin palace and commanded her to come with him. He'd given no explanation of where he'd been or what he'd been doing. Having no choice, Laaqueel had stepped through the dimensional door and ended up in this city only an hour ago.

"We're in Skaug," he replied.

The malenti knew of the city from her travels above the sea, but she couldn't imagine what would bring them there. "The pirate capital of the Nelanther Isles?" she asked.

The mainlanders along the Sword Coast feared the place, and merchant ships lived in dread of the pirates who found a home port in Skaug. Only the most vicious and fearsome claimed the city as home, and the Skaug Corsairs protected the shores viciously from even those who pursued the pirates for crimes committed at sea and in their own countries. The Skaug Corsairs turned them all back, charging fees to those who stayed there.

"Yes," Iakhovas said, turned, and grinned. "Little malenti, you've never known a time when you kept pace with any and all of my plans and machinations, but you're going to learn more now. I'm feeling generous." He grinned again broadly, full of self-confidence and purpose. "You're not to know everything, but more than you have been allowed to know in the past."

She refused to react to his statement because it was true. Of late, she'd been constantly reminded of how true that was. A newborn hatchling still trapped in its nursery with its voracious siblings had more control over its future.

"What are we doing here?" she asked.

"*I*, little malenti," he rebuked her in a voice that sounded as gentle as steel encased in silk. "What am *I* doing here?"

She bowed her head, breaking eye contact in true sahuagin fashion. "Of course," she said. "Forgive me."

"Now you may ask me your question more properly."

Anger flooded through the malenti priestess, but it wasn't enough to quench her fear, or to make her forget that she'd have nothing without him. "What are *you* doing here, most honored one?"

"Marshaling the forces of yet another army I direct," he told her expansively. "The sahuagin aren't the only ones who follow me, nor only the creatures of the seas. There are dark cults spread around this world, among the surface dwellers, that know aspects of me. I've spoken with them of late, given notice to those as well to help me recover all that was taken from me. My war is escalating, my little malenti, and I shall break and shatter the surface dwellers."

Laaqueel recognized it as the truth even as he spoke the words. She knew he'd had dealings with the druids of the Vilhon Reach, gathering more information in his dark quest and striking bargains. He also had an agent of sorts in the Sea of Fallen Stars, a pirate called Vurgrom. She had seen Iakhovas talking to the blustering pirate a handful of times through a crystal ball kept at the sahuagin palace. Most of the conversations had revolved around another pirate captain, a half-elf woman called Azla, who seemed determined to work at cross purposes to Vurgrom. Laaqueel had never been part of those conversations, though. Vurgrom had also delivered some of the items Iakhovas searched for by way of dimensional doors.

Iakhovas had a number of maps of the Sea of Fallen Stars in his private quarters. The few times she'd been allowed to view them only briefly, she'd seen notations scattered across the charts.

"Time to go," the wizard announced. "They're waiting for us and these are not men to be kept waiting." He gestured to the door.

Laaqueel went, but she kept the gifts bestowed upon her by Sekolah close to hand, fearing she would have to use them. Iakhovas followed closely behind her.

A carriage awaited them at the front of the inn. The inlaid wood and the draped windows advertised the presence of wealth. The driver was clad in sky blue and crimson finery and wore a cap. His eyes never met Iakhovas's or Laaqueel's. Two crossbowmen stood at the back of the carriage, their weapons naked and ready.

Laaqueel hesitated when the driver opened the door. Riding in the carriage would mark them instantly as wealthy targets in the pirate city. She didn't like the idea of being trapped in Skaug's streets in terrain that she was so unused to.

"My lady," the driver said, offering his hand like a proper gentleman.

"Get into the carriage," Iakhovas commanded. "No one who lives on this island will dare attack it."

Reluctantly, Laaqueel allowed the driver to help her into the carriage. She sat back on one of the plush seats and gazed out the window. Taverns, festhalls and boarding houses lined the street, rubbing shoulder to shoulder with trade shops and mercantiles that offered services and goods. The promontory the inn was on provided a good view of the docks, showing the general portage offered to the pirate vessels as well as the private docks for the corsairs. Many of the sailors and passersby gave the carriage a lot of attention, but none seemed willing to draw attention themselves. The malenti closed her hand around the haft of her long sword.

Iakhovas sat across from her, arms spreading across the backrest of the bench. He appeared relaxed and totally content.

The carriage tilted slightly on its springs as the driver pulled himself up into the seat. A moment more and the carriage rocked forward. The horses' hooves rang against the rocky street.

"Who are we going to see?" Laaqueel asked.

"A man named Burlor Maliceprow," Iakhovas answered. "He's called the Portmaster of Skaug, and even though this island empire knows no official ruler, Maliceprow's word bonds everyone who lives here. He's assembled the men we're to meet."

"Who are these men?" Laaqueel asked.

"Pirates," he answered. "The fiercest bunch of men I've been able to rally to my standard. Maliceprow has relationships with all of them."

"When did you arrange this?"

"Years ago." Iakhovas smiled at her with that disconcerting, two-eyed gaze. "I've been known, little malenti, by a number of names throughout my life. Some of the undersea races know me as 'the Taker.' You know me as Iakhovas, or One Who Swims with Sekolah. The sahuagin know me as a prince. Here I have adopted the identity of Black Alaric."

Laaqueel shook her head, struggling to believe everything he told her, yet knowing it was true.

"I must tell you, Black Alaric has had almost as many lives as I." Iakhovas looked out through the window. "The first Black Alaric died in the Year of Giant's Rage, over fourteen hundred years ago. He was the pirate king and captain who brought the pirates to the Nelanther after they were turned away from the Velen Peninsula, then there was the Black Alaric that brought down House Ithal in the Year of Scarlet Scourges. Other Black Alarics followed, each purporting to be the original and the legend continued to grow until it was believed he's a man who cannot die. He has united the pirates in seven major wars along the Sword Coast in the last fourteen centuries."

"You propose to become this Black Alaric?" Laaqueel asked.

Iakhovas took a black crepe bandanna from his pocket and tied it over his lower face. He pulled his cowl over his hair and the top of his face, cinching it tight so that only his eyes were revealed. "Little malenti, I *am* Black Alaric."

Laaqueel remained silent, thinking, realizing that his masquerade had them both at risk here in the pirate stronghold.

"It had been nearly a hundred years since the last Black Alaric was heard from," Iakhovas said. "Five years ago, after I'd decided what I was going to do about the Sword Coast and knew that the item I got from Serpentil was somewhere in that area, I found the newest man who dared to wear this mask and killed him." He smiled, cold and evil. "Not only am I a sahuagin prince, little malenti, but I am a pirate king."

The carriage came to a stop. Hurrying, the driver climbed down and opened Iakhovas's door.

The wizard stepped out in the mask, and the driver moved back in fear. "Black Alaric," he whispered before he caught himself.

Laaqueel climbed out of the carriage behind him, her hand never far from her long sword. She gazed in wide-eyed wonder at the great house before her.

It was set on a slope on the east side of the port. High walls surrounded the estate, enclosing grounds that had been well tended. Flowering shrubs and trees of every color covered the landscape, leaving room for inlaid brick walks that effectively divided the estate into various areas. From where she stood, Laaqueel saw one such meeting place that contained stone benches and a large stone table.

Standing four stories tall, the house loomed over the estate, carefully crafted so that many of the rooms had views out over the sea. Where most of the houses in Skaug had been built of wood, Maliceprow Manor and its stables and outbuildings had been constructed of cut stone elegantly laid. Guards stood at their posts.

Iakhovas led the way up the stairs to the main house, showing an easy familiarity with the place. Having no choice, Laaqueel followed, feeling out of her depth. She had no business there and felt the wizard should have left her at the palace where she could have gone about the preparations she needed to make for the upcoming battle.

"Alaric, join us over here, if you please."

Turning on the verandah, Laaqueel spotted the speaker. He was a wide man with hard lines and a life of luxury that had let him go to fat, but the way he moved to stand from the small table where he'd been sitting let Laaqueel know he was still quick on his feet. His hair had been soft brown but was now going to gray in streaks, cut squared off at his jawline. Hazel eyes swept over the malenti daring enough to almost make her blush, something she hadn't experienced in decades.

She thought perhaps it might be because she was aware of the illusion Iakhovas had wrapped around her with his glamour, knowing how her clothes revealed her upper body.

"Laaqueel," Iakhovas said in the politest tone the malenti had ever heard him use, "may I introduce you to Portmaster Burlor Maliceprow, our host and the controlling power behind Skaug."

Maliceprow smiled at the introduction and took Laaqueel's hands in one of his. The other hand, the malenti noted, had been replaced by a mithral hook that gleamed with a razor's edge.

"Such a charming lady you have with you, Alaric." Maliceprow kissed the back of Laaqueel's hand then released it.

"Thank you," Laaqueel said, but she'd not prompted her voice. Such courtly manners didn't come naturally to her. She realized her behavior had to have been caused by Iakhovas's glamour.

"I have someone for you to meet as well," Maliceprow announced. "Please sit and I'll be back with him, then we can get to our meeting."

Iakhovas sat at the table all laid out with meats and cheese and wines. Laaqueel followed his lead, sitting next to the verandah railing so she couldn't be trapped against the house. She looked at the sea, judging it to be close enough to run to.

"Relax, little malenti," Iakhovas said quietly. "You'll come to no harm here."

"What are we doing with these people?" she asked. "I didn't know you were going to be affiliating with surface dwellers."

He gazed at her with both his eyes, but she could occasionally see behind the missing one into the hollow where it had been. "Little malenti, I'll deal with anyone who can help me reach my goals. For now, that happens to be, in part, these pirates." He picked up a bit of meat and ate it. "In four tendays, I'm going to take Baldur's Gate, and these men are going to help me. When we leave that city, it will not be as Waterdeep. I will destroy everything in that city that touches the river, and a message will be sent that no one is safe. At no time, at no place."

Laaqueel heard the chill of menace in his words but she was still concerned. She didn't see how he planned on mixing the sahuagin and the pirates. Before she could ask any of the questions that were on her mind, Maliceprow returned with another man in tow.

The newcomer was a tall man dressed in a scarlet blouse tucked into charcoal gray breeches. A long sword hung at his hip, counterbalanced with three throwing knives on the opposite hip. His black hair was carefully combed, pulled back and held in place by garnet and ivory combs. Silver hoop earrings hung from each ear. His brown eyes returned her gaze with fire. The cruel turn of his features were partially disguised by the short goatee and mustache that were fastidiously trimmed, but left in plain view the tattoo on his left cheek. It depicted a sharklike creature with a black haired mane twisted in mid-strike.

"I've added another ship's captain to our roster and increased our strength," Maliceprow said with pride. "I'd like to introduce Captain Falkane, also called the Salt Wolf. His ship is *Bunyip*. I'm sure you've heard of it."

"Bloody Falkane," Laaqueel said, knowing the pirate for who he was.

Falkane took no offense at the use of his sobriquet. He smiled at her. "A name I've fairly won and proudly carry, wench. Make no mistake."

"Falkane," Maliceprow said, "will be joining us on the raid on Baldur's Gate, Alaric."

"Fine," Iakhovas said, "then join me in a toast." He picked up one of the wine bottles from the table and poured drinks all around. He raised his glass and waited until the others followed suit. "To the death of Baldur's Gate, by sword and by fire!"

31

Jherek sat in the morning sun in the small court off the temple of Lathander that overlooked the Athkatlan docks. He felt empty, totally dispirited. The low stone wall he sat on, already soaking up the sun, felt warm. His body was still filled with aches and pains from the fight in the tavern half a tenday ago, but he didn't give much thought to them. Only some of the swelling and little of the bruising had gone away.

Sabyna, despite Captain Tynnel's words, never came to see him. *Breezerunner* sailed that same afternoon. The ship's mage hadn't even left a note. That dealt Jherek a harsher blow than he had expected. Her absence, and the lack of a response about his lost passage, struck a hollow resonance inside him that he'd never before experienced, but there was nothing he could do about it.

Even when he knew *Breezerunner* had been about to leave, he hadn't been able to try to contact Sabyna. He'd hobbled down to the dock and watched in silence as the ship had sailed away, his new stitches tight in his flesh.

Now he watched the activity at the docks with a mixture of emotions, working hard to keep them all in check. If he failed to control any one of them: pain, rage, or confusion, he was certain he'd be lost. He felt homesick and thought often of returning to Velen and facing whatever awaited him there.

Live, that you may serve.

Those words, that command, belonged to someone else. He'd convinced himself of that. Perhaps a someone he might have been had the fates not conspired against him. His birthright was the tattoo on his arm, not some ghostly voice that echoed in his head.

The dockhands labored night and day, but they weren't just loading ships, they were packing goods onto barges and wagons that would be part of the numerous caravans traveling along the Alandor River or the River Road trade way to Crimmor. From there, the barges would off-load onto more wagons for the trip up the Bitten Road between the Fangs, into the Cloud Peaks, and on to Nashkel. Then began the increasingly dangerous trip north along the Coast Way, an overland trade route that had been only seldom used since the sea trade had opened. During his days of convalescence, Jherek had learned a lot about the overland trade routes that had become so heavily trafficked of late.

News continued drifting into Athkatla about the vessels and cargoes that were lost at sea, going down to sahuagin attacks and to leviathan creatures that erupted from the ocean bottom. Few ships reportedly reached Waterdeep or came from there. The other points north along the Sword Coast were just as dangerous. Paperwork, which had been only given lip service at many of the smaller ports, had become more sternly enforced.

More and more investors were starting to put their cargo on caravans. The losses at sea were too much. The overland trips took longer and grew increasingly dangerous as well. Orcs and goblins, and all too human bandits, passed information along about the caravans. Few, if any, reached their destinations unscathed.

A few cargo ships still attempted the sea trade north. Primarily ones that couldn't take the loss on the goods they'd agreed to deliver, and weren't able to find someone else to deliver it for them.

Jherek didn't like thinking about Sabyna traveling into those hostile waters, but he couldn't help himself. He'd failed her. If he hadn't gotten into the fight with Aysel, he'd have made the journey with her, could have been there to protect her.

He got frustrated with himself for thinking that one man could make such a difference. That only happened in the romances Malorrie started him reading. He heard footsteps glide softly along the stone courtyard.

"How are you feeling this morning?"

Jherek turned, finding Fostyr approaching. The priest wore the robes and vestments of Lathander, the Morninglord. Colored in bright yellow taken from a dawn morning, the robes had seen better days, and so had the temple. Lathander's beliefs weren't a prime pursuit in Amn.

"Better," Jherek answered. "Thank you for asking."

The courtyard held a small wicker table and three mismatched chairs. Berries grew along the south wall, against the small rooms where the four priests slept. Although he'd been invited in, Jherek had slept outside all five nights, wanting to be in the open and in the salt air.

The bedroll and pack that contained all of Jherek's possession was neatly packed and sitting in the corner of the courtyard. The priest's eyes flickered over them, and he sat in one of the chairs. He was a small man with skin the color of buttered rum. Only in his thirties, he kept his head shaved. His quick, dark hazel eyes surveyed Jherek.

"You've had morningfeast?" the priest asked.

"Aye."

"And your appetite, how was it?"

"Good," Jherek answered.

"You have to eat to keep your strength up."

"I know, Fostyr, and thank you for being so attentive."

"I worry about you, my friend. Kythel told me you were working in the gardens yesterday, and you washed your own clothes when we could have seen to it."

"I feel I have to earn my keep," Jherek said. "I'm not a man to sit idly by."

"Still, you have been wounded and should rest. You're here at the temple as our guest."

Jherek curbed his impatience. It wasn't the priest's fault that he hated lying fallow. Ilmater forbid that he should ever become a burden on anyone.

"Aye, I know that, and I thank you for your hospitality."

"But you will not simply accept that hospitality?"

Jherek shook his head. "I can't."

Surprisingly, Fostyr only smiled and said, "Such responsibility in one so young."

"Not so responsible," Jherek disagreed. "Otherwise I'd have never gotten into that fight in the tavern. That wasn't the course of a responsible man."

"According to my friend who brought you here you fought for a lady's honor."

"Aye, I suppose I did."

"Another responsible act."

"I'm not so sure," Jherek said. "What Aysel said were only words. I could have walked away."

"But where do I draw the line?" Fostyr mused. "That is your question isn't it?"

"Not mine," Jherek replied.

Fostyr nodded, then took another tack. "I saw you at the service this morning," the priest said.

"Aye."

"What drew you there?"

Jherek shifted positions gingerly, mindful of the aches and bruises he'd received. "I wanted to pay my respects to Lathander. You could have turned me away when I was brought here bleeding, covered in ale-reeking sawdust."

"Do you know of our religion?" the priest asked.

"Some," Jherek admitted. "I'm a follower of Ilmater."

"He is a good god to study, but Lathander might have something to offer as well. Lathander is the god of spring and the dawn, of birth and renewal, of beginnings. I've heard the nightmares that plague you, my friend, when you were in the grip of the fever that took you the first two nights you were here."

The priest hadn't mentioned that to Jherek before, and his face burned hotly. "What did I say?" he asked.

"You mean did you mention that you're the son of Falkane, one of the most feared pirates along this coast? Yes, you did."

Jherek shook his head in wonderment. "There's a price on the head of any man who sailed with Falkane," he told the priest. "You could have turned me in."

"No, I couldn't have," Fostyr said. "I prayed for you, that you might find peace and happiness, and that the fear in your life will depart."

Jherek didn't mean to sound harsh, but his voice was tight. "You've seen the tattoo on my arm?"

"Yes."

"It's a brand, Fostyr, and there's no getting rid of it. As long as it's with me, I'll be forever marked and my life won't be my own."

Fostyr was silent for a time, letting Jherek have time to regain his composure. "I just wanted to point out the possibilities," he said.

"At the temple?"

"Yes."

Jherek almost wanted to laugh in spite of the heartache that filled him. He shook his head and asked, "A pirate for a priest?"

"Stranger things have happened."

"No, Fostyr. What I need is a ship bound for Baldur's Gate."

"Why?"

Jherek thought about his answer, considered telling the priest about the voice that had plagued him, about the vision Madame Iitaar had had concerning that city, but he didn't. "Because I have to," he said. "I've been told that whatever calling I have in this life will be found there. At least some part of it."

"You seek the truth of that?"

"Aye."

"And if you find that it's not true?"

Jherek looked out at the rolling blue sea and said simply, "I don't know."

"The north is dangerous country now, along the trade routes."

"I know. Have you found a ship I can travel on?"

"No." Fostyr sighed. "Even with all the contacts I know, no one is willing to take a man on without papers. There's talk that some of the pirates are getting conspirators on board some vessels to sabotage them. If you're not known, they won't take you on."

The only people who'd know him, Jherek realized, would be sailors from Velen. They would have heard all about his heritage by now. That was no answer, either. He turned to the priest and said, "I've got to go."

"Now?"

"Aye. I feel as though I'm getting behind now." That feeling had been nagging at Jherek since the fever had broke.

"You're in no shape to travel," the priest protested.

"I suppose there's only one way to find out." Jherek stood and took up his pack and bedroll. The cutlass hung on his hip.

Fostyr watched him silently for a moment. "You're very driven, aren't you?" he asked finally as he too rose to his feet.

"Aye," Jherek answered, "only it's more like . . . haunted." He was relieved the priest wasn't going to try to argue with him further.

"Then I'll wish you godspeed," Fostyr said, offering his hand, "and provisions."

"No," Jherek replied. "I'll not take any more charity."

"You can't eat pride."

Jherek gave him a crooked grin, but didn't feel as brave as he tried to sound. "Pride's all I've got left, Fostyr, and not much of that. I'll have to work with what I've got." He took his coin pouch out and dumped all the coins inside onto the table, knowing the priest would never accept them.

"What are you doing?" Fostyr asked.

"I'm making it harder on whatever's driving me," Jherek answered, knowing the truth of his words. "All my life my ill luck has kept me from having things no matter how hard I worked. Well, now I have nothing but the clothes on my back. I've been told that if a thing is supposed to happen, a way will be made." He folded the empty coin pouch up and put it away. "I'm going to test that."

The priest nodded. "You may be surprised, my friend," he said. "Know that the door will always be open here should you need us." He offered his hand.

Jherek shook the priest's hand. "There's one other thing," he said, reaching into his pack and pulling out a folded sheet of paper. "I've written a letter. I'd appreciate it if you could have someone send it to Velen."

"Of course."

"Thank you for your hospitality. Tell the others good-bye for me." Jherek didn't think he had the courage to go through any more good-byes. They were getting to be a habit.

He walked out of the temple courtyard and turned his steps toward the docks.

Less than an hour later, Jherek stood in a ragged line with two dozen other men down by the docks, waiting as the caravan master walked toward them from the wagon he'd just drove up in. He stood as straight as he could, knowing that his face was still marked and his eye nearly swollen shut. At least his vision didn't appear to be harmed.

The caravan master was a big man, beefy and broad, burned by years of travel in the hot tropical sun. His clothing was sweat-stained and covered in grime. He wore a two-handed broadsword over his back. His leather armor showed signs of repair and of battle. Scars covered his body and marked his face.

"Listen up," he barked. "My name's Frauk. I got a caravan going out by evening so we can avoid most of the heat of the day. We're going to be traveling all night, so any man that don't think he can make that, step out now."

Three of the men swapped looks, then stepped out of the line, drifting back toward the taverns where most of them had come from.

"I just got back from a caravan coming out of Waterdeep," Frauk said, "and I want you to know what you're facing. Since the shipping's gotten so dangerous along the Sword Coast and the overland trade routes have opened up again, you might think you'll be traveling well-traveled roads. Well, I'm here to tell you that the orcs and goblins are traveling those roads too. You might be able to figure out which end of a horse is which, but if you don't know how to fight, if you're not *willing* to fight, you might as well cut your throat here before we leave and save the orcs and goblins the trouble."

Five other men left, grumbling to themselves, trying to act like the caravan master's words hadn't frightened them.

"Those of you still interested," Frauk said, "I can promise you long hours, short pay, and little patience. We're making a profit by getting shipments up and down the coast on time. I'll be dogging every step you make if you lag." He paused. "Now before I get a good look at you, are there any questions?"

Jherek looked at the man and asked, "How far north is this caravan going?"

"As far north as Baldur's Gate, boy," Frauk replied. "If things look prosperous enough, maybe on into Waterdeep. That suit you?"

"Aye, sir."

Frauk narrowed his gaze. " 'Aye, sir?' Are you a damned sailor, boy?"

Jherek hesitated, knowing that his bad luck was already showing again. Anger stole over him, giving his tongue a sharper edge than he'd have liked. "Aye, sir, and a good one."

"What the hell are you doing trying to sign up on a caravan?"

"I need the work, sir," Jherek replied.

Frauk came closer, taking long strides. "Can you sit a horse, boy?"

"Aye, sir."

Frauk stopped less than a foot from him, glaring at him with cold blue eyes. "Have you been in a fight, boy? It looks like you've been in a fight lately."

"Aye, sir."

Frauk glared at him and put his hands on his hips. "Do you know how to fight, boy?"

"Aye, sir."

Frauk spat on the ground and shook his head in derision. "From the looks of you it don't look like it. Bruised up, beat up . . . I need men who know how to handle themselves. Grab your gear and get the hell out of my line." He turned smartly on his heel and walked down the line to a big man. "Now you, you'll do just fine. Go put your gear on that wagon."

Embarrassment and anger flooded through Jherek. He shouldn't have been surprised. His luck had doomed him from the start. There'd never been a chance. He'd only made a fool of himself. He reached down for his packs and took them up, turned, and walked away.

Two other caravans had offered to hire him, but they'd both been bound for the south. None of the ones he'd found going north so far had needed men.

He trudged away from the line, listening to the caravan master hire another man. He tried to think of what else he could do, but he was out of options. The anger inside him grew until he couldn't stand it any more. He hadn't been fairly judged and he knew it. He rated more than an offhand dismissal from the caravan master, and he meant to have it. He wasn't just going to quietly go away this time. If that voice wanted to push him, then he was going to push back.

"You'll do too," Frauk told another man. "Go put your gear on the wagon."

Shouldering his pack, Jherek turned and walked back to the caravan master. The man stopped, watching as Jherek came closer.

"I've shipped with a captain who knew manners and who knew men, and had no dealings at all with someone like you, so maybe I'm out of place here," the young sailor said in a hard voice that could be clearly heard, "but I want you to know something. I've fought sharks and I've fought pirates. I've even fought sahuagin. I've fought in the day and in the night, on a ship's deck, on land, and in the sea. My face is marked up right now because I've been in a fight, but that was a fight I *won*. If you speak to me with such disrespect like that again, you're going to find out firsthand how well I fight."

Without another word, Jherek turned and walked away. His pulse was pounding in his head and he knew he should have been feeling guilty about his behavior, but he didn't. He'd stood up for himself and it felt good. He even thought Malorrie would have understood.

"Hey, boy."

Slowly, Jherek turned back to face the caravan master, thinking maybe the man intended to fight him after all.

The caravan master stood looking back at him.

"Aye, sir," Jherek answered.

"You still want that job?"

"Aye, sir."

"Then go put your gear up on that wagon. I'm hiring fighters today."

For a moment, Jherek stood frozen, not realizing for sure what the man had said. Then he nodded and said, "Aye, sir." He crossed to the wagon and tossed his bedroll and pack into the back.

Baldur's Gate was a long way off overland, but at least he was headed in the right direction. He tried not to think of what may lie ahead of him, taking comfort in this small victory.

UNDER FALLEN STARS

PROLOGUE

Flyys raked his webbed hands through the water and kicked out with his finned feet. The young triton knifed through the shallows of the ocean but knew it wasn't enough to escape his pursuers. Even though he tried not to, he glanced over his shoulder.

The morkoth swam after him. There were six of them now; too many for him to try to fight in the ocean. All of them were vaguely humanoid in shape, with bulbous heads that reminded Flyys of locathah, except for the squidlike beaks that filled their faces. The huge eyes on either side of their heads focused on him, moving independently. The dorsal fins on their backs looked like knife blades on edge.

They each had four arms, two of those arms equipped with thick pincers that identified them as the morkoth warrior class. Six tentacles flared out from their lower bodies, then pushed against the water. They looked deep purple in the light of the shallows, and iridescence flowed over them where the light struck, turning them almost pearl pale. Every now and again, the morkoth pulled the ocean brine through their gills and used it to propel themselves in the same manner as squid.

Flyys knew they could have easily overtaken him but had chosen to wear him down. His only solace was that they were evidently loathe to die capturing him. He knew he couldn't get away unless Persana chose to favor him. The Guardian of the Deep, creator of the triton people, couldn't ride with every tide, though. Sometimes those tangled nets Persana cast upon the water required sacrifices be made by his people so that greater works might be wrought. Persana was a master architect, not only of structures, but of fates as well. The young triton's belief told him this was so.

Glancing desperately at the ocean floor less than twenty feet below, Flyys searched for inspiration. Here in the shallows the morning sunlight gleamed down to the brackish silt below. Colorful fish, their hues given more life by the sun, darted in all directions as he neared them, but all of them avoided the greenish-gray claw coral mounds sprouting from the ocean bed.

The surface dwellers called the claw coral "hydra's stone" because of the seven collective offshoots that grew from its center. Sharply edged facets covered every inch of those coral fingers and even the slightest touch could open flesh to the bone. A number of the undersea races in Serôs used claw coral to make weapons.

Spotting a thick copse of the claw coral ahead, Flyys turned and swam for it. Ahead lay only open water and certain capture before he could ever get out of the shallows and into deeper Serôs.

Little more than five feet long, the young triton knew he wouldn't be a match for the morkoth warriors. One on one he felt confident he could have held his own, but the morkoth didn't fight that way. Flyys had heard stories that the morkoth in the outer seas lived solitary lives, much different than the morkoth who dwelled in Serôs. In the Sea of Fallen Stars, they lived in the Arcanum of Olleth, on the lowest reaches of the Hmur Plateau along western Serôs, a community that fought and conquered together.

He grabbed fistfuls of water again, altering his swimming stroke into a finfirst descent in the middle of the claw coral he'd chosen as his impromptu fortress. He drifted down to the soft silt below, carefully avoiding the sides of the claw coral. He nestled quietly into the coral like a hermit crab taking on a new shell, then he waited.

He gazed up, wishing he wasn't so frightened. A warrior wasn't supposed to be frightened, but he'd barely made it through his training before he'd been sent on his first mission.

His shoulder-length dark blue hair was tied back in a ponytail to keep it from his brilliant blue eyes. His skin was only a few shades of blue lighter. He was broad across the shoulders from living in the sea, and wore a shell-covered cloth girdle fitted with a belt because he'd been in the shallows, where surface dwellers, uncomfortable with nakedness, might see him. Still, he had appreciated the pockets in the girdle for carrying some small shells he'd found along the way.

Flyys drew the tapal from his belt as the morkoth gathered overhead. The weapon was uniquely triton. Formed of crystal, it was shaped into a curve like a surface dweller's fishhook. Two handles, set in the middle of the tapal and inside the curved end, allowed usage of either end of the weapon. A trained triton warrior could use the tapal as a long sword, dagger, or spear by spinning it around in his hands.

"Give up, longmane," one of the morkoth advised, "and your death will be mercifully swift."

Wishing he had a gallant reply readily on his lips, Flyys lifted the tapal in defiance. Sunlight caught the wide, curved end. "I know not to trust the word of kraknyth." Kraken were mortal enemies of the triton, and the triton considered morkoth to be kraken-kin.

The morkoth undulated in the water, their tentacles splaying out and curling reflexively in the currents. They carried spears, but Flyys knew it was the savage beaks and pincers he most had to fear. Sunlight gleamed over their bodies, creating hypnotic patterns on their purple skin.

"We'll have more time with you than we did with your fellow spies, longmane," the morkoth warned.

The death screams of the three tritons who had taken him with them echoed in the young triton's ears. They'd been discovered aboard a pirate ship near Dragonisle in the early hours of that morning. Junnas had immediately thrown Flyys overboard, instructing him to swim to Pumanath as quickly as possible and tell the nobles what they'd learned. Junnas and the others had stayed behind to die.

Flyys stared into the creature's eyes, having to switch focus often as it turned its head from side to side to view him. The morkoth drifted down closer. The claw coral extended beyond the young triton's reach even with the tapal.

"We can take time with your death," the morkoth promised, its gaze drawing him in.

The promise sent a chill down the young triton's back. Flyys remembered the stories he'd been told even as a child about the morkoth, about the ways they'd learned to rip flesh from their prisoners with their beaks and pincers, bringing death while extending the agony. They knew how an enemy's body was put together, and how best to take it apart.

"You've allied yourselves with the Taker," Flyys accused, glaring up at the morkoth. "According to the legends of Serôs, there won't be much time for anyone if he makes his way here."

"He's coming," the morkoth said, shifting in the current again, "but the legends also say that the Taker will offer death only to those who stand against him. We shall stand with him."

"The legends say he will bring nothing but death and destruction to Serôs." Flyys knew the legends, though he didn't much believe in them. Even though he'd been sent to investigate the morkoth interest in the Taker, the tritons had their own agenda. Persana had given them the task of watching over the great evil that slept at the bottom of Serôs.

"Wrong," the morkoth said. "The Taker comes to reshape the destinies of everyone in and around Serôs." The head continued turning from side to side, more slowly now.

Flyys felt himself going limp. He chose to go with it, knowing it might be his only chance. A warm lassitude crept through his limbs, relaxing his muscles. He kept his gaze locked on the morkoth.

"Your best choice is acceptance," the creature crooned. Its voice held a muted cadence that beckoned to the young triton.

Flyys relaxed his arms, letting the currents gliding between the edged fingers of the claw coral pull at him. The morkoth came closer. A tingle raced through the triton's legs, then they turned numb. Fear made his heart hammer inside his chest as he continued to take his chance against its hypnotic powers.

Swimming effortlessly, the morkoth descended till it could touch him. The creature slid its heavy pincer against the side of Flyys's face. He felt the hard chitin graze his cheek with almost enough force to break his skin. Still, it wasn't close enough. He stared into first one bulbous eye, then the other as the morkoth dropped down and seemed almost to embrace him.

Moving lithely, with all the skill he'd had the chance to acquire in his handful of years, Flyys gripped the tapal's center handle and spun the weapon around so that it lay along his arm. Before the morkoth could move, confident that it had him in its thrall, the young triton raised his hands with the keen blade wrapped around the outside of his arm.

Flyys punched forward with all his strength. He felt the tapal's blade bite into flesh, and blood swirled into the water around him, obscuring his vision. Still, he saw the morkoth's head leave its shoulders and float away. The head glanced off one of the claw coral spires, shearing away flesh in a long strip. Before it had a chance to settle into the silt, the nearby small scavengers were already at work.

The other morkoth gathered, drawing closer.

Flyys shrugged the tapal through the water to spread the blood cloud out farther and tried not to be sick. The morkoth was his first kill. The young triton had never expected to experience the nausea that filled him as his gills drew in the bloodstained water. The taint of old copper raced through his breathing passages. He glanced up at the approaching morkoth group and set himself. The numbness that had threatened to fill his body had left as soon as the morkoth died.

"Hold!"

The great voice filled the surrounding area. Immediately, the morkoth drew back, opening the way for another morkoth which descended upon the young triton's refuge.

Flyys studied the newcomer. The young triton's fear tripled when he noticed the human-shaped hands at the ends of the morkoth's four arms. Where the pincers signified the warrior class among the kraknyth, human-shaped hands nearly always denoted a morkoth mage.

Flyys's education included lessons in spellcraft as well as warcraft. So far he'd only learned the spell for identifying magical things, to better search the wrecked ships that the surface dwellers lost in battles and storms. All Serôsian races that worked magic raided the fallen ships surface dwellers didn't ransack themselves, or lose in the currents. Flyys had been told his own magic was strong and that his potential would be marked by the mages in Pumanath.

"Ignorant whelpling," the morkoth snarled in a voice hoarse with age. Taking a small piece of metal from the conch shell belted at its side, the morkoth mage gestured and spoke arcane words Flyys didn't know. The metal flamed despite the surrounding water, disappearing into a haze of blackened bubbles that roiled to the surface.

Flyys felt the spell slam into his body, vibrating along his bones. He couldn't move, couldn't blink. At first he thought he'd been struck dead, then he realized his heart still hammered in his chest and his gills still drew in water.

"Get him," the morkoth mage commanded.

One of the morkoth warriors swam down and wrapped two of its tentacles around Flyys's upper body. Though he fought against the spell, the young triton remained bound. Frozen in place, he watched helplessly as the morkoth swam to the surface with him.

The shadow of a ship lay heavily on the turquoise water, sketching its shape along the surface. He recognized it as a cog, a craft well designed for trading along the shores of Serôs. Turned to float partially on his back, Flyys saw sailors clustered along the side. A net was quickly lowered, then he and the morkoth mage were drawn up.

The young triton fought to regain the use of his limbs, but couldn't. He knew from his studies that the spell he was under wouldn't last long, but it lasted long enough for the sailors to secure him to the mainmast with loops of rope.

As the sailors finished their knots, feeling returned to Flyys's body. He pulled hesitantly against the ropes and found them too tight to escape. Under the glare of the morning sun and left out in the breeze, his skin started drying almost at once.

"Khorrch," a man bellowed.

The morkoth turned and gazed up to the ship's stern castle. "Yes, Vurgrom," it replied in the human tongue.

Flyys spoke the language himself. Everyone who traded in Serôs learned the human tongue. With the enmity that existed between the undersea cultures at times over Serôs's long past, it proved to be as common a tongue below the waves as above it. He also recognized the name.

Vurgrom the Mighty was chief of the pirates among the surface world. He was also the man Flyys and his companions had been sent to spy on. Though Vurgrom hadn't been on board the ship they'd invaded during the night, his minions had been.

"This is one of them?" Vurgrom walked down the steps leading up to the stern castle. He stood tall and broad, with a huge chest that sloped down to a massive stomach. Still, he moved lightly enough on the ship's rolling deck that Flyys knew the bulk would throw off most of his opponents. Vurgrom's reputation was fierce and savage, built on the number of deaths he'd ordered over the years. Many of them he'd taken part in himself.

"Yes," Khorrch answered.

The wind stirred the wild red hair on the pirate captain's head, ruffled the long, untamed beard. He stopped in front of Flyys. "He knows where the Eye is?"

The young triton tried not to let the fear inside him show, but he knew that the morkoth mage and the pirate captain both sensed it in him. He swallowed hard, feeling his mouth and throat dry as his gills sucked in air instead of liquid.

"I believe he does," Khorrch said. "When the Taker was banished all those thousands of years ago by Umberlee, stories and tales of him were passed among those who lived in the sea. No one race got everything, and each was given something to protect—something that would keep the Taker from regaining his full strength. Our legends of the Taker tell us the longmanes were given some of the secrets of the Taker's missing Eye."

Flyys struggled against the ropes that held him but still didn't find any slack. Though he was not a great believer in the menace that the Taker represented—primarily because the evil his people guarded against was even larger—he preferred death to talking.

" 'Some of the secrets'?" Vurgrom repeated irritably. "I thought they knew what we needed to find out."

The morkoth drew itself up to its full height on its six tentacles, but it still didn't stand as tall as the pirate captain. "They know where it is," Khorrch declared. "Without it, all the things we've gathered here in the Sea of Fallen Stars will be useless."

Vurgrom switched his glare back to Flyys. "I don't suppose you'd be willing to tell us on your own, would you, boy?"

Flyys wanted to answer but he didn't trust his voice. He felt certain it would crack and shake.

Vurgrom smiled, sunlight dancing from the gold hoops in his ears. "We could let you stay out here and dry out, boy." He hooked a thumb over his shoulder. "I got lads here wouldn't mind betting on how long it takes till your skin starts to peel off. Maybe we could even hang you out on the prow. The gulls, they get scent of you, they'd be down for a little snack."

Despite his best efforts not to, Flyys shivered at the prospect. He knew he wouldn't be the first triton to be treated in that fashion. However, it was preferable to being ripped apart by the morkoth.

"Time is of the essence," Khorrch stated.

Vurgrom crossed his huge arms over his barrel chest and said, "Aye, I know. Iakhovas is a harsh taskmaster."

"But his rewards are good," Khorrch pointed out.

Vurgrom smiled, a rictus of humor that belonged on a shark's mouth. "Get it done, then."

Expecting the morkoth to use its hypnotic powers or perhaps magically command him to speak, Flyys closed his eyes and prayed to Persana to deliver him from his fate quickly. One way or the other.

Khorrch spoke words of power that started small fires under Flyys's skin. The young triton's eyes snapped open, commanded by a force outside himself. He watched in swiftly growing horror as Khorrch took a small copper piece from the conch shell at his side.

The morkoth laid the copper piece on one of his human palms and continued his spellcasting. His voice rose, and he curled his fingers over the copper piece, holding tight. In the next instant the copper piece vanished in a brief burst of flame. Khorrch opened his palm, revealing unblemished skin.

Then Flyys felt as though someone had buried a spear in his head, bursting through bone and flesh. He screamed and shivered against the ropes.

"Tell me of the Eye," the morkoth ordered harshly. "Tell me of the Taker's Eye. Tell me where I may find it."

Gasping, fighting against the pain that filled his mind, thinking his skull must surely be peeling back like an onion against the creature's magical assault, Flyys tried to think of anything but the triton legends about the Taker's Eye. It proved impossible.

"The Taker's . . . Eye," Flyys heard his own voice saying, "is . . . kept . . . in Myth Nantar!" Once the words had been forced through his clenched teeth, the spell's force left him. He sagged weakly against the mast, hung there by the ropes.

"Myth Nantar," Vurgrom said. "I've never heard of it."

"You shouldn't have," Khorrch said. "The city is magical, something that wasn't for the eyes of the surface dwellers. If they had known, it would have been raided long ago."

"Aye, but who's to say this place hasn't been raided by another race?" Vurgrom demanded. "One that makes its home beneath these waters?"

The morkoth shook its head in a very humanlike gesture. "No. That's not possible."

"Why?" the pirate captain persisted.

"Because," Flyys croaked, feeling some of his confidence return, "Myth Nantar was lost to everyone thousands of years ago. It lies hidden and barred. No one may enter it. Now or ever."

"You're wrong, longmane whelpling," Khorrch snarled. "There is one who may enter."

"Not the Taker," Flyys promised. "Our legends tell us the walls will hold against even his might."

"Not him," the morkoth mage agreed, "but there will be another who will bring its walls down. One whose destiny lies with the Taker's, their futures so intertwined that one may not live on without the other."

Flyys wanted to rail against the morkoth's words, but he didn't have the strength. He had lost his friends, betrayed some of the legacy that had been left to him. Only the dying remained. He was certain neither Vurgrom or Khorrch would suffer him to live.

As if some of the mental bond that had existed between them still remained, Khorrch gazed into the young triton's eyes and hissed, "Ah, longmane, there yet remains one service you may do for my people."

Flyys tried to summon up enough liquid to spit, but his throat was already too dry from exposure in the wind.

The morkoth mage crossed to the ship's railing where the net had brought them aboard. The creature gestured. A moment later the net was hoisted again, lifting yet another morkoth to the deck.

"Stay back from her," Khorcch warned the ship's crew.

Immediately the sailors stepped back from the new arrival, some of them making the signs of their gods and calling out their names.

Flyys stared at the morkoth. It was noticeably smaller than the mage, and possessed only tentacles instead of hands. It swayed drunkenly across the deck as it approached the young triton.

"No!" the young triton yelled. He wrenched against the ropes again, but it was in vain. Instead, he concentrated on Persana and prayed. He couldn't close his eyes even though he knew what was going to happen.

The female morkoth's abdomen belled out, looking as though the creature had just eaten a big meal. Flyys knew that wasn't true. It came closer, reaching out tentatively with all four tentacles. The rubbery flesh slid syrup-sticky across Flyys's face and chest as it investigated him.

The morkoth mage stood nearby, though obviously not in any proximity. It clutched a long-bladed knife defensively. "Don't be fooled by his age," Khorrch told the female. "He's young, but the magic is strong in him."

The female morkoth seemed to nod in agreement. Its tentacles continued to rove over Flyys.

The young triton had never seen what was about to happen, but there had been plenty of stories about it. The event was only one more reason to make war against the kraknyth.

Slowly, the female morkoth's abdomen flexed. Scaled flesh peeled back, opening like a mouth. A wicked appendage with a spike at the end slid free. It wavered for a moment out in the open as if uncertain. Female morkoth never had the opportunity to practice the maneuver. It was only done once, and it was guided by instinct.

Flyys tried to move but couldn't. In the next heartbeat, the appendage flared out and stabbed deeply into the young triton's abdomen. He screamed at the pain and felt warm blood seep down his midsection and thighs. The appendage writhed within him, seeking out the various internal organs, not damaging any of them.

The female morkoth held him as if in a lover's embrace. The appendage pulsed as it began laying her eggs, scattering them among his internal organs. Flyys tried to fight against it in vain. He gazed into the female morkoth's black eyes, almost hypnotized, and watched as they dimmed, watched as life left it.

When all of the eggs were laid, the female morkoth fell backward, dead before she hit the deck. The appendage wrenched free of Flyys.

Filled with horror, the young triton gazed down at his wound. As he watched, it closed up and sealed, healing instantly as the final part of the cycle pumped into him. After all, it wouldn't do to have a host body die or become infected before the eggs could hatch.

"Get rid of it," Vurgrom commanded.

Reluctantly, his men came forward. They grabbed the dead female morkoth and heaved it over the railing. The splash barely carried above the ship's creaks and the sails snapping overhead.

Khorrch peered into Flyys's eyes. "You've been given a great gift, longmane."

"You've killed me," the young triton whispered hoarsely.

"Mayhap," the morkoth mage admitted. "Even should you live after the young hatch inside you and eat their way free, you would only be reimplanted with eggs or killed outright."

Flyys knew it was true. The morkoth young would feed on his flesh and tear their way out of his body. Even if he could get free of the morkoth, he knew of no spells or mendicants that would kill the morkoth young and let him live. Still, if he could get free, he might survive their birthing.

"You may know where the Taker's Eye is," the young triton said, "but you'll never get it."

"The Taker will."

"Your precious Taker," Flyys said, the certainty of his own doom freeing him from the fear that had filled him, "will turn on you in the end. He is only after those things that matter to him. You and the other kraknyth are only a means to an end."

Murderous rage gleamed in the morkoth mage's eyes. "You lie."

"You yourself said that no one undersea race knows all about the Taker's past or his future," Flyys went on, "but we know this. You will pay for your greed and for your mistakes. Myth Nantar shall never reopen."

"Enough prattle," Vurgrom declared. "We've got leagues to go if we're to get where we need to be." He gestured at his men. "Take the triton belowdecks and stow him."

Flyys waited until they untied him, then tried to break free. He preferred death now to birthing the morkoth young, but everything he'd been through had left him drained. One of the pirates slammed the flat of his heavy cutlass against his head and consciousness abandoned the young triton.

1

"Meat is meat!"

The roar of sahuagin thumps, ticks, pings and whistles that served as their communication filled the walls of the open amphitheater, almost deafening Laaqueel as she stood in the sahuagin king's retinue. It was pure bloodlust, fired from their king's promise of the coming deaths in the amphitheater.

As a malenti, an accident of birth among the sahuagin caused from being born too close to a community of sea elves, she immediately stood out from the hulking sahuagin around her. Even though she was only a few inches under six feet in height, all of the sahuagin nearby were at least a foot or more taller.

She looked supple and slender, and knew from past experience that she turned the male heads of surface dwellers as well as sea elves. It was cruel injustice that the form she wore was so hideous to her, yet so pleasing to the enemies of her people. She wore only the simple sahuagin harness, making even more evident the curvaceous form that set her apart from the other priestesses allowed at the king's side.

Her coal black hair lay in a long braid at her back, bound up by artificed fish bones and carved bits of coral. Instead of the usual blue or green skin coloring granted a malenti, her deformity had cursed her even further. She had the pale complexion of a hated surface dweller.

Standing in front of her, King Huaanton towered almost nine feet and was built broad with muscles sculpted and hardened from hundreds of years spent living under the sea's constant pressure. Sahuagin survived the harsh sea only by being the most feared predators there. Skin so green it was nearly black stretched across his back, showing a few scars from past battles. Rising to a kingship within the sahuagin culture was not without blood price. Keeping that office required even more blood be spilled into the salty ocean. The skin over his stomach was lighter green. The fins on his back, shoulders, arms, and legs were black, as was his tail.

He wore a combat harness with the seal of Sekolah, the sahuagin Shark God, decorated with shark's teeth and rare shells. His white gold crown flared up in four separate talons that cruelly hooked at the end. The crown rode low on his savage face, creating a half-mask that drew even more attention to the oily black eyes planted on both sides of his head. His mouth held razor-sharp fangs.

"Meat is meat!" King Huaanton roared again, lifting high the bone and inlaid yellow gold trident that was his seal of office.

"Meat is meat!" came the thunderous return cry from the hundreds of sahuagin seated out in the amphitheater. They shifted and waved their arms on the stone tiers that surrounded the center court of the structure.

"I bring to you," Huaanton went on when the response died down, "part of the spoils of our past victories against the surface world." The war against the surface dwellers along the Sword Coast was only two tendays old, but there had been many strikes, many triumphs. Waterdeep still reeled from the raid that had been their first blow. Huaanton gestured toward the center court with his trident.

Immediately, gates at the left side of the amphitheater opened, releasing a half-dozen humans. Laaqueel watched them with interest, noting the way they swam so clumsily. These, then, were true surface dwellers that had rarely entered the oceans. The malenti priestess knew several of the sailors who regularly crossed the Claarteeros Sea didn't know how to swim at all. These creatures possessed no grace and precious little skill at cleaving through the water. They fought the sea as if it were an opponent instead of taking grace and speed from the currents that constantly swept through it.

The sahuagin in the amphitheater made their displeasure known by slapping their webbed feet against the stone and emitting more thunderous clicks and whistles. Even though the humans didn't know the sahuagin tongue, Laaqueel knew the intent behind the cries couldn't be misunderstood.

The surface dwellers swam uncertainly, staying within a group near the coral-tiled floor. The builders had designed the floor meticulously, creating a swirl pattern of light and dark coral pieces. At something more than three hundred feet below the surface, little light penetrated the depths. None of it held the colors that were available in the dry world, but the light and dark pattern of the tiled floor showed clearly.

A sahuagin guard glided effortlessly among the surface dwellers and passed out simple knives. Before they'd been released into the amphitheater, Laaqueel knew the humans had been exposed to an aboleth's mucus cloud. After they'd captured the humans, Huaanton had demanded that an aboleth be captured as well, then ordered the creature's mucus used to give the humans water-breathing ability that would last for at least an hour and maybe as long as three hours. Until then, the surface dwellers had been held captive in special dungeon cells that had air.

Either way, Laaqueel knew, the humans wouldn't live long enough for the temporary magical effects of the aboleth mucus to wear off. Normally, the sahuagin hated magic and anything resembling magic, but Huaanton had made concessions in that area to promote the torture he had in mind. After all, the aboleth mucus was found in nature, not forged from it by some arcane means.

After the sahuagin passed out the next to last knife, the young human he'd given it to attacked the guard the moment his back was presented. The young surface dweller swam well enough and fast enough, but the sahuagin's lateral line, the sensory organ that allowed him to detect vibration and movement in the water, warned him.

Even before the young human could strike, the sahuagin flicked his tail and clawed the water with his free webbed hand and both webbed feet. The sahuagin rose steeply, ascending over his foe and drawing the trident in line. Wrapping both hands about the trident's shaft, the sahuagin brought the tines down quickly, driving them through the human's back and into his heart and lungs, splitting the flesh easily.

Blood erupted from the wounds, spilling a dark cloud into the water. The human struggled, trying to get away from the barbed tines, but he was solidly hooked.

The sahuagin spectators cheered lustily and slapped their huge webbed feet against the stone seating tiers in appreciation. Clicks and whistles rose in anticipation.

Laaqueel watched closely, knowing she would have enjoyed the festivities more if she wasn't facing fears of her own. But she knew her own fate might be as dismal as that of the surface dwellers—unless a miracle did happen here tonight. After all, Iakhovas had promised Huaanton a divine sign from Sekolah himself to prove that the raids the sahuagin staged against the surface world were what the Shark God wanted.

The other humans stayed back instead of going to help their comrade. The sahuagin guard pulled the corpse along by the trident's handle, streaming dark bloody strings after it that twisted in the currents. He flicked out his claws and carved great gobbets of flesh from the dead man, then hurled them into the crowd. "Meat is meat!" he cried.

"Meat is meat!" the crowd cried in joyful acceptance of the offering.

Small sahuagin darted forth to claim the unexpected treats. Some of them were fast enough to get the pieces they were after, but others ended up locked in mortal combat while the adults watched on in approval. The sahuagin life was supposed to be hard, and they learned to kill their enemies by first killing each other. That vicious cycle started in the domed nurseries with newborn hatchlings. Only the best and strongest survived to carry on their fierce race.

After slashing the corpse to chunks, the guard saved the heart for himself, shoving it into his great fanged mouth as he floated above the amphitheater. Blood gushed from his mouth and nose as he choked down the impromptu meal.

Her senses as acute as any sahuagin's, Laaqueel smelled the blood in the water. The scent caused further excitement within her. Though her appearance masked her true nature, the malenti was sahuagin.

"And now," Huaanton stated, "I bring to you a champion!" He pointed again.

On the opposite side of the amphitheater, another set of gates released a huge diamond-shaped manta ray that streaked out into the open center court. The combined noises of displeasure from the sahuagin spectators were even louder. Manta rays closely resembled the sahuagin's sworn enemies, the ixitxachitls.

The sahuagin guards immediately backpedaled through the water, pulling back and above the amphitheater. Getting its bearings almost at once, obviously starved for days, the manta ray flipped its broad fins and closed on the group of surface dwellers.

The sea creature was among them before they could scatter. It seized one of the surface dwellers in its mouth, swallowing the man in a single gulp as it cruised through. Another man of the surviving four attacked, gripping one of the leather wings in one hand as the creature passed, then pulling himself to its back. The manta ray flicked out its stinger and barbed a man. In seconds the stricken man succumbed to the tail's paralytic effects and hung motionless in the water.

The man clinging to the manta ray's back dug in with his knife. Laaqueel admired the man's tenacity. He was meeting his death with a bravery and anger a sahuagin could respect.

Wounds reluctantly opened up in the manta ray's back. Blood gushed in threads behind it, curling and fragmenting in the wake. Flicking its wings again, the manta ray increased its speed, obviously hoping to shake its attacker from its back. Graceful and desperate, the creature planed through the water, curling back to where it had first encountered the humans. Blood spilled out in a fog behind it as the human kept sinking his blade home.

As they watched the deadly duel taking shape in the amphitheater, the sahuagin seated in the tiers cheered loudly and slapped their feet encouragingly. Even though they hated the surface dwellers, the humans were the underdogs in the battle, and the sahuagin respected that all too familiar position.

Pride and hope flared anew in Laaqueel, driving away the fear that Iakhovas's promise for the day had instilled in her. This *was* Seko-lah's promise to his chosen people. Born and bred for battle, the death matches that played out in the amphitheaters of all the cities remained proof of their eventual destiny to conquer. She watched and prayed to the Shark God, begging for forgiveness for ever allowing even a shred of doubt to enter her heart. Whether Iakhovas's claim to be acting on the will of Sekolah was true or false, she would know in only a short time. However it turned out, she chose to put her faith in the Shark God. She watched the battle in rapt attention.

The manta ray scooped up the paralyzed victim on its next pass, gulping him down effortlessly as well. It flipped its wings again and swam for the outskirts of the amphitheater. Before it could reach the edges high over the gathered crowd, four sharks under the control of the sahuagin guards swam to meet it. Reluctantly, the manta ray turned back.

Taking a fresh grip on the leathery wing he held, the human on the manta ray's back pulled himself forward while the creature turned. The human slithered over the manta's wing, still maintaining his hold. On the inside of the wing now, a safe distance from the fanged mouth, the human dug in with his knife again, ripping through the manta's softer underbelly.

Angry and fearful, driven by irrational hunger as well, the manta returned for the two humans who had gone to ground against the coral tiles. Laaqueel noticed that the manta's movements were no longer as sure or as quick as they had been. The wounds robbed it of constitution, continuing to leech its strength away.

The cavernous mouth scooped up a third victim as the man tried to flee. Evidently encouraged by his comrade's success, the last human grabbed the manta's wing as well, but he didn't have enough skill to do more than simply hang on.

Long minutes passed and the struggle continued, but in the end there could be no doubt. Starved and weakened by its captivity, further depleted by the blood loss, the manta gave in to the wounds. It struggled only weakly as it drifted down and came to a rest against one side of the amphitheater's coral-tiled floor. With a final flicker of wing movement, the great manta ray died, leaving only the ocean currents to stir it.

Immediately, a thunderous swell of appreciation and encouragement rose from the sahuagin spectators. They pushed to their feet and filled the amphitheater with their triumph.

Laaqueel chose to view the battle as a sign. It was not a sign from Sekolah—the Shark God didn't trouble himself with the affairs of anyone, including his chosen people—but the victory of the surface dwellers over the giant manta ray, the small versus the large, represented the backbone of sahuagin ideals. Still, her heart pounded inside her chest at the anticipation of Huaanton's introduction of Iakhovas.

Slowly, the surface dwellers disentangled themselves from the manta ray, partly hidden from sight by the cloudy blood swirling around them. They swam fearfully, uncertain of what to do next.

Huaanton raised his great trident again, then turned the tines down.

Immediately the sahuagin guards closed in, fanning through the water with their webbed hands and feet. The humans tried to flee, but they didn't have the speed and there was nowhere to go. With a practiced toss, the closest sahuagin to each man snared their prey with the barbed nets they carried. They pulled the nets tight, sinking the hooked barbs into flesh and binding their prisoners.

Even winners didn't make it out of the amphitheater alive. It wasn't the sahuagin way. The spectators cheered again, bloodlust filling them.

The human who'd first attacked the manta ray was brought before Huaanton. The sahuagin king regarded the bound figure at his feet with contempt. The human spat out curses that Laaqueel knew few except her understood. She listened as the man alternately called out to his gods for help and for vengeance.

Huaanton ripped away the barbed net in a practiced fashion. Small trickles of blood ran from the dozens of wounds covering the surface dweller's body and mixed with the sea, creating a sensory explosion to Laaqueel. She knew the king's Royal Black Tridents, his personal bodyguards, and the other priestesses were affected by the taste in the water they breathed.

In a show of amazing defiance, obviously knowing what was to become of him, the surface dweller plunged his blade toward the sahuagin king's broad chest.

Before even the hardened members of the Royal Black Tridents could move to intercept the strike, Huaanton lifted the royal trident. After deflecting the knife, the sahuagin king reversed the trident and swung the tines at the human's neck.

Blood exploded into the water as the jagged edged tines ripped through the pale flesh. Even as death claimed the surface dweller, Huaanton grabbed the man's head, cracked the spinal column with his great strength, and finished the decapitation. Holding the head, he shoved the corpse back to the guards.

"Share the bounty of this brave warrior," the sahuagin king commanded. "Let his flesh impart to you his courage and cunning. Meat is meat."

"Meat is meat!" the crowd responded.

Huaanton stripped flesh from the head, savoring it with obvious gusto. He ate while the remains of both prisoners were distributed through the spectators. Other guards carved up the manta ray, then emptied the creature's stomach and disbursed the meat from its victims.

Laaqueel waited, but none of the flesh was offered to her despite the fact that nearly all of the king's personal priestesses got some. She bore her hurt and anger quietly. As a malenti she'd become accustomed to such treatment, but as senior priestess to a prince, there were few she'd accept it from these days. Joining with Iakhovas even though she had her doubts about him had benefited her in rank. Having to trust in Sekolah to guide her through the treacherous currents that lay ahead had made her even stronger.

Finishing with his impromptu meal, Huaanton threw the stripped skull from him. A shark hovering overhead glided down and snatched the skull less than an arm's length from the sahuagin king. Bone crunched as the shark bit its prize and swam away.

"We are come upon great times for our people," Huaanton stated. His clicks and whistles carried strongly to the amphitheater spectators. "Only two tendays ago, we staged the most magnificent raid ever in the history of our race against the hated surface world. Waterdeep, their prize gem, located in the stronghold of the humans, suffered our wrath. We killed them where we found them, burned their ships in the harbor, and—most of all—we taught them again what it is to fear We Who Eat."

Tridents rattled in the stone tiers, striking a syncopation and cadence that echoed through the water for a brief moment. Laaqueel felt the controlled revelry and took pride in her part in it. For good or ill, however events progressed with Iakhovas in the next few moments, she had helped bring these victories to her people.

"In past days," Huaanton went on, "we've continued raiding their ships and striking other small coastal villages and cities within our reach. Their sea trade has slowed and they no longer cross our waters as complacently."

More trident rattling punctuated by whistles and clicks followed.

"I chose these tactics," Huaanton said, "because I was compelled by the great Shark God, Sekolah, to go forth and spill the blood of our enemies, to eat their flesh and become strong again."

Another thunderous cheer sounded.

Huaanton looked out over the spectators. "I will ever do Sekolah's bidding that I might take my rightful place in the currents he has left for us to swim. I know these times will be turbulent and trying. We Who Eat were birthed to be tested under the harshest conditions, against the strongest of enemies. No weakness shall be permitted." He paused. "But now, I've had to consider where we go from here, and how far we should pursue our war."

Laaqueel saw a flurry of movement to the left of the king and knew instinctively it was Iakhovas. She started to move, but the cold quiver of the black quill Iakhovas had placed next to her heart when she had discovered him in the Veemeeros Sea all those years ago froze her in place.

Don't fret so, little malenti, his rough voice whispered in her mind as he confronted the Royal Black Tridents who blocked his path. *Else your own uncertainties about Sekolah will threaten everything you hope to do here. Look into your own heart and seize those convictions you so pride yourself on.*

Stung, Laaqueel stayed in place. Iakhovas's words challenged her uncertainty. As a malenti, she'd been cursed from birth, allowed to stay within the sahuagin city where she'd been born only because she could be raised as a spy. Her belief in Sekolah had been the only thing that kept her going through all those long years. Without her faith, she would be nothing.

"Do you think then," Iakhovas interrupted the sahuagin king, "that we should back down and fear retribution on part of the surface dwellers?" His words thundered over the assembly.

Instantly, the amphitheater grew quiet as death.

Huaanton turned to Iakhovas and waved the bodyguards away. Iakhovas walked up the steps. To Laaqueel, he appeared to be human, but she knew he wasn't. He stood a full head taller than her, but much shorter than Huaanton. He was broad, yet lithe, filled with long muscles that moved easily. His black hair hung past his shoulders, somehow unmoved by the ocean currents that cycled around the area.

Despite the scars that tracked his face, Iakhovas was handsome as humans considered themselves, but his features held cold cruelty. The short beard and mustache he wore covered part of his face and softened the effect of the scars. He wore a sleeveless deep green tunic that revealed the runic black tattoos that covered his arms, legs, and body. Laaqueel knew they covered his entire body because she'd seen Iakhovas naked the day she'd found him. Black breeches, boots, and a black cape completed his ensemble. A deep green patch covered his missing eye.

Although she'd tried for years to identify the bracelets, rings, and other adornments Iakhovas habitually wore and added to, Laaqueel didn't know anything more than that they were magical in nature. Most of them were weapons or defenses. Her own reticence in the matter had held her back because she was loath to touch them and didn't dare ask after them. All of them, she knew, had been recovered in the years since she'd found him. He and creatures in his service had sought them out. One of those items had been the sole reason Iakhovas had journeyed to Waterdeep.

If Iakhovas had appeared as a human to the sahuagin, Laaqueel knew they'd have killed him on the spot—or died trying. However, thanks to the spells he constantly wove around himself, the sahuagin saw him as one of their own, only slightly less in stature to Huaanton himself.

The malenti had even helped Iakhovas fake his own birth into her community after she'd brought him back. Once there, he'd quickly risen through the ranks by blood challenges and his sheer ferocity. Those traits, she'd decided, were as natural to him as any sahuagin, something no human she'd ever seen could match.

Now Iakhovas was prince among the sahuagin, a war chief they'd relied on heavily for the raid on Waterdeep. He still had his own agenda, and stopping the sahuagin raids conflicted with that intensely.

"Watch yourself," Huaanton warned softly. He flexed his muscles and intentionally set the trident between Iakhovas and himself. "You swim heavily over the largess I've granted you."

Iakhovas met the king's gaze directly, something no true sahuagin would do without starting a blood feud. Laaqueel was surprised when Huaanton didn't react to the obvious insubordination. She felt the fear ball up in her stomach and she started praying silently.

"Exalted One," Iakhovas addressed the sahuagin king in a voice that carried to the masses, "I am come here at this tide at your direction. A tenday ago, we discussed the possibilities of continuing our war with the surface dwellers. You challenged me to produce a sign from Sekolah that my words be proven true when I said the Shark God wanted us, We Who Eat and Sekolah's Chosen, to take the oceans back from the surface dwellers."

Low mutterings moved through the spectators and they shifted uneasily. Laaqueel continued her prayers, touching the shark-toothed necklace she wore. Her eyes flickered between Huaanton and Iakhovas.

"Yet now," Iakhovas continued, "I am here and I listen to you on the verge of canceling all further attacks on the surface dwellers."

"Our people shall not die needlessly," Huaanton announced.

"Sekolah has given me a vision," Iakhovas said. Only Laaqueel saw the mocking smile that played over his cruel lips. "There is a new tide upon us, a new time in which the sahuagin will be rejuvenated and made stronger than we've ever been before."

The spectators stamped their webbed feet in appreciation and yelled out their support.

"Words," Huaanton snarled. "You offer us only words. You carry on like some surface dweller who loves the sound of his own voice."

The smile dropped from Iakhovas's face, and deadly lights glittered in his single eye. "I offer only words of warning, Exalted One, because I was bade carry them to you as well. Sekolah has made me see the weakness in you."

Laaqueel stopped praying, knowing that Iakhovas had gone too far. Even an indirect accusation of cowardice among the sahuagin was enough to trigger a blood challenge.

"I told you of Sekolah's will," Iakhovas went on. "I told you how we are to continue raiding the world of the surface dwellers. Yet, you concern yourself with thoughts of their retribution. Sekolah says let them come, and let We Who Eat stand against them."

The spectators roared their approval.

"The tide of the Great Cleansing is upon us," Iakhovas stated, "and it shall see the weak and cowardly driven from us or dead as Sekolah wills it. The true warriors of the Shark God shall prevail against our enemies. We shall be unstoppable even though we fill the oceans with blood and drench the dry lands beyond!"

Huaanton raised his trident, instantly quieting all the noise around him. "You talk brave words, but they're only words. They ring as hollow as an abandoned hermit crab's shell, and are as fleeting as gulls feeding in shark-infested waters. I've seen no sign from Sekolah."

"How dare you," Iakhovas said bitterly, his voice cutting as surely as a spinefish's fin. "Sekolah has never owed We Who Eat anything, yet you choose to view him as one who should be at your beck and call."

Laaqueel took pride in the fact that the spectators all sat up and took notice of Iakhovas's words. It didn't matter that he'd borrowed them from her from the time they'd last met with Huaanton. They were true, and the sahuagin sitting in the stone tiers recognized them for that.

Huaanton reacted hotly. "You're putting words in my mouth."

"No," Iakhovas said, cutting him off. "Laaqueel has prayed about this matter ever since that time. And she fought you regarding this issue, telling you how out of place your demands were. You were out of line asking for a sign that we're carrying on as Sekolah would have us do. We survive, and we survive strongly and in numbers. That's all he's ever asked of us."

"Yet, if we were to follow you, all we would find is our deaths against the surface dwellers."

Iakhovas looked at him, fire dancing in his single eye. "Only the inadequate fail!" he shouted.

That was one of the core beliefs for the sahuagin, Laaqueel knew. All of them had been trained since hatchlings that it was true.

"The brave and strong shall flourish," Iakhovas went on. "The tide of the Great Cleansing is upon us!" He gestured across the amphitheater. "Should you want your sign that you so inelegantly demanded of we who choose to follow Sekolah's true way, then behold and tremble at the power of the Shark God!"

Every eye was drawn across the amphitheater. Laaqueel watched as well, noticing the huge mass that took shape out in the distance. At first it blended in with the deep blue of the sea, then it paled as it came closer. In moments, the great albino kraken hovered above the amphitheater.

The kraken's two longest tentacles drifted out at its sides while the other six coiled restlessly beneath its body. The single baleful eye on the arrow-shaped head, reminding the malenti of her master's, glared red even in the dark waters. Its tentacles were over one hundred and fifty feet long, making it the largest of its kind Laaqueel had ever seen or even heard about.

The malenti recognized the kraken as the one that had guarded the tunnels leading to the king's palace. Brought there as a young creature, the kraken had been fed by the royal guards till it was too big to get out through the tunnels it had been brought through. The guards had kept it on a regulated near-starvation diet that guaranteed it would eat anything that came within its reach.

Only it hadn't acted like that with Iakhovas when they'd encountered it a tenday ago. With Iakhovas, the kraken had acted totally docile.

"There is your sign, Exalted One!" Iakhovas shouted, pointing at the great kraken as it continued to drift closer.

Huaanton stared up at the huge kraken in enraged silence.

Every sahuagin in the amphitheater knew the creatures possessed an uncanny intelligence. A kraken wouldn't normally approach a sahuagin community, Laaqueel knew, especially one that had kept it captive. It had also gotten too large to get out of the caverns below by conventional means, leaving her no choice but to accept that Iakhovas had used his magic to arrange it. The kraken's presence was proof again of the arcane abilities Iakhovas wielded.

"Here is your proof," Iakhovas went on. "Proof that you demanded of our god."

"You stand there and claim the appearance of this beast is a sign from Sekolah," Huaanton thundered with deep clicks and thumps.

"Dare you claim it is not?" Iakhovas stretched his left hand upward. The kraken stretched one of its longest tentacles down at the same time, tenderly wrapping the huge, leaf-shaped pod around Iakhovas's arm. "Have you ever seen anything like this?"

Laaqueel knew the display left a distinct impression on the sahuagin community. Except for the guards who'd first seen Iakhovas with the kraken, no one else had ever seen anything like it either. The malenti priestess knew Iakhovas was treading a fine line between accreditation and accusation. Huaanton pushed it over the line.

"Magic," the sahuagin king stated. The charge echoed over the crowd, eliciting small clicks and whistles of quiet conversation.

Laaqueel's heart beat frantically in her chest. She took in fresh seawater through her mouth and flushed it out her gills. She held onto her belief in Sekolah with all her might.

Before the crowd had time to reach a decision on its own, Iakhovas raised his voice. "You try to denounce me? After all that you've demanded of Sekolah while giving so little of yourself?"

Huaanton shifted uneasily, knowing he was on dangerous ground himself. Laaqueel knew Iakhovas had led him there, carefully measuring each step.

"We've taken war to the surface dwellers for the first time in generations," Iakhovas said. "We've fought them and we've broken them. We challenged them in their greatest city and seen it burn, taken their ships and seen them flee from the seas. Now you seek to undo all that?"

"We've done enough," Huaanton replied.

"According to your will," Iakhovas agreed, "perhaps we have, but I've seen a vision of We Who Eat one day marching through the streets of Waterdeep and other coastal cities. The surface dwellers ran cowering before us, no longer able to claim any part of the seas." He paused, letting his words hang in the water. "*That* is when we've done enough."

"You seek to lead us to our deaths, Iakhovas," Huaanton said. "I know not why, but this I truly see. You were born less than fifteen years ago, yet you now hold the office of prince when most take three centuries to reach that position."

Laaqueel stood in silent panic, knowing if Iakhovas came undone, she came undone with him. Her prayers continued without cease, but as always in Sekolah's service, there was no true answer. Only the currents knew how things would sort out.

"Most of those positions," Iakhovas pointed out, "came from you."

"You fed off my own successes like a parasitic worm," Huaanton said. "I didn't see it then, but I see it now."

Iakhovas drew himself to his full height. Even in his human form as Laaqueel saw him, he was impressive. The Royal Black Tridents nearest him involuntarily drew back. The albino kraken hung over the group with its tentacles waving in the currents.

"Truly," Iakhovas said, "Sekolah does lay his hand upon our mission." Still only three steps down from the sahuagin king he turned to address the crowd. "I thought only one sign was going to be presented here today. Now, I see that I was wrong. In his generosity, the Great Shark has given his chosen people two." He gestured to the kraken. "We know that our war with the surface dwellers isn't over." He pointed at Huaanton. "And now we know that we have a king who is king of We Who Eat only in name and no true leader at all." He stepped toward Huaanton.

Instantly, the king's bodyguards moved to intercept Iakhovas. With a flicker of motion that ripped through the water, the kraken reached out and snatched up five of the guards in its tentacles, removing them from Iakhovas's path. Before the other guards could react, Iakhovas stood in front of the sahuagin king.

"Huaanton, false king of We Who Eat of the Claarteeros Sea," Iakhovas said in a loud voice, "I charge you with weakness, finding you unwilling to lead your people in this cause, and with impropriety for failing to carry out Sekolah's war against the surface dwellers."

The Royal Black Tridents closed in with their weapons raised, ready to chop Iakhovas down.

"As is my right," Iakhovas said, ignoring the weapons raised against him, "I claim blood challenge on behalf of the Great Shark."

Angrily, Huaanton waved his guards aside, brave enough to do so even in the face of the kraken as the gigantic creature cracked the bodies of his guards above him. "You lie," the sahuagin king said, taking a step forward, "and your death shall prove those lies."

"Your death," Iakhovas promised, "will prove your weakness and your failing."

Without warning, Huaanton exploded into action. He reversed the trident and thrust the cruel tines at Iakhovas.

Laaqueel watched helplessly as Iakhovas was caught off-guard. She didn't think such a thing was possible after having seen him in action against their enemies, but she remembered how she'd found him, trapped by magic and nearly dead. The scars were mute testimony that he wasn't as infallible as he acted.

The trident tines sank into Iakhovas's chest, drawing a spurting, murky cloud of blood. He screamed in enraged pain and reached for the trident's haft as Huaanton tried to shove it more deeply into him.

Watching on, Laaqueel knew it was a death blow. The tines had no doubt torn through Iakhovas's heart and only seconds remained before death claimed him. The black quill next to her heart quivered in response, signaling a cold flush of nausea that ran through the malenti. She wondered how tightly the quill tied to her Iakhovas, and whether she would die when he did.

A bloody grin warped Iakhovas's face, and touched even the dark hollow of his missing eye. He stood his ground and hooked his fingers between the trident's tines. Muscle rippled along his arms as he shoved the weapon back and pulled the barbed tines free.

Though the misting blood partially obscured her view, Laaqueel watched as the gaping wounds on Iakhovas's chest pulled back together, knitting the flesh, sinew, and bone. The ring she'd first placed on his finger when she'd discovered him glowed briefly, and she doubted that anyone but her saw it.

"Weak," Iakhovas taunted in a ragged voice that almost belied the injuries he'd sustained. He maintained his hold on the trident even against Huaanton's great strength.

The Royal Black Tridents stood back, unable to interfere in a blood challenge. It was one of the most sacred of the sahuagin practices.

Huaanton lifted a webbed foot and lashed out with the razor-edged talons on his toes. He ripped gouges across Iakhovas's face, narrowly missing his eye.

Fearful then, obviously in high regard of his remaining vision, Iakhovas reluctantly released the trident and stepped back. Still, the confident look never left his face as he set himself for another attack.

Huaanton launched himself up into the water, rising above Iakhovas. He was well within the kraken's reach, and Laaqueel knew the sahuagin king was no coward. He kept the trident before him. "Come, Iakhovas, come join me in our dance of death. Let the tides decide our fates."

Iakhovas leaped after the sahuagin king without hesitation. He eeled through the water with grace and speed that was totally unexpected. He slipped long-bladed knives from his belt and held them point down from his fists. Huaanton thrust the trident at him again. Iakhovas blocked the effort with one of the knives, then lashed out at the sahuagin king's midsection with the other.

Huaanton had to move quickly, but the knife slid harmlessly by. Before Iakhovas could recover, Huaanton swung a backhand at him filled with claws. Iakhovas got his arm up in time to save his face, but the claws sank deeply into his flesh, slashing to the bone. He maintained his grip on the knife, though, and brought it down and across in a move designed to disembowel the sahuagin king. The knife blade tracked a bloody furrow across Huaanton's stomach, but it wasn't deep enough to spill his guts.

Spreading the webs between his toes, Huaanton cut through the water, streaking behind Iakhovas. The sahuagin king levered an arm under Iakhovas's chin and popped his finger claws out. Before Huaanton could drag his claws across Iakhovas's throat, Iakhovas slashed the back of the sahuagin king's forearm, cutting through the ligaments that controlled the claws and fingers. Huaanton's claws recessed and his fingers unbent.

Iakhovas broke free of his opponent's grip while Huaanton was stunned by the severity of the wound he'd been dealt. If Iakhovas had used his magic, Laaqueel knew, the fight wouldn't have lasted this long.

Still in motion, Iakhovas swam around Huaanton. As the sahuagin twisted to confront him, Iakhovas drove one of his knives home between Huaanton's ribs, trying for the heart. He left the knife in place, and foggy blood spewed out into the water.

Even wounded as he was, Huaanton didn't give up. Laaqueel felt pride fill her as she watched the sahuagin king. Despite the fact that he didn't trust in Sekolah as he should, she felt Huaanton epitomized everything that was strong and good about the sahuagin.

Lashing out with the trident, Huaanton caught Iakhovas in the legs. He put enough force behind the blow to send the tines completely through one leg just below the knee, then nailed it to the other. With both legs pinned together, Iakhovas couldn't move to escape Huaanton's attack.

The sahuagin king pulled on the trident's haft, not hard enough to rip the barbed ends free of Iakhovas's flesh, but enough to turn Iakhovas in the water. Moving quickly, his fighting skill apparent in the economical grace he used, Huaanton yanked the blade from his side, then buried it deep in Iakhovas's back.

The kraken fluttered in the water. For a moment Laaqueel thought the creature was going to interfere in the battle. If it did, it would undermine everything Iakhovas hoped to win.

Don't count me out of the running yet, little malenti. Iakhovas's pain-wracked voice filled Laaqueel's mind. Torn between a king who refused to give as much credence to Sekolah as the Great Shark demanded and a mysterious being she'd inadvertently staked her future on, Laaqueel instead turned to her prayers.

Iakhovas tried to reach the knife in his back but couldn't. He struggled to free his legs but didn't seem capable of that either.

Even though he still bled copiously, Huaanton's combat instincts took over. He held the trident at arm's length and pinned Iakhovas to the stone floor of the amphitheater below him. He whipped the barbed net from his side, spreading it out with a quick, practiced snap. He threw it and the weighted ends flared out to encompass his struggling foe. He wrapped Iakhovas expertly, pulling the net tight so that the embedded barbs bit deeply into his flesh.

"Now," Huaanton warned as he turned to grasp the trident's haft more firmly, "now we'll see whose truth speaks more strongly." He yanked the barbed tines free of Iakhovas's legs, pulling a roiling boil of blood and shredded flesh after them. Gripping the trident, the sahuagin king held the haft in both hands high over his head, preparing to run it down into Iakhovas's chest.

The black quill next to Laaqueel's heart stilled its beating, froze the cycle of water through her gills. She wanted to scream in denial, but she couldn't honestly say if it was because Iakhovas's doom looked imminent, or if it was the grin on Iakhovas's face, so filled with fiery cunning.

Huaanton brought the trident down, arcing it fiercely. Iakhovas's movement was so swift that Laaqueel almost didn't see it. He thrust his right hand out, pushing against the constricting strands of the barbed net. His hand and arm blurred, becoming something else that was hard and sharp. The wedge-shaped appendage slashed easily through the net and plunged on into Huaanton's trachea and air bladder.

The impact staggered Huaanton's own attempt to stab the trident into Iakhovas. His life's blood poured out of him in a rush, flowing from the huge hole Iakhovas's blow had made.

When Laaqueel blinked again, Iakhovas's arm was back to normal. He fought the net as Huaanton's body went limp in the water near him. Barbs wrenched free of his flesh, leaving bloody tears behind. The malenti knew the effort hurt him; she felt part of his pain through the quill's magic that connected them.

Silence reigned over the amphitheater as the sahuagin spectators waited to see what would happen next.

Still only partially free of the ensnaring net, Iakhovas regained his feet and turned to face the amphitheater. He reached out and seized the trident from Huaanton's dead hand. He held it proudly thrust above him as the kraken spread out its tentacles and formed a loose but protective embrace around him, guarding his back.

"My people," Iakhovas said in a strong voice, "you have seen the Great Shark's will today. By right of blood challenge, and by right of Sekolah's ordained destiny for We Who Eat in our battle against the surface world to reclaim the seas, I name myself king! Let any who disagree with that stand and face me now!"

Laaqueel stared at the sahuagin, knowing none would come forward to stand against Iakhovas in his weakened condition. Sahuagin custom dictated against taking advantage of a wounded member of their community even for a blood challenge.

The response started, low at first, then continuing to gain power as the decision swept through the crowd. "Iakhovas, Exalted One of We Who Eat. Iakhovas, Exalted One of We Who Eat."

Iakhovas turned and grinned at Laaqueel. *Ah, little malenti, do you see the greatness we have wrought? We forge our new destinies from this point on. You and I, both castaways, have risen to the greatest positions among the largest and fiercest sahuagin in the Claarteeros Sea. No one may stop us now. No one!*

If it is what Sekolah wills, she replied.

His single eye burned into hers. *You have doubts?*

Not in the Great Shark. Perhaps in myself.

Then, little malenti, when you find yourself too weak to believe in yourself, believe in me. Iakhovas raised both hands above his head, holding the trident proudly. "I am *king!*" he roared. "None shall stand against us. The surface world shall quake in fear of We Who Eat, for they shall surely come to know that only their deaths await them in the seas we claim!"

The sahuagin cheered him, and Laaqueel watched as the fervor gripped her people. There was no turning back now, she knew. Iakhovas wouldn't allow it, and now he controlled everything.

"And our next victory," Iakhovas declared, "shall be at Baldur's Gate!"

The cheering rose in thunderous approval again.

Turning, Iakhovas hacked Huaanton's body to pieces and gave them up to the currents around him. The sahuagin surged from their seats, swimming to him rapidly to take part in devouring their last king.

"Come," Iakhovas invited as he continued to slash at the dwindling corpse. "We must be strong for our coming battles. Meat is meat!"

2

"You're pushing yourself too hard, old friend. If I could, I'd like to talk you out of this present course of action."

Taranath Reefglamor, senior High Mage of Serôs, the undersea world in the region known as the Sea of Fallen Stars, glanced at his companion and pierced him with his barbed gaze. Over the centuries, the look he gave the younger man was reputed to have withered even past Coronals who'd ruled over the sea elven kingdom where he lived. "If I'd wanted your counsel, Pharom Ildacer, I trust you know that I'd have requested it. As I'd have asked you to address me so casually, as if the station I've worked so hard to attain didn't matter."

Ildacer's round face blanched and his posture suddenly straightened. "Yes, Senior Reefglamor. If I've erred in any way, I offer my deepest apologies."

"Offer all you may," Reefglamor replied, "you cannot take back words once spoken. I know you learned that at my knee."

Inclining his head, Ildacer said, "It is indeed as you say, Senior Reefglamor."

Reefglamor leaned back in his chair, trying to find comfort in the seaweed padding it seemed he couldn't live without these days. He looked old and wizened, ravaged by time's ceaseless hand and the battles he'd undertaken while defending his people. The studies he'd conducted to become senior mage had been no less strenuous.

He possessed the thin build, pointed chin and pointed ears exhibited by so many of the *alu'Tel'quessir*. The blue skin with white patches further marked him with his sea elven heritage. His silver-white hair was bound back by a beaten gold circlet with carved glyphs and hung down nearly to his waist. Though shrouded by fatigue and red lines that seemed more like scars these days, his dark green eyes never wavered. He wore a pale blue diaphanous silken weave that bore the purple and black stripes of his office and the crystal clear dolphin that was the chosen symbol of Deep Sashelas for those few who didn't immediately know him by sight.

They sat at a round table in his sanctum. The room was generous but still filled to overflowing with the accoutrements and trappings of his chosen path. It was rumored, and rightly so, that he had almost as many volumes on magery in his home as were possessed in the temple of Deep Sashelas at Sylkiir. Shelves and bookcases covered every wall, designed to hold every tome whether it was inscribed on cut stone or on delicate gold foil. Round glass globes filled with luminescent pale blue lichens lighted the room.

Reefglamor ran his hand across the stone surface of the table. It hadn't always been smooth, but centuries of working at it, reading and studying, conversing with those few of whom he thought well enough to invite there, had worn away the roughness. Only his own contentious personality seemed to be unscathed by time.

That, he amended, and the ever-present threat of the Ravager.

"I shall need you at your best," Reefglamor said. "You may need to act with all the focus I've trained in you in order to salvage anything of this in case things go awry."

"Senior," Ildacer said quietly. He was rounder than most *alu'Tel'quessir* because he had an appetite for food and drink that was legendary in its own right. His blue skin was paler than Reefglamor's and his silver hair still yet held stands of black. He wore a deep purple silken weave. "I know I risk your considerable displeasure by venting my own thoughts in this matter."

"You risk far more than that," Reefglamor warned.

"You asked me here, Senior, and I think that means you believe you can't do this without me." Ildacer's gaze met Reefglamor's glare and only flinched a little.

"And you think this gives you some sway over me?"

"No, but I hoped that it might influence you." Ildacer hesitated. "If only a little."

Reefglamor waved a hand at him. A few minutes of the junior mage's prattle wouldn't mean much in the scheme of dangers that faced them. "Speak, but cogently and with brevity, and always with respect in mind. I lack even more patience than usual."

"Thank you, Senior. I believe you should rethink your decision to try to summon a vision about the Ravager. We've gone all these centuries without success in that regard."

"*I've* never before attempted it," Reefglamor pointed out. However, he hadn't with good reason. It was only the great danger he felt now that prompted him to make this decision.

"But others have," Ildacer hurried on. "Six that I can think of. Four were driven mad. One slew himself, and the final one was drawn into a gate that had never existed before or ever existed afterward. There have been no successes connected with attempting to learn more of the Ravager. It was those attempts that brought the number of High Mages so dangerously low in these past years."

Reefglamor considered the younger man's words. They carried only the truth. He spoke softly, persuasive instead of demanding for the first time in centuries. "The Time of Tempering is upon us. We've done as much as we can do in every other avenue we've had open to us. There lies ahead only this way."

"But you've outlawed this spell's use against the Ravager."

"Yes."

Ildacer appeared surprised. "You made the law."

"So it's only just that I break it." Reefglamor paused. "No one else had better dare."

Shaking his head in regret, Ildacer settled back in his chair and reached for the wine bladder on the table. He drank from it quickly, glancing out the cut crystal window that overlooked Sylkiir.

Reefglamor followed the other mage's gaze. Most of the homes glowed with the luminescent lichens. Though only two hundred feet below the Sea of Fallen Stars, not much light got through to the depths, and when night fell even elven vision didn't help much.

His house was built on the side of the hill overlooking the underwater valley where the city had been built. From there he could see the twisted coral spires of Deep Sashelas's temple where he'd spent so much of his life. He'd designed the god's temple, and helped shape the magics that had encouraged the coral growth that created the structure. Long-bodied fish and other sea creatures traversed the currents throughout the city, but no predators that would dare attack the sea elves finned through those depths. Sylkiir had been well warded against those.

"Do you remember how long it took us to grow the temple?" Reefglamor asked.

"Centuries," Ildacer answered. "And I remember all the hard work that went into the construction of it, all the mistakes that we made till we had it exactly right."

"It's beautiful."

"Yes."

"Yet," Reefglamor said, "the Ravager could come among us and destroy it in heartbeats. Nothing would stand to show the strength of our worship of Deep Sashelas. I find that intolerable."

"As do I."

"The Ravager's free again." Reefglamor looked back at the younger man. "You and I have both known it since we heard of the attack on Laakos' Reef in the Shining Sea nine years ago." The attack had taken place fourteen years ago, but the story of it hadn't reached Selu'Maraar and Sylkiir till five years later.

"That could have been a tale made up by the mermen," Ildacer objected. "An undersea quake, or perhaps they hadn't built their reef as well as they thought they had."

"The mermen went from there to Waterdeep," Reefglamor said.

"You never told me that."

Reefglamor knew the other mage was little surprised by that. He told his juniors only what he felt they needed to know when they needed to know it. "I only found out these past few days from a merman called Thraxos, who has his own mission here in Serôs. A merman shaman named Narros sent him here to bring the message to me, but this Thraxos's journey was a dangerous one and he had to depend on a human girl to get the word to me. Remember, even our legends of the Ravager, handed down by Deep Sashelas, say that the mermen will be the first to discover the Taleweaver, the human singer who will unite the histories of the world above and world below. The one who will find the way into that which was lost to us."

"The City of Destinies," Ildacer whispered reverently.

"Yes. All that once was to us and one day will be again."

"That doesn't mean the mermen of Laakos' Reef were the ones meant to discover the Taleweaver. There are many others."

Reefglamor fixed his colleague with his stare. "Doubt if you wish, but you'll only be a hermit crab hiding in its shell."

"You don't have any doubts? It has been fourteen years since their city was destroyed."

"Of course I have doubts," the Senior High Mage responded. "Unlike yours, though, mine haven't gone away. They've only grown larger. That's why I want to pursue this course in spite of all the risks inherent in it."

"You've said from the beginning that attempting to work a divination on the Ravager would be risking certain death," Ildacer said, "and it has."

"The Ravager has many protections left to him despite the punishment he's been given in the past," Reefglamor agreed. "Seeking him out in this manner isn't something to be lightly undertaken. He may be able to strike back along the spell I use. However, we need to know something at this point."

"Chancing your own fate isn't a good idea."

Reefglamor regarded the junior mage coolly. "I should risk someone else then?" They both knew from past experience that he would—if he thought it worth the risk.

"That's not what I said," Ildacer said quickly.

"No, but given the parameters of your statement, that's what you meant. And I would. If I felt any were better equipped to attempt this than I." Reefglamor turned his gaze back out through the window. "We've already risked much by using the selu'kiira on Jhanra Merlistar, Keryth Adofaer, and Talor Vurtalis. The memory gems have wrought great magic to bring them up to the level of High Mages these past thirteen years." Even then, that decision had not come easily, but the High Mages had wanted to be at full strength when the Ravager appeared.

"I know."

"You've done a good job with them," Reefglamor stated. Ildacer had been responsible for their training.

Surprise momentarily stole Ildacer's words. "Thank you, Senior."

Reefglamor faced him. "You know it is my way to seldom give praise."

"I know it well."

"Yet you overlook the obvious praise you're given this night. I trusted no one else with watching over me while I attempted this."

Ildacer nodded. "I understood that, Senior. I thank you for your trust, but I'm afraid that even I'm not good enough to protect you should anything go wrong."

"Argue though you may, I won't shirk from this. Events have been put into play. According to the merman Thraxos, the Ravager has already taken action against the surface world. Though it is not widely known yet, above water or below, sahuagin attacked Waterdeep two tendays ago. They were accompanied by all manner of sea creatures."

"You believe this to be the work of the Ravager?"

"Could it be anyone else?"

Ildacer held his gaze only a moment before looking away. Fear stamped into his features. "No. Of course not."

"That's why we need to know," Reefglamor said softly. "If there is any way to foretell where the Taleweaver may soon be, or discover who he is, I have to try. And if there's a way to discover the Ravager's whereabouts, I have to attempt that as well."

"There's nothing, then, that I may offer as argument in this?"

"Pharom Ildacer, I've argued with myself for days," Reefglamor said sternly. "Can you imagine a fiercer opponent?"

"No, Senior, truly I can not."

"Then prepare your wards that we may begin." Reefglamor already had his own in place. He ran his fingers over the white pearls in the gold bracer adorning his right wrist, the hand he'd given in service to his god Deep Sashelas, also known as Dolphin Prince and Sailor's Friend.

Long moments passed as Ildacer prepared, digging items from the kit he carried. He marked different colored symbols on the stone floor with the selection of oily gels from the writing packs the alu'tel'quessir had created. Since they'd chosen to live in the Sea of Fallen Stars after the Crown Wars that had torn apart the empire of the elves they'd had to design many things that would help them with their undersea life.

When the younger mage was finished, he looked at Reefglamor. "What do you have to offer?"

Attempting a vision called for the sacrifice of an item the caster cared about. Reefglamor's hand almost trembled as he took a clam-shell from a nearby shelf. He opened it slowly, revealing the contents.

"This." He took out a common spined urchin's shell and placed it gently on the table.

"That?" Ildacer's effort to not sound disbelieving went unrewarded.

Reefglamor touched the spined urchin's shell. "This was given to me by my wife on the day I met her," the old mage said, his voice surprisingly tight despite the centuries that had passed. "She thought I was full of my own worth, pompous even."

Graciously, and perhaps wisely, Ildacer didn't comment.

"She gave me this shell, plucked from the ground at our feet, as a token that I should remember worth is only in the eye of the person who perceives it. Those who perceive it in themselves oft fool first themselves." Reefglamor smiled at the memory. Their time together had been short. She'd died at his side, fighting the enemies they'd found while questing for one of the legendary elven devices he'd learned of. For all the long lives of the elves, they'd had scarcely a dozen years together, a heartbeat in time, actually. He'd never loved another woman.

"I'm sorry I never got the chance to meet her," Ildacer said.

"She was a remarkable woman."

"Perhaps the gift you offer is too generous."

Reefglamor looked at the younger mage. "I treasure nothing above this simple shell. So common in Serôs, yet there is not another like it in the entire world, above or below. Yet, at this moment, I can only hope that it is enough. This is strong magic I seek to employ, against a foe more powerful than we have ever known. The threat—by the fins of Deep Sashelas—the threat against all of Serôs has never been as potentially devastating. You know that."

"Yes."

Reefglamor closed his hand briefly around the shell, then pushed it to the center of the table and left it there. "Make yourself ready. This should be done."

Without another word, Ildacer bent to the task. He took the needed items from the kit he carried with him, then inscribed a circle and powerful symbols on the floor around Reefglamor. The younger mage used the different colored oily gels and added the necessary basilisk eyebrow, gum arabic, and whitewash.

Finished, Ildacer put away his gear, then stood inside the circle as well. "The circle is as strong as I can make it, Senior. Still, there is no saying how strong the Ravager's forces may be."

"We shall find out." Reefglamor bent to his own task, having his spell readied as well. He called upon Deep Sashelas, then followed his magic.

For a moment, Reefglamor thought the power of the spell had struck him blind. When he could see again, he studied the scenery around him. It was a surface city, but one he didn't recognize that bordered a river. He knew it was a river because he'd seen a few of them upon occasion.

Green sahuagin bodies looked almost black in the moonlight. Men, dwarves, and elves fought them. Ships were locked in combat out in the harbor.

This is Baldur's Gate, a quiet voice spoke quietly into Reefglamor's mind, sounding like the calm surge of an incoming tide riding over rock. *This is what will soon happen. The Taleweaver will be there.*

Excitement dawned inside Reefglamor. He didn't know if the voice belonged to Deep Sashelas, but he knew he was hearing it because of his god's will. "Can you show him to me?"

The battle continued, filled with the screams of dying men.

I cannot at this time. You've been told this so that you will know. Here, the Taleweaver will learn of where he is to meet you and come to the knowledge of the Sea of Fallen Stars.

The view faded from sight. Slowly, like a luminescent worm just coming to light, the second scene cleared. Reefglamor instantly recognized the cluster of clamshell-like buildings dug into the silt in the ocean floor.

This place you know, the voice said.

Telvanlu, the capital city of Naramyr, the Artisan State of Serôs. The old mage had visited there a number of times. Because of the shared blood between the elven cities, Naramyr and Selu'Maraar maintained good trade relations.

The Taleweaver will be here soon.

When? Reefglamor asked.

No answer came at first. *The possibilities are hazy. Perhaps early in Heartsong. Perhaps later. Perhaps never at all if the Ravager has his way.*

What will he look like?

An image formed beside one of the clamshell buildings. Reefglamor knew the Taleweaver was human, but the man's advanced age was obvious and shocking. The Taleweaver dressed simply in brown breeches and a green doublet. His head was shaved, making the silvery eyebrows over his dark eyes stand out even more. His skin was nut-brown, carrying the mark of a man long used to the sun and the elements. He carried a backpack and a stringed instrument in one hand that was bowl-shaped on one end and stuck out straight and true on the other. Reefglamor thought he recognized it as a yarting. Strains of music, haunting and almost familiar, echoed around him.

Who is he?

The Taleweaver. That's all I'm given to know.

Accepting the vision's inability to render anything further, Reefglamor took another tack. *Can you tell me of the Ravager?* Instantly, Reefglamor felt an unaccustomed chill flow over him, filling his veins. Serôs carried an even temperature year round despite the seasons. He'd never felt so cold in all his long years.

Choosing that path leads to danger.

Which is more dangerous? Reefglamor pressed. *Trying to know, or living in ignorance?*

The seer takes all the risks.

Then let the decision be mine. Show me when the Ravager will enter Serôs to bring the death and destruction that are his companions that I may know when the time is come.

Oily black filled Reefglamor's vision. He started to suffocate, unable to draw sea water in through his gills. Then his vision cleared, revealing a section of ocean floor that he couldn't recognize. In the next instant, roiling red liquid flame burned through the depths. It washed over Reefglamor with cyclonic force and brought a rush of searing heat that cooked him. In that whirling maelstrom, he felt something else searching for him, but the effort was weak and Ildacer's spell brought him away.

Gasping, choking on the sea water that flooded in through his gills, Reefglamor opened his eyes back in his sanctum. He glanced down at his hands, finding small blisters over his pale blue skin. The Ravager's power was incredible. Even from that time in the future, the Ravager had been able to strike back along the vision. Only his weakened state had prevented it from being lethal, but was the Ravager weakened now? Or was it from that time in the future?

Ildacer looked at him worriedly, crossing over to the older man. "What is it?"

"The sea," Reefglamor stated with hoarse effort. "The sea was burning!"

4 Kythorn, the Year of the Gauntlet

3

Jherek stood on the twilight-shadowed docks of Baldur's Gate and drew in the dank air from the River Chionthar. He missed the salty tang of the ocean, but it was the first time he'd felt close to home since leaving Athkatla.

He stood nearly six feet tall, a lean youth of nineteen heavily muscled in the arms and shoulders from years of hard work. Dust still covered his breeches and shirt under the cracked leather armor he wore. Sweat and grit had plastered his light brown hair to his head, causing it to hang heavily to his shoulders. Pale gray fire lighted his haunted eyes.

Baldur's Gate occupied a crescent shaped section along the river. Four dry-dock slips held skeletons of ships under construction. Normally the crews knocked off at eveningfeast, only working occasionally on late jobs or specially commissioned ones.

Now, work crews filled all four slips. Jherek had heard they were working night crews by lanterns as well, trying to meet the demand for ships from merchants who'd lost vessels to sahuagin and pirate raids. The watch had taken over one of the slips as well, turning out ships for the navy.

The river lapped at the dock pilings and the cargo boats at anchor in the harbor. Men worked the ships steadily, cursing in loud voices while cargo chiefs and harbormasters yelled at them as well. The cacophony of sound made him feel homesick, made his heart ache, and twisted his stomach in sour bile.

His home lay upon the sea even more so than in the house where Madame Iitaar read her divinations and had given an orphan boy hearth and love. He missed her, and missed Malorrie as well. Now, with the harsh traveling behind him for the moment and no threat of goblinkin

274

roaring down on him, he felt that loss more strongly than ever. More than that, he felt lost.

As long as I have a home, you'll have a home.

Madame Iitaar had told him that shortly before she'd sent him packing on *Breezerunner*, a cargo ship bound for Waterdeep. Only the ill luck that had marked him since his birth had continued to follow him, and events had gone awry in the City of Coin. He'd gotten kicked off *Breezerunner* for fighting with a crew member, and was forced to join up with a caravan to make his way to Baldur's Gate. All that to follow the destiny that lay before him. Madame Iitaar had seen in a vision that he was supposed to go to Baldur's Gate. Now that he was here, he had no idea what to do next. In Athkatla, he'd had a goal. Now there was nothing, only the emptiness and uncertainty stretching before him.

He watched the boats plying the river. The smaller cargo vessels managed the docks with ease while barges worked the larger ships, off-loading the cargo then ferrying it to the docks. Lights from lanterns reflected from the dark waters, held by sailors moving across decks and hung from pole arms.

There weren't as many ships as Jherek remembered from other trips to Baldur's Gate. With the sahuagin activity still at a frenzied peak, though, that was to be expected. From the moment he'd arrived in the city with the caravan, he'd heard reports of ships that had been taken, and how Waterdeep was rebuilding from the attack on her harbor. Everyone held the opinion that the sea was quickly becoming an unsafe place. Many people swore they'd never venture there again.

Jherek couldn't imagine never again sitting in a crow's nest or hanging in the rigging with an ocean spread out around him, being pushed by the wind while fighting it at the same time. Yet, for now, that seemed to be his fate. For a moment anger burned away the heaviness in his heart, but it didn't last. The anger was never enough to burn away the sadness that often filled him. There was no one save himself that he could blame for his misfortune.

"Ye're a sailor, aren't ye, lad?"

Jherek's hand strayed down unconsciously to the long sword he wore in a sash at his waist. He turned toward the voice. With all the overland travel now going on between the cities to replace the lost shipping lanes, goblinkin, dopplegangers, and raiders had infiltrated the cities and the wildernesses between. Opportunities abounded for those on both sides of the law.

"Don't mean ye no harm, lad. Just making conversation."

The dwarf stood at the railing to the left and behind Jherek. He leaned on his elbows, working a pinch of pipeweed into the bowl of his pipe. He was short and broad, his face filled with unruly gray whiskers that stuck out in all directions. His breeches and shirt had seen better days, and the thin coat he wore against the night's chill had been patched repeatedly.

"My apologies," Jherek said. "I meant no disrespect."

He didn't take his hand from the sword. He was used to carrying a cutlass instead of the long sword, but Frauk, the caravan master, had insisted Jherek use the more conventional weapon because he'd wanted all his men armed similarly. Malorrie had schooled him in the long sword, but Jherek was most comfortable with the cutlass.

"None taken." The dwarf pulled a twist of straw from his pocket, shoved it into a nearby lantern on a pole, then used it to light his pipe. "Just noticed that hungry look on yer face. Mayhap I should have kept my big mouth shut. Sometimes a man don't need his thoughts interrupted."

"Not these thoughts," Jherek said. "I'm grateful for the interruption."

"How long since ye've been at sea?" the dwarf asked.

"Longer than I care to think about," Jherek admitted.

"Ye miss a ship. Ye get used to her, get used to the way she's always moving, always passionate with a wind that gets a sailor's blood up."

"Aye," Jherek said, immediately warming to the kindred spirit the dwarf exuded. "Are you with one of these ships?"

The dwarf shook his head. "Been a damn landlubber off and on for the last five years," he said, reaching down to slap his right leg. It thunked hollowly.

Jherek saw the wooden peg sticking out of the breeches.

"Lost it to a hungry shark what was a faster swimmer than meself, even properly spirited as I was at the time."

The dwarf grinned wryly and a chill that was more than the cool air coming in off the river ghosted across Jherek's neck and shoulders. During the trip up from Athkatla, he'd dreamed of a great shark that had pursued him until each dawn had awakened him.

"I'm sorry," Jherek offered.

The dwarf flashed him a tight, practiced grin that lacked mirth. "I yet live. The sages say that while a man still lives all things are possible. Mayhap I don't ship out as often as I've a mind to, but I still get to go. Right now, I'm working on one of the ship's crews down in the dry docks. Me shift just ended and I thought I'd smoke a bit before finding a bite to eat."

Jherek's own stomach growled in frustration. He'd lost weight while hard traveling with the caravan. The work taxed him and he'd not had much of an appetite.

"Is the Elfsong yet open?" The dwarf asked.

Jherek remembered that famous tavern from past travels. On the first night *Breezerunner* had put in to Baldur's Gate with Jherek aboard, Finaren had treated him to dinner at the Elfsong. Ilmater's tears, but Jherek missed the old sea captain too.

"Aye," the dwarf answered. "Though it might be busy come this time of night."

"I'll stand you to a bowl of stew if you'd like," Jherek said.

"I'm no cripple, lad, and quite able to take care of meself, thank ye kindly."

Jherek felt flustered. "I only meant it as an offer." He hesitated, not wanting to admit that he wanted the company. He'd bonded with none of the hard men in Frauk's crew. "I don't like to eat alone."

The dwarf squinted up at him and asked, "Where ye hail from, lad?"

"Velên," Jherek answered.

"Aye, the city o' ghosts." The dwarf nodded and ran his fingers through his beard in contemplation. "Seen a few of them there on occasion meself. Ye are flesh and blood, ain't ye, lad?"

"Aye." Having grown up with the ghosts in the city, and having been schooled by Malorrie, a phantom himself, Jherek took them as a matter of course.

"Just checking. I've grown somewhat more careful in me old age. I don't like to eat by meself either, so I'll let ye stand me to a bowl of Lady Alyth's famous stew if ye'll let me stand ye to a drink."

Jherek stepped over, held out his hand, and said, "I'm Malorrie of Velen, journeyman shipwright and able-bodied sailor."

He hated to lie, but was afraid that stories of the young sailor Jherek, who bore the tattoo of one of the Sword Coast's most notorious pirate crews, might have beat him to Baldur's Gate.

"Khlinat Ironeater," the dwarf replied, clasping Jherek's arm in a viselike grip, "of the Daggerford Ironeater blacksmith clan. Able-bodied sailor and gemologist. Proud to meet ye, lad."

"Aye," Jherek said. "I've heard of the Ironeater clan. The cargo ship I crewed on transported clasps, hinges, shields, and other things they turn out in Daggerford."

"That's them," Khlinat stated proudly, puffing out his chest. "Near to busted my old da's heart when he found I'd fallen in love with the sailor's life. Seafaring is not something most dwarves would be about if they followed their natures, ye know."

Jherek nodded. He'd only heard of a few dwarven sailors and seen even fewer.

"Well, come on then, swabbie," the dwarf said. "Time's a-wasting and we're going to need to shoulder our way in amongst sullen and starved hostiles if we're to get our victuals this night. Men are working hard here as a result of them sea devil raids." Khlinat turned smartly on his peg leg, the wood thumping against the docks. He called out to a passing lamp boy who held a lit lantern at the end of a stout pole. "Lad, we'd be after hiring ye to guide us to the Elfsong Tavern."

As Jherek followed the dwarf and the lamp boy through the dark streets of Baldur's Gate, he found he was looking forward to sharing eveningfeast with the dwarf.

Traveling with the caravan had been arduous work. They'd herded wagons through broken lands while racing the sun and pitching camp against the coming night. In between, they'd fought off the numerous orc and goblin hordes that had come out of the Cloud Peaks and the Wood of Sharp Teeth to prey on the fat caravans that were overfilled with cargo and understaffed by mercenary warriors.

Frauk, the caravan master, had told them that two out of every seven caravans were taking huge losses or being captured by the raids. Pirating took the wherewithal to get a ship, by purchase or by capture, but anyone with a knife in hand could become a raider on the land. Fewer warriors wanted to take the risks inherent in overland travel because it was getting as dangerous as the seaways.

That was why the merchants had been so generous to Frauk when they'd reached Baldur's Gate. After starting out in Athkatla broke and leaving the last of his coin with the priests of Lathander there for tending his wounds, Jherek now found himself quite flush.

They followed Bindle Street south along the docks as the lamp boy weaved in among the laborers and night crowd that had gathered around the smaller offices where black market business was done between the large warehouses. An uneasy feeling draped Jherek, and he stopped to look back into the harbor to his right.

In the distance he spotted the old Seatower of Balduran thrusting up on the opposite side of the harbor. It housed a barracks and naval base, part dungeon and part fortress. Men moved along the ramparts. The twilight dusk still showed a few yellow tendrils that looked like curdled eggs under the gathering black storm clouds. Ships cluttered the harbor, their masts naked of sailcloth.

"What's the matter with ye, swabbie?" Khlinat asked.

Jherek shook his head, not knowing, but definitely aware of the crawling sensation moving along the back of his neck. Then, against the shadowed line of the river, he spotted ships. He guessed by the cut of their shape that they were the small cargo ships and cogs that plied the River Chionthar. Their sailcloth didn't reflect the moonlight, colored black so they would be harder to see.

"Do you see them?"

"Aye," the dwarf growled. "These old eyes may not be what they once was, but they see them ships right enough." He hollered at the lamp boy. "Make haste, ye little vagabond, we've got to find a member of the watch."

The boy took the lead, saying, "They're keeping ships in the harbor." His quick steps left Khlinat behind.

The dwarf glanced at Jherek and said, "Have a smart step there, swabbie. If'n the watch hasn't spotted them scoundrels and thought about the chance of trouble, somebody needs to tell them."

Jherek nodded and ran after the lamp boy, catching him easily. The lantern jerked at the end of the pole, throwing shadows to race crazily around them and warning people ahead of them to step aside. The troubled feeling inside the young sailor increased, becoming a gnawing in the pit of his stomach.

The lamp boy raced onto the next dock leading out into the harbor. Prowling cats scattered before him, yowling and hissing their displeasure.

"There!" The youth flung a hand forward.

Jherek spotted the black watch flag with its vertical red stripe in the stern of a converted cargo ship tied up at the dock. Warriors clothed in the black armor of the Baldur's Gate Watch occupied the deck. A few of them had already noticed the black-sailed ships.

"Halt!" a watchman cried, vaulting from the ship to the dock. His sword cleared leather with a sibilant *whisk*. The lamp boy's light flickered over his nervous features.

Jherek drew up at once, lifting his hands at his side, and said, "I mean no harm. I only came to tell you about the ships out on the river."

"We've already seen them," the watch guard said. "They'll be addressed before they're allowed to put in."

As Jherek watched, two other watch ships unfurled their sails and skimmed out into the harbor like low-flying geese. Ship's crew quickly passed out lanterns, lit them, and hung them from the ship to make it more visible. They drew shouted curses from a barge that was nearly swamped in their passing. Sword steel gleamed on the deck.

The uneasy feeling grew stronger inside Jherek, but he controlled it as the two watch ships sailed on an interception course.

"Cast away!" someone called from the ship in front of Jherek.

The watch guard raced to the stern to the mooring cleats. He unwound the thick hawser ropes while another man unfastened the one holding the prow. Sailcloth cracked as it ran up the masts and filled with wind. The watch members threw themselves back at their ship and clambered aboard. The ship's crew quickly passed out lanterns, lighting their ship.

Jherek stood by and watched, feeling at a loss that he wasn't able to join the coming battle. If it came to that, he amended. He felt his sword already in his hand, though, hard and sturdy.

Khlinat thumped up beside him, his breath ragged from the effort. He carried two hand axes and scowled at the approaching line of ships. "Yonder blows an ill wind, I'll wager."

Jherek didn't disagree.

"At least them's good, honest pirates and not them scaled, black-hearted devils what's got the taste for man flesh."

4

Glancing around the harbor, Jherek saw that most everyone nearby had spotted the black-sailed cargo ships. The vessels still ran dark, carrying no lanterns at all.

"Gives a man the shivers," Khlinat said, "them running in the black. Heard stories of the seas giving up their dead upon occasion, lifting ships up from the bottom and crewing them with corpses out to sacrifice them to dark gods thought long lost."

A crowd started to gather along the dock. Men brandished weapons. At the far end of the dock on the eastern side a barge towed across the huge chain that was used to block the harbor against unwelcome ship traffic. The massive links glinted in the moonlight and torchlight as they twisted and trailed through the water.

Even as the barge got the chain up across the mouth of the harbor and the watch ships closed on the black-sailed vessels, a gray cloud gathered suddenly and scudded in from the west like a heavy, fast-moving fog. The mass whirled and turned outward, continuing to spread as it came.

Jherek had seen plenty of fogs roll in from the sea while he'd lived in Velen, and he was certain this was no ordinary one. Before he could voice a warning, the sky exploded into harsh yellow flames that raced outward and dropped in sheets onto many of the ships in the harbor.

As the barge carrying the heavy harbor chain was about to reach the Seatower, a giant moray eel erupted from the water. Lantern light from the watch members aboard the barge illuminated the great creature. Nearly twenty feet long, though most of its body remained below the waterline, the moray eel was covered in thick, mottled, brown, leathery skin. Lighter spots showed along the broad chin under a mouthful of wicked incisors that overlapped its upper and lower lips in a cruel, merciless grin.

Despite its unexpected arrival, the moray eel still moved slowly. The watch members had a chance to ready their swords and get a few blows in as it lunged forward. The great jaws gaped open and seized a man's head and shoulders. Continuing its forward lunge, the moray eel overturned the barge then dived back below the surface with its prize.

Men flew into the water from the overturned barge. Some disappeared immediately beneath the black water. Others tried to swim but didn't get far as jaws or claws seized them and savagely yanked them under. Several screams drowned out in horrified gurgles.

Hoarse warning shouts rose all along the docks, but Jherek knew it was too little, too late. The invaders were even now closing the distance on the docks.

The sky flared again, spreading fire over the harbor. Some of it fell onto ships and set the sailcloth, rigging, and decks ablaze. More pools of fire fell into the harbor and floated on the water. A cluster of flames hit a small knot of people only ten feet from Jherek and fed on them greedily. Bystanders tried to beat out the flames but appeared to have little effect. Men died screaming in agony.

"Damned magery," Khlinat yelped, covering his face with one arm.

Another patch of flames hit the dock so close to Jherek that he felt the heat. He'd caught sight of the flames plummeting toward them out of his peripheral vision and shouted a warning. Khlinat had no problem getting out of the way, but the flames splashed across the lamp boy and caught his breeches on fire.

Panicked, the boy started to run back down the dock but the air only fed the flames. The deadly wreath climbed his pants.

Moving quickly, Jherek caught the boy, wrapping one arm around the youth. Wheeling, he threw both of them over the dock's side, making sure they had the necessary distance from the pilings.

They hit the water and went under. The dark water took only a moment to extinguish the flames that fought against the dousing brine. Jherek kept hold of the boy in case he couldn't swim. Still holding onto his sword, the young sailor kicked them back toward the surface.

Jherek whipped his head, slinging the water and hair out of his eyes. "Are you all right, boy?"

"Yes. I think so." His voice quivered.

Glancing up at the docks, Jherek watched the foggy cloud breaking up. The damage to the docks was already extensive, and the fires weren't being put out very quickly. The boy struggled in his grasp, pulling at his legs.

"Are you burned?" Jherek asked.

"I don't think so."

"If I let you go, can you swim?"

"Like a duck," the lamp boy promised.

Jherek let him go, watching for a moment as the boy kicked away and swam in a crude dog paddle that seemed serviceable enough.

The boy turned around, his face going pale and even more frightened. "Behind you!"

Jherek tried to turn, feeling the malignant darkness behind him as well as the water rippling against his back. Before he could do more than start the motion, he felt the scaly sahuagin arm snake around his neck and drag him under the water.

Even as he went down, Jherek heard a familiar roar that triggered a wash of fear that filled him. The loud scream of anger and challenge was artificial, but it sounded enough like a bunyip that there could be no mistake. The hoarse roar told him one of the black-sailed ships carried his father, Bloody Falkane, one of the most feared and vicious of the cold-blooded pirates of the Nelanther Isles.

Fear ran through the young sailor, not of the sahuagin who held him, but of the man who'd sired him. He bore his father's mark on his arm, indelibly put there with magic and ink, and carried the cursed fate that resulted from his father's sins.

The bunyip scream sounded again as the thickly muscled arm tightened around Jherek's neck and pulled him farther down.

Laaqueel tried in vain to shut out the keening roar of the bunyip. The malenti priestess stood in the stern of *Bent Tankard*, the cog the sahuagin had taken only two days ago under their new king's orders.

Wind whipped through the rigging and the sailcloth fluttered as the captain called out orders to his trimming crew while still others prepared to board the watch ships that had come to intercept them.

A few of the sahuagin weren't completely unversed in handling surface ships. They'd taken some and used them as decoys to attack other ships in the past.

The bunyip roar blared again.

Glancing across the distance separating them from the lead ship, Laaqueel made out Bloody Falkane's tall frame striding across the deck. The pirate captain was a striking man, tall and slender but packed with wiry muscle. Even now his oiled black hair was neatly combed back. He wore a mustache and goatee. Moonlight glinted from the silver hoop earrings he wore in both ears, as well as the other bits of jewelry. He wore a silk shirt of darkest blue and black breeches tucked into rolled boots that matched his shirt.

Laaqueel knew the bunyip roar came from a device Falkane had ordered made and carried on his own ship. The bunyip was a freshwater creature that was at first glance very sharklike in appearance, but the shaggy black hair that covered its body and the long, flowing mane set it apart.

The malenti didn't know why the pirate had chosen the bunyip as his standard, except for the keening roar that instilled fear into most people who heard it.

She watched the fires scattered around the harbor spread only slightly. Baldur's Gate was constructed mostly of stone and usually stayed damp because of the climate. This city wouldn't burn as Waterdeep had, but it had less chance of standing.

The cog slid into the harbor, following Bloody Falkane's craft. Six other ships, all loaded with pirates from the Nelanther Isles, followed them. The deck didn't pitch much, but the movement was still foreign to her after spending nearly all her life working with the sea's currents instead of against them.

Sudden lightning flashed from the harbor, racing in a horizontal line until it touched the mainmast of Falkane's cog. Wood splintered with a thunderous crack and embers blew up in a flurry from the wood. Sheared, the mainmast started to topple toward the deck, then got caught up in the rigging and sailcloth.

"Cut that damned mast free!" Falkane roared, rushing up to the stern castle himself.

Sailors moved quickly to do his bidding, clambering into the rigging with long knives in their teeth. Leaping from the stern castle, the pirate captain caught hold of the rigging and climbed through it with the agility of a monkey.

Despite all the truly monstrous things Laaqueel had heard about Bloody Falkane, she had to admit the man was good at his chosen profession. She watched him hack at the rigging holding the mainmast, calling out directions to his crew. In seconds, the tall mast started toppling over the side, its descent controlled by the rigging the pirates cut expertly so that it didn't land on the deck.

An arrow thudded solidly into the railing, missing Laaqueel's hand by inches and drawing her attention back to her own affairs. She drew up the heavy sahuagin crossbow she held and sighted on the boatload of Baldur's Gate defenders bearing down on the ship she was on.

Carved out of whalebone and strung with braided gut, the weapon was cable of firing above or below the water. She gazed down the greenish-gray quarrel shaft that had been chipped from claw coral that grew in hard, straight lengths. Hard as the bronze the surface worlders used, it was also razor sharp even on the sides. The hollowed shark's tooth serving as the arrowhead was filled with poison and was designed to break off inside a target. Even if the sharp quarrel didn't hit a killing spot, the poison ensured the kill.

With the approaching boat less than thirty feet out, Laaqueel fired the crossbow. The quarrel flashed forward and filled a man's eyesocket. He screamed and went down, brushing at the blood gushing onto his face. When poison stilled his heart, his companions had to shove his dead weight from them.

"To me!" Laaqueel cried to the sahuagin behind her.

They bounded forward at once. Only a few of them had crossbows.

The claw coral quarrels embedded in the boat and the men, snapped off in shields, breaking the staggered ranks the defenders of Baldur's Gate had tried to form.

Laaqueel had enough time to reload and get one more shot off, striking a man and piercing his leather armor. The impact of the quarrel twisted him sideways and threw him from the boat. Instantly, a dorsal fin cut the water, zooming toward the flailing swimmer. The malenti priestess didn't know if the poison or the shark got the man first.

The boats collided with a shattering thump that brought the smaller one up out of the water. Some of the men were already in motion. They stabbed spears upward, tangling the sahuagin tridents.

Braced as she was and expecting the collision, Laaqueel nearly fell. She regained her footing with difficulty and tossed the crossbow aside. She also loosened the thigh quiver of quarrels and kicked it away. Taking her trident up, she turned to face the invaders.

One of the other pirate ships raced past. The archers aboard unleashed a brief volley at the men in the watch boat. Then it went on by, closing on the harbor. Even at eight ships, the pirates weren't strong enough to take apart the defenses of Baldur's Gate, but they weren't alone. Iakhovas's magery had seen to that.

Rubbery ropes of arms shot up from the water without warning, wrapped around the watch ship, and yanked it almost to a full stop. Men tumbled from the ship, pitched clear by the unexpected seizure. A mast-mounted lantern smashed against the ship's deck and splashed a long blaze of fire that ate into the wood. Before the ship's crew recovered, sahuagin surfaced and slit their throats with long claws. Most of the crew died without a chance to defend themselves.

On the docks, sahuagin slithered up from the port and ripped into the citizens gripped in the thrall of fear. In seconds they were walking over corpses, hunting out fresh kills. Their fierce cries of bloodlust and savage joy rang through the alleys of Baldur's Gate and over the port. Men raced forward trying to protect loved ones or friends, and died as sahuagin tridents knifed through their stomachs or ripped through their lungs. Other sahuagin threw fishhook-embedded nets over small groups, then pulled them into the water and beneath the surface to drown them like rats.

Even as Laaqueel faced the men trying to swarm up the cog, the malenti was aware of the dozen or more giant crayfish that surfaced near the west docks around the Seatower and wreaked havoc among the Flaming Fist ships that tried to put out into the harbor. It was the mercenaries of the Flaming Fist who ran Baldur's Gate, and they were coming to the aid of the watch.

Fully eight feet long and equipped with huge pincers nearly a yard in length, the crayfish plucked men from the docks and the ships. Their hard, mottled brown, chitinous carapaces stood against sword blade, arrow, and spear. Their huge antennae whipped the air in a frenzy. The great pincers cut into their victims, sometimes sawing them in half. Other creatures Iakhovas controlled through arcane means swam beneath the river, working with the sahuagin to take the harbor.

Holding the trident in both hands, Laaqueel thrust the tines into a man's face, forcing him back off the side of the cog. Blood spilled across the deck from the man she wounded as well as sahuagin and other surface dwellers. The planks grew slippery.

A large man in chain mail armor and a thick helmet heaved himself over the railing. Scars decorated his arms and face. He carried a huge warhammer in one hand and a lighted lantern in the other. He scowled at the sahuagin, fixing his hateful gaze on Laaqueel.

"By the precious left hand of Tyr Grimjaws, I don't know how come you to be with all these deep devils, elf, but you're gonna regret it."

The warrior swung the lantern over his head, then brought it crashing down on the deck. The oil ran in a pool, and the flame from the burning wick chased it, starting a blaze that stood a foot high. Startled by the flame, already aware of the way it was quickly drying her skin, Laaqueel backed away. The other sahuagin did too, leaving enough room for seven other warriors to clamber onto the deck.

The big warrior took his hammer in both hands and said, "I'm Fyidler Tross, a sergeant of the Flaming Fist, and I'm gonna send you back into Umberlee's cold embrace myself!"

He came at her, the hammer raised high over his head.

Even as the water closed over his head and the darkness sucked him down, Jherek tried to get a grip on the sahuagin's arm. The creature's strength was incredible, but Malorrie's training had included ways to make joints work against their owners, and made the young sailor aware of the weaknesses of a hold.

The moonlight pooled silver against the harbor water overhead, allowing him to see the sahuagin's hand as the sea devil flicked out its claws. Clicking and whistling sounded in Jherek's ears, warring with the thumping of his own heart. Two other shapes slid through the water, closing in.

The young sailor thrust his sword up, blocking the fierce sweep of claws at his face. The blade bit into the sea devil's forearm. Jherek brought the edge down, ripping into the flesh. Blood burst into the water.

The sahuagin whistled shrilly and clicked madly, giving voice to the agony that gripped it. Taking advantage of the moment, Jherek ran his empty hand down his side, then thrust up in the hollow inside the sea devil's restraining arm. The hold broke, allowing Jherek to go free.

The two approaching shapes glided into view, becoming trident-bearing sahuagin. They streaked for the dockside as they bore down on Jherek. One of them flipped in the water, making a full circle then coming down from above.

Jherek met the blow with his sword, angling it in between the trident's tines. He was aware of the second unwounded sahuagin streaking in for his stomach, intending to meet him if he avoided the attack of the first.

Holding the sword firmly, Jherek locked the blade against the trident and let the first sahuagin drive him down. The second sahuagin angled by overhead, moving quickly in his headlong rush. The trident missed Jherek by scarce inches.

At home in the water, twisting his body like a dolphin, the young sailor reached above and caught the passing sahuagin's harness. His fingers knotted in the woven seaweed strands. He kicked out as the sea devil's momentum carried him along, adding to his speed, disengaging his sword from the trident.

Before the sahuagin he'd caught hold of could turn, Jherek pulled on the harness and swam around behind the sea devil. He couldn't strike the sahuagin in the back, though. He couldn't bring himself to be so callous and so unfair. He waited for an opportunity.

His opponent clawed the water frantically, flipping over and stopping almost immediately. That turned out to be an even greater mistake. It allowed Jherek to plunge the sword into its stomach and rip upward. Still, as death claimed it, the sea devil managed to catch Jherek in the face with one foot.

The ebony claws raked fire along Jherek's face, narrowly missing his right eye. He recoiled, momentarily disoriented as blood swirled up and clouded his vision. The moon was nearly obscured by the dark water as it was, and the blood made it even harder to see.

The blood didn't blind the sahuagin, Jherek knew. They had the ability to sense movement. He kicked against the dead sea devil, pushing himself toward the surface. His lungs ached for air.

Past the blood cloud, Jherek spotted the wounded sahuagin trying fitfully to stop the flow of blood from its stump. The sea devil's shrieking whistles pealed through the water. The young sailor kicked out again, nearing the surface, glancing around to try to find the third sahuagin.

Only moonlight kissing the crystalline facets of the sea devil's chipped-coral trident saved Jherek's life. He spotted his attacker closing in from the right, shoving the trident forward. Knowing that grabbing the weapon would only lacerate his hand, the young sailor twisted violently in the water, knowing in his heart it was too late and he was about to feel the trident buried in his stomach.

The tines grazed his sodden leather armor, ripping through it and branding his stomach with cold pain. Jherek continued to move, wrapping himself around the sea devil in a wrestling hold with his legs twined around his opponent's. He looped his free hand under the sahuagin's arm and locked his palm behind the creature's head even as the sea devil locked his clawed fist around Jherek's sword wrist.

Instinctively, wanting to take advantage of the power it held in the water, the sahuagin dived, going deeper quickly.

Jherek's lungs burned from lack of air and everything in him cried out to let go of the sahuagin and swim for the surface. As fast a swimmer as he was, though, he was fairly certain he'd never make the distance before the sea devil overtook him. He bent to the task at hand, putting more pressure against the sahuagin's head. The neck bent slowly, like working iron, proof of the sahuagin's great strength.

The sahuagin's whistles became strained. Jherek felt his vision fading, knowing he didn't have much longer before the lack of air started draining his strength. He kept the pressure on, finally feeling the sahuagin's neck muscles give.

The sea devil's neck broke with a crack that echoed dully in the water.

Releasing the limp corpse, Jherek turned and swam for the surface. His vision closed in on itself, starting to blot out the patch of moonlight he aimed for. His hand broke through the water and he kicked himself after it.

Light swept toward him as soon as his face cleared the water. He had a brief impression of men standing along the dock, then a gaff pole shoved toward his head. He jerked away, letting the cruel gaff hook slice into the water near him.

"Umberlee take yer eyes, ye thickheaded mutton!" Khlinat roared.

Treading water, Jherek saw the dwarf push his way through the crowd.

A surly man with graying side whiskers shot the dwarf a nasty look and said, "I saw a sahuagin down there, I tell you."

"Mayhap ye did," the dwarf agreed vehemently, "but that there ain't no slithering sea beastie." He crouched, offering his hand to Jherek. "Come up here, swabbie, and let's be after having ye out of the drink now."

Jherek caught the dwarf's hand, then found himself almost lifted from the water by Khlinat's strength alone. He scrambled, finding his footing on the dock with his water-filled boots.

"You did see a sahuagin," Jherek told the man. "There were three of them."

"Three, swabbie?" Khlinat said, peering into the water and fisting his axes. "And ye did say *were*."

The crowd along the dock drew back.

Jherek nodded, locking his hands behind his head to get his breath back more quickly. He glanced out in the harbor and saw the scattered fires. The pirate ships had invaded the harbor now, fanning out in a practiced move that put their onboard archers within range of other ships as well as the docks. Fire arrows blurred through the air, striking ships and occasionally breaking through building windows to land inside. Twisting clouds of smoke above several of the buildings showed that fires had started inside.

The surly man with the gaff hook shook his head and said, "That's a pretty tale you weave, boy, but I'm not going to believe a stripling like you could kill three sahuagin—and in the water yet."

"Only two," Jherek replied. "I cut the hand off another."

He took a fresh grip on his sword. Out in the harbor, a giant water spider clambered up from below and attacked a dock crew trying to cast off lines. Twelve feet across, the spider reared up on its four back legs and seized two victims with the front four. Before it had a chance to completely devour its screaming prey, ten more spiders bobbed to the surface and scurried over the docks.

A squad of sahuagin warriors rose up from the water and grabbed hold of the pilings. They pulled themselves up while others treaded water and threw javelins into the crowd. Propelled by the powerful sea devils' muscles, the slim, chipped-bone javelins often penetrated more than one victim. Still more sahuagin leaped up from the water long enough to throw their deadly nets. Over a dozen people were pulled into the water and sank without a trace. Two of the nearby water spiders dived after them.

Pressing forward, Khlinat engaged the first sahuagin to place a webbed foot on the dock.

"Have at ye, then," the dwarf growled.

He whirled the hand axes before him, gripping them midway up the hafts. His furious onslaught battered through the sea devil's defenses and turned the trident aside. In another moment, he stretched up and buried one of the hand axes at the base of the sahuagin's throat. The lights dimmed in the oily black eyes, but there were plenty more to take that sahuagin's place.

Jherek joined Khlinat, lending his sword arm, feeling his wounds burn. Blood still flowed from the cut beside his eye, threatening to blind him. He wiped the blood from his face with his sleeve.

Khlinat kicked his peg leg up to the center of the dead sahuagin's chest, then pushed his opponent off the hand axe and back into the water.

"We can't hold this position," Jherek told him, blocking trident thrusts with his sword.

The motions came swiftly and certainly to him as they always did. Malorrie had trained him well, giving him one of the first instances of confidence he'd ever known.

"I know it, swabbie," the dwarf replied, "but we'll hold it long enough mayhap for them what's got heart to set up a skirmish line we can fall back to. Just don't go getting yerself killed afore we've got a chance to make our grand escape."

Jherek gave himself over to the battle, fighting past the homesickness and uncertainty. If the destiny he'd been given was to die here, this night, then he was going to see that it was done rightly and well. Malorrie had trained him to always sell his life dearly.

He batted a trident aside with a deft move of his wrist, setting himself up for a lightning riposte that spilled the sahuagin's life's blood from its throat. When the creature grabbed its throat, suddenly more interested in staying alive than in fighting, Jherek grabbed the dying sea devil and used it as a shield.

"Now, swabbie!" Khlinat yelled.

Taking a step back, getting a brief respite from the other sahuagin by hurling their dead comrade among them, Jherek glanced at the end of the dock where men had shoved cargo crates into a defensive line.

"Quick as you can!" Khlinat turned and followed his own advice, sprinting for the crates.

Jherek didn't hesitate. He deflected a pair of thrusts from two different tridents, took a step to the side, and cut the hamstrings of both legs on a third sea devil as the creature tried to turn and face him. Wheeling, drawing his blade back, he strode forward, putting a shoulder into the sahuagin's midriff and knocking it back into the others.

Slipping in the blood covering the dock for only a moment, Jherek got his feet under him and ran.

A dozen more sahuagin climbed over the railing behind him. Glancing down the quay, he saw the swarm of sea devils pulling up onto the docks. Weapons gleamed in the moonlight and from the fires that were spreading through the warehouses.

Praying to summon the power given her by obedience to Sekolah, Laaqueel held up her palm and thrust it toward the big surface dweller rushing at her with his upraised hammer. She felt the molten heat leave her hand. It only caused a slight visible ripple as it passed.

The spell struck Fyidler Tross with physical impact and dropped the big Flaming Fist mercenary to his knees. He screamed in pain, trying desperately to hang onto his warhammer. Huge blisters covered his flesh, bursting as they filled to capacity, then filling again the way the malenti had seen surface dwellers fry their eggs.

He called on his gods in a faltering voice, then crumpled to the deck, already dead. The other mercenaries gave his death no heed, absolutely fearless in their attack. They engaged the sahuagin with bloodthirsty enthusiasm, yelling curses and impugning their heritage.

Laaqueel set herself, regretting that the battle had to take place on the ship's deck. She was much more at home in the water where she had the opportunity to attack from above or below instead of merely in a horizontal line. Most surface dwellers never knew how truly intricate the act of battle could be.

Holding the trident in both hands, she blocked a swordsman's overhand sweep. The blade struck sparks from her trident haft while another man closed in from her left. He'd intended to take advantage of the diversion his comrade created. Instead, Laaqueel ducked under his sword swipe, tangled his legs with the trident haft, and pulled him from his feet unceremoniously. The first man thrust at her, putting all his weight behind his sword.

The malenti glided to the side, missing the familiar feel of the ocean around her. The sword slid through her hair. Before the man had a chance to protect himself, she spiked him with the trident, twisting viciously to tear the wounds open further.

Other mercenaries trampled over their fallen comrades in their zeal to get to her. Laaqueel retreated before them and reached into her harness pouch. She took out a straight piece of iron she kept there. She prayed over it as the men charged her, then released the energy through it. The iron dissolved, consumed by the spell.

Four of the attacking mercenaries froze in place, becoming a momentary blockade for their comrades. The four affected mercenaries fell like statues, their limbs locked around their weapons. Five mercenaries pushed over the other men, still not losing the courage they displayed.

They weren't like other humans, Laaqueel knew. After seeing the power she wielded, most other surface dwellers would have broken off the attack.

Those men you see before you are Flaming Fists, little malenti, Iakhovas said in her mind. *Warriors tried and true. They make up fully a tenth of this city's population, and they'll give their life's blood to see Baldur's Gate stand. They'll gladly spill yours for the same reason.*

Laaqueel blocked a sword slash, maneuvering to use the remaining five against each other so they couldn't all attack at once. She kept her trident before her in both hands, blocking rapidly, then burying it in one man's chest. Letting go of the trident, the malenti priestess popped her retractable claws from her fingers and toes. When it came to close-in fighting, few were naturally more dangerous than the sahuagin.

5

Dodging another sword thrust, a prayer to Sekolah already on her lips, Laaqueel reached into her pouch and removed a small portion of oak bark. As she finished the prayer, the bark was consumed in a small burst of heat. Instantly she felt the effects as her skin tingled. A sword she couldn't stop in time rattled against her side with the dulled thunk of an axe hitting a tree, but it didn't break her skin.

Confident of the new protection she'd summoned, secure in her belief in the Shark God, Laaqueel gave herself over to the blood frenzy that was her heritage as a sahuagin. She dived into the mass of surface dwellers, using their proximity to each other as a weapon. Hand and foot claws slashed at the five men, turning their flesh to ribbons. Daggers found her, and the occasional sword's edge, but none of them did any real damage to her.

In seconds it was over. She stood on the blood-spattered deck above the dead and the dying, her gills flaring as they tried to meet the increased demand of her body. She glanced around the deck, seeing that the other sahuagin had successfully beaten back the Flaming Fist attack. There were already other boats in the water streaking for that ship as well as the other pirate vessels. She saw their standards now, a red fist wreathed in yellow flames emblazoned against a red spearpoint.

The cog sailed on into the harbor, cutting through water filled with sahuagin, sharks, sea snakes, giant water spiders, dragonfish, giant gar, and smaller crustaceans that scurried across the ocean floor at Iakhovas's bidding.

"Where were you while we were fighting these men?" Laaqueel demanded, turning her gaze to the stern castle where the man stood looking out over the carnage spread before him.

Dressed in black and aquamarine, a long sable cloak drifting in the storm winds behind him, Iakhovas appeared pleased. The black sapphire circlet he wore had small shark figures chipped into it twining about each other. She knew it gave him the power he needed to control the sea creatures that had invaded Baldur's Gate.

Iakhovas turned his hard face toward her. A cruel, mirthless smile touched his lips and he said, "Little malenti, do not presume too much. I am and will be your master."

Deep within her, Laaqueel felt the black quill spin and prick her heart. Pain and nausea drove her to her knees and she voided her stomach.

"Favored one," a nearby sahuagin shouted, coming to her aid.

"No," Laaqueel said, holding up a hand to halt the warrior's attempt to reach her. She didn't know what Iakhovas would do to him for interfering. She regained her feet with difficulty, making herself remember that everything she was involved with was at Sekolah's bidding. She locked eyes with Iakhovas. "Forgive me. I spoke in haste."

The pain clutching her heart disappeared. She inhaled through her gills more easily.

"Never forget, little malenti," Iakhovas warned. "Too many things are coming together now for me to worry about you and your indiscretions. I am king of your people, and I suffer your presence only as long as it is in my favor."

"I understand."

"You will address me as Exalted One," Iakhovas commanded. "I am your king, and you will recognize that as well."

"Exalted One," Laaqueel said.

Arrows ripped through the rigging as archers at the Seatower of Balduran got the range. Sahuagin crossbowmen knelt and returned fire.

"Subservience in a menial is a good trait," Iakhovas said. "Don't forget it. As to helping you, remember that in helping you I am also helping myself. I've been giving aid in ways that will be known presently, and I've been inconvenienced over the last few tendays."

She knew he was talking about the injuries he'd suffered at Huaanton's hands when he'd become king of the sahuagin. Though he hadn't shown it at the time, Laaqueel learned it had taken more out of him than he would admit.

"I'm going," Iakhovas said.

"You're leaving the battle?" Laaqueel couldn't believe it. He'd done the same thing in Waterdeep, though, so it shouldn't have come as a surprise.

In the distance, a flaming warehouse collapsed in a rush of fire and smoke. People who'd taken shelter inside it from the invaders were crushed or burned to death. The high-pitched keening coming from the few survivors barely penetrated the agonized screams of fear that rolled over the docks.

"They don't need me here," Iakhovas said. "Man, dwarf, elf,

sahuagin, and sea creature, they all know how to kill each other without any guidance on my part."

"But, Exalted One, you're their king. They'll notice your absence."

Iakhovas smiled. "I don't think so. Even should they look for me, little malenti, I am here for them."

He gestured, releasing something from his hand that suddenly swirled around on its own axis. In the blink of an eye, a huge, fierce looking sahuagin appeared beside Iakhovas. Laaqueel understood immediately that the replica was how he looked in his sahuagin form to the rest of her community. Gazing at the harsh features, she realized Iakhovas had deliberately made himself handsome by sahuagin standards. He hadn't done that at Waterdeep, and Laaqueel thought it was mute testimony that his powers had dramatically increased since then.

"Now," Iakhovas said, "we can go."

"Where?"

"To pursue my own interests."

Iakhovas released a sea gull feather into the wind, then he leaped into the air and hung there for a moment. Fear ran like ice through Laaqueel's veins. If the sahuagin saw Iakhovas openly doing magic, he would lose their trust immediately. Even most warriors regarded a priestess's powers with suspicion.

"Don't panic," Iakhovas said. "I've taken precautions. None of those around you can see either of us anymore. Come."

He gestured again, pointing at a place near the malenti as he glided above the deck. He flicked his finger, and a silver blob was flung off. Laaqueel watched as the tiny silver blob sailed through the air, then splashed against an invisible surface three feet above the ground. It glimmered and disappeared, consumed by the spell.

"Get on, little malenti," Iakhovas ordered.

Hesitantly, Laaqueel moved in the direction of where the silvery blob had disappeared. Even though she guessed that it was there, she was surprised when she bumped into an invisible object. Running her hands around it, she discovered that it was circular in shape but only had two dimensions, curved slightly concave like a clamshell.

"Hurry," Iakhovas urged.

Only the fear of his disapproval made Laaqueel climb onto the magic platform. Her weight shifted it only a little as it floated, but it quickly righted itself.

Without another word, Iakhovas flew forward, staying low over the water as he aimed them northwest toward the city proper. Glancing below, she spotted another Flaming Fist ship as it was boarded by sahuagin. The ship's defenders held the line for a moment, then broke as the sahuagin grabbed them in claws and jaws.

Laaqueel stayed hunkered down on the platform, praying to Sekolah to guide her. She wasn't surprised that Iakhovas had his own agenda tonight—he always did—but Baldur's Gate hadn't been taken quite as much by surprise as Waterdeep had.

"We can make a stand here, damn ye!" Khlinat roared as he chopped at a sahuagin hand that reached across the crates blocking that section of the harbor. Sea devil fingers splattered to the dock.

Standing beside him, Jherek concentrated on his swordplay, batting aside the trident thrusts. Other men stood shoulder to shoulder with him, making a tight line to hold back the sahuagin attackers. So far they'd managed to hold their position despite the mass of sea devils on the other side.

Only now a bearded man in chain mail with the Flaming Fist standard on his tabard was trying to get them to break ranks. He carried a broadsword in one scarred fist.

"Stand down and fall back!" the man roared.

"Who the hell do ye think ye are to be giving us orders?" Khlinat demanded. Several other sailors echoed his sentiments, adding various curses.

"I'm Sergeant Hobias Churchstone," the grizzled man said, "of the Flaming Fist Mercenary Company."

Spotting a familiar shape at the base of the crates he defended, Jherek stooped and caught up the boat hook that had been abandoned there. It slid into his hand naturally, curving up from between his spread fingers.

"Get some oil!" one of the sailors yelled. "We'll get us a proper bonfire going."

Out in the harbor, the distinctive bunyip roar sounded again. A thousand fear-filled memories charged through Jherek's mind, whipping by like a school of startled fish, shaking him to his very core. Everything he remembered about his father scared him, from the memories he actually had of the man to what he'd later learned of him in stories.

He'd been four when his father had lashed a man to the mainmast then made Jherek stand by while he whipped him to death. The man had stolen from his bunkmate, a crime that Bloody Falkane didn't put up with. Steal from anyone else and it was all right, but never from *Bunyip*'s crew. The only blood spilled aboard *Bunyip* had been with Bloody Falkane's blessings.

After the man had died, the pirate captain ordered the body hung from the mast by its feet, a grim reminder to all the crew about where their loyalties lay. It had taken weeks for the carrion birds that regularly followed ships at sea to finish stripping the meat from the corpse.

A sahuagin thrust at Jherek again, shoving a trident across the stacked crates. Jherek twisted and slipped the blow, then captured the trident's haft behind the fork with his hook. Yanking the sahuagin off-balance, he swung his sword, cleaving his opponent's skull.

"Fall back!" Churchstone ordered. "You can hold this position for only a few minutes more. They're starting to close in from the sides."

Glancing over his shoulders in both directions, Jherek knew the pronouncement was true. The sahuagin had battled across other boats and sections of the docks, climbing onto the mainland in front of the shops and warehouses that lined the harbor district. Fire claimed the interiors of more buildings.

"Where would ye be after leading us?" Khlinat roared.

"To the warehouse behind you," Churchstone said. "We're better prepared for them there."

Jherek risked a glance at the warehouse, noting its disheveled appearance and the open bay doors. The interior was dark and immense. He turned to the dwarf, knowing Khlinat had fallen into the leadership role for the group of dockworkers surrounding them through his prowess and loud voice. The Flaming Fist sergeant had recognized it as well.

"Khlinat," Jherek said, blocking another trident thrust and pinning the weapon against the crate. Before the sahuagin had a chance of pulling the trident back, the young sailor flicked the hook out and caught his opponent through the gills. Jherek gave a twist and a yank that tore the sahuagin's throat out. "Retreating does make sense. We made this line and we held them. Now it's time to fall back and meet them again."

The dwarf fought gamely, avoiding a thrown javelin, then batting aside a trident thrust and slamming home another hand axe into the sahuagin's thorax. "Aye, swab, ye have the right of it." He blocked another blow and missed one of his own. "At times, I'm a prideful man. I don't like backing away from no fight."

"By Tymora's favored smile and grace, you sawed-off runt!" Churchstone roared. "You're not retreating from a damned fight. You're moving to better wage it."

"Have a care as to how ye address me," the dwarf roared back. "Else, if ye should survive the blades of these sea devils, ye will soon have another fight on yer hands."

"Khlinat," Jherek said, wanting desperately for the dwarf to listen to him. Even though they'd fought the arriving sahuagin to a standstill, they were losing men.

The dwarf nodded. "Aye, swab, and I hear ye." He raised his voice from a roar to a bellow. "To the warehouse, damn ye lazybones! Regroup and let's show these beasties the color of their gizzards!"

Jherek hung the hook from the sash at his waist and reached out for a lantern hanging from a nearby pole. Holding it by the wire handle, he smashed it against the crates.

At his side, Khlinat did the same. Flames twisted up with a liquid *whoosh.* "Them what owns them crates," the dwarf said as they gave ground together, "ain't going to be any too happy seeing how we treated their goods."

"If they live after tonight," Jherek grimly pointed out.

"Aye, swab, and ye have the right of it."

Jherek turned and ran, spotting the two groups of sahuagin closing in from the sides. Another moment and their position would have been overrun.

They fled into the warehouse, going all the way to the back of the cavernous structure. The warehouse was two stories tall. Crates occupied space on either side, leaving the middle section clear. The scarcity of crates offered mute testimony about the way shipping had slowed since the attacks on Waterdeep and the sea lanes. On either side at the back, steeply angled wooden steps led up to the second floor.

"Don't stop till you reach the back!" Churchstone ordered.

Jherek and Khlinat ran at the back of the group with the Flaming Fist sergeant. The young soldier couldn't help noticing the grin on Churchstone's face. Glancing back over his shoulder, Jherek saw that the sahuagin had no compunctions at all about following them into the building. At least thirty-five or forty sea devil warriors ran after them.

Churchstone wheeled suddenly and lifted his sword. "Now!" he shouted.

Jherek only caught the flash of movement overhead, then a huge cargo net dropped down, snaring the sahuagin. Several of them dropped to the warehouse floor, hammered by the great weight of the thick hawser ropes. The sea devils struggled to get up. A few of them sawed at the ropes with bone knives fashioned with chipped edges. The ropes slid away greasily, twisting from the sahuagin's grip as well as against the knife edges.

Then a pair of flaming torches dropped from the overhead floor as well. From the way the cargo netting caught fire, running in rivulets as it greedily consumed everything it touched, Jherek knew it had been soaked in oil. The sahuagin whistled shrilly in pain.

It was a hard way to die, Jherek knew, and he felt bad for the creatures. It wasn't a way he'd have killed them. Malorrie had trained him to be a warrior, to fight the right fights for the right reasons. This was more like extermination. He felt the warmth of the flames against his cheeks as the men around him hooted in triumph and pleasure.

Jherek glanced away, catching Khlinat's eye.

"A bad bit of business," the dwarf commented. "But 'twixt a rock and a hard place, a wise man makes do and lives for the morrow."

"I know," Jherek replied.

Khlinat slapped him on the shoulder. "Buck up, swabbie, we've a city yet to save should the gods prove willing."

Out in the harbor, the bunyip roar pealed again.

The chill of dread raced through Jherek when he heard the sound. Resolutely, he steeled himself. Come what may, he knew he had unfinished business with his father. He followed the dwarf, skirting around the dead and dying among the sahuagin as they cooked. Archers on the floor above feathered any that appeared on the verge of escaping.

Out in the fresh air and clear of the smoke trapped inside the warehouse, Jherek stared across Baldur's Gate harbor. The battle ravaged the city along the docks. Flames twisted up through the roofs of buildings that would be nothing but ash by morning.

His destiny, he thought grimly, was supposed to be found somewhere in the chaotic debris, but he had no idea how he was going to find it.

* * *

"Pacys! It's happening—Baldur's Gate is under attack!"

Snarled in the layers of bedding, Pacys strove to come awake. As always, the bard reached first for his yarting. It lay on the floor beside the bed, barely fitting the hollow between the furniture and the wall in the small room. Until late, the yarting was the only thing of real value he'd carried in years. His fingers slid over the strings and the smooth wood out of habit, then he opened his eyes.

"What?" he croaked.

"We're being attacked by the sahuagin." Delahnane Kubha stood on the other side of the small bedroom and peered out the single open window. The flimsy pale green drapes blew over her naked body, illuminated by the lone taper on the small nearby table.

She was forty and still lushly curved, bursting with womanly charms that had warmed the old bard's bed for nearly a tenday. Her blond hair had strands of gray in it now, but her confidence in herself kept her from coloring it. She worked as a serving wench in the Blushing Mermaid tavern only a few streets back of the room she kept here. Pacys had enjoyed a friendship that was more than friendship with her the last twenty years whenever he was in the city.

Holding onto the yarting, not bothering to cover his nakedness, Pacys rushed to the window. His hard life was mapped across his lean body in scars and wrinkles, creating highlights on his nut-brown skin. He kept his head shaved, and went whiskerless as well. Jutting silver eyebrows arched over his light hazel eyes. He was thin, his long bones overlaid with stringy muscle.

Pacys had been in Baldur's Gate almost two tendays since arriving by ship. After the attack on Waterdeep and his talk with the merman Narros, he'd come to the city hoping to find more mention of the prophecy he'd been told of, more of the song he was chasing.

Since arriving in Baldur's Gate, he'd only experienced a few times when the song he searched so desperately for—had been promised—had come to him. They'd been troubling pieces, crammed with trepidation and the iron smell of blood.

Now, as he gazed out over the battling groups below and out in the harbor, the song filled his head. It was an extension of the piece he'd unconsciously played in Narros's home after having been invited to the merman shaman's dwelling. Pacys knew it was the piece concerning the hero of the tale.

The music was strong, vibrant, but there was a trilling uncertainty about it, a tremor that didn't ring quite true. Relieved and excited, he fit his hands to the yarting, then guided his callused thumb across the strings. The resonance between what he heard in his mind and what he produced on the yarting was perfect. The sleep fog that clung to him from too many late nights and too much wine lifted instantly.

"He's here," Pacys declared, smiling. The music filled the tiny room.

Delahnane glanced at him, light glinting in her eyes. "The hero you've been charged with seeking?" She wasn't as happy about the situation as the old bard was. There was every chance that someone she knew from the tavern, perhaps even someone she called a friend, would be dead before morning.

"Yes." The certainty that filled him surprised Pacys. At his age, there seemed to be so many doubtful things. He'd seen seventy-six years come and go, and had learned much in his unceasing travels across Faerûn as a wandering bard, not all of it good, but it all had fed his talent in one way or another. Every emotion he'd ever experienced had burned through his mind and into his fingers in thousands of bars, taverns, inns, and castles across Faerûn.

He closed his eyes, concentrating on the music. His fingers moved fluidly across the strings, seeking the notes now without hesitation. He added to the small store he'd brought with him from Waterdeep. No matter what song he'd played or how long it had been since he'd last played it, the old bard had never forgotten a tune he'd written or borrowed.

He gave voice to the song, his smooth baritone filling the room.

"He stood with the men of Baldur's Gate,
"This boy not yet become a man.
"He followed his heart, not knowing the plan,
"Of his destiny to stand before the Taker's hate.
"With naked sword steel tight in his hand,
"And fear filling his belly as he eyed
"The black-hearted sahuagin warrior pride,
"The Champion fought to keep the defenses manned.
"Steel rang and sparked as blood ran from wounds untended,
"As the Taker took up the malevolent war that had not ended."

The words stopped coming, but the music didn't. It became repetitive. Unable to stand idly by while the city fought back against the invaders, or to miss the chance to meet the young man Narros had said it was his destiny to find, the old bard hurried back to the bed.

He pulled his plain brown breeches from the chest where Delahnane kept her personal things and quickly stepped into them. As a raconteur of duels, battles, and wars, he'd learned to keep clothing close to hand and to dress in a hurry. During a war, the battle lines moved even while men slept.

"What are you doing?" Delahnane turned from the window and faced him.

"Only what needs be done, fair lady," Pacys replied. "I'm no man to lay abed when there's fighting to be done." He pulled on the faded green doublet, then stepped into his boots. His feet slid into them comfortably. He hung the yarting by its strap over his back and picked up the wooden staff he'd carried with him almost as long as the instrument.

"You're going out there?"

"I have no choice."

"Men are dying out there," Delahnane said.

"Yes, and my place is with them."

"You're an old man."

The statement, even though it was true, hurt Pacys. He was well aware of his advanced age. Elves, mayhap, had all the time in the world, but not him. He crossed to the woman and took her by the arms, staring into her green eyes. "Ah, and if I had my choice of deaths, O vision, I'd choose to die by your hand, knowing your willing love and your tender caress upon my brow as you urged me to greater rapture."

A small smile lighted her face, followed by an instant blush.

"But, dear lady," Pacys went on, "I fear I don't have my choice of deaths, and I must follow my nature."

Delahnane pulled him to her and hugged him fiercely. Her bare skin brushed against his hand. "I know, dear Pacys, and even should that nature of yours damn you to die this night, I know it has ever made you the man I've loved when happy occasion permitted us to be together."

Pacys stroked her face with the back of his fingers. He felt a pang in his heart. He didn't think he would die, though he knew it was possible, but he did know that the loving times they'd shared, and the quiet hours he'd spent reciting poetry to her, thrilling to the way she'd responded to every verse, were over.

"Should we not see each other again this night—" he began.

She swiftly covered his mouth with her hand. "No," she whispered. "Do not speak of dying."

After a moment, Pacys gave her a nod. It hadn't been his intention, but he felt she knew he was about to tell her he wouldn't be back. It was her way of avoiding that. He'd left her many times in the past, and both of them knew that with his station in life what it was, there could only be pleasant interludes between them.

She removed her hand. "Do you really think the boy you're searching for could be out there?"

"I have to believe," Pacys answered. "All my life I've felt I was destined for greatness, to pen and sing a song that will forever be known as mine, to take my place among the bards whose works achieve immortality. That has never happened. Until now. Oghma's blessing upon me and my craft has seen fit to put me on that path now. I can't step away from that."

"I know." With genuine effort, she released him and took a step back.

Pacys leaned in for a final kiss, tasting the wine yet lingering on her lips. Of all the women he'd known in his long life, she was a favorite, but settling down and leaving the traveling bard's life was as unthinkable as taking a wife to travel with him who wasn't a bard herself. The road was home only to those who could call no other place home.

He reached inside his doublet and took out the coin pouch he'd been saving. Deftly, with all the skill of a thief, he placed it in her hand and curled her fingers up over it before she saw it.

Delahnane didn't say anything. She already knew how generous he was from past times he'd stayed with her.

Whenever he spent time with Delahnane, he always filled his own coin purse and one for her from the fees collected in the taverns he visited. With the caravans bringing men into the city as well as the needed laborers for the shipyards and the usual sailors, the old bard had done well during his stay. Both coin purses held a lot of copper and silver pieces, as well as the occasional gold piece. He'd learned long ago never to get too attached to coin. Oghma had always found a way to pry it out of him by some means.

"Take care," she told him.

"And you." Pacys went through the door, memorizing the image of her standing there with only the candlelight blazing over her. His heart was heavy with the thought of leaving. At the same time, he was excited. The song played in his mind, nothing new yet, but he knew there would be something more.

Outside, he bolted and ran by the other apartment doors to the stairs leading down to the alley. He raced around the building and out toward the docks. The song thrummed in his head, growing stronger as he moved to the battle.

The tide of sahuagin flooding into the city seemed unbreakable.

Jherek stayed with Khlinat, aware that the dwarf knew the streets and alleys of Baldur's Gate much better than he did. If there was a stand to make somewhere, he trusted Khlinat to make it and to choose the proper place.

They raced down Bindle Street till it crossed Stormshore Street, then kept going. Few of the sahuagin had penetrated this far back the city as yet.

The peg leg coupled with his short stature helped Jherek easily keep up with Khlinat, but they moved quickly. Armed men, most of them evidently with the Flaming Fist, hailed citizens in the streets, urging them to join the efforts in the harbor. The young sailor guessed that less than half the efforts were successful. Men with families concentrated on getting those families to safety, not trusting that the sea devil invaders could be held.

The blood weeping from the cut beside Jherek's eye had finally ceased, leaving a hard crust that partially obscured his vision. It bothered him that they appeared to be running from the battle.

"Where are we going?" Jherek asked.

"Patience, swabbie, I've got a plan. Never ye fear." The dwarf's breath came in ragged gasps and he flailed his arms to keep up the pace. Two alleys further up, he pointed at a large building. "There."

The building stood three stories tall with a stone exterior. The bottom two floors contained what appeared to be a warehouse because there were no windows, while the third floor held personal living quarters with a large widow's walk facing the River Chionthar. A hand-painted sign stuck out from the building but it was too dark for Jherek to make it out.

Huffing and puffing from the run, Khlinat pounded the back of a hand axe against the door near the cargo bay. Hollow thumps sounded inside. The dwarf repeated his effort twice more, gaining intensity and frustration.

Suddenly a deep male voice called down from above. "What the hell do you want?"

Khlinat stepped back from the building and gazed up. "Yer city's under attack, Felogyr Sonshal, and there ye stand instead of taking up arms against them what attacks."

Sonshal stood in the shadows of the widow's walk, but Jherek could tell he was a big warrior who'd evidently enjoyed the successes of his life. Judging from his girth, he'd had several successes. Fierce mustaches stuck out from his lower face and dangled below his chin. He dressed well, but the thing that drew the young sailor's attention most was the long shape in the man's arms. It was pointed directly at Khlinat. Moonlight glinted from the dark metal.

During his time in Velen, Jherek had only seen a few weapons like the one Sonshal carried. It was an arquebus, a weapon as rare as the most arcane magic that took advantage of the explosive nature of the smoke powder made by the Lantans. The arquebus fired round bullets much like those a sling threw, but with far more destruction than either a sling or a bow. Also, the bullets weren't as easy for a healer to take out as an arrow or quarrel.

The dim glow of a slow match burned orange across Sonshal's face. "I'm on my way to help. I only just woke."

"Pulled yerself out of yer cups, ye mean."

Consternation covered Sonshal's face. "Do I know you?"

"Khlinat Ironeater. Aye, ye know me. From a time or two a round was bought at the Blushing Mermaid or the Three Old Kegs. Stories was swapped and lies was told, but I've never done business with ye. That blasted smoke powder ye sell is much too uncertain for a one-legged dwarf who's learned the value of the sure-footed path."

"Then what are you doing here?" Sonshal demanded. "Unless you're beating on doors and raising help."

"More than that," Khlinat roared. "That harbor yonder's filled with all manner of foul beasties, including no few sea devils. I've got me a plan, desperate, aye, and mayhap a trifle foolhardy, but Marthammor Duin keeps foolish wanderers ever in his blessed sight."

"Get to the point."

"Ye sell smoke powder," Khlinat said.

"I sell fireworks," Sonshal argued. "And torches, lanterns, and beacon pots. Things a man determined to go adventuring needs."

"Aye," the dwarf agreed, "and ye stock smoke powder that the Lantans make. The reason the four Grand Dukes don't run ye out of business here is because yer choosy about who ye sell to, and the fact that yer a rich man in these parts. Makes ye a good taxpayer, I'm told."

"What do you want? Do you figure an arquebus is going to serve you better than those hand axes you carry?"

Jherek listened politely to the conversation, staying out of it because he trusted the dwarf, but every instinct in the young sailor cried out to him to be at the harbor, helping where he could. Fighting men died while they stood there.

"No," Khlinat said. "I need that smoke powder ye have put away in the warehouse." He glanced at Jherek. "Steady, swabbie."

Jherek gave him a tight nod. Glancing at the harbor, he saw flaming catapult loads streak through the sky.

"I don't sell smoke powder to just anyone," Sonshal stated. "If you've heard anything, I know you've heard that about me."

"I wasn't intending to buy it," Khlinat said. "Just use it."

"For what?" Sonshal asked.

A broad grin split the dwarf's face. "Goin' fishing."

4 Kythorn, the Year of the Gauntlet

6

Laaqueel crouched lower on the invisible floating disc as Iakhovas guided her around a crowd of battling sahuagin and Flaming Fist mercenaries. Incredibly, the mercenaries were holding their own against the sahuagin, starting to push them back into the harbor in some areas. The sheer ferocity of the humans surprised her, and made her respect them as well.

Out in the harbor proper, ships burned. Three of them listed heavily in the water, burning down close to the waterline. Others were in the beginning stages of the same fate despite the efforts of dockworkers and sailors to halt it with water brigades.

The invisible disc stopped smoothly in front of a warehouse. Iakhovas alighted gracefully, pulling his cloak more securely around him. He drew his sword, revealing the runes carved into the shining blade. It was the first time Laaqueel had seen the weapon, making her realize the agents he had working around Faerûn to recover objects he claimed were his were still bringing things to him.

He grinned at her, his scarred features and eyepatch highlighted by a flaming catapult load that streaked through the night sky. "Come, little malenti. We have only a short time remaining that we may complete the assignations I've planned for our evening."

She didn't argue and she didn't point out that the sahuagin were dying behind them, shedding their blood for Iakhovas's machinations. Instead, she told herself that those were also Sekolah's machinations and followed Iakhovas to the warehouse.

The structure stood bleak and weathered, tortured by time, the elements, and ill use. The doors, leached gray by the sun working through the constant layer of moisture that hung over Baldur's Gate, stood only for a moment against Iakhovas's gesture. A thin green ray stabbed from his finger and caused the doors to glow briefly, then disintegrate into a whirling mass of fine dust.

Iakhovas strode into the warehouse. Laaqueel followed at his heels, marveling at the amount of magic he seemed capable of unleashing. She felt in her heart that he had Sekolah to thank for that. No matter what Iakhovas believed, she knew the Shark God's influence had put him back into the world and made him as powerful as he was.

"Hold!" someone shouted. "What in the Nine Hells do you think you're doing?"

Turning, Laaqueel gazed at the dozen agitated surface dwellers that came at them with swords bared. She saw them for only an instant, then Iakhovas stepped to her side and brushed her back protectively. He leaned forward, put a small bullhorn to his lips, and shouted with a deafening fury.

The shout drove the men back five paces, turning them like sediment stirred up from the ocean bottom. All of them survived, but they were injured and screamed in pain, clapping their hands to their bleeding ears.

"Hurry," Iakhovas said. He led her to the back of the warehouse, through stacked crates and shrouded items of all sizes and shapes. At the back wall he stepped into a small alcove and touched a panel. With a muffled creak, a section of the wall opened, revealing a long tunnel filled with shadows beyond.

Laaqueel held her trident ready, smelling old pain and death clinging to the tunnel. Iakhovas reached into his cloak and took out an amulet cut from a huge, flawless jacinth into a lens shape six inches in diameter. The device was set in platinum with a dozen diamonds on the left and a rune across the top. Holding it in his hand, Iakhovas spoke arcane words Laaqueel couldn't understand.

The gem's face glowed with lambent blue light. Instantly a map with a compass rose appeared. Gazing at it, Laaqueel recognized the warehouse, and the entrance to the tunnel they now stood before.

"A moment, little malenti," Iakhovas said softly, "while I orient myself."

The soft blue glow died, collapsing in on itself. He put the amulet back in one of the cloak's hiding places, then took out a jade-colored globe that looked almost black in the pale light streaming in from the warehouse. He spoke another word. The globe lifted from his open palm and floated into place behind his left shoulder. It glowed pale jade, illuminating the tunnel.

Laaqueel blinked against the sudden light even though it was soft.

"Now," Iakhovas said, "let's reap the rewards of the bold move I've made." He started down the tunnel so rapidly his black cloak shimmered like a waterfall behind him.

Having no other choice, and always curious as to his real purpose and the events he orchestrated, Laaqueel followed.

"You're crazy, dwarf."

If Khlinat harbored any ill feelings toward Sonshal for his pronouncement, Jherek didn't see it. They worked hurriedly inside the warehouse Sonshal had allowed them to enter after Khlinat explained his plan. "Hitch up them horses, swabbie," the little man said, "afore I have a chance to rethink much of what we're going to do."

Jherek brought the horses to the front of the wagon Sonshal had let them have as well. His hands worked quickly, buckling the traces into place. Khlinat continued rolling barrels of smoke powder into the wagon.

"You're going to blow yourself up is what you're going to do," Sonshal said, but helped the dwarf with the barrels. "That stuff's damned unstable if you don't treat it right."

"It's got me respect," Khlinat said dourly. "If I could think of some other way to handle this, I would. I'm only praying this works."

Finished with the horses, Jherek vaulted over the wagon's side and shoved the fifty-pound barrels up behind the seat. He handled them gingerly. Only three years ago in Velen, a local farmer had used smoke powder to clear stumps from some land he wanted to plow. Even Malorrie had been impressed by the carnage only a little of the smoke powder had done.

Khlinat shoved the last barrel into place.

"That's all of it," Sonshal said, twisting his mustache with one hand.

"Then I'll be off," Khlinat said, "and thank ye for yer kind donations." He offered his arm.

Sonshal took the arm, then shook his head. "Mighty Tempus watch over a thrice-blasted village idiot in the making, I can't let you go it alone, dwarf. If you've an extra seat, I'll be glad to accompany you. I may know more about fuse-cutting than you do."

Khlinat smiled broadly. "Aye, friend Sonshal, as long as ye keep in mind that one way or another, this is apt to be a one-way trip."

"I'll likely not forget." Sonshal took up a roll of fuse and a torch from the nearby stores.

Khlinat moved to the wagon's seat and grabbed the reins. "Have a ready hand there, swabbie," he said to Jherek. "Them sea devils see us coming, they ain't going to be very friendly about it. We start acting brave, they've to start asking themselves why."

Nervous about what the dwarf planned to do, Jherek sat on the bench seat beside him. Ever since he'd left Velen, his life had been turned constantly topsy-turvy, with certain death in every corner. The fear numbed him a little as he reflected on how he seemed to get caught up in the events spreading around Faerûn. All he could guess was that it was the ill luck of his birthright. He kept the sword and the hook naked in his hands.

The warehouse doors were open, revealing the confusion roiling out in the street as more mercenaries arrived and had to fight their way through the fearful crowds fleeing their homes. Lightning speared the sky, but there wasn't a storm cloud to be seen.

"These barrels get wet," Sonshal called out as he clambered into the back and sat, "all we're going to be doing is riding to our deaths. They get hit by that damned lightning those wizards are throwing around, and we'll go even quicker."

"I hear ye." Khlinat laid the reins across the backs of the horses in a practiced snap. The team hit the end of their traces at once, starting the wagon off quickly.

Sonshal cursed, warning about the barrels.

"Gangway!" Khlinat called at the top of his voice. The horses' hooves struck sparks from the cobblestones and the thunder of their passage cannonaded between the tall buildings on either side of Bindle Street. "Wild horses! Clear the street!"

People dived to the sides of the street, some of them just ahead of being trampled. Khlinat handled the horses expertly, slapping the reins and urging them to greater speed. The ironbound wheels whirred against the cobblestones.

Jherek braced himself, holding fast to his weapons and praying to Ilmater that their headlong rush hurt no one, and that they arrived in time to save something of Baldur's Gate.

Pacys's fingers twitched for the strings of the yarting. The music crescendoed in the old bard's head. He mapped the words and the rhythms, finding maddening pieces and partials of the lyrics that formed the song. The oppression and the sound of the battle didn't daunt his spirits or send fear into him at all. He felt more alive than he had in decades. His soul thirsted for the knowledge and the answers that he was certain lurked around the next corner.

He held his staff in both hands as he ran through the crowd in the street. He felt their pain of loss, their uncertainty of fear, and he worked it into the lyrics running through his mind as surely and skillfully as a silversmith working an intricate inlay assignation.

The music changed pitch, becoming the champion's song again when he heard the rough voice farther down the street.

"Clear the damned street, ye deaf lummoxes!"

The sea of people and mercenaries before Pacys parted. The music paralyzed him, stronger than he'd ever heard it before. He spotted the dwarf over the horses' laid-back ears as they pulled the wagon. Then his eyes rested on the young man beside the diminutive teamster.

Pacys knew he'd never seen the young man before in his life, but he felt he knew him with greater certainty than he'd experienced at any time in his long life. This was the one Narros had spoken of, the one who would challenge the Taker that brought death and destruction from the sea.

"Get out of the way, old man!" the dwarf roared, slapping the rumps of the horses yet again.

Getting his wits back about him, Pacys dived to the side, rolling to get more distance. The wagon thundered past him, and he memorized the cadence of the ironbound wheels across the cobblestones, figuring out how he could bring that sound to life with his fingertips against the yarting's bowl while strumming the strings with his thumb.

The wagon took the next corner and drove toward the harbor.

Pacys pushed himself up, watching as the wagon disappeared. Without a second thought, he pursued, running as fast as he could. When he turned the corner, he came face-to-face with the first of the sahuagin who'd battled their way farther into the city.

The bunyip roared out in the harbor as the lead sahuagin ripped trident tines toward Pacys's face.

Laaqueel followed Iakhovas through the darkness, the sounds of the battle out in the harbor far behind them now. She'd lost track of how many twists and turns they'd taken, how many other passageways they'd passed by, how many corpses they'd climbed over. She hated the enclosed atmosphere of the tunnels, especially the way she had to remain partially slumped over now that they'd wended their way more deeply into the undercity.

"Hold up," he ordered.

She froze in place, a prayer to Sekolah on her lips as she held ready the gifts the Shark God had given her as his priestess.

The globe floating behind Iakhovas's left shoulder pushed a dim jade glow across the distance, becoming brighter. At first Laaqueel didn't see the big man at the other end of the tunnel, then the glow crept over him.

He was tall and big-bellied, possibly the most massive surface dweller Laaqueel had ever seen. He looked even more so because of the way he was hunched over in the tunnel. Unruly red hair sprouted out from the sides of his head but nothing grew on top. He kept his beard shaved from his cheeks and upper lip, but it grew long and thick from his chin, hanging midway down his chest. He wore a dark red cloak over a sleeveless leather vest, high-topped boots and dark brown breeches.

"Lord Iakhovas," the big man rumbled.

"Captain Vurgrom," Iakhovas greeted, moving closer. Laaqueel was aware of the shimmer that took place around Iakhovas and guessed that he was altering his image again to fit the other man's perceptions.

"Quite a party you're throwing up above," Vurgrom said.

Laaqueel studied the man further, taking in the gruff manner and the tattoos that decorated his thick, beefy forearms. She knew from the cut of his clothing and the boots that he was a seafarer, and she guessed from his presence in the hidden tunnels that he wasn't there for good reason. He reminded her a lot of the other pirates Iakhovas had recruited for the attack on Baldur's Gate.

"I trust everything went well," Iakhovas said.

Vurgrom shrugged, the casual gesture made even harder by the tight confines of the tunnel. "I never cared much for river travel. Give me the openness of the Sea of Fallen Stars every time. The overland trip from Ilipur is not something I'm looking forward to repeating."

"You have the device I asked you to get?" Iakhovas asked.

"Aye." Vurgrom reached under his vest and took off a silver necklace that held a leather pouch. "Kept it close to my heart for safekeeping." He took the pouch from the necklace and dropped it into Iakhovas's outstretched palm.

"What of the man who had it?" Iakhovas asked.

"I did for him," Vurgrom said. "Split him from wind to water and left him like a grand buffet for the fishes to feast on. They'll not find him."

Iakhovas poured the contents out into his palm. The light of the hovering jade globe revealed a twisted metal piece no longer than Iakhovas's forefinger and less than half that wide. He closed his fist around it, covering the runic markings before Laaqueel had a chance to see if she could decipher them. "Very good, Captain Vurgrom."

"I lived up to my end of the bargain," Vurgrom said. His piggish eyes were surrounded by thick scar tissue, and the reflected light in them gleamed shrewdly.

"As I shall live up to mine." Iakhovas put the trinket away in his cloak, then removed a heavy coin purse and tossed it to the captain.

Vurgrom caught the purse with an ease that was surprising for one so bulky. He unfastened the drawstrings and emptied it onto his thick palm.

The glowing globe heightened its illumination a bit more, but the change was so gradual Laaqueel didn't think human eyes would notice as quickly as she did. Sahuagin eyes were meant for dim lights, though hers handled bright light better than her kin's did.

Red, green, blue, and amber fires burned inside the gems Vurgrom held. "Cyric's blessed avarice," the captain said in a thick voice, "that's a king's ransom there, Lord Iakhovas."

"You may think so," Iakhovas said, "but remember you well that even those baubles are but a pittance against what I'm prepared to offer you should you maintain your loyalty to me."

A small man came around from behind Vurgrom and fitted a jeweler's glass to his eye. He picked up a ruby, sapphire, diamond, and emerald in quick succession, eyeing them against the light of the glowing globe. He gave a short nod, never taking any of the gems from Vurgrom's sight, then nodded again and stepped back.

Vurgrom closed his hand over the jewels and made them disappear, splitting them up and putting them in various areas of his clothing. "Aye, milord, and know that ever my blade shall serve your will in any way that I might aid you. Would there be any other way tonight?"

"No. Take your men and go," Iakhovas directed. "I'll meet up with you in the Sea of Fallen Stars."

Vurgrom smiled, but Laaqueel didn't like the way the effort fit the man's face. "I'll look forward to seeing you there, milord. I and my crews have worked long and hard to put everything into play as you have designed. Until we meet again, Cyric keep you safe in his shadows that you might smite your enemies through no risk of your own."

"And you," Iakhovas echoed.

Laaqueel had no idea how Iakhovas had arranged for Vurgrom to see him, but she noted the obvious deferential treatment. After Vurgrom and his group had gone, she addressed him. "You're planning on meeting him in the Sea of Fallen Stars?"

"Yes." Iakhovas offered no explanation. He continued down the passageway they were in.

The thought bothered Laaqueel. Though she knew of the Sea of Fallen Stars from talks she'd had with surface dwellers and maps she'd studied, the idea of being in a sea surrounded entirely by land was unnerving to her. She didn't know whether she hoped Iakhovas left her behind or not.

"Ah, little malenti, for someone who evidences her faith so strongly, there remains much weakness within you," Iakhovas taunted. "You shall accompany me to the Inner Sea, and there you will see the culmination of all the prophecies that you're helping come true."

There was just enough truth in his words to ease her mind somewhat, but the knowledge that Iakhovas looked after himself first and only never left her thoughts.

They followed the passageway a little farther and found the end of it. However, when the globe got close enough, it revealed a break in the wall on the right. Iakhovas stepped through without hesitation.

Laaqueel followed closely, reluctant to lose the light. The smell that hit her when she stepped through the opening immediately told her they were in a sewer. She remembered when she'd first learned of such things, having never thought of surface dwellers living out their two-dimensional lives and such bodily functions being any kind of trouble. She'd been further disturbed and horrified to learn that most of the coastal cities and towns poured their waste directly into the ocean.

She avoided the running water in the center of the duct and was grateful she was sucking air through her lungs instead of water because the stench would have been even stronger. The glowing globe caught the attention of the long-bodied rats creeping through the duct and placed jade fires in their eyes.

Only a little farther on, Iakhovas stopped again. He gazed at the wall to his left.

With some effort, Laaqueel spotted the rune marked there. It wasn't a glyph with any power, but it marked an area of some importance. Iakhovas stepped off a measured distance, then stomped his foot down, creating a hollow thump. Moving quickly, he reached down and seized the slab of stone. With a show of incredible strength, he lifted the man-sized slab and shoved it to the side. The glowing globe obediently moved, providing illumination that looked down into the opening.

Stepping around him, her nose wrinkling in disgust from the bitter stench that erupted from the opening, Laaqueel peered down into it. Fully six feet or more down, the jade light reflected against a white powder floor and walls.

"A lime pit," Iakhovas explained. "It took me some time to find out the things I needed to know that brought us here, but I did. In the doing of it, I learned of this pit. A man named Nantrin Bellowglyn owns the Three Old Kegs, an inn nearby, and he prospers by renting out this as well. Lime breaks a corpse down faster than anything expect carrion eaters." He chanted briefly, his voice carrying power.

A moment passed, and when he finished, he gazed into the lime pit. Laaqueel watched as well, wondering what magery he'd wrought. A low, pain-filled groan escaped from the lime pit. Then, incredibly, the malenti priestess watched as a sticklike figure pushed itself up from the white powder around it.

Skeletal, half-formed bones constructing the basic framework of a human being pushed through the lime powder body. The thing glared up at Iakhovas through the hollows of the half-dissolved skull that sat on the bony neck. The thing's voice when it spoke was a mixture of hoarse, raspy anger and disgust.

"What do you want of me?" the thing demanded.

4 Kythorn, the Year of the Gauntlet

7

Jherek braced himself as Khlinat drove the wagon team into the irregular line of sahuagin blocking the mouth of the alley that let out into Baldur's Gate harbor. They'd passed most of them already, but the sea devils had taken refuge up against the buildings on either side of the alley, fighting hand-to-hand with citizens predominantly dressed in the Flaming Fist's colors.

The sahuagin group at the end of the alley was wedged too tightly to scatter, and Jherek knew if the dwarf slowed they'd be overrun in heartbeats. The young sailor blocked trident thrusts with his hook and hacked at heads and limbs that got close enough. He'd left at least four sahuagin lying behind the wagon.

The dwarf squalled in anger as a sahuagin grabbed hold of the wagon and tried to pull aboard. Sonshal's arquebus banged as Jherek went to Khlinat's aid. The big bullet cored through the sahuagin's head, punching it back off the wagon.

The horses kept to their pace, urged on by the dwarf slapping leather across their rumps. Their headlong run pushed the sea devils down before them, and their iron-shod hooves dealt grievous and mortal injury. The sahuagin clicked and whistled in pain and surprise, but two of them reacted quickly enough to catch hold of the animals. They popped their claws out and set to their bloody work.

"Swabbie!" Khlinat yelled.

Jherek was already in motion. With sure-footed grace, he stepped out onto the horse's back like it was a deck pitching in a wild storm. He kept himself centered, then dropped onto the horse's back and locked his legs with the skill he'd acquired riding up from Athkatla with the caravan. He swung the sword, coming down and cleaving the sahuagin from crown to chin.

The body twitched and fell away, but the moonlight glinted on the blood streaming from the horse's neck. Jherek realized the animal was dead already and didn't know it. There was no way to staunch the blood flow.

The young sailor turned his attention to the other horse. He reached out with the hook and caught the sahuagin in the muscles that joined the head and shoulder, tearing the flesh cruelly as he found a hold. He yanked and twisted, pulling the sea devil from the horse. One webbed foot pushed against the ground, and the sahuagin sprang at the young sailor more quickly than he thought possible.

Reacting instinctively, Jherek whipped his other hand across and caught the sahuagin in the face with his fist. Pain shot up his arm, but the sea devil went down under the horses' hooves.

They broke through the sea devils at the harbor. Khlinat whipped the horses one last time, hauling them away from the dock, and the carcass of a small cargo ship that had burned nearly to the waterline. The horse beneath Jherek stumbled and almost fell, but fear drove the creature over the harbor's side.

The wagon followed, and Khlinat yelled hoarsely in rebellion and fear, covering over Sonshal's own shouts.

Laaqueel stared at the resurrected dead thing in the lime pit with revulsion so strong it nearly caused her to empty her stomach again. She stood through willpower alone.

Dead things weren't meant to walk. Sekolah's teachings were clear about that. Dead things were meant to be eaten as quickly as possible, whether they were from outside the sahuagin family or from in it. She'd heard stories about the dead being brought back to unlife, about vampires and ghouls, and she'd once been attacked by a group of drowned ones while scavenging shipwrecks with a band of humans she'd spied on and eventually handed over to Huaanton when he'd still been baron.

Iakhovas glared at her and gestured.

Instantly, the quill next to her heart twisted and the nausea went away. At least, the physical effects of it did, leaving her stomach resting quietly. Mentally, she still couldn't stand the sight of the thing waiting quietly in the pit. Surface dwelling priests and priestesses had the ability to turn the undead, as did the hated sea elves, but as a priestess for Sekolah, she had no such ability. The drowned ones had nearly killed her before one of the humans she'd been working with turned them back.

"I would have something from you," Iakhovas told the thing.

"I have nothing."

"It was yours at one time," Iakhovas argued. "I was told it still resided with your body."

The thing ran its misshapen hands over its body. "I was killed and robbed. I don't even remember being brought here."

"Your name," Iakhovas said, "was Cuthbert Drin and you were brother to Halbazzer Drin, the owner of Sorcerous Sundries here in Baldur's Gate."

"I'm in Baldur's Gate?"

"Yes."

The dead thing moved uncertainly. Its face took on features as the rest of it sharpened into shape as well. Laaqueel realized whatever magic Iakhovas had laid on it was continuing to work.

"Release me," the thing ordered, knotting its crooked fingers and hands into fists. "This hurts."

"No," Iakhovas said.

"The lime *burns!*" The dead thing suddenly broke into a frenzy of activity, pacing and scratching itself. In places, the fingers penetrated the lime-covered skin. Tendrils of old blood wormed out, marring the white luster of the lime in the glowing globe's glare.

"Of course it burns," Iakhovas said. "It's a struggle to keep you alive at all."

"You can't keep me like this."

"Yes," Iakhovas said. "I can."

The dead thing moved faster, almost up to a run in the small area. It clawed at the walls of the pit, seeking some way to get out. "What do you want?"

"The ship you had with you on the day you were killed," Iakhovas answered. "It's mine, and I've come to claim it."

"It was taken," the dead thing argued.

"No," Iakhovas replied. "I traced your steps, Cuthbert Drin, through the ordinary means of agents planted here at Baldur's Gate, and through scrying and divining into the past. After I had the facts, I found the moment in time you discovered the bottle high in the Orsraun Mountains near the Vilhon Reach. You and your brother, Halbazzer, found mention of the bottled ship in scrolls that came into your hands at the shop. Even twenty years ago, his rigorous adventuring days were behind him, robbed by the poisoned knife of an assassin hired to kill him. The damage was so great he never fully recovered from the attack. You had the bottled ship the day you died, and your murderers didn't find it."

"How do you know this?"

"I found two of your murderers," Iakhovas said. "I took the time to question them, and I made certain of the veracity of their stories as I stripped their lives from them one layer at a time. Both stories, in the end, were screamed out and agreed on the fact that the killers hadn't seen the bottled ship."

"You know the mystery of the bottle?" the dead thing asked, picking at the lime-encrusted shreds of flesh hanging off it. "Though I tried any number of ways, I never succeeded in opening it. Even the glass wouldn't shatter."

"I know the secret of the bottle," Iakhovas said. "I petitioned the elemental beings who created it, trading with them for their services." He narrowed his single eye and deepened his voice. "Now give it to me or I'll leave you there like that, unable to ever escape the fiery kiss of the lime that ate away your flesh and bones."

"No!" The dead thing slapped and massaged at itself, still walking, still uncomfortable.

"Then burn." Iakhovas started to walk away.

"Wait," the dead thing whined.

Laaqueel watched as the dead thing dug down into the lime ashes and found a small bottle. The dead thing tossed it up to Iakhovas.

Stretching out a hand, Iakhovas said a word. Instantly the lime-encrusted bottle stopped, hovering above and not quite touching his palm. He took out a cloth from his cloak with his other hand, then wrapped it around the bottle and put it away without getting burned.

"I've done what you asked of me, wizard," the dead thing said, wrapping its arms around itself and rocking with the pain. "Where is my release?"

Iakhovas gestured and spoke.

Immediately the dead thing disappeared in a cloud of whirling white lime.

Iakhovas replaced the stone slab that covered the hole. "Come, little malenti," he growled in anticipation, "we've tarried here long enough." He turned and strode back down the passageway in the direction they'd come, the glowing globe keeping pace with him.

Still unnerved by her experience and not wanting to confront any undead in the tight tunnel by herself, Laaqueel hurried after her master.

As the horses and wagon tumbled the eight or ten feet to the black harbor water, Jherek gathered himself and dived from the horse's back. He plummeted toward the water and hit it cleanly, going under at once. Kicking out, he swam for the thrashing horses, aware of the sahuagin and the other sea creatures filling the water around him. Some of them changed course and headed for him.

He shoved the hook in the sash around his waist and closed on the horses with his sword. Grabbing the traces, he dragged the heavy sword blade across them, parting the leather in seconds. One of the horses swam away, but the other gave in to the wounds the sahuagin had inflicted on it and went still in the water.

Turning his attention back to the wagon, Jherek gratefully saw that it was tight enough at the sideboards and light enough to float—at least for the moment. Still, if the powder kegs had gotten too wet, Khlinat's plan wouldn't work.

The young sailor kicked out and swam to the wagon ahead of a pair of sahuagin. He grabbed the side with his empty hand and expertly pulled his weight aboard without tipping the wagon over. Sonshal worked among the kegs, stuffing fuses into their lids. The slow match coiled over his shoulder glowed orange more brightly when he blew on it to get the coal at its hottest.

Jherek dripped on the wagon. Two inches of water swirled around his boots as the impromptu craft took on water like a sieve. "We don't have much time," he told Sonshal.

"I'm aware of that, boy," the man said, "but if these fuses aren't measured off properly and cut right, we're not going to get the effect your friend is wanting."

Jherek glanced around. "Where is he?" He had to shout over the screams and hoarse yells of sailors and the men on the docks.

"I don't know." Sonshal took a brief respite to boot a sahuagin who was trying to climb onto the wagon, knocking the sea devil back into the water. "I lost sight of him when we hit the water and barely managed to stay with the wagon myself." He poked another fuse into the next barrel.

Concerned, Jherek peered into the water, uncertain if he'd see the dwarf for sure. Too many warring shades of light and darkness overlapped the dark harbor water, turning it alternately into a bright, reflective surface or into a dark and depthless one. Men died quickly out there, on sahuagin claws or tridents, broken and torn apart by the great creatures that had been summoned from the river.

A hand broke the surface only a few feet away.

Jherek reached out and caught the hand, then balanced his weight on the wagon as he took on the dwarf's weight and pulled him from the water. Khlinat's face was masked with fresh blood mixed with water that ran quickly down his chin and throat. He blew his nose noisily and freed his hand axes. Bellowing curses, the peg-legged dwarf hurled himself at their foes.

Jherek defended the other side, keeping the sea devils from Sonshal's back and from the wagon. He ignored the fatigue that filled him, and the throbbing pain that came from the laceration by his eye. In his mind, he imagined Malorrie there, guiding his hand by voice control.

"It's done!" Sonshal roared in warning. "Get overboard!" He dived over himself, setting the example. Khlinat hit the water next.

Jherek took a final glance over his shoulder and watched the smoke streaming from the fuses tucked securely in the powder kegs. He didn't know if the dwarf's plan was going to work, but he knew nothing else that would either. He said a prayer to Ilmater and leaped as sahuagin pulled themselves up into the wagon where water was already halfway up the barrels.

Jherek went deep, swimming for the bottom of the harbor. Khlinat had said he'd seen men use small amounts of the smoke powder to fish with. With the explosions, the concussive force rippled through the water and overloaded the sensitive lateral lines that ran the length of a fish's body, stunning the creatures. Since sahuagin were reputed to have lateral lines as well, which made them so deadly in their home territory, the dwarf had hoped the blast would have the same effect.

Traveling through the water, the sound of the detonations came in rapid succession to Jherek's ears. He held his breath tightly, knowing the blast force would only be a second or two after.

A heartbeat later, it hit him like a brick wall. He struggled to hold onto his consciousness but everything went black.

Pulling back in the alley quickly, Pacys let the sahuagin's trident rip the air harmlessly in his face. The old bard moved with fluid economy, echoing the triumphant cadence of the song that echoed within his head.

Lifting the staff, he blocked the sea devil's second slash then slid the weapon to the side and slammed the iron-capped end into his opponent's face. While the sahuagin remained dazed, Pacys twisted the staff in the middle. Foot-long blades sprang out of either end. He took another step back, set himself, and rammed one blade into the creature's thorax, penetrating the heart.

Still, the sahuagin remained determined to get to its opponent. It raked the air with its claws as Pacys held it back with the staff. The oily black eyes eventually dimmed and the sahuagin draped over the weapon.

Pacys shoved the corpse to the alley floor, aware that other sahuagin already crowded forward. He used the staff with lethal efficiency, clearing a space around him and winning the respect of his savage adversaries. Still, he burned inside to be moving, to pursue the young man he'd spotted on the wagon.

During a brief lull, he knelt down quickly and pinched up some sand from the cobblestones. "Oghma, grant that my spell be strong." He flicked the sand out as he said the words. When he finished, he thought he saw a shimmer wash over the combatants in the alley.

In the next instant, nearly two thirds of their number stumbled and fell, asleep by the time they hit the cobblestones. With the way much clearer, Pacys ran toward the docks.

At the end of the alley, the old bard spotted the sahuagin standing at the dock's edge and peering down, but he didn't see the wagon with the young man in it. The old bard went forward, drawn by the music that grew still stronger inside his head. Fearful of what might have taken place, he told himself that nothing could have happened to the young man without causing the song in his heart and his head to go away.

As long as the tune lived, so did the young man. He felt that had to be true, but he wasn't certain. Staying down from the clustered sahuagin, he raced to the edge of the dark quay and peered down into the water as they were doing. With the wavering light from so many of the nearby buildings and ships that had been torched, to say nothing of the docks in places, it took him a moment to spot the wagon.

It floated, although the amount of water it was taking on as its weight dragged it down testified that it wouldn't float long. The sahuagin jumping after it from the docks made that time even less. The old bard barely made out the gray streamers of smoke curling up from the small barrels in the back.

In the next instant, though, the barrels detonated one by one. The series of explosions threw up geysers of water, smoke, wood chips, and a wave of force that blew Pacys from his feet.

Live, that you may serve.

The cold, powerful voice filled Jherek's mind, snapping him back from the black void where his senses had fled. He woke in the harbor water, his lungs burning with the need for air and the cold claws of a sahuagin wrapping his neck.

Somehow he'd managed to hang onto his weapons. He let his anger at the disembodied voice that had spoken to him fill his mind. All his life, since he'd been a small boy, that voice had been a part of him. He didn't know where it came from, or from whom, or what he was supposed to serve.

He'd struggled for years to find out, thinking at first that he'd simply imagined it. But he hadn't imagined the dolphins that had saved his life that first time, nor the last time aboard *Finaren's Butterfly* when the unknown power had set him free from a sahuagin net during battle. Even Madame Iitaar with her skill at divination and Malorrie with all his book learning and knowledge he'd picked up over the course of his life and death hadn't been able to tell him what it meant.

But there was no doubt how that voice had influenced and shaped his life.

The echoes of the voice and the command were still in his mind when he moved. Despite the water surrounding him he moved quickly, going through it as if it wasn't there to block the sahuagin before the creature could scissor the flesh of his throat. The move would have worked above water but shouldn't have now—only it did, and he guessed that it had to be because the sahuagin was partially stunned by the exploding powder kegs.

Pushing away from his attacker, seeing the evil glint in its oily black eyes, Jherek shoved his sword into the sahuagin's throat with a quick flick, then twisted. Blood muddied up from the wound.

Jherek glanced up, aware of a number of sahuagin bodies floating limply in the water all around him. Several of them were slowly surfacing. Fire burned on top of the water where the wagon had been, and a spray of bright colors spread across the dark sky. He kicked past the dying sahuagin and stroked for the surface. Once his face was out of the water, he sucked in great breaths. He whipped the hair from his eyes and stared across the harbor.

The explosive force of the barrels had been considerable, greater than he'd expected, but he knew from Malorrie's teachings that water was denser and carried sounds more clearly. That was why a man swimming had to assume that anything in the water he tracked already knew he was there. The trick was to appear harmless. There was no slipping and hiding through the water unnoticed by one who lived there.

Sahuagin and sea creature bodies lay stretched across the harbor water, floating in islands of limp flesh. Some of them had been left conscious, though, and the ones on land hadn't been affected at all. However, those on the land suddenly experienced a lack of reinforcements and the Flaming Fist mercenaries noticed it. A rousing yell broke from the ranks of the citizens and the fighting began again in earnest as they recovered from the blast.

Not all of the concussive force had spread beneath the harbor. Several of the nearby buildings had only remnants of glass shards where windows had once been. Crates lay tumbled and scattered, and small boats used for servicing the cargo ships lay broken, overturned, or tossed out on the docks.

"Damn cure was almost worse than the disease," Sonshal growled from nearby. He gazed upward where the last of the fireworks spent themselves and winked out. "Couldn't resist that last touch. I've always prided myself on the quality of my fireworks."

"Where's Khlinat?" Jherek asked.

Sonshal shook his head. "Don't know, boy. I wasn't keeping track of things any too well there for a minute."

Jherek pushed past the limp body of a ten-foot long snake. He scanned the water hastily.

"Over here, swabbie." Khlinat sounded weak.

Tracking the voice, Jherek spotted the dwarf treading water with his face barely exposed. He swam to the little man. "What's wrong?"

"Can't feel me leg," Khlinat said hoarsely. "Marthammor Duin protect a silly old dwarf who's wandered so far from hearth and home to die alone." He cut his eyes to Jherek. "Swabbie, I think that blast done for me. I can't feel anything below me waist."

Jherek looked down at the water. The fires lighting the docks brought out scarlet highlights that floated on the surface. "What happened?"

"Don't know. Felt a powerful lot of pain after that explosion—then nothing at all." The dwarf's eyes rolled feverishly. "Getting awful cold, swabbie."

Sonshal swam up beside them. "Let's get him to shore."

"I've got him," Jherek said. He thrust his sword through the sash at his waist, then hooked an arm under the dwarf's chin from behind and swam for the docks. Khlinat's ragged pulse beat against his forearm. "Just hold steady, Khlinat. We're not going to let you go."

"Ye may not be given a choice," the dwarf croaked.

Reaching the dock, Jherek was challenged at once by the Flaming Fist mercenaries who'd established a beachhead and were in the process of beating the sahuagin back. More mercenaries arrived, and still others were putting out into the harbor in small boats and slitting the throats of the helpless sahuagin and other creatures that had been stunned by the blast.

Some of them helped Jherek and Sonshal get Khlinat up onto the dock and laid out. Jherek seized a torch from a nearby man and held it to study the dwarf.

Khlinat held his hands over his lower abdomen. Blood spilled between his fingers. "Got me betwixt wind and water, swabbie. Unless we can get a healer damned quick, I ain't going to live to see the morrow."

Jherek knew it was true. He turned to the Flaming Fist mercenaries. "I need a healer."

A grizzled old warrior with blood soaking up through his right arm and dripping from his bared blade crossed over to them. He looked down at the dwarf and shook his head. "You'd have to be one of Tymora's most favored this night to find one, boy, but I'll put the word out."

" 'Tis no good, swabbie," Khlinat whispered. "Ye did yer best, and there's no complaints about that." He managed a smile that looked terrible against his graying complexion. "We gave them damned sea devils what-for, didn't we?"

"Yes," Sonshal said, kneeling beside the dwarf. He'd seized a cloak from one of the passing mercenaries who still had dry clothes and spread it over the little man. "That was a piece of risky business you did there, friend, and I'll not begrudge the tale in the telling. I'm proud to have been at your side."

"Ah, 'twas ye," Khlinat said. "Ye stood there and lit them fuses while them sahuagin were about climbing yer backside. Takes a brave man to do that."

Gently, Jherek pried the dwarf's hands from his wound, finding it much easier than he'd thought. Tears burned at the back of his eyes for the little man, though he'd known him for only a short time. The innate bravery and honor Khlinat had shown touched him deeply.

The wound was two or three inches across on Khlinat's abdomen, and there was an exit wound on the other side just as large. Khlinat's breathing slowed and grew shallower.

"Looks like he had a spear rammed through him," Sonshal whispered.

"A spear didn't do that," Jherek said. He guessed that it had been a shard from the wagon, ripped loose and propelled through the water by the smoke powder blast. The wound seemed clear. "We need to get the bleeding stopped. That way he'll have a chance of lasting till a healer gets here." He felt panicked and responsible for the dwarf's situation though he didn't know why. He'd been as much at risk as Khlinat had.

Yet nothing had happened to him even when he'd woke with a sahuagin's claws at his throat.

Live, that you may serve.

Tears coursed down Jherek's face, released by the pent-up pain of watching the dwarf die, the frustration of not being able to do anything about it, and the anger at all that he didn't understand. He pressed his hands to the dwarf's wounds, stemming the blood flow. "Go find a healer," he told Sonshal.

"There's not one to be had," the old man said gruffly. He rested a hand on Jherek's shoulder. "You've done what you could for him. Sometimes all that remains to be done is to be with them when the passing comes. No man should be alone when that happens."

"No!" Jherek said hoarsely. "He's not going to die!"

"There's nothing you can do about that," Sonshal said. "A man's life runs the course his gods direct it on, and no man may stay the hand of death when it arrives."

"No! I won't accept that!" It wasn't right that the dwarf should save so many, yet lose his life in the attempt.

Live, that you may serve.

Jherek reached for that voice, wondering where it came from and how it dared seem to choose him when there were so many others to pick from. He willed the dwarf not to die. "Pray," he told the dwarf, "pray to your Marthammor Duin that you live, Khlinat, then believe with all your might."

Jherek knew that he didn't believe that strongly himself. He'd chosen Ilmater as his god because he most understood the religion. The Crying God based his ethos on enduring and persevering, things that the young sailor understood intimately. His whole life had been about those things.

Khlinat coughed and groaned in pain. Blood bubbled from his lips and ran down his cheek. Blue light dawned at his throat, partially obscured by his matted beard.

Without warning, Jherek felt a low buzz in his hands, like he'd brushed up against an electric eel. Smoky blue blazed under his palms pressed against the dwarf's side. He felt the changes taking place against his hands, but he couldn't move them.

The buzzing finished, and the blue light at Khlinat's throat winked out.

The dwarf's lungs filled in a rush, and he flicked his eyes open. "Swabbie, what have you done?" His voice sounded stronger, more certain.

"Nothing," Jherek said, as puzzled as the dwarf. He felt drained by the events of the last few minutes. His eyelids dragged as he scanned the little man.

Khlinat coughed. "Only if yer calling saving me life nothing, and I ain't ready to call it that. Whatever ye did, I feel better."

"It wasn't him," Sonshal said. "It was something at your throat."

Khlinat reached up and took up the shark tooth pendent at his throat, stretching it the length of the leather thong that held it. "This?" He shook his head. "This is nothing. A trinket left over from the shark what took my leg. Them teeth come out regular, and the healer what fixed me up found it in what was left of me leg. I've been carrying it as a good luck charm, nothing more."

"What else could be the answer?" Sonshal asked.

The dwarf looked at Jherek. "I don't know, but I do know I feel better. Let's have a look at me side."

Hesitantly, Jherek drew his hands away, afraid that the torrent of blood would begin again.

It didn't. Instead, the flesh appeared to have closed in both places. It remained raw and ragged looking, but it was obviously healing, reconnecting.

"Marthammor Duin save a wandering fool," the dwarf cried in astonishment. "Outside of a heal potion, or a healer's hands, I've never seen the like."

Jherek gave him a smile and settled back tiredly on his haunches. The blood was drying tight on his hands. "If I were you, I wouldn't loose that shark's tooth."

Khlinat reverently kissed the pendant. "I'll never feel as angry about that shark, I tell ye."

Glancing out at the harbor, Jherek saw that a rout of the sahuagin and their aquatic accomplices was in full swing. He had no wish in him to be one of the parties responsible for slitting the throats of the stunned sahuagin. Now that they were organized, the Flaming Fist mercenaries appeared to have things well in hand. He looked for his father's ship, but *Bunyip* was nowhere to be seen.

It was too late to save many lives, too late to save nearly all of the boats and much of the docks and some of the warehouses and buildings near them, but the docks thronged with men and women who fought enemies as well as fires.

He considered the battle. Madame Iitaar had sent him to Baldur's Gate after his heritage to Bloody Falkane's pirates was discovered on *Butterfly*. She'd had a vision that his destiny lay here in the city, but where?

He studied the narrow stone buildings and homes and tried to divine what he was supposed to find here. Dark thoughts intruded, and he had to wonder if it hadn't all been some kind of mistake. His life had never been simple or easy. He thought this could be a set of circumstances deliberately fashioned to lead him here and make an even bigger fool of him.

But who would do such a thing? And why?

He didn't know, but the voice he heard in his mind at such times was real. He had to believe at least that much because thinking himself mad was no option at all.

He heard someone come to a stop behind him and looked up to find a skinny old man with a bald head peering down at him with more interest than the young sailor had ever felt before. Carefully, he got to his feet.

"Can I help you?" Jherek asked.

"Mayhap we can help each other," the old man said. "My name is Pacys. I'm a bard. I wonder if I might have a moment of your time."

Jherek studied the old man but didn't feel in any way threatened by him. "Let me help my friend to a safe place, then I'll help you in any way I may." He couldn't turn down the anxious note in the old bard's voice, though he also didn't know why the man might think he needed him.

"Of course. Perhaps I could accompany you."

" 'Tis a long walk down some powerful dark streets," Khlinat said.

The old bard nodded. "I've seen hardships in life. Surviving this night has not been easy."

The dwarf harumphed as Jherek helped him to his feet. "One as aged as ye, I'll wager ye have seen some bad times."

The young sailor found aiding Khlinat in walking was an adventure in itself. The dwarf was too short to simply drape his arm across his shoulders, and too heavy to support easily.

"Well come on then," Khlinat growled. "I've a small place, but yer welcome to what I have. With Marthammor's sagacious blessing, mayhap there'll even be some victuals we can scrape together."

8

"Ye play a pretty tune on that thing."

Pacys glanced up at Khlinat, who lounged across the small table in the modest quarters he kept at a rooming house on Windspell Street just west of the Wide, the name of Baldur's Gate's bustling marketplace. "Thank you, my friend." His fingers strummed the strings casually, picking out the notes, making them ring true. The song lived inside his head, adding to itself by leaps and bounds. He was already working on the song of the attack on Baldur's Gate and the words came so easily.

A beeswax taper burned on the table between them, throwing up a thin streamer of smoke and illuminating the carving board with a loaf of bread and cheese on it. Felogyr Sonshal had begged off as soon as they'd reached the dwelling safely. The dwarf's fare on hand had been simple, added to by small journeycakes smothered in honey he'd had put away, a clutch of apples, and a jug of cheap wine.

The old bard had eaten, picking at the offered food mostly, and he'd watched Jherek of Velen, trying to see some sign that the young sailor was the one Narros had told him to look for. As he surveyed the young man, he tried to figure out how he was going to tell Jherek of the destiny that lay before him. How could one so young, so vulnerable, be expected to shoulder such a heavy burden as facing the wrath of the Taker?

Khlinat had eaten with the relish of someone who had recently ended a long fast, drinking the wine with zest. He cut up another apple with a small carving knife, glanced briefly out the window as a Flaming Fist mercenary group went by carrying lamps. "How came ye to know the swabbie?" he asked.

"I don't," Pacys said.

"Yet ye came over to him like ye knowed him." The dwarf's eyes narrowed in suspicion.

They spoke about Jherek because the young man had taken his leave of them only a few minutes ago. Pacys had been loathe to let him from his sight, but Jherek had been adamant about not leaving Khlinat to himself should something go wrong with the wounds. The young sailor had taken it upon himself to seek out an apothecary for balms to better treat and dress the wounds until a healer could be sent for.

Pacys put a hand over the yarting's strings, stilling their hum. "I was sent to find him."

Khlinat fisted the carving knife casually, but shifted in his chair to get into better position. "The swabbie's not wanted for anything, is he? I'll not harbor anyone saying bad things about him. He laid his life on the line for people tonight, meself included, and didn't say one word about it."

"I expect he wouldn't," Pacys agreed. He'd noticed Jherek's calm demeanor as well. "No, he's not wanted for anything."

"Good, for ye had me worried a moment." Khlinat stabbed the knife into the carving board. "I've not had blood spilt in me room before, but I'd not hesitate."

Pacys's fingers returned to the strings, playing the hero's tune that he identified with Jherek. "How long have you known him?"

"I only met him tonight."

Surprised lifted one of the old bard's eyebrows.

"He came up on a caravan from the south," Khlinat said. "I had that from him before them pirates sculled into the harbor and started their attack. He hails from Velen."

"I know the place," Pacys said.

"Lot of ghosts and such there," Khlinat mused.

"What do you know about him?"

The dwarf shrugged and popped a piece of apple into his mouth. "He's a sailor and a good man. Lot of sand in his craw, ye want my opinion. Not many would have stood up like he did tonight."

"You did," Pacys said. "Driving a wagonload of smoke powder into the harbor was no trivial thing."

"I had me reasons."

Pacys changed tunes, finding the one he'd selected for the dwarf as he wove his song about the attack on Baldur's Gate. It was somewhat hard and unpolished, much like the little man himself. "You mean the Harper pin you wear?" The old bard had spotted it on the other man earlier back at the docks. It was clipped inside his shirt, out of the way of the most casual glances. Harpers didn't readily identify themselves except to others of their group.

Khlinat didn't answer.

"It's all right," Pacys said. "I know about Those Who Harp."

"Ye wear the pin yerself?"

Pacys shook his head. "I was asked. I chose not to." The Harpers were a group spead thinly across the face of Faerûn that primarily worked for good. Individuals among the group also had their own agendas, though, and that was a problem at times and for some people.

"Being a Harper is an important thing," Khlinat stated.

"Some would call your group meddlers," Pacys pointed out.

"Mayhap, but we stand betwixt evil, them what would take away freedoms, and the common man." Khlinat returned his gaze levelly, the candle flame wavering in his eyes. "I can imagine no higher calling."

Pacys reworked the tune in his head, bringing out the true sound of it through his fingertips. "For myself, I can imagine no higher calling than my art. Belief is a harsh mistress, and you have to believe in one thing most of all in your life. Otherwise, you're compromised."

"Aye. Now that's the right of it." Khlinat drained the dregs of his wine cup. "Ye never mentioned what ye wanted with the swabbie."

Changing the melody again, going back to the piece he'd constructed about his visit with Narros the merman in Waterdeep harbor, Pacys told the tale in his best voice, trusting in the good nature of Those Who Harp, winning Khlinat over to his side. Also, he knew it would help to have Khlinat on his side if possible when he presented the story to Jherek. As he talked, the dwarf poured them both fresh cups of spiced wine.

"How can I help you, my son?"

Jherek looked into the priest's eyes and saw the fatigue there. "I'm looking for a healing balm for a friend if you've any to spare." He opened his coin purse. "I'm willing to pay."

The Rose Portal was a shrine to Lathander, also called Morninglord, who was god of the spring, dawn, birth, and renewal, of beginnings and hidden potentials. Like the other buildings along the north wall of Baldur's Gate, the temple was constructed primarily of stone but the windows inset in the walls were of the palest pink to reflect the dawn. Even the torch Jherek carried picked up the color in the night.

He'd tried the temple of Ilmater before coming here, but their resources had already been drained. He'd stayed long enough to say his prayers to the god and make his peace with the night's events. Remembering how well he'd been treated at Lathander's temple in Atkatla, he'd decided to try there when one of the people on the street he'd asked had mentioned it.

"Child," the old priest said as he stepped back from the door, "enter and we'll see what Lathander has seen fit to provide us. Even now new donations are being received to help with the victims." He was short and broad, with a belly on him that spoke of familiarity with wine casks. His red and yellow robes hung loosely about him, stopping just short of the smooth stone floor.

Jherek stepped into the foyer and felt some of the chill hanging over the city drain away from him. He hadn't taken the time to change his drenched clothing, and it clung to his body with the touch of ice and rough salt.

While the temple back in Athkatla had been modest, this place spoke of opulence. The decor was ornate, steeped in inlaid gold and silver, constructed of polished and burnished woods carefully fitted together. Beyond the foyer, rows of long benches filled the space, all turned toward the dais where a huge rose quartz disk almost ten feet tall occupied the back wall. Rendered in the glowing pink stone were rose-colored swirls centered around a pair of golden eyes.

Jherek flushed with embarrassment to think that the temple would need any or even all of the coins he'd been paid for the caravan work. Quietly, he followed the priest down the aisle.

Several people in agitated states sat in the benches. Many of them prayed out loud while others cried and wailed for lost loved ones. Other priests moved within the groups, offering solace or a healer's touch. As Jherek passed by one bench, he saw a young priest not much older than him on his knees reaching up to close the eyes of a Flaming Fist mercenary who'd stilled in death. Beside him, the dead man's wife and children clung to his legs and cried.

The young sailor quickly averted his gaze, not wanting to intrude on their grief. He knew none of the people, but he knew the anger and frustration and fear that filled them. In his life, he'd known little else until he'd escaped his father and reached Velen.

The priest led him to a back room where foodstuffs and other stores were kept. The room was large and generous, filled with well-stocked shelves and lit by candelabras. Priests worked with parishioners, sorting through the boxes and baskets of supplies that were being unloaded from a cart at the back door.

The priest called one of the acolytes and asked him to search for the things Jherek needed. In quick order, the young priest rounded up the necessary materials.

Jherek offered his coin purse. "Take what you feel is just."

The priest regarded him with renewed interest. "Pardon me for saying so, boy, but you look as though that pouch contains the last coins you have."

Jherek felt another sharp pang of embarrassment. The pouch in his hand looked pitifully slim, and he'd been so proud of it that afternoon when the caravan had arrived in Baldur's Gate. "If it's not enough, I'll bring more at another time if you'll trust me for it."

The priest shook his head, reaching out and curling the pouch back in the young sailor's hand. "You misunderstand me, boy. Lathander doesn't just take from a community; he gives back. Else how can he work the miracles with the new beginnings he speaks of?"

Still, Jherek felt bad. The priests at Ilmater's shrine hadn't dissuaded him of making a donation there, and he'd gotten nothing from them except apologies.

"Just remember Lathander, boy," the priest said. "The Morninglord knows the wheel turns. We all give and get alternately, each as to their needs. Every day is a beginning of some kind for everyone."

Jherek nodded.

"Stings your pride, doesn't it, lad?" an old man's voice croaked behind Jherek. "Taking things offered you is hard."

When he turned and saw the old man who'd addressed him, Jherek swallowed an angry retort. The young sailor couldn't guess how old the man was. Time had marched scores of hard years over him. The man's face sagged with thick wrinkles, and his fevered blue eyes peered up from gristled pits. A fringe of gray hair gnarled around his head. He wore deep scarlet robes that marked him as a priest. Both hands shook, whether from age or illness Jherek couldn't say, and provided him a precarious balance.

"Do you have something to say, lad?" the old man asked, his face stern in spite of the loose flesh on his face.

"Brother Cadiual," the first priest said, "what are you doing out of bed?" He sounded very concerned and walked over quickly to the old man's side. "I gave strict orders that you were not to be disturbed."

Jherek smelled the illness on the old man and breathed shallowly through his mouth to avoid it.

"I'm here doing Lathander's work," Cadiual snapped. "As I have ever done during my life."

"But you're not well."

"Ghauryn," the old man said in a hoarse whisper that stopped the other priest's objections immediately, "I was running this temple long before you ever suckled at your mother's breast. I'll not suffer your insubordination now."

The other priest nodded, taking a half-step back. "As you command and Lathander wills."

Cadiual eyed Jherek. "Who are you, boy?"

"I'm called Malorrie, a sailor from Velen."

The rheumy old eyes searched Jherek's face. "What brought you here?"

Jherek showed him the bandages and balms Ghauryn had given him. "I've got a wounded friend."

Cadiual waved the answer away in irritation. "No. Before that. What brought you to Baldur's Gate?"

"I came with a caravan from Athkatla."

"Yet you're not from Amn, and by your own professed statement, you're a sailor. What were you doing with a caravan?"

Jherek felt very uncomfortable, suddenly realizing he had the attention of many of the priests in the back room. "It was the only way I could get here."

"Again," the old man said in his cracking, hoarse voice. "Why did you choose to come here, at this time when the sea itself rises up against us?"

"I came because I wanted to learn more about myself."

"See," Ghauryn interrupted, "you've been under the influence of that fever again, Cadiual. He's given you your answer." He reached for the old man's shoulder.

Angrily, Cadiual swept his cane toward the other priest, making him step back again. He returned his attention to Jherek. "You came because you wanted to learn *what* about yourself?"

Jherek silently wished he'd never stepped foot into the temple of Lathander. He wished he could muster the ill manners it would take to simply walk away from the old man and his piercing gaze. "Where I should go from here."

"You were sent here, weren't you? By a divination that you couldn't possibly comprehend."

Jherek didn't reply, feeling that he was being the butt of some bit of humor he didn't understand. He tried to take a step and leave.

"You think I'm some foolish old man, don't you?" Cadiual said.

"No," Jherek answered politely. "I think perhaps you've got me confused with someone else."

"Nay. I was told long before you were born that you would one day find your way here. A sailor, I was told, shorn from the sea and bereft of home, a man hardly more than a boy who runs from the bloody shadow of his father. A boy seeking his future to outrun his past, who was needy, yet hated to take on any help from others. To accomplish his task, there was much help he'd have to take along the way. Learning to accept that would be only one of his lessons." He paused. "Though we think we live our lives alone, there is no one of us completely alone, boy. The gods overlook us all."

Astonishment froze Jherek in place. There was no way the priest could know all that, unless he truly was mad and his powers of divination were confused by his insanity.

"Still, there is one way to be certain." Cadiual reached inside his robe and took out a soft leather bag that showed decades of wear. He opened it and poured yellowed ivory bone splinters into his hand. "These are dragon bones. Lathander himself saw to it I was given these while still yet a child. They've guided me for years. Let me have your hand."

Reluctantly, Jherek stuck his hand out. When the priest's hand wrapped around his, he felt the shakes the old man was experiencing, and the thin finger bones as sticklike as the dragon bones the priest poured into his hand.

Cadiual gripped Jherek's hand in both his shaking ones, then closed his eyes and began praying to Lathander. The heat that suddenly flamed through his flesh surprised the young sailor. He tried to pull away, but the old priest gripped him more surely than he'd thought.

The old priest finished his prayer, and the priests around him echoed his final appreciative sentiments toward the Morninglord. The rheumy eyes gazed up at Jherek.

"You are the one," the old man said. "The one who has come to

Baldur's Gate at the time the sea has risen up against all of Faerûn. The one who will somehow find a way to stem the tide of dark reaping."

Jherek immediately shook his head, feeling trapped. "No. You've got me confused with someone else. That can't be right. You don't know who I am. Or what I am."

"I don't have to know," the old priest said. "All I have to do is believe in Lathander and let his hand guide mine. It's all I've ever needed. There is a final proof." He took back the splinters of dragon bones and put them back in the pouch, then he took from his robe an oval pearl encased in a gold disk nearly as large as Jherek's palm.

The gold was soft and buttery, showing numerous scratches and hard usage. As the old priest turned the object in his fingers, Jherek noted that the flat side of the pearl had been cut, raising a trident overlaying a silhouetted conch shell from the gemstone.

"I was told by the man who gave me this all those years ago," Cadiual said, "to give this to the young man who appeared in this temple on the night the sea powers wended their way into Baldur's Gate to strike against us."

"Why?" Jherek asked.

"You must stem the tide." Cadiual held the half-pearl out for him to take.

"No," Jherek said hoarsely when he realized the priest meant to give him the gem. "I'm not who you think I am. I can't be."

"Take the gem."

"I can't." But Jherek wanted to so badly he could barely restrain himself from plucking it up. Such a destiny must lie before the person that gem was truly meant for. He'd no longer have to be known as Jherek Wolf's-get, son of the bloodiest pirate of the Nelanther Isles. But to stem the tide of sahuagin that ravaged the Sword Coast? How was that going to be possible?

"It's yours," Cadiual said. "I felt it when I closed my hands over yours. You are the one." He grabbed Jherek's hand and placed the pearl in it.

Immediately, the young sailor thought the gemstone glowed soft pink but that could have been only a trick of the light. Still, it felt natural for him to hold it. He gazed into the pink-stained depths, trying to make sense of the trident and the conch shell emblazoned on the face of the pearl. If he were the one, wouldn't the secrets be unlocked for him? In the novels Malorrie had given him to read, things like that always happened to the heroes.

But he knew in his heart he couldn't take it. The gemstone was obviously meant for someone other than him. Someone better. The old man had gotten unbalanced with his age and the responsibility given him.

"What am I supposed to do with it?" Jherek asked, thinking that his lack of knowledge would be a clear indication that the wrong person had been entrusted with it.

"I don't know," Cadiual admitted. "Nor do I know for sure where it came from. The man who arrived here came from the east. I had a gemologist look at it once, and he said perhaps it came from as far away as the Inner Sea. There was something about the way the pearl was constructed, about the layering."

"Then why bring it here?" Jherek asked.

"Because this was where you were going to be, of course," the old man snapped. "You have so little faith. Why is that?"

For a moment, Jherek was almost moved to tell the priest everything, from his childhood to the tattoo revealed on *Finaren's Butterfly* that had cost him the only good life he'd known, but he couldn't.

He offered the gemstone back to the man.

"No," Cadiual replied. "I've not made the mistake here. It's you and your lack of faith, and that's something between you and your god. I can only offer guidance."

"You've made a mistake," Jherek said in a level voice.

"No," the priest said confidently. "I've made no mistake." He put his thin hand on Jherek's shoulder. "Go and find your destiny, young sailor. For though I don't know it, I feel it will be something truly grand. But the way will not be easy." The rheumy eyes locked with Jherek's. "Find your faith, boy, find your faith and cling to it so that it will make you whole." He turned and walked away.

Desperate, Jherek looked at the other priest, then offered the pearl to him.

"Ghauryn," Cadiual called without bothering to turn around, "I've carried that gemstone since before you were born and I've grown weary of its burden. I thought death was going to steal my life away before I had the chance to finish what I was given to do. Don't you dare touch it."

The other priest shook his head at Jherek.

Reluctantly, Jherek closed his hand over the gemstone. It felt warm and sure, and he was surprised at the confidence that seemed to radiate from it. He had no doubt that they'd given it to the wrong man. Perhaps, though, he could return in the morning and the old priest would have had time to rethink what he'd done.

He thanked the priest for the bandages and salves and walked outside. He belted the healer's items in a bag at his side, but he kept the pearl out, not wanting to release it.

"Are you his woman?"

Startled by the question but wanting to buy herself some time, Laaqueel stood in *Bunyip*'s stern and gazed at the western sky. The fires that had burned Baldur's Gate had dimmed somewhat, but an angry yellow glow like fresh broken seagull eggs still carved a pocket from the dark sky in the distance.

The malenti priestess kept her hands on the ship's railing, holding fast. The dark waters of the River Chionthar slid back from where she stood, cleaved by *Bunyip*'s prow.

Behind her, Bloody Falkane came closer, till he stood right behind her. He kept his voice soft and low. "I asked you a question." His tone held command.

Immediately, Laaqueel rebelled against that authority. She turned to face him, a prayer to Sekolah on her lips and her hand resting on the long dagger at her hip. Her trident was only an arm's reach away, but she knew he could move quickly and intercept her.

"You have asked a question," she replied, "and I have deigned not to answer it."

Bloody Falkane stared at her with hooded eyes. His foul surface dweller's breath fell against her cheek. She knew he was handsome in the way that surface dwellers counted themselves so, and there was a cruelty about his dark eyes and mouth that a sahuagin could appreciate.

His oiled black hair was pulled back, but strands blown by the wind leaked down into his face. Silver hoop earrings caught the moonlight and splintered it. His mustache and goatee were carefully trimmed, leaving the tattoo of the bunyip coiled in mid-strike on his left cheek. He wore a black shirt trimmed in scarlet open to his chest, and scarlet breeches tucked into knee-high boots rolled at the top. A long sword hung at his left hip, balanced by the three throwing knives on his right.

Falkane smiled. "I could make you answer."

"You could die trying," Laaqueel promised in a cold voice.

"Ah, Laaqueel, that would be such a wondrous thing to see. My skills against your skills." Moving slowly, Falkane touched her hair with his fingers, stroking it.

Not knowing how she was supposed to handle this situation according to Iakhovas's strictures, Laaqueel allowed his touch. Never in her life had a man, an elf, or a sahuagin touched her so.

"Do not," she warned, "think to overstep your bounds with me."

"Or what?"

Laaqueel had no answer. Iakhovas had joined with the pirates of the Nelanther Isles without her knowledge, only revealing the fact to her shortly before he'd killed Huaanton and proclaimed himself king. She didn't know what those alliances entailed, or how she was supposed to handle them. She stared hotly back at Falkane, hating the fact that she couldn't speak on her own.

"Do you know what generally happens to people who threaten me?" the pirate captain asked.

Laaqueel didn't reply. She'd heard a number of stories about Bloody Falkane, the Salt Wolf. His whole past was spun of violence and fear.

He dropped his fingers from her hair, tracing her jawline.

The malenti controlled herself, not flinching from his touch. He held no power over her. If anything, he might be considered her equal. So she didn't drop her eyes and defer to him as was custom among the sahuagin so no insult might be implied. She returned his full gaze hotly. What surprised her most was how her body reacted to his touch. Warm vibrations thrilled through her, and a bitter ache dawned at the core of her. She didn't know how his touch had incited such a reaction unless it could be blamed on her cursed heritage.

He traced her jawline with his forefinger, then brought it back to rest at her chin just below her bottom lip. He was a few inches taller than she was and suddenly seemed to envelop her.

"People who threaten me," he said, still in that soft voice, "die—in the most horrible ways I can think of. I assure you, I'm quite practiced at it."

Laaqueel tried to keep her thoughts centered on Sekolah, remembering that the Great Shark wouldn't put anything before her that she couldn't handle. If she failed Sekolah's tests, she would only prove her unworthiness. That was totally unacceptable. She only wished that Falkane's touch didn't have the affect on her that it did.

She shifted her attention to the deck over his shoulder. His men moved through the halyards with grim efficiency, some of them sporting bandages from wounds they'd received in the attack. Still, it didn't keep her mind from his touch.

"I've watched you," Falkane said, "these few times that we've shared company since first meeting in Skaug, and I've puzzled over your relationship with Black Alaric."

Black Alaric was the name Iakhovas had chosen to wear among the Nelanther Isles. The first pirate to wear the name of Black Alaric had appeared fourteen hundred years ago, then reappeared time and time again during periods of unrest.

Since learning of Iakhovas's chosen identity, the malenti priestess had researched the legend in her books of surface history. She'd first studied those to become adept as a spy among the sea elves and surface dwellers. The last Black Alaric had been active a hundred years ago. Iakhovas had claimed to take over the present identity five years ago, and had been plotting his strategies since that time.

"There is nothing to puzzle over," she told Falkane.

The pirate looked at her and grinned. "Until that day I met you, I'd never seen you in Skaug before."

Until that time, Laaqueel had never been in the capital city of the pirates before.

"I know I didn't because I would have remembered you if I had," Falkane said. "Someone so beautiful as you."

"You mock me." Laaqueel let some of the anger she felt drip venom into her words before she could stop herself. It was bad enough she had to so resemble a surface dweller and the hated sea elves, but her disfigurement also included dealing with some of the emotions that plagued them.

"No," he assured her. "I don't. I think you're a most enchanting creature." His eyes blazed as he deliberately looked at her from head to toe. "You're a beautiful woman. Don't you know that?"

"No," she replied. Even though she was fully clothed, she felt naked for the first time in her life. It was an unsettling experience.

"You have no man sequestered away somewhere?" he asked. "No lover?"

"No." In the sahuagin culture, possessions were to be admired and fought over, not mates. The reproductive cycle was a necessary thing. They didn't even raise their own children, turning the eggs over to the crèches responsible for rearing them.

"Where were you raised to be so uninformed about the power you have to turn a man's head?" he asked.

Laaqueel looked at him, thinking that she'd like to turn his head till it spun off his shoulders. She wished she knew where Iakhovas was. They'd taken passage on Falkane's ship when they'd fled the sewers under Baldur's Gate. Iakhovas had immediately demanded a cabin and went off to examine whatever treasure he'd captured from the lime pit.

"I've heard that Black Alaric is a satyr in bed," Falkane said. "I've paid women who've spied on him. They couldn't tell me much more because he's very secretive."

Laaqueel looked at the pirate captain in shock. Since she'd been with Iakhovas, she'd never seen that side of him. Among the sahuagin, he'd been uninvolved with the opposite sex, and among others he'd always been in control.

"You didn't know that?" Falkane taunted.

"No. He has a habit of keeping his business as his own."

"And what are your feelings about him?"

Laaqueel shook her head. "I have none. I follow him because I believe that's what I'm supposed to do."

"Don't you ever think for yourself?"

"Of course," she snapped.

Falkane tapped her chin with his forefinger, stroking her flesh. "Then what do you think about me?"

"Nothing," Laaqueel stated flatly, but she knew that was no longer true. His interest in her, even if it was for reasons of his own, could provide an advantage for her that she'd never had since entering Iakhovas's thrall.

"Then I'll make that my mission," he told her. "Starting at this very moment, I promise you that you'll have cause to never forget me."

"You'd only be wasting your time. I'll forget about you the second you walk away."

Before she could move, he slid his hand behind her neck with a quickness she hadn't expected. He cupped the back of her head and pulled her to him, crushing his lips to hers in a deep kiss.

9

The streets of Baldur's Gate remained busy as wagons went to and fro. Crews gathered the dead and piled them in community graves so sickness wouldn't spread from the corpses. Other groups concentrated on clearing the debris. The forlorn cries of women and children, and even some men, filled the streets. Clerics walked at the head of the death wagons, speaking prayers and waving censers filled with strong-smelling herbs.

Jherek couldn't keep his thoughts from the carved pearl disk in his fist. Everything it represented hung in his mind. Madame Iitaar and Malorrie had both felt his future had lain in Baldur's Gate, but he'd been offered no clue as to what it might be. He didn't even know where to go from here.

How was destiny found, or even pursued?

He had no clue, but holding the disk made him feel like achieving that was possible. He passed a group of men standing around a rose-red torch at a corner where the street he followed wound back toward the Wide. They talked quickly among themselves, voices high with emotion.

Earlier, he'd noticed the groups around the rose-red torches gathered for what seemed to be casual conversation. Cobble parties, Frauk had called them in a voice that gave no doubt how he felt about them. The caravan master wasn't a man to waste time.

The men had no light bantering of conversation between them now. Their voices reeked of angry frustration and pain. Jherek clung to the pearl disk a little more tightly, silently willing it to give up its secrets. Even though he knew he wasn't the one it was intended for, and that impression was very strong in him, he wanted to experience part of what it must feel like to be given something so important.

Instead, he remembered how *Bunyip* had looked out in the harbor. The lines remained as he'd remembered them, clean and tight except for the missing mast, and she'd looked defiant as ever.

Jherek wondered if his father would even recognize him now without seeing the tattoo on the inside of his left bicep. He became angry and frustrated with himself for even considering such a thing. His father had never cared about him, only about his own dark desires.

Black depression settled over Jherek, robbing him of even the small comfort the pearl disk had lent him. How could he dare to think even for a moment that such a thing might be intended for him, knowing where he'd come from?

No, what tonight had proven was that even the gods liked their cruel jokes. They'd placed the pearl disk before him, given him a hint of the legacy that lay ahead of someone more deserving, only to taunt him and make him recognize again the low station he'd been given in his life.

Despite the priest's words, the young sailor knew there was no escaping the past. His unmasking in Velen had proven that. He had been marked by fate as surely as Bloody Falkane had marked him with the sorcerous tattoo.

Jherek had been so deep in his thoughts that he hadn't noticed when the slim-hipped figure had walked by him, but he was aware when the person turned around. Jherek took a step to the side and his hand drifted down to the sword hung in his sash. Cold air chilled him through his wet clothing. He waited.

"Malorrie?" a feminine voice called out. Hands reached up and took away her cloak's hood, revealing the short copper tresses and wide-set eyes that he recognized at once.

In spite of the darkness that gripped him, Jherek's spirits lifted. A smile filled his face. "Sabyna?"

For a moment, Laaqueel was paralyzed by Falkane's sudden kiss. Nothing like that had ever happened to her. She felt the heat of him against her and her senses swirled, giving over to the otherness that had crept in with her deformity. Then she recovered, opening her mouth and intending to bite his lips, perhaps even chew them off before he could back away.

She felt the whisper of cold steel at her throat and knew he'd drawn one of his throwing knives. "No," he told her quietly. "Don't even try it."

She froze, knowing he could take her life between heartbeats. She closed her mouth, horrified to find only now that some instinct had compelled her to return his kiss. She breathed out, locking eyes with him. "From this day forward, watch your back, Bloody Falkane." Her voice sounded hoarse and uncertain.

He kissed her again, allowing her to flinch away but giving her no chance to escape. "From this day forward, lady, you'll think of me. I promise you that, and I keep my promises." He called over his shoulder, "Targ."

"Sir." Targ's brutish features, gray-green skin tone, sour odor, and nearly eight feet in height marked him as a half-ogre. The malenti priestess had noticed him around Falkane earlier, always hovering like a bodyguard. He wore a chain mail shirt over a leather rough-out vest and leather pants tucked into fishskin boots. Shells hung knotted in his stringy black hair. The hafts of the crossed short swords he wore on his back rose over his shoulders.

"Watch her," Falkane ordered.

"Aye sir." Targ's face split suddenly, revealing a mouth full of crooked yellow fangs. "Want her dead if she tries anything?" He raised a crossbow and aimed it at Laaqueel.

"No, but pain is just fine. She can always get a godspeaker and get it fixed." Falkane brought the tip of his knife to his forehead and saluted the malenti priestess. "Another time, beautiful."

Praying quickly, Laaqueel readied her power. When she loosed it, the air around Falkane would thicken and grow heavy, crushing him in seconds. She felt certain she could be over the railing before the half-ogre would know what was going on or could hit her with a quarrel.

No.

The quiet affirmation of power knifed through Laaqueel's mind, breaking the concentration necessary to launch the attack. It was echoed by movement of the black quill lying so near her heart. She looked to the cargo hold and saw Iakhovas come up the stairs onto the deck. *You— you saw what he did!* She wanted to spit the taste of Falkane from her mouth but she knew the pirate captain would only laugh at her.

Yes, but Falkane is necessary to me.

I will not be handled so by such filth! she told him.

My dear malenti, I know that part of you found that encounter quite stimulating. Iakhovas's dry chuckle rattled in her mind. *I find it quite fascinating, actually, because I've never thought of you that way myself. It opens up whole new concepts.*

Falkane walked by Iakhovas without even looking at the man, as if nothing had happened at all. The pirate captain moved confidently, as though he thought he was invulnerable. He called out orders to his crew in a loud, stern voice.

Targ gave a snuffling and disdainful laugh, then lifted his crossbow from her, turned, and walked away.

Laaqueel felt her gills flare in indignation.

You, Iakhovas told her, *will do exactly as I tell you to do. Would you deny the wishes of Sekolah as he seeks to lead his chosen children into greater power over the seas of Toril?*

Laaqueel had no answer. She had to believe that Iakhovas's way lay with the Shark God. It had been through Sekolah's direction after years of prayer that she'd been guided to the books that had given flesh to the legend of One Who Swims With Sekolah. If she stopped believing in Iakhovas, where would the disbelief end? What would be left?

With great effort, she turned and faced back in the direction where Baldur's Gate lay smoldering. Her belief was all she had. If that was lost, she was lost.

Good, little malenti, Iakhovas told her. *I need no further hindrances your lack of control might cause. I'll have enough problems justifying the loss of men and ships to these pirates. The Flaming Fist mercenaries got organized and held much more quickly than I'd thought they could.*

Laaqueel remained silent in her shame. Her way had to be hard. She knew the Shark God would demand no less. Even now she'd risen much higher in her station than she'd ever believed possible, thanks to throwing in her lot with Iakhovas.

She bent her head and prayed, knowing by her belief that the prayers she gave voice to fell ultimately on deaf ears. Sahuagin priestesses she'd known had consorted with other dark gods as well as Sekolah to get their powers, always holding the Shark God in a position of prominence. She had never done that, never entertained the possibility of worshiping another. Sekolah was the only god she'd ever followed. She'd been more true than anyone she'd known. Since her earliest days she'd been taught that only the inadequate failed.

Don't be so hard on yourself, little malenti, Iakhovas said. *You found me when no one else could, and I had been there thousands of years. Look at all we have wrought. The sahuagin are more feared than they ever have been.*

More hated.

Ah, little malenti, you forget that hate is merely an investment of power. Even the surface dwellers have to respect power. Measure their hate and you measure their respect—and in turn you measure our power. They wouldn't fear the inadequate—only the successful.

She lifted her head, knowing he was right. They had been successful. It remained to be seen how respected, and how feared, the sahuagin were going to be.

"Captain Tynnel only told me that you'd decided to stay in Athkatla," Sabyna Truesail said.

Jherek walked at her side, accompanying her down Dock Street to the harbor. He still couldn't believe *Breezerunner*'s ship's mage had ended up in the city at the same time he had. In a way, he supposed it was more a part of the cruel injustice the gods were determined to swing his way this night. There was no way Captain Tynnel would allow him back aboard the ship after the fight he'd had with some of the crewmen in Athkatla.

Though he had expected Tynnel to carry through on his offer to tell the ship's mage and let her see him briefly if she wished, a tightness centered in his chest when he thought he might never see her again after tonight.

The night's darkness wreathed the city and drew dense shadows through the street. She'd told him she'd been out searching for goods she needed to make repairs to *Breezerunner*. The cargo ship had been at anchor when the sahuagin and pirates had attacked. They hadn't been able to get their sails up in time to do much because most of the crew had been ashore on leave. Luckily the damage the ship had suffered had been minimal.

"I suppose it's true that I decided to stay," Jherek said cautiously. He found he couldn't tell her that the fight in Athkatla had been over the coarse words Aysel had said about her. He would have been ashamed, and he'd given up much that she not ever hear about the incident or the caustic things Aysel had said. It would be self-defeating and braggartly to tell her now.

"Why?"

"Why what?" The rapidity with which she changed tacks in a conversation confused him. Partly, though, he had to admit it was her beauty that he found so distracting. During every night the caravan had trekked for Baldur's Gate, his thoughts had been drawn to her. It would have shamed him to admit that too, and probably shame her as well.

Ship's mage she might be, and self-admittedly no highborn lady, but she was far beyond the reach of a man who was no more than a pirate's-get. Especially the son of Bloody Falkane, who'd killed her brother when Sabyna had been only a girl.

"Why did you stay behind?" Quick-witted and gregarious by nature, Sabyna never seemed to lack the ability to speak her mind.

However, that ability was now creating problems. When he'd first met her aboard *Breezerunner* he'd given her his name as Malorrie. It had been only the first lie. He'd lied about staying behind at Athkatla, and things seemed to get more convoluted the longer he knew her.

"I ran into a cousin," he answered.

"And you decided to stay and talk to him instead of voyaging on to Baldur's Gate with us?" Sabyna cut around a wagonload of burned planks, walking faster than the tired team could pull.

Jherek stepped up his pace to follow her. "He needed help. My help." He tried not to notice how tightly her blue breeches hugged her slim, womanly hips as her cloak flared. The sight made thinking hard, but he was aware that he made no real effort to draw even with her and lose that view.

"You could have come and told me," she said.

"He was sick." Oh Ilmater, this was turning out worse than he thought it could. Each lie piled more uncertainly on the other, all of them waiting to come tumbling down.

"So sick that you couldn't come tell me?" She glanced over her shoulder and caught his eye.

Luckily he hadn't been watching beneath the cloak's edge. "Aye. He had no one to stay with him."

Sabyna gave a very unladylike curse. "You're lying."

"Lady?" Jherek thought frantically, wondering which lie she'd caught him in.

"I live aboard a ship, Malorrie," she said, coming to a stop. "That makes for a very small world."

Breezerunner sat in the harbor over her shoulder. The sails were trimmed and men scurried about in the rigging with lanterns, repairing damage where they found it. They looked like busy fireflies moving through the upper sections of the ship. Jherek heard Captain Tynnel's voice crack orders.

"How long did you think I would go before I found out the truth?" she demanded.

Jherek wished he knew which truth she was talking about.

"Not long after we'd sailed from Athkatla," she went on, "I was told about the fight you had with Aysel—and why."

A burn of embarrassment spread across Jherek's face and he had to break the eye contact by pretending to check his pouch.

"What frustrates me," Sabyna went on, "is that *you* were taken from *Breezerunner* instead of Aysel."

"He's crew," Jherek said. "I wasn't." As ship's mage, she should have known that.

"You would have been crew once we made Baldur's Gate," she said. "You as good as had the job."

The thought pleased and excited Jherek. Traveling overland wasn't something he wished to do again. He shrugged. The fact still remained that Tynnel had made his choice.

"You also could have talked to me," she went on.

"I was told that wouldn't be possible," Jherek said.

"By who?"

Jherek hesitated, realizing that he'd said more than he intended. Evidently whoever had spoken to the ship's mage hadn't told her everything.

"Captain Tynnel told you that, didn't he?" she demanded.

Jherek considered his options. Lying again was something he was determined not to do. He stood close enough to her to smell the delicate lilac scent she wore. Most of it was gone, worn away by time and the smoke that wreathed the air, but enough of it remained that it stirred memories of dining on meals she'd prepared for them in her cabin.

"Never mind," she went on before he could reply. "I can answer that one myself. Tynnel *did* tell you to stay away." She muttered another oath, more virulent and descriptive than the last.

It wasn't that Jherek had never heard the curses before, though they weren't casual ones most seafarers would know, but rather the fact that Sabyna had called them out that stunned him.

"Look," she said, looking at him levelly, "first of all, I want to get a couple things straight with you. Then I'm going to see to Tynnel." She paused. "Don't get me wrong, I think the idea of you defending my honor is flattering, but I live at sea, a place where few women actually stay for long. When I became a ship's mage, my father protested, as did my mother. They both knew the coarse laxity of men at sea, and they knew how hard it would be to be the only woman on board a ship. Did you think Aysel's comments were the first of that kind that had ever been made?"

"I never considered it," Jherek said. Then he realized Sabyna must not have been told that Aysel was commenting on his feelings for her. He was quietly thankful.

"You should have," she said flatly.

A small group of Flaming Fist mercenaries approached them with drawn swords. The sergeant of the guard asked for their papers.

Before Jherek could explain that he had none, Sabyna produced hers, unfolding them with a flourish. "Read it and hit the cobblestones," she told the sergeant. "I don't have time for delays."

The sergeant held his lantern close to the papers as he read. Evidently he was chastised enough that he didn't bother asking for Jherek's. He thanked the ship's mage for her time and moved his group on.

"That wasn't the first time something like that has happened," Sabyna said. "I handle it when it does. That's how I maintain the respect of this crew. I won't put up with it, and I've got the means to make my displeasure known. If a sharp tongue won't get the message across, I have my magic. You stepping in like you did undermined that to a degree. By fighting you, Aysel now considers himself deserving of my attentions."

"I hadn't considered that." Jherek felt bad. He should have known the ship's mage could take care of herself. She'd faced pirates and storms at sea, and he'd discounted her independence. "I apologize."

"No," Sabyna stopped him. "There's no need to apologize. As I said, I found your defense of me to be very flattering. I wish I could have thanked you."

Jherek thought about that, feeling a little better. "You have a curious way of showing it." He'd seen Madame Iitaar go through mood changes that had confused him. Even Malorrie hadn't been able to understand them. The phantom's only words of advice were to remain as quiet as possible and offer only a small target till it passed.

"That was then. Now I'm mad." A small smile twisted her lips. "I was afraid I wasn't going to see you again. Faerûn is a big place, and so much is going on now."

Jherek played her words back in his ears again. She'd been afraid she wouldn't see him again. He worked hard to keep the smile from his own face. Unconsciously, he twisted the pearl disk in his hand, barely aware of it.

He was also unaware of the figures that had closed in on them until it was too late. He glanced up, noticing that Sabyna had seen them as well.

The ship's mage shifted, putting the dock and the harbor to her back as she moved to Jherek's left, leaving his sword arm free.

A dozen men surrounded them, all thick-bodied from indulgences in drink and food as well as hard work. Jherek marked them as sailors because of their dress, weapons, and the rolling gait that showed in their movements.

None of the Flaming Fist mercenaries were anywhere to be seen.

The leader was a huge man with fiery red hair that caught highlights from torches in the distance. He carried a battle-axe in one hand and wore a small shield on his other arm. The shield was featureless except for a score of scars from previous battles.

A smaller man stood at his side, cloaked and hooded, his narrow shoulders pinched and rounded together. He kept his hands in the voluminous sleeves of his cloak.

"Sabyna Truesail," the big man rumbled. "Ship's mage of *Breezerunner*."

"I don't know you," Sabyna said.

Jherek kept his hand away from his sword hilt, hoping he was overreacting. Still, he noticed Sabyna's hands moving, readying her spells.

The big man grinned. "I'm Captain Vurgrom, of *Maelstrom*."

"I don't know your ship either."

Vurgrom shrugged, the smile never leaving his lips and never quite touching his eyes. "It doesn't matter, lassie. It's a long way from here."

"What do you want with me?"

Jherek glanced around, but no one seemed to be paying them any attention.

"It's not you," Vurgrom said. "It's your ship I'm after. Piece of business turned nasty on us tonight, and we want to get out of Baldur's Gate before morning. Unfortunately, the ship we'd borrowed took a lot of damage. My crew noticed your craft fared better. Took a little bit of doing, but we found out about you. Figured your captain might be wishful of keeping you in one piece. I guess I intend to find out."

Leather hissed at Jherek's side. In the next instant, Sabyna held long-bladed knives in both hands. The young sailor hadn't made a move yet.

Vurgrom grinned. "You can come easy or you can come hard. If I have to, I can chop some pieces off and take your captain what's left. I'm still going to wager he'll be ready to deal."

"No," Sabyna answered.

Vurgrom waited just a moment, then nodded. He didn't wait for his men. He brought the battle-axe forward, holding well down on the haft so he'd get a full stroke.

The axe blade whistled as it cleaved the air and sped for Jherek's head.

10

Stepping to the side and twisting to avoid Vurgrom's battle-axe, Jherek slid his sword and hook free of his waist sash. His clothing still remained wet from his earlier dip in the harbor and constricted his movement. His muscles flared in protest at being forced to perform again without rest.

Vurgrom's axe missed him by inches, biting deep into the cobblestones and shattering some of them as the other men closed in. For the moment their numbers worked against them, though Jherek was sure that wouldn't remain so.

The young sailor moved aggressively forward, slashing at Vurgrom. The blade crashed fire across the mail shirt without penetrating. For a big man, Vurgrom moved surprisingly fast, bringing the shield around as Jherek hammered at him again. The sword struck sparks from the shield. While the young sailor tried to recover after expecting the sword to find a home in flesh, Vurgrom stepped forward and body-blocked him with the shield.

The massive blow slammed Jherek from his feet and knocked him back almost three feet. Shaken, the young sailor stumbled back and set himself again. Vurgrom lashed out with the shield again, expecting Jherek to still be off-balance. Instead, the young sailor slammed into the shield at an angle, rolling off it toward Vurgrom's front. He brought the sword around again, but this time barely succeeded in getting it up in time to block the battle-axe.

The impact rang along Jherek's arm.

Vurgrom came for him with the shield again. Anticipating the move, recognizing it as a favored one, the young sailor ducked and went low. The shield raked against his chest but lacked the force to knock him away. Reaching with the hook, he snaked it under the shield and hooked Vurgrom in the back of the leg. The big man yowled in pain.

With the hold secured, Jherek yanked. For a moment he thought the man's sheer weight would keep him from succeeding. If it had been strength against strength, Vurgrom might have held, but the hook was firmly embedded in the big man's flesh with tearing pain.

Screaming curses, Vurgrom stopped fighting the hook's pull. The leg came up and he went down.

Jherek didn't have time to capitalize on his success. One of Vurgrom's men came at him with a short sword. The young sailor abandoned the hook, unable to tear it free of Vurgrom's leg. Swiveling, he met the man's attack in a fencer's pose that Malorrie had taught him.

Steel rang on steel as the man sought to tear through Jherek's defenses. The young sailor gave himself over to his training, keeping his arm loose but strong, defending then attacking. The sword became a live thing in his hand, compelled by countless hours spent under Malorrie's demanding tutelage. Jherek moved ceaselessly, small steps that kept them in a tight circle, using the man's own body and attack to keep the others from them.

A man staggered away, grasping futilely at the throwing knife protruding from his throat. Evidently Sabyna's skills with a knife were considerable.

"Skeins," the ship's mage called from behind Jherek when he'd deliberately tried to protect her. "Attack."

From the corner of his eye, Jherek watched as hundreds of scraps of cloth flew from the bag of holding the ship's mage held open. They whirled and flew as if trapped in the eye of a hurricane, stretching out and growing longer until they reached serpentine proportions.

Even though he'd seen it before, Jherek's first impulse was to get away from the creature, and it took a lot of control not to act on that impulse. It was a raggamoffyn, a sentient creature that could strike or simply wrap around a human and take over that person's thoughts. The young sailor had seen it in action before.

There were some who said raggamoffyns were a race unto themselves, while others said they'd been created by a wizard with only evil intentions. Sabyna had created this raggamoffyn to be her familiar, taking the scraps that made up its physical body from her dead brother's burial shroud.

The raggamoffyn rode the breeze, nearly nine feet long now, coiling restlessly. Its initial appearance startled the attackers, driving them back. Sabyna threw a second knife, piercing a man's leg and eliciting a sharp yell.

The noise of the battle attracted a nearby group of Flaming Fist mercenaries. The four warriors sprang into action, shouting to the pirate group to identify themselves as they ripped swords from scabbards.

The thin-shouldered man with Vurgrom turned and gestured at them, saying words Jherek couldn't understand. Three of the men staggered and fell limply to the ground. The fourth appeared disoriented but that lasted only until one of Vurgrom's men ran him through.

The raggamoffyn streaked through the air and broke into its myriad pieces. It plastered itself to the man, covering him from the waist up in seconds, each piece locking into place securely. The man's mouth opened as he tried to scream but no sound came out. He dropped to his knees, letting go his sword as he struggled to tear the cloth away.

More knives glinted in Sabyna's hands as she avoided an attacker and partially turned the blade aimed at her head with one of the knives. Razored steel edges whispered together for a heartbeat.

Beyond the battle, Jherek saw men standing in the shadows, unwilling to take part in any fight that wasn't their own or where they couldn't tell immediately who was in the right. The young sailor fought deliberately, parrying, blocking, then riposting quickly, escalating the speed until he went from the defensive to the offensive. The sword was a blur before him and he stared through it, concentrating on the man across from him. He beat the man's shield down, knocking it from his numbed hands and causing him to step back.

"Damn you, Pharan!" Vurgrom roared as he pushed himself to his feet. He threw the blood-covered hook away. "I told you I wanted that woman alive. If you hurt her, I'll kill you myself!"

Pharan drew back. Taking advantage of his withdrawal, Sabyna lashed out with one of her knives, scoring a bloody line on his face.

"Zensil," Vurgrom shouted. "I want this ended now."

The thin-shouldered man nodded. Arcane words spewed from his lips, and his hands traced curious designs in the air. He drew a long length of small-linked chain from a pouch at his waist, stringing it out with quick movements.

Pressing his own advantage, Jherek slapped his opponent's sword aside a final time, then put a foot of steel through the leather armor and into the pirate's heart. The dead man started to fall, taking the young sailor's sword as well. Jherek faced the mage, not knowing what the man planned to do with the chain. Placing his foot on the corpse, the young sailor yanked his sword free. He breathed heavily, perspiring from his efforts in spite of the wet clothes.

The pirates drew back as the mage worked his magic. Even Vurgrom hesitated.

Jherek stomped on the abandoned shield at his feet, flipping it up in a trick Malorrie had taught him. He caught the shield, managing to run his hand through one of the leather straps on the back. Pulling it over his arm, he ran for the ship's mage.

Jherek caught her around the waist with his sword arm, pulling her into the crook of his elbow and into a run. He lifted the shield to block the man who swung at them. The sword crashed into the shield, almost coming free of his grip. He asked Ilmater's blessing as he powered forward, knocking the man down. Then no one stood in their way. *Breezerunner* remained before them.

"Run!" he told Sabyna. He gave her a final push to get her started, then turned to face Vurgrom and his men in order to buy her more time. He felt the weight of the pearl disk in his pouch and experienced a momentary pride. He might not have been the one the disk had been intended for, no hero with a lofty destiny awaiting his arrival, but he could sell his life with honor to protect the ship's mage if it came to that.

"Malorrie!" Sabyna called behind him.

"Go!"

"I'm not leaving you."

Jherek heard her shifting behind him, the leather soles of her boots grazing the cobblestones. "You've got a sinking ship here, lady, and naught but storm-tossed seas about you. Get clear while you're able."

The wizard wound the length of chain over his head, then threw it at Jherek.

The young sailor lifted the shield to block the mass of coiled links, thinking the chain was meant as a diversion more than anything. It clanked against the shield's metal surface. Instead of falling to the ground, however, the chain snaked over the shield and lunged at Jherek. It wound around him quickly, twisting and weaving to avoid the shield and the sword as he tried to block it.

The chain wrapped his chest twice, holding tight enough to squeeze the air from him, then it wound out and captured his arms, threading down to encircle his ankles as well, pulling them tight. Off-balance, Jherek fell. He watched helplessly as Vurgrom closed in and swung the battle-axe. His last thought was that he'd failed to protect Sabyna. Then the battle-axe hit him.

By the time Pacys had finished recounting to Khlinat Ironeater details of the battle of Waterdeep and his own meeting with Narros, the shaman of the mermen living in Waterdeep Harbor, the beeswax taper had burned down to its final inch.

"Ye have an incredible task ahead of ye, Pacys," the dwarf acknowledged, "but are ye sure there's no mistake about the young swab? Oh now, and he's a brave one, and some skilled at weapons. I've seen him in action this night, and I know how deadly he can be. I question whether ye have the right person even in spite of all the good qualities the swabbie exhibits. He's hardly more than a boy."

"I know," Pacys agreed. He glanced at the stub of the candle, the hot melted wax spilling over the sides of the holder. He turned and peered out the window, seeing the streets filled with people who were returning cautiously to their homes. Occasionally during their conversation there'd been cries of warning about sahuagin, pirates, or some foul creature lurking in the shadows. The old bard hadn't known if those really existed, or were the product of overactive imaginations. They hadn't seen any on the trek back to Khlinat's home. "How far away is the apothecary?"

"Not far," Khlinat said, "but I'll wager me good boot that the swabbie hasn't found anything there. The Flaming Fist would have descended on all them places and taken what they needed already. Maybe he's giving a look 'round and seeing what he can turn up. Betwixt ye and me, I think he needed some time to himself to think."

Pacys nodded. Still, the creeping feeling that something might have happened took root in his mind. He'd come so far to find the boy, and had so much riding on the finding of him.

"So why do ye seek the swabbie?" Khlinat stuffed the bowl of his pipe with pipeweed and set fire to it. "Them mermen could have found anyone to deliver the message."

Pacys deliberately hadn't revealed his own part in the prophecy. "You mean someone younger." His fingers continued to stroke the yarting's strings, and to his great joy, he found additional chords as he sought them out. They were notes and measures that normally signaled traveling. It was confusing.

"If ye insist on being so indelicate," the dwarf said with an unabashed nod, "then aye."

Pacys smiled, showing he took no offense at the suggestion. "I don't know. All I can say is that I was told this was meant for me. Tell me, friend Khlinat, have you heard of Thoreyo?"

"Him who sang 'Short-Hafted Hammer and the Wizard's Tall Black Tower?' "

"Yes." Pacys had chosen the song deliberately.

"As a dwarf, how could I not know of that song? It is one of the most popular dwarven brawling songs—harkening back to the days when the dwarves warred with one another to build their empires across the Far Hills."

"What about Yhitmon?"

There was no hesitation in the dwarf. "Ah, 'Strangled Leaves of Lily-Grass and the Goblin-King's Betrothal.' I've hoisted a few pints of bitters and sang along with that one meself." He grabbed his cup and held it high.

"*And would-be noble, himself a worthy warrior among goblinkin,*
"*In his own eyes,*
"*Did take upon himself to find a wife.*
"*So sword to hips*
"*And prayer to lips,*
"*He did ride, so boldly ride,*
"*To the House of the Rising Sin.*"

At the end of the stanza, the dwarf burst into laughter that turned into a coughing fit.

Pacys waited patiently till it passed.

"Now there, by Marthammor Duin's watchful eyes," Khlinat swore, "is a drinking song made for men who love the taverns."

"Yes," Pacys said, "and when you think of Pacys the Bard, what songs come to mind?"

Khlinat looked embarrassed. "Ye have caught me at a bad time, singer, otherwise I'm sure I would know of one."

"No," Pacys said quietly. "I've written songs, and good songs at that, but never a song that has captured the hearts of Faerûn the way the ones we've mentioned have. I was drawn to the music early. Now I am in the winter of my years and I find I have no legacy to leave."

"Ye believe the story of the Taker is yer legacy?"

For a moment, Pacys felt uncomfortable. Part of him felt embarrassed about making something so grandiose about his part in the dark war rising from the seas of Faerûn, and part of him felt silly for believing so easily. But the song had existed, so he believed.

"I've been told that it will be."

"And ye believe?"

Pacys hesitated only a moment before saying, "Yes."

Khlinat nodded. "Belief is a strong thing. And song, by the gods, there's something to forge a man's belief to his dream, make him reach for something that he never thought would be his. There's such power in songs."

Pacys felt pride at the dwarf's description.

"I remember a tale," Khlinat said, "told me by me old grandda, and it twice-told at least a thousandfold ere he ever gave it to me. About Twahrm Kettlebuster, a hidden dwarf of the Far Hills."

"I've heard of it," Pacys said, remembering the little known song. He didn't play it much except in front of a select dwarven audience, and there had been few of those in recent years.

"Now mind ye," Khlinat went on, "old Twahrm weren't no trained bard, nor was he gifted in any way. Them what heard him sing said it was punishment should be set for only the most black-hearted of folks. But one day while wandering, scouting for a new vein of metal for his village where he smithed, he come upon a hunting party of ogres."

Unconsciously, Pacys's fingers found the yarting's strings and played an accompaniment to Khlinat's words. The dwarf picked up on the rhythm, became trapped by it, and fell into cadence with it.

"They had him outnumbered, and surrounded in a trice. So Twahrm hit his knees and began singing of how he'd courted Haela Brightaxe, also called the Lady of the Fray, and goddess of dwarven warriors. She'd spurned his love, he said, and he was ready to greet death. He sang of how much he would love to die and how pleased he was to see them. Meaning that he wouldn't have to die alone."

The bard's plucked notes flowed through the room.

"And the strength of his song was such that the ogres believed him and grew afraid. When he finished and took up his great battle-axe, the ogres left. See, they believed him about him being ready to up and die, and they didn't want to get taken with him."

"It's a good tale," Pacys agreed, "and it's exactly what I was talking about. I've been chasing this song for fourteen years. I came across part of it the night Narros and the other mermen came to Waterdeep after the Taker destroyed their city. Since that time I've wandered what seems like all of Faerûn pursuing it, never able to get more than a few scraps of it here and there."

"But now there's more."

"Every day," Pacys agreed. "It led me to Narros, and it led me here, to the boy."

Khlinat shook his head. "It's a powerful lot for a man to think on, but have ye given any thought to what if yer wrong?"

"No." Pacys, who was never at a loss for words because it was those words that kept food on the table, tried to find the right ones.

"The swabbie's just a boy," Khlinat said. "If he's to go up against this thing ye call the Taker as ye say, he's got a lot of growing up to do."

"I know," Pacys admitted, "but this search for him, and finding him here at a time when this attack happened, and him being part of the effort that turned the tide of battle, it all sounds right."

Khlinat's tired eyes sparkled with merriment. "Ye mean to say old Khlinat Ironeater's going to be in yer song?"

Pacys smiled gently back at him. "My friend, you're going to live forever."

"Hopefully well and handsome in them verses, singer." Khlinat raised his cup in a toast.

Pacys toasted him and they drank. He put his cup down and searched the yarting for any new chords for the song.

At that moment, the candle guttered, reaching the end of the wick and drowning in the pool of melted beeswax. Pacys thought again of the long time that Jherek had been gone and wondered if something had happened to the boy. Then, for the first time that night, he hit a discordant note. A chill settled over the old bard as he put a hand over the strings to quiet them.

"What is it?" Khlinat asked.

Pacys pushed up from the table and settled his yarting over his shoulder. He picked his cloak up from the peg on the wall. "I have to go find the boy. Something's happened."

The dwarf tried to get up, but the pain drove him back to his seat. "Damn me for a weakling. I'd go with ye, but I can't. Let me know, will ye?"

Pacys nodded and let himself outside, hurrying down the stairs. He paid attention to the sounds around him. If a person only listened to the noises around him, he'd know music was being made all the time.

Now, beyond the street noise made by the wagons and Flaming Fist mercenaries filling the city, a discordant resonance hung over all of Baldur's Gate. The old bard knew he was probably the only person who heard it, but it told him that no matter what efforts he made, he was already too late.

348

He felt the rift between himself and the younger man, but he quickened his steps anyway, trying to find the direction, frustrated because the young sailor's tune seemed lost to him, a distant whisper of what it had been.

11

"Have a care there, lad. You took a pretty good knock to your melon."

Rough hands steadied Jherek, holding him down. He knew from the weakness filling him that it didn't take much effort. The liquid motion beneath him told him he was on a ship, though that motion was somehow off. The movements were too quick and sharp. The stink of stale sweat and sickness filled the air he breathed. His stomach rolled and rumbled in protest.

"Easy there," the deep voice advised. "Else you'll be throwing up everything we've managed to put down you the last day or so."

The back of Jherek's throat was raw. He cracked his eyelids open, feeling a sticky and gummy substance binding them. Sunlight stabbed into his eyes and exploded with the ferocity of smoke powder, blinding him. He groaned and his stomach rolled again.

"You still live, lad, and Selûne willing, that's a good sign. Come on around and let me see if you've still got your wits about you." A big, callused hand patted his cheek sharply enough to sting without jarring his head. "I've seen such blows as you've taken leave a man addled for the rest of his life, not knowing much more than a child."

Jherek tried his eyes again, squinting against the harsh light. Tears ran down his face but he kept them open. He quickly discovered he was on a ship, but he was in the cargo hold, in a portion that had obviously been set up as a makeshift brig. Iron bars above let the sunlight in but he couldn't tell if it was morning or afternoon. The sound of rigging creaking in the wind and someone calling out sharp orders reached his ears.

"Don't know if you remember me, lad, but the name's Hullyn." He was a short man, but nearly as broad as a dwarf, with thick sloping shoulders heavy with muscle. His skin carried a permanent windburn red from weathering the elements. He wore his graying blond hair tied back, letting his great beard and mustache roam free.

"I remember you," Jherek said. Hullyn was part of *Breezerunner*'s crew. That gave the young sailor some hope. "Where's Sabyna?" He sat up with assistance, putting his back against the bulwark for support.

Hullyn scowled. "She's topside with those thrice-damned pirates what's got our ship. They're using her as blackmail to keep us in line." He reached to a small bowl and took out a damp cloth, then pressed it against Jherek's head.

Jherek winced in pain, but he looked around the brig. From his previous experience aboard her, he knew *Breezerunner* carried a crew of twenty men. All of them appeared to be there, including Captain Tynnel.

The captain stood leaning against the iron bars that separated them from the empty ship's hold. His arms crossed his chest and he looked disapprovingly at Jherek. He was short and had a small stature, but fierceness showed in every inch. Blond hair the color of bleached bone was tied back from his hatchet face. Bright blue eyes held the cutting edge of diamond. For the first time ever, his clothing appeared disheveled.

"You going to live?" Tynnel asked.

Jherek nodded, then regretted it immediately when pain shot down his neck and back. "Aye sir."

"You're a lucky man," Tynnel commented. "Vurgrom and his people were going to kill you, but Sabyna talked them out of it."

"They came looking for her."

"I know. From what I've gathered, they were in Baldur's Gate on bad business. Perhaps they even had something to do with the sahuagin raid as Vurgrom claims. I'm not certain."

"They took the ship?"

Tynnel blew out a short breath. "Would have been nine or ten of them against us, but they had Sabyna. If we hadn't cooperated, Vurgrom told me he would kill her. I believed him."

"Bastards like as not will kill us all afore it's over with. We'll have just put our necks in the executioner's noose for nothing."

Jherek turned his head slightly, spotting Aysel against the left side of the brig. Large and hairy, Aysel resembled an ape trying to pass itself off as a sailor. He was broad shouldered and heavy bellied, covered in scars. His shaggy black hair hung to his shoulders, almost covering the finger-length daggers that hung from ear hoops. He held his hands one on top of the other, two digits missing from his left hand. A soft leather shoe encased his right foot.

Looking at the leather shoe, Jherek took small satisfaction from the knowledge that the fight that had cost him his berth aboard *Breezerunner* hadn't left Aysel unmarked.

"Is Sabyna all right?" Jherek asked. He tried not to think about

Sabyna being alone topside with Vurgrom and his pirates, or what could have happened to her.

"Aye," Tynnel replied. "So far. She's a mage, though still fairly new to her craft, but enough of one that none of Vurgrom's curs has tried to touch her." The captain's hawk's face tightened, and white spots of anger showed in his cheeks. "She could probably have gotten away from them if not for us. Vurgrom told her if she left, our lives would be forfeit. Likewise, if we try to escape, she'll suffer."

"We're not at sea," Jherek said. He assembled the information he had, working through the pieces as Malorrie had always trained him to.

"No," Tynnel agreed. "We're on the River Chionthar, heading east."

"Why?"

A pirate walked by the iron-barred hold above, never even glancing down into the cargo area. All of *Breezerunner*'s crew watched the man, and no few curses and epithets were muttered.

A sour look darkened Tynnel's face and he asked, "You've never heard of Vurgrom the pirate, self-styled Vurgrom the Mighty?"

Jherek shook his head. From his exposure while on his father's ship, he'd learned names and stories of most of the pirates of the Nelanther Isles. Vurgrom was new to him, as was any reason why a Nelanther pirate would head inland across Faerûn.

"If you get a chance to talk to the arrogant son of a bitch," Tynnel said, "he'll tell you all about himself. As he tells it, he's the Pirate Lord of Immurk's Hold in the Sea of Fallen Stars. He's planning on taking *Breezerunner* as far east as she'll go."

"That's not possible," Jherek said. "The River Chionthar doesn't run all the way to the Sea of Fallen Stars. It branches out at the Reaching Woods, going on north and south and ending in the Sunset Mountains and the Giant's Plain, respectively. Both are still leagues from the Dragonmere and the Sea of Fallen Stars."

Tynnel eyed the young sailor with renewed curiosity. "You seem to be well aware of the lay of the land here. Most of the men aboard *Breezerunner* couldn't have told you anything more than that the River Chionthar was where Baldur's Gate was."

"I've never been there," Jherek said. "I had a harsh schoolmaster who had a love of cartography. He taught me how to find my way around by the heavens at night, and the places those star readings could take me."

"An education is a wonderful thing," Tynnel said. "If you've had one, I have to wonder why you've settled for the life of a sailor."

"Settled?" Jherek echoed. "Captain Tynnel, living out on the sea is all I've ever aspired to do."

"She's as harsh and demanding a mistress as ever was," Hullyn said, interrupting the tension that had come up between Tynnel and Jherek, "ain't she, Cap'n?"

Tynnel remained quiet for a moment, eyeing Jherek suspiciously. "Quite right, Hullyn."

The pounding inside Jherek's head was unrelenting. He cradled his head in his hands and wished the pain would subside while Hullyn continued ministering to him. A momentary lightness touched his senses. He waited it out, then took a deep breath, feeling some of the pain seem to leave when he exhaled through his mouth, controlling the pain the way Malorrie had taught him.

"Steady, lad," the big man said gruffly. "Now that you're awake and the bleeding seems to have stopped, let's see about getting you cleaned up."

Breezerunner suddenly came about, throwing everyone off-balance as she crested the river flow.

"She's against the wind," Jherek said. "He's tacking her from shore to shore to get any distance from her sails."

Tynnel nodded. "Aye, and she's fighting the magery Vurgrom's forcing on her."

"What magery?" Jherek asked.

"Using Sabyna to keep us in check was only one of the reasons Vurgrom kept her. He took us so we couldn't report to the watch in Baldur's Gate and maybe stir up some kind of pursuit. He knew he couldn't kill us outright because she'd have fought him, but Vurgrom's using her to power *Breezerunner*."

"Some damned demon device," Hullyn growled as he made the sign of Tymora over his chest.

"A chair," Tynnel stated. "I don't know where Vurgrom got it, but I saw it being set up before they put me in the hold. Sabyna and Vurgrom's own ship's mage take turns using it. The chair pushes *Breezerunner* far faster than any normal wind would. That's the strangeness you feel about the ship's movements. When we come to a sharp bend in the river, you can feel her shuddering through the turn, chopping across the water, but she doesn't slow down. Whatever course and destination Vurgrom's got laid out, we're going to get there damned fast."

Jherek thought desperately while Hullyn continued cleaning his head. "How far have we come?"

"We're two days from Baldur's Gate, boy," Tynnel stated gruffly. "You've been unconscious that whole time. It's anyone's guess as to how far we've come. I don't know this territory."

Jherek couldn't believe it. In two days time with the speed he felt the ship was moving at, they would be miles from Baldur's Gate even having to sail against the current. As he recalled, the shores along the River Chionthar inland were virtually empty of ports or towns. The countryside was infested with orc and goblin hordes who'd staked out territorial claims.

"Bastard could have died," Aysel said, glaring at Jherek. "Maybe should have." The big man sneered, shifting gingerly around his injured foot. "Always sensed something about you that reminded me of a bad copper that keeps turning up."

"Stow that bilge," Tynnel commanded sternly. "Whatever problems the two of you have with each other, they're not allowed on my ship."

"Begging the cap'n's pardon," Aysel said, "but things ain't quite the way they were aboard old *Breezerunner*. I'm thinking part of that is because of this snot-nosed pup here."

Tynnel glanced at the man with his burning gaze. "If I want any lip from you, Aysel, I'll let you know."

The man looked like he was going to say something further, then apparently thought better of it.

"That goes for both of you," Tynnel finished. "Whatever problems existed back at Athkatla stay at Athkatla."

Jherek nodded tightly, his thoughts centering on Khlinat and the old bard who'd appeared so mysteriously. He'd left them waiting back in Baldur's Gate. He wondered how the dwarf was.

"That's odd," Hullyn said, peering closely at the back of Jherek's head. "I looked at the split you took back here earlier and I could have sworn you'd needed some healer's stitches, but as I get it cleaned up now I see it's not bleeding anymore and seems to have closed up more than I'd have expected. You're a fast healer, lad."

Taking another breath, Jherek realized he did feel better. He attributed it to Hullyn's ministrations, then turned his attention to Tynnel. "So, what are they going to do with us?" Jherek asked.

Tynnel shook his head. "I don't know."

Sitting up straighter, Jherek went through his clothes, wondering if there was something he could use. Unfortunately, Vurgrom's pirates seemed to have been quite thorough. He'd been robbed, of course. They'd even found the fishing knife he kept tucked inside his boot.

Frantically, he searched his clothing again, having remembered the pearl disk the Lathander priest had given him.

"What's wrong?" Hullyn asked.

"There was a disk," Jherek said. "I had a pearl disk with a carving on it." Thinking about the priest's words, of how an important destiny was tied to the disk, made him grow even more afraid. He tried to remember if he'd lost it somehow during the fight on the dock.

"Aye," Hullyn said. "Them pirates went through your clothing out in the hold when they brought you down. They robbed us all, but I remember seeing that piece you describe. Vurgrom spied it himself as one of his men tried to be off with it without notice."

"Vurgrom has it?"

Hullyn nodded. "Was it worth much? Something that belonged in your family?"

Jherek wondered what destiny cost, what price could be placed on it. Some, like his, were cheap, but the one tied to that pearl disk he was certain was a great one.

He'd lost it when it wasn't even his to hold. Despair settled over him, made even worse when he scanned the heavy iron bars keeping them caged.

Pacys sat on a bench inside the Unrolling Scroll, the shrine in Baldur's Gate devoted to the worship of Oghma, the Binder of What is Known. The god was also known as the Patron of Bards, and Pacys had walked within his service ever since discovering his affinity for music. Always before, the old bard had found visiting the shrines, temples, and churches of Oghma to be an uplifting experience, but for the past three days, he'd known only darkness that had chipped away at him until he'd dwindled into the core of himself.

The boy he'd come to find was gone, disappeared into the night. Though he'd searched then, and had Khlinat's help in the following two days, there'd been no clue as to where he'd gone.

It had also been the day the music had gone.

Searching back, Pacys had found he could call up all the notes and fragments and tunes he'd pieced together over the years, most of it coming during the attack on Waterdeep and in the days that followed, but there was nothing new. Every time he went to the well of creation that had always been within him, it was dry. That scared him more than anything ever had in his life. To him, a bard didn't just live to play old tunes, tunes that had already been added to his repertoire. No, it was the search and the finding of new music that made life worth living.

He found himself unwilling and unable to work on even other pieces that had nothing to do with the epic he pursued so diligently. He held his yarting in his lap, but his fingers couldn't coax from the strings any series of notes that lasted for long. Nothing made him want to lift his voice in song.

"You seem distressed."

Blinking, surprised that the priest could get so close to him without his knowledge, Pacys looked up.

The priest showed signs of experience at his chosen vocation, deep-set wrinkles and faded gray eyes that had seen too much, but he was still little more than Pacys's age. His dark hair was shot through with silver, and his beard had gone mostly to gray. He wore a white shirt and trousers, and vest with black and gold braid. A small, boxlike hat sat atop his head.

"Pardon me for interrupting," the priest said, "if I am."

"No," Pacys said, "you're not. Actually I'm grateful for the company. Too much solitude is never good for a man with much on his mind."

The priest gestured toward the empty space on the bench next to Pacys. "May I sit?"

"Of course." The old bard put the yarting aside.

The priest sat and offered his hand. "I'm Father Duhzpin," he said. "I lead this temple."

"You've got a nice place," Pacys said, then introduced himself.

"Blessed Oghma does," Duhzpin agreed. "Though before the Time of Troubles things were much better."

Pacys knew that. He'd crafted songs about the Time of Troubles himself. During that time when the gods themselves had walked the lands, Oghma's chief patriarch Procampur had disappeared. As a result, the churches worshiping Oghma had splintered, no longer a cohesive whole.

"I've noticed you in here the last two days," Duhzpin said, "and though I don't recognize you as a regular parishioner, I felt moved to speak to you." He gazed around at the church. Modestly outfitted, the room was still near to overflowing.

Most of the people prayed for guidance, or for the souls of those who had been taken from them or were on the steadily shorter list of those that were missing since the raid. Great sadness had hung over the church both days Pacys had visited it.

"I appreciate the time," Pacys said, "but I know there are people in here who have much greater problems than I do."

"Maybe," Duhzpin said, "but I've learned to listen to the dictates of Oghma. He placed you in that seat for whatever reason, so I took my own seat. Why don't you tell me of your troubles? They always get lighter when they're shared."

Pacys considered the offer, knowing it was true and remembering how often he'd been the one listening. He knew from experience it was much easier to listen than to talk, though. "All right," he agreed.

He told of his troubles with skill, something he felt guilty about taking pride in as he went along. Oghma forgive him any vanity as he struggled to find the music within him.

"Now this boy can't be found anywhere?" Duhzpin asked when Pacys had finished. If he was shocked at the far-reaching impact of Pacys's tale and what it could mean to all of Faerûn, the priest didn't show it.

Pacys figured the man thought he was the biggest liar he'd ever seen, or Duhzpin was so strong in his belief he could handle anything. "No," the old bard said. "I've looked for him."

"Do you think it's possible he's dead?" Duhzpin asked.

Pacys started to say he didn't know, then he changed his mind about the answer. "No," he said, "I don't think he's dead."

"Why? That seems to be an obvious conclusion to draw."

"Because it doesn't sound right," Pacys said.

The priest lifted his eyebrows. "Doesn't *sound* right?"

Surprised himself, Pacys nodded. "That's exactly what I mean."

"And what are you listening to?"

Pacys pondered the question. "Myself." He felt the ache of desire fill him, and the frustration of not knowing. "Father, all my life I've searched for the legacy I was destined to leave. I know this is it."

"Finding this boy and singing of the Taker and his war against the surface world?"

"Yes."

"What makes you so certain of this?"

"My faith."

"In what?"

"In Oghma," Pacys answered. "He's seen fit to give me what little gift I have for music."

"You expect Oghma to work great things with it?"

"Yes." Pacys considered his response. "That sounds vain, doesn't it?"

"No," Duhzpin answered. "That sounds like conviction."

"Conviction?"

The priest shrugged. "I'm in a business of convictions."

"I thought that was a judge," Pacys bantered, wanting to break the string of somber words, "or a lawreader."

"Or career criminals," Duhzpin added, proving himself worthy of the diversion. "However, in this business, I've learned to hear the truth that people say—the things they believe in—and sometimes those things they believe in aren't the same things other people see."

"Are you questioning my belief, Father?" Pacys asked. The possibility shocked him to a degree.

"No," Duhzpin replied. "That's what you're doing. It's all you've been doing for the last three days. In fact, not only have you been questioning it, you've been agonizing over it."

"That's not right." Pacys didn't want to argue with the man in the temple he was responsible for, but neither did he think the man was correct.

"Then what have you been doing?" the priest asked.

"I'm trying to figure out what to do next."

"All by yourself?"

Pacys became somewhat irritated by the man's constant barrage of questions. "I've prayed about it, several times, and made offerings."

"Good," the priest said in happy satisfaction. "We can always use anything we get, but what have you been praying for?"

"That I might know where to find the boy again," Pacys said, "before it's too late."

"I see." The priest smoothed his beard. "But what if learning the boy's location isn't exactly what you're supposed to do next?"

"That doesn't make any sense." Pacys watched the younger priests moving through the crowded seats, offering prayers and assistance with prayers. Suddenly he wished he'd gotten one of them instead. They tended to give answers rather than demand them. "What else would I be doing?"

The priest beamed like a teacher who'd gotten through to a particularly dense student. "Exactly."

The old bard started to object, then he realized what Duhzpin was getting at. Pacys leaned back in the bench, feeling a weight lift from his shoulders. He hadn't considered that. He'd locked in totally on finding the boy.

"If Oghma has put something before you as you believe," Duhzpin said, "then he will find a way for you to do it. That isn't within your realm. It's up to you to provide the faith and the strength to see it done, and Oghma will help you with the strength."

"You're right," the old bard agreed. "If now had been the time for me to find the boy—"

"—it would be done."

"I know he yet lives," Pacys said. "If he didn't, I'd know that too." He lifted his yarting and settled it across his lap. His fingers found the strings without hesitation. "Thank you for your time, Father."

"You're welcome," Duhzpin said. "Should you need a friendly ear again. . . ."

Pacys shook his head, feeling some enthusiasm for the first time in days. "I don't think I'll be staying much longer."

"Probably not." Duhzpin stood, looking around the room, and said, "If I could ask something of you, I'd be in your debt."

"I'd be only too happy to answer any request you might have. I'm in *your* debt."

Duhzpin nodded at the room. "The other priests and I have been helping people for days. I fear we're running short on strength ourselves, and I don't know if our flagging reserves are up to handling today. Perhaps you could play something uplifting."

Pacys stayed where he was, but he pulled the yarting to him with the skill of an old lover and the passion of youth. The strings rang out, strong and true, and filled the room. He sang, reaching back through the years for a song of praise for Oghma, one that hopefully everyone in the room knew.

In short order, the church filled with the sound of voices lifted in praise. Pacys clung to the sound, letting it fill all the empty places he'd chiseled away inside himself for the last two days, knowing that response was the best a bard who truly loved his work would ever know. As his fingers found the strings, his mind found an answer.

The vision came to him in perfect color and crystal clear. When he saw the gleaming black double doors equipped with white many-toothed gears that were the symbol of Gond Wonderbringer, he knew they could only belong to one place in Baldur's Gate.

He also knew he had to go there.

12

"The attack on Baldur's Gate didn't go the way you'd promised."

Laaqueel felt the weight of the accusation even though the words were spoken softly. The malenti priestess shifted uncertainly in Iakhovas's shadow. She prayed silently, pulling Sekolah's gifts to her, wondering if her power and his would be enough against the men that stood against them.

Iakhovas spread his hands. The illusion he wove over himself was so strong that Laaqueel couldn't even pierce it. As Black Alaric, he was a legend among the pirates, a man who'd lived for fourteen centuries and fought in every war that touched their shores.

In his present guise, Iakhovas was taller than any man there, dressed in azure and black garments complete with a cloak that carried the colors, black on the outside and azure on the inside. He wore rolled-top black boots that gleamed. A black crepe bandanna covered his lower face and his cloak hood was pulled tight so that only his eyes were revealed. It was the presence of those two eyes that let Laaqueel know the appearance was at least part illusion.

They stood in the spacious galley of *Grimshroud*, the flagship of the Nelanther Isles pirates. The sahuagin army Iakhovas had led into Baldur's Gate was already far from them, sent on ahead while Iakhovas ventured on to Skaug, the pirate capital of the Nelanther Isles.

"The attack didn't go as well as I'd hoped," Iakhovas admitted.

Laaqueel felt a chill when she heard that admission. Iakhovas wasn't one to admit mistakes. Not without someone else's bloodshed.

Bloody Falkane hung uncharacteristically back out of the limelight. The malenti priestess tried to keep her eyes from his, but they still touched upon occasion. It was awkward, and she got the sense that the pirate captain enjoyed her discomfort.

Burlor Maliceprow sat in an ornate chair at the head of the long table. He was the only person in the room allowed to sit. His given title was Portmaster of Skaug, but he was the controlling power of the Nelanther Isles. In his youth he'd been a wide man with hard lines that had gone to fat through his successes. His soft brown hair, sheared off at the jawline, carried gray streaks in it now. Hazel eyes glinted with the hardness of a newly minted coin. His clothes, despite his size, fit him well.

"You convinced us of this strike," Maliceprow said in his soft voice, barely heard above the ship's creaks and groans.

"I merely pointed out the opportunity," Iakhovas replied. "You convinced yourselves."

Maliceprow's eyes narrowed. "You say you don't accept the blame for this?"

Iakhovas reached out and pulled back a chair, ignoring the four guards around Maliceprow who moved to defend him. Iakhovas sat across from the portmaster, every eye in the galley on him. "I only accept my share of the blame. You knew there would be risks."

"I thought there would be less risk involved," Maliceprow stated, waving at his guards to stand down. He hadn't achieved his position by being afraid. "You said those damned sea devils and their creatures would chew up more of the city's defenses than they did."

Laaqueel felt her face grow hot at the disrespect the man obviously held for her people.

Easy, little malenti. You have even less respect for him.

Only the discipline Laaqueel had learned through serving Sekolah helped to keep her mouth closed and harsh words unsaid.

Iakhovas replied easily. "They incurred even greater losses than your pirates, Portmaster."

"And there's a balance to be struck here?" Maliceprow demanded.

"They went there to go to war with their enemies," Iakhovas said. "You went there out of greed to sack Baldur's Gate. Even with the losses you took, you made a profit."

Maliceprow said nothing.

"I'd call your attack a success."

"Except that every city and country along the Sword Coast is going to be more interested than ever in the Nelanther Isles," Falkane said.

Iakhovas smiled at the pirate captain. "I thought you took pride in the amount of the bounty offered for your head, Captain Falkane. Surely that amount will go up once the Sword Coast learns you were involved in the attack."

A smile spread across Falkane's thin lips. The yellow light from the lanterns mounted on the walls painted shadows on the wall behind him. He gave Iakhovas a small salute, fingers briefly touching his forehead. "A pirate's reputation is worth its weight in gold."

"Exactly," Iakhovas said. "After the attack on Baldur's Gate, all of your reputations have been enhanced, and you've made a profit."

"Not enough of one," Maliceprow growled. "I don't give a damn that you're supposed to be some kind of unkillable legend, Alaric. There will be an accounting here—or mayhap we'll see the evidence of those myths."

"I'm not a man to be pushed," Iakhovas said quietly, maintaining his steady gaze on Maliceprow.

For a moment Laaqueel's breath caught. She felt certain that violence was about to erupt in the galley.

After a long breath, Maliceprow leaned back in his chair and said, "Your alliance with the sea devils is of benefit to us."

"Of course it is," Iakhovas replied. "So far none of the pirate ships from the Nelanther Isles have been attacked by the sahuagin, or any other creature from the sea."

Laaqueel watched as the threat rolled over the gathered captains. She saw that they understood Iakhovas wielded more power over them than they'd before believed.

"Our arrangement guarantees your continued safe passage on the seas," Iakhovas went on. "You're free to continue to plunder the Sword Coast, secure in the knowledge that whoever decides to pursue any of you will become targets for the sahuagin. You yourselves have no cause to worry about them."

Maliceprow nodded slightly, but Laaqueel knew he didn't like his position and perhaps suddenly realized how untenable it was.

"Surely that's worth something," Iakhovas pointed out.

"Maybe it is," Falkane stated, "but you have to ask yourself, what's it worth to you to walk out of this galley alive?"

Laaqueel's heart sped up at the bald-faced threat.

Turning his head, Iakhovas stared at the pirate captain. "Your absence wouldn't go unnoticed. You'd be a hard man to replace."

Silence stretched in the galley, filling it. Laaqueel watched Falkane, knowing the pirate captain was fully confident enough to act.

"We want more," Falkane said. "Your precious sea devils took things from Baldur's Gate as well. We want a share. They don't need all that they took."

Maliceprow glanced at the younger man in irritation, obviously unhappy at having his authority or decisions questioned.

"Perhaps," Iakhovas said smoothly, "it would be interesting to humble you."

"You speak as though it could be done," Falkane interrupted.

"But not today," Iakhovas went on. "There's still need of you." He reached under his cloak and took out a green velvet bag. "All of you will have your share." He loosened the drawstrings on the bag and poured.

Gold and silver coins spilled to the galley floor, bouncing and rolling when they hit. Gems and jewelry followed them. The bag was obviously magical because it continued to pour even though it had already emptied more than twenty times its own ability to hold.

The pirates scrambled forward, each searching through the treasures that cascaded across the floor. Only Maliceprow and Falkane didn't move.

Iakhovas tossed the bag to one of the nearest pirates. "Hire more pirates to take the places of those you've lost. Build, buy, or steal more ships to replace those sitting at the bottom of Baldur's Gate's harbor."

Disappointment marked the man's face when the bag appeared to have emptied at last. When he upended it again and more valuables tumbled out, he shouted out in glee, joined by others.

"I pay my debts," Iakhovas said, "but I also call in the favors that are owed me. Beware some of the items you find there. They're magical in nature." He smiled cruelly. "You wouldn't want to destroy your ship before you return home."

Laaqueel relaxed somewhat, surprised yet again by how easily Iakhovas manipulated those around him. Sekolah was surely watching over him, even though the Shark God had never watched over anyone.

Maliceprow watched the wealth spilling across his ship's floor and said, "I shall look forward to continued business with you, Alaric."

Iakhovas pushed himself up from the table and turned toward the door. "Of course you do, Portmaster. I knew there'd be no other answer."

As Iakhovas left the room, Laaqueel lingered. She told herself it was to guard Iakhovas's back, but she couldn't resist a final glance into Falkane's dark eyes. They haunted her, and she'd come to enjoy the slight shiver that look gave her.

Then she turned and went out the door as well. Despite Iakhovas's generosity, the malenti priestess knew no love was lost between Iakhovas and Bloody Falkane.

Jherek dreamed, trapped by fatigue and by the fever that gripped him off and on still. Part of him knew he lay in *Breezerunner*'s hold and that Tynnel and most of the crew sat around him. They constantly moved and grumbled among themselves, ill at ease at being trapped in the ship's belly where no seafaring man would want to be. He felt sunlight across his legs where it streamed down from the bars overhead.

In the dream, he was five again, running across *Bunyip*'s decks with a bucket of wet sand. The pirates had surprised a cargo ship that carried a surprise of its own in the form of a passenger who was a mage of some renown. It was the first time Jherek had ever seen fireballs shoot through the air. Fear filled him again, but it was more than just the fear he'd known as a five-year-old. Even though everything seemed the same, he knew it was subtly different.

362

The voices and sounds blurred as they sometimes did in dreams, but the images were clear, full of color. His father stood on the stern castle, calling out orders to the men working to cut the flaming rigging free to save the sails and to the men he'd assembled for the boarding party.

Jherek ran as fast as he could. Despite all the activity taking place on both decks, his father would know how he performed. Flames hugged the deck near the port railing in front of him, already blistering the finish. He threw his bucket of brine-soaked sand over it, then raced back to the large crate amidships where more was kept.

His bare feet slapped against the deck, hard and callused from not wearing shoes and working the ship. At five, he already knew how to mend sails and nets. He also worked on the cleaning crews and in the galley. Days went by in those times when he'd never spoken a word. Even then it was mostly a quickly bellowed, "Aye sir!" followed by the smart salute his father had taught him.

He dipped the bucket into the crate of wet sand, scraping it up, then hurried back to the fire. The first bucketful had smothered some of the fire, but it was still in danger of spreading.

Bunyip caught a wave crossways, wallowing in the trough of rough water for a moment. Jherek stumbled at the railing, nearly spilling the bucket of sand overboard. He fought to keep hold of it, knowing his father would punish him if he didn't.

The pirate ship bore down on the merchantman. *Bunyip* closed rapidly when she got behind the other vessel and stripped the wind from her. Jherek's stomach twisted when he realized the killing would start soon. They had more buckets of sand for any blood that was spilled on *Bunyip*'s deck, and a stiff-bristled brush to scrub it away before it dried in.

Jherek tossed the sand over the fire. As he turned, *Bunyip* slammed into her prey with an explosive, hollow *boom* that splintered wood. *Bunyip* heeled over from the impact, then caught another crossways wave that tossed her high for a moment.

Without any chance to save himself, Jherek went over. He plummeted, splashing into the ocean. As he went under, he saw the shadowy shapes of the two ships come together again above him. Another boom, this one altered by its passage through water, crashed around him.

He kept his hand locked around the bucket. If he lost it, Bloody Falkane would whip him. Out of reflex, he tried to swim, but he was caught in an undercurrent, one of the vast movements that constantly shaped the undersea. Unable to use his other hand, he couldn't make any headway in the water.

In *Breezerunner*'s brig, Jherek felt the fever cover him in a sheen of perspiration. He struggled to wake from the dream, but was trapped by it. Waiting in the back of his mind, he knew what would happen next. At five, he'd given up, unwilling to release the bucket.

Bubbles streamed from his mouth as his vision darkened. Still, he kept himself from breathing. Then, in the distance, he saw a gliding gray shape streaking toward him. All those years ago, that shape had belonged to the dolphin that had turned up out of nowhere and saved him. He'd heard the mysterious voice for the first time in his life then.

Live, that you may serve.

Now, it wasn't a dolphin. Even though part of Jherek knew it was only a dream, part of him also knew what he was experiencing was something else as well.

The shape came closer, dolphinlike in its first appearance. It knifed through the water, and Jherek saw the hard lines of it. He remembered seeing it before, when he'd been held prisoner in *Butterfly*'s brig after the Amnians had discovered the tattoo he wore.

The shark was at least forty feet long, hard-muscled and gray as three-day-old death. Black lines etched its body, looking like scars at first, then becoming runes carved deep into the flesh. One eye glared at him coldly, but the other eye was gone, ripped away by claws or teeth. Still, the hollow raked him savagely with its gaze. The shark stopped, hanging motionless in the sea, the silhouettes of the two ships farther away as they continued sailing.

Don't think to fool yourself, boy, the shark told Jherek in a cold and malevolent voice that echoed inside his head. *I know about you. I've always known about you. Turn back while you still can.*

Jherek wanted to ask the shark what it was he was supposed to turn back from, but he couldn't. The dream had him in its thrall and fear closed his voice. He still held the bucket, unable to let it go even now. His father's rules still controlled him.

The shark opened its mouth, revealing rows of sharp teeth eight or nine inches long. It flicked its tail, speeding around him in a circle. Without warning, the shark dived for him, letting him know it was going to take him in one gulp.

Then die, boy, the shark said, *that you might be eaten!*

Blackness blotted out Jherek's consciousness.

Coming to in the brig, Jherek wheezed and fought for his breath, drawing in great rattling draughts. He sat up, drenched in sweat from the fever. He blinked at the sunlight, finding everything too bright.

Across the brig, Tynnel looked at him but didn't say anything.

"Are you well, lad?" Hullyn asked gruffly, leaning forward to drop a big hand across the young sailor's shoulders.

"Aye," Jherek croaked. "Fever took me. I'll be fine." The chills settled in then, racking his body. He wrapped his arms around himself.

"Here you go, lad. Have a sup of water." Hullyn handed Jherek a metal dipper filled to the brim.

"Thank you," Jherek said, taking it gratefully. With them traveling along the River Chionthar, freshwater wasn't a problem. Over the days of their travel, they'd kept a barrel of water in the corner. Vurgrom's pirates topped it off every day. Everyone knew they wouldn't have done it on their own so the general consensus was that Sabyna had something to do with the arrangement.

"Damn blackhearts," Hullyn grumbled. "What you need is a decent meal and some rest abed. Your melon's coming along right fine, but being down here in this pestilence hole isn't doing you any good."

Jherek silently agreed. He drank the water slowly, enjoying the clean taste of it, but afraid his stomach would rebel if he gulped it down.

Food was another problem. The pirates weren't as generous with it. *Breezerunner*'s crew complained about the lack of meals, but Jherek knew Vurgrom was intentionally half-starving them to keep them weak. All they got was a thin gruel twice a day. It was lowered in a big pot from topside, and the men used cups they'd been given to drink it. Even at that, there was never enough. Tynnel rationed it out himself, seeing each man got his share.

After slaking the fever-induced thirst, Jherek thanked Hullyn again and passed the dipper back. He tried not to think about the dream, but there was nothing else to think about. He'd dreamed about sharks before—every sailor did—but this was twice he'd dreamed about this monster shark.

Silently, he rested his head and forearms on his folded knees while he prayed to Ilmater, seeking solace in the Crying God's words. Only there was no solace. He sat trapped, and that was unbearable.

The despair in the brig soaked into him, ground into him with the filth that had accumulated after days of captivity. A large kettle from the galley served as the communal chamber pot and the smell from it pervaded everything. None of them had been allowed baths.

For some, Jherek knew, that was no real hardship because they didn't bathe often anyway, but he did. After having escaped his father's ship when he was a boy and making his way to Velen, he took pride in his cleanliness and manners. Those had been acquired things, things the wolfish boy who had run *Bunyip*'s decks with sand buckets had never possessed.

The shark's voice echoed in his mind again. Why had it warned him? And turn back from what? There wasn't anything he could do about his present course.

He pushed the thought out of his mind but found himself occupied with the missing pearl disk. He'd been wrongfully given it and hadn't made sure the old priest had taken it back.

Then he'd lost it.

"Hey," someone said, "look."

Attracted by the prospect of a diversion, Jherek glanced up. Above them, a rat clung to one of the iron bars covering the hold. Short black fur covered it except for the pale pinkish-gray tail, resembling any of the rats that were the bane of cargo ships. It wasn't unusual to see them aboard ship after spending any time in a city. Most of the time they crawled along the hawser ropes and onto the vessels.

"Foul creature," Aysel snarled as he stood.

The rat only eyed him curiously instead of running. The behavior gained it even more of Jherek's attention.

Aysel limped over to the center of the hold and took off one of his dagger earrings. Gripping it in his hand, he leaped up the short distance and caught hold of the bar with the other hand. Jherek already knew first hand how strong the man was, so he wasn't surprised when Aysel was able to hang onto the bar and prepare to strike the rat with the tiny dagger.

"Leave it alone," one of the men said.

"To hell with you," Aysel spat. "That there's meat on the hoof, way I look at it."

The thought almost turned Jherek's already feverish stomach.

Aysel swung the dagger, but the rat hopped to another bar and avoided the blow. Instead of running, it stuck its nose down to the bar and walked along its length in agitation.

A chill touched Jherek as he realized what must be going on. Fighting the weakness and the fever that clung to him, he pushed himself to his feet and slammed into Aysel as the man prepared to strike again.

Aysel fell off-balance and started cursing. He pushed against the wall and came back at Jherek with the small knife clenched in his fist.

Jherek blocked the blow. "Don't! You don't understand."

"I understand plenty!" Roaring in rage, Aysel tried another blow, this one coming from underneath.

Jherek stepped outside the blow and slapped Aysel's hand away. From the corner of his eye, he spotted one of the pirates approaching the hold. The man had a cutlass in his hand. When he spotted the rat, the pirate swung the blade.

"Jump!" Jherek said.

The rat flung itself from the iron bar, dropping into the brig. The pirate's sword knocked sparks from the iron. Reaching out, Jherek caught the rat in his arms.

The pirate leered down into the hold. "See you bastards are keeping proper company, ain't you?" He cackled at his own joke and walked away.

Aysel came at Jherek again, but Captain Tynnel caught the man roughly by the neck and yanked him off his feet. Aysel fell against the wall, squalling in anger.

"Don't move," Tynnel ordered Aysel.

"Bastard took my rat," Aysel said.

"That's no rat," Tynnel said calmly.

In the next instant, Jherek had both arms full of lithe feminine flesh.

13

"Leaving, are ye? And just like that? With no fare-the-well?"

Pacys looked up from securing his backpack and saw Khlinat standing in the doorway. The dwarf had been generous enough to loan him the couch while they searched for the boy. The old bard had put the bedding away and packed his things. "Yes. I was going to leave a note."

Khlinat's eyebrows climbed. "Oh, and ye are in a hurry too."

"Yes."

"Do ye know where the swabbie is?"

"No, but I've found out where I'm supposed to be," Pacys replied. He pulled the backpack up and settled the straps over his shoulders. "I have to trust that our paths will intersect again as they're supposed to."

"I've continued poking me nose into places around the city, but I've yet to find a solid lead."

Pacys shook his head. Music raced through his mind again, traveling chords. "I don't think you will. However he got out of the city, he's not here any longer."

"Aye, and I know that's true enough." He looked troubled. "Where are ye off to?"

"I don't know. While I was at the church, I got a vision. It told me where to go, but not where I'd be going. I guess I'm supposed to figure that out after I get there."

"Ye make this sound mysterious."

"The gods do tend to move in that manner," Pacys said.

Khlinat ran a hand through his tangled beard. "Ye going to be all right on yer own?"

"I always have been." Pacys rummaged in his coin purse, trying not to notice how light it was for a man possibly traveling a great distance.

"I know you've not been able to work at the shipyards since you've been injured. Let me pay you for letting me bed here."

"Faugh, and that would be a laugh. Don't think yerself so high and mighty, old bard. I'm a steady working man and no traveler from place to place depending on the generosity of strangers. I've got silver enough to do me awhile."

Pacys closed his purse, knowing it would be better to keep his meager coin as long as he could. As long as he stayed within a civilized area he had no doubts about being able to sing for enough to eat and put a temporary roof over his head, but if he was out in the wilderness things might be different.

"I got a question to ask ye," Khlinat said, looking a little uncomfortable.

"Yes."

"While ye are out and about, who's going to watch yer back? I mean, it's going to be powerful hard to find the swabbie if yer fertilizer for some lonely patch of forest."

"I've always watched out for myself," Pacys answered.

"Aye, but things seem to have greater stakes at the moment. I've a mind to go with ye meself, kind of keep ye out of trouble and it away from yer door. If ye would have me."

Pacys looked at the dwarf, realizing the warrior's nature that resided in the short, powerful frame. Despite missing a leg and the wounds he'd suffered only three days ago, Khlinat seemed prepared to leave during the next drawn breath.

"I don't know how far I'd have to go," the old bard stated. "Nor how long I'll be gone."

Khlinat nodded. "Something put me there where that boy was. I still feel its pull on me now. I never been a coward, no dwarf worth his salt is, but that night with that boy, I felt like I was fighting the good fight, the kind a warrior would want to sell his life at if blood price was demanded for participation. I ain't too willing to let that feeling go. Losing me leg, I've felt like half a man for a lot of years. With him, facing them sahuagin claws and jaws, a true axe in me hand, I felt like me old self. I want that back." He paused to clear his voice. "I ain't one to go begging, but if ye will have me, I swear by the anvil and hammer of Moradin to look over ye, be the shield over yer back should ye need it till I see ye clear of this mess."

Emotion choked the old bard. Riffs of music, carried on the unmistakable basso that marked many dwarven songs, echoed inside his head. "You truly feel that this is what has been put before you?"

"With all me heart," Khlinat responded. "I went down to the apothecary and bought meself a dram of heal potion to get meself more right for if ye should have need of me. Don't be telling me I wasted me coin."

"Get your gear together," Pacys said. "I've already wasted two days when I was supposed to be doing something."

Pacys led the way into the Hall of Wonders, between the black doors that floated in the air in front of it. The white many-toothed wheels on the doors looked exactly as they had in his vision.

The Hall of Wonders sat on Windspell Street, across from the High House, its parent temple. Stone gargoyles clung to the roof on clawed feet. The building stood three stories tall and ran straight back, a hall as its name implied. It was immaculately clean and the windows were scrubbed, shining glass.

A watchpriest greeted them dressed in a wheeled hat and a robe with a sash at the waist that contained gears, locks, hooks, and bits of tin, steel, and wood. Pacys paid the priest eight silvers, the entry fee for Khlinat and himself.

The old bard's feet made only slight noise against the waxed stone floor. Tall stone pillars ranged on either side of them under the vaulted ceiling. Between the pillars, display cases held the inventions and instruments for sale. Duplicates were kept and manufactured in the building's cellar.

"Have ye been here before?" Khlinat whispered, overtaken with the expansiveness of the hall and the tidy surroundings.

"Many times," Pacys replied. "I've purchased some musical instruments here over the years. While functional, I found them to be lacking in intrinsic quality. There's nothing like an instrument you've made yourself."

"Aye, and a certain satisfaction as well."

Despite the attack on Baldur's Gate only a few days ago, the Hall of Wonders still held numerous gnomes openly gawking at the displayed devices. Even Khlinat's attention was captured by some of them.

"Ah, the Ironeater clan I'm from would like to see this place," the dwarf said. "If they haven't already."

Halfway down the Hall, Pacys found what he was looking for.

The mirror was perfectly made, nine feet wide and nine feet tall, framed in red lacquered wood. The unblemished surface gleamed, offering a faultless reflection of the old bard, the dwarf, and the section of the Hall behind them.

Khlinat scowled at his image, running fingers through his tangled beard. "Ooch, now there's an ugly brute for ye."

"Gond Wonderbringer's blessing be upon you," an unctuous voice stated. "Is there any way I may be of service to you?"

Pacys glanced at the young priest that approached them, then looked back at the mirror. Except for its size, he didn't see anything out of the ordinary about it. For a moment he doubted the vision he'd been given in Oghma's temple.

"Tell me about this mirror," Pacys requested.

"It is beautiful, isn't it?"

"Yes," Pacys replied, "but Gond isn't known for his taste in beauty."

"I could disagree," the young priest pointed out. "The beauty of the gifts Gond bestows upon us is not inconsiderable."

"My apologies," Pacys said. "Forgive me for being so blunt, but what I referred to was the fact that Gond never built anything that wasn't functional in some way."

"And you're wondering how this is functional?"

"Yes."

The young priest approached the mirror. "It was ground as all mirrors are, and polished to its present sheen here. The sand it was made from came from a fallen star in the Inner Sea. Chosstif, one of the High Initiates of the Mysteries of Gond here, paid mermen in the Inner Sea for its recovery, then had it shipped here fourteen years ago."

"Fourteen years ago?" Pacys asked. The time frame fit in with Narros's story of the Taker destroying the merman village. "I don't recall seeing it when I was here before. The last time I visited was less than two years ago."

"It was only just finished less than ten weeks ago," the priest said. "It's surely one of the largest undertakings we've ever done. Chosstif was moved by a vision from Gond himself and made to carry out the construction of this mirror. It has very special properties."

"Like what?" Khlinat asked doubtfully.

The priest walked to the mirror and put his palm against it. "A mirror this size is usually hard to get from place to place. Yet, once you have one in your home, you must admit how much it brightens up the place. Purchasing a mirror this big is not much of a problem, but the transportation is. With Chosstif's collapsible mirror, transportation is no longer as difficult." He pushed gently.

Seams formed and tiny hinges revealed themselves. The mirror seemed to come apart, folding in on itself in foot-sized sections. The *clink-clink-clink* of the sections landing on each other produced a noticeable rhythm inside Pacys's head. In less than a moment the mirror had been reduced to a two-foot square that was only a little less than that in depth. It stayed hooked on the wall. A slim length of black cord hung down from the mirror. The young priest pulled on the cord and kept pulling until all the tiles once more appeared as a single, seamless unit nine feet square.

"Amazing," Pacys said. "I've never seen the like before." He stared into the mirrored depths

"Yes. As you can guess, it's one of our more popular items. Well worth the price. Though you will have to wait for it, you understand."

"Actually," Pacys said, "I'm not here to purchase a mirror."

The priest appeared surprised and perhaps a little disappointed. "By the way you approached it, I was certain you'd heard of it or seen it and come to purchase one."

"No." Pacys reached out to the mirror. It was cool to the touch, almost liquid.

"You'll find none like it and none finer," the priest guaranteed.

"Mayhap." Pacys was puzzled. The mirror remained yet a mirror, though in his vision it had been something else entirely in addition to being a mirror. He took his hand back and studied the fingerprints he'd left there.

"Is something wrong?" the priest asked.

"I don't know," the old bard answered, more to himself than the other man. He studied the mirror from different angles, drawing irritated glances from the priest who looked like he'd rather be somewhere else.

"What is it?" Khlinat asked.

"I was shown this mirror in my vision earlier," Pacys explained, "yet now it appears I was mistaken."

"Don't let yer faith be shaken," the dwarf said. "If ye were given a vision of this thing, then there's a reason. Think about why it would be shown to ye. I think ye have the key. Ye just have to find it."

As he concentrated, Pacys also heard the rhythms around him. People's voices, the sounds of feet moving on stone, the clink and clank of items being picked up and put down, all blended. Unconsciously, he found the rhythm of the noises, and another piece of the song he pursued so diligently came into his mind. He pulled his yarting forward and strummed his fingers across the strings as he gave vent to his voice.

> "There they stood, Taleweaver and dwarven warrior,
> Who'd pledged his life against the Taker.
> They faced mirror-bright mystery,
> Flashing,
> Clouded,
> And empty of answers.
> Yet the mirror shone its truth,
> Crowned under stars
> Forged
> From the bottom of the Inner Sea.
> Gond Wonderbringer's desire and power
> Guided the hand of the High Initiate,
> Imbuing his work with
> Additional magic
> That worthy didn't know about.
> The Taleweaver captured
> The cadence
> From the crowds that filled the House of Wonders.
> And when he did,
> When his voice reached the perfect pitch,
> A way was made."

Holding the final note, Pacys stretched out his hand to the mirror. For an instant, he touched the glass again, but the surface quickly gave way to a wet fog that dissolved and became a forest.

The priest of Gond stepped back and made a sign of his god, a prayer already on his lips.

The music and the certainty of what he was doing filled Pacys. Slinging the yarting once more from its straps about his shoulders, he told Khlinat, "Follow me," and strode into the mirror.

He felt a brief resistance, then the mirror accepted him. Coldness swirled around him but quickly went away. He felt the dwarf moving behind him, heard the prayer he breathed. The music stayed alive in Pacys's head. A moment more and he stepped from the stone floor in the Hall of Wonders in Baldur's Gate into the forest. Turning, the old bard saw the nine-foot square of shimmering space that represented the mirror. It opened, like a window, back into the Hall of Wonders.

The priest was shouting, and other priests and potential buyers ran to join him, staring in awe.

Khlinat stepped from the window, shivering. "Ooch, but that was cold on these old bones." He gazed in wonder at the forest around them. "Do ye know where it is we might be, me friend?"

The opening vanished like morning mist before a harsh sun, taking away the vision of the Hall of Wonders and leaving only the forest.

"Where we're supposed to be, praise Oghma." Pacys took a deep breath and scented the brine hanging in the air. "Do you know that smell?"

Khlinat snuffed the air, then a broad grin split his craggy face. "The sea, by Marthammor Duin's wandering eye! And it's not far here. We've come a long way."

"Yes," Pacys agreed, "but there's more."

Khlinat snuffed again. "Are ye sure? All I smell is the sweet breath of the sea, but not that of the Sea of Swords or the Trackless Sea where I've spent all me sailing days."

Pacys moved through the tall trees and dense vegetation, coming upon a well-worn trail winding down through the hilly country. "Your nose is sharper than mine when it comes to that, but I learned a long time ago to pick up the scent of a cookfire. Let's go find whoever owns it."

"You can put me down now."

Dazed by the events happening so quickly and by the young woman fitting so comfortably in his arms, Jherek blushed furiously. A few of the sailors around them snickered. If their situation hadn't been so dire, Jherek knew he would have been made the fool of mercilessly.

"Shut up," Tynnel ordered.

While the crew quieted, Jherek carefully placed the ship's mage on her feet. "Lady," he apologized, "I didn't mean to be so familiar. I'd thought to release you while you were still a rat." His face was crimson, he knew, and the heat he felt wasn't all from the fever. "I mean, while you were still—not yourself."

Sabyna stepped away from him, taking refuge against the wall were she wouldn't be so easily seen from the deck. "You're all right?"

"Aye. Thank you for asking." Jherek noticed Captain Tynnel shift in irritation and felt the man was somehow angry with him.

"I thought they'd killed you," Sabyna said, grabbing his arm and pulling him toward her. Despite his protests, she parted his hair and looked at the wound. "It's infected and needs to be cleaned out." She wheeled on the men around them. "Why hasn't anyone been taking care of him?"

Jherek felt angry and embarrassed all at the same time. "Lady," he said respectfully, "I'm able to take care of myself."

"Right," Sabyna said sarcastically. "That's why you've got a head full of pus and you're burning up with fever."

Jherek sensed she was angry with him already and that knowledge kept him from making any kind of retort. He wasn't exactly clear why she was angry. Her fingers continued to poke around on the tender parts of his head, maybe with a little vengeance included. Still, he made no sound.

"I've been taking care of him," Hullyn objected. "I saw that it was infected. I've been keeping that scalp wound like that on purpose. Like my old da always taught me. You get infection set in like that, you let flies get to it. Then maggots will eat out the rotten meat so it'll heal up proper."

Jherek's stomach lurched. Malorrie's instruction had covered such things, but those methods were to be used only under harsh and difficult circumstances, when no recourse to a healer was available.

"That way would leave a terrible scar," Sabyna said.

"Lady," Jherek said patiently, "I bear scars from past times. There's no—"

"You're not bearing this one on my behalf," she stated with determination.

"I gather that shape-shifting ability you've suddenly developed isn't going to last forever," Tynnel growled. He was angry too, Jherek noted, but the captain's disfavor appeared to be shared between Sabyna and himself.

"No," Sabyna answered, turning to face the captain, "it won't."

"Then I suggest you use this time you've taken to risk your life. How many men are there aboard *Breezerunner*?"

"Twenty-seven," Sabyna answered.

"I never saw that many," Tynnel said.

"You never saw all of them," the pretty ship's mage replied.

Tynnel pulled a face. "How well versed are they in ship's craft?"

"They know their way around a ship," Sabyna said, "and they're all heavily armed."

"Do you know where they're going?"

"To the end of the Chionthar. After that Vurgrom plans on making his way back to the Sea of Fallen Stars. He came to Baldur's Gate to deliver an item to the man responsible for the attack on Waterdeep and Baldur's Gate."

"You mean the *sahuagin* responsible—" Tynnel started to say.

"The man," Sabyna repeated. "He's called Iakhovas."

The news slammed into Jherek. It was one thing to think of the sea devils rising up to strike along the Sword Coast in concert, but it was even more stunning to learn that a man had orchestrated those strikes.

"I've never heard the name," Tynnel said.

"I've got the feeling you will. Vurgrom rails on about what Iakhovas is going to do to the Sea of Fallen Stars."

"Vurgrom's making you use that chair he brought aboard, isn't he?" Tynnel asked.

Embarrassment flushed Sabyna's face with color. "I've never seen its like. When I'm sitting there, *Breezerunner* feels more alive than ever. She moves when and where I tell her."

"Then stop her," Tynnel commanded. "On your next shift in that chair, stop her dead in the water."

Sabyna shook her head. "That would only get us all killed. They tie me in that chair under guard when it's my shift. As soon as I did that, they'd slit my throat, then come kill the lot of you."

"They won't let us live anyway," Tynnel said. "Not when they're done with us and *Breezerunner*."

"Then I'm the only chance we all have," Sabyna declared. She swept the crew with her gaze and Jherek saw the care she held for them and the distress she felt for them in that glance. "I would have been here sooner to check on you but they won't let me near the cargo hold. I finally had the chance to get into my room and get one of the potions I had. Unfortunately, it was the only one I had. I'd intended to trade it in Lantan to a mage there who hasn't been able to learn the spell himself. This will be the only time I can get down here like this."

"Can you open the door?"

Sabyna shook her head. "Vurgrom keeps the key with him at all times."

"Can't you magic him, lass?" Hullyn asked. "Put him to sleep or fry him with a lightning bolt?"

"I've already considered that," Sabyna said. "The problem is if I fail, Vurgrom will execute two of you. If I get caught in here now, I'm sure two of you will be killed."

"Then what the hell are you doing in here risking our lives like this?" Aysel demanded.

"Because I don't know if your lives won't be forfeit anyway if I can't get you out of here," she told him.

Aysel gaped at her, then turned away angrily. "We put our necks in the noose for a petty little twit like her. Umberlee take her into the dark and deep. We should have took our chances back at the dock."

Jherek started forward and Aysel turned toward him, a malicious grin on his brutal face.

Before Jherek could get close, Tynnel seized Aysel by the shirt collar and yanked him into the wall. Aysel's head slammed into the hard wood with a dulled gonging sound. Stunned, the big man dropped to his knees.

Tynnel shifted his hold to Aysel's hair and yanked the man's head back. The captain ripped the sailor's other dagger earring out, splitting the fleshy lobe, and held the keen little blade against the corner of Aysel's eye.

"Another word out of you," Tynnel promised in a tight voice, "and I'll carve you a face to frighten young children with during Moonfest. Do you understand me? Nod carefully."

Slowly, Aysel dipped his chin. "Aye, sir."

"Another thing, when we get to the next port of call, civilized or not," Tynnel said, "you're no longer part of this ship's crew. I stand by those who stand by me, and I've given you considerable leave of your responsibilities."

"You can't do that," Aysel blustered. "I'm a hell of a sailor."

"Aye," Tynnel replied. "That you are, but you're not much of a man. Keep your mouth shut till I tell you to speak."

Aysel dropped into a crouch against the wall and glared heated rage at Jherek.

Tynnel kept the small dagger. He turned back to Sabyna. "While you've got this ability I want you to get clear of *Breezerunner.*"

"You *want* me to?" Sabyna narrowed her eyes at him. "Since when do I listen to what you want?"

Tynnel appeared somewhat taken off-balance, but he recovered quickly, staring hard at her. "Consider it an order, then."

"Were it an order while you were in command of this ship, and it made sense to me, I'd think it over. Neither of those is true at this moment."

"Damn your eyes, Sabyna, get off the ship like I told you to." Tynnel took a step forward.

Unconsciously, Jherek took a step forward too, setting himself to intervene on behalf of Sabyna if it looked like Tynnel was going to get physical with her. Both of them noticed his approach at once. Tynnel made an effort to calm himself and didn't move any closer.

"And if I do get off this ship," Sabyna challenged, "Vurgrom will start killing all of you down here."

"Lass," Hullyn said softly, "Cap'n's right. This ain't no place for a young lady like yourself. If you have the chance to get clear of this stumble, you should take it."

"There's nothing out there to go to," Sabyna said. "Give me the sea and I could live off it, but not those plains and sparse forests. The river might offer a better chance, but I'm not happy with that either." She plucked a tiny hourglass from her necklace and checked the swift-moving sands.

"It would be safer there than here," Tynnel argued, "and if we didn't have to worry about you, Vurgrom's hold over us wouldn't be as tight."

"Says you. There's safety in numbers, Cap'n. Or did you forget that?"

Hot spots of color flared on Tynnel's cheeks. "You're getting really close to insubordination."

"Draw a line," Sabyna told him, "and I'll step over it just to make sure we both know."

"Gods, you can be so stubborn at times."

"Only when I'm right, and you know that." Sabyna turned to Jherek. "I'll need help getting back up there."

"As you wish," Jherek said.

A smile dawned on her face as she heard his words, and the sight of it shot pain through Jherek's heart. She was so beautiful and independent, yet she was so far from anything he could ever hope to attain. If she saw the tattoo of Bloody Falkane that he bore, it would be enough to trigger undying hatred on her part.

"As you wish," she repeated softly. "I'll try to get some heal potion down here, or at least some salve you can put on that head of yours."

Jherek nodded. "Thank you, lady, but don't trouble yourself overmuch. I'm holding up fine," he said, though he knew he wasn't. He felt broken inside, and wanted nothing more than a bowl of the soup Madame Iitaar used to make for him when he was ill back in Velen.

Sabyna said something unladylike, which shocked Jherek. Curse words from the other sailors he was accustomed to, but not from the pretty ship's mage's tender lips.

In the next instant, she blurred. Her size reduced and her form changed until only a rat ran toward Jherek's boots. Unsteady from the fever raging inside him, Jherek leaned carefully down and picked her up. Gently, he grabbed the iron bar overhead and tried to pull himself up, but his strength failed him.

"Here you go, lad." Hullyn came forward and laced his hands together into a makeshift stirrup.

"Thank you." Jherek stepped into the big man's hands and felt himself lifted until he could reach the iron bar. In her rat form, Sabyna quickly scurried away, hesitating at the edge only a moment.

Vertigo seized Jherek as Hullyn lowered him. If not for the big man's hand on his shoulder, he would have fallen.

"There's something I want you to keep in mind," Tynnel told him in a dark voice. His eyes blazed as he regarded Jherek. "If you do anything that makes her choose to step in harm's way, you'll answer to me."

Some of the anger and fierceness that Jherek had come to know in Athkatla and during the caravan trek to Baldur's Gate hit the young sailor. "I wouldn't do anything like that, sir."

Tynnel seemed on the verge of contesting the statement, then he blew out a great breath and turned away. "We'll see."

Unwilling to let the man walk away so calmly, Jherek addressed him. "Captain Tynnel, back in Athkatla you told me you'd tell Sabyna that I wouldn't be coming with the ship. I knew you wouldn't tell her about the fight, but you explained it so that it sounded like I didn't even take time to tell her good-bye."

"And what did you tell her?"

Jherek hesitated. "I carried on with your lie, sir."

"Why?"

"Because I didn't want to tell her the truth."

"Neither did I," Tynnel told him. "I knew if I told you different you might feel you had to see her again."

Jherek knew it was true.

"Also," Tynnel went on, "I think somewhat like Aysel in that you *are* a bad copper that keeps turning up. If you hadn't been here today, and hadn't gotten wounded trying to save her, I might have been able to convince her to jump ship and save herself."

Jherek didn't agree. He didn't believe Sabyna would have left any crew member aboard *Breezerunner.* He didn't understand why Tynnel laid so much of the responsibility for Sabyna's actions now on his shoulders.

Weak and shaking, the young sailor walked slowly back to the place he'd been sitting before Sabyna had arrived. His head throbbed and the light lanced his eyes. He closed them and laid his head on his arms, feeling the heat and oily slickness that clung to his skin.

Jherek suffered in silence, from the physical discomfort as well as the mental anguish he subjected himself to. He remembered Malorrie's teachings, part of the platform he'd built for himself to get him through the dark years since leaving his father's ship. The phantom had always told him to do what needed doing when it needed doing, not to borrow trouble, and to plan for what could be accomplished and not for what couldn't.

After a time, he slept, and the shark haunted Jherek's dreams, hunting him ceaselessly.

14

Laaqueel swam in Iakhovas's shadow, having trouble keeping up with him. In the last month since healing after his fight with Huaanton, Iakhovas seemed to become even stronger. The malenti priestess suspected that newfound strength came from one of the items his spies and lackeys constantly searched for. No human could swim as fast as a sahuagin, or a malenti, and no sahuagin could swim as fast as Iakhovas.

She continued to struggle as they arched through the tunnels beneath the sahuagin palace. Sahuagin homes always had numerous entrances, following tunnels that branched in all directions. Mazes were an entertainment as well as a defense for the sahuagin, and the most complex labyrinths were those constructed under the palace.

The malenti struggled to remember the route. Iakhovas never took the same one twice, and she knew there was some deliberate overlapping and repetition in his routes. It was a constant reminder that, though they were joined by Sekolah's will and the quill next to her heart, Iakhovas would always go his own way.

Make haste, little malenti, Iakhovas taunted. *I don't want to keep my people waiting. It would be unseemly if the Royal High Priestess wasn't at her station when I made my announcement.*

What announcement? Laaqueel swam harder, flaring out the webbing between her toes and fingers to better catch the water. Still, she couldn't close the distance. It was unsettling seeing him in his human form easily setting a pace she found grueling.

Patience, little malenti. I know events in Baldur's Gate sapped some of our reserves and even the savage nature of the sahuagin is daunted. I've made preparations to fix that. Trust me, they will be reinspired today.

Suspicion shot through Laaqueel. Since his meeting with the Nelanther pirates, Iakhovas had been brimming with energy and mystery. He took a final turn in the tunnel he was following, waiting until he was almost upon it.

Drawn by the wake he'd left, Laaqueel strove to make the corner but couldn't. She slammed into the rough wall, abrading her skin. Biting back a cry of pain, she pushed off the wall and continued her pursuit of Iakhovas.

Another turn and he shot straight up, coursing through yet another tunnel. Laaqueel watched him leave the opening above, flashing swift as an arrow.

As soon as he cleared the opening, Iakhovas spread his arms. Knowing he looked like a sahuagin male to her people, Laaqueel recognized the bit of posturing on his behalf. A sahuagin's fins would have flared out, standing briefly at attention. His arrival was graceful and impressive, showing that he was every inch the predator.

Laaqueel left the tunnel and entered the large chamber behind the amphitheater throne. She heard the clicks and whistles of the crowd and knew that the gladiatorial games that had been scheduled were underway. She'd been informed of them but had chosen to stay in her chambers until she'd been sent for.

Iakhovas alighted on his feet. Instantly the Royal Black Tridents closed in around him, barely giving Laaqueel room to take her place at his side. Iakhovas glanced at her with his single eye. Down in the dark pit of the empty socket, she thought she saw something metallic.

"You've changed your attire since our raid," Iakhovas said.

"Yes." Laaqueel didn't explain why she'd started wearing the hated human clothing. She couldn't really explain it to herself. Most of it had to do with how Bloody Falkane had flaunted his sexual aggression, and how it had affected her. It had, however, served her to notice that Iakhovas was aware of her nudity even though he'd never tried to act on it. The feeling was extremely awkward. She'd never before experienced any of the emotions or confusion the two men now generated within her.

There was something about Bloody Falkane, though, that had stayed with her. Sometimes at night she felt his lips still on hers, burning like the poisonous touch of a vinanquelt. It wasn't enough to cause pain, but it had disrupted her sleep patterns. Only prayers had ever done that before.

The possibility of an alliance with him was never too far from her mind. It could put her on more equal footing with Iakhovas. Though she knew attempting such an alliance would anger Iakhovas, she also thought the cunning and cruel part of him would respect her efforts.

Iakhovas led the way out to the terrace overlooking the amphitheater. He took his seat and the Royal Black Tridents spread out around him. Laaqueel stood at his side.

Below, on the swirl pattern of the amphitheater floor, nine captured surface dwellers fought an afanc. The blue-gray beast had a vicious wedge-shaped head and a mouthful of teeth, made even more distinctive by the long whiskers. Resembling a fish in structure, it was nearly fifty feet long and often was mistaken for a whale because of its size.

Laaqueel knew Iakhovas had chosen nine humans on purpose. The number meant much among the sahuagin culture. There were nine barons, and power was assumed to come from that number.

The humans fought because they had no choice. Armed with tridents, they tried to stay low to the ground. If they'd tried to swim up, the afanc would have easily picked them off.

Finning itself into a frenzy, the afanc began swimming in circles above the group. Faster and faster it sped, until a whirlpool took shape in the water. The funnel danced across the checkerboard amphitheater floor, twisting with quick, darting leaps that scoured the tiles. Debris formed bands inside the whirlpool.

The humans tried to flee, seeing the danger too late, but the whirlpool caught them. The suction ripped them from the floor, pulling them up into the open. As the humans whipped around the outer edges of the dancing whirlpool, the afanc swam in quick lunges and ripped them free in its jaws. When the creature crunched its prey, blood flowed into the water. In less than a minute, all nine surface dwellers were gone.

The sahuagin in the stands shouted out in savage glee.

Iakhovas let them have their moment, then he stood and held his hands out for attention. He waited until every eye was on him, then said, "My people, long have I prayed over our future. I have asked not for mercy from Sekolah for We Who Eat, for that would be foolish. I have asked for strength. We need to be strong, stronger than we have ever been before. Our destiny lies before us, shrouded in human flesh and human death. It is from them that we must rip what is our due according to the will of the mighty Shark God."

His words carried powerfully over the amphitheater. Laaqueel felt moved by them, and was certain that no matter what Iakhovas thought he was doing, Sekolah was working through him.

"Our losses were great at Baldur's Gate," Iakhovas said. "Many of our warriors fell in battle, but that, too, is the way Sekolah wills. Our path cannot be easy, not if we are to remain worthy of our heritage. Sekolah found us and shaped us into warriors." He paused. "No, he molded us in his wisdom into the *best* warriors."

A resounding cheer went up in the amphitheater. Laaqueel watched her people, knowing Iakhovas had them in the palm of his hand.

"We strike fear into the hearts of any who dare stand in the way of We Who Eat," Iakhovas continued. "As we should for now and for always. We took their lives that night, just as we did in Waterdeep, and we've become stronger because of our losses."

Out in the amphitheater, the afanc finished chasing down the stray bits of bodies left floating in the water. None of the sahuagin guards ventured forth for any of the choice morsels so tantalizingly close.

"Some of you may think we should halt for a time in our war against the surface dwellers," Iakhovas said, "but that would only be giving in to weakness."

Silence reigned in the amphitheater, and Laaqueel knew no one dared dispute Iakhovas's words.

"We were born to fight and die." Iakhovas looked out over the gathered sahuagin. "To do any less would be forsaking all that we know. So now I tell you that I've been told to guide you to a new battleground, a place where we can strike even more terror into the hearts of the accursed surface dwellers."

Laaqueel listened, trying to guess where Iakhovas would next send them. There were always the lands of the Shining South and the Empires of the Sands. Both of those regions conducted a lot of sea trade.

"I was given a dream," Iakhovas went on, "of a sea far from here. An inland sea held hostage by the hated humans."

Consternation spread throughout the ranks of the sahuagin. Laaqueel felt her heart slow, but the quill pricked it and it resumed its normal rhythm.

Be at ease, little malenti. I know what I'm doing.

"And in this inland sea, called Serôs by those who live there, I have seen thousands of our people held captive in subjugation. It falls to us to find them and free them from the trap the humans laid for them."

More noise erupted through the ranks, and Laaqueel knew Iakhovas was dangerously close to losing the crowd. Hardly any of the sahuagin had ever heard of an inland sea. To hold the very sea itself captive was unthinkable, an aberration they would struggle to even understand or believe.

"It's true!" Iakhovas roared. "No one may doubt my word, the word of your king!"

Instantly, most of the noise died away, but Laaqueel knew the implied threat didn't quell the confusion within her people.

"I will lead you there," Iakhovas said, "and we will find our people. A way will be made for us to achieve this, our greatest of destinies. Once again, our people will be made whole, no longer separated by the ignorance the hated surface dwellers would wish on us. I give you this, my promise, and I stand on it in the blood of combat to prove to you that Sekolah watches over our actions."

Before anyone knew what was going on, Iakhovas leaped from the terrace and swam out into the amphitheater. The afanc noticed him at once and began finning toward him.

The royal guards mustered quickly to go to his aid. Laaqueel reached for the gifts Sekolah had bestowed upon her, wondering if any of them would truly be enough to stand against the monster even now gliding toward Iakhovas.

"No!" Iakhovas shouted. "Do not interfere. Trust in the will of Sekolah."

Laaqueel rushed forward to the terrace railing. Fear pounded through her as she wondered what would happen to her when Iakhovas was killed by the afanc.

Iakhovas hung motionless in the water, floating well above the tiled courtyard. He spread his arms out, claws wide on his hands and feet.

The afanc streaked straight for him. It opened its mouth, knowing its prey couldn't escape.

Jherek woke from a troubled slumber, never free of the nightmarish shark that pursued him. Pale moonlight streamed through the iron bars of the hold overhead, letting him know it was still in the dark hours of the night. The familiar creak of *Breezerunner*'s rigging and planks sounded around him. Two men's voices talking casually to each other came from above.

Nearly all of *Breezerunner*'s crew were asleep around him, rolled tightly into themselves against the chill of the night that filled the hold. Only Tynnel was awake, sitting across the hold and staring up at the iron bars overhead. Jherek made brief, uncomfortable eye contact with the man, glancing quickly away. He closed his eyes and leaned his head back against the bulwark. Since their confrontation a few days ago, they'd had little to say to each other.

Slight fever still coursed through Jherek, but it wasn't as bad as it had been. At least now it burned and kept his sleep erratic, but it didn't leave him shaking all the time. The chill bit into him with jagged fangs, though, and he wished he had a blanket so he wouldn't wake up feeling stiff all the time.

Breezerunner still sailed through the River Chionthar as it had every night that Jherek had been aware of. Old Captain Finaren, who'd never liked even the idea of river travel, told him that normally a ship tied up at night on a river. There were too many dangers, unseen shoals that could rip a keel out from under a ship, or twists that could be missed in the night that would leave the ship run ashore, to risk sailing in the dark. Even the merchantman's necessary four-foot draft could prove challenging for the ship's pilot. The young sailor knew there must have been some reason for Vurgrom's haste, and he wished he had some clue as to what it was.

The fever left his mouth dry. Quietly, not wanting to disturb those around him, Jherek made his way to the water barrel. He used the dipper hanging on the side and drank deeply.

"Malorrie."

The whisper drew the young sailor's attention up. For a moment, he thought he'd imagined Sabyna's voice, a product of wishful thinking and the fever.

"Malorrie."

He glanced up, thinking perhaps he saw a slight shimmering against the star-studded night above. "Sabyna?" he said softly.

"I have the key to the brig lock." Her voice seemed to come from the air itself.

"How did you—"

"Vurgrom sleeps occasionally. I waited till his mage was deep in his own studies, then took my chances."

"That was foolish," Jherek said. "You could have been hurt."

"Quiet. I've heard them talking that we'll reach the end of the river tomorrow. If we're going to have a chance at all, it has to be tonight."

Jherek nodded. "I agree, lady. Once you give me the key, get yourself off the ship."

"I can do more good here."

"No," Jherek said softly.

"We don't have time to argue. Even invisible, if any of the pirates look in my direction at the right time they could figure out what's going on. If Vurgrom should wake up and find his key missing, all hell will break loose."

"Of course."

"Stretch your hand up."

Jherek did, standing on tiptoe. The hard metal key brushed his fingertips for a moment, and he seized it. He felt the warmth of Sabyna's hand close around his briefly, and he wished the touch could have lasted longer. He felt an immediate wash of shame and guilt. He was in no way deserving of her. His face burned and he hoped it was too dark in the hold for the ship's mage to see.

"As soon as you are ready," Sabyna said, "you should make your move. It's only a couple hours before dawn now, and most of the pirates are asleep."

"Aye, lady."

"I told you not to call me lady," Sabyna admonished.

"As you wish."

" 'As you wish,' " she repeated. "I do like the sound of that."

He heard the smile in her voice, and his heart ached that he wasn't able to see it. When he realized how selfish he was being, both for wanting to see her and for keeping her there any longer than she had to be, he whispered, "You should go before you're spotted."

"All right. Tymora's favored blessings of good fortune to you and the crew, Malorrie of Velen, that you may be seen safely through this night."

"And you, lady." He didn't know if she'd heard him. Even though he didn't hear her footsteps, he felt that she was no longer there.

"Let me have the key, boy," Captain Tynnel said in a rough voice.

Jherek crossed the floor and gave the key to the man. Whatever slight friendship that had existed between them when they'd first met seemed to have vanished. The young sailor still didn't know how or why that had happened.

Tynnel pushed himself to his feet. "Let's rouse these dogs. Quietly. We've got my ship to take back, and in one damned piece, Selûne willing."

In moments, they had the crew awake. All of them were full of fear and nervous energy when Tynnel slid the key home and twisted the lock. The tumblers instantly fell into place.

They went through the door and into the pitch black filling the center of the hold, moving by memory and by feel. Jherek went first among them, followed by Tynnel. He breathed rapidly, from fear and the fever filling him. He ran his hand along the wall, located the steps leading up to the main deck, and started up toward the lighted rectangle of the hatch.

Tynnel gripped the young sailor's wrist. "Once we get up top, things are going to get confusing. No matter what else, we have to seize control of the tiller—else *Breezerunner* will be run aground."

"Aye, sir." Despite the tension between the captain and himself, Jherek knew he'd carry out the orders to the best of his ability. He continued up the steps, going slowly, rocking his weight smoothly so the steps wouldn't be as likely to creak underfoot. His heart pounded and he was drenched in the sweat of the fever.

He peered out at the deck before his head ever cleared the hold. He glanced only briefly at the dark shore speeding by, almost overwhelmed by the actual sight of *Breezerunner*'s magically enhanced speed. He turned hurriedly away.

Two pirates were talking at the nearby railing. From their conversation, Jherek knew the subject was Sabyna and how Vurgrom had promised the ship's mage to them once they reached the end of the river in the Sunset Mountains.

The young sailor's anger came upon him full strength at the graphic nature of their discussion, but he kept himself in check. Malorrie had always instructed him in the dangers of anger, and Madame Iitaar had never put up with it.

Two more men stood at the stern castle manning the rudder. Vurgrom's ship's mage occupied the bronze-colored chair mounted there. Moonlight glinted darkly against it. Sailcloth above moved and cracked occasionally, but left great wells of shadow that a clever and surefooted person could use to his benefit.

The land on either side of the River Chionthar here bore scrub growth, short, stocky trees and an abundance of brush. Only a few trees of any real height lined the bank and leaned out over the water. The ship's mage piloted *Breezerunner* in the center of the river, and she glided smoothly along against the sedate current even with all the arcane speed she mustered.

"Move," Captain Tynnel ordered.

Jherek pushed out of the hold and stayed hunkered down as he crossed the deck. He placed his feet rapidly but carefully, staying within the pools of shadows created by the sails overhead. He heard the crewmen behind him, though, as they came up on the deck, and so did the pirates.

"Hey, what the hell?" someone yelled.

Giving up all pretense of getting across the deck unheard and unseen, Jherek sped for the stern castle. He pushed the fever and the uncertainty to the back of his mind. Live or die, it all came down to the next few minutes.

The man standing beside the seated ship's mage came forward, peering down at the deck and trying to find the source of the commotion.

"The prisoners have escaped!" someone screamed. "Sound the alarm!"

Swords hissed from leather. Halfway up the steps, Jherek lunged for the man leaning over the railing, catching him by the shirt front. The young sailor pulled as hard as he could, yanking the man over the railing and toward the deck below. As the pirate screamed and fell, Jherek stripped the cutlass from the man's hand. The young sailor heard the bone-splitting crunch of the man impacting against the deck at the time he had his foot on the top rung of the steps leading into *Breezerunner*'s stern castle.

He raced toward the ship's mage, grimly aware of the battle that had broken out behind him.

15

Incredibly, at the last moment before the afanc reached him, Iakhovas moved enough to avoid the beast's jaws. He buried a handful of claws in the side of the afanc's face, locking himself onto it. While the afanc swam faster, startled by the effrontery of the creature that dared challenge it, Iakhovas used his hand and foot claws to pull himself to the great creature's back.

Seated behind the afanc's wedge-shaped head, Iakhovas locked his foot claws into the creature's body, then began rending it with his hand claws. Great strips of flesh peeled from the creature, floating away in ribbons. Iakhovas didn't toy with it, going for the kill immediately.

Watching him ride the giant creature to its death, Laaqueel was reminded of the stories of Daganisoraan, the hero and villain of so many sahuagin tales. She knew that was exactly what Iakhovas was after.

Working in a frenzy, Iakhovas raked through one of the afanc's eyes. The creature whipped back and forth, giving vent to screams of pain that sounded very humanlike. Laaqueel had heard the afanc had learned to speak some human tongues and often lured sailors to their own deaths.

Once the eye socket was empty, Iakhovas shifted on the afanc's face. He clung with his toe claws and one hand, reaching his other into the bloody socket. He ripped past the soft tissues that did little to protect the vulnerable brain beyond. He had to shove his head and one shoulder into the socket to get the depth he needed to reach the brain, but he didn't flinch in doing it.

Laaqueel had never seen such savagery, and she knew Sekolah had chosen well his instrument of war against the surface dwellers. The sahuagin in the stands roared in savage anticipation, no longer fearing for their king. They cheered him on instead.

The afanc's movements became erratic, evidence that Iakhovas had damaged the brain. A shudder ran its full length and it died. Withdrawing from the wound he'd made in the eye, Iakhovas leaped from the corpse and swam high into the space above the amphitheater.

"I am Iakhovas!" he roared. "I work the will of Sekolah, the Shark God, to strike fear in the hearts of the enemy of We Who Eat! I will not be denied!"

The sahuagin stood in the stands and slapped their finned feet against the stone. Thunder, spread even more quickly in the water, crashed all around the amphitheater.

"Come eat," Iakhovas invited. "Sekolah has seen fit to give us this bounty. Meat is meat!"

The sahuagin swam from their seats, so close together they looked like a school of fish. The dim light shone from their wriggling scaled bodies as they closed on Iakhovas's kill and fed in a frenzy.

Laaqueel felt moved to join them, to revel in her heritage, but she knew that could never be fully a part of this world. She would always be an outsider, a freak among the sahuagin, but she took pride in them nonetheless.

Iakhovas floated above the scene for a moment, then swam over to join her.

What do you think now, little malenti? he asked as he swam down to stand beside her.

I think you follow the currents given by the Shark God more closely than even you would admit.

Iakhovas laughed. *Ah, little malenti, you profess such faith, yet you have so many doubts. I will teach you to believe.*

Laaqueel considered telling him that he was the only thing she doubted, not the will of Sekolah. She chose not to. The way looked hard before them. She was convinced they were being divinely led. The sahuagin were going to take back the sea coasts, including the abomination of the inland sea.

Join me, Iakhovas said. *I would call others to our cause.* He lifted his voice then, launching into the deepsong that the sahuagin used to communicate over enormous distances. He sent forth a song of vengeance and bloodlust, of battle and victory, drawing forth sahuagin as well as all manner of creatures that could heed the sound of his voice.

Normally a deepsong wasn't entered into so easily. Time was required to set up the message, to arrange the way it was sung, but Iakhovas's song was simple. It was an invitation to a slaughter, to a bloodletting that would make histories above and below the waterline of Faerûn.

Laaqueel joined him, lending her power to his. The royal guard followed suit, then all the voices out in the amphitheater joined in. As she sang, joy thrilled through the malenti. Usually a king and Royal High Priestess would lead five hundred singers in deepsong, and the words would reach as far out as fifteen hundred miles, but now there were thousands. The whole village sang. Laaqueel knew it was impossible to guess how far the deepsong could be heard, but she knew those who heard it, those for whom it was intended, would answer.

"Friend Pacys, what is it that ails ye?"

The old bard blinked, staring at the forest around him. When he and Khlinat had first arrived, he hadn't known exactly where they were, but the woodchopper whose fire they'd found had told them they were in the Gulthmere Forest north of the Orsraun Mountains. The forest was on the western coast of the Sea of Fallen Stars, with Turmish to the southeast and Starmantle and the independent city of Westgate to the northwest. They had begun trekking toward Starmantle rather than crossing over the Orsraun Mountains.

Khlinat stared at him in consternation, backlit by the glow of their campfire.

"What's wrong?" Pacys asked, not understanding.

"Ye were moaning and groaning," Khlinat told him, "like a man being pulled to his grave by a pack of hungry ghouls."

Reluctantly, Pacys sat up. In his older years, he knew sleep no longer returned so casually as it had when he was younger. Some nights sleep had to be wooed like an uncertain lover, and this night he was certain it wouldn't return at all.

"A dream," he told the dwarf.

" 'Tweren't no dream, I'll wager," Khlinat said. His hair hung in shaggy disarray, leaves twisted among it from sleeping on the light pallets they carried.

"A nightmare then."

"Come over here and sit by the fire," Khlinat entreated. "Warm up yer bones a bit and it'll get rid of them nightmares."

Pacys moved a little closer to the fire they kept burning to stave off the chill of the night. Khlinat threw a few more of the branches they'd gathered onto the fire. Stuttering yellow flames licked up anxiously for the dry wood.

"Maybe a bit of that stew I made earlier," Khlinat suggested. "Get your innards warmed up a bit too."

"No, thank you," Pacys said. "The fire will be enough." He held his hands out to the fire, marveling again that they were still in such good shape after all these years. He'd known several bards who'd lost their skill to arthritis or accident.

"So what was this nightmare?" the dwarf asked.

Pacys shook his head. "There were no images. At least, none that I can remember." He hesitated. "There was a song, though, something I could barely understand."

He reached for the yarting in its protective cover beside his pallet.

Despite his age, he sat with crossed legs. He'd spent decades on the ground, on tables in taverns, on hassocks in royal chambers, and on ships' decks. The position was natural for him.

Khlinat sat silently beside him, his hands never far from the axe hafts. The rough country had been hard on the dwarf because of his peg leg, but he'd never complained.

It was good, Pacys knew, to be in stouthearted company when the things that lay ahead appeared so uncertain. He slid the yarting from its cover, stroked the strings and tuned it briefly, then reached out for the song.

He closed his eyes, surrendering himself over to it. Since they arrived in the Gulthmere Forest the songs had stayed constantly in his thoughts, almost too many of them to keep track of, yet when he fitted them together, they wove tightly. His fingers found the notes easily, and he wasn't surprised that some of them were new. It was like mining a mountain shot through with veins rich with ore. Despite how many new things were coming to him, he knew there was much more that was not yet his.

Eyes closed in concentration, the old bard smelled the sweet scent of Khlinat's pipe as it smoldered. Though he hadn't thought of it before and didn't know why he hadn't, Pacys reached out for the scent, felt the smooth, wispy nature of it, and blended it into the song as well.

"That's me part," Khlinat said in surprise.

"Yes," Pacys told him, smiling. The music was so vibrant and true, even after hearing only brief pieces and snatches of it in the middle of so many others, the dwarf was able to remember the different verses. He cut out the other music for a moment, leaving only the notes he'd blended for the pipeweed smoke.

"Me pipe?" Khlinat asked.

Pacys smiled and opened his eyes. "You knew?"

"How could I not?" the dwarf asked. "By Marthammor Duin's long strides, how can ye capture pipe smoke in a song? I've heard bards doing that for people's voices and animals and the like, but not this."

Pacys shook his head. "It's as I've said, my friend, this song is truly meant for my hands and ear alone. I am come into my own." The old bard's heart trip-hammered as he recognized the truth behind the bold statement. He calmed himself through the music, playing out his excitement until he brought it to a steadier place.

The only thing that bothered him was knowing what he was supposed to do next. Narros's story hadn't included that. He paused in his playing, watching embers caught up in the rising smoke die only a short distance above the flames. Moonlight kissed the breakers rolling against the shoreline only a short distance away. He pulled their sound into him and made it his.

"Oghma help me," Pacys whispered to the dwarf, "but I have never in my life felt so alive. It should be sinful to feel this good."

"Aye," Khlinat agreed. "But ye and me, we know the truth of life, songsmith. That every day you trod upon this earth, a bit more of ye dies. Ye soon run out of new things, new places, new people. A wandering man, that's what I always wanted to be, but I've stayed in one place for far too long. This quest ye be upon, now there's a true calling for the measure of a man. That's part of why I wanted to tag along with ye, to sup the dregs from your adventures. Marthammor Duin willing, there'll be no few of those."

Pacys touched the yarting's strings, exploring all that was new to him. "I only wish I knew better where we were supposed to go. Starmantle is the closest city of any size."

"Ye worry too much about things that will take care of themselves," Khlinat said. "When it's a quest ye be following, why ye are the compass rose on the map. Ye can't help but go in the right direction no matter how wrong it may seem at the time. Ye mark me words, songsmith, and mark them well."

The old bard believed in his new friend's confidence, melding it with his own, but a cold tingle touched him as well. With a sense long born of traveling and being on his own, Pacys knew they were being watched. He caught the dwarf's eye and said, "We've attracted attention."

The dwarf slid one of his hand axes free and ran a thumb across the sharp blade. "I thought I felt something nosing around. Maybe I'll go take a look."

Pacys put a hand on the little man's arm. "No. I don't think that will be necessary."

A shadow stood in the forest, lean and somehow regal, part of the dark landscape, yet somehow apart from it as well. Moonlight flashed from the shiny surface of what Pacys believed to be the man's clothing.

When the man first stepped forward and his dark skin and silver-white hair glistened wetly in the campfire light, Pacys thought they'd drawn the attention of a drow elf. The man had the easy, liquid movements all the elves exhibited. He went naked save for a harness that supported a brace of knives and shiny leggings. He carried a long-bladed spear in his right hand.

Khlinat swore fiercely and bounded to his foot, swiveling on his peg as he set himself with axes in both hands. "All right, ye black-hearted backstabber, let's have at ye!"

16

As Jherek rushed the mage in the enchanted chair, the pirate behind him leaped forward and went for the sword scabbarded at his waist. He had it out before Jherek reached him.

The action attracted the ship's mage's attention. The man threw himself from the chair. Abandoned without a strong hand at the keel, *Breezerunner* listed out of true, wallowing against the river current now instead of cutting through it cleanly. The wind and sails warred with the push of the river, rocking the ship with bigger and bigger swings.

Jherek moved easily with his stolen cutlass, parrying the helmsman's blow and listening to the yells of the pirates as they woke the ship. Still not quite back to his fighting trim, the young sailor moved too slowly to get his return blow back on time after a successful parry. The pirate blocked it inches from his face.

Swearing, calling on darkest evil to descend on Jherek, the pirate slid his steel along the young sailor's and stepped inside his guard. Before Jherek could anticipate it, his opponent headbutted him in the face. Blood streamed from Jherek's nose, leaking the salty taste down into his mouth, and it felt like the back of his head was exploding all over again.

Jherek staggered back, barely able to get his cutlass up in time to keep from having his leg hacked by a foul blow that he wouldn't have tried himself. Steel rang, clear and strident.

"Get that damn rudder, Malorrie!" Captain Tynnel roared. Two pirates blocked his way up the stairs to the stern castle. He fought them with a belaying pin he'd taken from the ship's railing. "If you don't get control of her, *Breezerunner*'s going to end up as a pile of kindling on one of those riverbanks!"

Jherek knew it was true, and the thought filled him with fear. He didn't know where Sabyna was, but he thought first of the ship's mage. He wouldn't allow himself to fail. He leaned into his swordcraft, pulling up all the tricks and shortcuts Malorrie had taught him.

His fever and his weakness felt like they put him a half step behind what he tried to do. Perspiration burst out on his body from his efforts, and it made the night chill ghosting across the ship's decks even more harsh. A flurry of furious clangs sounded across the deck and the river, held in close by the overhanging trees. *Breezerunner* listed again, starting to come broadside into the river current. If it did, Jherek knew the ship could be lost from control forever until they ended up smashing somewhere.

Redoubling his efforts, Jherek concentrated on his foe, fighting the other man's skill as well as the effects of the fever. Everything from the waist up was a target. The young sailor allowed himself no foul blows, fighting his battle fairly and with honor. He tried a slash of his own every fifth blow, turning aside the pirate's frenzied attacks. His forearm and shoulder ached with the effort, then gradually warmed, responding better.

He stepped up his own pace, cutting now once for every three parries. He circled the deck, staying in close to his opponent, forcing the man to keep his blows short and not use his strength. When the man tried for the young sailor's head, Jherek dropped to the deck. His senses reeled enough that he had to catch himself on his empty hand. He brought the cutlass around in a sideward slash under the man's elbow that cleaved into his ribs.

The pirate yelled hoarsely, gazing down at the cutlass buried in his side. Blood spilled down his waist. Jherek locked eyes with the man, both of them knowing the mortal blow had been struck. The young sailor stepped back and pulled his cutlass free, feeling ribs grate along the sword. Holding his blade before him, he circled around the dying pirate who struggled to stay on his feet.

"By all the pirate's blood in me, and all the blood of my forefathers before me," the pirate croaked in a hoarse voice, "I curse you to never know peace, to never know a time when death isn't lurking at your door."

A chill fear raced down Jherek's back as he moved to the stern and captured the tiller. As a seafaring man, the young sailor knew to give credence to a pirate's curses.

Still, it wasn't as frightening as it might have been. He already wore his father's tattoo on his arm. "You're too late," he told the pirate. "I was cursed at birth by a man much more powerful than you."

With a howl of rage, the blood loss already weakening him, the pirate rushed at Jherek and swung his blade. Jherek hauled on the rudder, trying to pull *Breezerunner* back to true. The ship fought him, rising and falling like a wild animal. He held the rudder in the crook of his left arm so he could put all his weight into the effort. He parried with the cutlass, standing his ground as the pirate rushed into him.

The pirate's weight slammed Jherek back into the railing, knocking the wind from his lungs. The man clamped his free hand around the young sailor's throat and forced him back over the railing.

"Die!" the pirate screamed, drawing his blade back. Moonlight shimmered along the length of the sword as he raised it high and readied himself to bring it down.

Shifting, Jherek shoved his sword arm under the man's grip, hooking him solidly in a wrestling hold. He swept the man's legs from him with a foot, twisting at the same time to lever the pirate over the railing.

The man fell with a great splash into the River Chionthar. The dark water, trimmed in whitecaps trailing after *Breezerunner*, sucked the man down.

"Cut the damn ship hard to starboard," Captain Tynnel roared. "Cut her now!"

Turning back, Jherek watched as the rough and rocky riverbank on the port side came up fast on *Breezerunner*'s prow. Branches from the overhanging trees clawed at the rigging. Rope shrieked with the pressure, then parted with loud snaps as a cacophony of breaking branches accompanied the sounds. Limbs and leaves showered the cargo ship's deck, while other branches ripped through the sailcloth.

Jherek dropped his cutlass and grabbed the rudder in both arms, aware of the two pirates streaking up the starboard steps leading to the stern castle. The young sailor set himself, pulling at the rudder with all his strength, getting his back against the railing. The ship, the current, and the wind all fought him, and *Breezerunner* twisted violently like a live thing. She crested the current, then listed wildly on the other side, throwing everyone on deck from their feet.

Hanging on fiercely, Jherek manhandled the rudder, keeping it in the river by standing up with it. Grudgingly, *Breezerunner*'s prow came starboard, away from the riverbank. Branches and leaves continued hitting the deck, and sections of sailcloth came spilling down. A lantern slid from the mainmast and smashed against the deck, igniting a pool of fire that whirled up in blue and yellow flames.

"Fire!" someone yelled, and Jherek didn't know if it was ship's crew or pirate.

The young sailor pulled hard on the rudder, knowing he couldn't let go or he'd lose the ship. He watched the two pirates running up the steps, hoping that they'd see the danger all of them would be put in if they attacked him and knowing it was in vain.

The pirates topped the steps, rushing onto the stern castle deck and coming right at him.

Sabyna Truesail raced across *Breezerunner*'s main deck. She'd planned on finding Vurgrom and his wizard, thinking that she stood the best chance of interfering with the man's spellcraft. For days she'd helplessly watched the mistreatment of the crew she'd sworn to defend and care for as ship's mage, telling herself that biding her time was the best decision to make.

Now there was no waiting, no need to hold back, and everything she cared about was at risk.

She pulled her power close to her. Most of her training and learning she'd done on her own centered around the care and upkeep of ships, not waging war against other mages. She loosed the bag of holding at her side. "Skeins," she commanded, "guard."

Immediately, the raggamoffyn spewed free of the bag of holding in a flurry of cloth pieces and took shape in the breeze that flowed across *Breezerunner.* The creature formed a serpentine shape, coiling restlessly around her.

She stood against the cabin under the forecastle. Normally Captain Tynnel lived there, but Vurgrom had seized it upon taking over the ship. Fear clawed at her stomach, turning it slightly sour but she mastered it and kept her wits. The battle raged across the deck, and swords reflected the wavering light from the fire charring into the wood.

She ran to the railing near the fire and lifted the top from the water barrel. It was half full, sloshing with the ship's uneven movement. She glanced at her familiar. "Enter," she ordered.

Obediently, the raggamoffyn sailed into the water bucket and thrashed in the water.

"Out," she commanded.

Unable to float on the wind now, the waterlogged familiar crawled out of the bucket and plopped onto the deck at her feet.

Sabyna concentrated on the fire. The raggamoffyn's intelligence was about that of a well-trained dog, so complicated instructions were impossible. "Attack," she told it.

The raggamoffyn slithered across the deck toward the fire, wriggling through men's feet. Reaching the oil-based fire, the creature unfolded its myriad pieces and sloshed across the flames. The water and the creature's own mystical nature served to keep the raggamoffyn from harm. Gray smoke curled up from the fire as the flames were extinguished.

Sabyna heard Tynnel's shouted commands to Malorrie. She glanced up and saw the young sailor in the stern, fighting the rudder, then she spotted the two pirates climbing the starboard steps to the stern castle. She knew he couldn't handle them and steer the ship.

"Skeins!" she called, running for the ship's mainmast. She knew she'd never get through the men fighting across the deck in time.

The raggamoffyn sped across the deck, leaving oily black residue in its wake. It reached her by the time she got to the mainmast. She extended an arm down and Skeins curled around it. The creature was already partially dried from exposure to the fire and the wind.

As the raggamoffyn spread its weight across her shoulders, Sabyna climbed the mainmast. Her feet slipped in the rigging twice as *Breezerunner* rocked from side to side, but she kept pulling herself up.

When the two pirates reached the top of the stern castle, the ship's mage stopped halfway up the mast, hoping she had enough room to maneuver. Holding onto the mast with one hand, she slipped the leather whip from her side. She uncoiled it with a flick of her wrist. Drawing the whip back, she cracked it forward, aiming for the rear mast rigging.

The whip snaked across the distance and curled around a yardarm. Pulling it tight and saying a quick prayer, fully aware of the twenty-five foot drop that might land her on the ship's deck or in the river with the way *Breezerunner* was swinging, she grabbed the whip handle in both hands and leaped. Her father, Siann Truesail, had never approved of her mode of travel in ship's rigging, considering it not only risky but too showy as well. Her brothers were envious because none of them had ever quite mastered the skill.

She dropped almost three feet, then the give in the leather and the yardarm played out. She arced toward the stern, pulling her feet outward and forward to gain more momentum. At the apex of her swing, practiced in the maneuver, she popped the whip and relaxed the hold on the yardarm. The whip came loose immediately.

Sabyna somersaulted in the air, letting her momentum carry her, and gained an extra two feet that placed her securely on the stern castle. Still, she'd missed her chosen mark by a good eight feet or more.

The pirates closed on Malorrie, who still hadn't given up his death grip on the rudder. Only the young sailor knew she was there.

"Attack," she told her familiar.

Skeins uncoiled from her shoulder, breaking apart into a swirl of pieces that glided toward the pirate on the left. The creature was on the man before he knew it, wrapping around his upper body and stripping his self-control, reducing him to a zombie state.

The other pirate raised his arm to strike the young sailor, who ducked around the rudder for protection and set himself to attack. Sabyna cracked the whip, coiling it around the pirate's sword wrist. Grabbing the whip in both hands, she pulled it taut, then yanked the pirate from his feet before he could react.

The pirate's face darkened with anger as he pushed himself to his feet again and cursed her. He tried to shake the whip from his arm, but Sabyna yanked on it again, pulling him off-balance. Jherek took one step forward and kicked the man in the head, sprawling him unconscious to the deck.

"Sandbar!" someone shouted.

"Where away?" Jherek yelled, getting a fresh hold on the rudder.

There was no time for an answer. In the next instant, *Breezerunner* ran aground. Forced up and out of the river by the current, the wind, and the magic that pushed her, the cargo ship heeled over hard to port. Men tumbled from her deck, some into the water and some onto the long, quarter-moon shaped sandbar.

Sabyna tried to grab the railing but missed. She fell only inches, dangerously close to getting pulled under the stern section as it whip-sawed around. She felt a hand wrap around her wrist, tightening and halting her fall.

"I've got you, lady."

Looking up, Sabyna saw that Malorrie had grabbed hold of the railing with one hand and her with the other. She watched helplessly as *Breezerunner* shifted and jolted across the sandbar. The deck hammered Malorrie and her mercilessly, and she didn't know how the young sailor managed to maintain his hold, but he did, even pulling her in close to him. She grabbed him around the waist, fisting the sash around his slim hips and helping him hold her weight from dangling. He still supported both of them from one arm. His pale gray eyes, gleaming like new silver, met her reddish brown ones.

"Lady, I'm sorry," he said. "I did my best."

"I know," she told him. "No one could have done any more."

He looked like he wanted to say something further but couldn't.

With a shriek of tortured wood, *Breezerunner* came to a rest on her side on the sandbar. The river current slapped at the mired ship, and the sound echoed inside the empty cargo hold.

"Lady," Malorrie said quietly, "I fear I can't hold any longer."

Her arms wrapped around his waist, her cheek pressed to his stomach, she felt the tremors vibrating through him. Yet, somehow she knew he wouldn't release the hold until she told him she was ready. "It's all right," she told him. "Let go."

"As you wish."

He released his hold and they dropped into the river.

17

The elf looked at the dwarf in obvious disdain, dismissing him in a glance. Upon closer inspection, Pacys realized the elf's skin color wasn't ebony as a drow's was, but a very dark blue with infrequent white patches.

"You're him, aren't you?" the elf asked. "The one who will come to be called the Taleweaver?"

Pacys listened to the accent the elf used, finding it like none other he'd ever encountered. As a bard, he'd trained his ear for dialects and accents. They were part of the most colorful tools a bard had, able to carry emotion and character in a monologue. It was softer and more sibilant, as if used to carrying great distances with very little effort.

"I am Pacys the Bard," he replied, "and I've been called many things."

"But soon to be the Taleweaver."

"Maybe. No man may know exactly what lies in his future." Pacys played his cards close to his vest. Narros had also spoken of those who would try to prevent him from attaining his goals.

"No," the elf replied, "but a few are sometimes chosen by the gods to get a glimpse of those possible futures." He paused, then added, "You have no need for alarm."

"Aye, and ye speak prettily," Khlinat spat roughly, "but meself, I've found a man sometimes talks differently when he gets the chance to hold a knife to yer throat."

"I heard your song," the elf said. "I knew I had to come see you for myself—to discover if you were the one."

"You knew me from my song?" Pacys asked.

The elf nodded. "I'm something of a minstrel myself, and I was

397

brought up on the lore of my people. Your presence has been predicted in our histories."

"Whose histories?" Pacys asked.

The elf smiled at him haughtily. "I am Taareen, of the alu'tel'quessir. More directly of late, I am of Faenasuor."

Pacys laid a hand on the dwarf's shoulder. "This is my good friend Khlinat Ironeater, a sailor and traveling companion on this journey."

Taareen inclined his head slightly. "A pleasure to meet you, warrior."

"Aye," Khlinat replied gruffly. "I guess we'll be after seeing the truth of that, eh?"

The elf took no offense. "May I come closer?"

Pacys gestured toward the campfire.

Taareen smiled. "Not too close. The flames can be hazardous to one who dwells in the embrace of Serôs."

"Serôs?" Khlinat asked. "I thought ye said ye were of Faenasuor."

"Serôs," Pacys told him, digging into the lore he knew of the Sea of Fallen Stars, "is what they call the Inner Sea."

"Actually, it's the term for the world under the sea," Taareen stated as he sat on the ground across the campfire from them. "It came into use after Aryselmalyr fell—over a thousand years ago. In our language it means 'the embracing life.' "

"Aryselmalyr was the empire of the sea elves," Pacys told Khlinat when the dwarf looked up at him with suspicion on his broad face. "Several of the elves took up the sea life after the Crown Wars."

Harumphing in obvious displeasure, Khlinat sat apart from Pacys, giving himself a clear field of action should it become necessary. He laid his axes on the ground in front of him.

"Do you know of Faenasuor?" Taareen asked.

"I've heard of it," Pacys replied. "The city was thought lost when Aryselmalyr was destroyed."

He had heard songs of the elven empire's destruction when an undersea plateau shoved up without warning from the sea bottom and killed nearly eighty thousand inhabitants. The city lay covered over at the bottom of the Sea of Fallen Stars for a thousand years, until it was excavated seventy years ago.

"I've never been there," Pacys said.

"No," Taareen replied. "As a culture, the sea elves are friendly enough to humans, but only relate to them when there is need."

"Doesn't sound much different than elves anywhere ye go," Khlinat offered.

"I wouldn't know. I've never left Serôs." Taareen's eyes fell on Pacys's yarting. "May I?"

Pacys nodded, then rose and passed the yarting over.

The sea elf took it gratefully. His hands searched out the strings a little unconfidently, then he fit his fingers into the frets and stroked the strings. Music filled the campsite, and it was clear and true. After a moment, evidently feeling more at home with the instrument, Taareen lifted his voice in song.

The words were alien to Pacys's ears. He knew some of the elven dialects and languages, but this one wasn't familiar to him. Still, the emotion of the song was raw and throbbing, speaking of loss and redemption, of brighter days ahead. He finished quietly, but the words still echoed through the trees, vanishing the way the bright orange embers from the campfire did when they tried to touch the sky.

"That was beautiful," Pacys said.

"Aye," Khlinat said, tears glittering in his beard. "I've not had the pleasure of hearing the like before. Ye may be an elf, Elf, but ye have the heart of a dwarf."

Taareen bowed his head in thanks, then glanced up at Pacys. "That was your song, Bard Pacys. The song of the Taleweaver's arrival in Serôs."

"You just composed that?" Pacys asked in astonishment.

"No. I've but mean skills, and songcrafting takes me a long time. That song is ancient," Taareen said. "It is one of the few things that was carried from Aryselmalyr when so much of our history was lost."

A feathery chill touched Pacys between the shoulder blades. "How could they know all those years ago?"

"How could they not?" Taareen asked. "The Taker existed thousands of years before that. Knowledge of him has not come to us only recently, as it has to you."

"You said you knew me by my song." The thought troubled Pacys "Does that mean the song is not new as I thought it to be?" The possibility of him simply rewriting a song that had already been in existence ate at his confidence.

"No, your song is new," Taareen answered simply. "In our stories, it was said the Taleweaver would appear near reclaimed Faenasuor. Imagine the horror of those who lived then who realized that Faenasuor would first have to be lost in order to be reclaimed."

Pacys did, and the weight was staggering.

"When the empire was lost, it was believed that by leaving Faenasuor buried beneath the rubble the Taker wouldn't be allowed to return to the world." Taareen shook his head and his fingers began to pick out a soft, low tune on the yarting. "As if that would seal him in whatever limbo he'd been in."

"They realized in the end it was a false hope at best," Khlinat said.

"Yes, but the Taker wasn't the only reason they left Faenasuor buried. Part of it was because no one wanted to see what had been lost. They didn't want to remember. After a thousand years, the realization that if Faenasuor *didn't* exist, if the archives that were buried there *weren't* reclaimed, the Taleweaver would never be able to arrive there."

"But just hearing my song," Pacys said, "that couldn't be the only thing that led you to believe I was the one legend names as Taleweaver."

"Do you have your doubts about who you are?" Taareen asked.

Pacys thought about the question. To answer no was almost egotistical, but to say yes was to acknowledge the possibility existed that Narros had been wrong. The song Taareen played echoed in his head, summoning up images of Waterdeep and Baldur's Gate, and the young sailor he and Khlinat had only just met who'd had such considerable influence on their lives.

"No," he answered finally. "I don't doubt."

"And neither do I," the sea elf said, handing the yarting back across. "In the legends, we were told the Taleweaver could swim beneath the oceans as easily as he strode across the land. It was the only way he could witness all the battles to come. I see that you're a surface dweller."

"I have a gift," Pacys said, extending his arm and displaying the emerald bracelet Narros had given him back in Waterdeep. While wearing the bracelet, Pacys could breathe underwater, never feel the pressure of the depths, and move as easily as he would crossing a room.

"And your friend?"

"Has none," Khlinat growled. "And why would something like that be necessary?"

"Because," Taareen answered, "I must take you to Faenasuor that you may learn the legends of the Taker as we know them. It has been foretold."

Excitement flared through Pacys. If there had been any humans ever to enter the city of Faenasuor, there had been precious few.

"We can take care of your friend," Taareen offered. "Some of the things we trade with the surface world are potions which allow surface dwellers to breathe underwater. It would be our honor to aid you."

"When could we go?" Pacys asked.

Khlinat shifted uneasily, obviously not happy about the thought of visiting an undersea city.

"We can continue on to Starmantle by land," Taareen said. "I know a man there who deals in such potions. It won't be hard to strike a deal for one. After we are in Faenasuor it won't be a problem to keep your friend well supplied."

"Then let's break camp," Pacys said. "I know I won't be getting any more sleep tonight anyway, and dawn can't be more than an hour away."

He was left with the feeling that time was running out. How much difference did days, weeks, or months make when faced with an opponent who had thousands of years to plan?

18

Jherek kept his eyes on Sabyna when they hit the water. Both of them went under at once. The current wasn't overly strong and wasn't a real challenge that would keep them from the riverbank. He knew the ship's mage was a strong swimmer, but the possibility remained that *Breezerunner* might rip free of the sandbar and become a danger.

Despite the fatigue and dizziness that filled him, he waited underwater until she had her bearings, then followed her up. He broke the river surface little more than an arm's reach from her. "Lady, are you all right?"

"Aye," she replied, blinking water from her eyes. "A little worse for the wear, but I'm holding my own."

Treading water, Jherek glanced around, seeking out *Breezerunner*'s crew and the pirates. Men scrambled through the water like rats trying to escape drowning. A lot of ship's crews, the young sailor knew, had few men who could swim well, and even a good number of them that couldn't swim at all.

He spotted one man flailing nearly twenty yards away. The young sailor struck out at once, slicing through the water like a fish. He grabbed the man from behind, sliding his arm under his chin. "Lie still," Jherek ordered. "I have you."

The man choked and spat, and clung desperately to Jherek. "Don't let Umberlee take me, lad." He kicked frantically, spitting automatically whenever water touched his chin.

"Save your breath," Jherek advised. Fighting the current and the man was difficult. The young sailor swam backward, pulling the man after him toward the riverbank. In a short time, he could touch bottom. He got the man on his feet, then turned to survey the river again.

"Those that made it are already here," Captain Tynnel said as he walked up to Jherek. "The others washed down the damned river. Maybe we'll get lucky and they'll make their way back to us by morning, and maybe they'll wash all the way out to the Sea of Swords." He turned on Jherek. "Didn't you see that damned sandbar out there? It's as big as an island."

Jherek looked at *Breezerunner* tilted over nearly sideways on the huge sandbar. White-capped water rushed around her. From here, the sandbar did look impossible to miss.

"No," he said. "I didn't see it." He knew it was his own ill birth at work again. He had a chance—for a moment—of being the hero, but it had been stripped from his fingers.

"Never sign onto a ship to be a pilot, boy," Tynnel advised coldly. "Takes too long to build a ship for them to be sunk so quickly."

The words bit into Jherek, but he didn't argue. He deserved them.

"It wasn't his fault, Tynnel."

Jherek turned, surprised that Sabyna had approached in his defense.

The captain gave her a dark look and shook his head. "I should have guessed you'd be taking up for him."

"Taking up for him?" Sabyna looked about to explode. "He almost gave his life hanging onto that rudder. Two pirates were practically on top of him when I got there, and he hadn't turned loose of the rudder."

"She's right, Cap'n," Mornis, *Breezerunner*'s first mate, said. "I saw the lad standing there myself. Tried to get to him, but there wasn't anything I could do. If Sabyna hadn't reached him, I think he would have died holding onto that stick."

A muscle worked in Tynnel's jaw, but arguing with both his ship's mage and first mate didn't appear profitable enough for him to continue. He said nothing further and turned away sharply.

"You didn't have to do that, lady," Jherek said quietly after Tynnel had gone. "What the captain said was true. I should have seen that sandbar."

"No one could have seen that sandbar from back there," she replied angrily. "I didn't. Or are you going to tell me I should have seen it too?"

"No," he said, shaking his head. "I wouldn't do that."

"Then don't do it to yourself."

"She's right," Mornis said. "Cap'n's just not himself right now with everything that's going on. He'll be better come morning when he gets a chance to look at *Breezerunner* and know she's not hurt as bad as she could be. If you hadn't straightened her up like you did and we'd hit that sandbar side-on, like as not that ship would be kindling by now, and us down the drink with it." He laid a hand on Jherek's shoulder. "You did a fine job of it, a job to be proud of."

Jherek listened to their words, but the voice in the back of his head that he'd fought with all his life didn't let up on him. Guilt filled him. He'd grounded *Breezerunner* and he'd lost the pearl disk.

When memory of the disk slid into his mind, he glanced around the riverbank. "Where are the pirates?"

"Ran off into the forest," Mornis rumbled. "We got numbers on them. While you was pulling Torrigh from the drink, they took to nose-counting and realized they'd come up short in a free-for-all. They hit the brush like a covey of quail."

"We've got to go after them," Jherek said. Maybe Vurgrom's lead wasn't too extensive yet.

"No," Sabyna said. "There's nothing to be had in that." She glanced out at the river. "Our job now is to get *Breezerunner* secure before she tries to drift off that sandbar and ends up smashed somewhere farther down the river, then we need to fix any damage that's been done to her."

Jherek scanned the dark forest, feeling the pull in him to go after Vurgrom and the stolen pearl disk. Guilt filled him to the bursting point. The disk had to be returned to Lathander's church in Baldur's Gate.

"It's too dark, lad," Mornis said quietly. "If those pirates don't set up and take you down somewhere, there are things out in that forest stalking the night that will. It'll be a lucky man who gets through that of a piece."

Quietly, Jherek let go of any hope of finding and overtaking Vurgrom. He joined the others as they gathered around Tynnel and listened to the plans the captain had for securing *Breezerunner*.

"Lad, that's some rough country you've got ahead of you."

Jherek gathered the ends of the cloth he'd been given, tucked the rations he'd been parceled out from *Breezerunner*'s stores, and tied them together to fashion a crude pack. "Aye, but I've got it to do."

Mornis looked uncomfortable. "I feel guilty about letting you go on alone."

"I lost something that wasn't mine to lose, my friend, and I've got to return it if I can."

"Like as not," Mornis warned, "you may be spending your life foolishly."

"Dying with honor isn't a foolish death." Jherek told him sternly.

"No, lad, but any kind of dying is still dying. Myself, I'd rather keep both oars in the water as long as I'm able. A man going with the sea stays afloat a lot longer than a man going against it."

"I was told," Jherek said, "that it always matters how you go against it."

Mornis nodded. "Mayhap, but if you ever find yourself around *Breezerunner* again and in need of a berth, come see me. If the Cap'n won't take you on, I'll help you find a ship."

Jherek smiled and took the man's arm in a strong grip. "Till we meet again."

"Aye," Mornis said. "And may Selûne always favor you with her good graces."

Jherek took a final look around. Most of the ship's crew were aboard *Breezerunner* already working on the broken rigging and ripped sails. A few others stood in the river filling water barrels. It had been a hard, full day's work getting the ship off the sandbar and secure in the water again. Jherek's hands still burned from the work he'd done with shovels and picks, both freeing the ship and burying her dead. His legs were dotted with the red welts left by leeches.

He noticed Sabyna striding purposefully toward him down the riverbank, the early morning sun shining from her hair. Tynnel walked at her side, his jaw working fiercely.

The ship's captain turned his hard gaze on Jherek. "Talk her out of it."

The young sailor looked at them both. "Talk her out of what?"

"I'm coming with you," Sabyna said calmly.

Jherek glanced at her, noticing she'd changed clothes. She had no pack, but he knew she had a bag of holding she kept the raggamoffyn in. "Lady, you can't come with me."

Sabyna's eyebrows shot up. "I can't? So now *you're* going to try to tell me what to do?"

Hastily, sensing the rough waters he was venturing into, Jherek changed tacks. "No, lady, I wouldn't dare to presume to do that, but coming with me isn't a good idea."

"Neither is going after Vurgrom and his pirate crew by yourself."

"I have no choice." Jherek looked deep into her eyes, feeling like everything was suddenly beyond his control.

"Everyone has a choice," she told him. "You've made yours and I'm making mine."

Tynnel glared at Jherek. "This is your fault."

Sabyna wheeled on him, blood dark in her face. "No. None of this is his fault. He got caught up in this whole situation because he was talking to me in Baldur's Gate, taking care to walk me back to *Breezerunner*. I'll not see him suffer for his kindness and care."

"So you'll suffer for yours?" Tynnel asked.

"This isn't kindness. This is a debt."

"No," Jherek said in a stern voice. "There'll be no debts between us, lady. Especially not something like this."

"Stay out of this," Sabyna told him, then turned her attention back to Tynnel. "You left him in Athkatla and didn't tell me the real reason. You lied to me. If I'd had a voice in the matter, I'd have cut Aysel loose instead."

"It wasn't your choice to make," Tynnel said coldly. "I'm master of that ship."

"And you still are," Sabyna agreed, "but you're no master of me. Not then. Not now. Not ever."

Tynnel lifted his head and glared at her more severely.

Sabyna glared back at him hotly. "I signed on with you because I felt I could make a difference on *Breezerunner.*"

"Begging your pardon," Mornis interrupted hesitantly, "but you do make a difference on her."

"Stay out of this, Mornis," Sabyna ordered sharply.

The big man took a step back. "Yes, ma'am."

"I felt that I owed you something for taking me on," Sabyna told Tynnel, "because there were other ship's mages better trained than me. But no matter what, you owed me the truth, Captain. Somewhere in there, you obviously forgot that."

"You're not going," Tynnel said.

Sabyna drew herself up. "You can't stop me."

"Yes," Tynnel said, reaching out suddenly to grab Sabyna by the arm, "I can, and I will if I have to. I'm not going to let you squander your life so foolishly."

Sabyna struggled to get free but the captain's grip was too tight. Pain tightened her eyes.

Before he was aware of moving, Jherek stepped forward and seized Tynnel's thumb, breaking the grip the captain had on the woman's arm. Continuing to pull on the man's arm, the young sailor pressed it back against Tynnel's chest, shoving him back and making space between him and Sabyna. Jherek stepped into the space between.

Out of control, Tynnel swung a fist up.

Jherek didn't try to defend himself, and he didn't duck because it would have put Sabyna at risk. The blow caught him on the chin, snapping his head around. Dazed, he dropped to one knee for just an instant, but pushed himself back up immediately. He stood a little uncertainly, but he felt Sabyna at his back, trying to get around him. He put out an arm and didn't let her get past. He faced Tynnel. It went against ship's contract and conduct for a captain to strike a crewman without just cause, but Jherek knew he wasn't part of *Breezerunner*'s crew.

Tynnel stepped back and drew his sword. "Pick up a sword, boy!" He brandished his blade.

"I won't fight you," Jherek said calmly, not believing things had spun so wildly out of control.

"Then you're an even bigger fool than I thought. I'll cut you down where you stand!"

"No," a calm, stern voice filled with thunder interrupted. "If you try to touch that boy again, Captain, you'll deal with me. And by Lathander's sacred covenant, you'll not find me an easy man to deal with."

The speaker sat on a horse just beyond the treeline that surrounded the riverbank where they stood. The horse was a large, handsome animal covered in copper-colored barding. The man was in his middle years. A bronzed face, framed by a short-cropped black beard, peered through the visor opening of his helm, and his plate armor held the same copper color as his horse's barding. A scarlet cloak flared out behind him, flowing out over the horse's rump. A shield bearing a scarlet hawk in mid-flight hung over his left arm.

"Who are you?" Tynnel demanded, turning to face the man.

"You can address me as Sir Glawinn, a paladin in the service of Lathander, the Morninglord," the man said proudly. "Now step away from that boy and that young woman or I'll run you down where you stand." He kicked his heels into the horse's sides, urging it forward.

Reluctantly, Tynnel gave ground.

19

Jherek stood in the cool shade of an elm tree and looked back at the sparkling blue River Chionthar snaking through the hilly terrain. *Breezerunner* had vanished from sight hours ago and he found he missed the ship.

He was dressed in his leather armor, which stank badly. He hadn't been able to care for it while in *Breezerunner*'s brig and it hadn't quite dried out from its earlier drenching. While they'd walked the remaining hours of the day, the wet leather had chafed him. He worked at the sore spots, trying to find some degree of comfort.

"You'd be better served taking those things off, young warrior," Glawinn said. "They'll take longer to dry with you wearing them, and we've a long way to go tomorrow. If you press on too much like today and ignore that chafing it's giving you, you're going to get blisters and sores."

"I don't know that I'd be much more comfortable out here without armor," Jherek said, turning toward the paladin.

Glawinn had shed his helm and upper armor, hanging it from a rack one of his two packhorses carried. He'd fed and cared for the pack animals first only so he could devote more attention to the great warhorse he rode. While the big animal crunched noisily in the feedbag over its head, the knight painstakingly scrubbed the horse down with a currycomb. Without his armor and next to the horse, the man looked smaller than Jherek would have expected a paladin to look.

"It's a wise man who plans for tomorrow while taking care of today," Glawinn said.

"Meaning you think I should take the armor off?"

Glawinn faced him, a good-natured twinkle in his green eyes but steel in his voice. "Meaning I insist that you do exactly that."

"No disrespect intended," Jherek said, curbing his anger and surprised at his own impertinence, "but I hardly think you're in a position to tell me what to do."

Glawinn put the currycomb in one of the saddlebags near the tree he'd claimed as a sleeping area for the night. "Ah, now there's anger. That can be a warrior's truest weapon, you know, provided he makes it serve him instead of him serving it. A man who's righteously angry ignores pain and guilt and second thoughts, and glories himself in doing the right thing."

Jherek swallowed hard. "I'm sorry. I was out of line. After all, you've been nothing but generous with us."

Glawinn started stripping out of the rest of the armor. "Actually, you weren't out of line," he said in a softer voice. "I know it's the woman that you worry about most. You don't know me, yet you and she find yourselves somewhat dependent on me."

"We didn't mean any hardship for you," Jherek quickly said. "If we're imposing, I know we can make it on our own."

After the paladin had intervened between Tynnel and him, Jherek had readily agreed to the knight's offer to accompany them for a time, and he'd even lent one of the packhorses for Sabyna to ride, having to sacrifice some of the supplies he'd carried with him. Jherek had kept up walking, but only just, and he'd had to argue with Sabyna several times about sharing the pack animal. She'd stubbornly insisted on walking beside him a few times, but she didn't have the strength or stamina he did.

"Nonsense," Glawinn said, sitting down and putting his back to the tree. He crossed his legs and sat with his broadsword resting across both knees. "If I'd thought you were going to be that much trouble, I'd never have offered."

Jherek sat across the campfire from the man and lifted an eyebrow in doubt. "Leaving a woman out in the forest to fend for herself? That doesn't seem very knightly."

Glawinn laughed, and the honesty of the sound made Jherek feel good, safe despite the forest surrounding them and twilight coming on.

"And what would you know of knights, young warrior?" Glawinn asked.

"I've read about them in books."

"What books?"

Jherek named some of the books Malorrie had given him to read over the years. For a phantom, Malorrie had always seemed to have an extensive library.

"Ah, the romances," Glawinn said when he finished. "I've meandered through some of them myself. I find them very prettily written and good for a few evenings' entertainment but as far as training a paladin how to think?" He shook his head. "No, young warrior, a knight listens with his heart, the greatest gift his chosen deity has seen fit to equip him with. Have you ever read 'Quentin's Monograph ?' "

Jherek nodded. That had been one of the first things Malorrie had put before him. "It speaks about the virtues a paladin should have."

"Yes, and it's a very concisely written piece, with some practical information on the care of weapons and animals, and a few of Quentin's own adventures." Glawinn ran his fingers down the spine of his sword blade, hardly touching it. "Modestly expressed, of course."

"Aye."

Glawinn smiled. "But you prefer the romances, of course?"

Jherek grinned bashfully. "Aye."

"No worry, young warrior, there's no shame in holding to an ideal. I just hope that you aren't too disappointed by the things you see outside those books."

Jherek nodded. "I know the difference between the books and real life." He tried to keep the bitterness out of his voice. Almost everything in life was different than what was shown in those books.

"I can tell by the markings on your face and body that you've been traveling the rougher side of life for the last little while."

"Aye. I was at the battle of Baldur's Gate."

"Baldur's Gate?" Glawinn sat up straighter. "I am only lately come from Cormyr. I've no news of Baldur's Gate."

Jherek glanced toward the copse of trees not far distant from them where Sabyna had gone to study her spellbook. He'd been hesitant about letting her go off but in the end he hadn't had a choice. She'd been adamant about not missing her studies, though Jherek also thought she wanted to be alone to deal with what had happened with Tynnel and *Breezerunner.* He quickly brought the knight up to speed on the events at Baldur's Gate and Waterdeep, and the ships that had been taken in that time as well, because Glawinn hadn't heard of that either.

"The sahuagin are uprising?" the knight asked when he finished. "Does anyone know why?"

Jherek shook his head.

"Surely no one believes these are unrelated events?"

"I don't know," Jherek answered. "Sabyna and I were kidnapped from Baldur's Gate the night of the attack."

Glawinn gazed into the campfire for a moment, obviously thinking about what he'd been told. "You and your mates only just escaped the pirates from the Inner Sea who took part in this attack?"

"That's what Captain Tynnel told me the pirate captain Vurgrom said. You could probably ask Sabyna for more in-depth information."

"Have you ever heard of Vurgrom before?"

Jherek shook his head.

"So he could be telling the truth and he could be telling a lie?"

"Aye, and I wouldn't know the right of it."

"Then why do you pursue him?" Glawinn asked.

"Personal reasons."

"With the demeanor and focus you're wearing, I wouldn't have thought it was any less," the knight said sagely.

Jherek didn't feel comfortable not telling the knight all of it, so he did. He tried to trim down the way he'd felt about being the recipient of the pearl disk, but he found he couldn't do that completely either.

"So you don't think the old priest was right in giving that disk to you?" Glawinn asked.

"No."

"Why?"

Jherek shook his head and forced a smile he didn't feel. "If you knew me better, Sir Glawinn, you wouldn't even need to ask that question." He felt the burn of his father's tattoo on the inside of his arm.

"Ah, the wisdom of youth."

"What do you mean by that?" Jherek asked.

"To be young and think I know so much again," Glawinn said. "That would be properly painful. I'd much rather know for certain there is much I still yet need to learn." He looked at Jherek. "Meaning no disrespect, young warrior, but you've hardly put in enough years to give any real weight to the guesses you make about what the gods would or wouldn't do."

"One thing I do know and am sure of," Jherek said, "is that they wouldn't have anything to do with me."

Still, Jherek remembered the voice that had haunted him since childhood. He almost asked the knight about it, but stopped himself. Once he'd dealt with one fantasy, he didn't need to start working on another.

Glawinn let the topic slide. "So now you pursue Vurgrom to the Inner Sea?"

"That's where he's got to be headed. He told Tynnel he was from the Pirate Isles, and even claimed to be the pirate king of Immurk's Hold."

"Oh, I agree entirely, young warrior. Have you ever been to Westgate?"

Jherek shook his head.

"That will be the first city Vurgrom heads for," Glawinn confidently. "He may pass through Teziir, but it'll be Westgate that's his destination. It's a pirate's haven, and he's sure to have men waiting for him there."

"You've been there?" Jherek asked.

"A number of times. None of them pleasant or particularly long. Nor were they in any way uneventful." Glawinn fixed him with his green-eyed stare. "Which begs the question of how you think you're going to get something back from Vurgrom if he doesn't want to give it back?"

"I don't know," Jherek admitted.

"The trip to Westgate is at least a tenday's ride, young warrior, even at the pace we've been pushing these poor horses and with the shortcuts I know from having journeyed there before. You'd better give your actions some thought."

"I will," Jherek said, then added: "I am."

"And Westgate is no place for a lady."

"Aye," Jherek replied. "I tried to get her to listen to reason and go back with *Breezerunner*, but she'd have none of it."

"I gathered that from the way she was acting toward the captain when I arrived."

"I still don't understand Tynnel's behavior."

"You don't?"

"No."

"And you read those fantasies?"

"What do those—"

"It's as obvious as the nose on your face," Glawinn said. "Captain Tynnel is in love with her."

The paladin's words hit Jherek like physical blows. Now he understood better why Tynnel hadn't told Sabyna about the events in Athkatla. He tried to let nothing of the sudden aching pain and fear that threatened to consume him show on his face. He tried to understand why he felt the way he did. Images of the voyage from Velen to Athkatla flashed through his mind. He remembered the times and conversations he'd shared with the pretty ship's mage, and the meals.

"I see you have some feelings for the girl yourself," the knight said.

Jherek forced himself to speak. "I like her."

"And that's all?"

"It's all I know," the young sailor said.

"But you enjoy reading those fantasies of yours," Glawinn said. "How can you not want to be in love? How can you say only that you like her?"

"Because it's all I dare," Jherek answered. "I'm no high-born prince or liege man or warrior of high renown."

"You're a warrior. You stood at the battle of Baldur's Gate, and you stood up to that ship's captain without a sword in your fist."

"I'm no warrior," Jherek said, uncomfortable with any confusion that placed greatness on anything he'd done. "I'm just a man who's fought for his life."

"Most soldiers feel the same way."

"As for Tynnel, I couldn't have fought him."

"You would have let him kill you?"

"I don't think he would have."

Glawinn reached into his saddlebag and took out two apples. He tossed one to Jherek and kept one for himself. He polished the fruit on his shirt, then took a bite. "He would have killed you," the knight stated flatly. "Men in love sometimes do foolish things."

"I could not have fought him," Jherek said. "He wasn't my enemy."

"Tynnel saw you as his because you were taking away the woman he loves."

Jherek felt uncomfortable. He rolled the apple between his palms, but the anticipation of taking a bite had already tightened his mouth. "I didn't take her away."

"You were the reason she left."

"I didn't ask her. I asked her to stay."

"And if you did," Glawinn said, "that had to have angered Tynnel even further."

"She's stubborn," Jherek said. "And willful."

"Qualities that can work for good or ill in a man or woman."

"If she loves him," Jherek said, "she should have stayed with him. She owed me nothing that would come between them."

Glawinn bit off a piece of his apple and offered it to the war-horse. The animal took it daintily from his palm and whickered in satisfaction. "You don't listen very well. I said that he was in love with her. I said nothing about her being in love with him."

Hope flew in Jherek's heart, but it only took remembering that it was his father who slew Sabyna's brother to quash it. Even if that had not stood between them, what did he have to offer her?

Glawinn hesitated. "Perhaps I presume on territory that I don't belong in, but have you told the lady that you . . . you *like* her, young warrior?"

Acting on the small amount of irritation he felt, Jherek asked, "Why do you keep calling me that? I have a name."

"Malorrie?" Glawinn shook his head. "That's not your name."

Jherek's face colored and he felt shamed by his continued lie. Perhaps he could have told the knight his real name if they'd met alone, but Sabyna was there. She already knew he hadn't told her the truth about his name, but he couldn't give it, either, in case she'd heard about him being unmasked as one of Bloody Falkane's pirates.

"It's the name I choose," he replied.

"Yet hide your true name? I have to wonder what else you hide."

Jherek returned the man's level gaze. "I must ask you to judge me on what you see, not what a name may contain. If you choose not to trust me, I ask only that you take the lady to safety."

Glawinn held up a hand. "I'll not desert you, nor her. For all I know, you're why I'm here."

"Why are you here?" Jherek gladly shifted the conversation away from him.

"I'm on a quest, commanded by Lathander himself."

"He speaks to you?"

"Not in words," Glawinn admitted. "He found me when I was lost and brought me into his temple. I was not always as you see. As a young man I was uncertain and lacking. My love and understanding of the Morninglord, and my eventual dedication to him has made me what you see now. Not that you should be impressed. A paladin's life isn't exactly what you read in those romances." He chuckled.

"But to serve a god," Jherek said. "That would be—"

"A humbling experience, let me assure you. Though I serve him with my convictions, my teaching, and my sword arm every day, we don't converse. He fills my heart with a wanderlust that is as true as any compass, and I ride. When I arrive, then I discover where I'm supposed to be. It doesn't take long before I figure out what it is I'm supposed to do."

"Now you're bound for Westgate."

"Yes, and perhaps beyond. I don't know yet. I only know that I itch to travel, and that's the direction I must go."

Jherek tried to fathom that. "But you don't know why?"

"Not yet." Glawinn gave more of the apple to his horse. "What are you to do then?" Jherek asked, not really expecting an answer.

"I'm no teller of fortunes, young warrior. I'm much more a man of action. Like yourself."

Jherek shook his head. "I'm no man of action."

"Sure you are," Glawinn said. "I can see it in the way you hold your eyes, the way you balance yourself on your feet when you move. You're no stranger to the sword, are you?"

"I've had some training," Jherek admitted.

"You must have to have survived the wounds I see on you now."

"I've only a mean skill at best." Jherek felt bad about that because it undercut all the training Malorrie had given him over the years.

"Then strip out of that wet armor and let's have a look at it." Glawinn got lithely to his feet.

"Now?"

The knight took a long sword from his saddle and tossed it to Jherek. "Of course now. There's no better time. When we arrive in Westgate either your quest or mine may see us crossing sword blades with others. Perhaps I'll even need someone to stand at my back."

Jherek flushed with the honor he was being given. He took off the leather armor and hung it carefully from a tree so it would better dry. He also took off his wet shirt, not wanting it to slow his movements and so that it wouldn't get torn any more than it was because he had no other clothes. He also took off the kerchief he'd had tied around his head, being careful not to let the paladin see his tattoo when he lifted his arm.

"You've a wound on your head," Glawinn said. "Have you had it tended?"

"Aye."

"It doesn't appear to be healing well."

Jherek felt self-conscious, remembering that the wound was the reason Sabyna was there. "Circumstances haven't allowed it to heal at its best."

"Let me see it." Glawinn crossed over to him and examined it more closely. "It's healed some, but I can help still more if you'll allow me."

Jherek remembered the tales he'd been told, of how a paladin could heal and cure diseases with but a touch. He smiled and said, "I guess not everything in those romances are fantasy."

"A gift from Lathander, young warrior, and no doing of my own." Glawinn placed his hands on Jherek's head.

The young sailor experienced a moment of disorientation, a flicker of pain, then he immediately felt better than he had in days.

Glawinn stepped back. "How's that?"

"Good," Jherek answered. "Thank you."

"Your thanks may be premature, young warrior." Glawinn grinned and paced back to the center of the clearing. He raised his broadsword into an en garde position. "Move too slowly or awkwardly and I may bequeath you another rap on the skull for your trouble."

Jherek saluted him, then cut with the long sword to get the heft of it. The balance was good and it moved well, like it had been made for his hand. "All right," he said.

The paladin came at him without a word, and the sound of steel on steel rang out. Hesitant at first, Jherek held up a defense, then he started in with his attack, pushing at Glawinn's defenses.

After long moments, the knight stepped back, a smile on his face. He saluted the young sailor. Jherek saluted back, startled by the sound of clapping. Glancing over his shoulder, he saw Sabyna standing there. Her copper-colored eyes held the glitter of excitement.

"Very good," she complimented.

"Lady," Jherek said, bowing slightly. Then, aware that he was shirtless, he went to the tree to get his clothes. He pulled his shirt on with his back to her, covered with sweat and breathing hard from his exertions.

"The boy is good," Glawinn said, sheathing his sword with a flourish. "With the proper training and time, he stands a chance of becoming an accomplished swordsman."

"I see. While the two of you were so gainfully engaged, did either of you happen to think about dinner?"

Jherek glanced up, noticing the deep plum color darkening the eastern sky where Westgate lay. "No, lady, I'm sorry. I'll take care of it straight away." He felt embarrassed, knowing he should have remembered how hungry she would be after getting no sleep last night and traveling all day.

"Actually," Sabyna said mischievously, "there's no reason to worry. I've already taken care of it." She held up a stringer of catfish. "I took a little time off from my studies."

A grin split Glawinn's short-cropped beard. "And a profitable time it was too, lady. You have our humblest appreciation."

"I caught them," Sabyna announced, "but I'm not cleaning or cooking."

"I'll take care of it, lady," Jherek offered.

He studied her face as he took the fish, noticing the fatigue clinging to her features. She hadn't said anything about Tynnel's actions or what they meant to her. She and Tynnel had been together for awhile. He couldn't help feeling that he'd torn them apart. If he hadn't shipped aboard *Breezerunner* none of the resulting confusion would have happened. He carried bad luck with him, just as Aysel and Tynnel had said.

"Are you all right?" she asked him.

Jherek smiled at her. "I'm fine. I'll be back as soon as I can."

"I could help. I really don't mind cleaning fish."

"No," he said. "You've done enough, and I'd like some time to myself. Maybe when no one's looking I could grab a quick bath."

She nodded and turned away from him, walking back to the knight and the campfire.

Too late, Jherek realized he might have hurt her feelings by rejecting her offer. She'd just walked away from everything she'd known out of a debt she felt she owed him. He thought of calling out to her, then decided not to. If she grew angry with him, maybe she would accompany Glawinn while he pursued Vurgrom the Mighty. Maybe he could even persuade the paladin to see her back to the River Chionthar and find a ship that would take her back to the Sea of Swords.

He walked down the hillside where the stench of the fish cleaning wouldn't overpower the campsite. One thing he was certain of: Where he was headed was no place for a woman.

20

"Come, little malenti, you wished to see what your people spent their blood on. Now I will show you."

Hesitantly, Laaqueel crossed the throne room of the sahuagin palace, walking past the throne carved of whalebone, its jaws distended to hold the seat. Images of sharks and sahuagin stood out in bas-relief on the limestone blocks that made up the walls. She'd stood gazing through one of the windows overlooking the amphitheater.

Sahuagin warriors had assembled there to work on the fliers they'd gathered and built to undertake Iakhovas's latest mission. The fliers were seventy-five feet across at their widest and two hundred feet long, tapering at the ends. Salvaged wood from shipwrecks and surface dweller buildings on shore contributed to the construction. Each flier could hold up to six hundred sahuagin. Currently, there were fourteen fliers in various stages of preparation, and more were supposed to be coming soon. The deepsong had reached sahuagin everywhere—and they had come.

Iakhovas strode to the opposite end of the room where the huge image of Sekolah meeting the sahuagin occupied the wall. The image showed the Great Shark with the clamshell that had contained the sahuagin in his teeth, shaking out the sahuagin and releasing them into Toril's oceans for the first time. When Iakhovas touched the image, it shimmered and vanished.

Fear filled Laaqueel as she watched it vanish. Though she'd never been to the palace before the last year, she knew it had existed for thousands of years. "What have you done?"

"Relax, little malenti. Do not overconcern yourself. Your precious wall is intact. I'm merely using it at the moment for other purposes. Now come."

Woodenly, Laaqueel joined him, watching him step through the wall and vanish. Her gills flared as she drew in more water, then she pushed it through and calmed herself. She took a step forward, and in the next moment she was high in the shallows. Harsh sunlight glimmered silver across the sea surface only a few feet overhead.

"Where are we?" Laaqueel asked.

"Above the sahuagin city," Iakhovas answered. "Don't worry, little malenti, I haven't taken you far from home yet." He reached inside his cloak and took out the bottle the dead thing in the lime pit under Baldur's Gate had given him. "This is our prize."

Curious, Laaqueel swam closer to better see the bottle. It had been cleaned since she'd last seen it, the surface now bright and shiny. Brass capped both ends, gleaming in the sunlight penetrating the shallow depths. Inside was a tiny model of a great galley, one of the long ships the surface dwellers used for trade and war. The three sails were unfurled to catch the wind and tiny oars stuck out the sides in double rows.

"A ship in a bottle?" Laaqueel let acid drip into her words. Before she could say anything more, Iakhovas gestured angrily. In the next instant they both flew out of the water and came to a stop hovering forty or fifty feet above the surface.

"Do not mock me, little malenti," Iakhovas snapped.

He turned from her and threw the ship-in-the-bottle out toward the sea. It twirled and sparked sunlight as it descended. Before it touched the water, Iakhovas shouted a single word. The bottle burst into a spray of a thousand gleaming shards. In the next instant a full-sized great galley floated on the ocean below. Purple and yellow striped sails flared out from the three masts.

"Not just a child's amusement, little malenti. This is a weapon, a weapon I'm going to use to bring the surface dwellers of the Sea of Fallen Stars to their knees."

He gestured again and they floated to the deck. Laaqueel touched down lightly, feeling the ocean rub up against the ship.

"A great galley," Iakhovas stated, walking around the deck. He stroked the butt of one of the large crossbows mounted on the railing on the port side. The starboard side had them too. Racks held the harpoon-sized quarrels the weapons used for ammunition. "One hundred thirty feet long and twenty feet wide, it's a fortress, a place where I can command armies and rain destruction down upon my enemies. It takes one hundred and forty oarsmen, and can comfortably carry another one hundred fifty warriors. There are various other additions I mean to make."

"What?"

"Surprises," he told her, walking the length of the deck.

Despite the fact that she didn't want to, she followed him. She had no way of knowing how long the ship-in-the-bottle had been in the lime pit under Baldur's Gate, but it had weathered the time well. The wood grain of the deck was finished and smooth, showing no signs of warpage or wear.

"She's a mudship, one of only seven in all of Toril. Her name is *Tarjana*, which translates from an old and almost forgotten tongue to 'Fisherhawk on Wing.' "

Fisherhawks were oceangoing birds of prey. Equipped with a fourteen- to sixteen-foot wingspread, sharp talons, and fangs like a snake, fisherhawks were known to raid seabound vessels of small children, women, halflings, and the occasional dwarf as well as the fish it stripped from the sea.

Iakhovas pulled back his sleeve and revealed the gold bracelet he wore. Laaqueel had seldom seen it, but most of the slots on it that had been empty now appeared to be filled. Iakhovas plucked free the diamond and pink coral talisman they'd gotten in Waterdeep. "And this bauble that I got from Serpentil Jannaxil gives me control over her."

Laaqueel tried to get a better look at it, but he put it away quickly.

"*Tarjana* is able to run on land and sea," Iakhovas said proudly, "above and below the water. This will be the flagship of the navy I'm going to take into the Sea of Fallen Stars."

"You can't take the sahuagin there," Laaqueel said, unable to stop herself from speaking.

His single eye narrowed to a thin line of malevolence. Despite the patch he wore over his empty eye, something golden shone in its depths for an instant. "Don't presume to tell me what to do. I can lead the sahuagin there, and I will. They're mine to do with as I please. Or haven't you noticed?"

"They think you're working the will of Sekolah." Laaqueel made herself stand her ground as he approached. She squeezed her fear into her belief in the Great Shark, but she trembled inside.

Iakhovas placed a long-nailed finger under her chin, tilting her head back to face him. "Ah, and little malenti, how can it still be that you have any doubts at all that I'm not working the will of Sekolah?"

"Because I don't understand," she told him, wanting desperately for an answer. "Nothing in my training taught me about any of this."

"Your training led you to the legend of One Who Swims With Sekolah."

"Yes."

"It led you to me."

She had no answer.

"Now you falter, when you should be enjoying your greatest success. After all, it was through your efforts you became royal high priestess, a position you would never have attained without your efforts to find the truth your training led you to. You doubt, yet there is more now than ever that should offer you conviction."

"I don't understand why we should involve ourselves in the Inner Sea. Our place is here."

Iakhovas hooked her chin with his talon hard enough to nearly bring blood. "Because it is as Sekolah wills. You're a hypocrite, little malenti. You took Huaanton to task because he wanted a sign from the Great Shark that what we were doing was as Sekolah willed it. Now, here I am, proof of that sign, and yet you refuse to believe. You want still further proof."

"I don't see what the Inner Sea—"

Enough! Iakhovas roared in her mind.

Laaqueel's knees buckled from the pain of the mental shout, and she fell to the deck.

"Do you want proof?" Iakhovas demanded. "Or do you want to believe? One is not the same as the other."

Tears came to Laaqueel's eyes because she knew what he said was true. The difference between knowledge and faith was the first lesson Senior Priestess Ghaataag had taught her when she took her into Sekolah's temple. So often as a child Laaqueel had drawn Ghaataag's wrath for doubting.

"You can have proof standing before you, little malenti, and still doubt what you see. As for belief, once you can weigh it and measure it, that belief becomes knowledge. Belief is something that can't be proven in this world of physical restraint, but it can't be broken either. Yet it is the strongest of things that exist in the world. Believing is much stronger than knowing."

Laaqueel continued crying silently, remembering all the times Ghaataag had made her go pray on her knees on a bed of broken coral until she was able to excise the doubt that had touched her then. She was so, so weak.

"No, little malenti," Iakhovas said more gently. "You're not weak. You're stronger than you know, but you're fighting yourself and you're finding yourself to be a more formidable opponent than any you've ever known. You stood the test of your priesshood, and you found answers to questions that no one even knew existed until you came along." His voice grew fierce with pride. "How dare you call yourself weak."

His words calmed her a little, and they gave her back a measure of self-respect she'd been missing.

"I saw you stand up to Huaanton when he doubted in Sekolah. He could have taken your head then, claiming you to be mentally unbalanced by the aberration of your birth. You believed Sekolah would spare you then because you were right and you were standing up for him."

"I didn't know that he would."

Iakhovas smiled down at her. "That's what I said, little malenti. You didn't know. You believed. I only ask you to believe now." He offered her his hand and helped her to her feet.

Laaqueel regained control over her emotions with effort. Despite the fact that she wanted him to be wrong, Iakhovas was right. Belief was all she had in her life.

"I am the source of your greatest strength, little malenti," he told her softly. "I shall push you and goad you and shape you into your belief. Because I, by my very nature and the things we must accomplish together, will strip away everything in you that does not believe. Every weakness in you will be worn away by my actions, by the things Sekolah would have us accomplish. Your doubt shall forge us both into our destiny. Mark you that I only mentioned one such destiny. We shall arrive there together, and it will be glorious."

It was so easy to believe his words, but she had no choice really. What was she without her belief? She had the gifts Sekolah had given her, powers that no male sahuagin would ever know. What was there to doubt, except the man who stood before her?

He reached for her, touching her cheek with the back of his hand. It felt smooth and strong, and she found herself drawing away out of embarrassment. The feeling wasn't just out of the familiarity with which he chose to approach her, but because of the feeling his touch stirred within her.

"Ah, little malenti, you find the hungers of the alien flesh you wear have awakened." Iakhovas smiled darkly. "Bloody Falkane must have had quite an effect on you."

"What do you want?" she asked.

"From you, little malenti? Only your assistance. I find myself invulnerable to the charms you possess. Unlike Bloody Falkane, I find myself in no need of a spy within my ranks."

"I don't think his interest was purely for those reasons. He has loathsome habits."

"His reasons, whatever they are, I can guarantee you are anything but pure. So beware his charms, little malenti, because I'm told they're quite considerable."

Angry and embarrassed, Laaqueel turned away.

"Now I've offended you."

"No."

"You can't hide your true feelings from me. You should know that by now." Iakhovas spoke a word.

Instantly, the ship disappeared beneath them and Laaqueel dropped into the ocean. The water closed over her, taking her down and holding her close, the truest and only companion she'd ever known.

Across from her, Iakhovas caught the ship-in-the-bottle again and swam down. "Let's go check on my navy, little malenti. I've got an invasion to get underway."

21

"Something I can help you with, boy?"

Jherek bridled at the man's tone but calmed himself quickly. Emotion wasn't going to get him any closer to his objective. "I'm looking for someone."

The bartender set down a mostly clean glass and picked up another one, treating it to a quick bath in the dirty water in front of him, then drying it with the threadbare towel over his shoulder. He was broad and thick, with muscle that had marbled to fat over the years. A long gray fringe surrounded his gleaming pate, and an axe blade scar dented his forehead.

Behind him on the wall were rows of bottles containing different colored liquids. Two tapped ale kegs lay on their sides on rolling carts, and gruesomely displayed above them were seven koalinth heads. They'd been poorly mounted, and the piggish faces and floppy ears of the marine hobgoblins wrinkled and stretched hideously. The light green skin flaked off in several patches.

"This someone's got to have a name before I can help you," the bartender said. "That's how it usually works best."

Jherek flushed with embarrassment. Subterfuge was something new to him and he wasn't very good at it. He guessed he'd about strained his limit while keeping his identity secret from Glawinn and Sabyna.

"He calls himself Vurgrom," the young sailor said. "Vurgrom the Mighty."

The bartender looked at Jherek thoughtfully. He picked up a wooden splinter from the counter and worked it between his teeth for a moment. He never blinked.

Jherek met the man's level gaze, knowing he and his companions were in danger.

The Bent Mermaid had the reputation of being one of the worst taverns in Westgate—both in provender and clientele. It stood three stories tall and looked out over the neck of the Lake of Dragons. Docks stabbed long fingers out into the sea and ships from a dozen and more countries occupied the slips and stood at anchor out in the harbor.

"What business do you have with Vurgrom?" the bartender asked.

"Personal," Jherek said.

The bartender looked over the young sailor's shoulder. "Him too?"

Without glancing back, Jherek knew the man was talking about Glawinn. The knight stood out in the dark den of the tavern. When he'd first entered, sailors standing close to the paladin had drawn back and found other tables and places to stand.

"Aye," Jherek answered.

The bartender shook his head. "Don't know no Vurgrom."

Jherek looked the man in the face, hard, knowing it was a lie. "We were told he'd be here."

"By who?"

Jherek ignored the question. The old sailor who'd given them the information had no love for the pirate leader. "We were told Vurgrom arrived here three days ago."

According to the old sailor, the pirate captain had taken a ship in from the River Tun, sailing in from the Storm Horn Mountains while Jherek and his companions had been forced to cross the distance overland.

"Somebody told you wrong," the bartender said.

Anger flared through Jherek. The journey had been hard and made even harder by the tension that seemed to exist between Sabyna and him. Glawinn had noticed it, the young sailor had been sure, but had refrained from making comment.

The only times he'd really felt relaxed during the journey had been when he and the knight had practiced swordcraft. The young sailor had gotten sore from the daily exertion at first, but had quickly come up to speed, surprising the knight with his skill. Still, there were skills and tricks that Glawinn had taught him and continued to teach him.

"Malorrie."

Jherek heard Sabyna's voice at his side, then felt her touch upon his arm. "Aye, lady," he said, turning to her because he didn't want to be disrespectful.

"Leave it."

The young sailor thought briefly of arguing. Returning the pearl disk was his task to accomplish, and no matter how she felt about helping him because of what he'd done for her, she obviously didn't feel as strongly about it as he did. He knew the pirate was inside the tavern.

"Please," the ship's mage said in a soft voice. Her copper-colored eyes held his.

Jherek let out a deep breath. "Aye. I'm done here, anyway."

"You going to be drinking anything?" the bartender asked.

"Not if I wiped those glasses myself," Jherek told him, venting a little of the hostility he felt.

"Then you need to clear out of my tavern," the man told him. "I got a rule about people coming in to take up tables and not spending any coin."

"Do you have any rules about the clientele you serve?" Jherek asked. "I definitely see no scruples." He was aware that his words drew the attention of a dozen men around the front of the bar.

The sailors shifted in their chairs, taking offense. Jherek didn't feel badly because he knew no honest sailor would patronize the Bent Mermaid, but he was afraid for a moment he'd overstepped his bounds and endangered Sabyna recklessly.

Glawinn strode forward and glared harshly at the men. The paladin carried his shiny helm in the crook of his arm, but his hand rested casually on the hilt of his broadsword. "I'd not," he said in a low, steady voice.

For a moment, the group of sailors held his gaze, then they turned away and hunkered back over their drinks.

"I only got one rule," the bartender said, deliberately looking Jherek from head to toe, making the young sailor aware of his shoddy appearance. "I don't serve vagrants."

The men who'd backed down from Glawinn laughed contemptuously, slapping the table. Jherek's face flamed in embarrassment. Glawinn had offered clothing, but none of the knight's fit the young sailor's bigger frame. Jherek wished he had something clever to say, a cutting remark that heroes in the romances always seemed to have at the tips of their tongues, but he didn't.

Sabyna tugged on his arm and he went, suddenly aware how she looked leading him away. Gently, he tried to disengage himself but she kept her grip fast. Glawinn covered their backs as she led them from the tavern. She didn't stop until they were half a block away, standing at one of the railings overlooking the docks and cattle yards below.

"The man back there was lying," Jherek said.

"Aye," Sabyna answered. The wind blew her jaw-length copper tresses around her face. She had her arms crossed, standing an arm's length away from him to create distance even though they were close. "And what were you going to do? Beat it out of him with a whole room full of men watching on?"

Feeling himself willing to visit some of his anger on her, Jherek got control of himself. "Lady," he said softly, "I apologize for my behavior. You deserve my thanks. You probably saved me from making a serious mistake."

"Yes," Glawinn agreed, "she did."

Jherek looked back at the Bent Mermaid, feeling angry at the obscene sign that hung so large and proudly over the door.

"Vurgrom is inside," Sabyna asked. "He has ten men with him. They're waiting on his ship, *Maelstrom*, to arrive."

"How do you know that?"

The ship's mage smiled. "I asked one of the serving girls. If you want to know something, ask someone who has the most reason to tell it. The bartender's major profits are made from the pirates, but most of the girls despise Vurgrom and his ilk. None of the women work there very long. If you've been around taverns like the Bent Mermaid, you know that."

"Aye," Jherek said, feeling chagrined. He hadn't been around taverns much, not good ones or bad ones, and not even the ones in Velen more than enough to be marginally social with *Butterfly*'s crew. "I hadn't thought of that."

"It doesn't make it any easier," Sabyna said. "Vurgrom's on the third floor and I was told he has it sealed off. He's conducting some kind of business there."

"What business?" Glawinn asked.

"The girl I talked to didn't know."

Jherek studied the building, feeling the anger in him dissipate as he recognized the new course of action open to him. "The building next to the tavern is as tall," he pointed out.

"You're thinking of crossing over to get Vurgrom now?" Sabyna asked.

"Aye," Jherek answered and saw Glawinn smile.

"Do it," he said.

Glawinn prayed to Lathander, gesturing Jherek to bend his head as well, then inscribed designs in the air. When the paladin finished, Jherek felt as though he'd suddenly gone deaf .

He looked up and tried to speak but no words came out.

The paladin shook his head and drew a hand across his throat, letting the young sailor know verbal communication was no longer possible. The spell even took away all the sounds coming from the docks, the pinging of rigging against masts, shouted commands, and the slap of the surf against the shore and pilings. Glawinn waved toward the other building.

Gathering himself, Jherek leaped across the distance from the flophouse roof to the Bent Mermaid next door. When his feet hit, there was no sound at all. He turned and watched as the paladin, then the ship's mage jumped across the distance as well. The roof trembled beneath his feet, but there was no noise.

He hunkered down and went around the roof to the harbor side. Clinging to the roof's edge, forty feet above where the ocean smashed up against the side of the Bent Mermaid, he lowered himself and peered through the windows along the wall.

A dozen men sat around tables inside the large room that ran the length of the building's harbor side. Pitchers of ale sat on tables burdened with platters of food. Jherek recognized Vurgrom at one end of the center table.

Confusion spread throughout the room as the pirates stood, each gesturing widely and trying to clear their throats. Jherek understood that Glawinn's spell of silence was affecting the pirates as well, and he knew he had to act swiftly while surprise remained a possible weapon.

The young sailor glanced over his shoulder at Glawinn, finding the paladin in the process of knotting a climbing rope around the chimney sticking up from the center of the peaked roof. The knight gave it a final pull, then stood and nodded.

Without another word, Jherek flipped lithely over the roof's edge, holding the rope in one hand, and grabbing on with the other as he dropped. He turned his downward momentum into an arc, holding tight with his hands, and drove his boots through the window in front of him. He followed the broken glass inward, releasing his hold and throwing himself forward to regain his balance.

There was no sound of the shattering glass, only the sight of it spinning away in shards. Jherek landed on one knee, drawing attention only from the men who were looking in his direction. They opened their mouths, probably shouting warnings, but no sound came forth.

Jherek pushed himself to his feet and filled his hands with the cutlass and hook at the same time Glawinn broke through another window and landed only a few feet away. The paladin swept the broadsword from its scabbard, and the room became a battlefield.

Jherek blocked a long sword with the cutlass, feeling the shock of the blades meeting but hearing none of the usual clangor. The pirate drew back quickly, seeking to draw the young sailor after him so one of his companions could slip behind him.

Instead, the young sailor swung his hook toward the floor, biting into the stained rug across the wooden floor but not the floor itself. He yanked hard, pulling the rug from under the other man and sending him tumbling back.

Sliding to the side, Jherek dodged a cutlass blow that would have taken his head from his shoulders. He set himself and turned again, cutting forward with his own cutlass and splitting the pirate's chest open.

The mortally wounded man's face writhed in a scream, but Glawinn's spell blanked out the sound. The pirate dropped to his knees, trying to hold himself together.

Across the room, Vurgrom moved his huge bulk toward the only exit.

Already in motion again, Jherek sprinted to the nearest table. He blocked a sword thrust with the cutlass, turning it aside only inches from his leg. The young sailor threw himself into the air, skidding feet first across a buffet table and knocking dishes, food, and candelabras from it. He caught the table's edge with the hook, tipping it over after him.

The table was big and heavy, a thick oaken slab that had been crafted well but not treated with respect. Still, it held up.

Sliding the hook around the side, Jherek caught the end of the table, then put all of his weight into the pull-then-push that sent it skidding across the floor toward the exit. Uninterrupted, the table slid in front of the door, blocking Vurgrom's departure.

The pirate captain pulled the battle-axe from over his shoulder and slammed the bit into the table. The force split the table asunder and he kicked his way through the two halves. He yanked the door open and hurried out, obviously working on the theory that discretion was the better part of valor.

Jherek stood, glancing back at his companions. Glawinn, broadsword in one hand and shield in the other, held his own, staking out a whole corner of the room. One of the pirates rushed him, battle-axe held high. The paladin dropped slightly and stepped forward into the charging man. Catching him on his shield and avoiding the axe head as it came across with the intention of hooking onto the shield and pulling it away, Glawinn twisted and stood. The motion hurled the pirate through the smashed windows high over the harbor.

Sabyna's knife flashed out, driving an opponent back. Her lack of formal training in swordplay held her back some, but her skill with her throwing knives was deadly. She blocked another sword slash and stepped inside the blow, then raked her blade across the man's face. Blood flew as the pirate threw himself backward. At her side, the raggamoffyn swirled into a sudden mass of whirling cloth fragments and sped at another pirate.

Parrying a sword thrust, Glawinn screamed soundlessly at Jherek, yelling at him to *go*.

Hesitation held the young sailor only for a moment. He didn't want to desert his friends, and didn't like the idea of leaving Sabyna to fend for herself at all, but in the end if he didn't reach his objective, he'd risked their lives for nothing.

A pirate came at him, sword splintering the afternoon light. Jherek parried with the hook, then brought the cutlass down onto the man's head, splitting his skull. He kicked the dead man backward into another pirate, knocking them both clear of the door. At a dead run, the young sailor caught the doorway's edge with the hook and pulled himself around it.

On the landing outside, Jherek peered over the railing and watched as Vurgrom bounded around the second story landing where the steps switched back the other direction. With the surefooted grace of a man used to navigating rigging in hostile winds and blinding, storm-driven rain, Jherek leaped over the edge and landed on the railing slanting down toward the second story.

When he hit, the wood cracked ominously and he knew it wasn't going to hold him even as he realized he was past Glawinn's arcane silence. He fell forward, caroming off the second story landing wall only a few feet behind Vurgrom. He heard voices then, people calling out to one another from the tavern proper downstairs.

A bare-breasted serving wench carrying a platter of food and a pitcher of ale cursed at Vurgrom as he went by, then she turned into Jherek. Already a victim of his downward momentum caused by the treacherous railing, Jherek couldn't stop. He thought quickly enough to throw the cutlass and hook out to the sides so he didn't endanger her, which left him going face first into her.

There was a moment of confusion as they fell in a tangle at the foot of the landing. The platter of food went flying while the ale pitcher shattered against the wall. Jherek ended up face first against the serving wench's well-cushioned charms. He managed to prevent his full weight from falling on her by catching himself on his knees and the fist around the hook handle.

He pulled his head up from her breasts, the fragrant rose scent of them filling his nose. His face flamed in embarrassment.

"Lady," he apologized as he pushed himself up, "I'm truly sorry." Awkwardly, knowing there wasn't any time for anything else, he pushed up and resumed his chase, drumming his boots against the steps.

At the base of the stairs, Jherek ran through the coral shell stringers that made a partition from the steps leading into the main tavern. Vurgrom stood near the entrance, his face showing agitation and the fact that he recognized Jherek. The pirate captain leveled a thick forefinger in the young sailor's direction and shouted, "A hundred gold to the man who guts that bastard!"

Instantly, nearly every man in the tavern surged to their feet and drew weapons. Vurgrom grinned, the effort like a rictus in his round moon face.

"Been nice knowing you, boy, but you signed your own death papers coming here after me." He made an obscene gesture, then pushed through the door out onto the street.

Nearly half the tavern got up and followed Vurgrom, letting Jherek know the pirate captain had stationed men downstairs as well as upstairs. At least forty men came at Jherek with drawn swords, eager to cash in on the pirate captain's offered bounty.

Jherek watched helplessly through the paned windows as Vurgrom disappeared, heading down the incline toward the harbor. Stubbornly, the young sailor held his ground with the beaded strings covering the doorway at his back.

A woman to his left cursed and stood suddenly, sweeping back the hooded cloak that had covered her face. Tall and slender, her silky black hair hacked off evenly just below her shoulders, her pointed ears visible, she wore a rough green shirt that was loose enough to disguise her sex, and scarred leather breeches tucked into high-topped boots.

She grabbed the chair she'd been sitting in and hurled it toward the front of the crowd gathered in front of Jherek. The chair hit two men and knocked them backward into the others.

"Back, you damn slime-sucking bottom-feeders, or I'll fillet you myself!" she cursed as she drew a scimitar and dirk, then rushed toward Jherek.

The young sailor turned to face her, lifting his cutlass.

"Not me, you brain-dead ninny," she told him sharply. "I've come to take a stand with you, though by Fenmarel Mestarine's kindness, I don't know why. You've cut yourself enough trouble for a small army, much less one sailor boy."

Jherek kept his blade up, wary that she could be attempting to trick him to get close enough to put a blade between his ribs. " 'Ware now, lady," he warned. "I don't trust so easily."

"Azla!" someone in the crowd shouted. "Azla of *Black Champion* is here!"

"Kill her," another man roared. "Vurgrom's bounty on her head is a thousand gold pieces!"

The half-elven woman's brows arched in anger. "You'd better pick sides quickly, boy." A half-grin played on her face, but it was cold as a moneylender's heart. "I'm worth more dead than you are and I don't intend to die without trying to escape. You're standing in the way."

"Aye," Jherek replied, watching as the crowd regrouped, "but there was a mess left upstairs as well."

Azla glanced back at the tavern crowd and knocked a thrown dagger from the air with the flat of her scimitar. "Our chances of escape have got to be better there than here."

Jherek nodded, hating to lose Vurgrom and not certain what they were going to do even if they made it back up the stairs. He pulled the beaded strands to one side.

"No," Azla said. "You first." She spoke like one used to command.

"Aye." Jherek turned and raced back to the steps, waiting for her.

Azla reached for the pouch at her side and stuck enough of her arm inside it that Jherek knew it was a bag of holding. She removed a small flask, handling it carefully.

"Keep moving," she ordered, then flung the flask at the doorway as two men shoved their heads through.

The flask tumbled end over end and struck the floor, shattering and spreading slow moving oil in spots and a pool. Immediately, the oil caught fire. The flames spiraled up at once, and the spots that had landed on the two men charred holes in their clothes. They yelled in terror and pain and began beating at their clothing, but it only served to spread the flames. The fire in the doorway rose up four feet high.

"Run," Azla directed. "I don't have any more of that ensorcelled oil with me."

She sprinted after him as they ran up the first set of stairs. Three pirates were coming down, fleeing from Glawinn. The lead pirate raised his sword, yelling hoarsely to warn his mates of the danger.

Jherek reached the corner of the landing first and blocked the man's sword with his cutlass. The other two men ran into the first, and all of them struggled to keep their balance. The young sailor kicked the first man in the chest, pressing his own back against the wall to get everything into the effort he could.

All three pirates slammed against the railing, snapping the supports off and tumbling amid screams to the floor below. They'd only just landed when the first of the pirates from the tavern area burst through the oil, stopping only long enough to slap the few flames from his clothing. Now that the oil had nearly exhausted itself, other pirates followed.

Glawinn gazed down through the maze of switchback staircases. "Company?" the paladin asked calmly.

"Aye," Jherek answered, breathing hard from his exertions, "and plenty of it."

"Who's she?" Glawinn asked.

"A friend," the young sailor said, glancing at Azla again. Despite her unexpected appearance, he got a good feeling about her. "For now, at any rate."

The half-elf smiled and shook her head. "From the looks of things," she said, "I may be the only friend you people have in Westgate."

"Not the only," Glawinn snapped. "Begging your pardon for my abruptness, lady."

"That's *Captain* Azla," she growled.

"I stand corrected."

Jherek glanced back down the stairs and watched the pirates getting themselves organized. "Maybe we should sort that out later."

"The boy's right," Glawinn said. "What's your plan?"

"The harbor," Azla answered. "We jump."

"I've been pursuing Vurgrom for years," Azla told them.

Jherek sat in *Black Champion*'s galley nursing a cup of hot tea. For the moment, Glawinn, Sabyna, and he were guests of Azla. After jumping from the third floor of the tavern, they'd been pulled from the water by some of Azla's crew, who had been waiting in a small skiff for just such an eventuality. They sat at one of the long, rectangular tables where her crew messed. All of them had dry clothes from supplies the ship's captain had on hand.

Glawinn sat at one end of the table working on his armor. It was a job he'd told them couldn't be put off, and a job he didn't want anyone else doing. Jherek didn't blame him. A knight lived and died by the care he showed his weapons and armor. Having to pull it off quickly to keep from drowning after jumping into the water, made Glawinn even more thankful it wasn't lost to the harbor bottom.

"Why?" the young sailor asked. He'd been impressed by the caravel. *Black Champion* was a tight-run ship, and one of the cleanest he'd ever seen. That effort was reflected in the galley's spotless floors and cooking area. Three cooks were already at work on the next meal and the smells made his stomach rumble in anticipation.

Azla sat across from him, dressed in a somber black that seemed to fit her mood. "Vurgrom and I have been at odds with each other for years," she explained. "He's declared himself king of Immurk's Hold, while there are no few who think I should hold that office."

Jherek almost choked on his tea, realizing for the first time that he'd accepted the invitation of a pirate. He glanced at Sabyna. The ship's mage had a personal vendetta against pirates since her own brother was slain by Bloody Falkane. No emotion at all showed on Sabyna's face, nor did she return Jherek's look.

"Vurgrom has seen me as a threat ever since, and taken steps to eliminate me and my ship," Azla said. "I've returned the favor upon occasion. Lately, through spies I've got in Westgate and other ports, as well as in Vurgrom's crew, I found out he's been stealing and buying artifacts scattered all across the Sea of Fallen Stars. He's made deals with traders in all the nations, as well as bargains with some of the undersea races."

"Do you know what that's about?" Glawinn asked.

Azla shook her head. "I've heard that he's got a contact on the Sword Coast that he sells them to regularly. Now you tell me he was in Baldur's Gate the night it was struck by the sahuagin attack. It makes the whole situation I've been following even more suspicious."

Jherek silently agreed.

"I'd found out from my spies that Vurgrom had been out to the west and was going to be returning through the Lake of Dragons sometime during the last week. It was the first time he'd been off the sea in months. He owns over half of the Bent Mermaid and I thought to take him there."

"Until we showed up," Glawinn said, brushing at the fittings on his chest plate.

"Aye," Azla said. "I had a team of men waiting outside. If Vurgrom had been with a much smaller group, we could have taken him outside the tavern and spirited him away through the sewers under the city till we got him back to *Champion*." She scowled darkly. "With a little time, I'd have found out soon enough what he was up to."

"And now?" Jherek asked.

"Now," the half-elf captain said, "I'll have to do it the old-fashioned way. Follow him until I get an opportunity to find out what he's up to and move against him when I can."

"I'd like to accompany you if I could," Jherek asked.

"To get back the trinket he took from you?"

Jherek grimaced. "Aye, but I'd prefer it if you didn't talk about it so casually."

"From what my spies tell me, Vurgrom was quite pleased to get that pearl disk. It was one of the things they'd hoped to acquire in Baldur's Gate."

The announcement shocked Jherek, and it must have shown on his face. How had Vurgrom even known about the disk if it had been hidden away for so many years? And what was it?

"I have room aboard for extra crew," she said. "If you'd like, you're welcome. As long as you understand that I'm captain of this ship."

"Aye," Jherek said.

"There must be one other stipulation," Glawinn stated, turning to face her. "As long as we're aboard, there is to be no taking of prize ships, no piracy."

"Making demands like that goes against the acknowledgement of my being the captain," Azla stated.

"Yes," Glawinn admitted, "but you don't know yet how we may help you in your own agenda. As you've seen from the disk and all that this boy has been through to get it here, our fates are tied up in it. I'd think it's better that we worked together."

"You're shipless," Azla pointed out.

"Today," the paladin said, "but not in a day or so. There are some here in Westgate who claim Lathander as their deity. I would be able to find a ship, I promise you."

"Then why want to join me?"

"Because I think you know Vurgrom better than anyone else we'd likely find. If anyone can keep up with him, I'm betting that it'll be you."

Azla pushed her tea away and stood. "All right," she agreed. "You have your bargain. A combination of our talents, skills, and destinies. I won't take any ships while you're aboard, but what do I get in return?"

"If we can manage it," Glawinn answered, "Vurgrom's head on a pike."

"I'll hold you to that," Azla said, then turned and walked away.

22

Pacys sat on an outcropping of rock overlooking the sea elf city of Faenasuor. The old bard gave no thought to the two hundred feet of ocean above him, nor to the bluish hue it seemed all the world had taken on. The folk of Serôs called all depths between one hundred fifty feet and three hundred feet the Gloom. The Sea of Fallen Stars itself served to stratify civilizations and undersea worlds.

A few tall towers, mute testimony to the hubris of the elves of the ancient empire, stood up from the sea floor, rising over the other recovered structures and the new dwellings that had been built. The city sprawled unevenly across the irregular seabed the elves called the Hmur Plateau. Despite seventy years of reclamation efforts, much of the city yet remained in a state of disrepair. Excavation teams harnessing pilot whales, narwhals, and giant crabs worked to clear more debris in an effort that had been ongoing during the days Pacys had spent there. Brackish clouds of debris and silt, exploded upward from avalanches of resettling rock, sifted constantly in the currents, eventually drawn away.

Besides being an acknowledged center of sea elven history, Faenasuor was also surrounded by oyster beds. Pacys watched sea elves out harvesting pearls from the oysters, clams, and other mollusks that created them. They worked in groups, gathering the sea's bounty, then used the pearls to trade with other undersea races and surface dwellers. The last few days spent there had been highly instructional regarding all of Serôs and some of the Taker's legend, but it had also served to remind Pacys of just how much he didn't know.

He turned his attention back to the instrument Taareen had given him. Despite the magical bracelet he wore, he couldn't play the yarting underwater. Communication was fine, but the yarting's notes all suffered. So he'd put the instrument into his bag of holding and decided to wait until he returned to the surface to play it again.

The song kept coming together in the old bard's head. Thankfully, his musical skills weren't limited to the yarting. Over his life he'd found nothing he couldn't play with some skill.

Taareen had given him a saceddar, an alu'tel'quessiran musical instrument Pacys had never seen before. Mounted on a chest plate that hung over the player's neck and shoulders, the saceddar had thirty crystals of various sizes and thicknesses across it. To play it, Pacys wore platinum finger and thumb caps on both hands. The metal was more durable than gold and struck a truer note.

He played the saceddar by striking his fingers and thumbs against a single crystal or a combination of crystals at the same time. Striking a new crystal or combination broke the vibrations of the last ones, effectively silencing them and providing for long and short notes.

When Taareen had given it to him, Pacys had been fascinated. That fascination had grown even more when the old bard discovered how easily playing the instrument came to him, and how parts of the song he'd been working on seemed to knit themselves to the new medium. He'd composed new parts over the past days, as well as learning the songs from Taker legends.

Scrabbling to his right, the sound dimmed by the water reached Pacys's ears at the same time as the vibrations from the stone shelf he sat on. He turned and saw Khlinat pulling himself up through the twisted coral growth.

"Ye got up early this morning," the dwarf commented as he settled himself across from the bard. The potions the sea elves kept him supplied with allowed him the same free movement and breathing ability as Pacys had from his enchanted bracelet.

"I couldn't sleep," Pacys said.

Khlinat wiped at his face, and the old bard knew it was because even though the potion protected him from the harsh nature of the sea, it left the dwarf feeling like he was wet the whole time. "I didn't rest too well either, songsmith, but I know it's 'cause I ain't never going to get acclimated to this way of living. What's yer excuse?"

"Restlessness, I think." Pacys pulled on the saceddar and fastened the straps. He took the finger and thumb caps from the small fish bladder bag that hung around his neck and fitted them on.

"Oh, and ye mean yer through prowling through them sea elf books, then?" Khlinat asked hopefully.

"I don't know that I could ever be satiated with that, my friend. The wisdom of the ages resides in those tomes. Magic, history, travel, philosophy, worlds await any adventurer with the skill to read."

"Aye," the dwarf said, "and a goodly pouch of gold, I'm thinking, for any man clever enough and brave enough to make off with some of them books. Like as not, nobody's ever seen anything even kin to them topside."

"I'd say you're right. Even skilled as I am in languages, when trying to read ones that should be open to me, I found them hard to decipher."

Most of the books were written in special pastes that hardened and adhered permanently to pages that were cut from the shells of giant clams. A lot of time went into the creation of each book, so they were highly prized. Some of them were even tonal books, pieced together with crystals like the sacedder and designed to be struck by a tiny mallet in order to be read. Still others were merely books ensorcelled to withstand the sea.

Khlinat waved irritably at a small school of fish that seemed determined to find hiding places in his beard and hair. With the constant immersion of living beneath the Sea of Fallen Stars, his peg had started to show signs of distress. Taareen had asked a local smith to help out, and the dwarf had been issued a new peg made of green-gray coral Taareen had called claw coral and hydra's stone.

"So what are we to do?" the dwarf asked.

"I don't know." Pacys's fingers wandered across the saceddar's surface, pinging crystals. Before he knew it, he'd started a new song weave. The notes from the struck crystals cut through the water like a knife, pouring out into the sea.

The music surged through him, building, and he gave himself over to it. The sound was haunting and evil, at turns strident and threatening. It stabbed Pacys deep within his heart with an icy finger, yet he found he couldn't let go the song.

Sharp, poignant notes echoed across Faenasuor and floated toward the surface. Movement, barely sensed in the currents and then only because the old bard had attuned himself to listen for vibrations because of the saceddar, swirled around him. He knew from the feel that it was something large.

In front of him, Khlinat's eyes rounded in horror. "Get down, friend Pacys!" The dwarf pushed up quickly, reaching out for the old bard's robes and yanking him to one side.

Pacys flailed in the water, recovering quickly as he remembered to swim instead of trying to walk. He turned as Khlinat threw himself at the monster that swam up from the murky depths behind the rocky shelf.

The creature was a wide-jawed fish eighteen feet in length and nearly half that in width. Gray-blue, iridescent scales covered it, darker at the top and lighter at the bottom so it would gray out against the surface when looked at from underneath. Most sea predators possessed similar coloration for exactly the same reason.

Already in attack mode, obviously about to seize Pacys before the dwarf yanked him out of the way, the giant fish swam for Khlinat. It opened its mouth, blowing out fist-sized chunks that whirled around the dwarf.

Khlinat gave vent to a dwarven war cry and attacked the giant fish with both hand axes. Before he had the chance to land a blow, though, the giant fish opened its mouth, darted forward, and gulped him down whole.

Pacys watched in disbelief as his friend disappeared without a flicker of movement, then he noticed that the fist-sized chunks the creature had vomited up were swimming in his direction. Their bright teeth caught his attention first. Fully a dozen of them, as vicious looking as their parent, closed within striking distance.

Acting quickly, Pacys spoke a command word and gestured at the approaching fish. A shimmering filled the water in front of him just before the first of them reached him.

The fish smacked up against the invisible shield that formed in front of him. It stopped the next two as well, but the fourth one got through. Finning close to the old bard, the fish sank sharp teeth into his flesh.

Watching the blood stream into the water from his wound, Pacys voiced another word, traced a ward with his forefinger, and touched the fish attacking him. Electricity sparked in the fish's eyeballs. The predator released its hold and rolled over on its side, floating limply.

Pacys retreated, watching as the fish battered against his shield. He summoned his magic around him again and crafted another spell. Throwing his hand straight out to the side of the shield, he released energy bolts that darted from his fingertips.

Five greenish bolts of light streaked through the water away from the invisible shield, then curved back around and struck five of the remaining eleven fish, tearing their bodies to pieces. The others descended upon the spilled entrails and ripped flesh in a frenzy.

Taking advantage of the moment, Pacys swam to the bottom and stood on the rocky shelf. He took his staff from his back and flicked the razor-sharp blades out. He glanced at the parent fish, seeing that it had turned to face him. His heart was torn over Khlinat's fate.

One of the fish found its way around the invisible shield.

Pacys swept the staff around and neatly sliced the fish's head off. The pieces floated in separate directions for a moment, then were seized by its brethren.

Blood streaming from the giant fish drew the old bard's attention for a moment. Crimson mist poured from the creature's gill slits and it moved as though in agony. Pacys whirled the staff again and gutted another one of the fish. Shifting, he spotted movement in the distance, recognizing it as sea elves riding giant seahorses. They sat crouched down over their undersea mounts, barely skimming above the kelp and seaweed lining the ocean floor.

The next fish through the shield evaded the old bard's staff and sank its teeth into the flesh just below his ribs. He groaned in pain and elbowed the fish away, but it was on him again, tearing savagely, before he could take a full step.

The old bard drew a knife and drove it through the fish's head, through the gaping jaws and stilling the biting teeth. Though the tiny brain refused to accept the idea of death, it could no longer tear at him. It bumped him, rubbing its rough scales over his side, enveloped in the blood clouding the water.

More crimson suddenly spilled from the giant fish that had belched its offspring to the attack. Its jaws widened again, revealing Khlinat striking at the creature's upper mouth with both hand axes. Chunks of bloody flesh floated out of its mouth.

"Khlinat!" Pacys cried. "Get away from that thing, that I might aid you."

Spinning, the dwarf looked for Pacys and found him. Almost reluctantly, as if he had his terrible foe exactly where he wanted it, Khlinat swam from the creature's mouth in the ungainly dog paddle he'd managed over the last few days around Faenasuor.

Pacys dug his hand into the small meal pouch he'd taken from the sea elf city after deciding to spend the afternoon getting to know the sacedder better. One of the tidbits the elven chef had foisted upon him was octopus tentacle. It had been good, but the woman had been overgenerous with her portions, and there was some left.

The old bard pinched a portion off, said another command word, gestured, and pointed at the giant fish only twenty-five yards away. The octopus tentacle chunk disappeared from his hand, consumed by the spell.

Instantly, a mass of black tentacles formed under and around the giant fish. Over ten feet in length, the tentacles coiled in exploration, finding the giant fish almost at once. They ensnared and wrapped the fish, constricting around the creature and pulling it to within reach of still other tentacles.

One of the tentacles snaked out and wrapped around Khlinat's good leg. Reacting quickly, the dwarf swung both hand axes repeatedly, finally cutting through the rubbery flesh and severing the tentacle. He swam toward Pacys. Overcome by his wounds and the effort of casting the spells, the bard watched helplessly as the magic shield ceased its shimmering and went away. The remaining three fish swam for him eagerly, their jaws open wide in expectation.

Pacys covered up as best as he could, protecting his throat, face, and eyes with his arms. The fish went for the soft tissues of his stomach and under his arms. The old bard tried to knock them away with his elbows, but he'd run out of spells he could easily cast, and the staff didn't give him the room or time to use it that he needed to protect his face and throat.

In the next moment, Khlinat was there, roaring great dwarven curses and calling on his god. Pacys felt the shudder of the hand axes cleaving flesh through the connection he had with two of the fish that'd sunk their teeth into him.

The dwarven warrior threw his arms around Pacys protectively, holding the old bard up. "Speak to me, songsmith! Don't ye dare be dying on me shift. Not while ol' Khlinat's got his eyes peeled and made ye the promise I did!"

Pacys opened his eyes, fighting the exhaustion and pain that threatened to consume him. "I still live, my friend. You've not gone back on your promise yet."

"And I won't either," the dwarf declared fiercely. "Ye will see I'm a man of me word." Blood seeped from wounds on his body as well, mixing with the bard's in the salty water.

Taareen arrived foremost among the elves mounted on seahorses. He flung himself off the creature and swam toward Pacys.

"Taleweaver!" the sea elf cried, eeling toward him in the particular undulation the sea elves used for cutting rapidly through the water.

"I'm here," Pacys said.

Taareen surveyed him, taking in the damage done with a grimace.

"It's not as bad as it looks," Pacys said, though he felt that it was.

"We should have had guards over you," Taareen said. "We knew how important you were, and that the Taker would strike at you if he could. Now that he's found you here, we're going to have to move you somewhere else."

The other elves mounted on seahorses rode around the giant fish struggling against the black tentacles Pacys had summoned. They fired repeated crossbow bolts into the giant fish, taking care to stay well away from the reach of the tentacles.

"What makes you so sure the Taker has found me?" Pacys asked.

"The ascallion isn't a normal Shallows or Gloom predator," Taareen said, pointed at the creature that had attacked the bard. "Usually that monster is only found in the Twilight depths."

Pacys knew from his understanding of the stratification of Serôs' depths that the Twilight was the depth between three hundred to six hundred feet. "Maybe it found its way up here by mistake."

The black tentacles disappeared in the next moment as the magic sustaining them became exhausted. The ascallion tried only a feeble escape. More than a dozen quarrels stuck out of its face, and more were shot into it as the old bard watched.

Taareen shook his head. "There's no mistake. The Taker found a way to send that creature here, and we're lucky that you escaped with your life. By the Dolphin Prince, the things we would have lost had we lost you."

23

Laaqueel stood on the deck of the royal flier as it glided through the ocean, powered by sahuagin rowers. She'd never traveled on one of the craft for long distances before, and never at all until Iakhovas had become baron.

She felt proud as she watched the four hundred rowers working in rapid tandem, pulling the sahuagin craft through the underbelly of the ocean at a normal pace that more than doubled anything a surface vessel could do, even with rowers and a favorable wind. A two hundred forty-mile day was a normal average for the fliers. The other two hundred sahuagin that made up the rest of the crew rotated in, taking a shift at the oars as well while spelling another team.

Laaqueel scanned the deep blue of the ocean around them, looking back at all the fliers that followed. Though she couldn't see them all because even her eyes couldn't penetrate the gloom, she knew there were more than two dozen in all.

Satisfied that there was nothing she could do to make the journey more safe, she tried not to think about the possible dangers waiting at the Lake of Steam, where Iakhovas had said they were headed. With a final prayer offered up to Sekolah, she turned and walked the length of the flier to the cabin Iakhovas had ordered constructed in the stern as his personal quarters. None of the other fliers had such a thing.

She stood before the door and raised her hand to rap on the door.

Before she could touch it, Iakhovas's voice rumbled, "Enter, little malenti."

She let herself through the door, having the brief but certain feeling that it would not have opened at all if he hadn't allowed it.

Iakhovas occupied a chair constructed of whalebone that was

thronelike in its dimensions. Seaweed draped it, creating a cushion. Lucent algae hung in irregular strips across the ceiling. Shelves held some of the items his spies and troops had gathered since the attacks against the coastal lands had begun.

Laaqueel could sense the power that clung to most of them but didn't know what any of them were.

A crystal brain coral sat in the middle of the table, as tightly furrowed as its namesake. Though she was familiar with all the corals that formed along the Sword Coast, the malenti priestess had never seen anything like it. Motion slithered and twisted in the brain coral's depths.

Iakhovas sat back in the seat, his attention riveted on the crystal brain coral. Some of the glitter on the crystalline surface reflected through the patch covering his empty eye socket.

"What do you want?" he asked, sounding distracted.

"Only to see what it was that took up so much of your attention," she told him. "Our people need to see their king out among them more if they're going to follow him into areas not meant for We Who Eat."

Iakhovas fixed his single eye on her, but she felt something else—a cold and alien glare—settle on her from his missing eye.

"Not meant for We Who Eat?" He shook his head. "Little malenti, there are sahuagin in those waters, and we are on our way to set them free. Come. Let me show you." He gestured toward the brain coral.

Moving closer, Laaqueel stared into the brain coral's depths. Lights spun and glittered there. She knew it was an underwater location from the color around the figures revealed to her. No sky ever held that shade of blue, and no patch of land ever looked like the silt bed of the ocean floor.

One of the figures was an old surface dweller riding in front of a sea elf on a seahorse. They rode toward a city that had parts that looked as ancient as anything Laaqueel had ever seen. Even though she knew she shouldn't involve herself, the malenti priestess couldn't help asking, "Who's this?"

Iakhovas considered her question for a moment. "In all your studies about One Who Swims With Sekolah, did you ever hear the name Taleweaver?"

"No." She didn't remember reading the name, but something turned over in her memory.

"The sea elves have legends about me too," Iakhovas said. "All marine creatures that had a means of recording history when I was last in these waters had stories of me." He laughed, and the sound echoed within the cabin. "All of them are lies. Lies built on misconceptions and prejudiced hatred. Some of them I even started myself through various agents."

"This man is the Taleweaver?" Laaqueel asked.

"Yes," Iakhovas admitted.

Laaqueel scanned the man again, trying to find anything of

significance about him. "What part is he supposed to play in all this?"

"In the little drama the sea elves are trying to establish?" Iakhovas asked. "He is supposed to find their savior."

"Their savior?" Laaqueel felt a little uneasy talking of saviors. Her own beliefs were strong, and she knew that other religions, other gods, exercised considerable power across Faerûn as well.

"Someone who will stand against me and defeat me," Iakhovas explained. "You know how these legends are. Humans and elves all believe in these great romances of men and elves that are able to triumph against great and overwhelming odds."

"Is it true?"

"Their myth of the savior?"

For a moment, Laaqueel hesitated putting voice to her reply because she didn't know how Iakhovas would react. "Yes."

Iakhovas shook his head and laughed again. "Little malenti, I helped create the myth of their savior. There is no savior. Any human they find who believes he is this one is only a fool one heartbeat away from death."

"Why did you do that?"

Iakhovas raked a talon against the crystal brain coral, causing a tiny, high-pitched ring and said, "Because I could. Because it amused me. Most of all, because it served me. If they didn't have the legend of their hero, they wouldn't do the things I need them to that will insure my success."

"What do you need from them?"

He raked her with his harsh gaze. "You know more than any other at this time, little malenti. Don't get any greedier than I can tolerate."

Laaqueel felt a surge of anger thrill through her. Only days ago he'd helped her rebuild her faith, now he was pushing her at arm's length again.

"At ease," Iakhovas told her. "I only want you to remember your boundaries for your own benefit. Not mine."

Carefully, Laaqueel pushed water through her gills and dropped her eyes in deference to his authority. In many ways he was correct. She had her faith, and that would be enough. That strength would serve her as she served Sekolah.

"And to answer your question, the elves believe the Taleweaver will help them rebuild their histories and allow them some measure of a chance to defeat me once the savior is found. However, as the Taleweaver moves to the ripples they feed him, so does he serve the undercurrent I've had in play for thousands of years."

Listening carefully, Laaqueel filed the information away in her mind.

"There are, in the Sea of Fallen Stars—or Serôs as they call it there—beings who are unlike any of those elsewhere in all of Toril. They can prove to be somewhat difficult to deal with. And if I—if we—do not move cleverly while we are there, the Sea of Fallen Stars can become a trap. I have no intention of allowing that to happen."

Laaqueel tried to listen to any sign of fear or anxiety in his voice, but there was none. Only the confidence he always exuded sounded in it.

"Now come, little malenti, and let me show you the brethren to We Who Eat that I've spoken of. They are there, and they are kept behind a wall that is meant to keep them from taking over all of Serôs, as is their right."

"Sekolah would never allow such a thing," Laaqueel said. The idea of sahuagin penned up, being made to stay in one spot was unthinkable.

"The Great Shark will tolerate it no longer," Iakhovas said. "That's why you and I were brought together here and now. We will bring them their freedom, and the people of Serôs will know what it means to have doom suckled to their breasts like a vampiric child."

Curious and a little afraid to find what he was saying was true, Laaqueel peered into the crystal brain coral.

The image of the sea elf and the old surface dweller astride the seahorse floating down into the ancient city faded from the crystal's depths. In seconds it was replaced with the image of a sahuagin hunting party armed with nets and tridents.

"They are different," Laaqueel breathed, surprise filling her and driving away her own fears and doubts. Their anterior fins radiated from the sides of their heads as did the ones in the outer seas, but they flowed longer, reaching back along the skull until they merged with the dorsal fin at the top of their shoulder blades. Also, their coloring tended more toward blue shades than green. In fact some of those Laaqueel saw were teal and turquoise colored. A great number of them had speckles and stripes, like the markings they had as hatchlings.

Iakhovas touched the brain coral and the image changed again. When it cleared once more, it showed a massive wall lying under a stretch of ocean, only a short distance from the surface. The wall looked smooth, obviously manmade and constructed with care. She knew how massive it was from comparing the fish and the hated sea elves swimming nearby.

"We Who Eat of Serôs are held captive in a tiny portion of all that is available. The elves and surface dwellers call the area the Alamber Sea. None of the sahuagin trapped inside it have ever been allowed to leave that area in any great numbers. Only hunting groups in twos and threes have escaped through the sea elf guards that man the wall."

Laaqueel was horrified. "But if they're not allowed to migrate, how do they live? If they're not careful, they could over-hunt an area—"

"And die?"

Laaqueel said nothing. It was too ghastly to put into words. When sahuagin over-hunted a region—which was seldom—there were whispered stories of how they'd turned on each other, eating the young and the weak until the region repopulated and the hunting was good again.

It was one thing to eat another after death, or after a blood challenge, but preying on each other as a food source wasn't permitted except under the harshest of circumstances.

"Yes, little malenti. Those of your brethren have had to be careful over the years. The horrors you imagine, they've had to live through. That wall is over a hundred miles long, sixty feet tall, and a hundred feet thick. The sea elves and their allies have kept garrisons along it two miles apart to patrol. They call it the Sharksbane Wall."

Laaqueel burned the name into her memory, knowing it would forever live in infamy among the sahuagin.

"Until now, the elves and their allies have believed that wall to be impenetrable, but no more. I'm going to change that."

"You must tell the others," Laaqueel said, knowing the outrage would fire the blood of the warriors.

"I will. When the time is right. Now I am telling you."

"When we free them, what then? They will be hunted."

Iakhovas nodded. "Yes, they will. Probably more hunted than anything ever before in the history of Serôs. The sea elves and most of the other underwater races fear nothing more than We Who Eat."

"That is as it should be," Laaqueel stated proudly, "but they will have many enemies."

"Only the inadequate fail, little malenti."

Laaqueel looked at the long wall revealed in the crystal brain coral. "It is as you say, as Sekolah wills."

"Don't be so taken aback," Iakhovas suggested. "I've not come this far merely to free them from their prison that they might be killed. I've arranged allies for them. Other races in Serôs who would like to see the haughty sea elves brought to their knees. The elves have a city there—Myth Nantar."

Cold dread closed in around Laaqueel. She'd heard of the city, and of the dangers that lay there. "The lost city of the elves?"

"One of them," Iakhovas acknowledged. "Myth Nantar is special to the Serôsian sea elves. What have you heard of it?"

"That its elves were driven from it by wild magic they and their allies unleashed during one of their wars."

Iakhovas gazed into the brain coral. "When Myth Nantar began its fall and the magic ranged out of the sea elves' control, the sahuagin who are now trapped behind that wall raided there often. They helped drive out the last of the sea elves and claimed many treasures as their own."

"Still, they fell against the greater numbers of the sea elves and their allies."

"Yes, but then We Who Eat stood alone. It's not that way now. According to the prophecies of the sea elves, Myth Nantar will be returned to them in time to usher in a new period of greatness for their culture. They even believe they have a weapon there that will defeat me."

"Defeat you?" Laaqueel asked, trying to absorb everything she was being told. "We have no reason to journey to Myth Nantar."

"We will, little malenti. You'll see." Iakhovas gazed at her, resolutely and calm. "We can't free our people without taking the war we'll be waging to Myth Nantar. The sea elves must be broken again."

"What about the weapon they have?"

"That weapon . . ." Iakhovas mused. "I depend on that weapon of theirs, little malenti, and I depend on their faith to use it against me."

Laaqueel controlled her fears through discipline learned in her calling. Her lack of faith in Iakhovas himself was lessened as he revealed everything to her so calmly. He was undertaking the effort to free the other sahuagin in spite of all the odds against him. There could be no greater task that Sekolah would put before him.

Or her.

The realization of that made her proud. The Great Shark had tested her in the past, given her a birth defect that should have caused her death either as a hatchling or at any time growing up, and he'd given her all her massive doubts to overcome. Now that she knew what it was all for, she realized it had only been to make her stronger—strong enough to go to a land-locked sea and free those who'd never known freedom, to fulfill the future of her people while shattering the prophecies of the hated sea elves.

"Most Exalted One," Laaqueel said, assuming the open and defenseless stance of a sahuagin facing another in a position of authority, spreading her arms out to her sides to leave herself open to attack. She kept her eyes down out of deference to him. "In the past I've been doubtful and borderline rebellious toward you. I now pledge to you my complete allegiance and my promise never to work against you."

"And your doubts? Will those continue to plague you?"

"I swear by Sekolah the Uncaring that I will struggle with those," Laaqueel said. She stared at the wall, and her hatred grew anew for all the surface dwellers. This wall was blasphemy.

"That's good enough for me," Iakhovas said. "In return, I promise that through us the Great Shark will find a way to destroy that wall and free those who have been trapped there for so long." He touched the crystal brain coral.

Slowly, the image held inside dimmed, but Laaqueel knew she would never forget that hateful wall.

Iakhovas pushed himself up from his chair. "Come, Most Sacred One."

The malenti was surprised to hear him use the title with such respect. She straightened herself, accepting the responsibility of the office she'd been thrown into. Her doubts could no longer confine her, no longer take away her strength. She was a child of Sekolah, and the Great Shark had designed a grand current for her to ride. She would follow it with straight fins and without hesitation. Anyone who tried to stop her would die.

"Let us allow our warriors to see us in our coming glory that their hearts may be strengthened before we take them into the land of fire. We have many plans to make."

She followed him, certain with every stroke that she was going toward her destiny.

24

"Your lady doesn't approve of you working on this ship. I think she believes you should only be a passenger."

Jherek felt a flush of embarrassment when he realized Azla was standing beside him. The ship's captain wore tight black breeches with flaring cuffs over boots and a black leather vest with silver embroidery. Her scimitar and dirk hung at her side.

"She's not my lady," Jherek replied, "we're merely friends."

He glanced up at the stern castle where Sabyna stood and felt guilty. Sabyna definitely didn't like the idea of the young sailor working around the pirate vessel. However, Sabyna had been working with Azla's own ship's mage, an old man named Arthoris who'd spent his entire life on the Sea of Fallen Stars. It took both their efforts to keep *Black Champion* racing after Vurgrom's pirate ships. The small pirate fleet consisted of four vessels, headed up by *Maelstrom*, Vurgrom's personal ship. So far, none of the pirate vessels had seemed to spot them. *Black Champion* trailed out of sight, locked onto its prey by a spell Arthoris had cast.

Azla crossed her arms over her breasts and glanced up in irritation at Sabyna. "Aye, I hear you," she said, "but that's not the understanding I get when I look at her. Either I'm wrong or you're mistaken." She turned her dark gaze back on him. "Would you care to put a wager on which likelihood is more correct?"

Jherek flushed again. "No, lady."

He tried to return his attention to the sail he was mending. The cloth was in fairly good shape, showing some definite time put to hard use at sea, but it was serviceable. At least, it would be after all the great rents were repaired.

"No, *Cap'n*," Azla corrected without rancor but with definite steel in her voice.

"No, Captain," Jherek said. He drew more of the thick thread for his needle, measured off a length, then knotted the end of the twin strands. He returned his attention to his sewing.

"I'll tell you now," Azla said, dropping a hand to her scimitar, "I've never suffered the presence of anyone on my ship who made me feel ill at ease."

"She doesn't mean anything by it." Jherek fumbled for words, desperately seeking some answer to the problem the two women had presented him. Over the past few days, both women had sought him out and talked to him about the other. When he'd asked Glawinn for advice, the paladin had only smiled at him and lifted his sword to begin Jherek's training anew. The young sailor had been thankful for the swordplay. At least for a time it had taken his thoughts from the friction between the two women, even if it left him bone-tired afterward.

"I don't see how that could be true," Azla snapped. "Her disapproval of me isn't unintentional."

Jherek blew out a tight breath, wondering if he was about to make matters worse. "It isn't you she disapproves of, Captain. It's pirates in general. Her brother was killed by one."

Azla returned his gaze.

"Sabyna was just a child when it happened," Jherek explained. "She saw the whole thing. She'll never forget that."

Surprisingly, Azla's face softened. She looked away from Jherek and back up at the young woman standing in *Black Champion*'s stern. "Aye, then she'll never forget or forgive."

"No," Jherek said, knowing it was true. "I don't think she will."

Azla was quiet for a moment, alone with thoughts that captured all of her attention. She shook her head slightly and grimaced. "Who was the pirate?"

Jherek focused on mending the sail again. "A man named Falkane. He's called Bloody Falkane and the Salt Wolf."

"I've not heard of him," Azla said.

"Falkane's well known along the Sword Coast." Jherek took up another stitch, pulling the sailcloth neatly together. The spacing was important if the sail was to fit correctly again.

"He's still alive?"

"Aye." Jherek remembered seeing *Bunyip* in Baldur's Gate, and the eerie wail echoed again in his mind. He shivered in spite of the balmy heat that lay over the Sea of Fallen Stars.

"That must be a hard burden to carry," Azla commented, then called out briefly to her crew, ordering sails trimmed.

"Anything associated with Falkane is a hard burden."

Jherek tried not to let too much bitterness sound in his voice, but knew he failed. He hadn't even intended to speak his thoughts, but they'd been too strong to remain mute. Thankfully Azla seemed so busy with her crew for the moment that she didn't notice. He took out more of the thick thread.

"You've got a steady hand with that needle," Azla told him a moment later.

"Thank you." Jherek took up another stitch, gathering the material. *Black Champion*'s speed increased and she slid across a large swell that lifted her up and set her back down quickly enough to roll the young sailor's stomach slightly.

"You're a sailor then?" she asked him. "Not like your paladin friend?"

"Aye. Nearly all I've known is the sea."

"And you like it here?"

"More than any other place I've been."

Her line of questioning made Jherek believe that she hadn't always known the sea. Yet, with the grace and certainty she displayed on the deck, he couldn't imagine her not in command of a ship. As Finaren often declared, ships' captains were born and made, hammered into shape by events rather than through book learning.

Azla nodded and said, "But you're young. There are probably few places you've actually been."

Jherek tied off another stitch as he gave consideration to what she'd said. "I've been up and down the Sword Coast a number of times. I've been to Waterdeep, Baldur's Gate, Athkatla, and a number of cities to the north. I've seen my share of things."

"And now you're here in the Sea of Fallen Stars to see yet more."

"As the gods will it."

An icy chill touched Jherek again as he remembered the great voice that had haunted him upon occasion since he was a child.

"Personally," Azla informed him in a flat tone, "I don't believe the gods take an interest in anyone."

Jherek shrugged, then touched the praying hands of Ilmater hanging on the thong around his neck. "I have my beliefs."

"Do you find your god shading the luck and opportunities you have in your favor?"

Jherek considered the question gravely. Religious matters were important and he wanted to answer the question most correctly. "At times I have thought so."

"But you don't know?"

"No."

"Then how can you profess to believe?"

"Because believing is different than knowing," Jherek answered. "Once I know, how can I believe? Knowledge isn't faith."

Azla regarded him in silence. "You've been talking to soothsayers far too long."

Jherek shrugged, taking no offense. "Captain, I learned a long time ago that each man has to build within himself the things he'll need to get through life. Part of that is a way of thinking, certain skills that are meant to put food on the table and a roof over his head, other skills that keep him free from the tyranny of other men. Belief has to be in there as well, to shape a man's destiny and lead him forward."

"And what if that destiny is a bent or broken one?" Azla asked. "Where does belief fit in then?"

The question lit a new fire under all the doubts that Jherek tried to keep buried within him. He hesitated for a moment, then gave her the answer Malorrie had always given him. "A man's belief helps him through, helps him remain himself in spite of the trials around him."

"What about you?" she asked him. "Is your belief helping you so far?"

"Aye." Jherek's answer was given with far less confidence than he would have liked to admit.

"Good, then maybe it'll be enough for us all."

25

Laaqueel stood on *Tarjana*'s deck and looked out at the Lake of Steam. Thick, heated gray mist hung over the lake and clouded the surrounding lands with perpetual fog. Ahead of them in the distance, she could barely see Arnrock Island, which was the major source of all the volcanic activity in the area. Gray-white smoke with searing orange embers belched continuously into the air, creating the black cinders that swirled endlessly over the lake and filled the water with dark speckles.

She wrapped her arms around herself, already feeling her skin drying out from exposure to the steam. The other sahuagin stayed underwater on the mantas. Even there, the temperatures were hot enough to be uncomfortable and would tend to encourage parasitic growth inside gill tissue. For some of the spells Iakhovas had to do in order to open the gate for them that would take them to Serôs, he needed to be out of the water.

He'd also needed the things he had stored aboard the mudship. He'd summoned it after they'd entered the lake, praising it to the sahuagin as an item taken in battle from Baldur's Gate.

Laaqueel prayed constantly, clinging to her belief so much easier now that she'd discovered why Iakhovas had come among them. Freeing the captive sahuagin had preyed upon her mind since he'd told her about them, allowing her to focus on something more than her own doubts.

"Priestess."

Laaqueel turned, hearing unaccustomed fatigue in Iakhovas's voice. "Yes, Most Exalted One."

He walked out onto the deck from the cabin where he'd been

working. "It's done. All the preparations have been made. The gate will open as soon as Vurgrom has his piece in place in the Alamber Sea."

"Is there anything I can do, Most Exalted One?" Looking at him, Laaqueel wished she could take away some of the tiredness that clung to him. He'd worked hard for the last week, never stopping even to sleep.

"No, but thank you for your kindness, priestess. Now all that may be done is the waiting."

Despite the low burning that covered her skin, she went to stand beside him.

"He's dropping his sails," Jherek said, staring through the telescope he held.

He stood on *Black Champion*'s foredeck, the bright blue-green of the Alamber Sea spreading out around him. Vurgrom's flagship, *Maelstrom*, dropped anchor after another few moments, flanked by the three smaller craft floating around it. They all flew the skull and crossbones on a field of black. In the distance behind the pirates, the volcanic island that was called the Ship of the Gods spewed vile smoke into the air.

"That's foolish," Azla snapped, looking irritated. "Sitting out here like this, he'd be a target for any sahuagin who chose to attack. This is the Alamber Sea, and it literally crawls with them."

She scanned the sea in all directions, as if expecting some proof of her statement. The farther Vurgrom had led them from Westgate, the wilder their speculations had gotten about where he was going and why. They tried guessing at possible allies the pirate had in the coastal nations around the Alamber Sea. Finally they'd had to give up and admit defeat. None of the nations Azla could name would have aligned themselves with the sahuagin.

"What now?" he asked.

The half-elf shook her head. "I don't know." She turned and gave the order for her own crew to strike *Black Champion*'s sails. "I'm not going to get close enough that they can overtake us before we get the wind behind our sails again. All we have over Vurgrom's ships is speed."

Glancing back amidships, the young sailor saw Sabyna and Glawinn standing close together and talking. A pang went through his heart as he thought about how little he and the ship's mage had seen each other during the trip out from Westgate. He'd spent every morning and every evening practicing swordcraft with Glawinn. The paladin seemed to be made of iron.

His absence from Sabyna, Jherek knew, was because he took an active part in the care and maintenance of *Black Champion*. The ship's mage chose not to do anything other than give aid in summoning the winds that kept them at *Maelstrom*'s heels. The young sailor hadn't known how hard the trip was going to be on Sabyna.

"There he is," Azla said.

Jherek spotted the big pirate captain walking across *Maelstrom*'s deck. Even at this distance, the young sailor could see the glint of gold in Vurgrom's hand. The pirate captain threw the object out to sea. It twinkled in the air and vanished below the surface. Jherek had no idea what the thing was, but anxiety spread across his shoulders and shot up the back of his neck.

It's time.

Laaqueel glanced up at Iakhovas, watching as he rubbed the token that gave him command over *Tarjana* between his fingers.

Iakhovas walked back to the great galley's steering section and took the wheel. Under his command, the mudship dived, gliding beneath the heated waters. Even as she felt the too-hot caress of the currents closing over her, Laaqueel was grateful for them, too. They soaked tissues that had gotten too dry from exposure to the heat.

With Iakhovas at the helm, *Tarjana* sped to the front of the sahuagin armada. The fliers rested on the bottom of the lake amid the kelp fronds. When they saw the mudship gliding forward, powered by the rowers that Iakhovas had ordered aboard, the fliers lifted from the lake floor and started after it, having no problem matching the slower craft's speed.

Laaqueel peered through the murky lake depths, uncertain how Iakhovas had known it was time to start the voyage. She stood beside him, holding onto the nearby railing. Iakhovas guided the craft to within feet of the irregular bottom with more skill than she'd known him to have. As she watched his hands upon the wheel, she noticed that some of the tattooed scars inscribed on his forearms and chest glowed, showing through his clothing.

"Relax, priestess. No one else can see what you can see. You of all people see me most clearly."

They sped toward the base of Arnrock Island. Thinking perhaps a cave somehow existed in the thick column of rock, Laaqueel peered more closely, but only craggy rock remained in view. Even if there had been a cave, she couldn't imagine it being anything but superheated.

Still, Iakhovas maintained his course. The rowers aboard *Tarjana* hesitated. The malenti priestess felt the decrease in speed.

"They cannot stop," Iakhovas commanded. "We need the speed if we're to get through the gate in time for all the others to follow."

"I will attend to it," Laaqueel promised.

Staying low, she hooked her toe claws into the deck as she made her way down the railing and to the main hold opening into the rowing compartments. She went down the ladder, stepping out of the current.

One hundred and forty sahuagin manned the oars, and all of them looked up at her expectantly, only going through the motions of rowing instead of pulling with all their strength. Laaqueel glared at the sahuagin on the timing drum sitting on a deck up above the rowers and said, "You've slowed the beat."

"Most Sacred One," the sahuagin said, "I've been told we're speeding for the volcano itself."

"You're questioning the will of Sekolah?" Laaqueel's eyes flashed with anger. Gathering her power around her, she touched the Great Shark symbol she wore between her breasts and prayed quickly. She threw out her hand.

Bones snapped as a paroxysm seized the drum beater. Within a twenty-foot cube around him, the pressure in the water had suddenly increased to what it would be two thousand feet down. Without having a chance to acclimate, the sahuagin's air bladder exploded in his chest, followed quickly by the other soft tissue areas including the eyes and inner organs. The drum he'd been beating also caved in. Blood pooled up and spread out above the crumpled sahuagin. His corpse floated away from the deck and rose to the ceiling above the rowers.

Priestess, Iakhovas said into her mind.

"Row!" Laaqueel ordered. She struck the side of the ship with her trident's hilt, creating a bonging noise. She repeated the effort, setting the cadence for the rowers. "Fear is not for We Who Eat! Succeed or fail! Live or die! Row!"

The sea devils bent to the oars, pulling them lustily, and Laaqueel felt the difference at once. She pointed at another of the sahuagin in the hold who'd been responsible for spelling those rowers who needed it. "You are the new beater. By Sekolah's unkind smile, don't make me find another to replace you."

"No, Most Sacred One. We shall row for the Great Shark, and for you. We shall not fail." The man took up his trident and started beating it against the wall, keeping up the rapid cadence the malenti priestess had started.

Satisfied, Laaqueel climbed the steps back to the main deck.

"Now, priestess," Iakhovas said. "Now it begins!"

She looked forward and saw the trunk of Arnrock Island filling the view before the prow. They were too close now, going too fast to avoid cracking up on the rocks and coral. Only a small twinge of fear twisted through Laaqueel's stomach, but she quickly put her doubt away. The quest they were on was real. Even Sekolah the Uncaring would want his chosen children free as he'd first freed them so long ago.

"There, Laaqueel! Do you see it?" Iakhovas stood at the wheel, the tattoos all over his body lighted by lambent green fires.

A shimmering took place in front of *Tarjana* just as her prow reached out for the rock. A portal opened in the rock, tall enough and wide enough for the fliers that trailed after them.

"Hold on!" Iakhovas warned. "With all your might, hold on or you'll be forever lost and even I won't be able to protect you!"

Still gaining speed, *Tarjana* flew into the portal.

"They've raised their sails again," Jherek said as he watched the crews aboard *Maelstrom* and the other pirate vessels work their rigging with all due speed.

The sailcloth spread along the yardarms, then belled out, greedily catching the wind. Azla gave the order for her own crew to run the sails up. Rigging whined and creaked overhead as they hurried to follow her orders.

"They're doing something else, too," she said. "Can you make out what it is?"

Jherek strained to see through the spyglass, riding out the rise and fall of *Black Champion*'s deck. He spotted the coarse leather tarps the crew was spreading out across the decks.

"Tarps?" Azla repeated, pushing herself to the railing and hanging onto the rigging above. "What in the Nine Hells would they do that for?"

"Look!" Sabyna called from below. She pointed. "Something's happening to the volcano."

Jherek turned his attention to the smoldering tower of rock behind *Maelstrom*. Thicker and darker smoke, filled with fiery debris that could be seen even at the distance they were at, belched from the Ship of the Gods.

"It's going to blow," Azla stated quietly, and Jherek didn't doubt that for a moment.

⇒⊢———⊣⇐

T'Kalah, royal guard of King Kromes who ruled Aleaxtis, the kingdom of We Who Eat beneath the Alamber Sea, stalked his quarry with a patience born of relish for the kill.

He stood just over nine feet in height and was built broad and strong, a warrior who was feared by his own people as well as the surface dwellers. His scales held a deep emerald green so dark it was almost black. Legend said that was once the color of all sahuagin before they'd been trapped in the Alamber Sea and put in such close proximity to the sea elves of Serôs. Those same sea elves were reputed to have been different colors in ages past, but they had passed on their skin changes through the malenti and their proximity to the warriors of Aleaxtis.

Despite his size, T'Kalah slid quietly through the kelp lining the ledges where he'd spotted the sea elf only moments before. He'd been quietly occupying a cave in the area that overlooked Vahaxtyl, the sahuagin capital of Aleaxtis, dreaming of the day when he would be king.

Of course, that wasn't going to happen unless opportunity manifested itself. Still, it was a good ambition, and one that he'd pursued. After all, he'd waited and watched, made blood challenges as they became possible, and killed his way into a position as captain of the royal guard of King Kromes.

Success or failure had been the driving force in his life, the thing that had driven him to live in the hatcheries when so many of his brothers and sisters had been out to eat him. Yet sitting in the cave, thinking of that day, had ignited the black rage that often consumed him because he didn't think of patience as a virtue.

The amputated stub of his lower left arm served to remind him that patience was sometimes best given some degree of heed. But then, he still had three more arms. He'd been marked from birth as a four-arm to follow stronger currents than most of his people could fin. Since losing the arm, he'd worked to make the other three even stronger.

Thank Sekolah's uncaring grace that the sea elf had wandered into the area to provide him some distraction. T'Kalah undulated through the water, gliding through the kelp. From the changes in pressure along his lateral lines, he knew exactly where the sea elf was. The sahuagin royal guard closed the distance, knowing from the lack of movement that the elf had come to a stop. Whether because he'd seen T'Kalah or just wanted to observe the city wasn't clear.

T'Kalah parted the kelp with two of his hands while holding a trident in his third. He spotted the sea elf ahead of him, hunkered down behind a ridge of rock and sparse growths of gold-and-brown striped tiger coral. He was blue all over, with only a few white patches. T'Kalah guessed that the elf was there trying for one of the shipwrecks in the area that had been left by his people.

The sea elves often tried to raid the shipwrecks in the area controlled by We Who Eat. King Kromes had even taken to seeking out magic items himself, identified by the priestesses, and hoarded them as further temptation to the sea elves and surface dwellers alike. T'Kalah knew for certain that the number of magic items stored at the palace was considerable.

Spreading his fingers and toes so the webbing would better catch the water, T'Kalah swam for the sea elf.

Something must have given away his approach because the elf tried to turn and bring up a bone knife. "Black Claws!" the elf said, calling the big warrior by the name the surface world knew him by.

T'Kalah showed the elf no mercy, placing the trident before him and shoving it into the sea elf's chest. It was a quicker death than T'Kalah had intended. He would have preferred to make the elf beg for a time, taste the salt of his tears mixed in with the ocean before he'd ever tasted his victim's blood. Still, he held the elf at the end of the trident and shook him viciously until his death was apparent.

Climbing to the top of the rocks overlooking Vahaxtyl, T'Kalah shoved the end of the trident into a crack so that it supported the elf's corpse. He sat on a rock beside the dead man, popped his claws, and cut chunks from his unexpected feast.

T'Kalah shoved the gobbets of flesh into his mouth and swallowed them nearly whole. The blood scent in the water would draw other predators soon. Though the sharks knew better than to bother him, it was the little fish with all their darting around that annoyed him most. No matter how quickly he tried to eat a meal, they were always there scrounging for whatever they could get. He ate the soft parts first, knowing the little fish would go for those first as well.

His lateral lines picked up the changes in pressure even though he didn't immediately recognize what it was. He did know it came from the direction of Vahaxtyl.

The city was built on a shelf of rock it shared with the volcano the surface dwellers called the Ship of the Gods. His people called it Clii-taan, Cursed Fire. Besides the changes in pressure, his delicate olfactory senses also picked up the stench of sulfur. Scents spread quickly in the water much as sound did. As he watched, a red glow seemed to center midway up the Ship of the Gods. It grew rapidly, turning redder.

T'Kalah watched, mesmerized, wondering if Sekolah had started a new current—one that would change his life.

Laaqueel lost her footing when *Tarjana's* prow slammed into the left side of the opening at the bottom of the Lake of Steam. Though the ship itself wasn't hurt by the collision, she was lifted from the deck and tossed into the current that hurled her toward the stern.

All around her, filling the tunnel the mudship plunged through, molten lava glowed orange-yellow. The heat crisped fish that had been unlucky enough to be sucked in after them. Her senses were moving so quickly that even while she was turning in the vicious current herself she could see the flesh peeling back from the fish while they still lived, baring the skeletons beneath.

Just as she thought she was lost forever and about to share a similar fate as the fish, a strong grip wrapped around her left ankle.

"I've got you, my priestess." Straining, the effort pulling horribly on Laaqueel's ligaments and muscles, Iakhovas drew her beside him. He kept her curled protectively in his arms when he returned her to the deck. "Are you well?"

Overly aware of Iakhovas's body next to hers and its effects on hers, Laaqueel said, "Yes. Thank you." She didn't try to push away from him, letting him shelter her in his embrace.

Iakhovas remained standing, facing the wild current and staring into the heart of the liquid fire tunnel they followed. "We're traveling through the lines of volcanic fault. It was the fastest and truest way to gate into Serôs. When we reach the end of this tunnel, we'll be in the Alamber Sea."

Glancing over his shoulder, Laaqueel saw the line of fliers speeding after them. The sahuagin aboard them were shielding their eyes from the bright magma swirling around them.

"Will this gate remain open long enough for all of them to get through?" she asked. She'd never before heard of the mode of travel they were using now.

"Probably."

Laaqueel thought of what it would be like to be suddenly boiled alive when the lava closed in.

'If that should happen," Iakhovas told her, "be assured that it will be over before they know it. There are some risks that we must take, and some losses that we must endure."

"To become stronger," Laaqueel said, "as Sekolah has so designed."

"Yes."

Looking ahead again, Laaqueel kept herself strong in her faith, not thinking about the potential for failure, but for the promise of success. At the other end of the tunnel, made bright by the whirling lava walls, she saw the dead end. A roiling mass of lava and hard rock blocked the way.

"Isn't it supposed to be open?" she asked.

"Yes." Iakhovas's tattoos glowed deeper green, looking like they were burning into his flesh. "It will be."

Tarjana bore down on the blockage and Iakhovas kept his hand steady on the wheel. Laaqueel felt the rush of heat when the ship collided with the end of the gate.

26

Pacys the Bard sat in the small sea elf tavern down in the heart of Telvanlu and almost felt at home. The sea elves, he'd found, were a quieter lot than he was used to, but as it turned out they appreciated his music.

The bar was like a lot he'd played in on the surface world and the crowd wasn't that much different, but none of the sounds were the same. Voices echoed through the water much more easily so the listeners had to be more polite, and there was no shuffling sound of feet across a sawdust-covered floor. After having been in the water for so long he was getting accustomed to feeling the currents change around him, and how someone passing nearby could affect them.

He sat, at the owner's invitation, at the end of the bar. The bartender passed out drinks packaged in fish bladders treated so they were clear enough to see the contents. A patron drank from the bladder by squeezing the bottom and opening the seal at the top. It had taken some getting used to when he'd first arrived in Faenasuor, but now the bard drank quite easily. Learning not to lick his lips afterward still took concentration, though.

Telvanlu was the capital of Naramyr, the sea elven lands in the Lake of Dragons in Serôs, and was located two hundred feet down and forty miles southwest of Suzail. The city was moderately sized as elven dwellings went, but the architecture was definitely inspired by the sea.

Clamshell-like buildings hugged the silt, deliberately low to avoid the shipping that took place constantly between the coastal cities overhead. The architecture hadn't been all that agreeable to the elves. Some of them wanted taller buildings so they wouldn't have to be spread out. Many of them didn't like the fact that they had to live more or less two-dimensionally as the surface dwellers did. The trade with the surface dwellers was good, so though a lot of complaining was done, none of the buildings went any taller.

One of the things that surprised Pacys most had been the laws regarding weapons and armor. None were allowed in the elven city, and it was strictly enforced. Aravae Daudil, Coronal of Telvanlu, made sure her guards carried out her orders to the letter.

Pacys tapped the crystals of the saceddar, picking out the notes for "Lady Who Shed Golden Tears," an old elven song about the flight from Cormanthyr after the fall of Myth Drannor. Despite whatever cultural differences now separated the surface elves from their aquatic cousins, the song found favorable response among the listeners by tying into their common history.

As the last note faded away, passing through the open windows cut into the coral walls, they hooted their appreciation. Clapping took up too much energy to fight the water and stirred up currents that moved wildly within a contained area.

"Another song, Taleweaver," someone called from one of the tables.

"Nay," the bartender interrupted. He was pale and thin, with only a scattering of blue speckles across his body. His silver-white hair floated around his face, kept back by a band chipped from pink quartz. "The man has sung long and strong, and he's entertained you layabouts for free long past time enough. Now I'm going to stand him to a drink that he may rest his voice. What will you have, Taleweaver?"

"An ale, my kind friend," Pacys answered, stripping the saceddar from his body. "Nothing heavy, for I'll not be early to bed tonight."

Since Taareen had accompanied Khlinat and him there after leaving Faenasuor, the old bard had stayed busy with Telvanlu's lore-keepers, learning as many of their legends of the Taker as he could. He was only taking a short break now to rest his mind and gain some perspective on what he'd learned.

He took the ale bladder to a back table where Khlinat had camped out. From where he sat, the dwarf had a full view of the tavern and the street outside. The streets, Pacys had discovered, were there primarily for the surface dwelling traders that visited and didn't feel comfortable with a three-dimensional world.

"Ye sang well," Khlinat greeted. "Hard to see any of 'em crying in this watery deep, but ye could see the painful joy in their faces as ye called up the ghost of Cormanthyr past."

"It's a favored song," Pacys said.

"To yer health," Khlinat said, hoisting his ale bladder.

Pacys unsealed his own ale bladder, fixed his lips over the opening, blew the remnants of salt water from his mouth, and squeezed. The ale tasted bitter and strong, a Cormyrean brew that he was readily familiar with. Evidently the balance of trade included beverages.

He swallowed, then nearly choked as a convulsion tightened his body.

Harsh music created a cacophony of strident songs in his mind, making his head feel like it was about to split open. The refrain remained steady in his mind, hammering as viciously as a dwarven blacksmith marking out the preliminary shaping on a hard piece of metal. The song gave form to the smell of rankest sulfur and savage heat.

"Pacys?" Khlinat asked worriedly.

Understanding what the song meant, the old bard looked at his friend and said, "He's here, Khlinat. The Taker has arrived in the Sea of Fallen Stars!"

The wind kicked into *Black Champion*'s sails, driving the caravel into motion. Her prow slammed into the white-capped waves, burying down, then moving to rise again over the next trough.

Jherek clung to the rigging in frustration, unable to bring the spyglass into use when the ship was fighting the ocean so much. At his side, Azla continued to yell orders, putting up some sails and trimming others.

Vurgrom and *Maelstrom,* accompanied by the other pirate vessels, sailed at them. Jherek was beginning to believe that the pirates weren't chasing after them so much as they were fleeing something else. The tarps pulled tight across their decks still intrigued him.

Behind them, the Ship of the Gods increased the volume of smoke pouring out of the volcano. Thunder rent the air, slamming hammer-like blows that took away all other sounds. The concussions reached Jherek, rocking him in the rigging.

In the next instant, the volcano spat flames and burning rock into the air. They spread like fireworks, coloring the blue sky and blue-green water with reds and yellows. The sky faded, quickly lost in the thick black smoke that streamed from the volcano. Around the island where it projected above the waterline, the ocean boiled.

Even as another explosion rocked the area, throwing more burning debris skyward, the first of it started descending. Huge chunks of flaming rock slammed against the ocean, sending up twisting spirals of water. Other rocks hammered against *Black Champion*'s deck, shattering and skittering crazily when they didn't penetrate. More of the barrage knocked holes in the deck.

The falling rock smashed through the sails and set them afire in places. Two men went down, battered by the rock and sprawling out dead or unconscious.

Sabyna went to the aid of one sailor, grabbing him by the arm and dragging him to the relative safety provided by the prow castle. Glawinn joined her, holding his shield up over them and protecting her and the sailor. A large rock rolling in yellow flames and trailing smoke struck the shield but the paladin's strength held and it flew away in fragments.

Black Champion wallowed through another trough, but her gait wasn't as sure. She turned crossways, leaning hard over to port. She stuttered as she went over, loose and not working with the pull of the wind powering her.

Jherek glanced back at the wheel. The pilot lay stretched out on the deck, blood staining the wood around him and a gaping hole in his chest. Without a steady hand at the wheel, the young sailor knew *Black Champion* would be at the mercy of the cruel sea stirred by the raging volcano. He considered dropping to the deck and trying to get back to the wheel but he knew he'd never get there in time.

While he hung in the upper rigging, one of the large flaming boulders rolled into view without warning. He heard the sizzling heat of the boulder as it passed ponderously by.

Tumbling end over end, the boulder slammed into the mainmast only three or four feet up from the deck. The treated wood, hardened by processing and spells, shrieked as it exploded from the impact. The boulder sunk into the deck, burying itself in the wood and smoldering.

Sheared in two, the mast fell heavily to starboard, tangling itself in the suddenly slack lines of the rigging. Jherek fell with the slack, his fingers still hooked in the rigging. He hung on, watching the deck come up, knowing if he fell all the way and hit he'd be gravely injured if not killed outright. Even trying to angle for the sea beyond the sides of *Black Champion* would only leave him either in the water or at the mercy of Vurgrom's cutthroat pack.

When he hit the end of the slack hard enough to almost wrench his shoulders from their sockets, the young sailor said a brief prayer of thanks that he'd had the strength to hold on. He got his bearings quickly and started climbing through the rigging again, aiming for another section as the mainmast continued to roll around, threatening the other sails and rigging. He already felt *Black Champion* slowing, losing speed as readily as she lost her sails.

"Cut away!" Azla ordered from below.

Glancing down, his fingers cramped from the agony of keeping his hold and from the drop, Jherek saw the ship's crew lurch across the deck to follow their captain's command. Knives glinted in their fists as they sawed at the ropes holding the rigging. A small group of men lifted the broken end of the mast and guided it toward the port side of the ship, intending to slip it over the side.

The rigging Jherek had hold of alternately tightened and loosened as the crew cut the mast away. He kept climbing, knowing Azla wouldn't order them to stop while he got clear. Every heartbeat the broken mast stayed tangled up with the rest of the sails and rigging put *Black Champion* at risk.

He knew there wasn't enough time to go down, and the nearest rigging was still too far away to make the jump possible. Even as he realized he was running out of options, he spotted one of the smaller pirate ships racing up on them from starboard.

" 'Ware the ship!" Jherek called out in warning, listening as *Black Champion*'s surviving crew rapidly took up the cry.

But the warning came too late. Pirate bowmen let fly and arrows found targets among Azla's crew. The second volley that raked the deck had fire arrows among them that started blazes in a handful of areas in the deck and in the surviving sails.

Jherek positioned himself at the edge of the sagging rigging, feeling *Black Champion* foundering beneath him. The ship turned sideways, floating loosely with no hand at the wheel. In the next instant, the ship heeled over the top of a deep trough stirred up by the exploding volcano. Her masts dipped, raking the tips through the advancing wave curling over to replace the trough.

Water swamped *Black Champion*'s deck, washing away at least two screaming sailors. Jherek felt certain the ship was going to disappear beneath the waves as well.

T'Kalah stood on the ridge overlooking Vahaxtyl and stared in disbelief as heat washed over him. Red-hot lava burst from the Ship of the Gods to consume the city where he'd been born, fought, and lived. It flowed, a heavier liquid than the sea around it, and settled over the city. The lava was tens of feet thick, perhaps even hundreds.

The extrusion kept coming, piling deeper. As the chill of the sea settled into the lava, it cooled and turned solid, becoming gray. Still more flowed from the broken mouth.

Currents whipped across the seabed, ripping kelp free of the silt and sending it rushing away. T'Kalah stood against it, battered unmercifully, seeing if it meant to take his life as well. He embraced it, knowing if it didn't kill him it would only make him stronger.

27

Miraculously, *Black Champion* caught a gust of wind that righted her long enough to pull out of the downward plunge the caravel had taken in front of an approaching wall of water. Jherek held onto the rigging as the wave overtook the ship. The caravel shuddered when the wave slammed into her, twisting violently. Men's screams echoed over the crashing thunder of the impact. Azla snarled orders, trying desperately to rally her crew to meet the challenge of the pirate vessel that stalked them so easily now that *Black Champion* had lost over a third of her sails.

A ragged line formed along the starboard side. Only three men had bows and they struggled to bring their weapons to bear while trying to hold onto the railing as well. A curling wave peaked and raked brine fingers over them, tearing one of the bowmen from his feet even as he loosed a shaft. The cascade of water shoved the sailor across the deck and hammered him up against the stern castle then carried him on. Only Glawinn's quick grab and strength prevented the man from being washed overboard.

The salt spray from the waves crashing into *Black Champion* drenched Jherek and burned his eyes. The rough rope of the rigging sawed into his fingers and felt slick and unsure at the same time as it sagged.

Thankfully, the high waves smashed against the pirate vessel as well, stripping control from her for a time. Azla continued calling orders as she took up her own bow. She put a shaft to the string and threw a leg over the railing, threading it into the railing with her foot braced to hold her steady. *Black Champion* rode high on the next wave, towering over her pursuer. In that time, the half-elf sea captain put two shafts through pirates.

Black Champion dropped again, fast enough to trigger a feeling of vertigo in Jherek's stomach. The young sailor turned his attention back to the stern deck and started clambering through the rigging.

Below, Sabyna made her way across the slick and treacherous rise and fall of the deck toward the stern as well. Skeins slid across the wooden planks near her, darting out to smother flaming arrows that stood upright from the deck. With the sea spray whipping over the railing, Jherek doubted that any fire would take hold above decks, but the threat remained to the belowdecks. *Black Champion* would remain wet outside, but her belly could turn into a firepit.

The caravel plunged downward again, riding out the back side of the fast-moving wave and dropping into the trough it left. Without warning, the pirate ship slid down the wave as well, careening down the slanted water.

" 'Ware the ship!" a man bellowed. " 'Ware the ship!"

Jherek, locked into the rigging, watched helplessly as the pirate ship sped on a collision course with the caravel. "Sabyna!" he yelled, not knowing if his voice would carry through the violent sea lashing around them.

The ship's mage whipped her head around. Spotting the approaching vessel, she sprinted toward the rear mast and locked her arms around tightly. Her raggamoffyn familiar blew apart into hundreds of pieces, then flew after her. When the creature reached her, the whirling pieces reformed and wrapped around her, helping secure her to the mast.

The pirate vessel slammed into *Black Champion*, its prow riding hard against the starboard side and sending Azla's crew scurrying for cover. Wood splintered and Jherek prayed that it was the other ship or the railing and not anything below the waterline.

The shudder of impact rippled through the caravel, knocking it loose from the death grip the sea had on it for a moment. Choosing the moment of opportunity or perhaps torn free from their own ship, a handful of pirates leaped aboard *Black Champion*. Even as the pirate ship slid away and the caravel rose from beneath the other vessel's weight, a clash of swords surged up from the deck as well. A crashing wave splashed over the combatants before they barely had time to cross blades. They spun away, tumbling head over heels, grabbing onto whatever they could.

Before any of them could get to their feet, another onslaught of fiery rocks cannonaded against the decks with hollow, thunderous booms and pelted the ocean around them. White-capped water spiraled up from the impact areas.

Black Champion turned sideways in the following trough, completely out of control. Jherek knew the ship was a wreck waiting for the brine to drink her down. He turned in the rigging and waited while the ship righted herself again. Timing the slow roll back to starboard, he threw himself out toward the rear mast, free of the rigging in an all-or-nothing gambit.

Jherek slammed against the taut sail covering the rear mast's mid-section. He skidded down almost immediately and narrowly missed a section of sailcloth on fire from one of the rocks. He pushed off again and hooked his fingers in the support rigging above the steering section. Rigging strands parted and sagged as more rock sliced through the ropes.

As *Black Champion* briefly rose again, the young sailor spotted *Maelstrom* and Vurgrom's other ships in the distance. They were well separated from each other, evidently not taking any chances of being thrown together by the storm lashing the Sea of Fallen Stars. All of them seemed to be faring well.

Swinging his body to get momentum, Jherek swung forward again and released, sailing through the distance and dropping on the stern castle near the wheel. A large wave sluiced through the railing and washed across the deck, fast enough and strong enough to take the dead pilot's body across the planks to the railing on the other side. Debris continued peppering the caravel, filling the air with punctuations of thuds and pings.

Jherek was hit in the shoulder hard enough to knock him down. He glanced at his arm and saw an eyeball-sized rock smoldering in his flesh. Fighting back the pain and shock, he slipped his knife from his boot and pushed the rock from his arm with the blade. He tested his grip and found he could still make a fist, but most of his arm was numb.

He got to his feet with effort and launched himself at the spinning wheel as *Black Champion* wallowed in another trough. He seized the wheel as they went over into the trough, fighting the ship and the sea. The young sailor's muscles strained and burned with agony, but no matter what he did, the caravel seemed determined to founder. The ship fell hard to starboard and looked like it was going under.

Sabyna lurched to the top of the stairs leading up to the stern castle, holding on again as *Black Champion* slid across another water wall. To Jherek, it felt like the ship had suddenly hit a patch of ice. The caravel seemed determined to race to her doom.

This time the ship's prow pointed straight down into the black water at the bottom of the next trough and the wall of water rushing up from behind her seemed destined to push her end over end. The young sailor felt certain they were going to plunge into the unforgiving heart of the dark sea like an arrow finding its mark.

There'd be no survivors.

Jherek lacked the wind he needed to straighten her up and he wanted to cry out in frustration, knowing there was no way he could save Sabyna from the harsh death that lay before them all.

Then the cold, powerful voice filled his mind. *Live, that you may serve.*

A wind blew hard and clean from behind him, coming from a different direction than it had only a moment ago. The surviving sails filled, twisting *Black Champion* from the deadly course she was on.

Jherek pulled the ship into the wind, guiding her with an unforgiving hand. His injured arm burned and ached and felt numb all at the same time, hardly giving him any strength at all. But *Black Champion* came around into the wind, her holed and flaming sails capturing enough of it to pull her on course, turning her to face the oncoming waves. She met the next wave with her prow and cleaved it cleanly. The new wind stayed with her, pulling her out of the wallows, and it seemed as though less debris struck her.

An awestruck look filled Sabyna's face as she gazed around.

"Who are you?" Jherek shouted into the wind. "Who are you and what do you want?"

He felt scared and mad all at the same time. Despite all the good the voice had done over the years, he felt certain he was at risk and had taken his friends there with him because that voice wanted him there. Whoever owned that voice had saved him only to take a firmer hand in his destiny. Was he pawn or prisoner?

Only silence answered him above the creak of the rigging and the crashing waves.

Then an answer did come. *Soon, my son.*

"Tell me who you are!" Jherek shouted again.

"Who are you talking to?"

Jherek glanced to port and saw that Sabyna had joined him at the stern castle. Her short-cropped hair lay plastered against her skull, and a half-dozen bloody scratches covered her left cheek. Her eyelids blinked tightly against the salt spray continuing to come over the railing. The young sailor only shook his head, having no words—only the frustration that filled him.

Skeins coiled protectively around the ship's mage, barely holding its pieces together.

Jherek gazed at her, taking in the wounds he saw.

"I'm all right," she told him.

Black Champion continued to pitch and plunge across the uneven ocean, but the supernatural wind that had captured her guided her safely through the troughs. Startled shouts rang across her decks. The sailors cheered as they felt the ship come about under her own power despite the duress she was under.

Without warning, sails punched up into the sky, cresting the next roiling wave that was spurred on by the volcano. At the top of the mainmast, the skull and crossbones on a field of black crowned the pirate ship as it continued its pursuit. The cheers turned to dismay.

"I'll take the wheel," Sabyna said.

Jherek stepped back, breathing hard. He drew the cutlass from his sash and pulled the hook into his free hand. Pushed by a full complement of sails, the pirate ship closed quickly. Red-eyed pirates clamored for blood as they stood at the railing. They clanged their swords together and sang a sea chantey. Jherek only heard a few words, but he recognized it for what it was.

"They're ensorcelled," Sabyna yelled out to be heard.

Jherek nodded. No sane man would take the risks those dozen pirates had lined up for. The young sailor set himself, pushing the pain in his injured arm from his mind as well as he could.

In the next moment, catching the crest of the wave that overtook them, the pirates sprang from their ship. Propelled by magic, the men spanned the twenty feet separating them from *Black Champion* and landed on the caravel's deck. Immediately, the pirates pushed themselves to their feet and rose to do battle.

"Go below!" Jherek yelled at Sabyna, knowing he couldn't hold a dozen armed pirates back.

"If I let go this wheel, we'll go down!" she shouted back at him.

Knowing it was true, Jherek felt torn. She stood in harm's way, and yet he couldn't protect her if she abandoned the wheel. He concentrated on the possessed pirates who moved at them with single-minded purpose. With the way the stern castle's steering section was left so open, the pirates would surround them quickly. The red-eyed men already moved to flank them.

Jherek swung the cutlass, feeling the impact of blade meeting blade when the pirate automatically blocked. Before his opponent could withdraw his weapon, the young sailor reached out with the hook and caught the man in the shoulder.

The curved hook bit deeply into the man's flesh, skidding for just a moment across the shoulder blade before sinking into his back. Under the spell that held him, the pirate didn't make a sound, but tried to pull his weapon into Jherek's exposed arm.

Shifting quickly, Jherek blocked the weakly aimed cut, then stepped to the pirate's left and yanked on the grappling hook. Getting his weight into the motion, the young sailor pulled the pirate over his hip in a wrestling throw Malorrie had taught him.

Off-balance and at the mercy of the brutal hook, the pirate stumbled over Jherek's hip and sailed into the next man behind him. With a crashing thrash of limbs, the two pirates tumbled over *Black Champion's* stern railing and splashed into the dark sea below.

Pulled nearly off his feet by his own efforts, the hook lost to him because he hadn't been able to free it from the pirate, Jherek caught himself on his free hand and pushed up. He blocked a cutlass blow that had been intended to take his head from his shoulders, then launched a kick that caught the pirate wielding it full in the chest.

Bone snapped and the pirate stumbled back, knocking down two others.

"Well met, young warrior," Glawinn growled as he stepped in at Jherek's side. The paladin's blade gleamed despite the darkness of the sky. "Now let's rid ourselves of these vermin."

As the paladin and the young sailor engaged the pirates, Skeins blew past them in a violent flutter. In heartbeats, the raggamoffyn chose a victim and covered him, possessing him even in spite of whatever spell had already claimed him. The pirate lifted his blade against his brethren and attacked from the rear.

Jherek's breath burned deep in his lungs, gusting out in uncontrolled bellows. His trip through the rigging had taken a lot from him already. He fought fiercely, stepping into the rhythm Glawinn set up. Or maybe the paladin stepped into the rhythm Jherek had established. The young sailor wasn't certain. All the days they'd spent as sparring partners stood them in good stead now.

Ducking low beneath a wildly swung cutlass, Jherek saw Glawinn rip a backhand blow across a pirate's throat. Blood dribbled down the man's chest as he fell backward. Jherek surged up, holding tight to the hilt of the cutlass as he drove it into the chest of the pirate in front of him. Though the cutlass wasn't normally a thrusting weapon, it split the man's heart and killed him instantly.

Jherek shoved the corpse from his weapon, aware of Azla racing up the stern castle steps to join them. Her scimitar rang, a death song hammered out in steel. Jherek fought fiercely, defending Sabyna from the pirates who tried to take the fight in her direction. The footing became even more treacherous than the storm had made it, as blood spilled quickly across the brine-stained deck.

Despite his efforts and the fact that his life hung on the eyeblink of time between the slashing and parrying of the cutlass, Jherek played over the voice's words.

Soon, my son.

There'd been no promise of how soon, and no indication again of whom the voice belonged to. The young sailor was only dimly aware of the fight ending. He'd known the odds were lessening, but he didn't know the battle was over until Glawinn grabbed his arm.

"Easy, young warrior," the paladin advised. "It's over."

Jherek struggled against the man for just a moment, then realized the caravel's crew was even now beginning to throw the dead pirates overboard. The young sailor took a deep breath, feeling his heart hammering at his ribs and his body shake with exhaustion. Blood streamed down his face and from half a dozen other cuts across his body where his armor hadn't protected him. He let the cutlass hang like an anchor at the end of his arm.

He glanced at Sabyna as Azla assigned a man to relieve her. The ship's mage met Azla's eyes briefly, then Sabyna turned and walked away.

Jherek wanted to go to her, but he knew it wasn't right. Sabyna was capable of standing on her own, and if she wanted his company, she was capable of asking for that as well.

She didn't.

Uncaring of the debris that occasionally struck the deck around him, he walked to the railing and watched the pirate ship that had trailed them break off pursuit as the supernatural wind continued pushing *Black Champion* away. In moments, it was tacking back toward Vurgrom's other ship.

Jherek stared back at the spewing volcano in the distance, watching as more lava poured into the Alamber Sea. He didn't understand the forces that had pulled him there. He reached out for the voice inside his head, opening himself up to it, wanting it to fulfill its promise.

Only emptiness rang inside his skull.

Jherek gazed down at the deck, watching Sabyna walk away. The ship's mage had her arms wrapped tightly around herself. She never looked up at him. A heaviness he'd never felt lay on the young sailor's heart. He couldn't make sense out of anything, and in that moment, knowing how little control he had over anything that happened to him, he let go the faith he'd tried to cling to for so long.

Ilmater the Crying God, the god to whom the young sailor had given himself, shed no tears for Jherek Wolf's-get. The young sailor's heart turned cold and hard. No matter what happened, he promised himself silently, once he got the pearl disk from Vurgrom, he would be free.

Covered protectively in Iakhovas's grasp, Laaqueel watched the fiery red of the volcano channel give way to the cool blue of the sea again. Huge boulders spun through the water, wreathed in flames that wouldn't die, until they dropped out of sight.

Iakhovas gripped the wheel sternly, altering his course. "See, priestess. We are arrived hale and whole. If you have faith, all things become possible."

"You have my thanks, Most Exalted One. If not for you, I would have died."

"You cannot die. I won't let you. Our fates are strongly wound together—as long as you acknowledge them."

Laaqueel stepped away from him, no longer feeling the pull of the currents sweeping *Tarjana*'s deck. She stood easily on her own. "Where are we?"

"In the Alamber Sea."

The water around *Tarjana* roiled with boiling bubbles that raced for the surface. They were so thick, so tightly compacted together, that they created a misty curtain that limited visibility to no more than a few feet. Only the magic surrounding the mudship yet protected them.

Laaqueel looked behind, making sure the fliers trailing them had made it as well. Miraculously, the cone of protection that extended over *Tarjana* weaved back through the roiling water. She couldn't see if all of the fliers were there, rowed from the belly of the volcano that had burst underwater, but she got the sense that most of them had.

"Where are we going now?" she asked.

"There is much to do now that we are here," Iakhovas said. "First, we will find a place that will serve as our base of operations. If I'm to free the forgotten clan of We Who Eat from this place, I must find the tools to do it."

"Do you know where these items you need are?"

"Yes. There is an ancient place that lies far from here. It's called Coryselmal, a broken city that once housed the cursed sea elves. I shall reap from its corpse all that I need to destroy the Sharksbane Wall, then I shall recoup all that is mine."

Laaqueel gazed at the water, knowing the titanic forces that warred in the ocean were somehow kept separate from them. She started her prayers to Sekolah, asking that their voyage be successful, and that it try the spirits of the sahuagin so the Shark God's chosen might become even stronger.

It was better, she knew from her experience as a priestess, to pray for the things that were sure to happen. It helped to remind her that those trials weren't unexpected or without reason.

She knew her people would pay in blood.

28

"Are you sure you want to do that, young warrior?"

Glawinn's quiet words startled Jherek. He hadn't known the paladin was there. Immediately, he felt guilty about what he was doing. He'd thought he was going to be alone long enough to do what he planned.

"Aye," the young sailor replied, his voice thick with his own doubts and fears. "It's what I have to do." He peered at the long black sea stretching out to the east as *Black Champion* made her way west again.

Vurgrom and his pirates had lost sails during the volcanic eruption stemming from the Ship of the Gods, but they'd brought extra sails. After the turbulence had finally died down in the Alamber Sea, Vurgrom's pirates had simply rehung their rigging with the new sails and continued on with their journey. The pirate captain had paused to throw a few taunts Azla's way first. Azla had ignored him, but in stony fury. The half-elf obviously had a long-standing feud going with the pirate that wasn't going to end until one or the other was dead. Evidently *Black Champion*'s captain and crew were too well respected for the pirates to think they could take them without loss.

In the hours since the eruption, Azla and her crew, with help from Jherek, Sabyna, and Glawinn, had worked to repair the sails. However, there was no replacing the lost mainmast, not at sea. Jherek had sewn and cut and spliced sailcloth until his hands ached, but he hadn't complained. Neither had he talked with Sabyna. He'd also avoided Glawinn's offer of lessons with the sword, working on the sails until it was well past dark.

"Why do you think you have to do this?" Glawinn asked in a soft voice.

Jherek listened to the man's words but found no challenge in them, nothing he could take offense at and use to leverage an argument that would end the unwanted conversation. "Because I'm tired."

"We're all tired."

"It's not the work," Jherek snapped, his voice almost breaking with the emotion that filled him. With all the rage inside him, he felt like demanding that someone understand what was going through his mind. "It's the hope, Glawinn. I'm tired of all the hope."

"A man can't live without hope."

"Well," the young sailor challenged, "I'm going to have to see about that."

Glawinn stepped closer, coming within Jherek's peripheral vision. The young sailor didn't turn to face him. "You have no thoughts of a future?"

"I have no future," Jherek declared.

"You're not dead."

Jherek clung to the cold rage that had filled him since the voice saved the ship. "I was born dead, and I've died a little more each day, till I owe Cyric at least three or four other lives." A chill touched him when he mentioned the god of death's name. In all his life, he never had.

"You really believe that?"

Turning, Jherek glared at the paladin. "You don't know anything about me."

Glawinn crossed his arms over his chest and drew himself up to his full height. "Such wisdom in one so young, to be knowing all these things that you do."

"You taunt me." Jherek's eyes blazed, but he restrained himself. Glawinn didn't deserve his wrath and he knew it, but that emotion was so ready to be released.

"The opposite," Glawinn disagreed. "I marvel at you."

"This is my decision."

"I've not tried to alter it."

"You asked me if I was sure about doing this."

Glawinn let out a slow breath. "I only thought that someone should. I've known something was bothering you. I waited, thinking you might come to me for help. Or talk to Sabyna about it."

Jherek's throat hurt when he tried to talk, and his eyes burned from the effort it took to keep his words from breaking. "I can't talk to her about it."

"Why?"

"Because it would hurt the friendship I have with her."

"Is it so bad, young warrior?"

Jherek looked past the paladin, making sure none of the sailors were close by. Troge, the first mate, was making his rounds, checking his night crew and the lanterns that hung from *Black Champion*'s yardarms and masts to light her and to mark her for other ships in the water at night.

Closing his fist over the object in his hand, Jherek pulled up his left sleeve, baring the flaming skull tattoo masked in chains. "Do you know what this is?" he asked.

Glawinn only had to glance at it briefly. "It's the mark of Bloody Falkane the pirate, also called the Salt Wolf."

"Aye," Jherek said bitterly, "and known widely abroad enough that even someone from the Dalelands has heard of him."

"You're not old enough to have been one of his crew."

"No," Jherek agreed. "My fate is worse than that. I'm his son."

Glawinn didn't let any surprise show. He said, "I never knew he had a son."

"It wasn't," Jherek replied, "something he seemed especially proud of." He rolled his sleeve back down. "And what do you think of me now, Sir Glawinn, when you think back on those nights you've spent training me with a sword? Did you ever think you might be training a pirate captain's son who might someday hold that sword and all that skill at your throat?"

The paladin's eyes narrowed. "That's not something you'd ever do."

Jherek shook his head. "How can you be so sure about that?"

"I know you."

"You don't know me. The tattoo proves that."

"I know you," Glawinn said, "I admit the tattoo is something of a surprise. Tell me about it."

Standing there gripping the railing, his fist tight about all that he was about to abandon, Jherek did. He told the story of his life on *Bunyip*, and of what little he knew about his father. He spoke of the sea battles he'd seen, the deaths he'd watched, and the tortures he'd seen inflicted.

And he told of the time when he was twelve and his father had first placed a cutlass in his hand and told him he was going to be part of a boarding crew. He'd escaped in the night and somehow made the long swim in to Cape Velen fourteen miles away.

"When I got to Velen I was starving," Jherek said, "but I couldn't even steal food. Instead, I lived on berries and eggs I found down by the beach. I hired myself out first working the docks to move cargo, then any job I could get in Velen. Eventually I got a job with a shipwright. I love working wood, and I've got a talent for it. That's what got me the job of repairing Madame Iitaar's roof."

He told the paladin of Madame Iitaar, how she'd taken in an orphan boy who was sleeping in an extra room in the shipwright's building during the months it took to repair her roof.

"Months?" Glawinn asked. "For a roof?"

"It started out as the roof but it moved on to other things. A new fence. A new porch, front and back. New tables and chairs. Madame Iitaar has a list of projects she always wants done. I'm a good woodworker."

"You must be."

"I lived in her house for years, and she wouldn't have treated me any better if I'd been her own son." As he said that, Jherek was surprised to find that he still believed that.

"Why did you end up in Baldur's Gate?"

Jherek told him of *Breezerunner* and the Amnians, and how Madame Iitaar seemed certain that whatever destiny he had lay in Baldur's Gate. "Even Malorrie thought so."

"Malorrie's the man who taught you your skill with the blade?"

"Actually, Malorrie's a phantom," Jherek replied. So he told of how Malorrie had been the first to really find him living on the beaches. He'd broken his leg a short time after arriving in Velen and it had been the phantom that'd taken care of him. He told of the nights they'd spent in the shipwright's building learning all the combat skills the phantom knew.

"You don't know who this Malorrie was when he was living?" Glawinn asked.

"I never asked. It's like that between us. We just accept each other for the way we are. Without trying to change anything." Jherek's voice turned bitter. "You don't get that out of many people."

"I know. So why give up now?"

Jherek glanced at his fist, thinking of the object inside it, what it had meant then and what it had ceased meaning since. "I'm not giving up. I'm acknowledging my inability to control whatever destiny I may have."

"It sounds like quitting to me."

Jherek shook his head and laughed. "Call it what you will. I've had enough."

"Enough of what? Disappointment? Everybody faces disappointment."

"Not disappointment," Jherek answered. "I've been betrayed."

"By whom?"

"I don't know."

Glawinn let him have some time, then asked, "How have you been betrayed?"

"What does 'Live, that you may serve,' mean to you?" the young sailor asked.

"Nothing. Should it?"

"Probably not, but for years I've been wondering what it meant for me."

"Why?"

"Because I've been told that."

In a shaking voice, Jherek told of the voice, how it had said that the first time and he'd been saved by a dolphin. He also told him how the voice had spoken again earlier that day, just before the freak gust of wind had powered them out of capsizing.

"For all my life," he finished, "I've wondered what that's supposed to mean."

"Maybe it's not time," Glawinn replied.

"No," Jherek said in a loud voice. "I'm tired of waiting. I'll tell you what I think now. I think whoever that voice belongs to has been trying to destroy me, to destroy my hope. I've fought it. I lived when I wanted to die. I escaped my father, risking my life against the sea, rather than take up a blade against an innocent man. I starved because I wouldn't steal. I worked because I had to take care of myself and not throw myself on the mercy of others. I've lived, but I've had no life." His voice broke.

Glawinn, thankfully, kept his distance and let Jherek regroup on his own.

The young sailor spoke carefully when he could. "The closest I've ever come to a life was in Velen. In risking my life to save a rich, spoiled girl, I saw all that taken away from me. My reward. No, it should have been 'Live, that you may suffer.' " He shook his head. "I'm done with that, and I'm done with this."

The young sailor opened his hand and revealed the small pair of white clay hands bound at the wrists by a blood-red cord that lay on his palm.

"You follow Ilmater the Crying God's teachings," Glawinn said.

"Aye. I did."

"He teaches endurance and perseverance. Good qualities for someone who's had to learn to accept."

"I've accepted," Jherek said. "I had accepted—even the voice—but I'm not going to accept any more."

"What are you going to do?"

"I don't know."

Glawinn paused for a moment, then his eyes opened wider. "You're afraid that the voice belongs to something or someone evil, but that could never be, Malorrie. You aren't an evil person."

"I'm not?" Jherek laughed bitterly. "You just called me Malorrie. Don't you understand that was my teacher's name? I've never told you my real name. I lied, and I would never have done something like that until now. As it is, I'm not even able to live my own life. That's been stripped from me as well."

"Maybe you're only being shown to your new life." Glawinn shrugged. "I don't know how these things work, young warrior. I only trust the weave that I follow."

"I can't," Jherek said. "Not any more. I only fooled myself into believing that I could."

"Have you spoken with Sabyna?"

Jherek said nothing, the pain in his throat growing larger and harder to swallow. "No."

"Why not?"

"Why should I?"

"Because she seems to have a vested interest in you."

"She's under the mistaken impression that she owes me something."

"Ah, young warrior, there are so many things you still don't see in life."

Jherek's anger turned him hot even in spite of the cool night breeze blowing around him. "What's that supposed to mean?"

"Only that time will make you wiser, but I can see that the learning won't come easily to you in certain matters."

"I can't tell Sabyna."

"Even though you love her?"

Jherek shook his head. "You don't know that I love her. *I* don't know that I love her."

"You were willing to abandon your quest for the pearl disk because of her."

"It's foolish for her to die for my mistakes."

"She didn't let you walk away. She cares about you."

"I know," Jherek said thickly, "but I'm afraid to let that happen either. If I foolishly ever thought that it might. She deserves someone much better than me."

"Why haven't you told her about your past?"

"Because," Jherek said, "my father killed her brother, and I was on *Bunyip,* hanging in the rigging and watching when he did it."

Glawinn cleared his throat. "I see. That does present some difficulty."

"And there again," Jherek said, "is the ill luck that has been bequeathed to me in this life. I find a woman and feel something for her that I've never known, never allowed myself to feel except in the occasional fantasy of a story I was reading, and my father has murdered her brother. That's why I've made my decision."

He curled his fist around Ilmater's symbol, then threw it far out to sea. The white clay hands caught the light for a brief moment, then disappeared from sight. Jherek felt empty, but he filled it in with the newfound cold rage that had claimed him earlier that day. Live, that you may suffer. From here on, any suffering he experienced was going to be on his terms.

"Now what, young warrior? You have no hope and no god. What are you going to do with yourself?"

"Hope only got in my way," Jherek replied. "I'm going to be a realist. I have no god because I've never had one. I'm going to get that pearl disk from Vurgrom or die trying because I don't know what else to do."

"Is that it? Or is part of it because you still believe returning the disk to the temple of Lathander in Baldur's Gate is the right thing to do?"

"Azla pursues Vurgrom," Jherek said. "I'll ship with her and see that my part of it is done. When everything in my past life is dealt with, I can begin anew."

"Then where will you go?"

"I'm not even going to think about it," Jherek declared, trying to imagine such a time. "I'll eat when I'm hungry. I'll sleep when I'm tired. I'll work when I have to. I'll settle with that out of life until I'm dead."

"What a bleak, hard life you've set for yourself."

Jherek shook his head. "There'll be no false expectations."

"So you choose to believe in nothing?"

"Aye."

"We'll start with small beliefs, then," Glawinn said, drawing his sword. "Get your weapon out and I'll begin with trust with your eye and your sword arm, young warrior. Your eye and your sword arm—and we'll let your heart take care of itself." He waved his broadsword about in invitation.

"It's dark."

"Do you think every fight you're going to wage will be well lighted?"

"No." Jherek already knew that.

"Then draw your sword and show me your best. Or do you think you have anything better to do?"

Jherek stepped back and drew the cutlass from his sash. His left arm still hurt and was healing slowly. Dark shadows limned the paladin's face. In the next instant, the sound of steel ringing on steel filled the deck and echoed over the Alamber Sea.

Glawinn pressed him hard, driving him backward, coming closer than he ever had in practice to actually cutting him. "Come on, young warrior, show me what you have. Or has your disbelief exhausted your strength and skill as well?"

Growing angry but tempering it with the cold rage that filled him, Jherek beat back the attacks, stepping up his own retaliation.

"You'll believe in your eye and your arm," Glawinn promised again. "The heart will take care of itself. You'll see."

Jherek drove him back, circling closely to turn him to his weak side. He wished Glawinn would shut up.

They fought until Jherek's arm trembled and he was covered in sweat. The young sailor tried to beat back the paladin's offense, tried to chew through his defense, and tried to overpower him at every turn. Jherek fought until the rage filled him and slipped past his control. His blade moved faster. He no longer thought of any restraints.

"That's it, young warrior," Glawinn said softly. "Get it out. Let it all out."

"Shut up!" Jherek said.

"Get it all out. All the frustration and fear and anger. Give it to me. Once you get rid of it, you'll fill up again. You'll see."

Glawinn fought even more fiercely, his blade moved like a live thing hammered into the steel. Jherek couldn't even see the blades any more, only the red fog of anger that clouded his vision in the darkness. He was vaguely aware of the crowd of sailors that had been attracted to the duel.

"Give me your anger," Glawinn coaxed.

Jherek swung harder, faster, and sparks shot from the blades. His legs quivered from the strain of keeping up with his arm as they moved him across the deck. He concentrated all his hate on the paladin, just wanting the man to shut up.

Then, without the least indication of what he was going to do, Glawinn dropped his sword point to the deck, leaving himself totally defenseless. Jherek checked his swing with difficulty, missing a diagonal cross-body slash that would have cut Glawinn from right shoulder to left hip if it had landed.

"What are you doing?" he shouted. "I could have killed you!"

"Proving to you that you can trust your eye and your arm," Glawinn stated calmly.

"And what if I hadn't been able to stop myself?"

"Then I'd have been wrong."

Suddenly overcome with emotion, Jherek threw the cutlass down and turned to walk away.

Glawinn sheathed his own weapon and grabbed him by the shirtfront. "Where are you going?"

"Away," Jherek answered. "Away from you and this madness." He tried to push away, but the paladin held him too tightly.

"No. You must realize what you were able to do. What skills you have."

"I could have killed you," Jherek said hoarsely, not believing the man couldn't understand him.

"But you didn't. Don't you see that?"

"No," Jherek answered. "No, I don't. You took a fool's chance with your life."

"I trusted your skill so that you could trust it too. Your eye and your arm, Jherek. I'll teach you to believe, but we'll begin there."

"I could have killed you."

The image of the knight with his chest and belly split open filled Jherek's head and made him sick. Nausea boiled up inside him and Glawinn helped him over to the railing. Later, when he was finished and there was nothing else to give up, Glawinn pulled him back. Jherek's mouth was filled with the sour taste.

"And what if you had killed me, young warrior?" the knight asked in a ragged whisper. "Would it have mattered?"

"Aye."

"If you're so empty of caring, it shouldn't have. You may think your heart's empty, but it's not." Glawinn held him at arm's length, both of them breathing hard and covered with sweat. "It's not completely empty. Trust what's within your reach and the rest will come." Tears ran down the knight's face as he held the young sailor's face between his callused hands. "I give you my promise."

Jherek wished desperately that he could believe, but he couldn't. There'd been too many lies.

29

Tarjana cleaved steadily through the water, deep into the territory of Aleaxtis. Vahaxtyl, the sahuagin capital, lay in ruins less than five hundred yards away, riven by the volcano's explosion the day before.

Standing on the enchanted mudship's prow, Laaqueel stared out at the destruction scattered over the bed of the Alamber Sea. It was worse than she had expected. For a time she'd feared none of the sahuagin community had lived through the fiery blast.

Huge, jagged rocks lay strewn across the blasted terrain. Dead fish floated in the dappled turquoise water and glinted silver where the weak sun's rays touched them. Small scavengers that had finally returned to the area worried frantically at the unexpected feast, concerned that larger predators would come at any moment. More rubble covered the skeletal remains of ships that had fallen to sahuagin savagery, battles, and deadly storms.

Dozens of sahuagin bodies floated in the currents as well, prey to the flesh-eaters also. The malenti priestess knew that those weren't all that had been killed. Many more corpses had surely remained trapped inside their dwellings when they caved in. Other bodies had been swept away by time and tide.

The living sahuagin worked among their dead, sharp claws and huge teeth stripping meat from the corpses for meals. The scent and taste of scalded blood and boiled meat hung in the water, constantly touching Laaqueel's nostrils.

"You are troubled, priestess?"

Slowly, not knowing how to properly broach the subject, Laaqueel turned to face Iakhovas. Her eyes met his even though she still wanted to show him deference. No matter what, she knew she couldn't lie. He would know and she didn't want that between them.

"Yes," she said simply.

Iakhovas walked to the railing and closed his hands over it. His face remained stern and hard. "Why?"

"So many lives of We Who Eat have been forfeited." She gestured out at the seabed. "They have lost their homes."

In the distance, the Ship of the Gods still simmered. White, foamy bubbles from superheated water spiraled to the surface. The currents threaded hot waves in with the cool ones that coiled around Laaqueel. Still, the volcano appeared to be in little danger of spewing deadly lava again.

"Ah, little malenti, your perception of things is off and you don't even know it."

A sudden flush of anger flooded Laaqueel. She turned to him.

"You forget, my priestess," Iakhovas continued before she could speak, "they didn't choose to make their lives here." He gestured at the heaps of rubble. "That's no home, no village lying out there strewn about and destroyed. This parcel of unwanted land is what the sea elves and mermen grudgingly gave this tribe of We Who Eat after the First Serôs War over ten thousand years ago. They drove them here, then penned them in, and they've kept them here ever since." He held her eyes with his solitary one. "This was no home, priestess. This was a prison."

In her heart, Laaqueel knew he spoke the truth. Everything around her, including the Alamber Sea, was a cage. The Serôsian sahuagin had lived very small lives.

"I had not intended for so many to die," Iakhovas stated quietly. "In truth, I didn't know that our arrival here would cause such an upheaval."

Despite his flat tone and the fact that she knew he wouldn't have wanted her to know much of his private thoughts, Laaqueel believed the note of regret she heard in Iakhovas's voice was genuine.

"It was not your will, Most Exalted One," she said, speaking with the certainty of faith. "It was the will of Sekolah. These deaths are the result of the fury of his claws and teeth reaving the weak from the tribe, making his mark on his chosen people."

He stayed silent for a moment, not looking at her, as if weighing her words carefully. It was the first time Laaqueel could ever remember him doing that. "Do you truly think so, Most Sacred One?" His voice was almost a whisper.

Laaqueel shoved aside the tiny seed of doubt that stayed relentlessly within her. Even by Iakhovas's own admission he hadn't known the explosion was going to happen, but it had. Her training taught her that it had to be by the Great Shark's will.

"Yes," she said. "The sahuagin who lived here have stayed in one place for so long, it would have been hard to convince them to leave."

"Or to convince them to challenge the sea elves and mermen who sentenced them." Iakhovas glanced at her, a small smile twisting his lips. A dim golden light gleamed in the hollow of his missing eye. "I find your words, your thinking, very comforting, my priestess."

Laaqueel bowed her head, not prepared for the onslaught of emotions that whirled within her. She had never thought in her whole life that she'd be completely accepted. She was too much of a freak to expect that. She could only hope, and even then that hope was always dim. A surge of embarrassment filled her, one of the few times that it came from something she'd accomplished instead of something she'd fallen short on. She tried to think of an appropriate reply but couldn't.

"Thank you, Most Exalted One," she said simply.

Tarjana floated closer to the destroyed sahuagin city, powered by the oars of the rowers below. The ship's approach had drawn attention in the form of a dozen fliers that suddenly skimmed from hiding on the sea floor. All of them carried sahuagin warriors.

"Ready yourself," Iakhovas warned. "We won't be greeted gratefully."

Laaqueel knew it was true. As she'd been trained, she pushed her emotions away. It was so hard this time, though, because there was so much pleasure in how she felt as a result of Iakhovas's unexpected praise. That confused her because generally her emotions were filled with pain. Bloody Falkane had left her feeling the same way.

Tension twisted her stomach as she watched the fliers quickly flank *Tarjana*. The fliers the Serôsian sahuagin used were smaller than the ones the malenti was accustomed to, but they moved quickly and powerfully through the sea.

Iakhovas called orders out to stop the mudship. Quietly, *Tarjana* sank to the sea floor, settling deeply into the loose silt, crunching against the lava rock thrown out from the volcano.

The smaller fliers rode the currents above them. Coral spears and tridents bristled over the railings of all the Serôsian fliers. Crossbowmen peered over their weapons.

Iakhovas stood before them all, his arms at his sides. He took no cover and he offered no outward threat. Laaqueel glanced at him, then had to turn quickly away. Whatever spell he was using to disguise himself as a sahuagin had gained power. Even though she normally saw him as human, the malenti's vision clouded painfully, giving different views of human and sahuagin that overlapped so quickly one blurred into the other.

Occasionally, the view was of something else—something she couldn't clearly recognize.

The sight of Iakhovas's other self sent fear thrilling down Laaqueel's spine. Nausea twisted her stomach relentlessly. She wasn't certain if the ill feeling came from the spell or the sight of his misshapen other self. Her curiosity made her want to look again in spite of her reluctance.

Instead, her attention was riveted to the large sahuagin who strode to the forefront of the closest flier. He wore a prince's insignia, recognizable even though the markings were different than what Laaqueel was used to. He held a royal trident in one gnarled fist. A three-armed sahuagin in a royal guardsman's war halter flanked the prince on his left.

The royal guard beside the prince held Laaqueel's attention. The guardsman gazed at her with bold viciousness, no hesitation in him at all.

"Who are you?" the guard bellowed.

Silently, the other sahuagin aboard *Tarjana* who weren't at the oars swam up to take a stand behind Iakhovas. They bared their weapons as well, but Iakhovas waved them still.

Even with all the fliers they'd brought with them, Laaqueel knew they didn't have a chance if the Serôsian sahuagin attacked. Despite the awesome destruction the volcano had unleashed, Iakhovas and his followers wouldn't have been able to stand against them. Unless Sekolah wills, the malenti amended to herself. She kept her gifts at the ready, certain Iakhovas was doing the same.

"I am Iakhovas." His voice thundered through the water, punctuated by the shrill clicks and whistles of the sahuagin tongue. "I am king of We Who Eat in the Claarteeros Sea."

"Liar!" the black-clawed royal guard roared. "That place exists only in myth."

"Most Exalted One," a sahuagin baron among *Tarjana*'s crew said quickly, "let me claim the right of blood challenge against this offender. I swear by Sekolah's blessed fins that I will bring honor to your name."

"No," Iakhovas answered calmly. "No blood will be shed unless I command it. They need every warrior they can muster." His words resonated and carried through the water.

Laaqueel quivered inside. Not responding to the royal guard's accusation could be construed as cowardice. It was an open invitation to attack.

A four-armed sahuagin, missing one of his arms, who floated next to the Serôsian prince opened his mouth to speak.

"Silence, T'Kalah," the prince commanded without looking at the warrior.

T'Kalah swung on the other man, displeasure evident in his body language. Laaqueel knew if the prince had noted the movement he would have punished the warrior for insubordination.

The prince studied Iakhovas with his measured gaze. "You are a king."

"Yes," Iakhovas answered shortly but politely.

Laaqueel watched T'Kalah, feeling that if any attack was launched it would come through that sahuagin first. During her inspection of the royal guard, she noted the fact that the anterior fins on the sides of his head flared back over his skull and merged with the dorsal fin on his back. The anterior fins of the sahuagin in the outer seas didn't connect. His different coloring had already been noticed. Even as strange as the

Serôsian sahuagin looked to her, she knew they fit in more securely with her own people than she did despite Iakhovas's influence.

"Among your own people, perhaps," T'Kalah growled, "but not here."

Iakhovas pinned the sahuagin warrior with his glance. "I made myself king through blood, three-arm, and if need be, I will remain so by spilling more. Make no mistake about that."

T'Kalah's black eyes burned with hostility and he stared hard back at Iakhovas. It was not something most sahuagin would ignore. Instead, Iakhovas looked back to the prince, dismissing the sahuagin warrior as if he were nothing. Laaqueel watched the muscles bunch across T'Kalah's chest, and the amputated stub of his arm jerked involuntarily.

"No," she stated forcefully. She held her hands up before her, feeling the power of her gifts. "I am a priestess of Sekolah, warrior, and you would do well to heed my calling and the authority of the Most Exalted One."

The prince looked at T'Kalah as well, then moved his trident to face the other sahuagin. "If you move, you shall have to get through me as well."

"I seek only to protect you," T'Kalah argued.

"Then do it by serving me," the prince ordered.

Angrily, T'Kalah held his trident upright in one hand, then folded his other two arms across his chest. "These are ill currents, Maartaaugh."

"If so," Maartaaugh said, "we shall swim through them." The prince turned his attention back to Iakhovas. "What are you doing here?"

"I came to see your king," Iakhovas said.

"King Kromes is dead. He died when the volcano exploded."

Iakhovas remained silent.

"His death," Laaqueel stated to fill the uncomfortable void that followed, "was by the will of Sekolah."

"Liar!" T'Kalah cried. "He's dead by your hand! Killed when you came through the volcano!"

Maartaaugh looked at the royal guard. "They couldn't have come through the volcano."

"I tell you, Exalted One," T'Kalah stated, "it is as I say. Would you call me a liar?" He took a step away, setting himself into a fighting stance. "I won't take such an accusation without demanding blood honor."

"We came through the volcano," Iakhovas told them.

The sahuagin prince faced Iakhovas again. "How?"

Laaqueel heard the uncertainty and fear in the prince's voice. She knew Maartaaugh was thinking of the magic involved with such a thing. "We were brought here by the Great Shark's will."

"They spout still more lies," T'Kalah said. "All true sahuagin know that Sekolah doesn't meddle in the affairs of his chosen. He expects them to fend for themselves."

Maartaaugh's face grew stony. Laaqueel felt the prince slipping away from them, saw it in the way he folded his arms and closed in on himself.

"Why," Maartaaugh asked, "would Sekolah do such a thing?"

Laaqueel stepped forward, taking her place beside Iakhovas. She lifted her voice and made it strong. "The Great Shark has established certain currents within Most Exalted One Iakhovas. Sekolah started a ripple within the Claarteeros Sea, and through the strength and forethought of Iakhovas, that ripple has spread even unto Serôs."

"Brave words," T'Kalah snarled, "but words are cheap."

"He brought an army here," Laaqueel said.

"And killed our king." T'Kalah stepped toward her. "Tell me why the Great Shark would choose a malenti to speak for him."

The words stung Laaqueel.

"Because," Iakhovas snapped, "her faith is stronger even than your thick-headedness."

T'Kalah swam up from the flier's deck, cutting through the water swiftly. The currents he started slammed against Laaqueel.

"Most Sacred One," Iakhovas said softly, "don't kill this one yet."

T'Kalah arrowed toward them, disregarding the prince's commands to return to the flier.

Summoning her power, Laaqueel shot out a hand, praying to the Great Shark that her control be strong and sure.

Little more than halfway between the vessels, T'Kalah's smooth stroke suddenly shattered. His arms and legs twisted in a vicious convulsion. He flailed out against the sea as if it was closing in on him.

Laaqueel held the sahuagin warrior in the spell's thrall, knowing the pressure she'd created was so great he wasn't able to breathe properly.

"Enough," Iakhovas said.

Silently, Laaqueel dismissed the spell, feeling terribly fatigued. It was one thing, she knew from experience, to unleash a spell, and quite another to attempt to curtail it and shape it once it had been loosed.

Released from the crushing pressure, T'Kalah finned weakly in the ocean, barely able to control himself. Weakness showed in every move he made. Angrily, he retreated back to his flier.

"What do you want?" Maartaaugh asked.

"If your king is dead," Iakhovas asked, "who leads?"

"The remaining princes. We serve as council. For the moment."

"How many are you?"

"Five," Maartaaugh answered.

"Then I will speak to them."

Glints of anger stirred in Maartaaugh's black eyes. "Why should I allow it?"

"You would be foolish to try to stop me," Iakhovas declared. "I've come from an ocean, a world away, and I've come here for one thing only. I've traveled to Serôs to free you from your prison."

Laaqueel stood at Iakhovas's side as he spoke at the public forum he'd demanded. She felt the currents eddying around her, tracked by the lateral lines that ran through her body. She watched the five princes gathered at the makeshift table that had been hastily cobbled together by laying a section of flat rock over two stacks of rock in one of the cleared areas in the center of Vahaxtyl. The table was more a show of authority than any furnishing. The princes wore their halters of rank and held their tridents.

All of the princes were grim-faced. They didn't even talk among themselves at Iakhovas's announcement.

The malenti priestess knew they were of one mind. Maartaaugh had already spoken to them. Even then, Iakhovas had agreed to come to their offered meeting unarmed, with only Laaqueel and a dozen Black Tridents as a token show of force.

If the princes voted against Iakhovas's offer, Laaqueel had no doubt that they would all be dead before the sun stabbed down into the water again. She averted her gaze from the princes' table out of deference, and more nervousness than she wanted to admit.

Most of the populace of Vahaxtyl ringed them, sitting on broken terrain over the underground sections of the city. Huge gray lava rocks piled high all around. She knew Iakhovas's voice carried well in the water, but messengers were on hand to relay what was spoken. She heard Iakhovas's words passed on again and again.

Most of the sahuagin crowd's body language registered disbelief and anger. They knew that the outer sea sahuagin had come through the exploding volcano and had emerged unharmed while so many of their city died. That crowd was only a step away from reaching out for vengeance. The rubble of the city lay scattered around them, and the twilight gloom of the depths filled the water above them.

Laaqueel didn't know what Iakhovas had been thinking to agree to the princes' terms. She drew water in through her gills, held it for a moment, then flushed it out again.

Steady, my priestess, Iakhovas stated calmly in her mind. *Trust in your faith. Everything is going to be as it should.*

As it should for them, or for us? she asked.

Iakhovas didn't answer.

Toomaaek stood at the center of the table. He was tall and thick, his body covered in scars from sharp edges and flames, testifying to how closely he'd fought the surface dwellers over his years. "You are responsible for the deaths of our people," he said.

"Am I?" Iakhovas demanded. His voice was hard and cutting as coral. "In my belief, only the weak die in mass graves, and those are taken by Sekolah's sharp fins and ferocious fangs. He wants his people strong."

"You twist our beliefs," Toomaaek said.

"No." Iakhovas's denial was flat, unarguable. "I only embody them with my actions. Sekolah sent me here, gave me the ship that made this possible. He destroyed the inadequate among your people to leave those who would be willing to die fighting for their freedom."

A rumble of angry clicks and whistles echoed in from the crowd. Laaqueel studied the sahuagin around them. She'd already overheard several comments about her own heritage and the fact that she was a malenti. Iakhovas's words struck the crowd harshly, fanning the anger in them to fever-pitch intensity.

Though the sahuagin didn't believe in the same concepts of family as the surface dwellers and sea elves did, they did stand for the community as a whole. Refusal to accept the loss and make someone else responsible was natural to them. She felt Iakhovas should have known to handle things better. Silently she prayed, knowing they were only inches away from death.

"You dare!" Toomaaek thundered.

"By Sekolah's blessed wrath," Iakhovas roared back, "I do dare!"

Toomaaek slammed the butt of his trident against the stone table. The sound echoed harshly, racing through the water.

"I dare to stand up for your people against those who would keep them in shackles," Iakhovas said, finning toward the princes' table. "I dare to travel here in a manner that I don't understand, listening to the guiding hand of the Great Shark as he speaks to my priestess, and trusting in the fact that I'm doing Sekolah's will."

"We don't know that." Toomaaek remained gruff.

"I do." Iakhovas kept swimming.

Laaqueel fell into motion automatically behind him. The guards around the princes started forward. One of them lowered his trident level with Iakhovas's chest.

With blinding speed, Iakhovas snatched the trident's tines away from his chest, then shoved the sahuagin guard back half a dozen paces. The show of strength caught the attention of everyone watching.

"Where are you guiding your people?" Iakhovas demanded. "What plans do you have for We Who Eat in Serôs?"

Toomaaek tried to speak after a moment, but Iakhovas spoke loudly over him.

"For ten thousand years and more," Iakhovas said, "you and the barons, princes, and kings before you have let your people languish in this prison built by the hated sea elves and mermen."

Another guard stepped forward and thrust his weapon, ordering Iakhovas to halt.

As if shooing away a bothersome fingerling perch, Iakhovas shoved the trident aside with one hand and caught the sahuagin warrior by his war harness with the other. Iakhovas yanked, and the guard spun back into two sahuagin behind him, knocking them all off their feet so they floated out of control for a moment.

"Why have We Who Eat not been freed from this place?" Iakhovas demanded.

"There is no escape," Toomaaek stated.

Laaqueel heard the buzz of conversation streak through the crowd of onlookers.

Iakhovas sounded as if he couldn't believe it. "Have you not looked at the Shark God's teachings? Sekolah teaches us that all things are possible if enough blood is shed. They happen more quickly if most of the blood belongs to the enemies of We Who Eat."

Toomaaek stood his ground but clearly wasn't happy about it. Iakhovas leveled an accusatory finger at the table of sahuagin princes.

"With that kind of thinking," he said, "*you've* become the jailers of your own people. Not the sea elves and the mermen. You teach your young not to struggle against that perversion of our nature called the Sharksbane Wall." He shook his head in rage. "Our very natures cry out for struggle and adversity to test us and shape us into the most deadly warriors we can be. We're supposed to teach our own lesson in turn: that We Who Eat are meant to be the most feared creature in any of the seas."

"We have fought against those that man the Sharksbane Wall," Maartaaugh argued. "For ten thousand years, we've shed blood over that construction."

"And still you've not shed enough," Iakhovas accused. "When has Sekolah ever declared the price too high to improve the sahuagin people?"

Unbelieving, Laaqueel listened as some of the anger started to drain away from the crowd's murmuring. They sounded more interested in what Iakhovas had to say.

"Instead of tearing that accursed wall down," Iakhovas went on, "you and those rulers before you have chosen to accept it and live with it as though it were meant to be. It wasn't! We Who Eat were born free and meant to die free."

A few scattered cheers sounded from the crowd. Laaqueel drew in a deeper breath and took heart in the reaction. No matter what else, Iakhovas was right about the sahuagin heritage.

"The Sharksbane Wall can't be torn down," Toomaaek declared. "The sea elves and mermen guard it without reservation. The sea elves use their magic to make it strong."

Iakhovas stood across the table from the sahuagin prince. "It can be torn down."

Toomaaek shook his head. "It's been tried."

Iakhovas gazed at him fiercely. "Not by me."

Pride at Iakhovas's display of courage and conviction whipped through Laaqueel. He stood before the whole city, sounding as if he was prepared to take them all on. She held onto the feeling as she watched him, praying the whole time to Sekolah. Awe filled her at the audacity Iakhovas showed. He was more sahuagin than any she'd ever met before.

"You can't break that wall," one of the other princes stated.

"I can," Iakhovas replied hotly, "and I will. I won't sit back and quietly be a coward while pretending to be a prince."

"You go too far!" Toomaaek roared.

"I'm going far enough to tear that wall down," Iakhovas promised, "and I won't stop short of that. Any sahuagin warrior who wants to take up arms and follow me to freedom is welcome."

"The sea elves are too powerful," Maartaaugh said. "They have magic and numbers and allies."

"Then we'll get our own magic and our own allies." Iakhovas didn't move away from the table, but Laaqueel knew he was no longer talking only to the princes. His words were for the ears of the crowd. "Those things are out there. Sekolah gives power to his priestesses, and there are others out there who resent the sea elves controlling so much of Serôs with their machinations. The sea elves have grown fat and lazy, complacent in the inability of We Who Eat of the Alamber Sea to do anything other than send a few groups of warriors across the Sharksbane Wall every now and again."

Hoarse, ragged cheers started up from the crowd intermittently. Laaqueel struggled to keep a smile from her face. The knot of fear still sitting sourly in her stomach made it easier.

"I will raise up an army," Iakhovas vowed, "an army the likes of which Serôs and the lands around it have never seen before. That army will spend its blood and that of its enemies, and the sea will run red because of it." He turned and raked his eye over the crowd, his posture proud and erect. "For those of you who will follow me, I will lead you to greater glory than you've ever known. I will teach you again what it means to be a warrior, to truly be one of the Great Shark's chosen."

The crowd came alive, and the cheering clicks and whistles echoed everywhere. Sahuagin picked up fist-sized rocks and slammed them together to make even more noise. The poundings punctuated the cheers.

The smile broke through Laaqueel's defenses and spread across her lips. She gazed across the crowd in wonderment. Surely this was a sign. No one could have walked into Vahaxtyl and claimed the city's populace in so short a time.

Iakhovas flung a hand back toward the princes' table. "Warriors, blood of Sekolah's chosen, up until now you have been robbed of the heritage to become true members of We Who Eat as the Great Shark would have wanted. These princes and others like them have held you captive here like prawns in sea elf farms."

Toomaaek tried to silence the crowd but failed. Laaqueel watched as the sahuagin whipped themselves into a frenzy. Fresh anger fed off the fear and confusion that had been left over by the destruction of their city. Iakhovas offered them enemies and a chance to strike back at those enemies at a time when they felt the need to do something. War came naturally to the sahuagin.

"If you continue to follow them," Iakhovas went on, "you'll

overpopulate these waters in time. Or you'll curtail the population so that won't happen, kill your young yourselves and deprive yourselves of the army you will need in the future to conquer Serôs."

The cheering turned thunderous, but somehow Iakhovas could speak over it even though the Vahaxtyl princes couldn't.

"Sekolah found the sahuagin," Iakhovas said, "and he freed them from the shell that was their prison then. Do you think he freed you to find another prison in which to live?"

"No!" filled the water from the throats of thousands of sahuagin.

"We Who Eat were born free," Iakhovas said. "Our heritage is to die free, cleaving the hearts of our enemies and gnawing the flesh from their broken bones!"

The cheering drowned out all other sound. Toomaaek swam over the table and finned down beside Iakhovas, stirring silt with his splayed feet. The prince raised his trident in an open threat.

Instantly, the cheering started to subside.

Slowly, Iakhovas turned to face the Vahaxtyl prince. He stared at the warrior and waited silently. All voices from the crowd had died away when Toomaaek spoke.

"I say you speak lies, Iakhovas of the Claarteeros Sea. Whatever brought you here, it wasn't Sekolah. Your purpose isn't to guide We Who Eat to a greater destiny. You seek only to make our people throw their lives away."

"I speak the truth," Iakhovas replied.

"Then pick up your weapon and defend yourself," the sahuagin prince ordered. "I claim blood combat against any champion you care to name."

Iakhovas regarded the warrior. The sahuagin prince was head and shoulders taller than Iakhovas and weighed nearly half again as much. His skin was dark blue with places that looked almost black.

Since someone of lesser rank was challenging him, Laaqueel knew according to sahuagin custom that Iakhovas could pick one of his guards to fight for him. The priestess waited tensely, knowing how Iakhovas was going to handle the situation.

"I will stand as my own champion," Iakhovas said, "that the truth of my words be more accurately measured."

"Then pick up a weapon." Toomaaek stepped back, his great feet raking up silt in small clouds from the ocean floor.

Iakhovas raised his hands. Bony claws fully six inches long protruded from his fingers. "The only weapon I'll need are these."

"Fool!" Toomaaek snapped.

He backed out into the center of the impromptu meeting area. Without hesitation, Iakhovas followed, gliding up a few feet above the ocean floor with the grace of an eel. He smiled.

"I'm proud of you, Prince Toomaaek," Iakhovas said. "You're a fine sahuagin warrior. My only regret is that you can only die once, but it will be for the good of your people."

Toomaaek didn't waste words. He became an explosion of action. Pulling his barbed net free of his hip, he expertly flung it out at Iakhovas. The net splayed out and sailed true, wrapping around its target. Toomaaek pushed the trident forward and swam after it, driving it before him.

For a moment Laaqueel thought Iakhovas was dead. Her heart almost stopped its frantic beating. Iakhovas hooked his fingers in the net that had wrapped around him. He'd protected his single eye with one arm. Tugging fiercely, he ripped the net off him, tearing the barbed hooks from his flesh at the same time. He screamed in rage and pain.

Toomaaek closed quickly, the trident aimed directly at Iakhovas's heart. In motion almost too fast to be seen, Iakhovas shoved his feet against the water. He shot up, curling gracefully over his attacker as the trident tines missed him by inches. Continuing the roll through the water, Iakhovas flipped behind Toomaaek as the sahuagin prince passed. Cruelly, Iakhovas dug his claws lightly across his opponent's neck, leaving bloody scratches. The claws also sliced through the anterior fins, freeing them from the dorsal fin.

Blood streamed out into the water from the superficial cuts.

Toomaaek threw out his free arm and kicked hard, finning himself into a roll of his own. He tucked forward and under, coming up with the trident again as he faced Iakhovas. The move was designed to catch an enemy from underneath, driving the trident deep into the stomach or crotch. Either would have been a debilitating wound.

Turned as he was from his own flip through the water, Iakhovas had his back to Toomaaek. Though he didn't see the sahuagin warrior's move, Laaqueel knew Iakhovas must have sensed it in some fashion. As the trident sped toward his back, Iakhovas swept out a hand and pushed himself sideways in the water.

The trident tines missed him again by inches. As Toomaaek swam by, already aware he'd missed his opponent, Iakhovas raked claws across the back of the sahuagin prince's lower leg. The sharp edges cleaved flesh easily, drawing blood in a gust.

Laaqueel watched Toomaaek as he tried to turn. His leg was obviously hamstrung, the foot flopping loosely as the current pushed it. Stubbornly, the sahuagin prince turned in the water again. He appeared surprised to see that Iakhovas hadn't pursued him.

"You're wounded," Iakhovas said, still floating in nearly the same spot he had been since the fight had begun. "Stop now and live to help me set your people free."

"No." Toomaaek shook his head. "I'm going to kill you to show them the lies you've promised them."

Laaqueel watched the sahuagin prince. She felt certain it was obvious to the crowd that Iakhovas had deliberately stopped short of tearing Toomaaek's head from his shoulders on the first pass. She watched Iakhovas, marveling at the strength and skill he displayed. When he'd killed Huaanton, Iakhovas had struggled in that fight. Toomaaek was even bigger than Huaanton had been, and Iakhovas was handling him easily.

"They're not lies," Iakhovas told him. "There is greatness coming to We Who Eat. A rebirth. You can be part of it."

"No one can do what you say." Toomaaek finned toward him again, more slowly this time because of the injured leg.

"You have time to reconsider." Iakhovas stood his ground, finning down a couple feet to stand in the silt. "You can heal and still fight the battle that should be yours."

Toomaaek adjusted his approach and sped at his opponent.

Iakhovas ran out of time to move, standing loosely before the sahuagin prince.

Cheers and shouts of anger battered Laaqueel as she watched. She couldn't believe Iakhovas was doing nothing to defend himself. He couldn't use his magic, not without turning away the sahuagin crowd he'd won over.

At the last moment, Iakhovas raised his hands and grabbed the approaching trident. He hooked his fingers over the tines and rocked back slightly as the impact pushed against him. He dug his feet into the ocean bed and shoved as hard as he could.

The trident stopped no more than a finger's width from Iakhovas's chest, but the haft knifed through Toomaaek's heart, spearing him. Blood clouded the water. Triumphantly, Iakhovas lifted the quivering corpse on the end of the trident above his head. He gazed at the princes' table in open challenge. "Is there anyone else who wishes to dispute my words?"

None of the princes answered.

"Then, by the power of blood and combat," Iakhovas said, "I declare myself Deliverer of We Who Eat of Serôs."

Sporadic cheering came from the crowd at first, then grew in intensity until it filled the area. Laaqueel was surprised when Iakhovas simply didn't declare himself king. The malenti knew he could have and also knew that no one there would have challenged him for that right after seeing what he'd done to Toomaaek. The decision seemed to shock the four remaining princes as well.

When the cheering died down a little, Iakhovas swam up, pushing the corpse at the end of the trident above him. "I will deliver you from this captivity," he shouted. "I will find you allies to fight your most hated enemies. I will teach you and mold you into the fiercest army Serôs has ever seen."

The cheering started again, but somehow Iakhovas was able to speak loud enough to be heard.

"I also promise you glory." Iakhovas held steady in the currents, high enough in the water to be seen by everyone. "I will give you the chance to live and die as true sahuagin warriors. Blood will demand blood, but we will drink our fill of it from the skulls of our enemies."

Laaqueel watched Iakhovas, feeling as mesmerized as the Serôsian crowd. He'd won them over and made them his, just as he'd done with her own people. He truly was a gift from Sekolah. The Shark God had answered all her prayers from the time she'd been a little girl to this very day. She *was* something important to her god and her people.

"I *will* break the abomination that is the Sharksbane Wall!" Iakhovas shouted. "You will be free, forever free, to run the course of Serôs."

Laaqueel noticed even Maartaaugh was shouting his support, caught up in the tide of what was happening to the crowd. However, T'Kalah stood in the shadows of the rubble, a dark scowl on his face. Still, she didn't let the royal guard's presence touch her celebratory mood. Iakhovas had triumphed, and she was part of it.

"Born free!" Iakhovas yelled.

The crowd took up the chant. *"Born free!"*

"Die free!" Iakhovas followed.

"Die free!"

"I will take you from this prison that is the Alamber Sea," Iakhovas shouted. "Together we will descend upon the sea elves and destroy them where we find them. I will see Myth Nantar, the sea elves' most sacred city, razed and driven deep into the ocean floor before we are done!"

"Destroy the sea elves!" someone yelled. The crowd took up the chant. "Destroy the sea elves! Raze Myth Nantar!"

"We are born *free!*" Iakhovas screamed to the crowd, using both hands to wave Toomaaek's corpse at the end of the trident haft like a banner.

"We will die free!" the crowd screamed back at him.

"Born free!"

"Die free!"

Laaqueel felt Iakhovas's voice inside her mind. *What do you think, Most Sacred One? Do we have an army?*

Yes. Laaqueel looked around at the thousands of sahuagin standing around them cheering.

I will break Serôs, Iakhovas declared, *and I will forever change the lands of the surface dwellers. No one will avoid my touch or the carnage I will have wrought. I am their destiny!*

Laaqueel knew with certainty that his statements were true. Iakhovas reached up and used his claws to shear Toomaaek into bloody gobbets. He flung the flesh chunks outward, drawing up the closest sahuagin sitting around him.

"Come and eat, warriors. Let us take Toomaaek into battle with us. He stood for what he believed, though he believed wrongly. He can still nourish us. Meat is meat!"

"Meat is meat!" the crowd roared back. "Born free! Die free!"

As Laaqueel watched Iakhovas stripping the flesh from the dead sahuagin, then swimming out to feed the crowd, she knew there was no turning back. Iakhovas had raised his army.

And the Sea of Fallen Stars would fill with blood to pay the butcher's bill.

THE SEA DEVIL'S EYE

The Alamber Sea, Sea of Fallen Stars
4 Flamerule, the Year of the Gauntlet

PROLOGUE

A man's dying scream drew Pacys's attention. To his right, the Sharksbane Wall extended across the sea floor until it disappeared in the gloom. Below and to the left, for as far as Pacys could see, the wall lay in ruins. Chunks of stone and coral lay in a fan shape, as if a huge hammer had shattered the wall.

"Marthammor Duin," Khlinat breathed somewhere above and behind the old bard, "watch over them what wander far and foolishly." The dwarf was thick and broad. Unruly gray whiskers stuck out around his wide face and his hands caressed the hafts of the two hand axes at his waist. He kicked out with his good foot. A gray-green coral peg took the place of his lower right leg.

Elf, merman, and sahuagin all warred below. From this distance, they looked tiny against the wall, but Pacys felt their terror and courage. Those emotions transmuted to musical notes in his mind. He carefully braided and twined them, piecing together the songs that haunted him.

The hum of sahuagin crossbow strings rolled over the sharp clash of coral tridents against stolen or salvaged spears. Even the whisk of the sea devils' barbed nets echoed across the terrain, picked up by the old bard's heightened senses.

For the moment, Pacys *was* the battle. He was the life and death of every one of the hundreds of warriors at the Sharksbane Wall. He wore only a sea elf's diaphanous gown of misty blue. The magic of the emerald bracelet on his wrist allowed him to breathe underwater and kept him comfortable even from the occasional chill. Though he kept his head and jaw shaved, his silver eyebrows hinted at his age. The bard was seventy-six years old, still vigorous but in his waning years.

"Hallowed wall, prized from death,
Built on blood and mortised by fear,
Stood broken, shattered, crumbled,
No longer protecting those here.
  The loyal warriors warred, sinew against sinew.
They fought, and they died,
Clamped tight between unforgiving fangs
Of those who followed the Taker's dark stride."

It wasn't a song of victory. Despite the excitement at having found another piece of the song he'd searched for, the old bard's heart grew cold and heavy.

His trained eye noted the whitish colors of the rock, nearly a dozen hues that he could pick out at a glance, all colored by pearled iridescence from the millennia the wall had stood. The blue sea had texture, the color of a sky rent by gentle summer rains. The uneven terrain at the foot of the Sharksbane Wall spilled in dozens of cliffs and gullies where schools of brightly colored fish cowered.

Through it all, clouds of blood twisted and spun, caught by the shifting ocean currents and the movements of those who fought and died. Even though the bracelet gave him the ability to breathe underwater, it didn't remove the harsh metallic taste of iron.

In the land engagements he'd witnessed, Pacys had smelled the stench of battle, spiced by the fear and anger of the men and women who sold and bought lives with a sword stroke. But here, in the underwater realm of Serôs, the kingdoms scattered across the bottom of the Sea of Fallen Stars, death had flavor.

Pacys steeled himself, gaining control over his lurching stomach. Bright blue light flared like a dying star to Pacys's left. The old bard turned and spotted Taranath Reefglamor, Senior High Mage among the High Mages at Sylkiir. The old elf mage wore his silver hair loose. Blade thin, his blue and white flecked skin hung loose on him. The pointed chin and pointed ears made his face seem harsh and angular. He thrust a hand out at a knot of a dozen nearby sahuagin that swam toward them.

In the blink of an eye, shark's teeth seemed to form in that part of the water. The teeth were etched in silvery gleams, bare sketches that still left no doubt as to what they were.

The cone of shark's teeth grew to twice Pacys's height in width and nearly five times that in length. The sorcery ripped through the sahuagin, shredding flesh and breaking bone. Severed limbs and heads exploded out from the corpses, and mutilated torsos came apart in chunks.

Surviving sahuagin swam at them, clutching their tridents to their chests. Fangs filled their broad mouths to overflowing, showing bone-white and ivory against the teal and pale green of their skins. Fins stuck out from their arms and legs, sharp-edged appendages they used to slice open their prey.

Built broad and squat, hammered into near indestructibility by the pressure of the uncaring ocean, the sahuagin moved gracefully through the water. Webbed feet and hands pulled at the sea. Their magnetic black eyes sucked the light from the depths, black holes that held no mercy.

Pacys brought his staff up. There wasn't time to run.

"Die hu-maan!" the lead sahuagin snarled.

"Friend Pacys!" Khlinat cried.

From the corner of his eye, Pacys watched the dwarf struggling to swim through the water to reach his side. They'd met in Baldur's Gate, at the time of the attack that destroyed the city's harbor, and they'd remained together since.

Pacys struck with the staff, lodging it in the tines of the trident his opponent carried. The old bard pushed away from the attack.

The sahuagin flew past him, streaking toward the dwarf who was clawing up to an even keel.

Pacys reached into the bag of holding at his waist, took out a piece of slate and a fingernail clipping, and held them in his fist.

Pointing with the forefinger of the fist that held the ingredients to his spell, Pacys scribed a powerful symbol in the water that flared pale violet for a moment. He mouthed half a dozen words, then felt the explosion in his fist as the spell claimed the materials in his hand.

Gray ash spilled from his hand as a shimmering wall formed in the water before him. A dull roar blasted out from the other side of the shimmering wall.

The sahuagin trapped there writhed in agony. The sahuagin, like many sea creatures, had lateral lines that ran the length of their bodies. Those lines sensed vibrations in the water, and the roar was agony to them.

Pacys swam for Khlinat.

"Foul devilspawn," Khlinat roared in a voice only a dwarf in full battle frenzy could muster. "I'll keelhaul ye and have yer guts for garters, I will. I'm one of the Ironeater clan, one of the fiercest, fightingest dwarven clans ever blessed by Marthammor Duin!"

"Die!" the sahuagin replied in its raspy voice.

The bard gripped his staff in the middle and twisted. Foot-long, razor-edged blades shot from both ends.

The sahuagin released its hold on Khlinat's hand axe, then ran its talons down the dwarf's arm.

Yelping with pain and surprise, Khlinat brought his knees up, then shoved his claw coral peg into the sahuagin's chest. The peg burst through the sahuagin's back. Blood roiled out and settled in a cloud around the creature's upper body.

"I done for ye," Khlinat declared, putting his other foot on the sahuagin's face and kicking out. "Behind ye, songsmith, and be right quick about it, too."

Moving with the fluid grace of a dancer, Pacys whipped the staff around. The razor-edged blade sank into the sahuagin's shoulder next to its thick neck.

The creature's momentum and speed shoved Pacys back and down as he held onto the staff. The old bard ripped the staff free, and let his momentum carry him around. The staff flashed as the sahuagin swam over his head. The keen blade ripped across the creature's stomach, spilling its entrails in a loose tangle.

Two sahuagin who'd been close to the one Pacys disemboweled were overcome by the bloodlust that fired their species. Their predatory instincts sent them after the easier prey of their own kind rather than the bard. Their jaws snapped and clicked, biting into the tender flesh released into the sea. They followed their dying comrade toward the seabed below.

Pacys moved the staff in his hands, keeping himself loose, but his head played the song that would be part of the fall of the Sharksbane Wall. It was not a song of victory. The music was a dirge, a song of defeat and death.

A dozen sahuagin surrounded the bard and the dwarf. Pacys swam toward Khlinat, putting his back to the dwarf's.

One of the sahuagin in front of the bard lunged forward.

"I've got 'im, songsmith," Khlinat said. "Mind you watch yerself."

The dwarf sliced his right axe across, shearing off two of the sahuagin's fingers. Before Khlinat could recover his balance, another sahuagin threw one of the barbed nets over him.

Khlinat bawled in rage and pain. He slid his fingers through the openings in the net and tried to pull it away, but succeeded only in sinking a dozen or more of the bone hooks into his own flesh.

Pacys ripped free the keen-edged, dark gray coral knife from his belt and raked the blade at the net strands, parting a handful of them.

A sahuagin swam across the top of the net, grabbed the loose line floating at the top of the seaweed hemp, and dragged Khlinat easily after it.

Another sahuagin swam up from under the net and rammed its trident into the old bard's right thigh. The sahuagin swam backward and yanked hard on the cord. The pain hit Pacys with blinding intensity.

Suddenly, a fan-shaped spray of bright red, gold, green, and red-violet lanced through the water. Pacys experienced a sudden vertigo, then the feeling passed and he only felt slightly dizzy. The sahuagin pulling him lost its bearing and started flailing helplessly in the water.

"Easy, Taleweaver."

The old bard recognized Reefglamor's voice and turned in time to see the Senior High Mage swim toward him. A group of mermen and sea elves were with him. They moved among the disoriented sahuagin and stabbed their swords and knives through the creatures' gill slits, then ripped all the way through, bleeding them out.

Reefglamor laid his hand on the trident that impaled Pacys's leg. He spoke a few words, and a pale green fire leaped from the High Mage's fingers and quickly enveloped the offending trident. In the next heartbeat, the trident was gone, leaving only gray-black ash to drift along the ocean's currents. Two mermen freed Khlinat from the net.

Further down below, the battle raging across the fallen section of the Sharksbane Wall continued.

"We are losing this fight," Reefglamor stated in a low voice.

"Yes," Pacys agreed reluctantly.

"Senior," Pharom Ildacer called. His fondness for food and drink made him more round than most sea elves. Black strands still stained his silver hair and he wore a deep purple weave. Anxiety colored his features. "We can't stay. The guards here can't hold their positions."

"I know," Reefglamor said. "Gather who we can, and let's save as many of them as we are able."

Ildacer nodded and swam away.

The music inside Pacys's head continued, mournful and hollow. He was certain the song would stand in the memories of its listeners as strongly as the fall of Cormanthyr and the flight of the elves.

"There! Do you see it then?" one of the nearby mermen asked, pointing with the trident he held. "That's the Taker's ship."

Pacys spotted the great galley cutting through the water. It was strange to see the big ship completely submerged, yet moving like a great black shadow.

And somewhere aboard her, Pacys knew, the Taker savored his victory. The threat from the sea was a threat no longer, and death now traveled through the world of Serôs, powered by sharp fins and devouring fangs.

1

"What you want here, boy? Is it enough for ye to take a man's rightful belongings, or are ye gonna cut an honest man's throat too?"

Jherek pressed the older man up against the back wall of the Bare Bosom and held a scaling knife hard against the man's bewhiskered throat.

The man was in his early forties and his breath stank of beer. A skull and crossbones tattooed over his heart advertised his chosen profession.

Jherek breathed hard, and struggled to keep his hand from shaking. Full night had descended over the pirate city of Immurk's Hold hours ago. Clouds covered all but a handful of blue-white stars. Shadows filled the narrow alley behind the tavern.

Even at nineteen, Jherek was bigger and broader than the pirate, his muscles made hard from years of working as both shipwright and sailor. His light brown hair caught the silver gleam of the stars in the highlights bleached by the sun, and hung past his shoulders now. His pale gray eyes belonged to a wolf living in the wild. He wore leather armor under a dark blue cloak that reached to the tops of his boots. A cutlass hung at his side.

"If it's me purse ye want," the pirate offered, swallowing hard, "yer gonna find it light tonight. I been swilling old Kascher's homemade beer and dallying with them women what he keeps upstairs."

"I'm not after your purse," Jherek whispered. The very idea of robbing the man turned his stomach.

"Slice his damned throat."

Jherek cut his gaze over to the left, startled by the harshness of the words.

Talif stood near the building, fitting in neatly with the shadows. A sharp short sword was in his fist. He was one of Captain Azla's pirate crew. The ship's hand had stringy black hair and a triangular face covered with stubble.

"He lives—or we live. Which is it going to be?" Talif sneered.

Sabyna Truesail sat at a table in a hostel across the cobblestone street from the Bare Bosom and tried to relax. Nothing worked; she still worried.

The hostel was small, and at this time of night most of the guests meandered over to the Bare Bosom for more ribald festivities. The rest had called it a night in favor of an early morning. Sabyna, Captain Azla of *Black Champion,* and Sir Glawinn—a paladin in the service of Lathander—were half the crowd in the common room of the hostel. The scents of spiced meat and smoked fish warred against the stench of pipeweed and bitter ale. The tavern crowd could be heard easily from across the street, screamed curses mixed in with shouts of glee.

"I believe your attention would be better served elsewhere," Glawinn stated softly.

The paladin was middle aged but only a couple inches taller than Sabyna. He possessed a medium build, but carried himself with confidence, every inch a soldier. His black beard was short-cropped. Tonight he wore leather armor with a dark gray cloak over it. He used a brooch with Lathander's morning sun colors to hold the cloak around his shoulders.

"Where should I look?" Sabyna asked.

She stood a little more than five and a half feet tall, with copper-colored curls shorn well short of her shoulders. Seasons spent with the sun and sea had darkened her skin, but a spattering of freckles still crossed the bridge of her nose and her cheeks. Light from the big stone fireplace that warmed the hostel against the wet chill of the sea ignited reddish brown flames in her eyes. Her clothing was loose and baggy, worn that way so it wouldn't draw attention to her femininity.

Beside them, Azla wrinkled her nose in distaste. She held a half-drunk schooner of ale curled neatly in one gloved hand.

"He means you need to stop looking out that window so much," the pirate captain stated. "You're going to draw attention." Azla was a half-elf, bearing the characteristic pointed ears and slender build of her elf parent. Her features were beautiful and dusky, made even darker by a dozen years and more in the sun and wind. Silky black hair hung just to her shoulders, cut straight across. She wore a green blouse so dark it was almost black, and leather breeches dyed dark blue.

"The thing that worries me," Sabyna said, "is that he doesn't seem to be himself."

"No," the paladin said, "our young warrior is torn."

"By what?" Sabyna asked.

She risked another glance at the Bare Bosom, watching a sailor stride drunkenly from the establishment in the company of a serving wench doing her best to prop him up. The girl's fingers found the man's coin purse.

"There are things I feel a man should be willing to discuss on his own without having others discuss them for him," Glawinn answered.

"He could get killed over there tonight," Azla warned coldly.

"True enough," Glawinn replied, "but sometimes you have to rely on faith."

Azla snorted. "Faith isn't as certain as cold steel."

"It is for some." Glawinn's words were soft, but strong.

"Faith has never done well by me," Azla went on. A trace of bitterness threaded through her words.

Sabyna knew the captain hadn't always been a pirate. Azla had grown up in the Dalelands, but events and her own guilt forced her down to the Sea of Fallen Stars and into a pirate's life. Glawinn had no way of knowing that.

"The problem could be that you're not supposed to expect faith to do well by you," the paladin said. "You're supposed to do well by your faith."

"I am a mage," Sabyna said. "My faith is strong enough, but I'm no cleric to be led around by looking at a chicken's entrails to figure out what my chosen god wants me to do. I believe in knowledge. Our gods choose what knowledge to put in our paths, but it's up to us to learn it and choose what to do with it."

"My faith is not that way," Glawinn said. "I choose to let Lathander set me upon a path, trusting in the Morninglord that I will know what to do when the time comes."

"More men have died from conflicting beliefs than over gold and silver," Azla said. "Trusting a god is a very dangerous thing."

"On that issue, Captain," Glawinn said gravely, "I fear we'll have to disagree."

Sabyna pulled her cloak more tightly around her against the night's chill. More than anything she wanted to be up and around, doing something but not knowing what. "He's changed so much since I first met him," she whispered.

"How so?" Glawinn asked.

Across the street, a handful of cargo handlers deep in conversation walked across the uneven boardwalk in front of the Bare Bosom. One of them carried a shielded candle hanging from a crooked stick that barely beat back the night.

"When he first came aboard *Breezerunner,* there was a quiet desperation in him," Sabyna said. "I didn't understand that, now I understand his feelings even less after seeing how he handled himself aboard *Breezerunner.* He stood up against Vurgrom and his pirate crew in the middle of a maelstrom and never faltered. Now he seems . . ."

"Afraid?" A faint smile twisted Glawinn's lips. "He's a warrior, lady."

"Then why should he be afraid?"

"So that he might live, of course." Glawinn sipped his drink. "Warriors live with fear as they might a lover. They never forget that fear, else they step closer to Cyric's cold embrace."

The ship's mage wrapped her arms even tighter around herself, losing the battle against the night's chill creeping in against the banked coals filling the hostel's fireplace.

"Then where does that leave him?" she asked.

"He's dangerous," Azla commented. "He's dangerous to himself and to us."

"I don't think that's entirely true," Glawinn said.

The pirate captain shook her head. "I don't mean to disparage your beliefs, Sir Glawinn, but men believe what they want to believe. Sometimes purely because they have nothing else to believe in."

"And to live a life with nothing to believe in?" The paladin looked directly at her and asked, "What kind of life is that?"

Azla broke the eye contact, put on a deprecating smile, and said, "A very profitable one. If you're a pirate."

"Gold and silver assuages a wounded heart?"

Azla's eyes turned cold and hard. "You step over lines here, paladin."

"Forgive me, lady," Glawinn replied, though he showed no remorse, "I do indeed."

Sabyna watched the exchange in silence. She didn't know how Glawinn knew so much about the pirate captain, but she was aware how close he was to the truth. Azla's own life was filled with tragedy. The ship's mage reached for the hot tea she'd ordered and sipped it only to find that it was now cold.

"The thing that most concerns me is that your young friend didn't come here to take that pearl disk back from Vurgrom," Azla said.

"Then what?" Sabyna asked.

Azla kept her voice quiet and still. "I think it's very possible that your young friend came here to die as nobly as he can."

"I can't kill him," Jherek said. He stood in the alley, his body pressed up against the man, and silently damned all the events and the false pride that led to the point of holding a man's life at the edge of his knife.

"Then let me." Talif stepped forward and lifted the short sword.

The man in Jherek's grip tensed, on the verge of fleeing and taking his chances.

Jherek swung his empty hand, balling it into a fist and rolling his shoulder to get most of his weight behind the blow. His fist caught the pirate on the point of his chin and dropped him.

Talif knelt and grabbed the man by the hair. He swung his short sword toward the man's exposed throat.

Jherek kicked Talif in the chest, knocking him back across the hard-packed earth of the alley. Talif rolled instantly, coming up from the ground like a trained acrobat. His triangular face was a mask of rage. The short sword came around in a glittering arc.

The young sailor stepped in close and brought up his left arm. His open hand smacked into Talif's wrist and blocked the sword strike. Talif grunted in pain and anger. Before the mate could recover, Jherek slipped his free arm under the man's outstretched one and flipped him over his shoulder.

Carried by his own weight and momentum, pulled by Jherek's strength, Talif landed hard on the ground on his back. Murderous rage gleamed in his black eyes. "You're a fool," Talif snarled.

"That remains to be seen," Jherek said, "but I do know I am no murderer."

Talif struggled a moment to get free but couldn't.

"You knocked that man out, boy, but I've seen men knocked cold like that before. Sometimes they come around in just minutes, none the worse for it. He could still come into the tavern after us and let them all know we're among them."

"He doesn't know who we are," Jherek said quietly.

"By Leira's razor kiss, you fool, that man has seen me. He'll know I sail with Cap'n Azla."

"So you say." Jherek shook his head. "Maybe that's just your pride talking. We'll take our chances."

Talif cursed him soundly, using invective that would have shamed even most sailors.

Jherek maintained his grip even though Talif sought to shake out of it. "You think me a fool for letting this man live, but keep in mind that should a man attack me willingly with a sword in his fist, I'll not be so generous."

"A man doesn't always see the sword that cleaves him, boy," Talif threatened.

Jherek nodded. "But Glawinn would know." Azla's pirates walked lightly around the paladin.

"Umberlee take you both," Talif snarled. "The two of you think you're so high and mighty."

Jherek felt even more embarrassed. Glawinn was a paladin, a noble and courageous man who lived for honor and served a god who put quests and challenges before him. The young sailor knew he didn't belong in such company. He was only a foolish boy with misbegotten pride and an ill luck that followed him all his life as a birthright from his pirate father.

"Standing among men such as yourself," Jherek said in a harsh voice, "Sir Glawinn has no choice but to shine. I'd keep a civil tongue in your head, otherwise I'm going to feel that you're questioning his honor. That's something I won't allow."

Talif started to say something, but he glanced into Jherek's eyes, swallowed his words, and looked away.

Jherek released the man and stood with easy grace. He slipped the scaling knife back into his boot, then turned and walked toward the tavern's back door. He knew Talif thought about attacking him, but he counted on his own hearing and the dim shadows that moved on the alley wall to warn him if the man tried. And, truth to tell, maybe he didn't care.

Talif straightened his clothing and followed him a heartbeat later. A short flight of steps led up to the tavern's back door. The door was narrow and made of scarred hardwood that showed years of abuse by guests and thieves and the neglect of uncaring employees.

Azla proved most resourceful as a pirate captain, though, and had provided Jherek a key that let him pass. He opened the door and stepped inside. A mixture of spicy odors tweaked his nose, almost drawing a sneeze. The aroma filling the room also held the scent of jerked beef and the strong odor of seafood. The stink of smoky grease overlaid everything.

Sand covered grease spills on the stained wooden floor. Grit rolled and crunched under Jherek's boots as he walked toward the narrow door on the east wall. He found the latch with his fingers and slipped it open with a tiny screech that he knew wasn't heard over the uproar in the tavern's main serving area.

Quietly, he went up the narrow and winding staircase, making himself go when every thought in his mind was to turn and leave. Kascher, Azla had assured him, used the hidden passageway to serve meals to guests who preferred to remain incognito. The man the young sailor was after was such a man.

Kascher's Bare Bosom tavern stood three stories tall, shouldered between the warehouses along the natural harbor at the center of Immurk's Hold.

On the top floor, Jherek paused at the door, listening. Muted voices echoed in the hall as footsteps passed.

The young sailor let himself out into the passageway. His eyes narrowed briefly even against the dim brightness of the small oil lamps hanging on the walls.

He glanced at the door on the right, reading the numbers. According to the information Azla gave him, the room he wanted was at the end.

The door at the end of the corridor was heavy oak, reinforced with bands of beaten iron.

"One side, pup," Talif said arrogantly. "Let a man do his job."

Grudgingly, Jherek stepped aside, leaving the door open to Talif. The thief moved to the door with a small smile curling his thin lips.

"Ah, pup," he whispered, "there's nothing like the sensation of being someplace you ought not be." Thin pieces of metal glinted briefly in his gloved hands. "Gladdens a man's heart, it does. The chance to prowl through another's secrets, steal kisses from another man's woman . . . there's nothing more sweet."

Shamed and furious, Jherek turned away. He heard the thin scratches of metal and tried to ignore them. The subtle arts Talif practiced went against everything Jherek believed in. Yet here he was, depending and hoping on the man's skills that he might set a greater wrong right.

The young sailor glanced out a window at the city. Torches gleamed brightly along the wharf. From the tavern room, Jherek saw ships at anchor, men scurrying about aboard them, carrying crates and other prizes they'd no doubt taken from some luckless merchanter. His father, he knew, would have been perfectly at home here.

Farther into the interior of the city, fewer torches gleamed. The houses were ramshackle affairs for the most part, places cast together by seafaring men for families formed more by desperation than any emotion.

The men who worked the night were down by the harbor and the others lay abed or in the dozens of taverns throughout the city. Shadowy figures crossed the narrow, twisting streets below, some of them in groups but most of them alone. Thin wails of bawdy pirate chanteys drifted over the rooftops. The only thing that seemed normal to Jherek was the salt smell that lingered in the air.

"I'm done, pup. Do you want to join me?" Talif's whisper barely carried to Jherek's ears.

"Aye."

The young sailor drew his cutlass, the razor edge sliding free of the sash he used to bind it to his waist. He filled his other hand with the wickedly curved boat hook.

Pausing, Jherek nudged up the thin glass protecting the oil lamp's wick and flame. He blew it out, then replaced the glass cover. That end of the room darkened immediately.

"You have more skills at this kind of skullduggery than you'd think, pup," Talif said as he eased the door open. "Maybe you're not so honest as I thought, or you'd like to believe."

Jherek didn't argue, but he felt a sick lurching inside his stomach. Pirate's get and thief—he didn't really deserve any other label. Except maybe fool.

Talif led the way into the room, and Jherek covered his back. The young sailor heard the hoarse rasp of deep breathing as he gently closed the door.

Reaching back, Talif pressed a finger against Jherek's chest. "Wait," the man hissed.

Jherek breathed shallowly, taking in the sour odor of unwashed flesh and old rotgut whiskey. The stench of pipeweed clung to the room, salted with the flavor of cheap perfume.

"Not alone," Talif whispered. "I smell a woman."

For a moment, Jherek considered leaving the room. Catching the man they were after, even with everything Azla had ferreted out, had been difficult and risky enough. Endangering an innocent wasn't something he was prepared to do.

Talif's finger left his chest and the man glided silently across the room, a swiftly moving shadow.

Jherek moved immediately. His own vision quickly adjusted to the dark. The room was spacious but held only a couple trunks, an armoire that listed badly to one side, and a four-poster bed shrouded in mosquito netting.

"Alive," Jherek warned.

Reluctantly, Talif nodded. He moved to the left of the bed, while Jherek moved to the right.

Jherek put the hook back in his sash, then reached for the sleeping figure, brushing aside the mosquito netting with the blade of the cutlass. He clamped his hand on a face that he suddenly realized was too small, too smooth, and without whiskers.

At the other end of his arm, the young woman he'd grabbed by mistake opened her eyes wide in fear. She tried to sit up in bed. Jherek was so surprised by the turn of events that he didn't resist, watching in horror and embarrassment as the sheets fell away from her bare breasts.

The other form in the bed lurched up, a wickedly curved scimitar sliding free of the space between the feather-filled mattress and the carved headboard. Jorn Frennik was a large man, broad shouldered and beefy from a dozen years and more of living the savage life of a pirate.

Like the woman, he was naked, but he wore his calf-high boots. Bed covers flew as the pirate forced himself to his feet in the middle of the bed, yelling in rage and fear. He drew his scimitar back to swing.

2

Jorn Frennick's scimitar cleaved the air sharply, and Jherek met the yelling pirate's steel with his own. Sparks flared from the blades.

Despite the shadows and darkness filling the room, Jherek read the pirate's moves. Keeping track of the woman on the bed was harder, but he managed.

"Kill him!" Talif croaked hoarsely as he jockeyed for position.

"No," Jherek ordered. "We need him alive."

Frennick shifted on the bed, kicking at the frightened woman and forcing her away from him. She screamed in pain and covered her head with her hands.

Moving swiftly, Jherek raised a booted foot and slammed it into the center of the man's chest as hard as he could, getting his weight behind the thrust.

Frennick flew backward off the bed and crashed against the wall. Plaster shattered as he burst the inner wall and dust roiled up in a great cloud.

Jherek pursued the man, striding across the bed and barely avoiding the naked woman cowering in the twisted bedding. He slipped through the mosquito netting.

Wheezing, his face a mask of rage, Frennick struggled desperately to push himself up from the wreckage of the wall.

The young sailor feinted, drawing out Frennick's attack. Jherek stepped back just enough to let the wickedly curved blade pass by him. He slammed his cutlass broadside against the pirate's scimitar, trapping it against the left side of Frennick's body.

"I'm gonna kill you, whelp!" the pirate roared. "Gonna have your guts for garters, I am!"

The young sailor ducked his head forward, slamming the top of his skull into Frennick's face. The pirate's nose broke with a snap. Blood gushed over his beard. Before Frennick could recover, Jherek drew back his left hand, balled it into a fist, and slammed it against the man's jaw twice. Frennick staggered. Still in motion, the young sailor grabbed a handful of Frennick's beard and slammed the man's head up against the wall. He lifted his knee three times in quick succession, driving it into Frennick's stomach.

Vomit streamed suddenly from Frennick's mouth, a gush of noxious liquid that spilled down his chest and stomach. The stench of soured hops almost gagged Jherek, but the young sailor breathed shallowly through his mouth.

The strength drained from Frennick in a rush as he struggled to regain his breath. Jherek kicked the scimitar from the man's hand. He placed a foot on the back of Frennick's head to hold the pirate in place, then turned back to the woman on the bed.

Talif leaned over her, holding a pillow over her face. The woman struggled, kicking her feet and scratching with her fingernails. Talif cursed her in a quiet voice.

Jherek slipped the knife from his boot and threw it. The effort wasn't hidden by his body as Malorrie and Glawinn had coached.

The knife spun and cut the air.

Cursing, Talif leaped to one side so it wouldn't spear his face. "Umberlee take you," he snarled.

The woman on the bed sucked in her breath in ragged gasps. She peered at the young sailor with rolling, frightened eyes, not bothering to cover her nakedness at all. Tears tracked down her face, and she shivered.

Still cursing him, Talif turned his attention to the small chest at the foot of the bed. "If she leaves the room, she'll warn the tavern—maybe call his mates up here on us."

Jherek gazed at the woman. "Lady," he said softly enough only to be heard over the noise coming from the tavern below, "I ask that you not leave this room."

Slowly, the woman sank more deeply into the bedding. She shook her head in a small motion that stirred her dark curls and said, "No, sir. No, I won't try to leave."

The term of respect, applied in such a situation, stung Jherek. He dropped his eyes from the woman's in shame. To have come so far pursuing what he hoped would have been a clue to his destiny, only to end up like this, making prisoners of frightened women, it was almost too much. If it were up to him, he would have left then, but the pearl disk Vurgrom took was not Jherek's to leave.

Talif ransacked the room with quick, knowing movements. Small drawers came out of the chest at the foot of the bed. Each was checked, inside and under, before being discarded. The thief even went on to disassemble some of the bigger pieces, checking for hiding places within them.

Frennick remained dazed, sick drool oozing occasionally from the corner of his mouth.

Jherek bound the man's hand behind his back with strips torn from the stained and faded sheets. He yanked the man to his feet. Frennick swayed drunkenly, like a storm-tossed cog riding out a stiff crosswind.

"Lady," the young sailor said, "I have one more task to ask of you."

"Yes, sir." She looked at him in bright fear.

"Could you dress him, please?"

Talif's derisive snort filled the room.

Cautiously, the woman climbed from the bed. She left the bedding behind and stood naked, embarrassing Jherek further. She took the pirate's clothing from a pile beside the bed, choosing the breeches first.

"At least have the common sense to go through his clothing first," Talif called out as he helped himself to the coins inside Frennick's duffel.

"Search his clothing then," Jherek told the woman. "Leave his personal effects. I'm looking for a gold disk that looks very old. At its center is a pearl with a carved trident overlying a conch shell."

The woman knelt and began searching the pirate's clothing with experienced fingers, easily finding hidden pockets sewn into the material. Coins and small gems scattered on the floor before her, barely catching the dim light. Two small, very sharp blades that couldn't be properly called knives slid across the floor as well.

Frennick stood straighter, growling under his breath. "You've signed your own death warrant, boy. You do know that?"

"My death," Jherek told the pirate, looking him calmly in the eye, "was guaranteed the day of my birth. The only thing that remains to be seen is the how of it."

"At the end of my sword," Frennick promised, "with your guts spilled before you."

The young sailor glanced down at the woman, who was busy making some of the coins and gems disappear.

"No, lady," he said gently. "Don't rob him. You don't want him looking for you later."

The woman looked up and said, "He owes me a night's wages."

Embarrassed, knowing what the wages covered, Jherek gave her a tight nod. "As you will," he said.

"The night's not over," Frennick grumbled. "She didn't earn all her wages."

"The night was over for you," the woman rasped. "Once you've gotten so deeply into your cups and sated yourself like some rutting goat, you never wake again until well after morningfeast."

Frennick snuffled, drawing in phlegm and saliva, preparing to spit.

Jherek yanked the pirate's head back as he spat. Frennick succeeded only in spitting into his own face.

"No," he told Frennick softly, hating that he was taking part in any of the night's events.

The pirate growled in rage.

"Take a fair price, lady," Jherek said. "No more, no less."

Jherek watched as the woman hesitated, then dropped most of the coins and gems back to the floor.

"I can't find a disk like the one you described, sir," the woman said.

"Please dress him," Jherek replied.

Frennick kicked at her, but the woman quickly dodged away. Jherek rapped the man's ear with the flat of the cutlass blade, splitting the skin.

"Conscious, or dead weight," the young sailor promised, "I'm getting you out of here tonight. How things go after that will depend on how you act now."

Reluctantly, Frennick stood, then stepped into the breeches the woman held ready for him.

"Watch her," Talif advised from the other side of the room. He pried at the facing along the bottom of the wall, searching for hidden places. The wood pulled out easily. "She may act like she hates that bastard, but she may try to slip him a knife all the same."

Jherek didn't respond. He was already aware of that possibility. He watched carefully, trying to ignore the embarrassment he felt at watching the smooth, rolling nakedness the woman presented.

"Put back everything you've taken," the young sailor said.

"What?" Talif demanded.

Jherek spared the man a hard glance and said, "I won't be party to robbery."

"What do you think we're doing here tonight?"

"Taking something back that Frennick has no right to," Jherek answered.

Talif glared at the young sailor, trying to intimidate him. Jherek met the other man's gaze.

"I mean what I say," the young sailor said, "and I'll know if you lie and try to take something."

Despite his own show of will, Talif melted before the younger man's gaze. "Cyric take you," he said. "Are you afraid for your soul?"

"No," Jherek answered, knowing that the birthright passed on by his father already doomed him, "but I will stand accountable for my actions."

"These are *my* actions."

"You wouldn't be here if it weren't for me."

"Foolish, prideful stubbornness."

"Aye," Jherek responded without rancor. "Call it as you will, but you will not leave here with any stolen goods."

"Others will steal it in our stead," Talif protested.

"But we won't."

Uttering venomous curses, Talif emptied his pockets of coins, gems, and pieces of jewelry.

"I've not found your precious disk, boy, and I've searched every inch of this room."

"That disk is not here," Frennick said. He stood dressed in boots and breeches. With his hands behind his back, the woman hadn't been able to get a blouse on him. "Vurgrom has it."

Jherek faced the pirate more squarely and asked, "Where can we find Vurgrom?"

"If I tell you, Vurgrom will kill me."

Talif stepped closer, a wickedly curved blade in his hand, and said, "At least the death he hands out won't come as soon as the one we'll give you."

"There are things worse than death," Frennick said. "Vurgrom knows many of them."

Jherek grabbed a cloak from the foot of the bed. He checked through it quickly for weapons, turning up three knives, a sap, and a set of brass knuckles. He dropped the collection to the bed and draped the cloak over Frennick's shoulders, securing it with a brooch at the throat. Unless someone looked closely, they'd never know he went blouseless beneath it.

"You're even more of a fool than I believed to think you can simply walk this man through the tavern and out the building," Talif stated.

"He knows about Lathander's disk," Jherek replied. "I need to know what he knows of it, and Captain Azla wishes to know about Vurgrom's movements."

The young sailor placed a hand on his prisoner's shoulders and shoved him forward.

"You can't just leave my valuables out for anyone to take," Frennick protested.

Jherek kept the man moving forward. "I won't be taking them," he said.

The noise from the pirates gathered downstairs filled the hallway, echoing up the stairwells that led down to the tavern. They were noisy and they were drunk, but the young sailor knew every sword in the place would be turned against him if they figured out what he was doing.

Over thirty pirates crowded into the Bare Bosom tavern, seated on the long, rough-hewn benches on two sides of the uneven rectangular tables in the center of the large room. The wooden walls held scars that were obscene pictographs, fake treasure maps, and touchstones for tall tales told over tankards of ale when storms kept men from the sea. A fireplace built into the far wall held caldrons of fish stew and clam chowder.

Booming, drunken voices raised in song and tale-telling made a cacophony of noise. The soot-stained windows at the front of the tavern faced the empty, dark street outside.

Three serving wenches made the rounds of the tables, ale-headed enough now that they no longer avoided the groping hands of the pirates. Only one of the serving girls seemed determined to stay out of their grasps. She was thin and short, looking barely into her teens if the rosy glow on her cheeks was any indication.

Behind the bar, amid the clutter of shelves that held glasses and bottles, was the tavern's centerpiece. It looked as if the prow of a ship had smashed through the wall, leaving ripped timbers in its wake. The prow held a mermaid whose carved auburn hair flowed back to become part of the ship. Her proud breasts stood out above the narrow waist that turned to scales.

Frennick hesitated for a moment, and Jherek tightened his grip on the man's arm.

The young sailor kept his prisoner moving, using his body to press the man toward the broad oak door. Jherek and his prisoner were at the door when the girl screamed behind them.

At first Jherek thought it was the woman they'd left in the room above. He turned swiftly, stepping back and away from Frennick so the pirate couldn't turn on him.

A pair of the pirates caught up the young serving girl. Her long skirt and sleeveless blouse looked incongruous compared to the scanty clothes of the other wenches. Her blond hair fanned out over her shoulders as one of the pirates ripped her scarf from her head. She struggled in the powerful grip of the man who held her.

"Let's see what you look like when you let your hair down, you little vixen," the pirate said. "Old Tharyg believes you're a pretty little peach."

The girl tried to batter the old pirate with her fists but Tharyg seized them effortlessly. She shrilled in frustration and fear.

The bartender and bodyguards stayed back, thin, wolfish grins on their faces.

"Clear the room," Tharyg entreated. "Give a sailing man room to work."

The pirates pushed themselves up and staggered into motion. Bets were placed on Tharyg's ability after imbibing so much ale. " 'E'll never get the old Jolly Roger unfurled!" one man cried out.

The girl continued to scream and fight, but it was no use. She was outnumbered and overpowered. They held her at wrist and ankle, pinning her to one of the rectangular tables.

Jherek paused, knowing these events weren't uncommon in such a place as the Bare Bosom.

"No." Talif came up behind the young sailor and shoved him forward, adding, "Leave her to the jackals."

"I can't," Jherek said.

"You're a fool," Talif told him, his eyes hard.

"Get him to Captain Azla."

"Aye. Good-bye and good riddance," Talif grumbled as he prodded Frennick through the door.

Coldly calm, Jherek approached the group of pirates. He caught up a chair in his free hand and never broke his purposeful stride.

Laaqueel luxuriated in the swim to the mudship *Tarjana*. The water off the coast of Turmish was dirtier than she was accustomed to, but the brine was sweet relief after all the hours of overland travel.

She was malenti, a sahuagin trapped by the appearance of a hated sea elf. The dreaded mutation happened to sahuagin born too close to sea elves. Her life had been further cursed by the fact that her skin was the pink of a surface world elf, not the blue or green of a true sea elf.

Somewhat less than six feet tall, slender and supple, she looked weak.

She wore her night-black hair pulled back, bound with fish bones and bits of coral. Her clothing consisted only of the war harness worn by the sahuagin, straps around her waist, thighs, and arms that allowed her to tie weapons and nets so she could keep her hands free.

Iakhovas's mystical ship lay at anchor half a mile from shore, only a short distance for one born to wander the sea. *Tarjana* was one hundred thirty feet long and twenty feet wide, and took one hundred forty rowers, seventy to a side. There was enough room aboard to comfortably fit another one hundred fifty men. Huge crossbows with harpoon-sized quarrels lined the port and starboard sides. Purple and yellow sails lay furled around the three tall masts. Sahuagin warriors filled the deck as well as the water around the ship.

Laaqueel swam among the sahuagin without comment. As senior high priestess to the king, she demanded respect. She grabbed the net hung over the vessel's side and pulled herself up, regretting the need to leave the sea. She crossed to the stern castle and knocked on the door to the captain's quarters.

"Enter," Iakhovas's great voice boomed from inside the room.

The malenti priestess felt a momentary tingle when she touched the door latch and knew that Iakhovas had heavily warded the entrance. She stepped through into the large room and blinked, adjusting her vision against the darkness within.

"Did you find the item I sent you for?" Iakhovas asked.

"Yes, Most Exalted One, but I lost all the warriors under my command."

Laaqueel stood, waiting to be chastised.

"The druids are a cunning and vicious lot. Don't worry, Most Favored One, the Shark God smiles down on you without respite."

Iakhovas sat in a large whalebone chair that could have doubled as a throne. Though other sahuagin aboard *Tarjana* only saw him as one of their own, the malenti priestess saw him as human, though she wasn't sure if even that was his real form.

Iakhovas stood over seven feet tall, an axe handle wide at the shoulders and thick-chested. Black hair spilled over his shoulders, framing a face that would have been handsome if not for the ancient scarring that twisted his features. He wore a short beard and mustache. A black eye patch covered the empty socket. He was dressed in black breeches and a dark green shirt. A flowing black cloak hung over his shoulders.

The table before him was nailed to the ship's floor so it wouldn't move in rough seas. Dozens of objects littered the tabletop.

Laaqueel recognized some of them from the hunts Iakhovas had engineered over the years. Others were from recent finds made by Vurgrom and the other Inner Sea pirates. Sea elves and other creatures, as well as many sahuagin warriors, had died in the gathering of those things. Just as the sahuagin warriors that accompanied her that day had died.

Iakhovas worked diligently at his task. He picked up a curved instrument set with five green gems, each of a different hue. In his hands, the instrument grew steadily smaller, until it was a tiny thing almost lost between his thumb and forefinger. Satisfied with his efforts, he fitted the piece into a small golden globe in the palm of his hand. A distinct, high-pitched note sounded when the instrument fit into place.

"Give me the item I sent you for," he commanded.

The malenti reached into the net at her side and brought forth the slim rod she'd found in the druid's wooden altar. It was scarcely as long as her forearm and as thin as a finger. Carved runes glowed beneath the surface but none of them were familiar to her.

Iakhovas took the rod from her, running it through his fingers with familiarity. The rod glowed dull orange for a moment, then faded. He closed his hands over it and it shrank. With practiced ease, he slid the small version of the rod into the golden globe. It clicked home.

A thousand questions ran through Laaqueel's mind, but they were all prompted by her doubts about him. She forced them away as she'd done for months. Even if Iakhovas's motives and methods were questionable, he still followed the edicts set forth by Sekolah, strengthening and improving the sahuagin condition across the seas of Toril.

Iakhovas finished a final adjustment on the golden globe in his hand, then popped it into the empty socket where his eye had been. The orb gleamed. He stood, and his appearance seemed to shimmer.

A knock sounded on the wall and Laaqueel glanced at the spot. She knew the draft of the mudship put the knock below water but the sharp raps didn't sound hollowed out the way the sea would make them.

"Follow me," Iakhovas said, and walked toward the bulkhead without hesitation.

He reached back and captured one of her hands, then stepped through the bulkhead.

3

"Unhand the girl."

Jherek spoke softly, but his words interrupted the raucous voices of the pirates as they terrorized the frightened young woman. The closest pirates noticed him first. They stepped drunkenly backward, stumbling against chairs and tables. Snarled curses reached Jherek's ears.

The girl's rolling eyes met the young sailor's, and for a moment he felt her fear and weakness.

"Mind your own business," one of the sailors said. He took a threatening step forward, drawing a short sword from his hip.

Jherek hesitated only a moment. The man before him was drunk, as were most of the men in the room. Still, they remained fully capable of hurting the girl on the table, and they were just as capable of killing him.

"Help me," she cried softly.

Sparked by his own sense of justice, Jherek spun into battle. He whirled quickly, smashing the flat of his blade into the nearest pirate's face.

The man's nose broke in a bloody rush and an audible crack. He stumbled backward, cursing Jherek in Umberlee's name. His size and the drunkenness of his companions sent a small group of them reeling back for the short bar.

Pressing his advantage as the other pirates fell back and tried to bring their weapons into play, Jherek stepped forward. He swung the chair he'd picked up as he'd approached the group, breaking it across Tharyg's back.

The big man roared in pain and anger as he dropped to his knees on the floor. He turned his baleful gaze toward Jherek and reached for his sword.

Jherek focused on the two men who lunged at him from the left. He met their swords with his own, slamming the blades aside. He twisted the cutlass, wounding one of the men deeply across the forearm. Blood spurted on the man and his nearest fellows.

"Make way, you damned sot-heads!" one of the bouncers standing watch at the tavern called.

Turning to the right, Jherek overturned a table, then kicked it at the three armed men coming at him. The table skidded across the sawdust-covered floor and slammed into their legs. If they hadn't been so impaired by their drinking, maybe they'd have remained standing. As it was all three of them tumbled across the table.

Still in motion, Jherek set himself and met the blade of the man who came at him from the front. The young sailor was already aware that pirates were circling behind him, closing off his escape route to the front door.

"Kill him!" Tharyg ordered. "A gold piece to the man who takes that bastard's head!"

Jherek hardened himself, driving out all merciful feelings that remained within him. Despite their drunkenness, the men were all killers, skilled and experienced at their profession.

His cutlass leaped out like a thing alive, sliding along the man's sword and opening his throat in a tight riposte. Gurgling, dying, the man fell backward, clawing at his mates to help him.

Two men rushed at Jherek with long knives. The young sailor dropped almost to his knees and caught himself on his empty hand. He pushed forward, catching the man on the right just above the knees with his shoulder. Jherek drove the man backward, lifting him off his feet and hurling him into the pirates behind him. They collapsed in a staggering melee.

Recovering, Jherek ripped his cutlass up in time to block the overhand blow Tharyg directed at his head. The young sailor shifted his footing, parrying two more blows from the bigger man, then pushing the cutlass's point through the pirate's heart.

"Bloody hell!" Tharyg gasped, staring down at the steel blade thrust into his chest. "You've done killed me!"

Jherek pulled his sword free, feeling the steel grate along bone. The young sailor gave himself over to his training and to the blade. The cutlass whirled before him, striking sparks from the other blades that reached out for him, creating a rhythm of metal rasping against metal.

He sliced a man across the stomach, spilling the pirate's entrails onto the floor. The other pirates shouted in horror and disgust while the wounded man screamed in fear and struggled to hold himself together. Jherek whirled again, bringing the cutlass around in a flat arc that all but decapitated another pirate.

Seizing the moment when the area briefly cleared around him, Jherek reached the side of the young woman. He sliced the hand from a man who'd been slow in releasing his grip on the girl. With his free hand, the young sailor grabbed the girl's arm and pulled her from the table. The floor around them was slippery with blood in spite of the sawdust. The girl remained wild-eyed, trying desperately to hold onto the young sailor.

"No, lady," Jherek told her in a calm voice as his eyes raked the hellish destruction he'd wrought. "I need my arm."

He had to force her from him, hoping he didn't hurt her or accidentally steer her into an opponent's blade.

A pirate came up behind Jherek, blindsiding him by standing behind the young girl. He didn't see the pirate until the man almost ran him through, but a preternatural sense warned him. Unable to bring the cutlass into play, Jherek let the short sword skim past him when he took a step back. He locked his free hand in the pirate's blouse, then stepped in and pulled as hard as he could.

The pirate spun over Jherek's shoulder and crashed into another group of men, bowling them all down.

Jherek gazed around the tavern room, unwilling to believe he was somehow still alive. Over a dozen sailors were down, most of them never to rise again.

A blade drew in close before he could dodge. The edge kissed the flesh of his upper left arm, ripping through easily. Hot blood spilled down his arm and drenched his blouse and cloak. He managed to keep the few sword thrusts at the girl turned aside.

Whirling again, aware that the drunken pirates were starting to get organized, Jherek glanced up at the heavy wooden wheel depending from the ceiling. Glass-encased candles, most of them still lit, stood proudly around the wheel.

Tracking the line of rope that held the wheel in place near the ceiling, Jherek spied the support post the rope was tied to near the front windows of the tavern. He planted a hand in the girl's back, helping steady her over a broken table and scattered chairs.

"Run," he told her. "Don't look back."

The girl ran, staying low, both hands wrapped protectively over her head.

Jherek picked up a chair and hurled it at a pirate who moved after the girl. The chair smacked into the pirate from behind, two of the legs shooting by his side while the other two slammed into his back. Chair and pirate plummeted toward the floor.

"Get him!" one of the tavern's bouncers shouted, shoving the pirates before him like an incoming tide pushing flotsam.

Taking two quick steps, Jherek swung the cutlass hard into the support pole where the chandelier was tied. The rope parted at once and the wheel plummeted from the ceiling like a rock. The wheel was almost as wide across as a man was tall. When it hit, it carried half a dozen pirates to the ground, burying them under its weight.

Another pirate swung his sword at Jherek's knees. The young sailor vaulted the man easily, placing a hand on the back of the bent pirate's head and pushing off. The pirate skidded face first into the floor.

Jherek leaped to the next table, feeling it skid uncertainly for a moment before snagging on the rough-hewn floor. As it started to tip, he vaulted to the next table near the bay window, then folded his arms over his face and threw himself through the latticework and panes.

Glass shattered and wood splintered around Jherek as he plunged through the window. He landed on his feet, bending his knees slightly to keep his balance. As he stood, he saw Glawinn, Sabyna, and Azla run from the inn across the street.

"This way, young warrior!" Glawinn roared, waving his sword.

Before Jherek could get started, a pirate leaped through the broken window after him and landed on his back. Only a swift move of the cutlass prevented the pirate from raking his dagger across Jherek's throat. Grabbing the man's loose shirt with his free hand, the young sailor bent and pulled, yanking the man from his back. He ran, spotting Talif and Frennick moving quickly through the shadows toward the paladin.

A crowd boiled out of the Bare Bosom. Two of them had lanterns, filched from the tavern's walls. "This way!" someone yelled. Booted feet beat a rapid tattoo against the wooden slats in front of the tavern.

Jherek caught up with the thief and his prisoner easily. He grabbed Frennick by the arm and hurried him after Glawinn.

The paladin raced into an alley beside the tavern where they'd been waiting, Sabyna and Azla close at his heels. Jherek swung around the corner, still pulling on Frennick, who was yelling encouragement to their pursuers.

Glawinn pulled himself up into the bench seat of the freight wagon waiting in the alley. The rear deck of the wagon contained barrels, kegs, crates, and sacks of foodstuffs and other supplies.

"Get in!" the paladin yelled. "Pirate stronghold though this may be, they take care of their own. We've worn thin our welcome here."

Jherek wholeheartedly agreed. Azla and Sabyna easily vaulted into the back of the wagon. The half-elf pirate captain set herself to work at once, smashing open a keg of spirits with her sword hilt.

Glawinn had the wagon going before Frennick was up in the back. The pirate dropped to his knees in an effort to keep from being forced on.

"Leave him," Talif snarled, hauling himself aboard the wagon.

"No," Jherek said.

He sheathed the cutlass in the sash at his waist and hooked his hand under the pirate's wide belt. He heard the yelling approach of the tavern crowd and saw the yellow glow of the lanterns paint long shadows on the wall to his left as they rounded the corner.

"There they are!"

"Kill that salty young pup—and his friends!"

The wagon started out slowly. Old horses and a heavy load held them back.

Holding Frennick's belt and the back of the pirate's hair, Jherek lifted his prisoner to his feet and rushed toward the fleeing wagon. In three great steps, he covered the distance. He pulled Frennick over his hip and threw him into the wagon bed.

"They've got Frennick!" someone yelled.

"Or he's with them!" another said. "I never trusted him."

Jherek ran to the wagon and vaulted up. He turned immediately, seeing that the tavern mob was closing the distance. Desperately, he grabbed a nearby five-gallon keg in both hands and heaved it at the lead man.

The keg broke against the man's chest, scattering salted pork across the alley and knocking the pirate back. Four more men went down with him, breaking the pursuit for just a moment.

"Everything goes off," Jherek ordered.

He remained on his knees and tossed the wagon's load over the back as quickly as he could. Sabyna and Talif helped him, shoving things over the end of the wagon.

Sacks of flour burst and spilled filmy white clouds into the alley, soaking into the potholes of the uneven cobblestones. Nail kegs, broken bottles, and shattered jars created more obstacles in the path of the tavern crowd. Potatoes and beans rolled across the stones.

As the load lightened, the horses pulled more strongly. The iron-bound wheels rang against the cobblestones, knocking off accumulated rust and striking occasional sparks.

Glawinn yelled to the horses and pulled them hard to the left as they bounded out onto the street at the end of the alley. The new street plunged down and twisted crazily on its way to the harbor.

The crowd from the tavern made the next turn much tighter than the wagon. They were gaining. Other men walking along the new street joined in the chase. Jherek stared at the wolf's pack in dismay. Anything like a quiet escape was totally out of the question now. Flame suddenly flared at his side. He turned and watched Azla fit an arrow to the short bow she'd carried into town.

The pirate captain pulled the string back to her cheek and fired from a kneeling position. The arrow sped true, shedding sparks from the cloth tied just behind the barbed head. The missile found a home in a man's chest. Blue and yellow flames twisted up and caught his beard on fire, wreathing his face in flames. He fell back among his companions.

Azla picked up another arrow that held a scrap of cloth tied to it and drenched it in the keg of spirits she'd broken open.

"Talif," she called calmly, her black eyes searching the street for targets.

The thief held a green flame between his cupped palms. The strange fire emanated from a coin. Azla lit her second arrow from the enchanted coin and fired it into the thatched roof of a nearby warehouse. The flame spread quickly across the wooden shingles.

A cry of alarm sounded from the pirates. More than half of them peeled off and ran for the building. As tightly packed as Immurk's Hold was, and being constructed of wood, Jherek knew there was a real danger of the town burning down if a fire was left untended. He balanced on his knees, his fist curled tight around the cutlass hilt, rocking as the bumpy ride continued.

Azla shot two more fire arrows into buildings they passed, creating even more of a diversion. By then the horses were hitting their pace and the wheels rattled across the uneven cobblestones.

Laaqueel felt a moment of heated resistance, then she slipped through the wooden timber of the bulkhead behind Iakhovas. In the next instant, harsh sunlight and the unsteady deck of a ship lunging at sea greeted her. Iakhovas had set up gates in the sahuagin castle as well that let him travel immediately to different areas along the Sword Coast.

"Lord Iakhovas!" a loud voice boomed. "Welcome aboard!"

Turning, the malenti priestess spied the tall, big-bellied form of Vurgrom the Mighty. The pirate captain came down the stern castle stairs like a flesh and blood avalanche.

Vurgrom was a mountain of a man, no taller than Iakhovas but easily twice as broad. He had flaming red hair on the sides of his head but none on top, and long chin whiskers that thrust out defiantly. He wore scarred leather breeches and a sleeveless leather vest.

"You called me," Iakhovas stated.

The big pirate captain grinned, swaying slightly as the ship thundered across the ocean waves, pushed by a strong wind.

"Aye," Vurgrom said, "and it's because I've got some news you might be interested in."

The crew tried to get closer to him, but he waved them all away.

"What is your location?" Iakhovas asked.

Vurgrom shrugged and said, "A few days from the Whamite Isles."

"You will be there." Iakhovas's tone left no margin for misunderstanding.

The big man flushed a little. "Aye," he said, "and I won't let you down, Lord Iakhovas, but I have something else to show you—something you need to know about."

Vurgrom dug in a pouch belted at his prodigious waist and produced an oval pearl encased in a golden disk. Laaqueel watched sudden interest dawn on Iakhovas's face. He studied the disk in the pirate captain's fat palm.

"I hired a diviner to look at it," Vurgrom said. "She told me it would lead me to a weapon."

Iakhovas studied the disk. "So it will."

"I've been trying to get in touch with you," Vurgrom said. "The device you gave me wasn't working."

"It worked when it was supposed to," Iakhovas said sharply.

Vurgrom's face blanched. "Of course, Lord Iakhovas," he said. "I only meant that I would have spoken with you earlier if I had been able."

"It's a powerful piece," Iakhovas said.

"It guides us, lord. Place this trinket into a bowl of water and it floats like a lodestone seeking the north."

"The weapon," Iakhovas said, "lies on the Whamite Isles."

Surprise gleamed in the pirate captain's eyes. "You know this?"

"Yes."

Vurgrom laughed and said, "I should have come to you, lord, instead of paying the diviner."

"You took two days' travel from my schedule," Iakhovas said in a hard voice. "If it weren't for the wind that pushes you now, you wouldn't make your assigned destination on time."

With a shrug, Vurgrom said, "I've been fortunate."

Iakhovas held a hand up. The wind died suddenly and the sails hung limply from the lanyards. Laaqueel shifted her footing. The ship felt as though it had become mired in mud.

"It was more than fortune's good graces," Iakhovas said. "I am seeing to it that you arrive on time in spite of your bad decisions."

Iakhovas clenched his raised hand into a fist. The blast of wind that hit the ship staggered it, almost rolled it over on the cresting wave. The sails popped and cracked, sounding as if they were going to be ripped free. Some of the ship's crew went rolling across the deck, unable to balance themselves quickly enough. At least three men went over the side, screaming until they hit the water. The ship sailed on, having no way to come around for those overboard.

Iakhovas stood as if rooted to the pitching deck.

Vurgrom grabbed the rearmost mast only a few feet away, unable to maintain his stance. He roared and knocked away other pirates nearby. The ship continued to pitch and twist.

"You're going to tear her apart!" the captain shouted.

"The ship will hold," Iakhovas declared. "I won't allow you to be late, Captain Vurgrom."

"I won't be late, my lord." Vurgrom had to yell to make himself heard over the gale force winds. "I won't be late."

"See to it then," Iakhovas threatened. "If you are late, Vurgrom, after everything I've invested in you, you won't 'be' at all."

He gestured and the golden orb in his eye flared. The world seemed to ripple at his side, like a pool disturbed by a tossed pebble. He stuck his arm into the ripples and it disappeared up to the elbow.

The pirates looked on in superstitious awe. Magic was known to them, of course, but not so familiar. Many of them, Laaqueel knew, had seen more this day than they would in their whole lives.

"Get this weapon if you want, Vurgrom," Iakhovas said, "but I'll want it when you do. You belong to me until such a time as I release you."

Vurgrom held tight to the mast and said nothing.

Iakhovas held out a hand to Laaqueel. The malenti priestess was barely able to maintain her own stance as the ship pitched again and the canvas cracked overhead. Even during her spying days, she'd hated ships. She reached for Iakhovas and felt him take her hand. Her balance steadied at once and she stepped through the gate back into the captain's quarters aboard *Tarjana*.

"I sense conflict within you, little malenti," Iakhovas said flatly.

He moved behind the table again and resumed his seat. The king of the sahuagin studied her with his one good eye and the golden one, and the malenti priestess felt as though he could see her clearly with both.

"When we arrived here and you saw that things were as I promised regarding the imprisonment of the Serôsian sahuagin, your faith seemed to return to you, stronger than before. Now I feel that you are questioning yourself again."

"Faith," she replied, "lies in the ability to answer those questions."

"You are my senior high priestess, and you serve the will of Sekolah. There should be no questions."

"I am weak." The admission was as much to herself as to him.

"I need you strong."

"I will be," she promised. "Have I ever failed you? I returned from the dead at your call."

Not so many days ago in Coryselmal while searching for the talisman Iakhovas had used to sunder the Sharksbane Wall, Laaqueel was certain she'd died at the hands of a vodyanoi, or come as close to it as the living could without fully crossing over.

Iakhovas had been as close to panic as the malenti priestess had ever seen him. He'd worked to save her, using a black skull with ruby eyes he'd gotten from his artificial eye. Laaqueel still felt certain somehow that it hadn't been Iakhovas's efforts that turned her back from death. It had been another, someone with a soft, sweet, feminine voice.

Go back, the voice told her. *You are yet undone.*

Iakhovas raked her with his gaze. She felt the quill quiver tentatively inside her.

"Go then, little malenti," he said, "and attend to your faith. Answer your questions as best as you are able, but in the end you'll find that the truest belief you have is in me. You may have rescued me from the prison I was in, but I have made you more than you have ever imagined you would be."

Stung by the dismissal and the knowledge of her own uncertainty, Laaqueel left the room and strode back out onto *Tarjana*'s main deck. She walked to the starboard railing and peered over into the sea. For a moment she wished she could just leap in and swim away to leave all the confusion behind her.

Farther along the railing, a group of sahuagin hauled on a length of heavy anchor chain hanging in the water. Bodies—some of them sahuagin of the inner and outer seas, others sea elves—were hooked to the chain. All of them were relatively fresh kills.

Three of the sahuagin group doing the hauling reached down and began plucking off bodies, harvesting them for meals. Razor-sharp talons sliced through flesh and brute strength snapped joints. Gobbets of flesh were torn free and passed around. Crabs and other sea creatures that had taken up brief residence within some of the corpses, and they became part of the meal.

One of the sahuagin warriors turned to face Laaqueel, regarding her with his black gaze. "Join, Most Favored One," he said. "There is plenty for all."

He held out a forearm, not a choice section, but not food to be turned away either.

"I am not hungry," she declared.

The warrior looked at her with consternation. No true sahuagin passed up a meal. A warrior needed to consume huge quantities of flesh to give him the strength to make it through a day.

"I ate the fallen on my return," Laaqueel said.

She knew the warrior probably wasn't listening and didn't care, but she made the excuse so that she might hear it herself. In truth, she was nearly starving. Since her arrival, days ago, in the Sea of Fallen Stars, she hadn't eaten from either dead sahuagin or enemy. The thought repulsed her, made her stomach twist violently within her.

There was no reason that she could think of for that to be so, no malady that she'd heard of that so plagued her people. Sahuagin, even ill-born malenti, were born to eat.

She watched as the warriors who made up *Tarjana*'s crew ripped at the dead bodies and ate what they wanted. She sighed, trying not to think about what Iakhovas had told her, trying not to succumb to the doubts that filled her. Her faith was more fragile than ever, a hollow shell she wrapped around Iakhovas.

She leaped overboard, longing to find solace in the sea.

Black Champion sat at anchor in the harbor. Jherek stood on the ship's deck and looked up at the Earthspur. The huge tower of rock and windswept land stabbed more than a mile above sea level in the center of the Dragonisle, the island where Immurk's Hold was located. Even in the night, the mountain left a shadow across the black water.

Azla was below with the others, questioning Frennick. The pirate captain laid out torturer's tools on a small table, the metal gleaming from the lantern light.

Jherek hadn't been able to stay, nor did Azla permit it.

He struggled with his conscience, telling himself that Frennick deserved all that Azla could think to give him, but it was no use. Through it all, the young sailor remembered that it was his doing that placed Frennick in her hands.

"Young warrior."

Turning, Jherek saw Glawinn approaching him, two steaming cups in his hands.

"I brought you some soup," the paladin said. "I thought it might serve to warm you some."

Jherek didn't want the soup, didn't want to pretend that everything was normal. A man he'd captured was being tortured down in the hold. He couldn't help but listen for the screams he knew must come. Thankfully, the crash of the sea's waves was too loud.

He accepted the cup anyway and said, "Thank you."

"What an awful place this is," Glawinn commented quietly.

"There are people in Immurk's Hold who still maintain an innocence," Jherek stated, thinking of the girl he'd rescued in the tavern.

"That was a brave and good thing you did back there, young warrior."

"It was foolish," Jherek grumbled, then shook his head. "Come morning, the girl will still be on the island."

"You saved her from a bad night."

"Delayed, is more correct, I think." Jherek turned the cup in his hands, absorbing the heat. The soup smelled delicious, full of spices.

"You've got a headful of dark thoughts," the paladin said.

"I look out there, and I wonder how different I am from those men," Jherek said. "Did I ever tell you how I came to Velen from my father's ship?"

4

"I was twelve," Jherek said. "My father spotted a merchant ship, heavily laden so she was sitting low in the water and dragging down the wind. That night he announced to the ship's crew that we would claim it as a prize the next morning."

Glawinn listened in silence.

"My father is a hard man," Jherek said. "You know the stories they tell along the Sword Coast of Bloody Falkane, and you know that nearly all of them are true. He's unforgiving and merciless, as able to cut down an unarmed man as he is to fight to the death. There is no right or wrong in his world, only what he is strong enough to take."

The rattling of the rigging on the lanyards sounded hollow, echoing the way Jherek felt. Glawinn waited silently.

As he spoke, Jherek felt the heat of unshed tears burning his eyes. Still, even though his voice was so tight it pained him to speak, he had to.

"I loved my father."

"As a child should," Glawinn said.

"I remember how he laughed. It was a huge, boisterous sound. Even though I didn't understand much of what made him laugh, I laughed with him. As I grew older, I stopped laughing and learned to fear him. Then, one day, he saw that in me. My father told me that I had to learn to be hard, that the world was cold and would eat the weak. I believed him, and I believed I was weak."

"That's not true."

Jherek didn't bother to argue. "He had me taken from the small room off his cabin where he'd kept me all that time and put in with the men. They weren't any more gentle than he'd been, though they were careful not to leave any marks that he could see."

In the distance, another longboat drew up to a cog and lanterns moved along its length as the passengers prepared to board.

"For the next eight years, I lived in the shadows of my father's rage. There was never a day I felt peace between us, nor anything even close to love."

"To be the son Bloody Falkane wanted," the paladin said, "you'd have to have been born heartless and with ice water in your veins. Where was your mother?"

"I never knew her."

"Your father never spoke of her?"

"Not once," the young sailor replied. "Nor did the ship's crew."

He stared up at the dark sky and refused to let the tears come. How much of it came from what he remembered, and how much because he knew Frennick was down in the hold, he couldn't say.

"The night I chose to leave," Jherek continued, "my father visited me in the hold. He brought a cutlass and placed it in my hand and told me I would take a place in the boarding party in the morning."

"At twelve?"

"Aye. He told me I'd kill or be killed, and in the doing of that, I'd be dead or I'd take my first steps toward becoming his son."

"Lathander's mercy," the paladin whispered.

"I stayed up most of the night," Jherek continued. "I knew I couldn't be part of that boarding party."

"Because you knew it was the wrong thing to do."

His throat hurting too much to speak right away, Jherek shook his head. "No. I only knew I was afraid," he said hoarsely. "I was afraid I would be killed, but mostly I was afraid of what my father would do to me if I froze and could not move, could not make it onto that other ship. I was certain he would kill me himself. So I walked out onto the deck when no one was looking, threw the cutlass into the sea, and jumped in after it. *Bunyip* sailed on, leaving me in the ocean. I wanted to die, but I started to swim, not even knowing where I was heading. I don't know how long I swam, but I know it was well into the next day before I washed up on Velen's shores."

They were silent for a time and Jherek struggled to ease his thoughts back into the dark places of his mind where he kept them.

"Why are you telling me this?" Glawinn asked.

"Because you seem to see something good in me," Jherek said, "and I wanted you to know it was false. I ran from my father's ship that night."

"You didn't want to kill innocent people," Glawinn objected.

Anger stirred in the coldness that filled Jherek. "Am I any better now? I took a man prisoner tonight only so he could be tortured."

"It's not what you think."

"Isn't it?" Jherek demanded. "I am my father's son. When it came time to take Frennick, I took him and I brought him here."

"No, young warrior, you judge yourself too harshly. You did only what you had to do. You are meant for more than being a pirate's son, Jherek."

"How can you believe that?"

"That's the wrong question." A small, sad smile twisted Glawinn's lips. "After having heard everything I have from you, the question is how could I not believe that."

"I just want out," Jherek said tiredly. "I don't want any more false hope, no more dreams, and I'm sick of the fear that has filled me all my life."

"A way will be made," Glawinn whispered. "You must believe."

Jherek couldn't, and he knew it. He looked out over the black water, taking in all the emptiness that made up the Sea of Fallen Stars.

"It's done."

Almost asleep, Jherek blinked and looked up at Azla as she strode across the deck.

More than an hour had passed since Azla had gone below with Frennick. The young sailor pushed himself up from his seated position against the prow railing.

"And Frennick?" Jherek asked.

"Relax," Azla told him. "Frennick is alive and of one piece still."

Images of how the man must have been tortured ran rampant through Jherek's mind. The instruments the pirate captain had laid out with such familiarity looked vicious enough to come straight from Cyric's darkest hells.

"Nor have I harmed him," Azla went on, "so your precious honor and integrity yet remain whole."

Jherek shook his head. "I don't understand."

"Glawinn asked that no harm come to Frennick when we returned to the ship," Azla said.

"Glawinn didn't tell me he'd asked that," Jherek told her, confused.

"No, nor did he want you to know until it was over."

Jherek grew angry but pushed it away. That lack of knowledge was something he intended to deal with the paladin about. He should have been told instead of spending time worrying over it.

"Pirates are a superstitious lot," Azla commented. "Despite all his blustering and bravado, Frennick is not a brave man. My ship's mage bewitched him, making him think we'd immersed his hand in a pot of acid till the flesh melted from his bones. Actually, it was a pot of water."

Two of the ship's crew marched Frennick up from the hold. The pirate captain swore venomously, calling down the spiteful rage of Umberlee on Azla, her ship, and her crew. When the crewmen threw him over the side, both the splash and Frennick's curses echoed around the ship. Relief filled Jherek, but it didn't take away the anger he felt toward Glawinn.

"Where is the disk?" the young sailor asked.

"Vurgrom has it."

"Does Frennick know where Vurgrom is?"

Azla shook her head. "But he did know that Vurgrom used a diviner to learn what he could of the disk."

Jherek's heart sped up. "What did he learn?"

"Frennick wasn't allowed in the room. Only the diviner and Vurgrom were there. However, Frennick gave us the location of the diviner. She lives off the northeastern harbor of the Dragonisle."

"If we are not sailing there," Jherek said, "I need to know so I can make other arrangements."

Azla looked at him, her dark eyes flashing, and asked, "You would, wouldn't you?"

"Aye, Captain. I've no choice."

"You won't have to walk," she replied. "We're going to weigh anchor in a short while."

"Enter, young warrior."

Jherek slipped the lock on the door and let himself into the room.

Glawinn sat on the lowest of the bunk beds, crouched over so his head wouldn't bang against the upper berth as the ship gently pitched at anchor. An oil lantern hung from the ceiling over the small desk in the corner. The paladin was cleaning his armor, a task he tended to every day.

"You lied to me."

"No." Glawinn's eyes narrowed and became hard. Steel filled his voice. "You never accuse another man of lying unless you know that for a fact. Especially not a man of honor."

Shame burned Jherek's cheeks and ears. "My apologies." He tried to maintain his level gaze but had to drop it to the floor. "You didn't tell me that they weren't torturing Frennick."

"No."

"You let me believe they were."

"Yes."

"Why?"

"You were comparing yourself to the wretches and scoundrels that populate that island like that was your destiny. Suddenly you were seeing yourself as no better than they are, doomed somehow to follow in your father's footsteps."

"They say the apple never falls far from the tree."

"Then looking forward to a life as a pirate or a thief is something you deserve?"

"I never said that."

"Yes you did. You were pulling penance for Frennick. You looked out over Immurk's Hold and told me you couldn't see the difference between yourself and those men. Can you now?"

"Aye," Jherek said, his voice tight, "but I also see the difference between you and me."

"Do you believe that difference to be so great, young warrior?" Glawinn stood. Without his armor, he looked like only a man. Lantern light gleamed against the dark black of his hair and short-cropped beard.

"You're a paladin, chosen by a god to represent the covenants of his faith."

"Was I anything before I became a warrior for Lathander? Or was it Lathander who made me the man I am today?"

"I don't know."

"Tell me what is in your heart, young warrior," Glawinn said softly, his voice barely carrying across the small room. The waves slapping against the side of the ship outside the room underscored his words. "Tell me what you believe me to have been before I followed Lathander's teachings."

"You were a good man."

After a moment, Glawinn nodded. "My father was a knight before me, and my mother a good woman who learned the art of cheese making from her father. I am their get, and I wear Lathander's colors and fight the battles the Morninglord sets before me."

Jherek stared into the paladin's eyes, wondering for just a heartbeat if Glawinn was telling him this to make him feel worse.

"I was born one of twins," Glawinn said. "I have a sister. She was never a gentle child, and never easy on my parents. When she was seventeen, she left our home in Daggerdale and joined the Zhentarim."

Astonishment trailed cold fingers across Jherek's back. Even on the Sword Coast people knew the Zhentarim to be an organization of great evil.

"I was a boy when I fought at my father's side under Randall Morn against Malyk," Glawinn went on in a steady voice. "My sister, like many other Daggerdale citizens, felt that the Zhentarim would continue to hold the lands after the battles. Some thought only to hold onto their property, not caring who ruled them as long as they were allowed to follow their own lives. Cellayne—my sister—saw joining the Zhentarim as a chance to follow the dark nature that possessed her."

Footsteps passed beyond the door. Men's voices talked quietly. Eyes reddened with pain and glazed with memory, Glawinn turned to peer at the armor lying on the small bed.

"I've seen Cellayne twice in all these years," he said. "The last time she tried her best to kill me. Only by Lathander's grace was I spared. I lost two dear friends. Cellayne has immersed herself in the dark arts and become a necromancer. She's very powerful." The paladin tried to clear his thick voice but was unsuccessful. "As penance for daring to attack her in her stronghold near Darkhold, Cellayne . . . did something to my two fallen companions . . . set them on my trail. I destroyed the walking corpses of my friends. I know not what happened to their souls, though priests I've talked to since tell me that the good part of them knows peace."

"I'm sorry," Jherek whispered, knowing how feeble those words were.

"Lathander keeps me strong." Glawinn bowed his head for a moment, then turned to Jherek. "You need only believe, young warrior. Let your faith and your heart guide you, not your birth, not everything you've seen. Pursue that which you want, and a way of living that pleases and rewards you."

"There is nothing to believe in."

"So, for now at least, that is what you believe, young warrior, but to believe that there is nothing to believe in, is a belief itself." Glawinn smiled at his own circular logic. "Don't you see? If there was no belief in you, you would be like a piece of driftwood tossed out on the sea."

"Even driftwood finds a shore sooner or later," Jherek said.

A smile crossed Glawinn's face. "How much you know yet refuse to see. Truly, your stubbornness is as great as any I've ever witnessed." He crossed the room to stand in front of Jherek, then put his hands on the young sailor's shoulders and said, "When I look at you, I see a good man."

Unable to maintain eye contact, Jherek dropped his gaze to his boots.

"I only wish that you could see yourself through my eyes." Glawinn paused. "Or Sabyna's."

"I've got to go." Jherek couldn't stand there any more. It hurt too much.

The paladin pulled his hands away and said, "You won't be able to escape the doubts that fill you, young warrior. They only sound the emptiness that is within you. Belief is the only thing that will make you whole again."

Jherek held back hot tears. "If there was just something to hold to, I could," he said, "but there is nothing."

"Sabyna loves you, young warrior."

That single declaration scared Jherek more than anything else in his life.

"Even if that were true," he said hotly, "my father murdered her brother. She could never forgive me."

"For your father's sin?"

"A father's sins are visited on the son."

"Not everyone thinks so."

"I'd rather not talk about this."

"I told you I'd teach you to believe again, young warrior," Glawinn said, his voice carrying steel again, "and I will."

"You weren't able to rescue your sister."

As soon as the words were out of his mouth, Jherek regretted it. Pain flashed in Glawinn's eyes.

"Now is not the time to speak of this," Glawinn said. "I see that." He turned and walked back to his bunk, sitting and taking up his armor again. "Good night, young warrior."

Hesitating, Jherek tried desperately to find something to say, but couldn't. He had no head for it, and he didn't trust his tongue. His heart felt like bursting.

The sound of the scrubbing brush filled the room, drowning out the echo of the waves lapping at the ship's hull.

With a trembling hand, Jherek opened the door and left. There was nothing else to do.

5

Seated midway up *Black Champion*'s rigging, Jherek stared hard out at the sunlight-kissed emerald green waters to the west. The Dragonisle maintained a steady distance to the southeast as the ship sailed north over slightly choppy waves, but the Earthspur towered over all. Below Jherek's position, the pirate crew worked steadily under Azla's watchful eye.

Reluctantly, he returned his attention to the wooden plate he held. Over half of the steamed fish and boiled potato chunks yet remained of his meal, long grown cold. He picked at the morsels with his fingers but found no interest. The worry and the headache that settled into the base of his skull and across his shoulders left him with no appetite.

Giving up on the meal, he gripped the edge of the plate and flung the contents into the wind, watching them fall the long distance down to the sea. An albatross wheeled and dived after them, managing to seize one of the chunks before it hit the water.

The rigging vibrated, drawing his attention. When he peered down, he saw Sabyna climbing up the rigging toward him.

"I didn't expect to find you up here," she said. "You're usually laboring about the ship."

"I wasn't feeling well."

Sabyna huddled expertly within the rigging, hooking her feet and leaning back so that her elbows held her as well. She gazed at him with concern and said, "Perhaps you should have stayed in bed."

Jherek shook his head.

"I'm worried about you." Sabyna regarded him sternly with those frank, reddish-brown eyes.

Sabyna loves you, young warrior. Glawinn's words spun through Jherek's mind as soft as silk and as unforgiving as steel.

"I worry about you. Perhaps it is time you make your way back to the Sword Coast."

"Do you think I'm some kind of ballast you can just heave overboard?" Sabyna's voice turned icy.

Jherek felt as though his thoughts were winding through mush.

"No, lady," he said. "I worry only about your safety. This is not your fight, and I fear that things are going to get even harder from this point on. Last night has proven that."

"I remember a time when you spoke pretty words to me, and enjoyed my companionship," she told him in a cold voice.

"Lady, I have no hand with pretty words. My skills are with the sea, and with raising the ships that sail on it."

"Then you're telling me I heard wrong?"

Jherek felt as though he was being mercilessly pummeled. "No," he said, "I wouldn't tell you that."

"Then tell me what you feel."

Jherek hung his head. "I can't." He hated the silence that followed.

"Perhaps," Sabyna said in a softer voice, "I did hear wrong. Maybe I was wanting to hear something that wasn't there, nor ever offered."

She reached into the bag of holding at her hip and brought out two books. "I spoke with Glawinn this morning. He asked me to give you these."

Heart still hurting, Jherek took to the books, meeting her eyes and never even glancing at the titles. Normally books were a fascination to him, a promise of adventure and other lives he could share.

"Has something happened between you two?"

"Please," Jherek said, "I don't wish to speak of it."

"I'm sorry. I didn't mean to intrude. It's just hard watching the two of you have trouble when it's obvious you're so much alike."

"Alike?"

The comparison stunned the young sailor. He saw no way in which he and the paladin were alike.

"You're both proud, strong men. You're brave enough to face your fears, and you're a good friend."

"If I was such a good friend, Glawinn wouldn't be angry with me, and you wouldn't be so uncomfortable around me."

"I have no doubt that you and Glawinn will work things out," Sabyna told him. "That is the nature of men. And you're not responsible for my discomfort." Unshed tears glistened in her eyes. "That is caused by my own folly and foolishness. You have worries enough of your own. I only wish I could help you."

Without another word, the ship's mage turned lithely in the rigging and glided down the ropes, hard muscles playing in her arms, shoulders, and the small of her back.

Jherek almost went after her. It was only when he realized that he'd have to say something, but had no idea what, that he stopped.

He watched her, though, as she dropped to the deck and strode to the stern to join Azla. They looked up at him together, then they turned and walked behind the stern castle.

The young sailor felt shamed to have been caught watching after them and quickly turned his head. He'd never felt so alone or unhappy in his life. He glanced at the two books he held, wondering what Glawinn would have thought to send him—and why.

Both books showed signs of stress, as if they had been read a number of times. The first was a thick volume called *The Rider and the Lost Lady of Grave Hollow.* Jherek carefully opened the front cover and read the frontispiece, discovering the work to be a romance about a Ridesman of Archendale. He flipped through the pages, smelling the scent of the parchment and the ink and remembering all the hours of pleasure he'd received from the books Malorrie had let him borrow.

The second tome was *Way of War, Way of Peace* by Sir Edard Valins. The book was much slimmer and promised to be a treatise on the art and thinking of combat.

Jherek closed the books, wondering why Glawinn would have sent them to him. He secured the book on the strategies of war in the rigging and opened the romance. A few hours of sailing yet remained before *Black Champion* reached her destination and he felt it would be best if he could stay away from other people in the meantime.

Standing at *Black Champion*'s starboard rail, Jherek gazed out at the grotto of sea caves that made up the Dragonisle's northeastern harbor. The harbor sat back in the curvature of the rocky shoreline below and around the caves, creating a crescent of calm water scarcely able to shelter a dozen ships. Nesting pelicans and seagulls lined the craggy surface.

"These waters are filled with treacherous rocks and reefs," Azla said as she belted her scimitar around her slim hips. She tucked a fighting dagger down inside the rolled top of her left boot, then pulled on a cloak against the chill of the bitter wind. "I won't take my ship in there. We'd only be a target if two or three of the other ship's crews decided to take us as a prize. Out here, *Champion* can maneuver."

Glawinn gave a quick nod, accepting her judgment. He offered his hand to her at the ship's rail and said, "Lady, if I may."

The half-elf pirate captain seemed a little surprised at the offer, but she took his hand and said, "My thanks, but I am *captain*, not lady."

"Of course, Captain."

Azla made her way down the rope ladder hanging over the ship's side to the waiting longboat, and Glawinn followed.

Jherek hadn't noticed the change in temperature until they'd come closer to the harbor. The sun hung low on the horizon behind them, drawing long shadows over the emerald waters. He pulled his cloak more tightly around him.

Without a backward glance at him, Sabyna strode to the side and quickly descended the rope ladder. Jherek shifted hands with his wrapped bow and followed. He quietly made his way to one of the rowing stations and sat. No one seemed inclined to speak to him and that fact gladdened him at the same time it made him feel disappointed.

No one came to meet them when they reached the uneven shoreline, but there were plenty of eyes watching. Five ships sat at anchor inside the harbor proper. Pirates lined the railings and hung in hammocks beneath the yardarms. Others cooked fish over slow fires on the rocky beach. The beach butted up against the gray rock of the cliff face where the caves were.

They ran the longboat aground, then shipped oars. Jherek and three pirates leaped out onto the beach and grabbed the longboat's sides, pulling it easily onto the rocky sand. The wind ripped low howls from the caves as the breeze traveled across the mouths. Jherek looked up at the towering cliff face while the others stepped from the longboat. A few of the seagulls took wing curiously, swooping down within a few feet of him.

"Look at 'em," one pirate growled. "You'd think they was watchdogs close as they eyeball a body."

Azla assigned four of the ten men in the crew to guard the longboat. She took the lead with long strides, crossing the shoreline to the nearest group of men frying fish.

"I need some information," Azla told the strangers.

A hulking brute of a man standing nearby gave her an evil, gaptoothed grin. "Ain't nothing free here, wench. Mayhap you show me a little kindness—"

Before the man even knew what was going on, Azla ripped her scimitar free and touched the blade to his throat.

"How much," she asked coldly, "would you be willing to pay for your next breath?"

Color drained from the big man's features. "What was it you'd be wanting?" he asked.

Azla kept the scimitar at the big man's throat. "There's a diviner who lives here. Do you know her?"

"I know *of* her, Cap'n." The big man's Adam's apple slid across the blade's edge. "Name's Dehnee. She gives readings and such for them what want 'em."

"Where can I find her?"

The man pointed up the narrow ledge that wandered back and forth across the cliff face. Other branches led off to other caves, giving each a portion of privacy. The diviner's cave was halfway up and on the right.

"Take us there," Azla commanded.

"Cap'n, I'd rather not. The woman lives with a ghost."

"You'd rather not more than you'd rather try breathing through your neck?"

The man started walking, glancing in cold rebuke at his companions who sat without comment. Azla kept the scimitar's point at the back of the man's neck.

Jherek kept a ready hand on his cutlass hilt as he brought up the party's rear. They marched up the narrow, inclined path to the cave the big man indicated.

A handmade sign hung beside the cave mouth that simply proclaimed DIVINER. A thick carpet of sea lion hides stretched across the cave mouth, hung from a length of rope. The hides possessed the maned heads and forelegs of great lions, but the body and tail of a fish. The bottom of the carpet of stitched hides was rolled up and sewn around rocks that weighted it to the ground.

Azla dismissed the big man with a turn of her head. He went quickly, muttering beneath his breath.

"Dehnee," the half-elf captain called out. "I've got coin if you've a mind and skills enough to earn it."

The hides slid to the side, revealing the torchlit interior of the cave. A woman no older than her late twenties stood at the entrance. Her hair was mousy brown, long and pulled back in a ponytail. Gold eyes regarded the party and showed no fear, set deeply in a face that was chiseled and translucent as if she seldom saw the sun. She wore a gown of good material that showed age as well as care.

"I've always got a ready use for coin," she said, smiling, "but I'm not a desperate woman."

"I don't particularly care for the desperate," Azla said. "They have a tendency to tell you what you want to hear."

"It's the truth you're after then?"

"Aye, and we've come a far way to get it."

Jherek watched the woman, remembering the times he'd seen Madame Iitaar work at home in Velen over a man's hand or an object yanked up from the sea in a fisherman's net.

Diviners could tell of things yet to come upon occasion, as well as the past of objects that were brought to them. Those who lived on the sea, depending on the gracious bounty of the waters, learned to respect people like that.

Dehnee looked at them coolly and said, "My home is small, and I like my privacy."

"Only four of us." Azla pointed out Sabyna, Glawinn, and Jherek.

The diviner's eyes raked casually across the ship's mage and the paladin, but came to rest on the young sailor.

"Yes," she said softly. "I can see that the four of you are tied. Some in more ways than the one you came to see me about."

The announcement surprised Jherek, but he said nothing.

"Enter." Dehnee stepped back and held the folds of sea lion skins back.

Jherek entered last, his mind and eyes seeking danger everywhere. He hadn't forgotten the story about the diviner sharing her cave with a ghost.

The cave evidently divided into three or more rooms. Some of the division was natural but the young sailor could also detect scars and markings from tools and stone cutters.

More hides taken from sea creatures decorated the walls along with mounted fish on lacquered wooden plaques. Shells and bits of coral of different sizes and colors strung on sections of net in designs and patterns hung from the uneven ceiling. Red, blue, and green lichens clung to the walls in whirlpool patterns, evidently carefully directed in their growth.

Two clam shells more than a foot across hung upside down from more nets. They were filled with blubber and burning wicks to fill the cave with light.

Dehnee passed her hand over a small net with silver bells and shells that tinkled and rattled. The sensation of clawed feet crawled over Jherek, causing him to shift his shoulders.

"It's all right," Sabyna said in a soft voice. "The spell was intended as protection only."

"I have been hunted before," the diviner said. "I like to make sure that no one enters my home while bewitched by a charm, and that I have no unseen guests."

She sat cross-legged on a sea lion hide that had the creature's head still intact.

Jherek's hand tightened as he stared at the maned head. The itching sensation grew even stronger. Dehnee turned a hand palm up and offered seating on the piles of hides in the center of the cave.

"If you don't mind, lady," Glawinn said, "I'll stand. The armor becomes rather cumbersome."

"Of course, Sir Knight. I know merely being here must be troublesome to you. Some of the objects I use in my divinations would not be comfortable to you, but they are necessary in what I do."

"Thank you, lady."

Gazing at the paladin, Jherek saw that Glawinn was a little paler than normal and held his lips tightly as a man at rough sea might. The young sailor didn't feel well himself and was experiencing a throbbing behind his eyes.

Sabyna and Azla sat in front of the diviner.

Dehnee looked up at Jherek with dark, liquid eyes. "I can attempt this without you," she told him, "but my best chance of success will be with your assistance."

"I don't understand," Jherek said.

"You come here seeking an object," Dehnee told him. "Of all, you are the most closely tied to it."

Jherek hesitated only a moment, wishing there were some other way. "What do I need to do?"

"Sit."

Dehnee pointed to a place before her. The young sailor pulled his cutlass from the sash at his waist so that he could sit in comfort. As soon as the blade came free, the sea lion's eyes glinted with unholy light and tracked his movement. The massive jaws unhinged and loosed a coughing roar of warning. Skin prickling and heart hammering in fear, Jherek stepped back.

The sea lion's body rose from the carpet, magically transforming and coming fully to life.

6

Half formed from the diviner's carpet, the sea lion glared at Jherek with hot hatred in its emerald green eyes. In life the creature had been easily a dozen feet long. Light danced on the shiny scales that began just behind its forelegs as it slithered protectively in front of Dehnee.

"Narik!" Dehnee cried, tugging on the fierce mane. "No!"

Slowly, the sea lion shifted its attention from Jherek to the diviner. The coughing growls subsided and changed to a plaintive whining that filled the whole cavern.

"He means no harm," Dehnee stated, continuing to pull on the ensorcelled beast. "He thought you were going to hurt me. He's not been around many such as you."

As if in grudging obedience, the sea lion glided back to the cave's stone floor and became inert. The green eyes continued to follow Jherek's movements.

The young sailor swallowed hard, discovering he had a death grip on the cutlass.

"This is an uneasy place for us, young warrior," Glawinn said softly. "As you sense danger about this cave, so it senses danger from you. Trust the lady to hold the balance."

Jherek let out a tense breath, reminding himself why they were there. He sat slowly, offering no threat, watching the green eyes that watched him. He sat with crossed legs, his cutlass across his knees.

"Believe in me," Dehnee told him, offering her hands.

"Lady," Jherek said in a tight voice, "as much as I am able."

He held his hands out and she took them. Her touch felt almost too warm, too exciting. Emotions and desires that he kept carefully bottled up slapped at the sides of his restraint, threatening to explode. He tried to yank his hands away, feeling shamed.

Dehnee tightened her grip, but he pulled hard enough to bring her to her knees before him. He gazed into her gold eyes.

"It's all right," she told him. "Your feelings are natural."

"No." Jherek shook his head and kept pulling at his hands. Nothing that strong and heady could ever be natural.

"An innocent," Dehnee breathed in quiet wonder. "By Umberlee's favored sight, I've not touched an innocent in decades."

"Have a care with him, lady," Glawinn warned softly. "I'll not have him hurt in any way."

"I know what I'm doing, Sir Knight."

All Jherek's ability to struggle deserted him in a powerful surge that left him weak. He still felt the woman's hands on his, still felt the unaccustomed and unacceptable desire that flamed him, but he couldn't move.

Then Glawinn's strong hand dropped to his shoulder, anchoring him and putting some of the feeling at bay. "Patience, lady," the paladin said. "He's never been around one such as you."

"What did you come here seeking?" Dehnee asked, her eyes totally focused on Jherek's.

Jherek's thoughts ran rampant. It was hard to concentrate. "Lathander's disk," he said.

"Picture it in your mind."

Unbidden, Jherek's thoughts ranged only on the woman before him. He saw her naked, her body trim and gently rounded, her small breasts heavy with desire. He closed his eyes tightly against the vision and whispered, "No."

"What you're feeling is normal," Dehnee said.

Jherek didn't believe her. Nothing like this could ever be normal—or acceptable.

"Picture the disk."

Calming himself as much as he was able, Jherek built the image of the disk inside his head.

"Good," Dehnee whispered. "I can see it as well. What do you wish to know?"

"Vurgrom took it," Azla said beside Jherek. "We want to know if he still has it."

Lathander's disk tumbled in Jherek's mind.

"Yes," the diviner said. "It is still in Vurgrom's possession."

"Where?"

Filmy black patterns ghosted over Jherek's vision, like rotten spots on fruit. They cleared momentarily, revealing a glimpse of a ship. He managed to peer closer and see her name, then the image slipped away. He recognized the ship from the confrontation at the Ship of the Gods.

"*Maelstrom*," he gasped.

"Do you know where she is?" Azla asked.

Jherek shook his head, too weak to say anything.

"It is far from here," Dehnee replied.

"We want to find it," Azla told her.

"Of course you do. And you will. It is meant for this boy to find."

The diviner released one of Jherek's hands but not the other. The young sailor watched as she reached into the sea lion's open mouth and pulled out a complex device.

"An astrolabe. It's used by a ship's navigator," Azla said. "With it a captain or anyone learned enough to take readings from the azimuth of the sun, the moon, or certain stars can determine where a ship is on the sea."

"This is no ordinary astrolabe," Dehnee told them. She cradled the instrument in her lap with one hand. "This device is ages old, and its origin is almost completely unknown to me."

The whale oil light glistened off the astrolabe's surface. Only then did Jherek realize it was cut from some kind of yellowed crystal that held only minute fractures.

"I was given this by a sea elf in exchange for information," the diviner continued. "I can enspell it to track Vurgrom's ship for you."

"At what cost?" Azla demanded.

"Only that you bring it back when you're finished," Dehnee replied. "And I would ask a favor."

Azla's eyes narrowed. "What favor?"

"Not from you, Captain." Dehnee's eyes locked with Jherek's. "From this boy."

Glawinn interrupted before Azla could respond. "He is only a boy."

The diviner nodded. "And what he faces will make a man of him." She glanced at the paladin. "You know this as well as I. That's part of the reason you're here. I won't ask a favor of the boy. I will want a favor from the man."

"He's too young to know what you ask," Glawinn interrupted. "A promise from him—"

"Is all that I will settle for," Dehnee said. "Otherwise, you are on your own."

"You know of the portents and magic that surround the Sea of Fallen Stars," Azla said. "Some are saying that ancient prophecies are being fulfilled, that an old evil is descending upon us."

"That's not my concern." The diviner stared at Jherek and he felt the pull of her gaze. "What is your answer?"

"Young warrior," Glawinn said gently, "don't agree to these terms. Wait until a more proper time."

"Time is against us." Jherek spoke clearly, but his words sounded distant.

"There is much for you to learn," Glawinn persisted.

"It's only a favor," Jherek said. "I owe a debt to the temple of Lathander . . ."

"Do you accept?" Dehnee asked.

Dehnee took his hand back in hers, holding both of them again.

"Swear to me that you will honor my request, and that you will never lift your hand against me."

In the periphery of his vision, Jherek saw Glawinn's stony face and knew that the paladin didn't approve.

"Lady," the young sailor said, "I swear that I will honor your request and will never lift a hand against you."

"Swear by your god."

Jherek's throat tightened. "Lady, I'm sorry. I recognize no gods. I am adrift in my beliefs and hold no anchor."

The diviner's eyes studied his face, searching.

"He speaks the truth," Glawinn stated coldly.

"I can see that. Yet he's no stranger to falsehood."

Shame burned Jherek's cheeks. The only things he'd never been completely forthright about concerned his heritage and his true name—and those he'd hidden primarily from Sabyna.

"Not in this matter," Glawinn said.

"It's strange to think of one such as him without strong beliefs."

"As may be, lady," the paladin said, "but so it is."

Dehnee tightened her grip on his hands and said, "Then name something you believe in, boy."

An incredible weight seemed to descend on Jherek's chest. It felt impossible to breathe. He had confessed to Glawinn that he believed in nothing. The paladin swore to teach him to believe again, but hadn't told the young sailor what he was supposed to believe in. Only now there was a huge gaping emptiness where his faith in the gods had once been.

"My eye and my sword arm," he croaked in a tight voice, remembering what Glawinn told him he would believe in first. "I believe in those."

"No," the diviner said. "Those things you *trust* in, but that is no real belief. Search yourself, boy, tell me what you believe in."

Jherek thought furiously, trying to find some quote, some philosophy Malorrie had taught him that he could cling to in that moment. Memories piled in on him, breakfasts shared with Madame Iitaar, battle sessions with Malorrie, sunsets he'd seen sink into the waters off the western coast of Velen.

He recalled the smell of the blueberry pies Madame Iitaar made for him, the feel of the paper of the books Malorrie loaned him, the satisfaction he got the day he first finished mending Madame Iitaar's roof, already knowing the woman had more work for him and a bed as well.

He remembered the cake he'd gotten from Hukkler's Bakery to celebrate Madame Iitaar's first birthday since he'd gone there to live. An image of Madame Iitaar at her husband's grave filled his mind. The old woman had grown a special flowering plant, then planted it on the grave in remembrance. Her smile that day, both sad and joyous, was something he'd known he'd never forget.

And he remembered the first day he'd seen Sabyna. He avoided talking to the pretty ship's mage then, fearing himself too backward and too entrenched in lies about his own identity. He'd admired her from afar, watching how she managed *Breezerunner*'s crew so efficiently and effortlessly, the easy way she smiled and the graceful way she moved with the ship's roll.

"What do you believe in?" Dehnee asked again.

"These are troubling times for him," Glawinn said.

"He knows what he believes," the diviner replied. "All he has to do is give voice to it."

Jherek faced the woman, feeling scared and alone, but his thoughts kept focusing on the same images. Madame Iitaar hadn't been forced to take on an orphaned boy and make a home for him. Whatever drew Malorrie to him hadn't ensured the bond that grew between the phantom and the boy. He didn't doubt the way he felt about Sabyna. When he'd met her again in Baldur's Gate, his spirits soared. Even though he knew he could never be good enough for her, he knew how he felt about her.

"Tell me what you believe in," the diviner said in a softer voice.

"Love," Jherek whispered, knowing it was true. "I believe in love."

The diviner's hands suddenly shook as if palsied. Her eyes went wide. The sea lion beside her snarled irritably, one forepaw flexing, then drawing back.

"By the gods," the woman said in hoarse surprise.

Embarrassed, the young sailor risked a glance at Sabyna, not knowing what she might make of his answer. Her gaze didn't meet his, but unshed tears glittered in her eyes.

Jherek felt like a giant hand reached inside of him and tried to yank his heart from his chest. He sat up straighter, knocking the cutlass from his knees, his chest suddenly too tight to breathe.

The feeling of being yanked out of his own body passed as suddenly as it came, dropping Jherek back to the floor. He gasped, then his breath came back to him in a rush. Awareness returned to him, making him feel as though a part of him was gone, but he couldn't name which part.

"Your promise," the diviner stated in a strained voice, "is accepted."

"Lathander help you, young warrior," Glawinn said gravely, "as I will if I am able."

Jherek sat, stunned, unable to explain what had passed between the woman and him. He had no doubt that it would have consequences.

Dehnee took her hands from his and lifted the astrolabe from her lap. She spoke over the device, calling out in a language Jherek couldn't understand. A purple flame filled the yellowed crystal and threw a lambent glow over the room. A moment later and the light shrank back inside the astrolabe.

"It's finished," the diviner said, and offered the instrument to Jherek.

The young sailor reached for the astrolabe, his limbs feeling like lead. When he touched the polished surface, an icy chill filled him.

"All the readings you take from that astrolabe will give you the position of Vurgrom's ship and not your own," Dehnee said.

"You took a reading from the disk for Vurgrom," Azla said.

The diviner didn't try to deny it. "Yes."

"What did you learn?"

The diviner shook her head. "Not much," she said. "The disk is protected from the small skills I have."

From what he'd been through in the last few minutes, Jherek doubted the diviner's skills were in any way small. He wondered what brought her to the Dragonisle, and why to that place's most desolate harbor. Had it been through choice, or need? How would that affect the promise he'd made her?

"But you learned something," Azla said.

"The disk is designed to lead its possessor to a weapon," Dehnee said.

"What weapon?"

"I couldn't see that much, but I know it lies somewhere off the coast of Turmish. In the vision, I was able to see that coastline and the druids that care for the place. In the past, I've been there."

"You're certain of this?" Glawinn asked.

"Yes."

The paladin faced Jherek and asked, "Did the talisman ever try to guide you?"

The young sailor thought back. He had possessed Lathander's disk for only minutes. "No."

"Maybe the disk isn't guiding Vurgrom either," Sabyna offered.

"It is," Jherek told her.

"How do you know this?" asked Azla.

"Because," the young sailor said, "I felt it come alive in my grasp."

7

"You're keeping to yourself a lot these days."

Jherek looked down from his position in the rigging and spotted Sabyna. "Good evening, lady," he said, and immediately felt uncomfortable.

There had been much to do in the four days since they'd taken their leave of the Dragonisle. Jherek had taken care to stay involved in shipboard duties that the pretty ship's mage hadn't been assigned to oversee.

"I've gotten the impression you don't care much for present company," Sabyna said as she hauled herself up in the rigging and looked out over the curved horizon of the sea.

They were well away from land now, sailing by the mystic astrolabe. The canvas cracked and snapped as it held the wind.

"Not true," replied Jherek. He marked his place in the romance Glawinn had loaned him.

"I thought maybe I was the cause."

"Of course not," Jherek assured her. "Why would you think such a thing?"

"Because the last time we spoke I was so . . . forward."

"You merely said what was on your mind."

"Is that what you think?" she asked softly.

Despite the quietness of her words, barely heard over the crash of the waves below and the snap of canvas sails around them, Jherek suddenly felt as though he'd stepped into the jaws of a steel trap.

"Lady, I don't know what to think," he admitted. "These are very confusing times."

"For all of us." She held his gaze with her eyes and said, "When things get confusing, people who are together should be most truthful with each other."

"Aye."

Jherek's temples pounded. He hoped she wouldn't steer their conversation in a direction that would force him to lie.

"Your name isn't Malorrie."

"No. Malorrie is the name of a good friend and teacher."

"Your name is Jherek. I know you feel that you have reasons to conceal your identity. I promised you I'd never push you about it." Her eyes searched his and he saw the pain there. "But times have changed. I can no longer bide my own counsel. There are things I must know."

Jherek's stomach protested, wanting to purge its contents. Even though the wind raced over him to fill the sails, he felt like he'd come to dead calm inside, the last place a sailor wanted to find himself in an uncharted sea.

"Are you a wanted man, Jherek?"

"Aye."

Sabyna didn't bat an eye. She'd already been mostly certain of that, the young sailor knew.

"Is it for something you have done?"

"I've never done anything in my life to harm another soul out of greed or anger."

"I believe you," she said.

Relief flooded through Jherek.

"So your guilt, the price on your head, came from association with others?"

"Aye."

"So how did you come to be with these people that earned you the price on your head?"

"Through no fault of my own, lady," Jherek replied honestly. "It was ill luck."

"When did you leave them?"

"I was twelve," Jherek whispered.

"By the Lady's mercy," Sabyna said in a hushed voice, "you were only a boy."

Jherek remained silent, hoping she had probed enough. Every question she asked—skirting so closely to the truth he felt he needed to keep hidden—felt like a healer lancing an infected wound. Only in this there was no release from pressure and misery, only the promise of even more, sharper pain to come.

"What did they do?" Sabyna asked.

"Lady, please, I can't talk of it."

"Why? Jherek, don't you see that there doesn't have to be anything unsaid between us?"

Her question caught him by surprise. He shook his head, unable to voice what she wanted to hear.

"Lady, I would never have anything unsaid between us."

"But there is something?"

He couldn't answer.

"I told you before, when we first met on *Breezerunner*, that I could be very forward," Sabyna said. "Most men feel uncomfortable around a woman who knows her own mind. Sailors especially. They're not used to it."

"Aye, but that is not true of me. Sometimes," Jherek said quietly to give his words weight, "no matter how hard you struggle for something, it's not meant to be yours."

"Is that a threat?" Sabyna's voice hardened, but it was only a brittle shell over uncertainty.

The young sailor laughed when he wanted to cry. "No, lady. May Umberlee take me into her deep, dark embrace this very moment if ever there was a time I would intentionally hurt you."

"Back in the diviner's cave, she asked you what you believed in. You told her that you believed in love." Sabyna gazed deep into his eyes. "Did you mean that?"

Jherek hesitated, but in the end he knew she would know if he lied. "Aye," he said, "I believe in love. Perhaps, lady, it's the last thing I do believe in."

"So many things, evil as well as good, have been done in the name of love."

"There is no evil when the love is true," Jherek stated.

"How much do you believe that, Jherek?"

He shook his head. "Lady, with all that I am."

"Then how can you be so far from me? Surely you must know how I feel."

The question hammered Jherek like a fisherman's billy.

Tears trickled down Sabyna's face. "Never have I met a man," she said hoarsely, "that I've wanted as much as I want you. From the moment I saw you hanging onto *Breezerunner*'s side scraping barnacles, to the time we sit here together. Yet you don't acknowledge it."

Helplessly, Jherek watched her cry, not knowing what to do or what to say except, "I didn't know."

Her eyes remained steady on him and dark sadness clouded them, took away the merriment he always saw there.

"I know," she said finally, "and I think it's that bit of naivete that endears you to me even more. I look at you, Jherek, and I see a kind of man I've never known before. The puzzle of it all is that I don't know you."

"You know what you need to know, lady," Jherek told her.

"Do I?"

Jherek forced himself to speak, choosing his words carefully. "The other things you don't know, they are of no consequence."

"Then how is it we are apart? Unless I am wrong in your feelings about me."

Jherek tried to speak but couldn't. He dropped his gaze from hers, looking down into the deep waters below. How could his life be so twisted and so painful? What could he have ever done to deserve this?

"Tell me I'm wrong, Jherek," Sabyna said in a voice ragged with emotion. "Tell me I'm a fool."

"I would never call you a fool, lady," he told her.

"Tell me again how you believe in love, Jherek. Gods above, when I heard that timbre in your voice in the diviner's cave, I felt more confused than ever. The anger I'd been harboring toward you left me, and with it all of my defenses against these feelings. Tell me."

He raised his eyes to meet hers, seated across from her in the rigging. "As you wish, lady."

She gazed at him expectantly.

"I believe in love," Jherek said, "but I don't believe in myself. If I've learned anything at all in my life, it's that a belief in himself is what makes a man. I haven't yet become one."

Sabyna shook her head. More tears cascaded down her face. "Mystra's wisdom, I wish I knew some way to let you see yourself as I see you, and as others see you."

"It wouldn't matter, lady," Jherek said gently. "It's how I see myself."

"Why?"

"Because I know the true me that no one sees," Jherek stated. "Even now, you're in danger here on these seas because of a mistake I made. That weakness of pride I felt in accepting Lathander's disk at the Rose Portal has brought us all here."

"And what if that was no mistake?" Sabyna asked. "What if that disk is truly supposed to be here?"

"It's in evil's hands, lady. There's no way to make that right."

"You are so stubborn, Jherek," the ship's mage said in a harsh voice. "I would change that if I could."

"I know of no other way to be," Jherek told her.

"I know, and changing you would be so dangerous. Everything in you builds on everything else. Were one small part removed, I think the whole would somehow be changed as well. You are one of the most complete men I have ever known." Sadness carved deep lines into her face, draining her of the vitality he loved about her. "I'm sorry. I shouldn't have pressed you like this, but I couldn't go any further without letting you know how I felt. Forgive me."

"Lady, there is nothing to forgive."

"There is. I should have handled my own emotions better. I am a ship's mage, trained to handle battle, dying men, and the ravages of an uncaring sea and a fickle wind. I am no young girl to have her head turned so prettily. I have a heart, though, Jherek, and I've learned to listen to it. Selûne forgive my weakness."

Sabyna stood in the rigging and turned to go.

"Lady." Jherek stood too, catching her hand in his. It felt so slim and warm, so right in his. "It is not you."

Tears sparkled like diamonds on her wind-burned cheeks. "I know. I only wish I could be brave enough and strong enough for both of us. I wish I could help you trust me."

Without warning she leaned in, too quickly for Jherek to move away. Her lips met his, and he felt the brand of her flesh, tasted the sweetness of her tears. His pulse roared, taking the strength from his knees. In all his life Jherek had never known such a feeling, so strong and so true. For the moment, all his fears and self doubts were nothing. He felt whole.

She pulled back, breathing rapidly. The wind swept her tears away, sipping them in quick gusts.

"I do trust you, lady," Jherek said in a thick voice. He still held her hand, pulling it to him and placing it against his chest. The heat of her flesh almost seared him. "I swear to you, if it came to it, I would give my life to save yours, and you would never have to ask."

"I don't doubt you," she replied. She clenched her hand against his chest, knotting up his shirt and pulling him toward her with surprising strength. "You would give me your life, but can you give me your heart?"

10 *Flamerule, the Year of the Gauntlet*

8

At Iakhovas's bidding, Laaqueel stepped through the wall of *Tarjana* and out into the ocean. She only felt a moment's sensation of passing through the wood. Though it was not uncomfortable, she noticed immediately that the water on the other side was cold. The depth also blocked the penetrating light from the sea, turning the craggy ledges and canyons of the ocean floor black. She floated easily, adjusting the pressure in her air bladder to make herself weightless.

"Where are we?" she asked Iakhovas.

Silently, Iakhovas replied, through the connection made between them by the quill near her heart. *There are others here.*

Picking up on the tension in Iakhovas's words, Laaqueel grasped her trident more tightly and peered into the shadows around them. Her lateral lines picked up the small movement of fish nearby, and the coil of an eel shifting in its hiding place.

Who are we meeting? she asked.

Allies, Iakhovas replied. *That is all you need trouble yourself to know, little malenti.*

Unease swept through Laaqueel. Over the last four days, she'd seen little of Iakhovas. He'd remained within *Tarjana's* belly and hadn't allowed her to visit with him much. He watched over the princes in Vahaxtyl, and even though the malenti priestess told him they should return to the sahuagin city and change the currents that were passing through the minds of the populace as the princes spoke out against him, Iakhovas resisted. Clearly, he followed his own agenda.

She felt new movement. Something was slithering in from the left. The sensation pulsing through her lateral lines made her skin tighten in primitive fear. She turned to face it, dropping the trident's tines in front of her.

"Welcome," Iakhovas boomed.

He moved his arms and floated twenty feet down through the water to the sea floor. Puffs of sand rose up around his boots, then quickly settled again.

Three figures glided across the ocean floor from beneath a coral-encrusted arch. Laaqueel's senses told her more of them remained in hiding, but she could not tell how many more. She studied the figures, opening her eyes to their widest to use what little light the depths held.

They looked like surface dwellers, dressed in clothing rather than going naked as most races in Serôs did. There were three men, none of them possessing any remarkable features. They carried no apparent weapons, which surprised Laaqueel. The only surface dwellers the malenti priestess came in contact with who hadn't carried weapons were magic-users.

"Welcome," one of the men greeted. The word sounded foreign to his lips. "You have received word through Vurgrom of the Taker's Eye?"

"Yes," Iakhovas said. "I was told the eye resides in Myth Nantar."

"And so it does."

"I have brought gifts for the Grand Tor, a means of increasing his own armies," Iakhovas said.

He whirled the net above his head and it grew, increasing in size until it was as big as Iakhovas. He flung it away from him and still it grew. Something struggled within the strands.

When the net finished growing, it was huge. Tritons moved against each other inside it, striving desperately against the hemp strands.

The tritons were humanoid in appearance. They had the pointed ears and beautiful features of elves, long manes of dark blue and dark green hair. From the waist up, they could be easily mistaken for sea elves. From the waist down they were covered in deep blue scales. Their finned legs ended in broad, webbed flippers.

"How many?" one of the strangers asked.

"Thirty-four," Iakhovas said. "Four above the agreed-upon price. A gesture of good will to Grand Tor Arcanaal."

"He will be most appreciative," one of the men said. He gestured and shadows swam from the darkness, moving through the water smoothly, their arms at their sides. Two men swam to the net and grabbed it, then towed it back toward the gloom.

The tritons cursed and called on their god Persana but it was to no avail. They were doomed to their fates at the hands of the men Iakhovas gave them to. In only minutes, they were gone from sight and no longer heard.

The man gestured again. Another man swam from the shadows bearing a gold chest inlaid with precious stones, marked with sigils of power. He handed it to Iakhovas. The man turned and swam away.

Come, Iakhovas commanded, gesturing at the water and opening the gate again. *We have much to do.*

Shaken and mystified by the encounter, Laaqueel propelled herself after Iakhovas.

Look back, priestess.

The serenity of the feminine voice was startling. Laaqueel glanced at Iakhovas as he summoned the gate.

He does not hear me, priestess, the serene voice went on. *My words are meant for your thoughts alone.*

Who are you? Laaqueel asked. The voice was the same one that she had heard in Coryselmal as she was turned back from death.

Patience. All will be explained. For now, turn back and see the lies that Iakhovas has woven for your eyes to see.

Almost unwillingly, Laaqueel finned around, sweeping a hand through the water with the webbing open. The men were still in sight, only they weren't men anymore.

The three figures had deep purple skin that darkened to inky-black. Iridescent tips and lines marked the dorsal fin on their heads and backs. The heads were not oval like a human's or an elf's, but rather elongated and stretched out like that of a locathah. Their jaws formed cruel beaks.

Instead of two arms, they had four, all of them with humanlike appendages instead of the pincers or tentacles Laaqueel knew were also possible on the creatures. Their lower bodies ended in six tentacles.

Iakhovas lies, the serene voice said. *He's not as invincible as he would have you believe. You must watch yourself.* Then the voice was gone, a slight pop of pressure that faded from the inside of Laaqueel's skull.

"I am Myrym, chieftain of the Rolling Shell people, and I bid you welcome."

Pacys believed Myrym to be the oldest locathah he'd ever met. Cataracts clouded her eyes, but she gave no indication of missing anything around her.

The fin at the top of her head ran all the way down her back. Other fins underscored the forearms and the backs of her calves. The huge eyes were all black but were unable to both focus on the bard at the same time. The locathah turned her head from side to side. She wore a necklace made of threaded white and black pearls that would have been worth a fortune in the surface world, and a sash of netting that held a bag of different kinds of seaweed, coral, and shells. The old bard's own magical inclinations told him the net bag contained a number of items of power.

They sat at the bottom of the abyss in a grotto between a crevice of rock made easily defensible by stands of claw coral. Fist-sized chunks of glowcoral had been used to build cairns around them, punching holes in the darkness of the sea bottom. The tribe sat scattered about her, nearly three hundred strong, covering the ledges above them as well as smaller caves. The young in particular pooled together in schools, floating and watching with their big eyes.

Three days ago, the music had brought Pacys south and east of the sea elf city, drawing him toward Omalun and the Hmur Plateau at the base of Impiltur. The old bard couldn't lay name to what exactly pulled him, but he'd been insistent about going. Taranath Reefglamor had assigned guards to him and provisioned them well. The sea elf guard waited further up the Hmur Plateau with the seahorses they'd used as steeds.

Seated cross-legged only a few feet from the locathah chieftain, Pacys ran his hands over the saceddar, underscoring their conversation with a gentle melody that spoke of calm seas and the patience of her people, their willingness to sacrifice so they might live.

Khlinat sat only a little distance away, laughing at the antics of the foot-long locathah children as they swam close to him to investigate, then swam away with quick, darting movements.

"Thank you for your hospitality," Pacys said, listening to the music that crooned within him. "I didn't know what drew me out here, but I think I know now."

"We were drawn to each other," Myrym told him. "We've only been in this place two days. We have kept moving. The sahuagin have come into these waters, and the surface world has developed a strong distrust of anyone who calls the sea home. We have received word that our locathah brethren in the Shining Sea have allied with the Taker, an unfortunate choice that will affect us all."

"I know," Pacys replied.

Khlinat chuckled heartily as one of the small locathah children finally got the nerve up to touch his beard. The sudden explosive laughter sent the locathah child swimming for its life, threading under and between stands of rock thrusting up from the seabed.

"Oh, an' yer a quick lad, ain't ye?" the dwarf chuckled. "A-dartin' through them waters like that, it's a wonder ye didn't brain yerself."

The locathah child cowered behind the nearest adult, who laid a tender hand on the child's head. The other locathah laughed with the dwarf.

Even in that moment of levity, though, Pacys could sense the innate fear of the locathah tribe. They hadn't known peace and prosperity for generations, nor were there any reassurances now.

"What do you know of the Taker's beginnings?" Myrym asked.

"Nothing." Pacys paused his song. "All whom I have talked to have told me only that he was born long ago, when Toril was young. They didn't know if he was human or elf in the beginning, or what he would look like now."

Myrym nodded. "Someone once knew, but they have forgotten. However, that which others forget, the locathah hold close and treasure that it may someday benefit us. The other races have prophecies, parts they are to play in the coming battle."

Pacys changed tunes, finding one that played more slowly and conveyed menace. He recognized it as one of the Taker's alternate scores.

"Those thousands of years ago," Myrym said, "there existed a being unlike any that ever lived before. Some have said he was even the first man, the first to crawl from the sea and live upon the unforgiving dry. What made him crawl from the blessed sea, no one may know, but some say there was a longing within him to find another such as himself. The sea in those days was very green and had only recently given up space to the lands that rose from the fertile ocean bottom at the gods' behest."

Pacys listened intently, striking chords that would help his song paint the pictures of the tale.

"The Taker wandered the lands," Myrym said, "but of course, he found nothing there. The dry world was too new, and even the world of the sea was very young. While he was on the land, he talked with the gods. They were curious about him, you see, at this weak thing that dared talk to them and question the things that they did."

From the corner of his eye, Pacys saw that the locathah woman held the full attention of her tribe. The cadence of her voice pulled them in.

"With nothing to find on land, the Taker returned to the sea. It has been said that the Taker was there the day Sekolah set the first sahuagin free."

"Did he have a name?" Pacys asked.

"If he did, it has been forgotten," Myrym answered. "In those days, before people came to the sea, before some of them left the oceans and made their homes on dry land only later to return to the sea, names were not necessary. There was only one."

"Is he a man?" the old bard asked. "A wizard?"

"Not a true man, but again, not a creature of the sea either. He was himself, a thing unique."

"How did he come to be?"

"No one knows for sure, Loremaster. There are those who say his birth was an accident, created by the forces that first made Toril. Others say the god Bane crafted him to torture others. All agree that the Taker searched for love, for acceptance, for an end to the loneliness that filled him at being the one."

"But we all crave those things," Pacys said, not understanding. "How could this monster look for that which we all seek? I've been told the Taker is evil incarnate."

"He is," Myrym replied. "Are the wants and needs of good and evil so very different?"

"No," Pacys said. "Our stories are filled with those who fell from grace. Heroes and villains, only the merest whisper sometimes separates them."

"The Taker simply was," Myrym said. "His loneliness persisted till he drew the eye of Umberlee. The Bitch Queen in those days was softer. The gods had not yet begun to war over territories and the supplication of the thinking races that spread throughout the lands and seas of Toril. They existed in peace, each learning about their own powers, learning to dream their own dreams. Umberlee found the Taker, and she grew fascinated by him."

"Why?" Pacys asked.

"Because she had never known anything like him. He hurt and bled easily compared to her, weak in so many ways. Still, he held forth a joy and a zest for life that she had never envisioned. She grew to love him."

"And he grew to love her." Pacys's fingers sketched out a brief, sprightly tune that echoed in the grotto.

"As much as he could," Myrym admitted. "The concept of love, though credited to the gods, was a virtue of the elves, who knew loyalty and honor first. It was made bittersweet by the humans, whose lives ran by at a rapid pace and who could not maintain the attention and focus of the elves. In the beginning, an elf could love others, but only if he loved himself first. Humans, though, could love past themselves, love others more than themselves. They could love ideas, could love even the sound of laughter, which many thought was foolishness. No one, it is said, can love as a human can whose heart is pure and true."

Jherek gazed down into Sabyna's eyes and felt shamed. That she should have to ask him was his own failing. He held his hand in hers, feeling her fingers knotted up in the material of his shirt.

Her eyes searched his. "Can you promise me your heart, Jherek?" she asked again.

"Lady—"

"The answer can be so simple," Sabyna said. "Despite everything else you have on your mind, despite the other troubles that have your attention, there can be only two answers. Anything else would be no answer at all, and that wouldn't be fair to me after all I've revealed to you."

In the end, he knew what his answer must be, and why. He was not the man he needed or wanted to be, and she deserved far more than he ever could be.

"No."

Her fingers unknotted from his shirt and she pulled her hand back. Jherek made himself let go her hand, thinking he would never again have the opportunity to touch her.

"You tell me no, yet you made the diviner a promise not knowing what she might ask."

"There was no choice in that, lady."

"There's always a choice, Jherek. That's what life is about."

"Lady, I've never had the choices of others."

"No," Sabyna said. "I think maybe you've never been one to fight time or tide, Jherek. You gave your promise to the diviner even though that promise might take your life."

"Lady, I swore my life to you."

"Your life isn't what I wanted," Sabyna said. "A chance at a life with you is all that I asked."

She turned to go, tripping over a line in the rigging even though she'd been so surefooted earlier.

"Lady—" Jherek took a step forward, meaning to catch her, meaning to tell her—something.

The bag of holding at her side suddenly erupted and the raggamoffyn exploded from it. The bits and pieces of cloth wove themselves into a serpentine shape that struck like a cobra. The blow hammered Jherek's chest hard enough to knock him off balance.

"Skeins!" Sabyna cried, grabbing the raggamoffyn as it prepared to strike again. "No!"

Reluctantly, the familiar backed away, relaxing and floating easily on the wind.

Steadying himself, Jherek stared at the pretty ship's mage. Before he could find anything to say, a voice bawled out a warning from below.

"Slavers! Slavers off the port bow!"

9

Jherek turned to face *Black Champion*'s port side. Below, the pirates ran across the deck, following orders Azla barked out on the run. The pirate captain grabbed the railing of the prow castle steps and hauled herself up.

"Malorrie!" Azla yelled. "Do you see the damned ship?"

"Aye," Jherek replied in full voice. "She's off to port about a thousand yards."

"Her heading?"

"For us, Captain."

There was no doubt about her heading. White-capped breakers smashed against her prow as she cut across the green sea. Her lanyards bloomed with full canvas, harnessing the wind as she rose and fell on the great hills of the Sea of Fallen Stars.

"Is she riding high?" Azla demanded. "Or wallowing like some fat-arsed duck?"

"She's riding low, Captain," Jherek bellowed back between his cupped hands, "but she's coming hard."

He turned to glance at Sabyna but found the ship's mage was already climbing rapidly down the rigging. The young sailor's heart hurt as he watched her go.

He grabbed the book Glawinn had loaned him and quickly shoved it into the leather pouch where he stowed his gear. He left the pouch tied to the rigging, hoping it would be there when he got back. Out of habit he took the bow and quiver of arrows he'd brought up with him.

Glancing back at the approaching ship, the young sailor noted that it had gained considerably, pulling to within eight hundred yards and still closing. *Black Champion* held a south-southwesterly course, headed for the coast of Turmish. The slaver ship drew on due east, running straight ahead of the breeze as it swooped upon them.

"Bring her about!" Azla thundered. "Take up a heading due east. She's got our scent, boys, but let's see if the bitch can run!"

Black Champion came about smartly, taking up the easterly course. Deck crews sprang into action, bringing around the sails and running up new canvas. The caravel jumped in response to the wind, diving forward through the rolling brine hills. She dived into a wave, miring down, sliding back and forth like a hound trying to run up a muddy incline, then—when she broke through—she surged forward, her prow coming out of the water.

Jherek abandoned his place. Azla already had a man up in the crow's nest acting as a spotter. He pulled the bow and quiver over his shoulder, then ran through the rigging toward the bowline that ran from the mainmast to the prow.

He crossed the rigging without a misstep, pulling his cutlass free of the sash around his waist. He paused long enough to hang his hook from one boot, making sure it was secure, then he unknotted the sash. Shaking out the sash's length, he steadied himself on the rigging, then used the tautness of the ropes to spring up high. With the way *Black Champion* fought her way through the sea, the move was risky, but he trusted himself.

Holding the cutlass in one hand, he flipped one end of the sash over the bowline, then caught it in his fingers while holding the other. Squeezing both ends of the sash tightly, he hung from the bowline for just an instant, then began the long slide down to the prow. The sash sang across the twisted hemp. He lifted his feet to clear the canvas belled out from the forward mast.

Sliding across the bowline, Jherek glanced at *Black Champion*'s decks and watched the pirates taking their battle stations. They brought the prow and stern heavy ballistae around and fitted them with the ten-foot-long bolts. Two men began winding the winch that drew the great bowstring back.

The bowline was tied off at the end of the bowsprit sticking out from *Black Champion*'s prow. Judging the distance and the caravel's pitch, Jherek released one end of the sash. It unfurled from the bowline, and he fell to the prow castle, landing only a few feet from the forward ballista crew.

The young sailor rolled to his feet gracefully. He looped the sash back around his hips and slid the cutlass home, adding the hook from his boot a moment later. Taking the bow from his shoulder, he placed one end against his boot, took the greased string from his pocket, and strung it quickly. He unbound the strap that kept the arrows tight in the quiver and slid four shafts free. He nocked one to the string, then held the other three clasped in his left hand on the bow.

Azla stood at the prow railing, her scimitar naked in her fist. The wind tangled her dark hair. She took her chain mail shirt from a crewman and quickly pulled it on. The ringing chains on leather barely sounded over the crack of the canvas and the smashing waves.

"Who is she?" Jherek asked.

"I don't know the ship," Azla answered, "but I know the flag."

Jherek concentrated on the flag atop the approaching ship's main-mast. A feathered snake curled across a field of quartered black and red, mouth open and fangs exposed.

"They're of the Blood Tide," Azla said, "a loose network of slavers who work for the Night Masks in Westgate."

The slaver vessel was within four hundred yards, its advance slow-ing as *Black Champion* seized the wind. Jherek rode out the rise and fall of the ship, his free hand resting on the railing while the other held the nocked bow.

"Unfurl the spinnaker!" Azla shouted.

Crewmen rushed to the ship's prow. An instant later, the white sail billowed out, blotting the sky from forward view.

"Cap'n!" a mate squalled from the crow's nest. "Something just leaped off from that ship's rigging, and it ain't falling. Some kind of bird."

Jherek peered into the cloudy blue sky. The sun setting behind them turned the cloud banks blood-mist red, but he could make out half a dozen black shapes boiling out from the ship's lanyards.

The creatures swiftly overtook *Black Champion*, cutting through the air. The bat-winged humanoids had wedge-shaped faces and fangs that ran nearly to their lower jaws. A single horn sprouted from their narrow foreheads, curling back slightly. Grayish-white skin looked like marble in the sunlight, glowing with a rosy hue from the set-ting sun. Besides the arms and crooked legs, the creatures had long, spiked tails.

"Gargoyles," Azla breathed.

The gargoyles screamed, a raucous noise that filled *Black Champion*'s deck. They attacked the two men in the crow's nest first, swooping in to rip bloody furrows across the sailors' faces, chests, and backs with curved talons. Their blows also splintered the wooden cupola.

Tracking the nearest gargoyle , Jherek drew the arrow's feathers back to his cheek, led the creature a little, then released. The arrow jumped from the bow and struck the creature in the thigh.

The gargoyle screamed in pain, breaking the rapid beat of its wings for just an instant. It unfurled its wings and stopped its downward momentum less than ten feet above the main deck.

Horrid red eyes burned with rage as it spied Jherek. Screeching again, the gargoyle flapped its wings and gained height, streaking for the prow castle.

Standing his ground, Jherek fitted another arrow to the string. The other gargoyles in the rigging slashed the sails and smashed smaller lanyard supports.

"Kill those things!" Azla ordered at Jherek's side.

The young sailor released the bowstring when the gargoyle cleared the prow castle railing before him, less than twenty feet away now.

Even with the uncertain pitch and roll of the caravel, his arrow splintered the gargoyle's head.

Jherek sidestepped the flying corpse and watched the gargoyle smash into the bow railing, shattering some of the thinner decorative spindles. He already had another arrow nocked, searching for a target.

Pirates scampered through the rigging with swords in their fists to take on the gargoyles rending the sails. One of the creatures clung to the side of the forward mast with both legs, tail, and one hand. It struck out with the other, cleaving a pirate's face from his skull. Shrieking, the pirate fell from the rigging and smashed into the deck below. The screams stopped abruptly.

Releasing the bowstring, Jherek watched his arrow go wide of the mark, catching the canvas beside the gargoyle and sinking to the fletching. The young sailor nocked another arrow and let fly again.

The arrow sank into the gargoyle's thin chest, driving it back and nailing it to the mast it clung to. The wings fluttered as it struggled to get away. Before it could, three more arrows from the deck crew feathered it. The ship pitched across a breaker and snapped Jherek's shaft. The gargoyle dropped, missing the deck and falling over the side.

Jherek took four more arrows from his quiver, nocked one and locked the other three in his fist. He searched for other targets, missing twice as the gargoyles scampered and glided among the sails..

The mainsail came loose in a rush, snapping and fluttering as it dropped to the deck where it covered a dozen pirates. The loss of the sail had an immediate effect on *Black Champion* as the wind blew through her instead of against her.

Sunlight gleamed against copper-colored armor, drawing Jherek's eye. He put another arrow to his string as he watched Glawinn stride on deck, his long sword in one hand and his shield on his other arm.

The temptation proved too much for the gargoyles. Two of them swooped down from the rigging, flying directly toward the paladin. Pirates on the deck around Glawinn scattered, running for cover.

Pride swelled in Jherek's heart even as he drew back the bowstring. Glawinn's stance never faltered.

"For Lathander!" the paladin roared in challenge.

The young sailor launched his arrow, missing his mark by little more than a hand's width. The arrow thudded into the deck.

Glawinn stepped forward, striking the lead gargoyle in the face. Still in motion, he turned to the side, bringing his shield up and setting himself behind it as the second gargoyle hit him head on. The weight and speed of the creature staggered the paladin, but he held, turning the creature's momentum to one side.

The impact against the shield shattered bones in the gargoyle's arms and shoulders. It rolled across the deck, beating its wings futilely and howling in pain. As it tried to curl up and get to its feet, a nearby pirate ran at it and shoved a harpoon into the gargoyle's chest, driving it back against the starboard railing.

"They're going to overtake us," Azla said.

Jherek swung his attention back to the approaching ship. It was a hundred yards behind them, closing fast.

"Was Iakhovas immortal when Umberlee took him as her lover?" Pacys asked.

Myrym released the locathah child from her hands and smiled as it finned back among its brothers and sister. "Over the years they courted, the Bitch Queen gave him many gifts. Some merely of worth—gold and jewels and precious things—but many of them possessed powers that none but the gods had ever wielded before. When life began in the sea and took shape upon the dry lands, among the jungles and forests and swamps, Iakhovas was drawn to them. He wanted them to love him as Umberlee did."

"He was filled with his own conceits," Pacys said.

"Using Umberlee's gifts, he set about conquering the dry lands. There is a land where ferocious lizards still live till this day, unchanged for millions of years."

"Chult," the old bard said. "I know of the place." He had even visited there, seeing the dinosaurs for himself and carrying back tales of the adventurers who traveled there seeking fortunes.

"There Iakhovas caused to be built a huge palace," Myrym said. "They say it was more grand than any building on Faerûn. A man could walk it, I have been told, from one end to the other if he planned for a full day's travel. While Umberlee was away on other planes, Iakhovas warred incessantly, pitting one kingdom against another. He sent thieves out to take powerful items mages created, going there and taking them himself when no one else could do it. His greed knew no boundaries, no satisfaction. All he knew how to do was consume."

"And this was his true nature," Pacys said, understanding.

"Yes. The nature of the Taker is that he must take. His world was first the seas, remember, and those who live beneath the water have to move incessantly to feed. He was the chief predator among all the lesser species."

"What is he truly?" Pacys asked.

"Only the man who destroys him will know."

"Do you know this man's name?"

"No," Myrym said, shaking her narrow head, "but it is his destiny to become known to all through your songs."

"Can you tell me where to search for him?"

"No, but your path, his, and the Taker's will cross as surely as the limbs of a starfish have a common center. Learn what you need to."

Pacys nodded. "I have also heard it said that the Taker fell from grace with Umberlee."

"Twice," Myrym agreed. "The first time, it was over an elf woman the Taker took as his lover. By this time, his harems contained hundreds of women. Remember, gluttony was a way of life for him."

"Umberlee didn't know he had harems?" Pacys asked.

"The Bitch Queen knew," Myrym said, "but she didn't care. Physical relations were nothing to Umberlee, something to while away the time. What she wanted from the Taker was the way she felt when she saw her reflection in his eyes."

"Adoration."

"Yes. Nowhere else did she succumb to the draw of it. But she was gone too long to the other places she sought out for learning and conquering, and giving wasn't truly in the Taker's nature. His need was to take for himself. So he took this woman from his harem, and though he didn't truly care for her, he made it look like he did so that Umberlee would be jealous."

"Why?" Pacys asked. "Umberlee already loved him."

"But not as he wanted to be loved by her," Myrym said. "Her love for him was natural and good, as things are meant to be, but there was nothing natural and good about him. His appetites ruled his life. When she returned, she found this woman in the bed she shared with the Taker, not one of the harem rooms. The Taker pretended the woman put the shine in his eyes that he showed Umberlee. So great was the Bitch Queen's love for him that she did not see the truth."

Pacys listened to the story with sadness. He'd seen good love turn out badly as well.

"Umberlee killed the woman in a fit of rage," Myrym continued. "The Taker knew true joy as he saw in the Bitch Queen's face the pain and hurt her love for him caused. He thought he controlled her, then, and he mocked her for her weakness. Only he had no true accounting for how hurt Umberlee was. She'd never experienced pain like that before, and swore then that she would never experience it again. She lashed out at him, raking her claws across his face and ripping an eye from its socket, almost tearing the face from him."

Discordant music emanated from the saceddar as Pacys envisioned the fight, and words already came into his mind to paint the scene for his listeners.

"Umberlee left him there in his grand palace," Myrym said, "broken and ruined, no longer ever able to be what he once was. She did not suffer to kill him, but it was a near thing. The Taker brooded and banked his hatred for a thousand years and more.

"He began to build again," she continued, "to make himself stronger than ever before. He scoured all of Toril for powerful items, devices that he could use to control elements and men and magic. He scarred his body with sigils of power that allowed him to reach into other planes. In his mind, he was more than he had ever been or ever could be.

"He sought out Umberlee then, to take his vengeance."

Azla ran to the forecastle railing over the main deck and called, "Ship's crew, stand ready to repel boarders!"

Black Champion's crew numbered twenty-seven, Jherek knew, and a handful of them were involved in steering and trying to salvage what they could of the sails.

At least forty men lined the starboard side of the attack craft as it sped forward. They manned the fore and aft ballistae as well as the one on the main deck. The sound of running water filled the air.

A desperate smile played on Azla's lips, and Jherek recognized it as reckless determination.

"Ballista crews," she bellowed, "prepare your shots fore and aft! Make them count or I'll have the hide from your backs!"

"Aye, Cap'n!"

"Fire on my command!"

Jherek spied Sabyna making her way up behind Glawinn. Skeins drifted protectively over her shoulder.

"Ballista crews, ready."

"Ready, Cap'n."

"Fire!"

The two ballistae sang basso thrums as they released within a heartbeat of each other. The ten-foot shafts sliced through the air. One of them thudded into the slaver's wooden hull only a few feet from the railing, frightening the crew back. The other missile struck the foremast and broke it cleanly. The forward sails toppled, raining down on the crew below.

A ragged cheer burst from *Black Champion*'s crew.

"Belay that!" Azla roared as the caravel followed the next ocean rise down into a trough below the slaver's line of sight. "We've won no battle here yet. That remains for you to take it from their teeth!"

Jherek's heart beat rapidly. Here in this battle, there was no confusion.

"Archery crew," Azla called. "Stand ready!"

Black Champion's sails blew her forward, riding her up the next wave and pulling her back within sight of the slaver only fifty yards away.

"Fire arrows!" Azla commanded.

The crew fired, and Jherek bent his bow with theirs, aiming toward the knot of men standing in the slaver's amidships. Most of the arrows missed, striking the water or snapping into the canvas above. Jherek's own shot hit a man in the shoulder and drove him back and down to his knees.

The three ballistae aboard the slaver cut loose. One of them shivered into the stern castle and punched through. The second struck below the waterline, but the vibration that ran through *Black Champion* let Jherek know the shot struck home.

The third shot hit the railing near Glawinn. Splintered wood flew into the air as the ten-foot shaft punched an eighteen-inch hole dead center in a pirate's chest. Laden by the corpse, the shaft careened on, knocking down pirates like tenpins. It forced the body across the deck, then tore through the railing on the other side.

Cries of fear and prayers to gods filled the air. For a moment, the pirates' resolve seemed broken.

"Live or die, you damned brutes!" Azla yelled down. She hurled herself over the forecastle railing and landed in a crouch on the pitching deck. "The choice is in your hands and in your blades. Do me proud!"

A ragged cheer rose with her scimitar. "For Captain Azla! For *Black Champion!*"

The caravel dropped into another trough as Jherek heaved himself over the forecastle railing and dropped to the main deck.

"Young warrior," Glawinn called.

"Aye."

"If that's a slaving ship and she has a cargo in her hold, it may be that our attackers are holding a blade to their own throats. You understand?"

"Aye."

Jherek understood immediately. If the slaves were freed and given a chance at their own freedom, many of them would take it.

"I will stand with these men and lead them into the battle," the paladin said. "If you are able, perhaps you can raise us another army to even the odds."

"Aye," Jherek answered.

"Arthoris!" Azla roared.

The old ship's mage stepped forward. He was a gnarled man with long gray hair and a groomed beard. He wore robes with sigils and symbols on it and carried a staff. "Aye, Cap'n."

"Give them something to remember us by."

Arthoris raised his staff and chanted in a strong, clear voice. The heavens above him darkened as if a storm were coming.

"Ballista crews," Azla called. "Ready . . ."

"Ready, Cap'n."

"Fire!"

One of the shafts gutted the boarding party along the slaver's starboard side, breaking their ranks. The second shaft hammered into the mainmast a good twenty feet from the deck. For a moment the missile's fluted edges held it embedded in the wood, then the mast gave way with a horrific crack. The top of the mast listed to the side, bringing down more canvas and pulling the slaver hard over to port.

Black Champion's crew cheered again, calling out vile oaths at their attackers. The slaver crew shouted out in anger. Before they could recover, Arthoris launched his attack.

Three lightning balls leaped from the old ship's mage's staff and struck the slaver. Peals of thunder split the air. The lightning balls struck the boarding crew, burning them and knocking them from their feet, but only incapacitated a couple of them.

The slaver vessel pulled away, disengaging from the attack. With the two broken masts and only one remaining, she wasn't any faster than *Black Champion.*

"Cap'n!"

Azla turned, spotting one of her officers near the ship's hold.

"Come quickly!" the mate called.

All his arrows gone now, Jherek joined the ship's captain at the hold. Another man stood below with a lantern. The pale yellow light played uncertainly in the darkness as the ship yawed across the waves and reacted badly to the wind due to the tattered sails. There was no mistaking the heavy shaft that had broken through *Black Champion*'s side.

10

"The Taker thought he could defeat Umberlee?" The prospect astonished Pacys.

Myrym gazed at the old bard with her luminescent eyes and said, "Yes. She stripped his weapons from him, yanked the magic eye from his head and scattered it into its many parts, then caused storms to drive the weapons inland to the heart of Faerûn. The elves had only just abandoned Eiellur and Syorpiir during the War of Three Leaves to settle in the Selmal Basin.

"Then Umberlee reached into the heavens and caused stars to fall, crashing into the land and altering coastlines. It was almost enough, it is said, to drive the sea elves back to the surface, but they stayed. They became part of those whose destiny it was to cross paths with the Taker."

"In Myth Nantar?"

Myrym nodded. "All things above and below once passed through Myth Nantar. The elves named it City of Destinies because of the stories they'd been told about the Taker, but already they'd begun to forget some things."

"What is in Myth Nantar?"

"That I cannot answer, Loremaster. There are some events foretold that must be lived through."

"You never said what Umberlee did with the Taker."

"In her rage, the Bitch Queen thought she killed him. Umberlee broke her lover, shattered his bones, and spilled his blood."

"I was told the Taker's eye is in Myth Nantar."

"Only part of the Taker's eye is there," Myrym answered. "It is a key piece that the Taker will need to make his weapon complete again. No one knows where in the city it is. The Dukars took charge of the eye fragment when the Coronal at Coryselmal gave it to them after the birth of Myth Nantar."

"The Dukars?" Pacys repeated. "I thought they were only legends."

"No, Loremaster." Myrym's rebuttal was gentle. "Despite all your travels, there is much you have yet to learn. Tell me what you know of the Dukars."

"They were wizards," Pacys said, recalling the few, seldom heard stories he'd been told over the years. "At first they were brought together in Aryselmalyr. Some believe they were historians, and others thought they were warriors seeking to take all of Serôs as their own territory. It's been said that Dukars could speak to the sea and have it listen, and grow weapons from their own bodies. I always thought them to be purely myth."

Myrym shook her head in disbelief. "Ah, the tales of gods-struck humans and jealous elves. The Dukars are real."

Jherek watched helplessly as the sea cascaded into the hold around the ballista shaft stuck through *Black Champion*'s hull. Already the water was up to their ankles, swirling around the stores and crates in the cargo area.

"Damn," Azla swore at his side. "Umberlee is getting her tithing today." She raised her voice so the pirates in the hold could hear her. "Tear off your shirts and breeches, use them to plug up the hole around that damned shaft."

"What are you going to do?" the young sailor asked.

"I'm going after that ship," Azla declared.

"You could rip out *Black Champion*'s bottom in the chase," Jherek protested. "The currents are already gnawing at her."

Azla's eyes blazed. "Unless you can pull a chunk of earwax from your head, cast it into the water and grow an island out of it, I don't see that we have much choice." She marched from the hold to the boarding party.

"She's tucked her tail between her legs and run," one of the pirates yelled.

Jherek saw the slaver vessel limping away to the south, evidently trying to leave the area with no further confrontation.

"They're not going to get away," Azla said in a stern voice. "They've holed our ship and we're sinking. So we're taking theirs in turn."

Her crew turned to look at her in amazement, clearly not wanting to believe it.

"Bring us around," Azla ordered.

The pirates sprang into action, shifting what sailcloth was left after the gargoyles' attack and cutting free other canvas that only impeded their progress.

As he stood on the deck, Jherek could feel the sluggishness of *Black Champion*'s response as she came about.

Sabyna approached. No tears showed in her eyes now, and she acted as if what passed between them only a few moments ago had never happened. "What's wrong with the ship?" she asked.

"The hull's holed," Jherek told her in a low voice. "Taking that slaver is the only hope we have."

"As you say," Myrym told Pacys, "the Dukars were wizards. They found their beginning almost nine thousand years ago, in a small town then called simply Nantar. Nantar was located on the Lower Hmur Plateau, its population made up exclusively of sea elves. At first, the Dukars were lorekeepers only. There were four of them who joined together after being taught by their master, Dukar, from whom they took the name of their order. These were Jhimar, the triton warrior maiden; Kupav, the sea elf; Maalirn, also a triton; and Nunios, the female morkoth."

"A morkoth?" Pacys shook his head. "Chieftain Myrym, in the outer seas, the only morkoth that have been encountered are solitary creatures who dwell in caves and set traps for humans and elves, which they consider delicacies."

"You've heard of the Arcanum of Olleth?"

"Yes," the bard replied. "An empire of morkoth is something I'd have to see believe, though, and to accept the idea of a city of benevolent morkoth is harder still."

"The city is called Qatoris," Myrym said. "It is magically hidden by the Dukars who live there."

"How can this be?" the old bard asked.

"In the beginning, the Dukars recognized no oaths of fealty to the elven empire though pressure was put on them. Instead, they devoted their time to the development of their schools. Over the next three thousand years Serôs knew peace. More years passed, and more wars to go with them, and still the Dukars tried to serve the sea. They were captured and imprisoned many times in the struggles for power among the elves and other races. By the Year of the Druid's Wrath—six hundred and fifty-two years ago—the Dukars had pulled away from Myth Nantar, not wanting to take part in any of the Hmurran civil wars."

"What of the Taker's Eye?" Pacys asked the locathah.

"When Myth Nantar was built," Myrym said, "as I have said, the Coronal gave the eye to the Dukars for safe keeping. They hid it somewhere in the city."

"But Myth Nantar was lost," Pacys said. "That I remember."

Myrym nodded and said, "After the Dukars left, sahuagin warriors stole into the city and murdered the sea elves and merfolk who remained to stand guard. The sea devils destroyed much of the city, but could not stay. The mythal was designed to keep creatures like them out. They soon fled, but in later years, the magical shields around the Academy of the Dukars started growing till they encompassed all of fallen Myth Nantar. The water around the city became impenetrable even to those who built it. Some say it is haunted."

"And what do you say?" Pacys asked.

"Only that the city was properly named, Loremaster. It is the City of Destinies. For the Taker, for you, and for the young warrior you seek. Somewhere in that wreckage is the Taker's Eye, and it holds the key to all your destinies. I have one final gift for you if you will accept it."

"What is that?"

"You asked me in what direction the young warrior you seek lies. These water lilies may hold an answer of sorts for you." The aged locathah held the leaves out to him. "Simply put them under your tongue and think of him."

The bard opened his mouth and put the leaves under his tongue. He pushed the seawater from his mouth and waited. A pleasant tingling sensation numbed the underside of his tongue and his lips.

All at once it felt as if the top of his head exploded, and he was swept away on a cold, black tide.

Black Champion bucked and fought the ocean like a horse trying to keep its head above the waterline. Jherek peered down at the dark, green-black water little more than an arm's reach from the railing. Perhaps only minutes remained before forward progress became impossible for the caravel. Despite the slave ship's loss of two masts, *Black Champion* was barely closing the last hundred yards to her.

The caravel smashed through another wave. This time the cold seawater swept over *Black Champion*'s deck, drenching the assembled crew in spray. They didn't look hopeful even after the ship surged forward again.

The slaver tried to cut away as *Black Champion* came abreast, tacking into the wind. If the slaver had flown another sail, Jherek knew the maneuver would have cost them their last chance at overtaking their quarry. As it was, the single remaining sail only offered a token attempt at quickly changing their course.

"Come hard to starboard!" Azla ordered from the forecastle.

Jherek looked up at the half-elf pirate captain with respect. She stood there knowing she was losing her ship, yet she remained inviolate, totally in command.

"What are you thinking, young warrior?" Glawinn asked.

"Look at her," Jherek said. "Aboard a dying ship, about to take on a crew twice the size of hers, yet she knows no fear."

"You don't think she's afraid?"

"Maybe she is," he conceded, "but she overcomes it well."

"Fear isn't necessarily a bad thing, young warrior. It's meant to warn of uncertain situations and concentrate resolve, to give strength to flagging muscles and wings to thoughts. In the end it must be embraced and accepted, not conquered like an enemy blade. Aren't you afraid now?"

"Aye," Jherek said, continuing to watch the pirate captain as she ordered the grappling crew to the railing, "and it shames me."

"I'd rather see you afraid," Glawinn said, "and know that you are truly alive, than to see you the way I have seen you in the past days."

"I have done so many wrong things, made so many mistakes." He glanced at Sabyna, who stood on the forecastle deck with Arthoris and Azla. "I've hurt someone I would never have offered any injury." He turned his attention to the paladin and added, "I've even offended you, who have done nothing but try to help me."

Glawinn smiled, his eyes twinkling, and dropped his mailed hand on Jherek's shoulder. "Young warrior," he said, "if you made no trespasses, who would there be to say you'd ever been by?"

Black Champion smashed through another wave and took a while to right herself. Jherek held onto the railing, balancing himself easily while Glawinn struggled slightly with all his armor on.

"Keep something in mind, young warrior. A hero who has never known fear or want, uncertainty or anger, hunger or loneliness, is no real hero. It isn't their bravery that should impress you. That turns on a moment, marking an event that most people choose to recognize as heroic. It is in the journey that leads up to that moment, the persistence of vision, that makes a man or woman truly heroic. Do you understand?"

"Some of it."

Glawinn patted him on the shoulder. "The rest will come in time. For now we have a ship to take."

Jherek watched as the slave ship drew closer and closer.

The slaver's stern ballista crew swung the large weapon around. Even as they started locking the ballista down and getting ready to fire at *Black Champion*—a target scarcely more than seventy feet distant—a mass of writhing black tentacles suddenly sprouted from the deck.

The ballista crew turned and tried to flee, but the black tentacles whipped out blindly and wrapped the slavers up, snapping bones and squeezing the life from them. Their screams were lost in the rush of water and wind. The tentacles ripped the ballista from the deck and smashed it into a thousand pieces.

"Azla's mage," Glawinn said.

Jherek nodded and watched as the slaver crew attacked the tentacles with harpoons and swords.

Twisting tongues of flame suddenly ignited in the slaver's amidships. For a moment, Jherek believed the vessel was afire, then the flame blossomed hotter and brighter and shot toward *Black Champion*.

"Fireball!" one of the pirates squalled. As a man, the boarding crew ducked under the huge mass of roiling flames.

The wizard's casting was slightly off, and the fireball sizzled as it touched the water beside the pirate ship, then exploded into a wall of flames that rushed across *Black Champion*'s deck. Rigging and sail-cloth caught fire. Only the water washing over the deck kept it from burning as well.

Arthoris stepped to the edge of the forecastle railing above and extended his hands to the heavens, the sleeves of his robes falling back down his skinny arms. He cried out in a language Jherek didn't understand, his tone at once commanding and beseeching.

Dark clouds spiraled into the sky above the ships, spreading out for miles in all directions. The wind lifted and came howling across the choppy ocean surface. Rigging creaked above, and lanyards that were cracked but not broken through now gave way. A heavy, stinging rain smacked into *Black Champion* and her crew.

The flames atop the rigging were quickly snuffed.

"Grappling crew!" Azla yelled above the roar of the storm. "Ready on the line!"

The pirates surged forward to the railing again. Jherek stooped and picked up a grappling line, running the rough hemp through his hands. He measured back from the big, three-pronged hook and readied himself to cast.

A giant shape surged out of the water between the two ships. A webbed green foot with great claws slapped against the starboard railing. A huge head at least eight feet across, cut with a grim maw and gold-webbed spines along the back of its neck, followed the foot. Malevolent red eyes glared at the surprised crew. Another foot followed the first, and the great creature tried to drag itself aboard. The neck strained up from the dark green shell on its back.

"Dragon turtle!" a man screamed.

The grappling line crew surged back, breaking away from the deadly creature.

Pacys woke in black waters. Panicked, he struggled to get free of the ocean. He tried to find a way back to his own body.

Taleweaver.

The call wasn't from anything human. Pacys heard it in his mind, but the syllables were long and drawn out.

Do not be in such a hurry, the voice went on. *There is much to learn.*

Basso booming filled the water, stretching out into squeaks and squeals, turning again to a deep moaning sound like wind blowing over the neck of a bottle. The old bard listened to the sound carefully, drawn to its melodic nature.

Where am I? Pacys asked.

We call this the dreaming time.

Who are you?

Enemies of the Taker and his sahuagin.

What do you want with me?

We did not summon you. You came to us as it was foretold in our songs.

With surprise, Pacys realized that the booming squeals and squeaks were whale songs. *Are you here with me?*

In the only way that we can be.

I can't see you.

Open your mind, Taleweaver. All that we may tell you will be revealed.

Letting go the panic that vibrated inside him, Pacys immersed himself in the whale song. There weren't words or even tones especially. The sounds played upon the ear, but they touched the heart. He closed his eyes, and when he opened them again, the black water was sapphire blue.

He peered below, seeing the pale white-gray of the ocean floor a hundred feet or more below. Above him, sunlight kissed the surface of the water and turned it to too-bright silver. He glanced away, trying to peer through the blue-gray cloud that settled in the water before him.

Where are you? the old bard asked.

I am here, the slow voice replied. *Reach out and you will touch me.*

Tentatively, Pacys stretched out his arm toward the gray-blue fog. Only instead of penetrating it as he'd expected, the fog felt rough and solid. With that single touch, the bard's perceptions changed.

A great whale floated in the water in front of him. The gray-blue color partially masked it in the water, and his closeness prevented him from seeing all of it even now. Pacys knew some of the great whales grew to be four hundred feet long. This one was so long its tail flukes disappeared in the distance.

Who are you? Pacys asked.

In your language, I am called Song Who Brings Bright Rains. My mother gave birth to me after a storm, when a rainbow stretched across the sky.

By looking up, then down, Pacys could make out the familiar wedge-shaped head of the massive cetacean. He knew this was a humpback whale. The bard trailed his fingers along the pebbly skin as he swam down the length of its body. He found the creature's eye only a little later.

The eye was dark and bigger around than Pacys was tall. Instinctively, the bard swam away from the eye, wondering if the creature could see him from this close.

I see you, Taleweaver, the whale boomed.

Jherek stared at the huge beast clinging to *Black Champion*'s starboard side.

"It's not real, young warrior," Glawinn said, starting forward.

Jherek wanted to reach out and hold the paladin back, even put a hand on his shoulder. "Wait," he said.

Glawinn turned on him, his beard wet with gleaming diamonds from the salt spray and the rain. "Look at it. Look hard at it and you will know it's not real. It's just more magery, and a weak spell at best, not one that will hurt a man. Where is that thing's battle cry? Where is the sound of those claws rasping against the wood? How is it that the creature's weight doesn't tear the railing free?"

Pirates screamed at Glawinn to get back as the dragon turtle sighted him. The neck elongated and stretched forward. The mouth opened into a cavernous gullet that could swallow a man whole. The paladin stretched his arms out and smiled.

The dragon turtle struck, snapping its jaws closed over the paladin. Only instead of tearing flesh and breaking bone, the edged beak passed through the paladin. The illusion faded, leaving Glawinn standing untouched on the rolling deck.

"Magery," Glawinn shouted. "A child's trick meant to give them enough time to get away."

Jherek lifted the grappling hook again and raced to the starboard railing. The slave ship had gained twenty feet in distance, too far to make the cast good.

"Boarding party," Jherek shouted. "Make ready."

Snarling curses, the pirates gathered again and took up the grappling hooks. *Black Champion* came about at a crawl, the waterline no more than two feet below her deck. She moved forward slowly, overtaking the slave ship with flagging strength.

The distance closed as the pirate ship came abreast the slaver. The pirates jeered the slaver crew as they overtook them, then came alongside. Aboard the slave ship, crewmen stood ready with hatchets and axes to chop any lines that succeeded in grabbing hold.

"Steady, men," Azla ordered. "On my orders."

The slaver crew consisted mostly of humans, but there were a few half-ogres among them. The half-ogres towered above the human crew, standing eight and nine feet tall, dressed in bear skins and sahuagin hides.

"Arthoris," Azla barked.

"Aye, Cap'n," the old ship's mage responded.

"Ready the men."

Jherek felt a tingle pass through him and knew that the old man's spell had affected him. He felt curiously light, as if he weighed nothing. Understanding what was about to happen, he quickly wrapped the grappling line around his left forearm, holding the hook itself in his hand.

The ships closed to within twenty feet. Over-eager crewmen on both sides threw daggers, but none of them did any real harm.

A robed man dashed atop the stern castle and spoke harsh syllables. He gestured at the writhing black tentacles still holding onto the corpses of its victims and the tentacles disappeared in an explosion of crimson powder, the spell broken. He turned and pointed a wand at the crew aboard *Black Champion*.

As the slaver mage spoke, Jherek felt the hair on his head start to stand while energies gathered in the air above him. A lightning bolt from the wand cracked like a beastmaster's whip between the ships, and struck a pirate full in the chest.

The bolt lifted the man from his feet and held him in the air for a moment before ripping the flesh from his bones in bloody chunks that showered down over the crew. The charred corpse, white bones showing through burned meat, dropped to the deck. When a wave lapped over the side of the ship and rolled over the dead man, smoke rose from the body.

The slaver mage pointed again.

A flutter of movement speeding across the rain-streaked sky caught Jherek's attention. It took the young sailor a moment to recognize the bits and pieces of material as Skeins, Sabyna's familiar. Before the mage could unleash the power of the wand again, the raggamoffyn attacked. The living cloth plastered the man, sticking to him and covering him from head to toe in an instant, as tightly as a second skin.

The mage tried to fight the raggamoffyn, beating against his own breast and shouting in fear as the pieces wrapped over his face. His voice became muffled, then ended abruptly. The mage jerked frantically as he tried to escape, then even that stopped. Totally under the raggamoffyn's control, the mage ran for the side of the ship and threw himself over. He disappeared at once into the black water between the ships.

"Boarding crew, advance!" Azla shouted.

Stunned by the events of the last few seconds, *Black Champion*'s crew leaped across the twenty-foot span between the ships. The slaver rode the ocean a good eight feet higher than the pirate ship's deck. Though Arthoris's magic allowed them to leap the distance between the ships, most men only rose four or five feet.

Two pirates slammed into the bulwark and fell into the sea. Three others used their grappling lines to catch onto the slaver's railing. Jherek and the others managed to grab the railing and started hoisting themselves up.

A half-ogre stepped up to the railing as the young sailor started his climb. His eyes showed the white pupils of a true ogre. Scars tracked his ugly, pointed face bearing a nose that was too long and too broad for the rest of his features. The pockmarked skin was the color of butter gone bad. A single braid held his long black hair from his face, revealing pointed ears.

"Throg kill you, puny man," the half-ogre growled. He shoved his harpoon down toward Jherek.

The young sailor hooked an arm inside the railing, aware of the roiling sea below him and the waves crashing against the side of the slave ship. Even as well as he could swim, dropping into the ocean would probably mean death. He let go with his free hand, pushing himself against the ship in a half-roll. The ship's pitching hammered him against the side with bruising force.

Snarling in rage, the half-ogre drew the harpoon up to thrust again.

Swinging back into position, Jherek reached through the railing and caught the back of the half-ogre's foot. The young sailor yanked as hard as he could, counting on the unsteady deck to aid him. Slipping across the wet deck, the half-ogre's foot came forward and smashed through the railing.

Even as his opponent fell backward, Jherek planted his boots against the slave ship's side and leaped again, using what remained of Arthoris's spell. He flew ten feet into the air, over the heads of the slaver crew, his fist still tight around the grappling hook and line he carried. He landed, drew the cutlass from the sash, and turned to face his adversaries.

He swung the big grappling hook into the face of the first man who reached him, knocking the man to one side. Giving ground immediately, the young sailor retreated toward the broken stump that remained of the ship's mainmast. Moving lithely, he dodged around the mast, slammed a slaver's blade aside, then slashed the cutlass through the slaver's stomach, cracking ribs and ripping the man open.

Other pirates from *Black Champion* landed on the deck as well, and the brawl quickly turned bloody. Crimson stained the wet decks, sluicing through the rainwater pools that collected on the warped deck.

"Secure the lines!" Jherek yelled.

He beat aside another slaver's sword thrust with the flat of the cutlass, then stepped into the man and slammed his shoulder into his chest, knocking him back. The young sailor kept going forward, staying in close and using his elbows and knees to beat his opponents back as Malorrie had taught him. He slapped a knife stroke down, captured the wrist in his same hand, and buried the blade in another slaver's chest.

Taking advantage of the confusion and the tangle of arms and legs around him, Jherek ran to the slaver's port railing. He shook the line free of his forearm, thrust the cutlass point down into the deck, and readied the grappling hook.

A man charged at him from the crowd of slavers with an upraised sword. Jherek ducked under the angled sword stroke, then slammed the grappling hook into the man's chest, hooking the belt that crossed him from shoulder to hip. He yanked and twisted, putting all his strength and all the leverage he could muster into the move.

Instead of merely going over the side of the ship as Jherek intended, the ship pitched suddenly and aided in the throw, making the slaver go high into the air. As he came down, *Black Champion* surged into the side of the slave ship, crunching the man between the two massive wooden hulls.

The impact nearly drove Jherek from his feet. He stumbled and caught himself against the railing, staring down at the pulped smear that remained of the slaver trapped between the two ships. A wave crashed against the ships, and even that was gone.

Horror filled Jherek and he pushed nausea from his mind. He stood on the lurching deck and watched as *Black Champion* went up broadside against the slave ship again. He cast the grappling hook and watched as Glawinn made it fast. Dressed in his armor, the paladin would never have made the jump even with the magic spell Arthoris had woven.

The young sailor pulled the line taut when the two ships closed again, then wrapped it around the slaver's railing. Wood creaked ominously as the two ships started to slide apart, but the line and the railings held. The drag created by *Black Champion*'s flooded hold was immediately noticeable, pulling at the slave ship like a drowning man.

Jherek turned at the sound of footsteps behind him, catching sight of the half-ogre charging at him. The young sailor plucked his cutlass from the deck, wrapping his fingers around the hilt. He met the half-ogre's bastard sword as it descended. Steel clanged, and the impact shivered down Jherek's arm.

Parrying the half-ogre's next attack, the young sailor attempted a riposte, only to find that the creature was faster than his bulk implied. Jherek parried again to keep his head on his shoulders. Another slaver attacked from the young sailor's side, trying to drive a spear through his guts.

Jherek stepped back, letting the spear go by, then catching the haft in one hand. He jerked at the man, using momentum against him and easily pulling him off-balance. Throg swung again, but the young sailor stepped behind the slaver crewman. The half-ogre's weapon sliced into the man's chest, killing him instantly.

Shoving the corpse at the half-ogre, Jherek turned and sprinted for the main hold in the middle of the ship's deck. Water and blood made the deck slippery as the ship lurched and fought against *Black Champion*'s dead weight.

A slaver rushed at Jherek as the half-ogre screamed curses behind him. The young sailor dropped to the deck just ahead of the slaver's sword and skidded on his side. Jherek kicked and took the slaver's feet out from under him, knocking him backward. By the time the man stopped sliding, Jherek got to his feet and followed the steps down into the main hold.

11

Whale oil lanterns lit the cargo hold. The pale illumination barely lightened the shadows of the men, women, and children shackled in the hold. Jherek looked at them, unprepared for the sight.

Rough iron cuffs held the prisoners at wrists and ankles, connecting to an iron rod that ran the length of the slave ship. Foul odors filled the hold, and the young sailor knew the captives had been forced to sit in their own excrement. They looked at him with fear-filled eyes.

"Don't let us drown," a woman cried out in a hoarse voice. "If the ship is going down, at least give us a chance to save ourselves."

Pain welled up in the young sailor's heart. He'd never seen slaves before. No one should have to face what those people had been through.

"Look out!" a slave yelled.

Jherek sensed a big man stepping from the shadows behind him. The young sailor turned. There was no mercy in Jherek's heart.

The slaver carried a battle-axe in a two handed grip. The lantern's weak illumination glinted off earrings and a gold tooth. The slaver was a mountain of a man, rolling in muscle and fat. He swung the battle-axe with skill, making a short, vicious arc with the double-bitted head. Jherek fended it off, but the slaver followed up with a swipe from the iron-shod butt of the axe that could have crushed the young sailor's skull.

Jherek slipped the hook from his sash as he took two steps back.

"You done crawled into the wrong hole, rabbit," the brute taunted, grinning broadly.

Two other shadows stepped out behind the man, flanking him on either side. One of them carried a spear and the other wielded a short sword and a dagger.

Without a word, Jherek attacked. There was no one else to defend the people in the hold, no one else to set them free. Azla's pirates were shedding blood above so they might all live.

The young sailor swung the cutlass at the axe-wielder's head, expecting him to block it. The slaver followed up with another blow from the butt of his battle-axe. Jherek slammed the curved hook into his opponent's hand, nailing it to the wooden haft and blocking with the meaty part of his forearm.

The slaver shrieked in pain, looking at his impaled hand in disbelief. Before he could move, Jherek stamped on the slaver's foot and ran the top of his head into the slaver's face. Blood gushed from the man's broken nose as he stumbled backward.

Jerking the hook free, Jherek dropped low and slashed across the man's waist, spilling his guts. Even as the man dropped to his knees, the young sailor spun and slashed again, taking the slaver's head nearly from his shoulders.

The spearman came on, thrusting vigorously. The fluted blade cut across Jherek's left shoulder and the spear haft bounced under his chin. He brought the hook down savagely, driving the spear toward the wooden planking. The weapon caught and stopped suddenly, throwing the man who wielded it off-balance.

Before Jherek could attack, the swordsman slashed at him. Only the speed and reflexes Malorrie and Glawinn had trained into him kept the young sailor from getting his head split open.

The spearman drew his weapon back as Jherek parried the long dirk in the swordsman's other hand. Catching the dirk against his cutlass's crosspiece, the young sailor shoved his attacker back, causing him to stumble over the dead man.

Recovering his footing, the spearman thrust again, but Jherek dodged before the edged blade touched him. Blood ran warmly down the young sailor's shoulder. Letting the cutlass lead him, then leading the cutlass, Jherek never presented any undefended openings.

"Get the little wharf rat," the swordsman urged. "You've got the longer weapon."

The spearman feinted, thinking to draw Jherek out, then stabbed at his crotch when he sidestepped. The young sailor parried the spear, then moved quickly inside the man's defense. The slaver tried to bring the butt of his weapon around. Jherek slammed his cutlass through the spear haft, splintering the wood. Before the man could react, the young sailor swept the hook forward, knowing the swordsman was set up behind him.

The hook plunged through the spearman's temple and sliced into his brain, killing him instantly. Even as the lights in the man's eyes dimmed, Jherek released the hook and turned to face the swordsman. He let the swordsman's thrust slice by his face, drawing blood from his cheek, even as he brought the cutlass down in a hard sweep that cracked the man's head open from crown to chin.

He yanked the cutlass from the dead man's skull, not realizing the prisoners were cheering for him until he saw them. Their voices were strong and full.

Sheathing the bloody cutlass in the sash at his waist, Jherek took up the battle-axe dropped by the first man he'd killed. His breath came hard and fast, filled with the sour stench of the slaver's pit. He lifted the battle-axe and brought it down on the long chain that bound the prisoners' cuffs to the iron rod. Sparks flew from the iron.

Prisoners at either end of the rod pulled the two pieces of chain through the manacles. The sound of men fighting and dying on the deck above pierced the hold.

Jherek passed the battle-axe to a large man with broad shoulders and asked, "Do you know how to use this?"

The man smiled, yellow teeth splitting his grimy beard. "Like I was born with one in my hand, warrior," he answered.

Jherek gathered his weapons. He pulled the hook from the spearman's head, wincing at the gleam of splintered bone in all the blood. He looked at the prisoners, finding them gazing at him expectantly, as if he was supposed to lead them.

"I want no children on the decks above," he ordered. "Man or woman, if you've no fighting experience, stay below with the children. There's little enough space on that deck to begin with. The ship you'll see lashed onto this one, she's a pirate ship flying the Jolly Roger. Don't think that you haven't been saved. Captain Azla of *Black Champion* doesn't tolerate slavers." He paused, his voice thick with the anger he felt. "And neither do I."

"I've heard of Azla," a man said as he helped himself to the short sword. "As pirates go, she's not a bad'n."

"Are there any more weapons in this hold?" Jherek asked.

A woman took a lantern from a peg on the wall and said, "They keep swords and knives back here." She pointed to a small room at the back of the cargo hold.

"Those of you who want to join in fighting for your freedom," Jherek said, "get weapons and come topside. It's not going to be easy."

Jherek turned and dashed back up the steps leading to the main deck. The two armed former slaves followed him.

Pacys floated near the great whale. Generally the creatures were not overly friendly. They had their own agenda and didn't often give time to humans, elves, or anyone else.

How is it that you know me? the old bard asked.

By your heart. Just as the whale song fills all of Serôs, there are those among us who can identify individual heartbeats of any who live below and any who live above. Your heartbeat has been known to my kind for thousands of years. By now, after all you have seen and heard in Serôs, you shouldn't be surprised that you and the Taker are in our histories.

In truth, Pacys wasn't surprised. Every society he'd encountered in Serôs told tales of his arrival, as well as the Taker's.

What do you want with me?

To give you that which you seek.

Am I here, or am I still among the locathah?

You are safe among the locathah, Taleweaver. Only your mind journeys far at this moment. The locathah chieftain's herbs freed your thoughts. I merely captured them for a moment with my song.

You know I seek the boy, Pacys said.

Jherek. Yes, we know.

His name is Malorrie.

That is the name he gave you, Taleweaver, the whale replied. *He is in hiding, from himself and from the fears that have chased him since childhood. He is not whole.*

Pacys gazed into the great eye and saw the compassion there. *I was told he would not be whole.*

Your voice, your heart, Taleweaver, only these things can heal him.

Where is the boy? he asked.

He is far from here now, but he will be here soon.

Why?

It was foretold. The whales must help him forge his destiny.

Then I should be here.

No, the whale said. *Your time will not be then. You must journey to Myth Nantar. Your destiny lies in that direction . . . for the time being. When everything is as it should be, you will find Jherek.*

Wouldn't it be better if I found him earlier?

It would be easy to write a song in the heat of passion, but that should not be the only time you work on it. Passion and skill must both be applied to make it strong enough to stand in the hearts and minds of those who listen. Time is the glue that binds the two. When the time is right, you will find each other. The eye closed and reopened slowly. *Our time here grows short. My song only transports your thoughts here for a few moments. Like you, I am a bard to my people. It is my duty to record our histories, and to talk to you at this moment.*

You're a bard?

Yes. Who else do you think sang the first songs of Serôs, then gave music to the people above and below that they might spread it across the dry lands?

There are many stories . . . the bard admitted.

Even now, the whale went on, *my people gather along the Sharksbane Wall in an attempt to hold back the tide of sea devils overflowing into the Inner Sea. It is foretold that we will fail.*

Then why try? Pacys's heart ached to hear the quiet acceptance in the whale's voice.

Because we must all play our parts. We must all follow our destinies.

Topside, Jherek looked at the carnage littering the slave ship's deck and felt his resolve weaken. Blood ran in rivulets across the wood, watered down by falling rain. *Black Champion*'s crew formed a half-circle with Glawinn as their center. The paladin lunged forward, slamming his shield into one of the slavers, then running his sword through the body of a second.

With a cry of warning, unable to attack the men from the back without letting them know he was there, Jherek rushed the slaver crew. He caught one man's blade with the cutlass and stopped another with the hook. Striding forward, he kicked the first man, then used the cutlass to slit the throat of the second.

Bodies rolled on the slaver's deck, shifting with the pitch and yaw of the pirate ship tethered to her. The clang of metal on metal punctuated the sounds of screamed curses, prayers, and the wounded and dying. Footing became treacherous.

Arm aching with effort but never failing, Jherek fought on. Blood splashed into his face but he distanced himself from it, from all the death around him. Malorrie had trained him to think that way, to live past the moment.

Sabyna fought nearby, using twin long knives to turn attacks, then spinning inside an opponent's offense and delivering blows herself. She moved as gracefully as a dancer, sliding through the press of men around her and searching out opportunities. Skeins floated at her side, wrapped tightly into a whip that struck out men's eyes or tore their faces when they threatened its master.

"Fight, you dogs!" Azla screamed, urging her men on. "The first of you who turns tail on me now I'll personally deliver to Umberlee!"

She fought in a two-handed style, her scimitar flashing in her right hand while a long-bladed dirk was held in her left. She blocked a thrust from a half-ogre with her scimitar, then stepped forward and ripped the dirk across the creature's throat.

Incredibly, the slaver crew backed away before the onslaught of the pirates, giving ground steadily as they retreated to the stern castle.

A tall man strode to the front of the stern castle railing, above the trapped slavers. He was deep chested and long-limbed, dressed in crimson and gray clothing, a dark red cloak riding the breeze behind him. Gold and silver gleamed at his wrists, neck, and chest—plain bands with runes carved into them.

"I am Tarmorock Hahn, son of Jakyr Hahn, and I am captain of this ship," he declared. "Who is captain of that floundering pirate?"

The fighting broke off, and the two groups formed lines of demarcation.

Azla stepped forward, and three of her pirates and Jherek stepped with her, keeping a protective ring about her.

"I am Azla, captain of *Black Champion*."

Tarmorock grinned at her, gave her a cocky salute with the jeweled sword in his hand, and said, "You'll not be captain for long from the looks of her."

"I'm standing on my next ship," Azla stated.

"Confidence!" the slaver roared. "Gods, but I do admire that in a woman."

"As captain of a slaver," Azla retorted, "I find you offer little to admire."

"And a cutting tongue as well as good looks. Would that we had met under other circumstances, I'd have offered you a dinner by candlelight."

"It's just as well," Azla said. "Offered aboard a slave ship with the stench you find here, dinner wouldn't have stayed down."

Tarmorock glared at her, stung even more when Azla's crew hurled taunts at him. "I offer you the opportunity to duel for my ship," he said. "Captain to captain. I offer this as a man of honor."

"There's no honor in slavery," Azla said, "and I've no reason to fight you for anything. I've taken out your weapons, lashed my sinking ship to this one to drag about like a stone, killed over half your crew, and freed the slaves from the hold to fight against you as well. There's nothing here for me to fight for. Resist and we'll kill you anyway."

"I offer you honor in battle."

Jherek felt a response stir within him. Azla was correct in her assessment of the situation, but a need rose in him to recognize Tarmorock's challenge. He was barely able to still his tongue.

"I don't need honor," Azla stated. "Honor doesn't have sails nor cargo space. I have your ship in all but name. You offer me nothing I care for."

"Captain," Glawinn said, stepping forward. Blood stained his copper-colored armor and fresh dents and scratches showed. "If you don't mind, I'll stand him to his battle of honor."

"Ah, a true warrior among you," Tarmorock said. "You, sir, are a man of the blade?"

"Till the day I die," Glawinn said.

Pride welled up in Jherek as he watched the knight stand tall in front of the slaver captain.

"No," Azla said. "There'll be no battle for this ship. I've won her, fair and square, and I'll take her if I have to gut you down to the last man."

Tarmorock glanced at Glawinn and said, "Pity. Apparently there's no prize to be won, but what say you to honor itself? Will you be part and party to a bandit's approach to stealing my ship? Become a thief yourself?"

Glawinn's cheeks reddened, but Jherek couldn't tell if it was from anger or embarrassment.

"I'm no thief," the paladin said. "Nor shall I ever be."

"Those are harsh words that drip from your lips," Azla said coldly. "Especially from a man whose livelihood depends on stealing the lives of others."

"And you've never spent a life or three in the pursuit of your own wealth, Captain Azla?" Tarmorock hurried on before she could respond, switching his gaze back to Glawinn. "I was trained in the sword, and conducting myself honorably on the battlefield, long before fate handed me this vocation. You understand this?"

"Yes," Glawinn answered.

"Then you'll fight me?"

"Yes."

Tarmorock grinned. "And if I should win?"

"You'll have all I own," the paladin replied, "and your freedom from this ship."

"There will be no fighting," Azla stated, staring at Glawinn.

The paladin looked at her, gentleness in his eyes. "Lady, I have given leave to your ways though they are not my own, and I have stood in good stead when you needed me. I ask that you give me leave to stand by my own principles in this matter."

"You did the honorable thing by helping rescue the prisoners aboard this ship," Azla told him. "This isn't just about stealing something that didn't belong to you."

"There are times," Glawinn said in a patient voice, "when a man must stand or fall on his own merits, to be weighed and measured by the depth of his heart and the strength of his arm."

"You're risking this for nothing."

"On the contrary," Glawinn stated, "I'm risking this for all that I am." He looked at her. "If I may have your leave."

"Damn you for a fool, knight."

Glawinn spread his bloodstained hands and said, "If only I can be an honorable fool."

Azla waved her men back, clearing the space in front of the stern castle.

Tarmorock descended the stairs and stripped away his crimson cloak. "There is one thing further I'd ask of you." He rolled his bastard sword in his hands, causing it to dance and spin effortlessly. "Even should I lose, I want my men spared. The ones that yet live. I ask only that they be put overboard in lifeboats with provisions. This far out at sea, that's a grim prospect, and I know that, but it's the best I can do for them. They're a motley crew, but they are my responsibility."

"Done," Glawinn replied without hesitation.

The slaver captain glanced at Azla.

The half-elf gave a tight nod. "For the knight's honor, not yours."

"Of course." Tarmorock bowed.

"Do you have any armor?" Glawinn asked.

"No."

"I have an extra set aboard the ship," the paladin offered.

"Thank you, no," Tarmorock replied. "I was trained in the art of the blade without the benefit of cumbersome armor. My father felt I was destined for better things. Through no fault of his own, I managed not to find those things."

"Young warrior," the paladin called.

Jherek hurried over to Glawinn's side.

"This is Jherek of Velen," the paladin said as he began unbuckling his armor. "He will stand as my second."

Fear and pride swelled within the young sailor at the same time. He started helping Glawinn take his armor off and asked, "What am I supposed to do?"

"Take care of my armor," Glawinn said, "see to it that the promises I have made to this man are carried out, and stay with me as I die . . . should it come to that."

Myth Nantar must be open again, Taleweaver, the whale continued, *and made whole once more. You are the only one who can accomplish this. That which is secret must needs be known. Only then will the impenetrable wall that surrounds Myth Nantar be broken and the mythal once again protect those it was designed to protect to promote peace above and below.*

How will I do this? Pacys asked. *I am told the way is impassable.*

You are the Taleweaver, the whale replied. *This is your destiny. It will not be denied. Trust in the songs that are given to you. Now, there is one thing more. Stretch out your hand.*

Without hesitation, Pacys reached out to the whale. A warm tingle filled his hand. When he looked, he saw an ivory orb lying in his palm. It was as smooth as a pearl, no larger than the ball of his thumb, and with a slight translucence.

What is this? the bard asked.

It is your key to Myth Nantar, Taleweaver. This was created by the whales who first saw Myth Nantar lost to the Dukars, then to the sahuagin. When the mythal hardened and kept all out, the great whale bard of that time created this key, knowing it could only be used by you.

How could he know this?

She, the great whale bard corrected, *knew it the same way you know a song is strong and true, that it will wring joy or tears from its listeners. Do you question your muse, Taleweaver?*

No. Oghma be revered, I am thankful for the inspiration that comes my way.

The key is like a song that comes to you unbidden. The great bard drew upon her skill and magic and forged it, as was her destiny. You haven't yet understood why Myth Nantar is called the City of Destinies. It was created to knit the worlds below and above in harmony, to establish that which all the rest of Toril might follow. Those who live in Serôs know we are all of one. We must live as one if the seas are to survive. That is what we are taught, Taleweaver, and your efforts will help teach others.

Pacys studied the ivory ball in his palm, opening himself to it and feeling the magic inside. It felt very old and powerful, and it drew him to it like steel to a lodestone. The music that filled his heart let him know the talisman was his to use.

He closed his fingers over it, relishing the smooth surface and the confident way it made him feel. He was truly on the right path. The locathah hadn't been the only thing he'd been drawn to here.

Taleweaver, Song Who Brings Bright Rains said gently, *do not be overconfident. Things are written of the future from this point on, but they are more dreams than truths—plans that poke pools of light into the darkness of the waiting uncertainty of the Taker's War. It still remains up to us to find the strength, skills, and heart for victory.*

I know, Pacys replied.

The whale's eye blinked slowly again, as if the great leviathan was tired. For the first time, the old bard got the impression that the creature was immensely old.

It is time for you to go. May Oghma, the Lord of Knowledge, keep you close and watch over you as you bring back that which was lost.

And may Oghma grace your song and your skills, Pacys responded.

The sapphire waters grew dark around him, and when he opened his eyes again, he found he was in Khlinat's strong arms. The dwarf peered at him fearfully, holding him as he might a child.

"Are ye back among us then?" Khlinat asked.

"Yes," Pacys replied, finding that his tongue was still a little numb and his voice was hoarse. He was surprised at the weakness he felt, but the whale song still played at the edges of his mind.

Relief showed on the dwarf's face. "Ye were gone so long, I was beginning to fret maybe these folk had kilt ye kindly and out of ignorance but did the job all the same."

Pacys put his hand on the dwarf's shoulder. "I've been a long way, my friend, but we've still leagues to go before I die."

"Ye ain't dying," the dwarf promised. "I done give ye me promise, and I ain't gonna let ye back out of it. And ye ain't been nowhere, because I been with ye the whole time of it. Ye sat right here like some great lump."

Wordlessly, Pacys opened his other hand, revealing the ivory sphere. The polished surface caught the glowcoral light and gleamed.

"I've journeyed," the old bard said. "I've been there and back again."

In minutes, the paladin was stripped down to the sweaty, blood-stained clothes beneath his armor. He looked smaller than usual, and for the first time Jherek noticed that Glawinn's opponent was a head taller, at least twenty pounds heavier, and had a longer reach than him.

"Why are you showing this man honor?" the young sailor asked.

"Because some men show honor despite the circumstances they find themselves in. As I have told you, young warrior, it's so often not how low you may get in life, but how you conduct yourself while you're there. I only pray that you get a clearer understanding of this some day."

Glawinn took a deep breath and the sword the young sailor offered him. He turned to face his opponent and said, "This is as even as I can make it."

"On the contrary," Tarmorock stated, "I fear you make it too easy. I am quite good with the blade."

"We shall see." The paladin saluted smartly with his sword, bringing it down from his forehead and stepping easily into a swordsman's stance. "I am Sir Glawinn, a paladin in the service of Lathander the Morninglord."

Tarmorock bowed slightly, touching his blade to his forehead. "May your god keep you."

"And yours."

The slaver captain sprang into action, launching a volley of attacks, rolling off of each of Glawinn's defenses to launch yet another thrust or slash. Steel rang through the dead silence that washed over the ship.

Jherek found himself holding his breath. Tarmorock was an excellent swordsman. The blades moved almost faster than he could see, and it was only Malorrie's and Glawinn's training that allowed him to pick up every nuance. Instinctively, his body shifted and his hand moved slightly, following the paladin's quick moves.

Years of practice aboard the ship while it rocked at sea should have given Tarmorock the advantage on the heaving deck, but Glawinn's skill and focus with the blade stripped those years of familiarity away, putting the slaver on equal footing with his opponent.

The two combatants stepped forward and back, from side to side. Neither truly seemed able to press an advantage. Long minutes passed. Most sword duels between two men not on a battlefield, Jherek knew from both Malorrie and Glawinn, lasted only seconds at best. Unarmored sword fighting was an art form.

Tarmorock's attack became more loose, but Glawinn's remained tight, his moves compact but fluid. Without warning, Tarmorock lunged, and for once Glawinn's defense wasn't there.

Cold fear knotted Jherek's back as he watched the blade slide toward Glawinn. When the sword stuck through the paladin, the young sailor knew the knight was skewered. The paladin's own blade stabbed deeply into Tarmorock's chest, piercing his heart.

Tarmorock looked down at the blade through his chest in disbelief. His arm dropped and Jherek saw that the captain's blade had missed Glawinn by scant inches though he couldn't see that from behind. Nerveless, Glawinn dropped the sword.

Moving quickly, Glawinn caught the mortally wounded man before he could fall. Tenderly, he held him as he might a brother. Jherek stayed back, wondering what the paladin said to the man he'd just killed, but he didn't try to overhear.

A moment later and Glawinn gently laid the captain to rest on the deck. Reaching into his blouse, the paladin stayed on his knees and pulled out the rosy pink disk that was Lathander's holy symbol. There in the midst of companions and enemies, he prayed for the fallen warrior.

Touched by the moment, wishing he knew of something he could believe in so fiercely, Jherek dropped to his knees beside the paladin and bowed his head as well.

12

"Lady, may I have a moment of your time?" Glawinn asked. He stood with a bottle in his hand in the cramped doorway of Sabyna's cabin.

Surprised, Sabyna looked up from the spellbook she'd been studying. Arthoris, Azla's ship's mage, had given Sabyna two new spells that she believed she was capable of understanding.

"Is something wrong?" She stood up from the small bed. Her heart beat a little faster, and her first thoughts were of Jherek.

"Nothing's wrong," Glawinn told her.

Sabyna placed her spellbook into the bag of holding at her side and Skeins curled around it. Crossing her arms over her breasts, she walked to the window and looked down at the ocean.

The pirate crew stripped what they could from the skeletal hulk that had once been *Black Champion*. With her hold flooded and having her deck partly disassembled and hauled away, the ship listed even more heavily into the ocean, creating increasing drag on the slave ship Azla claimed as her prize. The deck tilted at an incline now and had for the last two days.

Ship's moldings and cleats, the rudder, extra sailcloth, and the remaining rigging were the first items the pirate crew reclaimed. They'd used a block and tackle to take even *Black Champion*'s two good masts to replace the broken ones on the slave ship.

They could not seat the masts while at sea, but after finishing the salvage operation, Azla planned to put into port at Agenais in the Whamite Isles to make the big repairs. Now they were down to taking the long, good planks from *Black Champion*'s corpse.

"What did you want to talk about?" Sabyna asked.

Glawinn hesitated. "The young warrior. I may be overstepping my bounds here, lady, but—"

"No," Sabyna said. "You're way over."

"Perhaps I should go. I thank you for your time, and I ask your forgiveness."

Sabyna pushed out her breath. "Wait." She sensed him standing there, rigidly at attention. "Has Jherek told you what I said to him?"

"No, lady," Glawinn answered, "he's not one to betray confidences. In fact, I think he keeps too many of his own."

"Why did you come?"

"To offer solace and share company." Glawinn held up the dusty bottle. "And to offer a glass of Captain Azla's rather fine port."

Sabyna was surprised. "I didn't know you drank."

"Rarely, lady," the paladin said, "and never in excess. May I enter?"

"Of course." Sabyna went to one of the small cabinets built above the bed and took out two wooden cups. "The service is rather humble."

"But adequate for our purposes. If I may." Glawinn took the cups and poured the dark red wine.

Sabyna returned to the bed and sat, accepting the cup the paladin handed her. "Say what you have to say."

Glawinn sat on the small bench under the window. "If you'll forgive me my indiscretion, lady," he said, "but you can be dreadfully blunt."

"I come from a large family whose lives were spent crowded aboard one ship or another," she explained. "I learned to speak my mind early. Perhaps you're a little sensitive."

"Lathander help me, but I knew this would not be easy," Glawinn said, shifting uncomfortably.

"If it isn't a pleasant task, perhaps it would be better if it were over sooner."

Despite her calm demeanor, Sabyna's heart beat faster than normal. Since she'd talked to Jherek and explained to him how she felt, they'd hardly spoken at all. The young sailor stayed busily engaged with the salvage work.

"It's just that I've become aware you aren't talking to each other."

"Have you talked to him about it?"

"No."

"Why talk to me first?"

"Because he won't listen to me."

"And you think I will?"

Glawinn's eyes turned sorrowful and he said, "Lady, you have no idea what that boy is going through."

"If he would talk to me, I might."

"He doesn't know himself," Glawinn explained. "Even if he did, he can't explain."

"Does he think I'm dense?"

"In his eyes he feels he isn't worthy of you."

"Because he is wanted somewhere for something?" she asked. "I told him that didn't matter."

"Maybe not to you, lady, but it does to him. In his own way, though, I don't think he quite fully understands it. He strives for perfection."

"I've never met a man who didn't have his faults," Sabyna said. "Though, I admit you've come closer than anyone."

"My faults?"

"You're a busybody," Sabyna told him. "I thought paladins knew enough to keep to their own affairs."

The knight blushed. "I beg your forgiveness. I struggled with this decision, and I'd hoped I'd made the right choice."

"You have," she conceded. "If I'd spent another day like this, with no one to talk to, I think I'd have gone out of my mind."

"I thought you talked to Azla."

"She doesn't understand Jherek any more than I do."

Glawinn smiled gently and said, "Probably not."

Sabyna looked away from the paladin. "It's never been like this for me. I've seen handsome men and wealthy men, and men who could turn a woman's head with only a handful of pretty words, but I've never met anyone like Jherek."

"Nor have I."

Tears stung Sabyna's eyes. "I've never pursued a man before. Climbing that rigging to tell him my feelings was one of the hardest things I've ever done."

"But, I wager, not as hard as the climb back down."

"No," she said. "Do you know what he told me?"

Glawinn shook his head. "I can only guess that it was as little as possible."

"Aye . . ." Sabyna didn't trust her voice to speak any further.

"If it helps at all," the paladin stated gently, "I believe he tells you everything he knows."

"There's a lot he won't tell me."

"*Can't* tell you, lady, not won't. There is a difference."

"You defend him very well."

"I didn't come here to help him, lady. I came to help you."

"Me?"

Glawinn nodded in resignation and said, "The Morninglord knows, I can't help him. He won't let me, and his course has already been charted."

"What course?"

"To becoming the kind of man he wants to be," Glawinn said. "The kind of man he has to be."

"Will he be that man?"

Hesitation furrowed Glawinn's brow. "I know not, lady. I've never seen someone come so far, yet have so far to go. I can tell you this: his path will heal him—or it will kill him."

The solemn way the paladin spoke pushed Sabyna's pain away and replaced it with fear.

"And what are we to do?" she asked. "What am I to do?"

"The only thing we can, lady. Give him the freedom to make the decisions he needs must make"

"What if it kills him?" Sabyna asked.

"Then we will bury him, lady, say prayers over him if that is possible, and be grateful for ever having known him."

Jherek strode barefoot across one of the broken beams still above water. *Black Champion* lay mostly under the sea now, her black bulk stretched like a shadow against the green water. Seagulls sat on the spars that made up her ribs and gave plaintive cries.

Rigging on the slave ship popped against the masts where she lay at anchor, heeled over hard to port as she supported *Black Champion*'s corpse. Six others worked the ship with him, seeking more timber to salvage before the sea took her to the bottom.

"Looks like she's been picked clean," Meelat called out.

Meelat was one of the prisoners rescued from the slaver's hold. Though he was scrawny, his narrow shoulders and thin arms were corded with muscle. Scabs showed at his bare ankles and wrists where the iron cuffs had been.

"Aye," Jherek agreed.

He mopped sweat from his face with his forearm, succeeding only in spreading it around. Nothing on him remained dry. He glanced up at the nets the ship's crew used to haul up the last load of timber.

"Comes a time when you gotta let her go," Meelat stated. "She's given up as much for the future of that other ship as she can. Spend much time aboard her?"

"No, but it was a time I'll not easily forget," Jherek replied.

Memory of his conversation with Sabyna in the rigging and of that kiss wouldn't fade no matter how hard he tried to push it to the back of his mind.

Meelat scratched at the scabs on one wrist, pulling them away so that blood flowed. He rinsed the wrist off in the water.

"If there are sharks around," Jherek cautioned, "that might be a foolhardy thing to do. They can smell blood in the water for miles."

Meelat grinned. "If there'd been sharks here, all that noise we been making in the water for days would have already drawn them. Besides, that comely young ship's mage has been keeping a potion in the water to drive away any sharks. Or haven't you noticed?"

Jherek shook his head.

"A pretty girl like that," the grizzled old sailor said, "I was your age, I'd be looking."

"She's a lady," Jherek warned quietly, "and shouldn't be talked about in a cavalier manner."

"Oh, I'm offering no offense, mate." Meelat shrugged. "My manners, maybe they need some brushing up, but a man at sea most of his life, he don't have much chance of that. Does he?"

Turning his attention back to the water, Jherek spotted a conflicting wave below and thought he detected movement.

"That's what I find confusing about you," Meelat continued. "You say you're a sailing man, but your manners put on like you been proper raised."

Studying the water around the bobbing remnant of *Black Champion*, Jherek tried to discern the movement again. Sahuagin prowled the Inner Sea now. Three passing merchanters two days ago had swapped supplies with Azla and offered up warnings concerning staying in one place or alone too long. Reports of attacks on harbors around the Sea of Fallen Stars—from Procampur to Cimbar—were becoming commonplace.

"I was a suspicious man," Meelat said, "I'd be wondering about you. Wondering what a man like you was doing running with pirates."

Jherek gazed at the man silently.

Meelat dropped his eyes. "Not that there's anything wrong with pirates. Been one myself a time or two, but you don't seem the type cut out for it."

"Thank you."

A puzzled expression filled the man's face, but it was quickly replaced by sudden and total fear.

Ripping his knife from its sheath on his thigh, Jherek turned and braced himself, aware that startled shouts had broken out on the slave ship's decks as well.

Less than twenty feet away, a creature broke from the sea and gazed at them. The triangular snake's face twisted slightly in the breeze, bringing one bright orange eye to bear on Jherek, then the other. Fins stuck out on either side of the head like overly large ears, echoed by the ridged fin that ran down its neck for a short distance. After a short space, the fin continued down the creature's back. Needle-sharp fangs filled the huge mouth and a pink, forked tongue darted out to taste the smells in the air. The gold scales glittered in the sunlight, some of them catching a slightly greenish cast, muted slightly by the water where the rest of the serpent body coiled.

Jherek thought it was beautiful. Four feet of the creature stayed above the waterline, but he judged it to be at least a dozen feet in length. The serpent's body was broader than a dwarf's shoulders at the neck, growing thicker toward the middle, then thinning out to a wide-finned tail.

"Selûne guide us from harm," Meelat whispered hoarsely. "That there's dragon-kin. Some call 'em sea wyrms. Dangerous beasties, lad, so don't do nothing to call attention to yourself."

The sea wyrm lowered its head toward the young sailor, then twisted from side to side again as if taking a closer look.

Jherek felt the ship's hulk bob against a wave and knew that one of the salvagers was moving along the beams behind him. He tightened his grip on the knife and slid his left foot forward.

"You try it," Meelat said, "and that thing will gobble you down where you stand. They're quicker than damn near anything you've ever seen in the water, and most things out."

In the next instant, Jherek got a glimpse of the creature's speed. Dipping its head into the ocean, the sea wyrm flipped its tail and pulled the ear fins in tight against its head. It cut through the water cleanly, gliding twenty feet in the blink of an eye.

The sea wyrm raised its great head from the ocean, water dripping from the edges of its open mouth. It rose from the sea until it could stare into Jherek's eyes with one of its own. The sea dappled it like diamonds.

Hypnotized by the fear that filled him as well as awe, Jherek held the creature's gaze. It was close enough to reach out and touch.

"You have a chance," Meelat stated. "Strike quick, if you can, and put that knife through that thing's eye."

Shifting subtly, Jherek reversed the blade, putting the point down. He stared into the orange eye, wider across than a pie plate. At the distance, he knew he wouldn't miss. Whether the blade was long enough to reach the serpent's brain was another matter.

The finned head moved closer, tentatively. Brine-flavored breath rushed over Jherek.

"Strike now!" Meelat urged. "That thing's going to have the head from your shoulders like a grape from the vine."

"No," Jherek said.

The forked tongue flicked out at the young sailor, missing him by inches. From the periphery of his vision, he saw the ship's crew armed with bows.

Afraid the pirates would fire at the creature, Jherek slowly sheathed the big knife.

"What are you doing?" Meelat demanded.

"I'm giving us the only chance we have. It's curious—nothing more." Standing steady, Jherek faced the sea wyrm.

The forked tongue flicked again, whispering through the air beside his ear, making light popping noises. The young sailor flinched, then steadied himself again. The forked tongue brushed against his face the next time, feeling wet, tough, and leathery.

The sea wyrm drew back out of reach. Its ear fins popped forward, and its large mouth yawned open. The orange eyes glinted. It hissed, yowling as if in anger.

Arrows sped from the pirate archers. Most of them dropped into the water around the sea wyrm, but three of them bounced from the golden scales.

"Stop!" Jherek commanded.

The sea wyrm turned its attention from the young sailor to the slave ship and back again. Sunlight gleamed from its sharp teeth. It hissed at Jherek again, then dived beneath the water, swimming deep and disappearing almost immediately.

"How did you know it wouldn't attack?" Meelat asked.

Jherek shrugged and said, "I didn't."

"Sails! Sails off the stern!"

Still shaking inside, Jherek turned and gazed back behind the slave ship at the cry from the lookout in the crow's nest. There, against the curve of the ocean's northern horizon, square cut white sails interrupted the line between smooth blue sky and green water. Judging the set of the sails, the young sailor knew the ship was headed for them.

"Where are we?"

On the other side of the gate they'd used to pass from *Tarjana*'s belly, Laaqueel spread her webbed hands and feet, stopping her descent toward the distant ocean floor. From the deep blue color of the sea around them, the malenti priestess judged they were in Serôs's gloom strata, the level of the sea between one hundred fifty and three hundred feet.

"Thuridru," Iakhovas answered without looking at her. He held a gem in his hand that glowed suddenly.

According to her studies of Serôs, Thuridru was a merfolk city along the Turmish coast. Located north of the Xedran Reefs where the ixitxachitl theocracy claimed the Six Holy Cities, Thuridru held a precarious position. Trapped near the ixitxachitl nation, Thuridru was also the sworn enemy of Voalidru, the capital city of the merfolk of Eadraal.

"The city of rogue merfolk," Laaqueel said.

"What do you know of Thuridru?"

"Little," the malenti admitted.

"Nearly four hundred years ago, there was a territorial skirmish between the mermen and the ixitxachitl nations over kelp beds west of Voalidru. Five war parties from the Clan Kamaar chose to ignore the Laws of Battle that have been in effect since the end of the Ninth War of Serôs and attack the ixitxachitl. As a result, Clan Kamaar was banished from Voalidru and driven out to make their homes in the abandoned caverns left by the defeated ixitxachitl." Iakhovas gazed into the distance with a satisfied look.

"What are we doing here?" Laaqueel asked, expecting to be assaulted for her impertinence.

"Ah, little malenti, your impatience truly knows no bounds."

"I would be more effective as your senior high priestess," she said, "if I knew more of what you were doing."

Iakhovas turned his malevolent gaze on her. Even the incomplete golden sphere in his empty socket gleamed. "This war is mine, and it is progressing exactly as I would have it."

"A small group of reinforcements from Vahaxtyl joined *Tarjana*'s crew this morning," Laaqueel hurried on, ignoring the threat in Iakhovas's voice. "I overheard them arguing among themselves and their brothers in our fleet. They say that your efforts have grown stagnant, that you no longer hold Sekolah's favor."

"You didn't champion me, or the cause I represent?"

"I wouldn't know what to tell them."

"Instruct them to believe. That's where your power lies. If you believe, they will believe."

Laaqueel let the silence between them build.

"Do not cease believing," Iakhovas warned. "That is the only worth you have to me. If you look to your heart, you know that it is the only worth you have to yourself."

"I know." Laaqueel's throat was tight when she spoke.

Without her belief, she was only a hollow shell. The voice she'd heard in her head created tremendous confusion.

"I'm aware of the surviving princes' efforts to undermine my control," Iakhovas said. "Just as I'm aware that the numbers of We Who Eat coming from the Alamber Sea are not as great as I expected after I shattered the Sharksbane Wall. I also know the Great Whale Bard has drawn a small army of his own to sing a barrier against the passage of more sahuagin."

"Only a few of them fight the magic of the songs," Laaqueel said.

"It will be dealt with, little malenti. In due time." Iakhovas grinned. "For now I conserve my strength and mask my presence. The high mages and the Taleweaver have learned about me. Perhaps they've learned more than they should have—but we will see. Despite everything they have heard, I am more powerful than they can ever possibly imagine."

Laaqueel dropped her gaze from his. Everything he said made sense, and it shamed her that she couldn't see it for herself. She loathed the insecurity that trilled within her, hated the way it took her straight back to the young malenti who knew only fear.

"For now," Iakhovas said, "we must gather our forces. Clan Kamaar will prove providential."

13

Jherek stood on the bobbing husk that remained of *Black Champion* and stared at the approaching ship.

"That's a Cormyrean Freesail from the cut of her," Meelat commented.

The privateers sanctioned by the kingdom of Cormyr were tall-masted brigantines crewed by hard men who took their prizes from the pirates they defeated. Most of the Freesails stayed around Suzail and Marsember, with a few others placed around smaller ports, but some of them took charters as trading vessels.

"She's seen us," Meelat said. "We're showing no colors and tied up as we are to this floundering ship, she'll be coming to investigate."

Jherek called to the rest of the salvage crew. The men climbed off *Black Champion*'s corpse and into longboats with the last of their salvaged timber.

At *Swamp Rose*'s side, Jherek and his crew shoved the planks into the waiting net, then held onto the net's sides as it was hauled up. The boom arm swung over amidships, cascading water across the tilted deck. The young sailor dropped to the deck and trotted back to the stern castle to join Azla.

The pirate captain stood with a spyglass in the ship's bow. "She's coming toward us. What was that thing in the water?"

"Meelat said it was a sea wyrm."

"I thought you were a dead man."

Jherek looked at the approaching ship, noting the ballistae and the number of men apparent on the decks. "She's rigged for war."

"King Azoun may see the release of the sahuagin from behind the Sharksbane Wall as a chance to further his own empire building. I wouldn't put it past Azoun to give the Freesails orders to bring in any suspect ships so they can be pressed into service." At the bottom of the stern castle stairs, Azla strode across the deck. "Tomas," she said, "your axe."

The pirate tossed the single-bitted axe through the air and Azla caught it easily. Pirates emptied the net attached to the boom arm, stacking the salvaged lumber. The ship's mages had magically straightened warped timbers and planks as they'd been recovered.

"All hands on deck," Azla roared.

The command was relayed instantly in loud bellows by the first mate. Men scrambled to the deck.

"Put some sail up on that mast," she said. "I want to be making some kind of speed by the time those Cormyrean dogs get here, and one mast'll have to do."

The pirates mustered out smartly, their ranks actually overfull from taking on men who were slaves only a few days ago.

Azla looked out at where *Black Champion* rolled, nearly submerged beneath the waves. "Umberlee take me for a sentimental fool," she whispered. A tear shone in her eye.

Jherek felt the woman's pain. Azla had lived aboard her ship for years. Since she was rarely on land, the young sailor realized that everything she'd cared about was on that ship.

Abruptly, Azla raised the axe and brought it down again and again, severing the ropes that held the shipwreck to *Swamp Rose*. As the ropes separated, the slave ship righted itself and *Black Champion* drifted further beneath the waves.

Glancing back at the deck, Jherek saw that several of the pirates held their hats in their hands. They'd shed blood aboard that vessel, dreamed quiet dreams, ridden out harsh storms, and learned to become one.

"Don't stand there like a bunch of heartbroken saps," Azla bellowed. "Pay your respects to the lady and move on. We may be fighting for our lives in a few minutes."

She flipped the axe back to the man who'd loaned it to her.

"Begging the cap'n's pardon," a pirate spoke up, "but we ain't got a name for this ship. Unless you want to keep calling her *Swamp Rose*."

"Boatswain," Azla barked, "fetch me a bottle of ale."

When the man hurried back, Azla took the bottle. By then the sails on the surviving mast had latched talons into the wind. The riggings creaked steadily in protest as the ship got underway. The half-elf pirate captain climbed to the top of the forecastle stairs and turned toward her crew.

"The brine took *Black Champion*, but before she went, she helped us win this ship. I'll give this lady a name, but it's up to you to pay the steel and blood it will take to make brave men fear the sound of it, and cowards run from her shadow."

She smashed the bottle against the railing, spewing broken shards and foaming ale over the deck.

"All right," Azla said, "you lump-eared, misbegotten excuses for proper pirates, I give you *Azure Dagger*. Long may she sail!"

Thunderous approval roared up from amidships. Standing there, Jherek felt proud. He turned his gaze to *Azure Dagger*'s stern and watched as the Cormyrean Freesail skimmed the water like a bird of prey.

"This is taking far too long," Pacys grumbled.

He swam at Taranath Reefglamor's side. The Senior High Mage inspected the caravan that assembled in Sylkiir the day after the Sharksbane Wall fell.

Below them, in a small valley behind a sheltering ridge of rock and kelp, the sea elves finished packing supplies onto flat sleds. The sleds were being pulled by narwhals and sea turtles on the journey to Myth Nantar.

The High Mage stopped and floated forty feet above the ocean floor. The incandescence from the sun lit the waters blue.

"Taleweaver," the Senior High Mage stated softly, though not with patience, "this journey will take as long as it will take. If we rush, we risk."

"Senior, I know. Truly I do." Pacys searched for the words to explain the anxiety that filled him. "The music fills me and drives me on," he said, "and I can't help feeling that we're progressing too slowly."

"And if we should fail after we've been given this chance?" Reefglamor eyed the old bard directly. "Who would be left to take up arms in this pursuit?"

"I don't know," Pacys admitted.

Coronal Semphyr, who commanded Aluwand, and Coronal Cormal Ytham, who commanded Sylkiir, both stood against any involvement in Myth Nantar.

Reefglamor clasped Pacys's shoulder tightly in his grip and said, "To most of my people, Myth Nantar is a corpse, better off left entombed by the mythal that surrounds it."

"But the Taker is headed there," the bard reminded him.

"And if you're wrong?" the sea elf asked. "If I and the other mages have left our cities, our people, undefended against the Taker?"

"If you could but feel the power of the songs that fill my heart near to bursting, you would know that what we do is the right thing."

"My friend," Reefglamor said, "I do believe you. That's the only reason we are here now. But even as I believe in you, you must believe in me. We must not just begin this journey, we must finish it as well."

One of the lesser mages swam to a stop nearby and waited patiently. Reefglamor excused himself and swam over to the woman.

"Trouble, friend Pacys?"

The old bard glanced up and saw Khlinat floating in the water only a few feet away. For the first time he noticed how tired and haggard the dwarf looked, then realized the whole caravan probably felt the same way.

With the regular military forces stripped from their ranks, men and women who served and believed in the high mages had volunteered for the journey. Many of them kissed their wives, husbands, and children good-bye on the day they left Sylkiir. No few of them, Pacys felt certain, would never look on their families again. For the first time, he realized the sacrifices they'd made.

"No trouble," Pacys said. "Only my own impatience at how slowly we travel."

"Aye, I been thinking on that meself," the dwarf grumbled, "but there's no way to increase our speed. Them people what's out there making up this ragtag army, they're doing all they can."

"And maybe more than they should be asked."

Pacys looked down at the long line of the caravan. Nearly three hundred sea elves took their breaks while the sleds were secured and the animals were changed out. They sat in small groups and talked. Weariness from the hard travel showed in the stooped shoulders and the lethargy that gripped them.

Glancing around, Pacys spotted a depression in the hillside of the sheltering ridge. It gave a view over the whole caravan. He swam to it and settled on the ledge at the front of the depression. As he took the saceddar from his back, he drew his skills to him, and listened to the music that haunted him all morning. He'd found no words for the music—until now. The music was lively but bittersweet, a tune that would live on.

> Torn from proud history,
> Forged in blood and love,
>   Come from the hand and eye and love of Deep Sashelas,
> No longer of the world above.
> They gathered at the behest of the High Mages,
> And descended into Serôs's deepest blue.
> They followed the course of dark prophecy,
> To discover what was right and true.
> They journeyed to far Myth Nantar,
> Still bound in wild and uncertain magic.
> The City of Destinies had a future unclear,
> And a history that had proven tragic.

Pacys played on, finding the words with ease. He let the music fill him and give power to his song. He knew they listened, every conversation brought to a halt by the majesty in his voice. He continued, finding the chorus.

> We are the alu Tel'Quessir,
> Our hearts build our home.
> Our blood is pure
> And our arms are strong.

Together we stand,
And never die alone.
We are the alu Tel'Quessir.
We march to right a wrong.
Our bodies may get weary,
But our spirits are filled with song.

The old bard stopped singing. The rest of the song was yet to be written. Verses would be added as they journeyed, but for now it was all he had.

"Don't worry, friend Pacys," Khlinat said quietly. " 'Twas a good song, strong and true, but mayhap them hearts out yonder aren't ready for something like that."

Pacys nodded, wondering what Reefglamor would have to say about his impromptu performance.

Then, with gentleness at first, the sea elves picked up the chorus, stumbling until a few of them found the meter and rhythm.

We are the alu Tel'Quessir,
Our hearts build our home.

More voices joined in, and the song became a thunderous, spirited roar. It was a song of defiance and pride.

Tears spilled from Pacys's eyes, plucked away by the sea around him. It wasn't just their belief he was rekindling and he knew it. The fear and anxiety sapped his strength as well, raked out hollow places within his convictions. Now he filled them up again. His fingers found the notes on the saceddar, pulling the group together until the song filled the valley. Khlinat joined in, adding his deep basso boom.

Our blood is pure
And our arms are strong.
Together we stand,
And never die alone.
We are the alu Tel'Quessir . . .

With only one mast in place, even with all the canvas it could support, *Azure Dagger* could not outrun the Cormyrean Freesail. Jherek clung to the railing next to Azla. Glawinn stood beside them.

"They're going to be suspicious of us," Azla declared. "We've obviously been in a fight, and this ship stinks of slavery when you get downwind of her."

Jherek watched as the Cormyrean ship cut through the water to within two hundred yards.

"Steady, young warrior," Glawinn stated softly. "They've yet to prove their intentions as anything other than honorable."

Gradually, the Cormyrean Freesail drew abreast of *Azure Dagger*'s port side. A slim man dressed in maroon with silver trimmings stood at the forecastle railing with a hailing cone in his hands. "Ahoy. This is Captain Sebastyn Tarnar of His Majesty King Azoun IV's ship, *Steadfast*. I'd like to speak to your captain."

Azla accepted the hailing cone one of her men handed over. "This is Azla, captain of the free ship *Azure Dagger*."

"We saw you had some trouble and thought we'd investigate."

"We're fine and sailing under our own power."

"Perhaps not as proudly as you could be," Tarnar replied, "but I'll grant you that. Can we be of any assistance?"

"Thank you," Azla called back, "but no. We're used to managing our own affairs and would rather others would do the same."

"What did for your ship, Captain?"

"We did," Azla answered. "We ran across slavers who thought to add me and my crew to their bounty. By the time we'd settled differences, I'd lost my ship. That was her you saw us cutting loose back there. So we took this ship in her stead."

"I thought I recognized the stench." Tarnar paused, then called, "Where are you headed? Perhaps we could share the wind for a while."

"Sometimes it's better to be by yourself than trust someone you don't know."

Tarnar put the hailing cone down and laughed. "You're a feisty one, Captain Azla. I would relish the opportunity to meet you at another time, the Lady willing."

"If chance and tide should allow you your wish, Captain Tarnar, I'll stand you to the first drink."

In the next moment, a wave of unaccustomed vertigo stole through Jherek. He leaned more heavily on the railing, struggling to stay on his feet. Just as suddenly the wind died.

Without warning, a plume of water stood up from the ocean, rising nearly twenty feet tall. In the still air, the twisting plume spun into the form of a man with outstretched arms.

"Jherek of Velen," the plume of water itself seemed to say, "your path lies in a different direction. Leave that ship and join the Cormyreans." The basso voice haunted the waters.

"No," the young sailor whispered.

"There is no choice," the water-being stated. "You are called to follow your own path. Sir Glawinn, warrior of Lathander the Morninglord, you must release the boy. He will no longer be under your guidance."

Jherek looked at Glawinn.

"I don't know what this is before us, young warrior," the paladin said. He stared out at the obviously magical creature. "You can see for yourself the power it wields."

"No." Cold anger and fear battered Jherek but they couldn't overcome the stunned numbness that filled him. His life was his own. He'd forsworn all gods.

Azla approached them, her face hard and chiseled. "This is sorcery," she said as she gazed around the two ships.

Jherek peered through the railing, looking at the eight-foot-high waves that seemed to pass all around them, leaving them in a hollowed bowl in the middle of the Sea of Fallen Stars.

"Young warrior," Glawinn said, "you must go. It is your destiny."

"No," Jherek argued. "This is my curse. I am finally among friends. Now I am being turned from them."

Nothing about this was fair. He looked over his shoulder and saw Sabyna. The ache in his heart worsened.

"Not a curse, young warrior. I sense this is part of your birthright. You must believe me."

Captain Tarnar shouted across the distance, clearly heard in the still air as he demanded to know what was happening.

A sudden banshee shriek ripped through the air above them, filling the sails hard enough to rip canvas free in places. *Azure Dagger* rocked violently, scattering men across the deck.

"What is going on?" Sabyna demanded as she joined them.

Glawinn looked at her and said, "Lady, he can't stay with us. His path lies in another direction."

Panic touched Sabyna's face for just a moment, but she got control of herself. "If that is true," she said, "I'm going with him."

The banshee wind shrieked again, ripping more canvas free.

"You can't go," Glawinn gasped. "I can't go. No one can go with the young warrior. We each have our parts to play in this tangling of threads."

"No," Sabyna denied quietly. "You have to be wrong."

"My friend, I wish that I was wrong." Glawinn took Jherek's hand tight in his. "Look inside your heart. Tell me if you feel that I am wrong."

Cold and adrift inside himself, Jherek found it hard to concentrate. He closed his eyes and took a deep, shuddering breath, searching within. No voice gave him direction, but he felt a tug eastward, a wanderlust that pushed him to go in that direction.

"There is no place for me here," he croaked as he stared into the paladin's eyes.

"How can you speak so surely?" Sabyna demanded.

Jherek looked up at her, trying not to see the tears that tracked her cheeks. "I can't say, lady."

"You don't have to go," Azla said defiantly. "This is my ship. I say who comes and goes."

Another powerful gust of wind slammed into *Azure Dagger*. Half her canvas ripped free and cracked in the wind. Pirates immediately worked the rigging, dropping the canvas.

"I have no choice," Jherek said. He forced himself to his feet. "What am I supposed to do?"

Glawinn shook his head. "I don't know. Trust the love inside you, Jherek. It is your strength and your belief. You must hold tight to that till you find your anchor and your forgiveness."

"There is no one to forgive me."

The paladin was silent for a moment. "There is one."

"Who?"

"It's not for me to say. When the time is right, you will know. Come. I will help you pack."

"No," Jherek said. "I'll take what I have with me."

"You have gear here," Azla said, "and we have supplies we can spare."

"Nothing." Jherek looked at the still water between the two ships.

"You're going then?" Sabyna asked.

Jherek looked at her, the pain in his heart almost too much to bear. "Lady, perhaps it is better. All I seem capable of doing is bringing you pain, and I am sorry for that. I'm sorry that you are so far from home."

"I am where I need to be," Sabyna said. "I have charted this course as much as you have."

Jherek started to shake his head.

"I'll not tolerate a pig-headed argument," Sabyna warned in a hoarse voice, "and you've no other to offer in this matter."

Before he could stop himself, Jherek took her hand in his and knelt. He pulled her hand gently to his chest above his heart.

"Lady," he said, "I swear that should you ever need me, should there be a way made that I can help you, I will be there."

She tightened her fingers in his shirt. "I know," she whispered.

Jherek turned and hugged Glawinn fiercely.

"Go with Lathander's mercies, young warrior."

Holding tightly onto his control, Jherek stepped in front of Azla. "Captain, requesting permission to disembark."

"Granted," the half-elf pirate captain responded. "May you know nothing but safe waters. If ever you need berth on a ship, my men will know of you."

"Thank you."

Jherek kept himself from looking back at Sabyna. He stepped to the railing and threw himself overboard. Only the certain knowledge that the ship and all aboard her would be sacrificed if he stayed gave him the strength.

He hit the water cleanly, completely submerging. The sea plumed white around him as he passed through it. For a moment he considered diving as deep as he could, until his lungs ran out of air and he couldn't make the surface again, but he didn't.

Whatever drove him from Velen and buried him with the ill luck that pursued him from the time he was born stayed with him. Whatever god, whatever demon, maybe it could make him leave his friends, but it couldn't control him completely.

In Athkatla, he'd given in to that force and to the voice that commanded him and made the trip to Baldur's Gate. After the Ship of the Gods exploded, he gave up. Now, he decided, he would fight that force until he was free of it or it destroyed him.

He surfaced and swam across to *Steadfast*. When he arrived, he pounded on the hull and called, "I need a ladder."

Captain Tarnar gazed down at him with suspicion. "I don't need to be berthing a curse," he shouted down.

Jherek gazed back up at the man, fanning the hurt and anger inside himself until it glowed white-hot. "If you don't take me aboard," Jherek said, "I'm willing to bet you don't make it out of here."

"We'll see about that."

Before Tarnar's words faded away, the water-figure spun quickly and winds whipped the ship, tearing rigging free.

Jherek pushed away from *Steadfast*, treading water until the ship settled again. The coiled rope ladder plopped into the water near the young sailor, and he wasted no time clambering up it. He stood on *Steadfast*'s deck totally drenched, water cascading around his feet.

"What manner of hell chases you, boy?" Tarnar demanded.

"I don't know," Jherek answered, "but there will be an accounting."

No sooner had the young sailor come aboard than the water-figure sank into the ocean and the wind returned, filling *Steadfast*'s sails and shoving them forward again.

Tarnar gazed upward, a wary look on his sun-browned features. "You think you can fight *that*?"

"Whoever I see at the other end of this trip," Jherek said, "who is in any way responsible for this will regret ever laying eyes on me."

Glawinn and Sabyna stood at the railing, looking out after him. He stared at them even after they were gone from sight, certain he would never see them again.

The wind flowed over him, bringing the sea's chill to his wet clothes. He ignored the cold, focusing on the hate that he'd finally allowed to take root in his heart.

14

The ixitxachitl swooped through the sea at Laaqueel with a suddenness that belied its great size. It resembled a manta ray, solid black across the top of its thin body and purple-white underneath. The wing membrane was fully eight feet across, not the largest of its kind the malenti priestess had seen, but close.

She kicked her feet, powering through the water and pulling her trident between her breasts. The lateral lines running through her body echoed the disturbance in the ocean around her. Spinning, one hand flaring out and catching the water in the webbing between her fingers, she avoided the demon ray's barbed tail. One of the Serôsian ixitxachitls' tactics was to snare an intended victim's neck or torso and hold it captive.

Laaqueel popped her retractable finger claws from hiding, raked them across the ixitxachitl's tail, and lopped off a two-foot section.

Blood streamed from the creature's tail stub as it curled its wing membrane and rolled over with deceptive ease.

"Hateful elf!" it cried in its gravelly voice. It sped at her again.

Leveling her trident, Laaqueel sprang at her opponent. The ixitxachitl's mouth opened, over a foot wide and filled with serrated teeth.

She shoved the trident forward, burying the tines in the hard, rubbery flesh between the ixitxachitl's malevolent eyes. The creature's greater bulk propelled her backward, but she swung at the end of the trident safely out of reach of its hungry jaws.

She popped her toe claws and raked her opponent from just behind its mouth all the way to the bleeding tail stump. The creature's entrails spilled into the water in long ropes. The ixitxachitl screamed as death claimed it.

Laaqueel yanked her trident free and raked the surrounding water with her gaze. War raged around her as the ixitxachitls battled sahuagin from the outer and inner seas. Blood filmed the sea the way a surface dweller's smoke choked an enclosed building.

With their greater speed, the sahuagin were making short work of the demon rays.

It feels good to be back in the fray, doesn't it, little malenti?

Laaqueel listened to Iakhovas's voice inside her skull and answered, *Yes.*

In truth, all doubt and fear left her for the moment. There was no uncertainty. She was a priestess serving the will of Sekolah to battle and destroy enemies of the sahuagin.

The ixitxachitls had set up their Six Holy Cities in the Xedran Reefs, south of Thuridru. They ran from just off the coast of Alaghôn on the Turmish coast to the shallows in the mouth of the Vilhon Reach.

A foraging party from the koalinth tribe called the Sea Hulks had been used as bait for the ixitxachitl military party Iakhovas staked out as a target. When the demon ray group attacked, the koalinth foragers fled east, leading their pursuers between the pincer attack of the combined sahuagin and Sea Hulk groups.

Driven before their ambushers, angered and confused—the Laws of Battle had not been adhered to—the ixitxachitls swam east, desperately trying to outrun the death that chased after them.

Her lateral lines warned Laaqueel of the attack coming from behind her. Praying to Sekolah, praying that her failing belief had not yet caused her powers to leave her, she turned and shoved her hand out.

Bright incandescence shot from her hand, causing steaming bubbles to form and dart rapidly for the surface little more than a hundred feet up. The ixitxachitl caught in the blast of power cooked, great blisters rising in a heartbeat, then bursting. The rancid taste of burned fat tainted the water Laaqueel breathed.

To the left, another sahuagin rode an ixitxachitl's back, holding onto the wing membrane with both fists as it took great bites from the screaming creature's back. Its shouts and prayers to Ilxendren, the Great Ray and god of the ixitxachitls, echoed in Laaqueel's ears.

Laaqueel pulled her weapon free and swam on, giving herself over to the chase. It was the closest she'd felt to normal in days.

The meeting with Vhaemas the Bastard had been five days ago. Now Iakhovas hoped to win the support of the Sea Hulk koalinth tribe south of the Xedran Reefs, completing a union of enemies around the ixitxachitls. The malenti priestess was present at only one of the meetings between Iakhovas and the koalinth chief, though she knew Iakhovas met with Dhunnir more times than that.

The fleeing ixitxachitls flexed their wings and skated only a few feet above the ocean surface, gliding over the clumps of coral that gave the Xedran Reefs its name. Sand ballooned out from under their great wings as they swam. Colorful fish darted from in front of them.

Ilkanar, the town the ixitxachitls were from, lay over a mile to the west. The attack was sprung far enough away from the devil ray city that no reinforcements could arrive quickly even if a messenger did get away.

The ixitxachitls swam through a stand of rocks and coral, hoping to escape their pursuers. Instead, they met *Tarjana* rising up from the ocean floor over the rise behind which it had been hidden.

The mudship's deck was filled with more sahuagin wielding crossbows. Even as the ixitxachitls turned to avoid slamming into the massive ship, the crossbow quarrels found their marks.

Iakhovas was among them. Laaqueel swam, watching as Iakhovas's arms became hard-edged with bone and dorsal edges that ran the length of the appendages. His finned arms and legs slashed through the ixitxachitls.

In minutes, the last demon ray had been executed. Sahuagin and koalinth alike made a meal out of their conquered enemies. Laaqueel swam above *Tarjana*'s deck and surveyed the battlefield that stretched for almost a quarter mile. Bodies of sahuagin, ixitxachitl, and koalinth alike littered the water, twisted into inelegant poses.

The survivors moved through the dead with large nets in their wake, gathering them up. Meat was meat, and none of it needed to go to waste.

Jherek was on *Steadfast*'s forecastle deck, whirling the cutlass and hook around him as he moved from attack to defense and back again.

Finished for the moment, standing on quivering legs, his arms trembling from the exertion, the young sailor took a deep breath and looked over the bow at the eastern horizon. *Steadfast* tacked into the wind now, rolling first port then starboard as she plowed through the oncoming waves. The Whamite Isles were two days back and she made for Aglarond.

When his legs were steady again, he stepped over the bow railing and stared along the thirty-foot bowsprit. The wood glistened with salt spray. Ratlines ran down from the forward and mainmasts, helping hold the lanyards square and in place.

Concentrating, anything to keep from thinking about what and whom he'd walked away from thirteen days before, Jherek stepped cautiously and steadily along the bowsprit. The long pole measured nearly a foot across where it buckled into the caravel and narrowed to something less than four inches at the end. Nearly halfway out, the ratlines dropped too low to be any good to him if he fell. Still, he continued, his knees bent as he rode out *Steadfast*'s rise and fall.

Long moments later, he stood within only a few short feet of the bowsprit's end. He reveled in the feel of the wind and the sea's uneven terrain. All around him, he could see nothing but the sea and the sky. He closed his eyes, turning his face up into the wind.

If he lost the anger that filled him, what would be left? The question had haunted him over the last few days. The answer terrified him. Whatever drove him wanted him broken. Perhaps it didn't know how close he already was. Perhaps it would have been satisfied if it had known. He'd even wished for a while that he could break, but he couldn't. He simply didn't know how.

"Jherek."

The call was soft, not meant to startle. The young sailor moved his feet carefully, turning to stare back at the ship. Captain Tarnar stood in the bow, arms folded across his chest.

"It's almost time to come about and tack into the wind the other way. I didn't want to lose you when we re-rigged the canvas."

"Thank you, Captain."

Carefully, Jherek walked back along the bowsprit, then hopped onto the forecastle deck.

Tarnar gazed at him in open speculation and said, "I've never seen a sober man try to do what you just did, and even drunk I never saw it accomplished."

Jherek flushed with embarrassment over drawing unnecessary attention. Since boarding *Steadfast*, he'd been the object of enough of it.

"Most of my crew is convinced that you're cursed, but a few think of you as some kind of holy man. Which of them have it right?"

"I'd say cursed," Jherek replied bitterly. "I don't know."

"Personally, I was thinking you might be blessed."

Jherek glanced at the captain to see if he was joking.

"All these days at sea, and us staring the Alamber in the teeth the most of it, and we've not suffered one sea devil attack. Most ships aren't finding passage that easy."

"The voyage isn't over yet," Jherek said harshly.

"You're not a man to ever see a glass half full, are you?"

"I've had reason not to," Jherek said. "Most days, it's not even been my glass to look at."

Shouts suddenly rang out from the port side of the ship. "Dragon!" a man bawled.

"Where away?" Tarnar demanded, turning and striding to that side of the ship.

"There, Cap'n!" The mate pointed at the sea.

Looking out into the blue-green water, Jherek saw the unmistakable gold scales of the sea wyrm forty yards out. Its serpentine body undulated through the sea, easily pacing the ship, not having to fight the wind.

"What is it?" a man bellowed in consternation.

"Dragon-kin," another man roared back. "Umberlee probably sent the great damned thing to fetch us and pull us under the salt."

A handful of the crew grabbed bows and drew arrows back.

"No!" Jherek ordered even as they loosed. The arrows raced across the intervening distance, but none of them found their mark. "Don't loose any more arrows!"

The young sailor stepped forward and pushed a man to the deck. The crew instantly formed a pocket around Jherek. Knives and cudgels appeared in their hands.

"Demonspawn," one of the men growled. "Shoulda tied an anchor 'round his feet and deep-sixed him!"

Jherek raised the cutlass to defend himself, but—looking into the angry and frightened faces of the men before him—his resolve left him. He knew there was no way he could fight them. They weren't pirates or slavers, nor any black-hearted rogues that he could recognize. They were simply men afraid of what was before them. A warrior didn't fight such men over anything less than honor or to save a life. Jherek couldn't fight them just to save his own life, not when he was the cause of their fear.

The young sailor dropped his cutlass and stood before the crew unarmed. The anger inside him kept his fear away. He waited. He wouldn't run.

"Run him through!" a crewman near the back yelled. "See if his blood's red or if you can read his befouled heritage in his own tripe, by the gods!"

One of the men lashed out with a cruel skinning knife. Jherek turned just enough to avoid the blow.

"Enough!" Tarnar roared. "This is my ship. As long as it remains my ship, nothing will happen aboard her that I don't sanction. That's the way it has always been, and that's how it shall be until I'm not fit to command her." He glared at the men assembled before him. "Is that understood?"

"Aye, Cap'n." The response was quick and came from the mouth of every man. All the oaths were grudgingly given.

"Then get back to work," the captain ordered. "Every mother's son of you."

The crew turned and walked away, grumbling.

Tarnar turned, his eyes wide as he studied Jherek. "By the gods, boy, what is it about you that you'd stare them in the teeth and not raise a hand against them?"

"They didn't deserve my wrath," Jherek answered. "They have no control over my being here."

"They would have killed you if I let them."

"Aye."

Tarnar shook his head in disbelief. "What is that thing doing here?" He pointed at the sea wyrm keeping pace with *Steadfast*.

"I don't know, Captain." Jherek turned to the railing and stared out at the sea wyrm. It disappeared beneath the waves. "I've seen it before. Back on *Azure Dagger*."

"Then it has followed you here," concluded Tarnar.

Jherek made no response to that, but his mind reeled with the implications of the dragon's presence.

"Boy, if something powerful enough to stop the winds and control the waters wanted you dead, it would have drank down the ship and you with it," the captain said. "You're still alive, so I have to ask why."

"I don't know," Jherek said with grim determination, "but whatever it is, it will regret it."

Tarnar shook his head. "A prudent man wouldn't presume to put himself above the gods."

"I'm beyond prudence," Jherek declared. "I will demand an accounting. My life has never been an easy one, and this force—this god if you wish to see it that way—has seen to that. It can kill me, strip the flesh from my bones, but I will not kneel before some heartless thing. I will have my battle, and I will acquit myself with honor."

Sabyna paused at the edge of the narrow, rutted street and watched a wagon pass.

The wagon was loaded with timber the driver was hauling to the sawmill down by the docks. The merry jingle-jangle of the horses' harnesses stood out in sharp counterpoint to the tired plod of the animals. The driver and the three woodchoppers with him looked worn out.

Agenais rumbled with steady business and men. Coin changed hands quickly, and prices marked on goods didn't mean a thing. If no one was interested in something, the price could sometimes be halved. Impromptu auctions went on all around her where there was more than one prospective buyer and a limited supply of goods. The roll of bids, accompanied by oaths and strident voices, remained as steady as the conversations and stories that were told.

Sabyna crossed the street, aware of the men's attentions. Some eyed her discreetly, and others stared at her with openly wolfish hunger.

On the other side of the rutted street, she stepped up onto a boardwalk under a badly listing eave in front of the apothecary's shop. Her boot heels rang hollowly against the wooden surface.

"Hey, little woman," a man called gruffly.

Sabyna kept her eyes forward. From experience she'd learned not to acknowledge speakers in such situations.

The man reached out and wrapped a beefy hand around her wrist. "Hey," he grumbled, "I was talking to you." The man was short of six feet but was as broad as the back end of a barge. He was unshaven and smelled of ale.

Slowly, Sabyna reached out with her free hand for the whip lashed to the big man's belt. She smiled, watching other men come join the first.

"You're lucky," she said in a soft voice.

The man grinned more broadly and asked, "How am I lucky?"

"Despite the mood I'm in and your own bad manners, I'm not going to kill you." Sabyna tapped the whip and said, "Bind."

The whip surged up from the man's side and uncoiled. Before he could do more than let go her wrist and take a step back, the whip wrapped around him, pinning his arms to his sides and trapping his legs together. He yelped in fear and surprise.

Placing a hand in the center of his chest, Sabyna shoved the man into the rutted street. She turned to face his friends, who weren't totally convinced they couldn't take her.

She opened the bag of holding at her side and called, "Skeins."

The raggamoffyn fluttered up through the opening and formed a striking serpentine shape that hovered on the wind. The men backed away at once, terror on their faces.

"Don't," Sabyna said coldly, "let me see you again."

Without another word, the men grabbed their friend from the rutted road and took off.

Releasing a slow, taut breath, Sabyna stepped into the apothecary's shop. Skeins retreated into the bag of holding.

The shop stood small and tidy beneath a swaying ceiling that had seen its best days pass it by. Wheel-shaped candelabras hung from the ceiling. Handmade shelves, added as needed and not with a uniform design in mind, stood against the left and right walls.

Glass bottles of all shapes, sizes, and colors mixed with jars, canisters, and small boxes to cover the shelves. Open vases held sticks of spices and rolled herbs. Cheesecloth pouches of pipeweed sat on barrels.

Some of the herbs had been dried and left in their original shape, lying in jars, in thick clusters, or hanging from strings strung around the room. Other herbs had been ground into meals and powders, grains separated from the chaff.

"Hail and well met, lady."

Fazayl stood behind the battered counter at the end of the shop. Long gray hair hung to his shoulders, but the top of his head was bald. Gray chin whiskers jutted out in disarray. He wore a homespun shirt and worn breeches. A long-stemmed pipe was in one hand, and the rich aroma of cherry blend pipeweed filled the shop.

"Hail and well met." Sabyna crossed to the counter. "You have the herbs and other things I asked for?"

"Aye," the man replied. "That I do."

He reached under the counter and brought out a small wooden box. Inside were a dozen vials, jars, and bottles of different colors. Bundles of herbs and incense sticks took up more space.

Sabyna took the bottles and herbs out one by one, checking each.

"I've gotten some new stock in, lady," Fazayl stated, waving his arm generously around the small shop. "If you'd care to take a look."

"Thank you. I will."

Despite the danger inherent in being in the town of Agenais by herself, Sabyna found she was reluctant to return to *Azure Dagger* so readily. While aboard ship she was consciously aware of Jherek's absence. She left the small box in the apothecary's care and crossed the room to the potions and oils.

Two small children, no more than six or seven, entered the shop amid gales of laughter. Dressed in made-over clothing patched in dozens of places, they pushed and shoved each other in playful sibling rivalry. The children stopped at the counter and peered up at Fazayl.

"And where do you rapscallions think you're off to?" the apothecary demanded.

The children didn't answer, simply peered over the edge of the counter with their big eyes. Dirt stained their wind-reddened cheeks, and they wiggled in excitement.

Smiling, Fazayl reached under the counter and brought out half a dozen hard candies. The children scooped them up, yelled quick thank yous, and scurried for the door. The old man laughed at them, then caught Sabyna looking.

"Bless the children, lady, for they see only the good things in this world."

"Are they your grandchildren?" Sabyna asked.

"No, lady. My boys and my grandchildren live in Chessenta. The Whamites turned out far too small to keep them from roving. Still, most of the children in town know I and the missus can be counted on for a few pieces of sugar candy without too much of a fight."

The shop door opened and two rough-looking men stepped through. Both of them walked with the rolling gait of professional seamen and wore cutlasses instead of long swords.

"Shopkeeper," one of the men roared. "I've got a list of goods here we'll be needing." He reached inside his blouse and took out a scrap of parchment.

"If I can," Fazayl replied. "Some goods are in short supply these days."

The two men swaggered to the counter and gazed around at the shop. One of them looked directly at Sabyna, and the ship's mage recognized him in an instant as one of Vurgrom the Mighty's crew of pirates that had captured her in Baldur's Gate and fled with her down the River Chionthar.

She readied her spells in the event that he recognized her.

After they gave their list to Fazayl, they turned to the barrels where the apothecary kept live fish, salamanders, frogs, and newts that he used to make some of his powders, potions, and oils.

Returning to the counter, still watching the two men, Sabyna quickly paid for her supplies, then shoved them into the bag of holding. Skeins sensed her tension and tried to ease from the bag. She pushed the raggamoffyn back inside, thanked Fazayl, and headed for the door.

Without looking back, she crossed the rutted street that cut through the heart of Agenais and took up a position beside a sail maker's shop. From the alley she had a clear view of the apothecary.

When they left, she followed.

15

"You're an excellent player," the captain said.

Jherek glanced at Captain Tarnar across the inlaid marble chessboard on the small table between them in the captain's quarters. The pieces were done in dark red and white, matching the board, carved in figures of king, queen, priests, horsemen, castles, and kneeling archers.

"You're very gracious," the young sailor responded.

Steadfast cleaved the water as she was named, pulling full into the wind now.

"No," Tarnar replied, "I'm not. I don't like to lose."

He poured another glass of wine for himself, then offered the bottle to Jherek, who politely refused.

The captain had invited Jherek to join him for dinner, and the young sailor had reluctantly accepted. Jherek preferred his own company, but he was loath not to show good manners in light of the situation.

"I find it more disturbing that you beat me three times in a row"—Tarnar paused to sip his wine—"in light of the fact that you're distracted."

"I'm not—"

"A woman?" the captain asked, interrupting politely.

Jherek didn't reply. To speak of Sabyna so casually would be dishonorable.

"Of course it's a woman," Tarnar said with conviction. His eyes bore into the young sailor's. "The only other interest to so bewitch a man's soul would be an object of greed, and you aren't the type to covet physical goods." The captain started setting up the chess pieces again. "You threw yourself into the sea without so much as a bag packed those days ago."

Jherek set up the pieces on his side of the board, appreciating the smooth feel of them.

"Is it the ship's captain I saw you with?" Tarnar persisted. "The half-elf? Or the young red haired girl that seemed so upset by your leaving?"

"I'd rather not speak of this," Jherek said.

"Nonsense. Men at sea always talk of women," the captain persisted. "First, they speak of their mothers, then of lovers, then of women they've left in different ports. When they start speaking of wives, you'd best start looking for another crewman."

Candles lit the room and filled it with the smoky haze of herbs that eddied out the open windows in the ship's stern. A generous portion of the room was given over to the large bed that extended across the stern a good eight feet. Shelves and closets occupied the remaining space along the wall on either side of the bed.

There was a large rolltop desk that held map scrolls and nautical plotting and marking tools. Ship's journals sat neatly ranked on one side. The current journal occupied the center of the table, open to the entry Tarnar last made. A quill and an inkwell sat nearby.

A shelf on the opposite side of the room from the desk held a row of books. Most of them, Jherek found upon inspection, were treatises regarding the worship of Mystra. Beside the bookshelves was a locked armory that held swords of different makes and styles.

Jherek nodded at the shelves and said, "I've noticed your interest in books."

"The worship of Mystra. Yes." Tarnar swirled the dregs of his wine. "I am a failed priest of her order."

Stunned that the man announced the fact so casually, Jherek opened his mouth to speak but found no words.

The captain grinned. "It's nothing I'm ashamed of," he said. "While I attended the Lady of Mysteries' schools and talked with her priests, I learned a great many things. All of them have helped me become a better man. I begrudge none of the experience, not even when I took myself from the order."

"Why did you?" Jherek asked.

"Because I felt the calling, but I never felt I could devote myself to the priesthood. Not the way I wanted to, wholly and without reservation. So I went to sea, which seemed as wild and as restless as any mysteries I might seek to uncover under Mystra's guidance."

"But your interest remains," Jherek observed. "Why would you keep the books otherwise?"

"Aye," Tarnar replied. "My fascination remains. Mystra is also known as She of the Wild Tides here in the Sea of Fallen Stars. I love her because she seems so much a part of this world, yet above it. Legend has it that during the Time of Troubles she even walked on this plane as a mortal herself."

Jherek remained silent.

"Today I tried to divine something of what lies in your future," Tarnar said.

Shaking his head, Jherek grumbled, "I don't want to know."

"There's not much to tell," Tarnar told him. "I never learned how to divine properly, though I was told by my teachers that I possessed some mean skills at it. I only got two impressions from the attempt. I know that something shapes your future—though you have a choice in that—and that the guiding hand does not belong to Mystra."

"What choice?"

Tarnar ran his finger around the rim of his wineglass and said, "I could not say. Have you any stronger feelings about where we're supposed to go? By the afternoon of the day after tomorrow we'll be at the mouth of the Alamber Sea. Providing the wind stays with us, the trip to Aglarond will not be long."

"No. I have just the steady need to travel east—and even that is not as sharp as it once was."

Even as the young sailor's words faded away, a low, mournful croon echoed inside the captain's quarters. Drawn by the sound, Jherek excused himself from the table and headed through the door.

Men stood out on the deck, lit by a few lanterns secured in the rigging to warn other ships of their presence and to allow them to see in the dark night. None of the sailors appeared relaxed.

"What in the Nine Hells is that?" one man grumbled.

"It's enough to wake the dead," another volunteered.

"You ask me," a third stated, "that's the cry of someone or something dead. Come to call us on home ourselves."

"Stow that bilge, Klyngir," Tarnar ordered as he followed Jherek up the steps to the stern castle.

"Aye, sir," the sailor snapped.

The mournful moaning continued, just loud enough to be heard over the waves lapping at *Steadfast*'s sides. It echoed on the wind, as if carried a great distance.

Jherek stepped up on *Steadfast*'s stern castle deck. The chill wind snaked icy fingers under his clothing, prickling his skin. His hair whipped about, blown forward from the stern. He scanned the horizon where the star-filled black sky met the rolling, green-black sea.

"I want men circling this ship along the railings," Tarnar roared as he stood overlooking the deck. "Those blasted sea devils are known to be thick in this area."

"Sounds far away, Cap'n," the mate behind the wheel stated.

"I don't want to take any chances," Tarnar snapped.

Steadfast creaked and the rigging popped in the wind, but the ship's noises never covered the mournful moans. Jherek listened to the sounds, finally recognizing them for what they were.

"Whale song," he said.

"Aye, Cap'n, it is," the mate at the wheel said. "I know it now, too."

The cadence of the whale song rode up and down the scale, sounding eerie and menacing.

"I've been told whales can sing the length and breadth of the Inner Sea," the mate said, "but I've never heard anything like this."

"Nor have I," Tarnar agreed. He glanced at Jherek.

"Wherever they are," Jherek said, "that's where we must go."

"You're sure?" Tarnar asked.

Men scurried along *Steadfast*'s railing, holding lanterns out over the sides as they scoured the dark water.

"Aye," Jherek replied. The pulling sensation inside him was growing, accompanied by an increased anxiety to get there.

"What direction?"

The young sailor listened, but the mournful moaning seemed to come from everywhere.

"I don't know," Jherek mumbled, frustration chafing at him.

Tarnar approached him and spoke soft enough that his words didn't carry. "Close your eyes, my friend. If this is a message for you, as you believe, it will be made known to you."

Filled with tense doubt, Jherek closed his eyes. The moaning continued to echo around him, faint and distant. He couldn't guess in what direction it truly lay.

He shook his head and said, "It doesn't help."

"That's because you're still listening with your ears," Tarnar said patiently. "Listen with your heart, Jherek, not your head, not your body. Breathe out slowly. Relax."

Jherek exhaled, concentrating on the sound.

"Your heart," Tarnar said, "not your ears. You're still trying to listen with your ears."

"I can't do it," Jherek whispered hoarsely.

"You can," Tarnar told him. "Think of some other place, some other time. Get some distance between here and now. Think of a place you like to go. One that has no bad memories, no pressure."

With difficulty, Jherek imagined Madame Iitaar's house at the top of Widow's Hill in Velen. He remembered the trails he'd raced up and down while working at the shipwright's shop and living with Madame Iitaar.

Breathing out, he recalled the cool breeze that lingered under the apple tree where he'd often stood and watched the ships out in Velen's harbor. He'd spent hours there, hungering after the opportunity to put to sea again. Out in the harbor, he watched *Butterfly* pull out of port, her sails popped full of a favoring wind, knowing that he had Finaren's promise that the next time she sailed he'd be part of her crew.

Whalefriend. The voice in Jherek's mind was rusty with fatigue. *You must come as quickly as you can. Time grows short. The Taker moves more swiftly than our legends foretold. He is already on his way.*

Who are you? Jherek knew the voice wasn't the one that had been with him for the last fourteen years of his life. This wasn't the voice that told him time and time again, "Live, that you may serve."

I am called Song Who Brings Bright Rains.

What do you want?

Only to do that which I have been given to do, Jherek Whalefriend. As we all must. The voice sounded weaker, farther away, like a light growing dim in a long corridor.

You are not the one who has talked to me before.

No. I am but a piece of the tapestry that is your destiny. Another's hand has wrought it.

Who's hand?

That is not for me to say, Jherek Whalefriend. It is not yet the time of choosing. Follow, and may all your songs be strong.

When the communication ended, Jherek opened his eyes. The wind blew cold over the perspiration that covered him. He stared hard into the darkness.

"Do you know the direction?" Tarnar asked.

"East," the young sailor replied. "We need to adjust four points to starboard." He felt the direction like a compass needle.

"Make it so," Tarnar told the mate.

As soon as *Steadfast* came about on her new course, the sensation within Jherek's breast felt a little stronger.

"How far is our destination?" Tarnar asked.

"I don't know."

The captain hesitated, picking up the small lantern near the plotting desk beside the wheel. He glanced at the compass, traced a map with his finger, and said, "If we stay on this course, we're going to end up in the middle of the Alamber Sea."

"When?"

"By the day after tomorrow. That's the very heart of the sea devils' empire. I can't ask these men to go there, and I won't order them to."

"I understand," Jherek replied. "If the time comes that you're faced with that, I'll go on alone."

Grim-faced, Tarnar folded his map and put it away. "Let's hope it doesn't come to that."

"There is another problem," Jherek said. "I was told we're not the only ones headed this way."

"Told?" For the first time, doubt showed on Tarnar's face. "Who told you this?"

"The whale who sings," Jherek replied.

The young sailor noticed the look the mate swapped with his captain and chose not to respond to it.

"Who else is supposed to be coming?" Tarnar asked.

"The Taker," Jherek said.

Confusion lit Tarnar's face in the glare from the small lantern he held. "Do you know what the Taker is?"

While Azla pursued Vurgrom, mention had been made of the Taker. In fact, some of the people the pirate captain questioned suggested that Vurgrom was somehow in league with this mythological terror.

"A story," the young sailor said. "I've heard a few legends about the Taker."

"And what if this thing is real?"

The possibility seemed overwhelming to Jherek. His life was troubled enough.

"How could the Taker be real?" he asked. "The Taker is a legend. No one has ever seen him."

"If you have spoken to a whale," Tarnar said, "then you know someone must have. Whales never lie."

16

Follow me more closely, little malenti, Iakhovas ordered as they swam through the currents around Vahaxtyl. *I would not have the princes know we are divided in any way.*

Laaqueel obeyed reluctantly, drawing two feet closer to Iakhovas. The sahuagin princes of Aleaxtis had sent warriors to escort them from *Tarjana.* The great galley sat at anchor above the ruined city. All around them, the whale song echoed.

No one in the sahuagin city seemed happy to see Iakhovas return.

How easily they forget, Iakhovas commented as they swam to the amphitheater. During their absence, the princes ordered the amphitheater cleared so meetings could once again be held there.

Crews of sahuagin women and children still labored to clear the city of debris, but Laaqueel knew the area would never be fit to live in again. Black chunks, shelves, and mountains of cooled lava covered the place where the city had once been. Here and there were pockets, mostly intact, that left a few landmarks to distinguish where proud Vahaxtyl once stood. Warriors stood guard and foraged for food to feed the populace.

The ringed seats around the amphitheater were only a quarter full but there were still thousands seated. The three surviving sahuagin princes stood in the center of the mosaic of black and gray stones. Fully four dozen guardsmen flanked them, outnumbering the warriors Iakhovas had brought four to one.

Iakhovas sank easily before the princes and stood to his full height.

As the malenti priestess gazed around, she saw that the princes were accompanied by their priestesses as well. Evidently it was hoped that all of their combined power might stand against Iakhovas's might.

Panic sailed through Laaqueel as she looked at the full-blooded sahuagin priestesses. They stood in stark contrast to Laaqueel.

Relax, the feminine voice whispered in her mind. *Make no untoward moves. For now, let Iakhovas have his way.*

Laaqueel glanced at Iakhovas, but his attention was on the princes.

"Honored Ones," Iakhovas addressed them. His voice boomed, carrying easily throughout the amphitheater.

Ruubuuiz, as most senior among the three princes, strode forward. He planted his webbed feet flat on the amphitheater floor and held his trident beside him. The prince wore his best combat harness, adorned with sigils representing Sekolah as well as his own station. Made of soft gold and adorned with finger bones taken from enemies as well as bits of fire coral, his crown gleamed.

"You have journeyed safely," Ruubuuiz stated.

"I have journeyed on a true sahuagin warrior's path," Iakhovas countered with a warning edge in his voice. "I have left broken enemies in my wake, feasted upon them that I might maintain my strength, eaten of my fallen brothers that they might forever stay with me, and created currents that will send all of our enemies cringing in fear."

Ruubuuiz shifted uncertainly.

"I came back here," Iakhovas roared, "to lead the army you were supposed to have readied in my absence. Instead, I find you and your people grubbing around the corpse of this city long after the marrow is gone."

Laaqueel held herself proudly, listening to the words Iakhovas spoke. Confusion vibrated inside her. As Iakhovas had stated, he moved more truly along the currents a sahuagin would, and he gave voice to thoughts only a sahuagin would have. She felt proud and shamed and conflicted all at once. How could he, who Laaqueel knew was not a sahuagin, be better at playing one of her kind than she was?

"Our people were not meant to live as carrion feeders," Iakhovas yelled. "In the days after the destruction of this city, you princes teach your people the way to live their lives. In turn will they teach their children. Now is not the time to be cautious."

"Now is not the time to foolishly throw away the lives of our warriors," Ruubuuiz countered. "We must rebuild, and—"

"While you are rebuilding," Iakhovas accused, "you're going to allow the sea elves and mermen time to rebuild the Sharksbane Wall. You might as well help lay the stones yourself."

"Carefully," Ruubuuiz growled, flaring his fins and puffing up his chest angrily. "Your words here this day will not be forgotten."

"I will have my priestess put them in a singing bundle for you to remember always," Iakhovas declared, referring to the strings of shells, rocks, and knots tied to bone or sinew rings that the sahuagin used as books.

Iakhovas turned to look at the amphitheater seats and called out, "I did not come to Serôs to free you only so you could trap yourselves again. The wall is broken, a world lies in wait out there to feel the caress of your claws and mighty teeth. Are you predators or prey?"

The crowd rose from their seats, clacking their claws against each other, shaking their tridents and spears. They hooted, whistled, and clicked their support of his words. Thousands made the cacophony almost deafening.

Iakhovas turned back to the three princes, strong and tall in triumph.

Maartaaugh stepped forward and gazed at the yelling sahuagin. "Don't be easily swayed by his words," he screamed at them. "Remember the thousands who have left this place already under his guidance, and remember that only hundreds of them have returned—or still may live."

Some of the audience's celebration died away.

"Those who fell in battle fell as true warriors should," Iakhovas rebutted. "With their claws in an enemy's heart or their teeth in an enemy's throat. Through me, they got the chance to die with nobility rather than live out their days behind a sea elf's wall."

Cheering started again, but it wasn't as loud as before. Laaqueel knew it was because there was a lot of truth in Maartaaugh's words. She eyed the other priestesses. Laaqueel knew that if Iakhovas fell out of favor suddenly, or made himself appear the slightest bit weak in the eyes of the sahuagin, the priestesses would kill her first, then turn on him. Their obvious resentment of her spurred her on, overcoming her own reluctance to champion Iakhovas. Her own dignity and self-worth was at risk.

Laaqueel strode forward imperiously, letting her anger bury any hesitation she felt about her actions. Every eye focused on her—she was so different from both the outer sea and Serôsian sahuagin.

"You shame me," she accused the priestesses.

"N'Tel'Quess," one of the priestesses snarled. She touched the holy symbol of Sekolah hanging over her ridged chest and threw out a hand.

Laaqueel braced herself, summoning her own powers. She felt the spell tingle over her body as she clasped the holy symbol hanging between her bare breasts. The tingle went away and the priestess who'd attacked her burst into green flames.

The priestess swam from the others, trying to escape the blaze that consumed her. The water boiled around her, giving off terrible heat that coasted on the currents sweeping over Laaqueel. The malenti priestess watched in quiet shock as white foam from the boiling sea water and green flames consumed the priestess. Seconds later, the priestess's blackened bones drifted to the amphitheater floor. Her flesh was entirely consumed.

Quiet reigned over the amphitheater.

Little malenti, Iakhovas said gently into her mind, *you have their complete and undivided attention.*

Gathering her own composure, Laaqueel saw that it was true.

Wariness gleamed in the black eyes of the priestesses before her.

"You, who are supposed to be the backbone of Sekolah's worship in your tribes, baronies, and kingdom," Laaqueel accused, "choose to be silent about Sekolah's teachings in this time of greatest need."

"Not true," one of the oldest priestesses stated.

Two of the sharks circling overhead under the control of sahuagin warriors broke ranks. Before anyone could say anything in warning, the predators ripped into the Serôsian priestess.

The first shark chewed the priestess's face from her skull in passing while the other disemboweled her. The sharks returned to their positions overhead.

Laaqueel glanced at Iakhovas.

It's no work of mine, little malenti. His human face, when she saw it, even held a trace of suspicious hostility.

Laaqueel had no doubt that he'd taken part in neither attack. It was something else, something divine. She was certain of it. Feeling more confident, she returned her attention to the priestesses.

"If you don't live and teach as the Great Shark would have you," Laaqueel preached, "live in fear of Sekolah's wrath. As always, the weak will be culled from true warriors. So shall it be for the priestesses who stand in the way of the path the Shark God has chosen."

With fierce gazes and open hatred, the priestesses bowed their heads in acknowledgment.

Savage pride burned through Laaqueel. As she took her place at Iakhovas's side, she held her head high.

You've acquitted yourself well, little malenti, Iakhovas sent her, *though I'd like to speak on this matter later, and at greater length. We are still not out of danger here.*

Even that did not dissuade Laaqueel from the joy she felt. Sekolah had defended her, stepping in and destroying the priestesses who challenged her. It was unheard of.

"Warriors make war," Iakhovas roared. "Leaders lead." He spun slowly in the amphitheater, his arms thrust straight out and his claws fully extended. "When I first arrived here, I declared myself as your deliverer, the one who would set you free. I have not done that yet."

Laaqueel glanced at the princes as they conferred among themselves. They knew where Iakhovas was headed as well as she did. There was nothing they could do to prevent it.

"I tore down the Sharksbane Wall," Iakhovas said. "I opened a path to the outer Serôsian world, to the seas the surface worlders depend on."

Clicks and whistles of agreement echoed around the amphitheater.

"But I failed to truly set you free," Iakhovas went on. "I left, handling errands of my own, taking the first steps to build We Who Eat a conflagration that would end the empires of our enemies, to leave them broken and shattered in our wake. I will not fail you again. I will be the king that you deserve, the one who will make savage warriors of you all in name and in deed."

The shrill sahuagin applause rippled across the amphitheater, growing steadily.

"No!"

The hoarse shout rang over the amphitheater. Laaqueel felt the movement along her lateral lines. She turned and found Maartaaugh striding toward Iakhovas.

"You will not be king here," Maartaaugh swore. "You are not from our sea. You are not of our heritage. You will not usurp our waters."

Silence immediately filled the waters as the sahuagin audience waited to see what would happen. Only the throbbing crescendo of the whale song continued unabated.

"Would you die then, Maartaaugh?" Iakhovas asked. "Would you challenge me and lose your life as Toomaaek did, unable to even fight for your people or the place they deserve in Serôs?"

Maartaaugh slammed the butt of his trident against the inset stones that made up the amphitheater's floor.

"I will not die," the prince said. "Aleaxtis will have one of its own as king."

"I would kill you," Iakhovas stated flatly. "I would rend your flesh from your bones and feed it to those you claim to lead."

"That remains to be seen."

Maartaaugh's courage held him despite the carnage he had seen Iakhovas do.

Laaqueel felt the tension in the water, could feel Maartaaugh's heart beating rapidly through her lateral lines. Surely Sekolah's will would be served now.

"If you wish to dispute my right to the throne," Iakhovas said in a soft, deadly voice, "then I will name the challenge."

Maartaaugh nodded.

Iakhovas swung to the crowd. "In order to prove my worth—to become your king, to take upon myself the right to lead you in your greatest battle—I will slay the Great Whale Bard who even now blocks passage through the Sharksbane Wall."

Excited conversation started up again.

"If I can't do what I say," Iakhovas went on, "then let me die as Sekolah would have me: clawing at the face of an enemy." With noble grace, he spun back around to Maartaaugh. "If you wish, I will give you the honor of trying to slay the Great Whale Bard first."

"No," Maartaaugh replied in a quiet voice.

"Then agree to my terms," Iakhovas said. "If I kill the Great Whale Bard and end the threat of the whale song that attacks this place, you will recognize me as king and serve as my grand champion, to renounce and combat any who would attack or challenge me."

Maartaaugh hesitated only a moment, and Laaqueel knew it was because the warrior tried to find a loophole in Iakhovas's offer.

"I will," the prince answered.

"Good," Iakhovas said.

"When will you attempt this?" Ruubuuiz asked.

"Now," Iakhovas said. "There is a war to be fought, and I will tolerate no waiting."

He turned and leaped away, pausing when he was twenty feet above the amphitheater floor.

Laaqueel swam up beside him, seeing him totally in the sahuagin illusion now. He was a proud warrior, his fins flared out and his chest puffed up, gripping the trident in one fist and his crown seated on his broad head. One eye held a golden gleam.

"I am Iakhovas!" he roared. "I am destined to be your king!"

The sahuagin crowd exploded into movement. They slapped their feet against the stones and whistled and clicked in full support. There were even comments from some that Iakhovas was Daganisoraan, the greatest sahuagin warrior of all, reborn.

"Iakhovas!" some of them began to chant. "Defender and king! Iakhovas!"

"I will bring you victory!" Iakhovas declared. "Meat is meat!"

"Meat is meat!" the crowd roared back.

⊐⊢――――⊣⊏

"It looks like they're waiting for something," Sabyna said.

She kept a low profile on the hill overlooking the stretch of coastline below her.

"Something," Glawinn replied, "or someone."

The paladin lay beside her on the hard, rocky ground. He wore hunter's leather instead of his armor and carried his sword in a plain scabbard.

"They could be waiting for Vurgrom to join them," Azla added. She lay in the tall grass on the other side of the paladin, the spyglass they'd been sharing pulled tight to her eye. "Or perhaps they're putting in to harbor for a few days to join him at a later time."

Irritated at the position they'd been thrust into, Sabyna glared at the pirates. The pirate ship *Brave Wager* rested at anchor in the small, natural harbor. Her sails were furled around her masts, looking for all the world like she was an innocent merchanter taking advantage of a brief respite before sailing dangerous waters again.

Part of the crew maintained lean-tos on the shore under broad-leafed trees. Blackened pits showed where they'd roasted wild pigs and deer they'd brought back from the forest surrounding the harbor. Fishing and crabbing were plentiful as well.

Azla's charts called this island, which lay to the southwest of Agenais, either Zagrus or Kloccbarn, as if the cartographer was unable to chose one name or the other.

After Sabyna returned to *Azure Dagger* and told her story of the men she'd seen at the apothecary's, Azla continued work on the ship. When *Azure Dagger* was fit for sailing a few days later, her replaced masts securely in place and completely outfitted, they'd gone sailing, using the enchanted astrolabe as a guide.

Vurgrom's ship maintained a steady route in the sea way between the Whamite Isles and Turmish, gliding as restlessly as a shark. Even as they prepared to set an intercept course for Maelstrom, one of Azla's crew spotted *Brave Wager* in the distance.

Rather than risk getting caught between the two ships they knew of, and perhaps more, Azla decided to wait *Brave Wager* out and see if they couldn't gather more information on what Vurgrom was doing.

While they'd been in port at Agenais, stories continued flowing in from new arrivals. Sahuagin, koalinth, morkoth, and other sea species continued to raid the surface world nations and take ships. Their goal appeared to be to rid the Sea of Fallen Stars of anything that traveled over the water.

Some of the sea captains even brought news that uneasy alliances between the surface world nations were starting to unravel as realms in turn accused other realms of being involved in the sea-spawned threat. Assassins were rumored to ply their trade on and off the sea. There were still others who insisted the assassins were hired by the different aquatic races.

Trade routes and communication lanes broke down. The Sea of Fallen Stars became a battlefield, something it hadn't been in over four hundred years.

"I've got to get back to my ship," Azla announced. "There's still some trim and other work I want to see to while we're here." She passed the spyglass over to Glawinn, who thanked her for the loan. "Let me know if anything develops."

"I will, lady," the paladin promised.

Sabyna rolled up into a sitting position, still behind the brush and below the ledge so the pirates couldn't see her. She wrapped her arms around her legs and held them tightly. "I'll stay here as well."

Azla nodded. "I'll have two men spell you when it gets dark." She turned and walked away, making her way carefully down the hillside.

Wanting to take advantage of the waning sunlight, Sabyna took out her book of spells and spent time trying to study. Glawinn lay across the ridge, as calm and still as any animal that made its home in the forest. The ship's mage found that irritating.

"Is something wrong, lady?"

"I want to know Jherek is all right." It had been nearly two tendays since she'd last seen him.

"You can look to your own heart for that."

"So you say."

"Trust me, lady. When you feel as drawn to someone as you do to the young warrior, you'll know when something happens to him."

"How do you know?"

"Because it has happened to me."

Startled and embarrassed at her own thoughtlessness, Sabyna glanced up at the paladin. His dark eyes were filled with old pain that time failed to erase.

"I'm sorry," she said.

"As am I." Glawinn returned his attention to the spyglass and said, "Sometimes, in order to love fully and completely, you have to let the other go. When they return, you'll find the bond between you is even stronger."

"I don't know that he will be back. There seems to be so much distance between us."

"Trust," Glawinn urged. "It's all you can do."

"I prefer a much more active solution."

"Then study, lady, that you may get better at your own skills," the paladin suggested. "Wherever you go, however this may turn out between you and the young warrior, you need to be as strong as you can be."

Reluctantly, Sabyna took out her book again and applied herself to her studies. Still, she felt as though she were on the edge of the world, peering down into a bottomless abyss.

"We've not seen the worst of this yet, have we?" she asked.

"No," Glawinn replied softly. "No, lady, I'm afraid we haven't."

Laaqueel stood on *Tarjana*'s deck and stared at the Great Whale Bard. The creature floated in the currents before the broken section of the Sharksbane Wall, flanked by other whales. The great whale was over four hundred feet long from its blunt head to its tail flukes. Gray-blue skin stood out against the blue-green sea so it looked more like a shadow than a solid thing. The whale song continued to echo in shrill squeaks and moans around Hunter's Ridge. *He knows you're coming,* she told Iakhovas when he joined her.

Of course he does. Iakhovas looked at her and grinned. *Can't you smell the fear on him, little malenti?*

Laaqueel said nothing. She couldn't smell fear from the great whale, but she sensed the anticipation from the sahuagin who ringed the mountains around her. Not far away, Maartaaugh and Ruubuuiz stood together, out of safe crossbow shot from the few sea elves that still manned the makeshift garrison.

Iakhovas held a harpoon in one fist. The thick shaft bore runes etched in black. The metal blade gleamed as though a fresh edge had just been put on it.

Why didn't you challenge Maartaaugh and be done with it? Laaqueel asked. *You could have beaten him easily.*

Little malenti, Iakhovas said patiently, *there is still much you have to learn when it comes to leading warriors. In Waterdeep, though our forces were turned away, we killed many of our enemies, destroyed their boats, and burned their buildings and homes. Though it was a loss in some respects, I taught We Who Eat of the Claarteeros Sea that they could win. They knew before that they could fight the surface world, but never before had they known they could win.*

The whale song continued unabated, throbbing through the water, racing with the currents. It was hard for Laaqueel to stand there and take the whale's abuse. A few of the sahuagin who came from Vahaxtyl to watch succumbed to the whale song's thrall and returned to their city.

Once I gave them that, Iakhovas continued, *Baldur's Gate could not stand against them. The Great Whale Bard will be Serôs' Waterdeep. It will teach these warriors here that anything is possible, and it will give notice to the sea elves and others that would stand in our way.* He grinned, and his golden eye gleamed. *What other creature can sing its death song the length and breadth of the Sea of Fallen Stars?*

Iakhovas signaled to one of the sahuagin warriors in *Tarjana*'s stern. The warrior started beating the drum brought up from below-decks. The basso booms echoed through the water, partially masking the whale song.

The sahuagin warriors aboard the mudship picked up the rhythm, slapping their webbed feet against the deck, creating hollow detonations that amplified the frenetic beat. Within the space of a few heartbeats, the sahuagin warriors along Hunter's Ridge picked up the rhythm as well, slapping their hands and feet against the ocean floor or banging rocks together.

Wish me well, little malenti.

Iakhovas leaped off the mudship. His illusion as a sahuagin warrior for the moment was complete. Not even Laaqueel could tell he was anything else.

He swam strongly, straight for the waiting whales as if propelled by the savage beat of the sahuagin. The long harpoon stayed close at his side.

Just over the broken section of the Sharksbane Wall, unchallenged by the sea elves who knew they were not his targets, Iakhovas halted in the water. He was less than a hundred feet from the Great Whale Bard.

"I am Iakhovas!" he roared. "And I will be your death!"

He swam straight at the great whale like a crossbow bolt.

17

Confusion consumed Laaqueel's thoughts as she watched Iakhovas close on the Great Whale Bard. The confrontation with the priestesses of Vahaxtyl weighed heavily on her mind. The closest Sekolah came to involving himself in his children's worship of him was when he sent avatars to inspire their blood frenzy, and that almost never happened.

Though she believed Iakhovas when he said he played no part in the matter, she couldn't help questioning whether her defense had come from Sekolah. She couldn't answer why the Shark God would choose to defend a malenti priestess. Malenti birth was only a sign that the sahuagin lived too close to the sea elves, their sworn enemies. There was nothing positive about being a malenti, nothing in their scriptures to suggest that Sekolah would show any kind of special interest.

Her line of thinking pointed her back to Iakhovas. Either he had engineered the priestesses' deaths and gotten away with lying to her, or he was as important to Sekolah's bloody designs as he said he was. Laaqueel's faith was torn in both directions. She was afraid to believe and fool herself, and afraid not to believe and take away the last vestiges of herself she had left, trapped by her own need for understanding.

She stood on *Tarjana*'s deck amid the sahuagin warriors as they kept up the frantic rhythm and watched Iakhovas approach the Great Whale Bard.

The whale song boomed through the water, partially obscured by the throbbing sahuagin beat. The Great Whale Bard shifted only slightly to face his approaching foe.

Taker.

The whale's voice rolled like thunder through Laaqueel's mind. From the way the sahuagin stopped slapping their hands and feet and rocks, the malenti priestess knew they'd all heard it too.

"Death," Iakhovas snarled, not slowing his pace toward the

giant creature. The great whale was nearly fifty times bigger than Iakhovas.

There is only belief. High Priestess Ghaataag had told Laaqueel that when the young malenti was first accepted into Sekolah's temple. Belief made a priestess strong, while knowledge took strength away. Never before had Laaqueel so fully understood that insight.

Two killer whales raced for Iakhovas. Their black and white bodies sped through the water, cutting across currents more swiftly even than sahuagin could swim. Iakhovas swam straight for them, never veering from the Great Whale Bard.

At the last moment, Iakhovas shifted, diving below the lead killer whale. He dragged his harpoon's edge along the killer whale's underside, splitting it open and gutting it in a bloody rush that fogged the water. Iakhovas disappeared, lost in the dark red haze.

When he burst through the bloody mist on the other side, the sahuagin warriors broke out in lusty cheers. They slapped the ocean floor with their feet and clapped their hands again, finding the savage rhythm of a raging heart.

Silently, Laaqueel prayed that Sekolah would take Iakhovas from them, prayed that the Shark God would allow the whales their victory, prayed that she would know now if Iakhovas was savior or slayer to her people.

The second killer whale finned around and streaked for Iakhovas again as sharks broke the tethers of their sahuagin masters and dived for the floating corpse of the first. Iakhovas turned once more, quickly overtaken by the killer whale. He dodged it, bumping his chest against his opponent's sleek underbelly. Iakhovas hooked the claws of his free hand into the exposed flesh, followed almost immediately by his foot claws.

Latched onto the killer whale like a barnacle, Iakhovas ripped through its flesh and pierced its heart. Convulsions wracked the killer whale as Iakhovas leaped from it toward the Great Whale Bard.

Other whales surged forward protectively.

Stay back, the Great Whale Bard ordered. *This has already been writ. We have done what we could. Those of you who can escape alive must do so.*

Reluctantly, the other whales ceased moving.

The Time of Tempering has come then, the massive voice proclaimed, *but you will not have everything you seek, Taker.*

"I will!" Iakhovas roared. "It will all be mine again!"

No. For all your plans and machinations, there is one you did not count on, one whom you could not know of.

Laaqueel felt the certainty of the Great Whale Bard's words in her mind.

"You lie!" Iakhovas screamed.

He reached the Great Whale Bard and slashed with his harpoon, driving it deep into the creature's blunt snout. The Great Whale Bard screamed in agony, disrupting the whale song. The other whales tried to continue, but without the Great Whale Bard to lead them and tie their voices together, the mystic enchantment lost most of its power. Laaqueel felt the change. The stomach-twisting nausea left her.

Still roaring in savage rage, Iakhovas dragged the harpoon free, tearing a large wound in the great whale's snout. The creature tried to move to avoid its attacker or to strike back, Laaqueel wasn't sure, but it moved far too slowly to escape Iakhovas's wrath. The harpoon buried into the great whale's flesh again and again, releasing clouds of blood into the water.

Even as she prayed, Laaqueel knew there could be no other end to the battle. With the blood in the water, not all the details of the fight were visible, but the malenti priestess watched as Iakhovas hooked his claws into the Great Whale Bard's side and clambered up to the top of its head.

The frenetic beat of webbed feet against stone and mud continued throbbing through the waters surrounding Hunter's Ridge. None of the elves dared leave their garrisons, and less of them were visible now.

Still hooked into the whale's flesh, Iakhovas pulled himself to the top of the head. He located the great whale's blowhole and shoved himself down inside. The creature continued to swim, but its movements quickly grew weaker. Blood fountained from the blowhole in increasing volume, like smoke from a surface worlder's campfire. The Great Whale Bard screamed in denial and fear. The sound echoed through the sea, and Laaqueel knew that Iakhovas had been right: the Great Whale Bard's death would undoubtedly be heard throughout all of Serôs.

The great whale's tail drooped, no longer moving. Only then did Laaqueel notice that the other whales were in full retreat. Their song had stopped.

The huge corpse turned slowly, like a ship combating an unfavorable wind. Incredibly, the small jaw hinged to the bottom of the huge blunt head opened. Blood spewed out in a violent rush, revealing the massive damage that had been dealt to the creature's insides.

When the currents washed the blood away, Iakhovas stood revealed, levering the jaw open by pushing against the whale's upper jaw. Still holding the Great Whale Bard's jaw open, he screamed defiantly, "I am *Iakhovas!* I am your king!"

The sahuagin warriors screamed with him, defiant and exhilarated.

"Meat is meat!" Iakhovas yelled. "Come eat of the feast I have laid before you!"

The sahuagin surged forward, filling the water as they streamed through the broken section of the Sharksbane Wall. They descended on the Great Whale Bard's corpse like carrion crabs.

Laaqueel stayed on *Tarjana*'s deck. She knew her absence among their ranks wouldn't go unnoticed, but she had no heart to join them. All she felt inside was a curious emptiness.

"All hail King Iakhovas the Deliverer!" one of the sahuagin warriors shouted as the feeding frenzy filled the ocean with blood. The other warriors took up the shout, and the sound filled the currents. They slapped their hands and feet against the whale's corpse, finding the savage rhythm again.

Laaqueel wrapped her hand around the white shark symbol that lay between her breasts and prayed. She found no comfort in an act that used to come so naturally to her.

"Aye, an' there's trouble afoot, friend Pacys."

Drawn from his work on the saceddar, the old bard glanced up at the dwarf. Khlinat's face was grim and hard. The last sweet notes from the saceddar died away.

"What is it?" the bard asked.

Khlinat pointed forward with his bearded chin and said, "It appears we've run afoul of a war party of mermen. They're refusing to let us pass through."

"Why?"

Pacys uncoiled from the flat rock on the sea bottom where he'd been working while the caravan took a brief respite. They'd crossed the outer edges of the Hmur Plateau a couple days back. At present, they were only a few miles east of the Pirate Isles.

"I'm figurin' the merfolk don't exactly take to what looks like a military group paradin' through their land. At least, that's the gist of what I heard afore I decided to come back for ye."

"What does Reefglamor say?" Pacys asked, securing the saceddar to his back.

"A whole lot," the dwarf replied, "but ain't none of it doing him any good. Him and that merman baron are both puffing up like toads. Me, I'm keeping a ready hand for me axe."

The old bard launched himself into the water, and Khlinat followed him. Pacys swam easily, making his way along the caravan line to the front. Undersea mountains around the Pirate Isles made their journey hard even for swimmers. Bands of raiding seawolves and scrags had attacked them during the nights, costing them nearly a dozen warriors before they were turned back. The mountains created too many potential ambush points, but the deeper water toward the center of the Hmur Plateau offered dangers as well. The depths also shortened even the sea elves' undersea vision to but a few feet.

The sea elf rangers among the caravan saw to the care of the narwhals and sea turtles that pulled the flat supply sleds. The warriors formed protective units around the steep hills, stationed in positions that allowed them to see in all directions.

Even with the bright sunlight streaming through the shallows, Pacys didn't see Reefglamor and the mermen until he was a hundred feet away. Twenty warriors floated behind the merman baron with their tridents in their fists.

Reefglamor stood on a small rise in front of the baron, "You must let us pass," he said.

"No." The merman baron studied Pacys as the bard approached. His tone turned derisive. "You even brought humans with you."

"This is not an ordinary human," Reefglamor argued. "This is the Taleweaver. Your people have legends of the Taker . . ."

"Yes."

The baron didn't appear convinced. He was broad and muscled. His long brown hair floated over his shoulders, following the path of the currents that swept over the area. Tattoos covered his arms and chest, and a spiral representing Eadro decorated his right cheek.

"Then you've heard of the Taleweaver, Baron Tallos," Reefglamor persisted.

The baron narrowed his eyes. "Those tales have been twice-told hundreds of times over," he argued. "I choose not to believe in them as much as some of my people do."

"Then your arrogance lends itself to ignorance," Reefglamor accused.

Tallos flicked his tail in irritation and shot a hand out to adjust his momentum. "Swim carefully in these waters, old fins," he warned.

The old sea elf drew himself up to his full height. "I am Taranath Reefglamor, Senior High Mage of Sylkiir."

"I was told who you are," the baron snapped. "Yet you still stand before me on two legs, sea elf, and I tell you that no one not blessed by Eadro with fins and a tail is a true creature of Serôs. Your people migrated here out of their own fear and prejudice. We have always been here."

Rage darkened the High Mage's features. At his side, Pharom Ildacer moved forward. Even as the merman warriors reacted by dropping their tridents toward the sea elves, Reefglamor placed a hand on his friend's chest. Ildacer stopped reluctantly.

"We only want to travel to Myth Nantar," Reefglamor said. "We must see to it that the Taleweaver arrives there safely."

"Not across my lands." Tallos glared at the old bard. "I'll not have a sea elf army moving through my city, or anywhere near it."

"We travel for the good of Serôs," Reefglamor protested. "If we don't stand against the Taker, all of our world may fall."

"The good of Serôs," Tallos echoed. "As I recall, the *alu Tel'Quessir* have long held that as a reason for their attempts to take over all of Serôs. How many have died as your people have tried to force their will on others? The Eleventh Serôs War was fought over the same beliefs. Well, we don't hold forth those beliefs. We don't even presume to know what's best for Serôs. We take care of our own, and life in these waters would be far better if others took care to do the same."

Reefglamor had no reply, visibly stung by the merman's hard tone and words.

"Myth Nantar was another vessel of sea elven conspiracy," Tallos continued. "Better it should remain buried behind the mythal that binds it than to return to this world."

"Prophecy has declared that the City of Destinies is the place where the Taker might be destroyed," Reefglamor said.

"So say you, elf."

"Your people have those prophecies as well."

"Mayhap you'd be surprised how few of my people are willing to trust the *alu Tel'Quessir* these days."

Reefglamor shook his head. "Unrest and strife stir the waters and echo on the currents," he said. "The sahuagin are once more free to roam all of Serôs. Surely you've noticed this."

"I've heard," Tallos answered coldly. "I've also heard that it was the sea elves themselves who shattered the Sharksbane Wall."

"Why in all the seas would we have done that?"

"Because to get to you, the sahuagin must first run through the Hmur Plateau—where the mermen live," the merman accused.

"Your King Vhaemas can't believe that."

"The king," Tallos admitted, "is more reluctant than some, but all are aware that there is no love lost between the sea elves and the merfolk."

"This is bigger than the animosity that lies between our people," Reefglamor said.

"If it were," Tallos countered, "wouldn't Coronal Semphyr or Cormal Ytham have sent you with more troops? Or approached our king first to request passage through our lands?"

"They, too, are blind to the dangers we face."

Tallos regarded the old mage, then said, "If your own people don't believe in you and your journey, why should I?"

"Because it is the truth," Reefglamor said.

"Not my truth."

Without another word, Reefglamor turned and motioned his warriors and fellow mages back.

"What will we do?" Jhanra Merlistar asked.

"We have no choice," Reefglamor answered. "We'll have to go around the plateau, along the western edge."

"That's insane," Ildacer stated harshly. "Those waters are filled with koalinth tribes who would waste no time attacking us. Only fools would swim there."

"The only other choice would be to head to the east and go through the deeper waters there," Reefglamor offered.

"Senior," the chief guardsman said, "I would prefer—"

"As would I," Reefglamor snapped irritably. "We're in agreement that the depths are too dangerous. We will go around to the west. Have someone inform your warriors and the caravan leaders."

Pacys thought about the proposed journey. It would add tendays, perhaps as much as a month to their time. That was just not acceptable.

Yet, as he looked at the merman baron's hard face, he knew the decision would stand.

Both the sea elves and the mermen turned suddenly toward the south, their weapons falling naturally into their hands. Pacys prepared himself, wondering what it was they sensed. His eyes revealed nothing but the murky water that took away his vision. All at once the currents swirling around him became a wave that rocked him.

Behind the wave came the death cry of the Great Whale Bard. Hearing it, the old bard knew it belonged to no other. Tears welled in his eyes as he remembered the great creature and the gift it had given so freely while calmly accepting its own fate.

"Taleweaver?" Reefglamor called out, swimming toward him. "What was that?"

"The sahuagin have slain the Great Whale Bard," Pacys replied. "Now there is nothing to hold back the sea devils."

Standing in *Steadfast*'s prow, his cutlass in his hands, Jherek stared at the huge, dark cloud that rode low over the ocean. The ship was ahead of the cloud, only a few miles southwest of Aglarond. The whale song stopped abruptly the day before, but the sense of direction that had dawned in the young sailor's breast remained constant.

He shaded his eyes with his hand. Perspiration cooled him in the sea breeze as his heart resumed a steadier beat. He'd worked himself hard the last hour, concentrating on the cutlass and hook as he went through the exercises Malorrie and Glawinn had shown him. The exertion kept his thoughts reined in, away from the memory of Sabyna and the sweet kiss they'd exchanged.

Tarnar ran up the steps, joining him. "I thought at first it was a cloud," the captain said, "but I'd never seen one settle so close to the sea and be so small. Thought it might be fog, then I thought perhaps it was a sail."

"No," Jherek said, tracking the jerky, fluttering movement visible within the mass now. "Those are birds. Scavengers." Even as he realized it, his stomach lurched and filled with cold acid.

Bringing his spyglass up to his eye, Tarnar swept the sky ahead. "You're right, but I've never seen so many."

Jherek hadn't either. Thousands of seagulls, pelicans, fisherhawks, and smaller birds skirled through the limited air space above the sea, eagerly seeking an opening. During a voyage on *Butterfly* last year, Finaren had spied a derelict at sea. Upwind of her, Jherek hadn't smelled the carrion stench of the ship until they'd thrown grappling hooks over the railing and prepared to tie on.

Birds had exploded from the decks and broken windows, frightened from the grisly repast they'd helped themselves to. The young sailor had never learned the reason why the crew had killed each other, but there was no doubt that they had. Finaren had guessed that some mage-inspired madness or a curse had overtaken them. No one had lived. For tendays afterward, Jherek remembered the bloated and beak-stripped faces in his nightmares.

"It means there's death waiting up there," the young sailor said hoarsely.

Tarnar didn't bother to disagree.

"Cap'n," the sailor in the crow's nest bellowed. "Got something off the starboard side."

Jherek stepped to the railing, the cutlass still tight in his fist. A sapphire whale, named for the blue flukes it bore, surfaced in the water only a few yards from *Steadfast*. Twenty feet long and easily eight feet in diameter at its thickest part, the sapphire whale could have been a formidable opponent for the caravel. It glided easily just above the water, making no move toward the ship.

"Lady look over us," the sailor in the crow's nest called out, "there are more of 'em out there, Cap'n."

As though appearing from nowhere, the whales rose to the ocean's surface, quickly flanking *Steadfast*'s port and starboard sides.

"They want us to stop," Jherek said.

"They've given us no choice," Tarnar growled. He turned and shouted orders to the first mate to drop their canvas. "The good thing is, if they wanted to, they could have already reduced *Steadfast* to so much kindling. I'm taking this as a good sign."

The caravel drifted to a stop, resting easily against the whales' broad backs. Tarnar gave the order to drop anchor. Crewmen spun the anchor chain on the drum, paying out the length.

Jherek peered across the hundred yards that separated the ship from the cloud of scavengers working at the waterline. They looked as though they were settling on a small island barely jutting up from the sea.

Tarnar put his spyglass in the sash at his waist and walked cautiously to the railing to peer down at the whales. Porpoises raced through the water around the whales, occasionally leaping up and disappearing beneath the waves again.

"What do they want?" the captain asked.

Jherek shook his head, then a ghostly whisper trickled through his mind. *Jherek, you must come with us.* The voice wasn't the same as the one that had contacted him days ago.

"They want me," the young sailor said.

"How do you know?" Tarnar demanded.

"They just told me."

The captain looked at him as if he'd gone mad.

"You can't hear them?" Jherek asked, amazed that the man could not.

"No."

Jherek, there is not much time remaining. You must accompany us.

Fear and wonderment touched the young sailor's heart. Even days ago when he'd felt the pull and heard the whale song and the voice, he hadn't been as moved. Gazing out at the scavenging birds, he felt the world close in around him.

"Why do they want you?" Tarnar asked.

"I don't know," the young sailor answered.

The sapphire whale swam alongside the caravel, bumping gently up against it. *Steadfast* bobbed in response.

Come, Jherek Whalefriend. Come and learn.

The young sailor peered down into the whale's eye, seeing the intelligence there.

"What are you going to do?" Tarnar asked.

Jherek clung to the railing, squinting against the wind in his face. "We have no choice. I don't think they'll let the ship proceed unless I find out what they want."

Tarnar was quiet for a moment. "If you go into that water, you're taking your life in your own hands."

"Aye." Jherek nodded.

"We're carrying Cormyrean dried pepper seasoning as part of our cargo," Tarnar said. "I can have the men ready the ship and dump a few pepper barrels into the water. It'll burn those whales—chase them away and give us a chance to run. The wind favors us."

"No." Jherek bent and pulled his boots off. "We've come all this way following the whale song. To try to leave without finding out where it led would be a waste of our time."

"Then I'll come with you."

"And leave *Steadfast* without her captain?" Jherek gazed at the man. "What kind of decision would that be?"

Tarnar looked out to sea. "You're talking to a failed priest, Jherek," he said. "If these creatures aren't here for your life, then this has got to be some kind of . . . divine experience. I wouldn't want to miss out on that."

Alone, the voice whispered into Jherek's mind. He repeated the request to the captain.

Tarnar clearly wasn't happy with the stipulation. His face hardened. "Go then, but I'm not going to leave you out here on your own."

"Weigh the risk if it comes to that," Jherek said softly. "One man isn't worth your ship and crew."

"Mystra keep you in her graces." Tarnar offered his arm.

Jherek took the captain's hand and shook it. Barefoot now, his dagger sheathed to one leg and the cutlass through the sash at his waist, he stepped over the railing and dropped into the sea. He hit feet first and slid through the blue-green water. From under the surface, where the largest portion of the whale's mass was, the creature looked even bigger.

No fear, the whale urged him, bumping up against him with her rough body. *You are the one to be known as Whalefriend.*

Why?

We will explain what we may. Please, climb on my back and I will save you the swim. The whale sunk lower in the water and came close enough to Jherek that they touched.

Hesitantly, the young sailor hooked his fingers over the sapphire whale's dorsal fin and pulled himself aboard. Jherek didn't look back, concentrating on the birds before him.

The whale swam swiftly, skimming along the ocean's surface while the other whales and dolphins opened the path. As they neared the mass in the sea, the cries of the feathered scavengers reached a crescendo, a vibrant clamoring of hunger and rage. The young sailor recognized the mutilated remains of the largest whale he'd ever seen.

The dead whale floated just below the surface, buoyed up in death. The sea rarely hid her dead unless they went down in ships or the scavengers got to them too quickly. Crabs scuttled across the corpse, hiding in pockets of pink-white flesh as they ate their fill and avoided the larger birds that would have eaten them as well. Fish of all sizes and colors darted about at the waterline, and Jherek knew there would be even more working the dead whale's underbelly.

An overwhelming sense of loss filled the young sailor as he surveyed the carnage. Fresh in death, the whale would float for a few days before the sea dragged it back down. Even then, it would be a long time before it was stripped down to its bones.

The sapphire whale closed on the corpse, nudging up against it tenderly. Crabs, fish, and birds fled from that small area.

This was Song Who Brings Bright Rains.

Jherek recognized the name. "What happened?"

The Taker slew him.

"Why?"

Because the whales joined together in song in an attempt to block the sahuagin from entering Serôs.

Jherek remained silent for a long moment, hardly able to think in the cacophony of sounds that filled the air. Fish bumped up against his feet and ankles in the water.

"Why have I been brought here?"

Because your coming was foretold in our legends. Song Who Brings Bright Rains had a gift he was meant to give you.

"Why?" Jherek tried desperately to understand, but he couldn't find a foundation.

You are the Whalefriend, the sapphire whale replied as if that answered everything.

"I don't understand."

We are here to help you understand, but you must claim the gift Song Who Brings Bright Rains had for you.

"Where?"

It is on the body. The Taker never suspected it was there. The magic that guards it is very strong.

"All my life," Jherek said numbly, "I have heard a voice in my head at times. Was it one of your people?"

No, Whalefriend, that was another.

"Who?"

That is not for us to say. We only have our part. If you live, you will one day know all. That is all we know. Go. Get the gift that has been held for you. You have far to travel, and there is much danger for you to face.

The whale's muscles rippled along its back. Taking the hint, Jherek lifted himself from the water and stood on the animal's back. Even walking barefoot was tricky. The whale's hide was slick. His stomach cringed as he stepped onto the great whale's carcass.

The corpse's buoyancy caused it to bob under his feet. Water rushed in and swirled over his ankles, mixing with the bright red blood. Birds took wing before him, revealing even more of the ravaged flesh. The young sailor steeled his mind and made himself go forward when everything in him wanted to turn back to *Steadfast.*

"What is my destiny?" Jherek asked.

You are to be the Whalefriend.

Jherek kept going, feeling the greasy flesh twist and turn beneath his feet.

"What am I supposed to do?"

You will be a friend to our people. In times of need, you will champion us.

Jherek tried to imagine anything the whales would need him to champion for and couldn't. Anything that could kill the creature he now walked on would be far too powerful for him to combat.

You have only just begun your revelations, Jherek Whalefriend. You do not yet know what you will be.

"Then tell me."

I cannot.

For a moment, the young sailor faltered. Was this going to be another false trail? Another game played by the voice that had haunted him? Or had he been lured to his death this time?

Look to your heart for strength and you will find it, Jherek Whalefriend. You have always been much stronger than you have thought. This is one of the things Song Who Brings Bright Rains has always told us of you.

"How did he know?"

With quiet determination, Jherek resumed his search. The sheer savagery that had torn the great whale continued unabated, and the young sailor knew the sahuagin had eaten their fill of the whale when the Taker had slain it.

He has always known. The whale bard that trained him told him, and the story came from the whale bard before him.

"They knew about *me*?" Jherek couldn't believe it.

They knew someone would come, the sapphire whale replied, *and they knew you would be recognized when the time came.*

Jherek struggled with what he was being told even as he skidded and slipped across the great whale's corpse.

"How could they know?"

The whale bards of Serôs have always been powerful in the ways of knowing. We choose to remain apart from most of those who live below and above because most ignore us. In times past, we have been ostracized for being harbingers, and even the surface folk hunted us for the ambergris. You are a sailor, Jherek Whalefriend, and you have ties to the sea. You can feel in your heart the twists and turns of wind and sea. How can you know these things?

Some of the larger birds challenged Jherek as he advanced. The young sailor drew his cutlass and used the flat of the blade to knock the more aggressive ones aside. He didn't want to kill them. The birds served a purpose in disposing of the body.

"Where is this thing I am supposed to find?"

You are looking for it. You will never find it that way. Close your eyes and feel for it as you felt for the whale song.

Doubt gnawed at Jherek's thoughts. He felt as though he was in a dream, that he might wake up at any moment to find himself in a hammock aboard *Steadfast*. If he'd really believed what was going on, what he was taking part in, he didn't know how he would have reacted. The numbness inside allowed him to remain focused.

The young sailor stopped and closed his eyes. It was hard to concentrate with all the angry cries of the birds around him.

Feel with your heart, Jherek Whalefriend. Your heart will always guide you if you listen to it.

Growing frantic with frustration, Jherek tried to relax. The birds distracted him, but the feel of the dead, rubbery flesh underfoot distracted him more. Still, with everything that had happened, how could he walk away?

He felt it. The small tugging pulled at the center of his chest. He concentrated on the sensation and slowly opened his eyes. Following the tug, he shoved his way through the large, ungainly birds, shooing them into the air.

Only a few feet farther on, he dropped to his knees, knowing whatever he searched for was below him. Water occupied pockets torn from the whale's flesh, mixed with ropes of congealed blood. A few hermit crabs occupied the small pools, drawing back tightly into their borrowed shells at his approach.

"It's inside the body," the young sailor rasped.

Yes, the whale replied. *That is where Song Who Brings Bright Rains carried it, as did the whale bards before him. You must cut it out.*

Jherek surveyed the dead flesh, knowing the whale was long past any suffering. He raised the cutlass and prepared himself to drive it down into the corpse. His hands shook with the effort, then he lowered the blade.

"I can't."

The birds shrilled angrily all around him, fluttering through the air above. Feathers flew as the scavengers battled each other for access.

Place your hand on the spot where the gift is, the sapphire whale encouraged. *Perhaps there is another way. The tie between it and you is very strong.*

Hesitantly, given strength by the numbness and desire within him, Jherek placed his hand over the spot where he believed the gift to be. Vibrations tingled against his palm. For a moment he believed it was only the ocean rocking the great carcass.

Iridescent tendrils shot up from the whale flesh and encircled Jherek's left wrist. Panicked, he tried to yank his arm back. On the third attempt, the tendrils still crawling around his forearm, a silvery mass of red, crimson, scarlet, yellow, and pink tore free of the whale's body.

Do not fear, the sapphire whale encouraged. *This is the gift—nothing more.*

Unable to get away from the wriggling rainbow-colored mass shifting along his arm, Jherek stared at it. His reflection in the polished sheen stared back at him. The mass smoothed out, becoming a thick bracer that covered him from his wrist almost to his elbow. A protective cuff flared out over the back of his hand to his knuckles. The colors twisted in stripes, each leading to the other. Instead of feeling cold and heavy, the bracer felt warm and light, like another coat of skin though it was nearly an inch thick.

"What is this?" he asked.

Designs surfaced on the rainbow bracer, distinct whorls and loops that looked like nothing the young sailor had ever seen.

It is your gift, Jherek Whalefriend. A gift that makes you one of our pod, a gift that will protect you in your direst need, and it is a weapon that will serve you against the Taker. It is also the first step you must take on the path to your destiny.

Turning his attention from the shiny bracer to the sapphire whale, Jherek demanded, "What destiny?"

Again, it is not for me to say.

"I won't accept that," Jherek declared.

He pulled at the bracer, managing to get a finger down inside the tight fit along his arm. Even then he thought the bracer only allowed him to do that so he wouldn't hurt himself. As he continued to dig, the bracer turned liquid under his questing finger—for just a heartbeat—and he pulled through. The bracer flowed back together almost instantly and was solid once more.

You have no choice.

"I will always have a choice," Jherek said.

You came here. You are the one, the sapphire whale told him. *You are the Taker's Bane. Every choice you make will be right for you and for your destiny. There is no wrong way for you to go. You have only to accept the power and responsibility that will be yours.*

"And if I don't?"

That will be your choice, and it will be the right one.

Jherek looked around at the dead whale and the scavengers covering it. The birds grew bolder, hissing and crying out as they closed on him. He beat them away with the flat of his blade.

"I don't understand," Jherek said. "I won't accept anything without understanding it first."

You have accepted the bracer, and it has accepted you.

Jherek barely restrained his angry frustration. "There was no acceptance," he claimed. "It attached itself to me."

If it had not been time, if you had not been right, that would not have happened. Only the One may wear Iridea's Tear.

Jherek held up his arm and the sunlight glinted off the rainbow bracer.

"Is this thing alive?" he asked.

No, but it will serve to help keep you living. It will shield you and be a weapon. As you become accustomed to it, you will find that you can shape it to fit your needs. Now be silent, for we must finish the Binding.

The sapphire whale lifted its true voice in song, an ululating chorus that echoed over the water. The other whales joined in and the prickly sensation of an approaching storm blanketed the area.

Questions flooded Jherek's frenzied mind, but before he could ask the first one, blinding pain flared along his left arm where the bracer touched him. Unable to stand, he dropped to his knees, certain that someone had set his arm on fire.

He howled in agony and crawled toward the edge of the whale's carcass, scaring birds from his path. As the song continued, he reached the edge of the corpse and thrust his arm into the seawater, sure the wound he was undoubtedly suffering would kill him—or cost him his arm at the very least.

After what seemed an interminable time, the pain lessened, then went away.

Jherek drew his arm from the water expecting it to be burned clear through the flesh down to the bone. Instead, his arm seemed perfectly healthy, as if nothing had ever happened. Even the multi-colored bracer was gone.

Not gone, the sapphire whale corrected. *The Binding has been completed. You and Iridea's Tear will never be separated as long as life remains within you.*

Still on his knees, the young sailor held his bare arm up for the whale to see. Water droplets clung to his skin.

Iridea's Tear will be your badge, Jherek Whalefriend. In time, you will come to be known by it. But there will be times that you won't want to be known at all. The Binding allows this to happen. Think of the bracer upon your arm.

Jherek didn't want to, but once the thought was in his mind he couldn't help remembering the image.

Crimson, scarlet, yellow, and pink strands erupted from his skin. The strands quickly wove themselves into the bracelet, again running from his wrist to his elbow, the iridescent surface showing no fractures or lines.

The bracer can be easily hidden again when you wish.

Jherek willed the bracer to go away, but it remained upon his arm.

There is much you have to learn, the sapphire whale said. *We will take time to teach you until you are ready to become.*

"Become what?" Jherek persisted.

That which you are destined to be. Nothing more, nothing less.

18

"To me!"

Laaqueel heard Iakhovas's thundering battle cry over the din of war even as she twisted from the path of an attacking ixitxachitl. The malenti priestess swept the barbed net from her hip and threw it at her attacker as it spun gracefully around in the ocean.

The weighted net flared out and enveloped the ixitxachitl, sinking barbed hooks into the creature's flesh. It screamed in rage and pain. Even as the net tangled its wings, Laaqueel drove her trident deep into its body. The ixitxachitl shuddered through its death throes.

"Most Sacred One, let me be of assistance."

Turning, Laaqueel found one of the sahuagin warriors from the outer seas swimming toward her, his movements already registering on her lateral lines. Bleeding from several wounds inflicted by the ixitxachitl fangs, the sahuagin warrior offered her another net. Bits of flesh clung to the coral and steel barbs woven into the strands.

"I will strip the net from this one," the warrior offered. "King Iakhovas will have need of you. The demon rays are attempting to rally their forces."

Laaqueel accepted the net and swam for Iakhovas. She gazed around the ocean floor, studying the buildings that comprised the ixitxachitl community of Ilkanar. Ageadren was the closest ixitxachitl city, but Ilkanar was an outpost town. The tallest structure in the community was the temple, built of coral and stones by the locathah, merrow, and koalinth slaves the ixitxachitls kept.

Iakhovas stood at the forefront of the invading sahuagin forces, ripping apart his foes with trident and claws. Corpses littered the city, including ixitxachitls and the slaves who hadn't quickly chosen sides. Iakhovas's wrath was unforgiving. As the invading army rolled through the resistance put up by the demon rays, the slaves scattered in full revolt, driven before sahuagin who would kill them if they tried to flee.

The oceans' currents darkened with blood.

Even as she drifted down and took her place at Iakhovas's side, he glanced up at her. Gold gleamed in his eye socket.

"Ah, little malenti, come to join the celebration?" he said, holding a bloody chunk of dead ixitxachitl out to her.

"I came to fight at your side."

A cruel smile twisted his lips in both his human and sahuagin guises as they flickered back and forth in Laaqueel's vision.

"As you can see," he said, "there are many who believe in me these days—many ready to fight at my side. I searched for believers, little malenti, and they have found me."

Feeling the spongy surface below the layer of sand at her feet, Laaqueel drove her trident down. Blood spewed up and the ixitxachitl crouched in hiding there flapped in pain. The malenti priestess slit its belly with a talon and watched it swim away to die.

Sharks and sahuagin finned by overhead, chasing all that fled before them that weren't of their kind. It was a whirling maelstrom of slaughter, a true vision of sahuagin power and savagery the like of which Laaqueel had never seen before. By rights, by her heritage, she should have been in bliss—or in a blood frenzy as so many of her brethren were—but she wasn't.

"What about you, little malenti?" Iakhovas asked. "Why do you fight?"

"I live to serve you," she answered. Fear filled her as she gazed at him, knowing he had the power to see through her and the lies she told.

"But do you believe?" Iakhovas asked. "Do you believe in me, or do you fight only to save your own life?"

Laaqueel gazed around them, aware of the fighting taking place. Sahuagin invaded buildings on either side of the thoroughfare, yanking ixitxachitls out and putting them to death where they found them. The slaves died as well. There was no rescue.

Even though the temple stood in the city, very few ixitxachitl priests stood against them. The sahuagin priestesses fought them spell for spell and emerged victorious even if they had to swim over the bodies of those who'd gone before them.

"I believe," Laaqueel replied, "as best as I am able."

She waited, thinking he was going to strike her down where she stood. Over the past few days, he'd been distant from her while plotting his intricate conspiracies.

"In Sekolah or in me?" he asked.

"In my eyes," Laaqueel answered, "you and the Shark God are equal. How could I believe in Sekolah's teaching if I didn't believe in you?"

If the Shark God had cared at all about what she did or thought, the malenti knew she'd have been struck down in that moment for the words of sacrilege she spoke. Instead, she prepared herself for the blow she fully expected from Iakhovas.

He gazed at her for a long time, as if the battle raging around them didn't exist. A disemboweled ixitxachitl drifted by them. Iakhovas angrily swept it away. His living eye showed malignant black as he surveyed her.

"You have changed, little malenti."

"We are all changed."

"I have grown and become more powerful."

"And I have become less so?" Laaqueel asked.

"No, it's not that . . ." Iakhovas waved the sahuagin warriors behind them onward. He paused to glance briefly at the carnage that was reaped in his name, grinning broadly enough to reveal the fangs that filled his sahuagin mouth as well as his human one. "It's just that I've never seen you without vision."

"I don't understand," Laaqueel responded.

"When I first met you all those years ago," Iakhovas said, "when I first saw you, I saw the hunger for power within you. It filled every fiber of your being, little malenti, a force so wild and powerful that for a moment I was afraid—tempted to kill you outright instead of using you."

Laaqueel stood in the middle of the battle waiting patiently. There was nothing she could say. Emptiness swallowed her emotions save for a trace of fear that kept her reactions on the edge.

"I thought I could control that hunger," Iakhovas went on, "so I let you live. In mastering you, though you may not see it that way, I shaped and strengthened that hunger in you."

Shame swept through the malenti priestess because she knew Iakhovas spoke the truth.

"I remember the way you stood up to King Huaanton after we brought Waterdeep to its knees." Iakhovas closed his fist, and it was at once human and sahuagin. "It was something you would have never done had I not entered your life."

Screams punctuated his words.

"I know," Laaqueel said, only because she knew some response was necessary.

"You would have tried to kill him for going against Sekolah's will."

"Yes."

"Then, only a few days ago, two priestesses who would have done harm to you were struck down before you."

Laaqueel knew that was a sore point for Iakhovas. Even though he'd questioned her at length about it, she'd been able to offer no reason why that had happened. That she had no explanation also undermined her own confidence. She didn't know why she couldn't believe Sekolah had acted on her behalf, but she didn't.

"At this point, little malenti," Iakhovas said, "I would think that your hunger would be about to consume you, that you'd want to stretch your talons and see how deeply you could cut into the world."

Laaqueel eyed him levelly and said, "To cut any deeper in this world I'd have to step from your shadow, and that would be dangerous."

For a moment Iakhovas held her gaze, then he tilted back his head and laughed. The deep, roaring bellow echoed through the ixitxachitl outpost, riding on the swirling currents that followed the path of the battle.

"Ah, little malenti, in truth, I had not thought about that. You think you have risen as far as you can go?"

"Yes," Laaqueel answered without hesitation. It was the truth.

"Then you truly have no vision," Iakhovas stated. "Before I am done, I will rule Toril. I will conquer its oceans and coastal lands, then I will find a way into the tender heart of the surface world. I will become the greatest emperor Faerûn—and beyond—has ever known."

"And will you be needing an empress?" Laaqueel challenged.

Iakhovas grinned cruelly. "No, little malenti."

"Then what am I supposed to envision for myself?"

Iakhovas was silent for a time. "Perhaps you are right. I miss the way you were, but should I see those hungry lights in your eyes again, I'll know to guard my back."

Laaqueel crossed her arms over her breasts and asked, "Do you fear me then?"

Cold anger froze Iakhovas's features. "You go too far," he warned.

"Yet you think I don't go far enough."

"Don't ever make that mistake."

Laaqueel shook her head. "What you saw in my eyes when we met wasn't just a hunger for power," she told him, "it was desperation. When I feel desperate, I've found I can do almost anything I need to do."

"And do you feel desperate now, little malenti?"

"No," she said quietly, again telling the truth. "For now, I only feel hollow."

"Perhaps," Iakhovas admitted, "that is a good thing. I will work to instill that hunger in you again, though. I want you to be all that you might be, Most Sacred One."

Laaqueel didn't know what to say. She sensed truth in his words, and that he cared about her in his own way.

"Come," he said after a time. "We have a war to win."

He leaped up and swam through the water, heading for the thick of the diminishing battle.

With nothing else to do, Laaqueel followed.

"To me!" Iakhovas cried with savage glee as he descended on the last rallying point of the ixitxachitl at Ilkanar. With all the priestesses around, he used his magic without fear, making sure no one could trace the efforts back to him.

The ixitxachitls holed up in the temple, holding their own at the doors and windows. Sahuagin clung to the stone walls with their claws, slashing savagely at any demon ray that stayed in the open too long.

Iakhovas battled through ixitxachitls that had been luckless enough to be caught out in the open. His attention riveted on the temple for a moment. Gold gleamed in his scarred eye socket and a thin green ray, almost lost in the swirling blue-green of the sea, stabbed toward the temple.

Without warning, the temple tower's base glowed green. In the next instant the glowing section of the tower turned to fine black dust. Shorn of part of its mooring, the tower fell to the ocean bed. It stretched out far enough to crush two more buildings, then threw a cloud of sand into the water. The hollow thump echoed, followed immediately by the clattering of stones as the temple went to pieces.

Laaqueel stared in disbelief. The ruined tower had killed not only most of the ixitxachitls hiding inside, but a large number of the sahuagin who'd been clinging to the walls.

The tower's destruction signaled the end of the battle. Dozens of demon rays remained, but they fled for their lives, only making the sahuagin and sharks chase them farther to kill them.

"To me!" Iakhovas cried, holding his trident triumphantly overhead. "I have brought you yet another triumph, as I promised."

"Long live King Iakhovas the Deliverer!" someone yelled.

The rest of the sahuagin quickly took up the cry. They slapped their feet against the silt-covered streets of the fallen ixitxachitl outpost, slammed their tridents against the stone walls of the buildings holding only dead and dying, and gave voice to clicks and whistles pledging their support.

Laaqueel kept her silence and her distance. Only she knew the truth of the beast the sahuagin had clutched to their breasts.

"Long live King Iakhovas the Deliverer!"

Jherek flexed his left hand and gazed at the brown skin of his arm, then he closed his hand and visualized the multi-colored bracer covering it. In the space of a heartbeat, the magic armor leaped through his skin and wrapped around his arm in a blur of color. It sparkled in the sun that shone down on *Steadfast*'s deck.

"Do you feel it?" Tarnar asked. The captain stood across from Jherek, sword in his fist.

"No," Jherek replied.

In the seven days that had passed since recovering the Great Whale Bard's gift, not a minute had gone by that the young sailor hadn't thought about Iridea's Tear.

"No extra weight?" the Cormyrean Freesail captain asked.

"No."

"Not even now, when it is manifested upon your arm?"

Jherek shook his head. "It's like it's a part of me," he said. "It's no more noticeable than the hair on my arm."

The caravel stood at anchor at a small cove south of Altumbel. They'd been met by a dozen caravan wagons manned by warriors who swore allegiance to the Simbul, the queen of Aglarond. *Steadfast*'s cargo was parceled out among the wagons even as the caravel's crew took on the goods the caravan had carried overland from Velprintalar, the closest thing to a port city Aglarond had.

Pirate activities in the eastern waters north of Aglarond had increased. Having no regular standing navy and only a small, desperate army, the Simbul had made arrangements with the merchants in Cormyr to avoid the waters with the overland caravan and make the exchange along the southern coast. It wasn't a tactic that would last long, but trapped as Aglarond was between Altumbel and Thay, the realm still needed the glass, iron, and food the merchant ships brought to trade for lumber, gems, and copper.

The southern coastline of Aglarond was harsh and uneven. Cliffs overlooked the Alamber Sea, broken only by the treacherous trails the wagoneers had used to descend to the rocky shore. Trees grew almost out to the sea's edge, kept at bay only by the saltwater that drenched the ground.

Foresters manned the wagons. All of them were hard-eyed men with the gruff manners of warriors constantly marching off to battle. They bore scars and memories, and their songs at night held sadness for things lost as well as hope for a brighter tomorrow.

Some of the wagons bore coast boats that many of the surrounding pirates feared. Though the coast boats were open, equipped only with lateen sails, oars, and poles, a group of them could grapple and board ocean-going vessels to kill pirate crews. According to Tarnar, they'd done that several times in the past.

For the last two days, only a ghost of a wind had threaded along the rocky coast, not enough to allow them to put out to sea. Jherek had spent most of that time with the captain.

"It's a wonderful thing you've been given, Jherek," Tarnar said.

"But I ask myself why." The question had plagued Jherek's mind constantly.

"Sometimes," Tarnar said softly, "things are meant to be accepted, not understood. So we practice, and the whales talk to you here, giving you what information they have. What follows will follow."

"I want to be back with my friends."

Tarnar grinned and said, "Good. Maybe that is a step in the right direction." He lifted his sword. "Prepare yourself."

Jherek squared off with the man, falling easily into combat stance. Though Tarnar wasn't as powerful a swordsman as Glawinn or Malorrie were, there were things the young sailor picked up from the captain. Malorrie and Glawinn had concentrated on raw power, complemented with quick, decisive strokes. Tarnar, however, moved from bold attack into feints that had upon occasion left Jherek open.

The young sailor watched his opponent's eyes, waiting for the captain's opening move. Tarnar slashed at Jherek's left arm. Jherek raised his arm and took the blow on the bracer, trusting it completely. Sparks flashed from the iridescent surface, but the bracer showed no signs of ill use.

Thrusting with his cutlass, Jherek came close to Tarnar's face but the captain parried the thrust with his dirk. Steel rasped. Jherek blocked again, this time causing the bracer to form a two-foot diameter buckler that he used to press up against his opponent. Even as they disengaged, he caused the bracer to form into a hook like the one he normally used. Each change was coming with less conscious thought now. The young sailor settled into the combat, trying not to think of Sabyna, Glawinn, Azla, or the pirate crew he'd come to know and care about.

Tarnar's crew had finally come around to him as well, after he'd walked upon the Great Whale Bard's body and retrieved the bracer. Over the days they'd spent traveling to meet the caravan in Aglarond, the crew seemed to accept him as one of their own. Tarnar had commented on that as well, stating that the young sailor had a natural affinity for drawing men to him.

Finally, after hammering away at Jherek's defenses for almost an hour, Tarnar called for a break. They drank sweet water the Aglarondans brought in wooden casks, and poured some over their heads to cool down in the murky summer heat.

"Never," the captain stated, "have I seen someone adjust so quickly to a new weapon."

"My teacher, Malorrie," Jherek explained, "schooled me in all manner of weapons."

Tarnar shook his head, spraying droplets to the wooden deck. "It's more than that, my friend. You are a true, natural born warrior."

Embarrassment flamed Jherek's cheeks and the back of his neck. He willed the bracer away, feeling only a tingle as it sank back inside his arm. "Perhaps I have an advantage with the bracer that we hadn't counted on."

"You mean that it enhances your skill?" Tarnar shook his head. "Even if that were so, it would perhaps only guide your arm, it wouldn't move the rest of your body or make you a better swordsman. I've seen people fight with magical—"

Jherek.

Responding to the quiet call inside his mind, the young sailor walked to the railing and peered down to find Swims Truly, the sapphire whale, in the water beside the caravel. Tarnar studied him intently, aware that Jherek could hear a voice he himself could not.

You will be leaving with the tide, Jherek Whalefriend, Swims Truly told him. *The wind will be with you then.*

"Where am I supposed to go?" Jherek asked.

Where you are supposed to go, of course.

"I want to rejoin my friends," Jherek said. "I still have to find the disk of Lathander that I caused to be lost."

Then, should you find your way there, that is where you should be.

Irritation stung Jherek. The whales' cryptic announcements contained truth, but what truth wasn't always apparent.

"How do I find them?"

As you may, Jherek Whalefriend.

"I don't know how."

Yes you do. Listen with your heart, just as you listened with it when you found Song Who Brings Bright Rains. Search inside yourself. The bond between you and your love is the most constant thing in your life. The ability to love and seek out love is your most whalelike trait, Jherek.

Jherek was suddenly glad Tarnar couldn't hear the whale's thoughts.

"I don't think I can do that."

Swims Truly twitched a fin in a gesture Jherek had come to learn signaled irritation. *You have not yet tried. How can you know what you can do and not do?*

Chastened, Jherek remained silent.

Close your eyes and let me guide your thoughts.

The young sailor closed his eyes, ignoring the inquiring look Tarnar gave him.

You have a gift, Jherek Whalefriend, Swims Truly said, *that comes from what you are, what you will be. Born upon the seas of Toril, destined to spend your life there, it has been seen to that you will always have a sense of where you are and in what direction people or objects lie from you.*

Jherek waited, trying to understand, trying simply to believe.

Paint the picture of your beloved in your mind. Open it to the special tie that will forever bind you to her.

Doubt clouded the young sailor's mind that such a thing existed.

You think too much, Swims Truly chided. *Build her face in your mind, remember her scent, then reach for her.*

Tentatively, afraid of failing, Jherek did as the whale suggested. He imagined Sabyna as he'd first met her, the wind blowing through her copper-colored hair. He imagined the lilac scent that she favored, then felt a familiar tugging within his breast. Another image of Sabyna, when she'd come to him in *Black Champion*'s rigging and dug her fingers in his shirt, filled his mind. It hurt him, remembering how he'd told her he couldn't give her his love. The feeling in his chest dimmed.

No. Do not doubt your love for this female, Jherek Whalefriend. Your doubts are in truth your greatest enemy. Try again.

Forcing himself to remain calm, Jherek built Sabyna's face in his mind again. He saw her smiling and his heart swelled within him. The tug in his chest returned, stronger than ever. He reached for her, knowing for sure in what direction Sabyna was: west, and a long distance away.

The love is true, Swims Truly said quietly. *You feel the connection strongly. It is how our kind finds our mates.*

"I can't—" Jherek started to protest.

Hush, Swims Truly instructed. *Jherek Whalefriend, no matter how much you doubt, you can never be other than what you were born and guided to be. Perhaps you can delay these things, but you can never make them go away. Whether you wish it or not, whether you feel entitled to it or not, at this time you love the female and she loves you.*

Abruptly, a wind came up from the east, flowing over *Steadfast* and rattling her rigging. Even with his eyes open now, Jherek could feel the tug urging him in Sabyna's direction. He closed his eyes again, imagining her and drinking her image in. He reached for her, calling her name.

The image sharpened and he saw her in one of the small rooms aboard *Azure Dagger.* She sat on a chair in front of Arthoris, the ship's mage. Her head turned and her eyes searched for him.

"Jherek," she called. A feeling of dread, of loss and confused pain, clung to her.

Startled, the young sailor lost his concentration. He dropped to his knees, suddenly weakened.

You put too much of yourself into the seeking. You must be wary of this.

Jherek gasped, gazing down at the sapphire whale. "She's in danger."

Of course, Swims Truly said. *All of Serôs is in danger. Your love follows the currents to the greatest danger of all.*

Anxiety filled the young sailor. "I should never have left her side," he said.

There was no choice. To be what you need to be, you had to come to these waters. If you had stayed with her, she would have been lost for certain. As you would have been, and all of Serôs as well. Now you are closer to being what you need to be so that most will be saved.

"Will she be saved?"

That remains to be writ, Jherek Whalefriend. We can see but a few currents from this point on, and all of those are not clear, nor without risk. Much death lies ahead for all of Serôs. No one may save them all. Perhaps, you will not even save yourself. If you do not complete yourself, you may not have even that chance.

"What do I need to do?"

Accept. Begin there and the rest will follow. May Oghma, Lord of Knowledge and Bards, keep you within his sight.

Without another word, Swims Truly dived deeply into the blue-green water and disappeared.

"Should we sail?" Tarnar asked. "Or do you yet have business with the whales?"

"No," Jherek said. "It's time for us to go."

He stared west, wishing he could be with Sabyna at that moment, facing whatever danger waited for her.

"Where do we sail?"

"West," the young sailor answered. "As fast as we are able."

19

"He hates you, my liege," Tu'uua'col said, "even though you are his father."

He swam easily at King Vhaemas's side through the palace in Voalidru. As usual, even though he'd been the king's advisor and trusted friend for years, all the other court personnel stayed away from him.

The merman king's face turned bitter, and his eyes wouldn't meet his friend's. Broadened by the sea and battle, a little more than eight feet long from head to tail, the old king's frame remained heavily muscled despite his sixty-eight years. His gold crown, inset with precious gems and rare bits of coral, held back his white hair. Scars decorated his arms and torso. Pink-ridged flesh scored the left side of his face from a koalinth attack years past.

"My blood is in him," King Vhaemas argued.

"And you denied it."

"Because I had to," the merman monarch replied.

"Yet you loved his mother."

Vhaemas put out a webbed hand and stopped his forward motion through the palace hallway. The nearest pages and court attendees scattered. Though he was one of the most favored kings in the history of the Serôsian merfolk, his temper was legendary.

"A nation," the king said, "cannot be compromised by a young man's indiscretion without proper perspective."

Tu'uua'col knew the king wasn't referring to his own illegitimate son, but to his own past mistakes.

"Your son does not see himself as an indiscretion, my liege, and I think he would take grave umbrage at your own insistence upon calling him that."

"He would not form an alliance with Iakhovas of the sahuagin."

"My sources suggest he already has."

653

"They're wrong," the merking snapped.

"Remember when your own court of advisors denied that you had made me one of them? Denied, in fact, the friendship that exists between us?" Tu'uua'col sighed heavily, hating the turbulence that formed between him and his friend.

The court rejected him for a number of reasons, and most of them still hadn't changed their minds. First and foremost among their complaints was that he was not a merman. He was a shalarin.

Tu'uua'col stood not quite six feet tall but seemed much taller due to the dorsal fin that started between his full black eyes and jutted up nearly a foot above his head before running all the way down his back to his buttocks. The jadelike sheen of his smooth, scaleless skin further set him apart from the warmer colors of the merfolk and their scaled tails. His gill slits were along his collarbone and ribcage.

All the merfolk knew him as a wizard, and a teacher of the royal princelings. That he had the ear of not only King Vhaemas but the royal offspring as well was enough to unnerve most of the other advisors. If the royal court at Voalidru had known he was a Blue Dukar of the Order of Kupav and interested in the protection of Myth Nantar, assassination attempts might have been the order of the day.

"They do not know you as I know you," Vhaemas stated irritably. "They think of you simply as a wild-tider."

The merman nickname came from the prophecy of Selana, the mermaid who rose to prominence after the Tenth Serôs War and the fall of Hmurrath, the merfolk empire. The mermaid predicted that the merfolk would one day ally with the shalarin. The wild tide referred to the magical force that brought the shalarin from their homes in the Sea of Corynactis, whose exact location had never been decided.

"Yet they will not listen," Tu'uua'col pointed out. "Sometimes the plainest of truths are the hardest to believe. They require acceptance rather than recognition."

Vhaemas shook his head wearily. "These are difficult currents we face, my old friend."

"That is why we must recognize and quickly deal with the dangers that surround us."

"Including Thuridru's king."

"Yes, my liege."

In all the years that they'd known each other, Tu'uua'col had never heard Vhaemas refer to his bastard child by the Kamaar clan as his son.

Vhaemas scoured the palace corridor with a jaundiced eye. As capital of the Eadraal empire, Voalidru was beauty itself, sculpted from the sea. The merman builders had combined stones dug from the ocean's floor with quarried rock lost in shipwrecks. The royal buildings were wide and generous, sporting shells and coral decorations in myriad colors and shapes.

"The ixitxachitl cities of Ageadren and Orildren, as well as their outposts, have fallen to the sahuagin. I have heard that Thuridru was instrumental in destroying Orildren and the outer temples."

"But to join with the sahuagin?" Vhaemas questioned. "Why?"

Tu'uua'col was silent for a moment, weighing his words. "Perhaps, the enemy of my enemy is my friend. Thuridru has no alliances in Voalidru and remains trapped between the demon rays and the morkoth, who also attacked the ixitxachitls with the sahuagin."

"The Taker is not to be believed. In our legends he only looks toward his own interests."

"I think that is true," the shalarin Blue Dukar replied. "Still, Thuridru's ruler is willing to set aside merman histories and beliefs in order to forge his own future. He is openly ambitious. This alliance is the only one open to him. At worst, he gets some of the ixitxachitl lands. At best . . ." Tu'uua'col shrugged. "Perhaps he even thinks to have a hand in humbling all of Eadraal."

"What would you suggest I do?"

Vhaemas started forward again, following the bend of the hallway to a balcony. The royal palace was built on the lower foothills of Mount Teakal. The vantage point allowed it to overlook Voalidru below.

Most of the citizens of Voalidru lived in stone houses and caves, though some of the merfolk took up residence in ships that had come to rest on the ocean floor. Once, centuries ago, a great naval battle had been fought along the coast of Chondath between the coastal and inland city-states during the Rotting War. Many of the ships had sunk around the Whamite Isles and drifted down to the Lesser Hmur Plateau.

Tu'uua'col hesitated, knowing the advice he was prepared to give wouldn't be well received. "I think you should take the first step in allying the merfolk with the sea elves and the shalarin. I have learned of a caravan journeying toward Myth Nantar. Locathah I have talked to have told me of them. They tell me the Taleweaver is with them."

Vhaemas's answer came immediately. "Never! I would rather cut my own throat than trust the accursed sea elves."

The Blue Dukar maintained his silence. Vhaemas could not be argued with on certain matters, and the *alu Tel'Quessir* was one of those.

"If they had the means and the power, they would take all of Serôs for themselves," Vhaemas said.

"But they don't. The Taker, however, has an army of sahuagin, morkoth, and koalinth at his beck and call that are already invading lands that can be used as staging arenas to attack Eadraal."

"Even with all of those, there are not enough to conquer these waters," the merking declared.

"We have not seen everything the Taker has planned. If you add Thuridru, you increase the threat even more."

"I refuse to believe that is possible," the king said.

"Perhaps the ixitxachitl felt the same way."

Tu'uua'col waited, remembering his friendship with the merman and all the years they'd shared between them. It was a lot to risk, and all on the next few words he had to say. "Denial is no defense, my liege."

Vhaemas did not look at him, drifting quietly in the current with his hands on the balcony railing. "Leave me for a time, Col," he said finally. "I need to think on things."

"Of course, my liege."

Pain shot through the Dukar's heart. He couldn't remember when he'd last been dismissed from the king's side so abruptly. He bowed his head and swam away, frustrated and embarrassed.

Pride, foolish, ill-afforded, and dangerous, was a sword pointed at the heart of the kingdom, and Vhaemas couldn't see it. But then, the Blue Dukar supposed, neither could anyone else. Though the High Mages journeyed from the sea elf waters, there were no ambassadors seeking a meeting with the merfolk or the shalarin. Nor were the shalarin seeking audiences to combine their forces.

He wandered alone and aloof from the other palace dwellers and those who had business within the walls. He knew the other advisors talked about what was going on in the Xedran Reefs, but none of them would take the tack he did. They believed themselves inviolate.

Sahuagin raiding parties had spread throughout Serôs, attacking coastal lands and ships, and more continued to come from the Alamber Sea, making the waters between there and the Xedran Reefs dangerously close to impossible.

Still, Tu'uua'col knew it would take even more before all parties involved would admit the extent of the peril that existed. It remained to be seen how much would have to be lost before they realized it.

Li'aya'su moved down the long line of shalarin eggs that incubated in the mud of the warm sea cavern of the Aya clan in Es'rath. As one of the provider caste among the shalarin, she was the Heart of her people. Unlike those of the servant or ruler castes, she'd been able to choose what she would work at. Her immediate decision had been caring for the hatcheries.

The cavern followed a twisting tunnel, widened by artificial means to more easily accommodate the eggs. It was twenty feet wide and almost that high.

Her glance roved over the eggs as she turned them in their nest of warm mud. She and three other providers were responsible for caring for and turning the six hundred eggs under their care.

Passing down the line, she turned each egg carefully, aware that her actions were necessary to keep her race healthy in this home they'd found away from home. Even though Li'aya'su had been born in Es'rath and had not been out of the deep waters her people called home, she still felt she was a visitor to Serôs. These waters were not her home, and she'd been told that since birth. One day the shalarin would be allowed to go back home, but until that time, she promised herself to make the best of it.

She studied the shells as she moved among them. The rough, dark brown shells would one day add to the ranks of the protector caste. Rust colored shells with striated surfaces signified new members for the scholar caste while the smooth, black shells would give birth to the seeker caste. The seekers swam forever among the currents and searched for meaning beyond the shalarin. The light brown whorled shells belonged to the provider class, and most of the eggs here were that color.

Working quickly and methodically, enjoying the nature of the work as well as the work itself, Li'aya'su touched each unborn child with love and prayed to Ri'daa'trisha, the Waverider, who was known as Trishina in Serôs, for the goddess's blessing on each. It was a simple task, but she had been doing it since she had been a girl forty years ago.

Screams broke her reverie.

Startled, Li'aya'su turned from the eggs and swam back toward the hatchery's entrance. Li'ola'des, another of the providers, stood at the entrance and gazed fearfully out.

"What is it?" Li'aya'su asked, joining her.

"The sahuagin," the other provider replied in disbelief. "They have come here to Es'rath."

Cold fear hammered the elder provider as she looked out over the shalarin city. She had heard about the war that raged the length and breadth of Serôs, but she had hoped her people lived too deeply for the sahuagin to bother.

Hundreds of the vicious sahuagin swam from above, engaging the shalarin protectors at once. Though the protectors fought bravely, there simply weren't enough of them. The protectors stood as the Hand of the shalarin, taught the ways of war and battle from the time they were newly hatched.

The providers and scholars couldn't help much even in their own defense. A warrior was a warrior and a provider was a provider. According to caste thinking and training, one could not be the other.

Long minutes after the battle began, Li'aya'su heard their battle cry. "Long live King Iakhovas the Deliverer! Meat is meat!"

Horrified, the shalarin provider watched as the sahuagin not only killed her people, but ate them as well. Blood tainted the water in a way she had never seen before.

A group of sahuagin swam toward the hatchery, clicking and whistling in savage glee.

Not knowing what else to do, Li'aya'su stepped forward, intending to somehow protect the hatchery and the defenseless unborn that lay within the cavern.

The sahuagin didn't pause at all. The lead warrior lowered his trident. Li'aya'su felt the impact of the weapon piercing her chest, but surprisingly she didn't feel any pain. The sahuagin's powerful legs drove her backward through the water. She slammed against the wall behind her, feeling the rock tear her skin but again there was no pain.

"Please," she gasped, feeling the incredible pressure squeezing the life from her. Her gill slits flared open in a vain attempt to breathe. "Please don't harm the children."

She lifted her hand in supplication. One of the sahuagin raked his claws against Li'ola'des's neck, ripping her throat out. The provider died without a sound.

Holding the trident to keep her pressed back against the wall, the sahuagin grinned at her and growled, "Meat is meat."

His great head snapped forward suddenly and his jaws opened to crunch down on Li'aya'su's wrist. When he pulled away, he took her hand with him, chewing it between bared fangs.

"No mercy, finhead."

Peering through a cloud of her own life's blood, Li'aya'su watched helplessly as the sahuagin ravaged the hatchery. They lifted the blessed eggs that nurtured the future of the shalarin race and ate them, one after the other. Pieces of broken shell littered the gentle currents that helped keep the cavern warm. The sea devils' terrible roars and laughter filled the cavern even as the shalarin provider's life was spent.

3 Marpenoth, the Year of the Gauntlet

20

"The sahuagin destroyed the Ola, Aya, and Yea clan hatcheries at Es'rath over a month ago."

Pacys felt the horror and helplessness of the tale the locathah female told him. She called herself Tyhlly. Music tugged at the old bard's fingers, sending them quietly questing along the saceddar's gems. Though he didn't touch the inset gems, the notes filled his mind along with the images.

He sat on the ocean floor on a rise that overlooked the valley the sea elf caravan had come through only moments before. Taranath Reefglamor had ordered a brief respite until the scouts returned. The three older High Mages—including Yrlimn Tidark who had remained to himself studying ancient texts written on specially treated shark-skins—and the three new High Mages, sat with the bard and Khlinat. They talked with the locathah who'd come looking for Pacys.

During their long trip around the Pirate Isles, the locathah had maintained contact with the sea elf caravan. Most particularly, they'd maintain contact with Pacys, bringing him stories from all around Serôs.

Despite the sea elves' initial resentment of the locathah habitually seeking them out, the High Mages had recognized their value and even commented on their valor and loyalty. During some of the skirmishes they'd had with groups of koalinth, the locathah had even pitched in and fought.

Though they maintained contact with mages back in Sylkiir who routinely monitored Serôs through crystal balls, there was much the sea elves missed. The locathah, however, were everywhere.

"Didn't the shalarin fight back?" High Mage Ildacer asked.

The locathah turned her attention to the sea elf and said, "Yes, Lord High Mage." Tyhlly's deference to Ildacer was obvious, reflecting the locathah attitude toward the *alu Tel'Quessir*. "They fought, and they died. Over a thousand of the unhatched shalarin died as well."

"A thousand innocent deaths," Reefglamor whispered in a hoarse voice.

Pacys studied the Senior High Mage. During the long months of travel, the journey had marked Reefglamor with fatigue.

"If the merfolk had let us travel across the Hmur Plateau instead of having to go around it, mayhap we could have prevented those deaths."

"Better that you had not," Tyhlly stated.

"How can you say that?" the Senior High Mage demanded.

The locathah blinked her huge eyes and hesitated.

"I'm sure," Pacys interjected gently, "that she meant no harm by the statement."

"No harm, Lord Senior," Tyhlly said. "No harm intended at all. I give my life to Eadro and to improving our world in ways that will benefit all. I would not wish such a terrible thing on anyone." She paused. "I only meant that since the deaths at the hatcheries and the attacks on Es'rath, the shalarin now openly take up arms against the sahuagin. You have more potential allies in your quest."

"Aye," Khlinat growled. "She's got the right of it there."

"Why would the Taker attack the shalarin?" Ildacer asked. "He's already engaged a host of enemies above and below the sea."

No one seemed to have an answer. Pacys let his fingers wander across the saceddar, listening to the notes in his mind. Excitement filled him—he knew the fabled city of Myth Nantar was only a short distance away—but doubt lingered with him, too. So far there had been no word of Jherek, the boy he felt certain was the hero Narros had told him about. He prayed to Oghma for guidance regularly, but there had been no definite course set other than the one he now followed.

Tyhlly broke the silence after a time. "There is a simple reason why he attacks the shalarin," she said.

"What?" Jhanra Merlistar asked.

"To take away further avenues you have open to you in the war against him," Tyhlly answered.

"What do you mean?" Ildacer asked.

"The Taker seeks to keep the races of Serôs divided." Though the locathah spoke softly, Pacys knew she had the attention of everyone there. "The merfolk wouldn't let you cross the Hmur Plateau to get here. The Taker's attack on Es'rath and occupation of parts of the Xedran Reefs has assured that their paranoia has increased. The elves of the Dragon Reach have erected battlements to keep out those potentially hostile to them."

Pacys knew it was true from the conversations he'd had with Reefglamor. The Dragon Reach sea elves stayed on guard against sahuagin attack, as well as hostilities from the nearby coastal lands.

"How do you know this?" Ildacer demanded.

The locathah ranger pointed at the dolphins that had accompanied her. "The whales sing of it, and we are friendly with the whales."

"What would you have them do?" Ildacer asked sarcastically. "Lay down arms and let the sahuagin death tide wash over them?"

"No," Tyhlly answered. "Freedom is precious—something that should never be easily given up. A bigger foe may threaten you or imprison you for a time, but you should always be looking for your first chance at freedom. My people learned this long ago, and at great cost."

Pacys's fingers stroked the keys, echoing the locathah's words.

"Now that the shalarin are put on guard," Tyhlly went on, "how do you think they would feel about another race invading their lands?"

"They wouldn't tolerate it," Jhanra said. "They would fight against anyone who wasn't one of them."

Tyhlly nodded, turning her head from one side to the other to fix her other eye on the young High Mage. "Exactly. You do see."

"I don't," Talor Vurtalis grumbled.

Unlike the other two newly made High Mages, Vurtalis wore his selu'kiira gem openly on his forehead. Over the months-long journey, Pacys had learned the choice was in direct opposition to elven tradition and propriety.

"The Taker has allied himself with the morkoth," Tyhlly said. "If he joins with them again and marches on Eadraal, successfully forcing the mermen from the Lesser Hmur Plateau and Myth Nantar, where will they retreat to?"

"Possibly the shalarin lands," Reefglamor said.

Pacys saw understanding light the Senior High Mage's eyes.

"And, after the attack on the hatcheries," the locathah asked, "what would the shalarin do?"

"They would attack. Vhaemas's army and his people would be cut down from both sides." Reefglamor's answer was sobering. He stared at the locathah with new respect. "You have quite an understanding of war."

The locathah ranger spread her hands. "It is just that we have been involved with them for so long, Lord Senior. We have come to understand war, and we have come to understand that unity often means our freedom. In times past, when the locathah were taken as slaves, we were particularly vulnerable when we fought among ourselves. We have learned from those experiences and vowed never to make them again. Working together, we understand that we are stronger than we would be if we stood alone." She hesitated, then added, "Some of our leaders, as well as the whales, feel that is something the other races of Serôs would do well to learn."

An uncomfortable silence followed her words.

Tyhlly rounded her shoulders self-consciously, making herself more vulnerable. "Forgive me if I have trespassed in my zeal to spread the news I have learned," she said.

"There's no need to apologize," Reefglamor assured her. "You have spoken fairly. Sometimes the truth is a hard thing to hear."

"Thank you, Lord Senior."

"Perhaps we should be thinking about a unity of some sort," Reefglamor suggested.

"With the mermen?" Ildacer scoffed. "They wouldn't even let us travel across their lands. An alliance will be out of the question."

"I take it you are not in favor of it?" Jhanra asked.

Ildacer's answer was immediate. "Of course not. With all the wars between us, how could anyone entertain such an idea?"

"In some of those wars," Reefglamor said, "the *alu Tel'Quessir* and the merfolk were allies, not enemies."

"That was a long time ago."

"Currents change," the Senior High Mage replied. "Things are not as they once were."

"Aye," Khlinat put in. "Dwarves are known for their warrin' ways. Don't know if ye get much stories about us down here, but I can tell ye that nothing sets a dwarf afire with passion the way a good battle can. Different communities battled orcs and goblins for caves where gems were mined and a dwarf could live if he had a mind to. They also fought one another for the same things. Now ye take a dwarf down to a tavern and him blowing the suds off a fresh mug and a human or elf get physical with him, why any other dwarf in the place would be the first to stand up for him if he got into more than he could handle."

"But if it was an elf or a half-orc in trouble, these dwarven feelings you praise so highly wouldn't be quite so ready, would they?" Ildacer asked sarcastically.

"Now there's a funny thought," Khlinat said without taking offense. "I seen mates on a ship, crew that had been together through some stormy weather and buckle to buckle against pirates what had tried to reeve them of their cargo—and they was a mixed bag, the lot of 'em. Aboard ship, they had their problems, but the cap'n set 'em straight. Mayhap on occasion they'd take an unkind hand with each other once they reached shore, but when it come to taverns and local roustabouts laying hands on 'em, why ye'd have thought they was long-lost brothers the way they took up for one another."

Everyone looked at the dwarf, who appeared suddenly as though he'd rather be elsewhere.

Finally Reefglamor broke the silence. "I've never heard you speak so much."

"I have me moments," Khlinat replied gruffly.

"Thank Deep Sashelas that you do, Khlinat. Your words ring true and I shall have to think upon them."

"I'm just saying there ain't no grand and perfect solution to how folks are to get along with one another," the dwarf said. "Neighbors ought to pay attention to who's in the neighborhood before they start picking fights with one another."

"The mermen will never listen," Ildacer argued. "You know how proud and haughty they are."

Reefglamor glanced at his second-in-command. "How very like the *alu Tel'Quessir* they are, you mean?"

"No, that's not what I meant to . . ."

Reefglamor sighed and looked out over Mount Halaath standing tall to the northwest. After circling under the Whamite Isles, the caravan had fixed on it and marched straight toward it. The City of Destinies lay between them and Mount Halaath.

"Senior, what I am saying is that we might be swayed by Khlinat's words while sitting here so far from our own homes, feeling perhaps a little lost and friendless, but King Vhaemas and his people are not going to feel the same. This place is the source of their strength. Even with the morkoth and koalinth adding to the ranks of the sahuagin, the Taker can't possibly hope to overrun all of Eadraal."

"From what I have pieced together," Pacys said. "The Taker only wants his eye."

"Have you found out what that is?" Jhanra asked.

Pacys strummed the saceddar. "Not yet. All that I am sure of at the moment is that it is some device the Taker had in his possession when Umberlee struck him down."

"Even so, to get the eye from Myth Nantar, the Taker will have to march through Eadraal," Reefglamor said. "As much as King Vhaemas hates the City of Destinies and all that it stands for, he won't see the Taker free to ravage it."

"Again," Ildacer said, "the Taker will have to raise up an army the like of which has never before been seen."

"And you have assurances," Reefglamor asked quietly, "that the Taker cannot accomplish this?"

"No, Senior."

"Good," Reefglamor responded. "So far the Taker has succeeded at everything he's attempted to do. We have no proof that we've set him back in any way at all."

"Except for the Great Whale Bard," Tidark commented in his whispering rasp. The High Mage was much older even than Reefglamor and usually given to his studies, not spending much time in the company of others.

Pacys knew it was true, but he didn't know what the whale bard had made his sacrifice for.

"We have every reason to believe that when the time comes," Reefglamor said, "the Taker will find the means to raise the army he needs to invade Eadraal."

The thought sobered all of the High Mages, Pacys noticed with satisfaction. The hardships of the journey, the turning away they'd experienced at the hands of the mermen, had tempered all of them.

A group of sea elf warriors approached from the north. Morgan Ildacer, young cousin to Pharom Ildacer and captain of the High Mages' guard from Sylkiir, came to a stop in the water. He bowed his head, his arms crossed at the wrist, and waited to be recognized.

"Captain," Reefglamor said, "your report."

"Our scouts have returned with good news, Senior High Mage Reefglamor. The way to Myth Nantar is clear."

"What of the merman guards?"

"If we move quickly enough, Senior," Morgan Ildacer said, "we'll be able to gain the city within the hour. Vhaemas's warriors seem to be concentrated to the south, prepared to defend their borders against the morkoth and koalinth. They're searching for groups much larger than ours."

"Very well," Reefglamor said. "Give the order, and let's get moving. Better this were done sooner than later."

"There are others of my kind in the area," the locathah ranger stated. "We can cover your backs in the event you are discovered. There are hiding places around here that not even the mermen know of."

"That won't be—" Morgan Ildacer started before Reefglamor cut him off with a raised hand.

"That would be very kind of you," the Senior High Mage said.

Tyhlly stretched to her full height and bowed, then turned her attention to Pacys. "Your gods be with you, Lorekeeper, for you shall soon be sorely tried."

"My thanks to you," the old bard said. He spread his hand and touched palm to palm with the locathah ranger. "May Eadro give you only pleasant and free currents."

She leaped up and was gone in seconds, disappearing into the darkness of the sea.

Turning to face Mount Halaath, Pacys strained to pierce the gloom that lay ahead. He made out the glimmering blue glow of the Great Barrier that sealed Myth Nantar off from the rest of the world.

He'd come so close to one of his goals. Now it only remained to be seen how things would play out.

Laaqueel stood on the sandy, rocky western shore of Graubunden, the largest of the Whamite Isles, and peered out at *Maelstrom* at anchor in the shallow waters. The pirate ship's sails were furled around the masts, and crew filled her decks.

Iakhovas stood beside the malenti, an imposing figure amid the sahuagin warriors he'd brought with him. The sahuagin lay in the shallow waters to prevent their scales from drying out. Though he had barely talked to her in fully two months, concerned with all the battles and alliances he'd made, Iakhovas had commanded her presence for the day.

Attention, little malenti, Iakhovas spoke into her mind. *You are about to see the first culmination of my labors here in the Inner Sea.*

Laaqueel turned her gaze to him.

Iakhovas smiled. He looked human at the moment, though she knew the sahuagin perceived him as one of their own.

Your astonishment astounds me, little malenti. Surely you didn't think I came here to conquer this place and never return to the outer seas.

The crew in *Maelstrom*'s longboat rowed into the beach with consternation showing on their faces. They'd been waiting since early morning, the malenti priestess gathered from Iakhovas's comments, after arriving in the night. When they gained the beach, the crew bailed out and pulled the longboat up onto the sand.

Vurgrom stepped from the boat and approached Iakhovas. The pirate tried to act courageous, as if he wasn't standing in the midst of a hundred sahuagin warriors, but his nervous gaze and white-knuckled hand on the haft of his battle-axe gave his uneasiness away.

"Lord Iakhovas," the burly pirate rumbled in greeting.

"Captain Vurgrom," Iakhovas acknowledged. "Are you prepared to finish your part in this bit of business?"

"More than ready," Vurgrom replied. "Carrying that disk around without knowing what it does is getting to be worrisome."

"I know what it is," Iakhovas stated, but offered no explanation. "You have the map?"

Vurgrom patted his shirt over his heart. "Aye."

"March inland," Iakhovas ordered. "Follow the markings on the map and be in position three days from now."

Vurgrom hesitated, then asked, "What then?"

Iakhovas glared at him. "Wait."

The big pirate's face purpled, and for a moment Laaqueel thought he might actually speak out angrily. The malenti priestess thought that would have been interesting to see. Evidently Iakhovas needed the man or he would have done whatever needed doing himself.

In the end, Vurgrom lacked the nerve to stand up to Iakhovas. "As you say," the pirate said, "Lord Iakhovas."

"What of the kegs I asked you to prepare?" Iakhovas demanded.

"All of my ships have been outfitted with them, lord."

For a tenday and more, Iakhovas had commanded sahuagin groups to hole up in caves with air pockets so they could make the poison their people used. Laaqueel was versed in it as a priestess. Usually the sahuagin used the poisons on their weapons, coating them every few days as they had need. Iakhovas had come up with a new design.

Once the lethal poison had been rendered in powder form, it had been packed in thin glass shells, then placed in weighted wooden kegs that would sink to the ocean floor.

By design, the thin glass shells collapsed under the pressure of the depths at three hundred to four hundred feet. The poison quickly diluted into the water, killing anything that breathed it. The effect might only last a few minutes, though, before currents would sweep it away.

Iakhovas had told the malenti priestess he planned to use the kegs to completely destroy Myth Nantar once their initial attack was finished. Laaqueel had seen the effects of the poison kegs and feared them. Once the poison was released into the water, there was no way to escape it.

With no further word, Iakhovas strode into the water and disappeared under the incoming waves. The only sound was the lapping of the waves against the shoreline.

Laaqueel followed woodenly, aware of the pirates' leering stares at her nudity. None of them dared offer any comment. Underwater, she swam quickly and fell into pace a little behind Iakhovas. He swam effortlessly, totally at home in the sea. The sahuagin warriors flanked them. Scouts immediately flared out to watch for the mermen guards that swam through the area.

The malenti priestess scoured the ocean floor. She knew from Iakhovas's statements that the sea elf caravan from Sylkiir should be in the area as well.

They are further to the north, little malenti, Iakhovas told her. *They believe their mission has met with success. They won't know any different until it is much too late.*

What will happen then?

His tone, even in her mind, was mocking. *I succeed, of course, and they'll find that their precious legends have ultimately betrayed them.*

High in *Azure Dagger*'s rigging, Sabyna studied Vurgrom and his pirates through her spyglass. The last of the sahuagin had disappeared into the sea some minutes ago, but the pirates didn't rush back to their vessel.

"Blessed Tymora," Azla said quietly at Sabyna's side, "those damned sea devils must not have swam under us. I thought we were lucky the first time they showed up and we weren't seen."

Arthoris had woven an invisibility spell that covered *Azure Dagger*, but there were drawbacks to the maneuver. Even though they couldn't be seen, the ship still made its usual noises, and those carried across the ocean. If they'd been too close to *Maelstrom* the crew would have heard the sounds and recognized them. They'd quietly dropped anchor during the night when *Maelstrom* was nearly a thousand yards away.

When they'd seen the sahuagin surface along the shoreline, they hadn't dared hope their good fortune would last. If one sahuagin warrior swam under *Azure Dagger* the ship would be sensed in the water or possibly seen against the sky.

Another drawback was that the ship's crew couldn't see each other or the ship. Despite being unseen, it was also a lot like being blind except that Sabyna could see the ocean and the island. Movement was done cautiously and only as necessary. Unaccustomed to moving about in the rigging, Glawinn remained below.

The longboat was rowed back to *Maelstrom* while Vurgrom and five pirates remained ashore. Sabyna wasn't close enough to see the pirate captain's expression, but she judged from the way he kicked rocks and gestured at his men that he wasn't happy. It was in direct contrast to the timid way he'd acted around Iakhovas.

Sabyna watched as provisions were lowered over *Maelstrom*'s side in a cargo net.

"Shore expedition," Azla said. "Maybe we're going to finally do something other than wallow around."

"Aye," Sabyna agreed.

In the months they'd followed Vurgrom and *Maelstrom*, they'd never had a proper opportunity to overtake the ship and board her. Even with the new crew that the voyages had given Azla time to whip into shape, Vurgrom's pirates outnumbered them two to one.

In frustration, Azla had limited herself to spying on the captain, hoping for a lucky break. During part of those times, Vurgrom had sailed with other ships under his command.

They'd become separated from *Maelstrom* three times during those months. Once they'd rescued a crew that had been attacked by sahuagin and barely escaped with their lives and lost a tenday getting the sailors to a safe port. Another time one of the freak storms that ravaged the coastal lands upon occasion had spun them into its clutches, then left them in a lull that lasted four days. Then, while in Ilighôn, the island port city in the Vilhon Reach, they'd nearly gotten Vurgrom in an ambush while he conducted a trade for unknown items. They lost him again, but each time the enchanted astrolabe had brought them back to Vurgrom.

All of it had added up to the certainty that Vurgrom had an assignment in the area that he hadn't yet finished. Now, perhaps the time had come. Though they'd seen the pirate captain with sahuagin one other time, they'd never seen him act so contrite.

"That sahuagin he talked to must have been Iakhovas," Azla said.

"That was no sahuagin," Sabyna said. "Vurgrom talked to a man. Very tall, with a beard and dark hair."

"I saw no men there other than Vurgrom and his pirates. You must mean the elf woman."

"No," Sabyna said deliberately. "I saw what I saw."

"They say the Taker is very powerful," Azla replied after a moment. "Perhaps one of the guises we saw was only an illusion."

"Perhaps both were."

During their travels, they'd added to the lore they'd heard about the Taker. They'd also learned about the war going on under the waves they sailed upon. Several times they'd sailed through small islands of dead morkoth, ixitxachitl, mermen, sahuagin, and koalinth being savaged by birds, crabs, and fish.

"We've seen enough," Azla declared. "If we're to keep up with them, we need to get to shore ourselves."

"Go on," Sabyna said. "I'll follow you down after you reach the deck."

She waited, clinging to the rigging as *Azure Dagger* heeled over repeatedly at the end of her tether. When slack returned to the rigging, she knew Azla had reached the deck. The ship's mage clambered down easily but paid more attention than normal to her efforts.

Once on the deck, she went forward, one arm before her and walking slowly so she wouldn't run into an unwary crewman. She ascended the steps leading to the forecastle and called, "Glawinn?"

"Here, lady."

Judging where the paladin was from the sound of his voice, Sabyna went over to the railing. "You've seen?"

"Yes. Captain Azla and I were just discussing when we should attempt moving the ship. Or whether we should just try swimming for the shore."

"We have the small boat," Azla said from nearby, "but there is the risk that we'll be seen once we leave the spell Arthoris has around the ship."

"We should wait," Sabyna said. "Vurgrom is moving a lot of supplies. He isn't planning on living off the land. I think he'll be easy enough to find."

"Then we wait till after dark and pick up his trail?" Azla asked.

"Yes," Glawinn said. "He won't get so far ahead of us that we can't catch him soon enough. If he's stocking supplies, what he is going to do isn't going to happen too soon."

"I'll see to our own supplies," Azla stated. "We're going in stripped down. I want to be able to move quickly if the need arises."

"Agreed," Glawinn said.

Sabyna listened to the half-elf's footsteps recede from the railing.

"Lady?" the paladin asked.

"Aye."

"You're quiet."

"I'm thinking."

"About the young warrior?"

Sabyna hesitated. Upon occasion she and the paladin had talked of Jherek, but those talks had never brought much in the way of satisfaction. She couldn't help thinking that he might be dead and she'd never know, but the feeling Glawinn had told her would come if that were so never did.

"Do you still feel him close to you?" Glawinn asked.

"Not now, but earlier this morning. I could have sworn I heard him say my name on the wind again. It was foolishness, brought on by too much anxiety and too little sleep."

"And, mayhap, love?"

She hesitated. "I don't know anymore, Glawinn. The way I feel has changed."

"Don't you still miss him?"

"Aye, but not like I did."

"That's a good thing, though, lady. There's only so much pain a heart can bear."

"I don't know. Not missing him so much scares me."

"Why?"

She smiled at herself, then realized Glawinn couldn't see the expression. "When I was younger, just coming into my teens, I fell in love with one of the sailors on a ship my father worked on. He was seven or eight years older than I was, and he was so beautiful. I wanted him so badly to love me—to just notice me—but I was Ship's Mage Truesail's daughter, and the crew knew to leave me alone. My father was very protective then."

"So this love went unrequited?"

"Not entirely. I followed him around like a guppy staying with its school. He couldn't ignore me, but he didn't say anything. My mother noticed. She talked to my father. My mother is the only one who has the ability to convince my father to change his mind. She persuaded him to let me eat eveningfeast with the sailor."

"Did the sailor live up to your expectations, lady?"

Sabyna laughed at the memory, but there was a bit of sadness in the effort as well. "No. It was horrible. We sat there at that little table across from each other and had absolutely nothing to talk about." She laughed again. "Well, I had nothing to talk about. All he did was talk about the things he'd done, the women he'd seen, and how he'd be captain of a Waterdhavian Watch warship someday.

"That was an infatuation, Glawinn. How am I to know this isn't?"

"I know love when I see it, lady."

She suddenly wished she could see the warrior's face. "How do you know it's love?" she asked.

"Close your eyes, lady, and imagine his face in your mind."

Sabyna pictured Jherek in her mind, as she'd first seen him aboard *Breezerunner*, then again as he'd fought for her when Vurgrom kidnapped them in Baldur's Gate. All the memories she had of him, of the way his chest had felt beneath her fingers, the way his lips had felt and tasted against hers, tumbled through her mind.

She seemed to see him again. His light brown hair twisted in the wind and a green-blue sea spread out behind him. White sailcloth fluttered overhead. There was a cut on his face, running vertically over his right cheekbone, half-healed and slightly red from inflammation.

Jherek?

Aye, lady. His lips moved, as though he spoke, but she couldn't understand any of his words.

Sabyna's heart swelled within her breast and ached so fiercely she thought she'd die. Then the connection blurred for a moment.

Come to me! she called.

He spoke again, smiling through the sadness in his pale gray eyes. She couldn't hear him this time either, but she read his lips. *As you wish.*

Opening her eyes, Sabyna remained somewhat confused. She couldn't see her own hands in front of her body due to the invisibility spell.

"Lady?" Glawinn asked.

"I'm all right."

"I called for you but you didn't answer."

"It was like I could talk to him, Glawinn," Sabyna said. "He felt closer than he'd been those times before."

"Maybe he is."

"I don't know whether to wish that was so or not."

"Why?"

"I hate not knowing if he's all right," Sabyna answered honestly, "and I don't like missing him—but we're so uncomfortable around each other."

"I know."

"I just don't see that changing."

"It won't," Glawinn said after a short time. "Not until the young warrior himself changes. But tell me, lady, when you imagined him, how did it feel?"

Sabyna thought about her answer. There were so many things she could say. "I like thinking about him."

"Then accept that as it is for now, lady."

"It's not that easy."

"No."

Sudden irritation at the paladin dawned in Sabyna, and her mind seized on something he'd said. "How did you know about my brother? I never mentioned it to you."

"Jherek told me," Glawinn said.

"Why?"

The silence drew out between them and Sabyna wished she could see the man's face.

"I would rather the young warrior tell you that."

"Is that part of the secret he won't tell me?" she asked. "How could it be?"

"Lady, as I said—"

"He's not here for me to ask him myself."

Sabyna grew more frustrated. If not for Arthoris's invisibility spell she could pin the paladin down with her gaze.

"The things I was told were told to me in confidence."

"Glawinn, I will have the truth. From you or from him, I will know what you both hide. I'm too deeply involved in this not to know." Sabyna made her voice harder. "Tell me, Glawinn. What is it about my brother's death that so concerns Jherek?"

21

Myth Nantar.

Even the name evoked magic and a sense of incredible history.

From the moment he saw the sea elven city in the shallows of the Lesser Hmur Plateau, Pacys was at a loss for words. Thankfully, music came to his fingers. Still a quarter mile from the City of Destinies, the bard stopped swimming and settled on the foothills of Mount Halaath.

" 'Tis a pretty thing, isn't it?" Khlinat, who swam to the bard's side, asked.

"Yes," Pacys whispered.

Around them, the sea elf caravan came to a stop along the foothills. From the behavior of most of the warriors, it was the first time they'd seen the city as well.

The pale blue glow of the ancient mythal illuminated Myth Nantar against the dark black of the sea. The City of Destinies sat on a tableland that rose up from the ocean floor above the Lower Hmur Plateau, three hundred and seventy feet below the surface.

During the centuries of its isolation, coral had invaded Myth Nantar. Thick clumps of aqua-colored cryscoral grew in crystalline plate formations and clung to the exteriors of the ancient buildings. Pale blue ice coral dominated the upper reaches of the city, strung together in knobby clusters that reminded Pacys of spiderwebs draped over the upper reaches of the mythal. Bright patches of glowcoral had set up colonies throughout the city, creating shadows that twisted and turned in the currents.

"By Marthammor Duin, the Finder of Trails," Khlinat whispered solemnly, "never had I dreamed I would ever see such a sight as this."

Pacys drank in all the sights, letting his fingers pluck notes from the saceddar. The music he wrung from the instrument was bittersweet

memories mixed with the sharp euphoria of hope and dreams yet unfulfilled. Tears came to the old bard's eyes as the song possessed him.

> *Elven city, pale and cold,*
> *Shaped by hands strong and bold,*
> *Vessel and shaper of destiny,*
> *Care-taker and leader of unity,*
> *Lost Myth Nantar lay wrapped in her own shroud,*
> *Broken but unbent, humbled yet proud.*
> *Promise of life had not deserted her,*
> *As proven by those who sought succor.*

The words and the notes flowed around Mount Halaath, and there
were none among the sea elves who weren't touched by the emotion
stirred by the old bard's song. After a short time for reflection and prayer
from the clerics among them, who asked for guiding and blessing from
Deep Sashelas, Reefglamor gave the order to swim to Myth Nantar.

The warriors went first, flanking the High Mages on all sides.

Pacys gazed at the city as the caravan closed on it. He heard the
haunting singing that came from somewhere among the city's empty
buildings. Some of the *alu Tel'Quessir*'s legends had it that the city
was now haunted by the ghosts of those who'd been slain during the
sahuagin invasion of the Tenth Serôs War.

As he got closer, the old bard was able to make out the four quarters of the city and identify them from the maps he'd seen. The Elves'
Quarter—a place of libraries and villas—lay in the northeastern corner
of the city, covered over by the thick layers of aqua-colored cryscoral.
What had been the Trade Quarter lay to the south of the Elves' Quarter.
The *alu Tel'Quessir* histories had it that markets and entertainment
had once ruled there, powered by the merchants who traded with
those above and below. Now tiger-coral reefs grew rampant, closing
most of the buildings from sight. The Law Quarter—the now-deserted
seat of the sea elf government—occupied the southwestern corner of
Myth Nantar. Tiger-coral grew from the roofs of the tallest buildings
in Myth Nantar, making them even taller.

The least devastated area of the City of Destinies was the Dukar
Quarter. Lucent coral street lamps lined the surprisingly clear streets.
Pacys easily recognized the Dukarn Academy by the arrangement of
four rectangular buildings facing the octagonal Paragon's College.
Crafted of opulent pearl, the Palace of Ienaron stood nestled up against
Mount Halaath along Maalirn's Walk and picked up the glow from the
lucent coral climbing the mountain. The Keep of Seven Spires stood
two stories tall, then branched into seven four-story towers all made
of green marble.

At the center of the City of Destinies, where Maalirn's Walk,
Chamal Avenue, the Street of Ser-Ukcal, and the Promenade of Kupav
all came together, the Fire Fountain shot twisting yellow and orange

flames into the sea. It burned hot enough to actually warm the currents within the mythal. Pacys had read that the flames had burned more than nine hundred years. Three Gates' Reef got its name from the arches over the three roads that exited the city. Maalirn's Walk ended at Mount Halaath.

The city's illumination made everything seem normal despite the crusty coral growth spread throughout the streets and buildings. The Great Barrier was invisible to the naked eye save as an occasional shimmering in the water. It looked as though Pacys could swim right into the city.

He saw the first of the advance warriors colliding with the Great Barrier. They drew back at once in stunned disbelief, then tested their tridents against the mythal's might. The impacts rang like steel on stone.

Pacys and Khlinat joined Reefglamor as the Senior High Mage swam toward the Great Barrier. The glow from the lucent coral washed the color from Reefglamor, lending him an ethereal pallor. Together, they sank toward Myth Nantar.

"It's a beautiful place," Pacys said.

"It was," Reefglamor said, his eyes sweeping the city. "It is my fervent wish that before I die I should be able to swim these streets, to touch the things that my ancestors once touched."

"Perhaps you shall."

Pacys stretched his toes down, fully expecting to touch the solid surface at any moment. Instead, he was surprised to find himself sliding on through where the Great Barrier should have been.

"Pacys!" Khlinat's startled yelp followed the metallic thunk the dwarf's peg made when it crashed against the Great Barrier. He made a quick grab for the old bard's hand but missed. "Marthammor Duin take me for a—"

The rest of the dwarf's expletive was cut off. Looking up through the shimmering haze that separated him from the sea elves and the dwarf, Pacys realized that he was on the other side of the Great Barrier.

More of the sea elf warriors descended on the protective shielding and tried to force their way through with their weapons. Pacys never even heard their efforts through the shimmering haze. The old bard swam upward but found the way blocked. He put his hands against the Great Barrier and tried to will himself through.

Instead, the barrier remained firm.

"You can't get out, Taleweaver," a deep voice rumbled.

Slowly, sliding his staff free of the harness that held it across his back, Pacys twisted it, flaring the foot-long blades open at either end.

"There are things you must be shown, things you must learn."

Above Pacys, the Great Barrier darkened, shutting out the view to the outside world. At the same time an impossibly large shadow stepped from the buildings below. The old bard recognized him immediately as a storm giant. The green skin, dark green hair and beard, and glittering emerald eyes gave room for no mistake. He stood something less than thirty feet tall with huge shoulders and a broad chest. In true Serôsian custom, the storm giant wore no clothes, though anklets, bracelets, and rings adorned his forearms, ankles, and fingers.

"Who are you?" Pacys asked, remaining near the top of the Great Barrier above the storm giant. Even as he looked at the huge warrior, the old bard could sense that there was a glamor around him. Skilled as he was, Pacys could almost see past it.

The giant smiled. "I am Qos, a Green Dukar. I am the Grand Savant of the Fifth Order and Paragon of the Maalirni Order. I have been waiting for you. There is much work ahead of us."

Floating well back of Iakhovas, Laaqueel watched as he reached inside his cloak and pulled something free. She felt the crackle of magic in the air as Iakhovas spoke strong words of power. The singsong cadence filled the currents ten miles north of Naulys, one of the chief cities of the merman empire below the western shores of the Whamite Isles. He spread the items he'd taken from his cloak into the water. Gold gleamed from his artificial eye. Bright purple sparkles danced from his palm when he opened his hand.

The malenti priestess recoiled from the new onslaught of magic that sped through the water. The purple sparkles spun and danced like tiny reef fishes evading a predator, whirling out in broader patterns around Iakhovas. At the center of the orbiting purple flashes, Iakhovas continued speaking words Laaqueel didn't understand.

When he was finished, the purple specks slowed, then floated calmly toward the surface. They also started to grow, stretching out into masses of leafy vines, floating against the currents under their own power.

Laaqueel watched them, aware of the eerie litany coming from the plant masses.

Whatever the spell, Iakhovas had been working on it for most of the last two days, devoting every moment and all of his energy to it.

Raiding by the sahuagin continued, gaining added momentum from the Sea Hulk koalinth tribe and the morkoth. Even with those allies, and the Thuridru mermen waiting in the wings, they weren't strong enough to take on Eadraal and the mermen of the Hmur Plateau.

She held her place and awaited him.

"It's done," he said.

Laaqueel nodded.

Only a little surprise showed in Iakhovas's dark eye. "You have no questions, little malenti?"

"I have learned," she replied, "that you only answer when you choose to."

Iakhovas regarded her with open disappointment. "I miss the zeal in you, little malenti, and I'm surprised by my own feelings in that regard." He glanced back in the direction of the masses of purple-leafed vines floating toward the surface and said, "Those are very old plants. They haven't been seen on Toril for thousands of years. No one in these waters has ever seen anything like them."

Laaqueel believed him. The eerie litany the plants voiced grew louder, pulling more strongly at her conscious mind with a bewitching attraction. She glanced up, noticing the first of the plants had reached the ocean's surface and still headed toward the southeast where the Whamite Isles lay.

"Even so," the malenti priestess said, "you lack the army you need to invade the merman empire. The longer we wait here, the greater the chance of our discovery. In time, even the bitterest of enemies in Serôs will join against you if you keep sending the sahuagin against them. Once joined, they will attempt to hunt you down."

Iakhovas laughed. "Little malenti, they have to join forces, otherwise everything I've done is for naught."

"I don't understand." If the worlds above and below the Sea of Fallen Stars joined forces, sahuagin lives would be forfeit.

"Only by their joining forces may the Great Barrier surrounding Myth Nantar be dropped," Iakhovas said. "I can't get through the Great Barrier alone, and I need access to the City of Destinies." He stared after the plants. "As for an army, little malenti, I'll be raising one of those soon now and it will be unlike anything you've ever faced before. That I promise you."

Laaqueel glanced up at the plants continuing to spread across the ocean's surface. She recognized them as a form of kelp she'd not seen before. The singsong litany grew stronger and stronger still.

"Let's go, little malenti," Iakhovas growled. "In your present state of fatigue and apathy, you might succumb to the kelpies' ensorcelment in spite of the protection I lend you."

It was true and she knew it. She hadn't prayed to Sekolah in days and only stayed awake because sleep would not come to her. Wordlessly, she followed him back through the shimmering gate he'd opened to bring them here.

Whatever Iakhovas had planned next, she knew the resistance in Serôs was growing. Sahuagin warriors had reported being attacked by shalarin east of the Whamite Isles, and there were even reports of morkoth battling morkoth along the eastern fringes of the Arcanum of Olleth. The surface world's response was the most sluggish, but even they were going on the offensive now.

Only the mermen of Eadraal had failed to attack, and their presence in the center of the Hmur Plateau prevented shalarin armies from marching against the sahuagin in the Xedran Reefs. Even the ixitxachitls couldn't be controlled now. Raiding parties of demon rays swept through the sahuagin rearguard in the two fallen ixitxachitl cities. The ixitxachitls weren't able to secure the cities, but losses were mounting, dividing the standing sahuagin army there.

On top of that, the surviving sahuagin princes from Vahaxtyl had started to foment rebellion due to the high losses among their warriors. Even Prince T'Kalah was cautiously hoarding his warriors instead of spending them as Iakhovas demanded. Iakhovas, though he knew of the resistance within his troops, ignored the situation.

Laaqueel knew that the sahuagin presence along the western reaches of Serôs was balanced on a knife's edge. Nothing could be completely controlled—especially if Iakhovas continued concentrating on his own missions instead of taking care of the armies he marshaled.

Taking on the merman empire in Eadraal wasn't something he should try to do. Laaqueel felt certain it would be the breaking point of the war. Yet, if the mermen couldn't stand against Iakhovas, the malenti priestess knew their defeat would demoralize the rest of Serôs.

She just didn't see how Iakhovas planned to raise a fresh army even with his mysterious kelpie.

Patience, the soft feminine voice whispered in her mind. *The time is near for all things. You have allies you've not yet seen, and the Taker doesn't know as much as he believes he does.*

Surprisingly, Laaqueel took a little comfort in the words. Ahead of her, Iakhovas disappeared into the gate that would take them back to *Tarjana.* She followed.

Sabyna lay low in the scrub brush that dotted the hilly interior country north of Agenais. Her breath stirred the red dust next to her cheek and a trail of black ants marched across her left hand. She held a dagger in her right.

Ahead, three of Vurgrom's pirates stood guard at the mouth of the cave the pirate captain and the rest of his group had entered nearly an hour before. Evening fast approached, stretching long shadows to the east while the red sun sank into a mass of purple clouds in the west.

"Lady."

The whisper almost startled Sabyna into movement. If she hadn't recognized Glawinn's soft voice she thought she might have screamed. She glanced down toward her feet and saw the paladin standing there.

"Aye, and—by Selûne's sweet grace—don't scare me like that again," she whispered hoarsely.

"I'm sorry," Glawinn said. Despite the plate mail the paladin wore, he moved almost as soundlessly as a shadow. "Azla and I have found another cave entrance that leads down to where Vurgrom and his men are."

"What are they doing?"

"It looks like they're waiting, lady."

"For what?"

"I couldn't say. I came back for you so that you could join us.

Whatever Vurgrom is here to do, this is the place he's going to do it."

Sabyna waited until the three pirates standing guard were talking again and not looking in her direction before she eased down the hillside, taking care not to disturb the brush. When they were safely out of sight, Glawinn offered his hand and helped her up.

The paladin took the lead, following the small ditch that zigzagged behind the rocky knoll where the cave was. Agenais lay to the south, not quite five miles away, about the same distance it was to the cover where *Azure Dagger* lay waiting, hidden from *Maelstrom*'s crew. From the way Azla had it figured, they stood near the heart of the island.

She trotted after Glawinn, avoiding the loose rock spills that had tumbled down into the ditch. The center of the island tended to be rockier than the outer edge. Loose limestone shale rose in pockets or showed in the parched, cracked land of the interior.

The limestone was a natural filter and removed the salt from the ocean in the numerous pockets and caves that formed in the island's heart. Rainfall added to the local water supply, trapped in natural and artificed cisterns. The limestone foundation also provided for the honeycomb effect of caves under the island. These caves were once the lair of brigands, who had been rooted out centuries before.

Her muscles ached from fatigue, short hours of sleep while they shared guard duty at night, and sleeping on the hard ground. Azla had decided that only the three of them would attempt to get close to Vurgrom's pirates. A dozen pirates from *Azure Dagger* waited at a hidden campsite half a mile away, providing them a position to fall back to if they were discovered.

Glawinn stopped ahead and pulled at a clump of brush that covered a narrow slash in the earth forming the knoll. It wasn't quite opposite the cave Vurgrom had entered, but Sabyna didn't think it missed by much.

The paladin turned sideways and fit himself inside. The slash extended up through the knoll, almost to the top, and allowed a narrow crack of the waning sunlight into the passage.

The ground was treacherous with loose rock and pebbles. Nearly forty feet into the passage, they lost the sunlight, and the air around them turned cool. Condensation chill to the touch glistened on the rocky walls and ceiling.

The passageway continued to go down and bear slightly to the left. Long minutes later, Glawinn waved her to slow down even more. They moved cautiously, deeper into the knoll.

Sabyna's hand trailed across the cracked surface of the passageway, feeling the jutting shale. The rock edges were sharp enough to cut if a person accidentally ran into them in the dark. Luckily, there was enough natural light coming from ahead to illuminate the passageway.

Azla, dressed in black chain mail and dark clothing, crouched on a narrow ledge ahead. She glanced at them briefly, a hand holding her scimitar across her knees, then returned her attention to the scene playing out before her. She wore a short bow and a quiver of arrows across her back. A spear rested on the stone floor at her side.

Glawinn touched a forefinger to his lip in caution as he hunkered down beside the pirate queen. He placed his shield against the wall at his side.

Sabyna crept closer, dropping to her knees between them to peer down into the cave below.

"Aye, and she was a feisty one," Vurgrom was saying. He sat on an ale cask in the center of a ring of seventeen pirates clustered around a campfire that poured oily black smoke against the cave ceiling thirty feet above. The cave looked at least three times that wide. He drank deeply and noisily from a tin mug, then wiped the ale foam from his lips. He touched a jagged scar on the top of his bald head.

"I had her," he said, "holding her down on the duke's own dining table and him crying for his life in the corner, preparing to take care of my business, and she reaches back for this damned great copper cook's pot. Next thing I know, the wench brains me with it."

The pirates laughed at their leader's story, but Sabyna noticed they waited until Vurgrom himself started laughing first.

"Like to split my head open, she did. If the wench had been swinging a slaughterman's mallet instead of that damned pot, why I'd a' been holding my own brains in."

"Bet you really gave her what-for then," one of the pirates stated.

"By the Bitch Queen's locked knees, are ye daft, man?" Vurgrom roared. "Wench liked to killed me. Had blood a-seeping down into my face and me three sheets to the wind and truly not knowing how bad a shape I was in. I took up a carving knife from a nearby roast bird set for the duke's own table and shoved it through her heart. I was done, she had no complaints."

Gales of cruel, ribald laughter ripped through the cave.

Sabyna shuddered, involuntarily remembering her own brother's death at the hands of Bloody Falkane. She glanced around the cave, wondering what had brought the pirates there. Other than the long and tall stalactites and stalagmites, a few patches of lichen that glowed soft blue and green, and a few threads of streams running across the stone floor, there appeared to be nothing of interest in the cave.

A shimmering haze formed only a few feet from the group of pirates. The grim-visaged man Sabyna had seen four days ago leading the sahuagin pack that met Vurgrom stepped through the haze, followed by the elf woman who had been there as well.

"Vurgrom," the grim man said.

"Lord Iakhovas." Vurgrom handed the tin cup to the pirate beside him and stood. "As you see, we stand ready. As we agreed."

"Do you have the pearl disk?"

Vurgrom reached inside his blouse and took a cloth bag from around his neck. He loosened the drawstrings and poured the pearl and inlaid gold disk into his hand, then tossed it to Iakhovas.

Azla quietly slipped the bow from her shoulder and nocked an arrow to the string, aiming at Iakhovas. Sabyna wasn't sure that such a move was wise, but she kept her own counsel, readying her spells. Glawinn took up his shield and found a new grip on his broadsword. He kissed the rosy pink quartz disk that hung at his neck and whispered Lathander's name.

"No!" Anger flashed in Iakhovas's voice. He gestured at the thrown disk as the inlaid gold flashed the campfire light. It froze in mid-tumble, then glided back to Vurgrom, who caught it gingerly. Iakhovas's scarred face twisted, and the tattooing showed even blacker in the shadows. "I will not touch that thing!"

"Beg your pardon, milord," Vurgrom said, turning the disk over in his fingers in open wonder. "I didn't know."

Iakhovas walked to the cave wall to his right. "Did you ever manage to find out what this disk was, Vurgrom?"

"No, milord."

"But you tried?"

Vurgrom hesitated only a moment. "Spent good gold on it, milord." He shrugged. "Maybe cut a few throats of them that demanded payment and them not telling me any more than I already knew."

"It's a key." Iakhovas drew back his fist and pummeled the rock wall.

Stone split and splintered more easily than Sabyna would have thought. She breathed shallowly, waiting for Azla to release the bowstring.

"To what, milord?"

"I don't know," Iakhovas said as he hit the wall again, deepening the crack he'd started. He gestured to Vurgrom, who walked forward and thrust Lathander's talisman into the hole.

The talisman rattled a few times, the sound echoing clearly in the cavern, letting Sabyna know the crack Iakhovas had created reached far deeper than she'd have thought.

"I only know that it contains power I can use when I destroy it," Iakhovas said.

A ruby ray jumped from one of Iakhovas's eyes. The sound of a powerful detonation deafened everyone in the cave.

Sabyna might have cried out in pain. She wasn't sure. In the next moment the ground quavered and rumbled, twisting and turning like a storm at sea. Despite her familiarity with rolling waves, she stumbled and would have fallen had Glawinn not steadied her.

Below, the pirates spread out and drew their weapons, crying out to their gods and cursing. Vurgrom bellowed and pulled up his battle-axe, but whatever he was trying to say was lost in the tremendous *cra-ack!* that suddenly filled the cavern.

A chasm opened in the floor, spreading quickly from a hand's-span to several feet. Stalactites fell from the ceiling, one of them crashing through a pirate's shoulder and driving him to the ground. Blood pooled around the man as he quivered and died.

Iakhovas strode through the falling debris untouched, keeping his feet with apparent ease even though the earth shifted dramatically under him. The elf who had arrived with him didn't fare so well. She fell and rolled toward the chasm's edge. Moving with inhuman speed, Iakhovas reached down and caught the elf woman, lifting her effortlessly.

At that moment, Azla released the bowstring.

Kellym Drayspout walked his rounds through Agenais's docks out of habit. He carried a heavy crossbow at full cock in his scarred and gnarled hand. The chain mail he wore had seen better days but remained serviceable. He was a stout man with a bigger belly than he cared to admit, and gray hair that showed how many years had passed him, but he was a warrior few would want to confront. His lined and scarred face threw fear into most folks he had stern words with.

The docks seemed less well lighted than he'd ever seen them, but he didn't pay it any real mind. Quiet was a good thing. The carousing and drinking that went on more nights than not meant a long shift.

More ships than ever anchored in the shallows around the port. Almost all were shattered and broken husks, some of which would never move again, just be plucked apart to salvage other ships.

Drayspout's feet thumped against the creaking wooden dock as he made the corner that led down to Verril's Tavern. He'd stood in at the tavern enough that the locals, and the sailors that had been in Agenais any length of time, knew better than to cause any problems on his shift. Verril proved generous with the tapped ale kegs in return. It had proven a good arrangement.

The still, black water in the harbor was as smooth as polished glass. Ships' rigging slapped against masts. Over all of it he heard a melodic tune almost hypnotic in its intensity. The tune was enough, he'd discovered, to raise the hackles at the back of his neck.

Instead of merely trusting the way tonight, he'd found himself raising his lantern on more than a few occasions to strip away the shadows and make sure some foul thing wasn't crouched there waiting for him. His nervousness made him angry.

Being a guard wasn't a new job for Drayspout. He'd been a mercenary along the Dragon Coast for Lady Nettel Thalavar of the Thalavar trading family in Westgate for twenty years, until a bandit's blade had nearly found his heart a few years ago. He wasn't quite as quick as he had been, and he figured he'd had enough of it.

He'd been too well known on the Dragon Coast to retire there. Bandits he'd slain often had kin who didn't believe in forgiveness. In fact, some of the rogues' bands had even put a price on his head.

So he'd come to the Whamite Isles to spend his last years. He'd even met a widow who owned a bakery and had three teenaged children he could almost tolerate. He'd surprised himself by settling so easily into the sort of domestic life he'd never expected to have.

That life meant yelling at those damned kids every day, occasionally helping out in the bakery, and a few free pints of an evening down at Verril's between rattling merchants' doors and seeing to it nobody broke into a warehouse or shop too easily. The ships provided their own security.

Come early morning, he could count on snuggling for a little while with that widow before they started the sweetbreads and cakes she sold for morningfeast.

He cursed the damnable haunting tune that lay heavily over the dock area as he stepped onto the boardwalk running in front of Verril's Tavern. The building was a run-down affair cobbled together from leftover ship's lumber that had been, upon lean times, stripped back off and sold to vessels seeking materials to make repairs.

Drayspout stepped through the single batwing door that hadn't yet been auctioned off to a quartermaster in need of lumber. He stared at the empty tables and chairs that filled the small room, not believing what he saw.

The pale, oil lantern light pooled weakly in the room, and the smell of burning milk and meat from the untended chowder kettle hanging over the fireplace stunk the place up. The dice cups Verril used for wagering with his patrons, slipping in the special set he kept up his sleeve when he need to, sat on the stained bar. The painting of naked sea elves frolicking around Deep Sashelas hung on the wall behind the bar. Waves lapped noisily under the wooden floor and echoed hollowly through the room, striking a counterpoint to the melody that streamed in from outside.

Drayspout's unease grew by leaps and bounds. Maybe the sailors might take a quiet night to rest up, but there was never a night when Verril's went empty.

"Dray."

The hackles returned to Drayspout's neck. Everyone in Agenais who knew him called him Dray, but the whisper that called his name almost unnerved him. He was certain he knew the voice, but he couldn't place it.

He lifted the crossbow and placed the butt against his hip so he could fire it one-handed. Turning, he gazed back through the tavern's entrance, the view partially obscured by the batwing door. Usually there was some ship's crew working by lantern light to repair their vessels and he thought one of them might have called out to him.

There was no one. The docks stood totally empty.

"Dray."

A figure rose up from the black water beyond the boardwalk. Raising his lantern so the beam fell over the boardwalk, Drayspout recognized the figure at once. "Whik?"

It was his wife's oldest son. Whik stood as tall as Drayspout and was only fifteen. He still lacked a man's growth and strength, but he had a temper that had earned him the back of his stepfather's hand on occasion. He was pale and blond like his mother.

"What the hell are you doing in that water, boy?" Drayspout growled. It wasn't the first time Whik had slipped out of the house at night. Drayspout had caught him before. "You'll catch your death and break your ma's heart."

Whik made no reply.

Irritated that the boy may have seen him acting nervous, Drayspout strode toward him and raised his voice. "You got water in your ears, boy? I asked you a question."

When Drayspout reached the boardwalk, Whik fell backward, letting the water close over him.

Thinking something was wrong, Drayspout hurried to the boardwalk's edge and raised the lantern again. The light played over the water, lighting the pallid oval of the boy's face gazing up at him. Whik made no move to swim, slowly easing more deeply into the dark water. The haunting melody seemed louder than ever.

Dropping to his knees, Drayspout laid the crossbow aside and placed the lantern nearby so he could see Whik. He plunged his arm and shoulder into the water, feeling the chill, and reached for the boy. With his face less than two feet from Whik's, Drayspout noticed how dead the boy's eyes looked. Living around the Sea of Fallen Stars all his life as he had, the old warrior knew what a man looked like who'd succumbed to Umberlee's endless embrace.

Whik was dead. Sure as Tymora hated two-headed coins, the boy was never coming home to his mother again after this night.

Even as Drayspout started to withdraw his arm, the dead boy lunged at him, coming up out of the water with a leering half-wit's grin. He roped an arm behind his stepfather's head, grabbing Drayspout's wrist with his other hand. He pulled the old warrior down into the water with him.

As they sank deeper into the harbor, Drayspout fought against the dead thing that held him. The boy's corpse was as cold as the water. The old warrior tried to fight his way loose, but his hands kept sliding off the dead thing's wet, flaccid skin.

Still clinging to Drayspout, the corpse lunged forward and sank sharp teeth into the old warrior's throat. As his life drained out of him, clouding the water the lantern light shined through, Drayspout saw dozens of other pallid faces surrounding him. He recognized many of them as regulars at Verril's.

All of them were dead, their open eyes staring at him with dulled intelligence. They floated easily, wreathed in the kelpie-beds that sang the eerie music and held them like favored lovers.

Even as his final moment of life fled, Drayspout watched as other citizens of Agenais—men, women, and children he could have passed on the streets—plummeted into the water and didn't even try to save themselves from drowning.

Something evil had come for Agenais, Drayspout realized, and it wasn't going to rest until it had them all.

22

Azla's arrow sped true, flashing through the rolling fog of dust that billowed up from the chasm that had opened in the cavern floor.

Iakhovas turned, fixing the ledge with his harsh gaze. Quicker than the eye could see, he snatched the arrow from the air, stopping it only inches from his heart. He snapped the thick shaft in his hand.

"You've been followed, Vurgrom!" he roared, dropping the broken arrow and pointing at the ledge.

Sabyna opened her bag of holding and released Skeins. The raggamoffyn surged into the dust-laden air and set up in its familiar serpentine shape. A pirate pulled a heavy crossbow to his shoulder and fired. The ship's mage dodged back, doubting she could get clear in the narrow passageway.

Glawinn was there, shoving his shield out. The crossbow bolt slammed into it. "Easy, lady," the paladin warned.

Coolly, Azla nocked another arrow and let it fly. The pirate with the crossbow looked down at the feathered shaft that stuck out of his chest.

"Get them!" Vurgrom bellowed.

As the earthquake continued, five pirates managed to get to their feet and race toward the ledge. More debris dropped from the cavern roof, pummeling one of the pirates to the ground.

Sabyna took a pinch of sand and rose petals from her bag of holding, crushed them together, and spoke. A light green haze spiraled from her closed hand as the sand and rose petals were consumed by the spell. The haze sped toward the rushing pirates, wrapping around them. All four dropped, asleep before they hit the ground.

Iakhovas pointed over the heads of the other pirates who had regrouped and started toward the ledge. A lightning bolt lanced across the distance.

Glawinn swept Sabyna back with one arm and stood to block the streamer of crackling energy. The detonation rolled thunder through the cavern and blew the paladin off his feet, knocking him back ten feet over the ship's mage's head.

Sabyna started toward the warrior's sprawled form, knowing in her heart he had to be dead. The colorful image of the scarlet hawk on his shield hung in tatters of peeling paint. She knelt beside Glawinn, who lay loosely, his eyes open and staring blankly.

"Glawinn . . ." she said.

The paladin's chest gave a convulsive heave as he sucked in a sudden breath. He groaned and levered himself up, picking up his shield.

"By Lathander's blessed eyes," he managed to say, "the magic in this shield is stronger than I thought."

He slipped the shield over his arm, coughed raggedly, and got to his feet with difficulty.

Face tight, Azla slipped her bow over her shoulder and turned to them. She drew her scimitar and said, "We can't stay here."

"Agreed," Glawinn agreed. He took a fresh grip on his broadsword.

Azla took the lead as they raced back toward the other end of the passageway. Night had descended since Sabyna had entered the cave, and she didn't see the opening she'd come through earlier until skeletal arms suddenly thrust through it.

The skeleton stepped into the passageway, moving jerkily and holding a rusty short sword in its bony fist. The ivory grin showed missing front teeth and black hunger burned in its eye sockets. More skeletons filed in behind it.

Glawinn moved in front of Azla, sliding his sword into its sheath, and thrusting forward his hand, palm out. "By the grace of the Morninglord," he said, "get you back, hellspawn."

The skeletons acted as if they'd hit a brick wall. Most of the creatures stopped their advance, but a few in the rear didn't. They were held back by the ones in front. Bones clacked as they collided with each other. Their jaws snapped open and shut in anger, but they turned and walked slowly back out the passageway, fighting with the others that hadn't been affected by the paladin's power.

Even turned away as they were, the skeletons moved too slowly to clear the passageway before Vurgrom's pirates overtook them. Sabyna glanced back toward the ledge as the first of the men scrambled up. The ship's mage ordered Skeins to attack.

The raggamoffyn swirled into action, wrapping itself around the man and possessing him. The pirate turned to attack the next man, swinging his cutlass at his comrade's head.

The pirate ducked and skewered the possessed man through the stomach. Blood drenched the raggamoffyn, staining it crimson.

Azla's scimitar flashed as she closed on the pirate while he freed his weapon from his possessed comrade. He stepped back, holding his slashed throat, and lost his footing over the ledge.

"This way," Azla called, turning to the right and following a narrow ledge that ran around the upper part of the cavern.

"After you, lady," Glawinn said.

Sabyna called Skeins to her and drew a pair of throwing knives. She followed Azla into the darkness. The light from the pirates' campfire was barely enough to illuminate the way, leaving long, dark shadows draped over the cavern walls and floor. Tremors still shook the cavern, causing minor avalanches around them.

Azla turned left and headed through an opening. Sabyna was at her heels, aware that the surviving pirates had climbed up onto the ledge and were after them. The passageway ran only a short distance before opening to another cave.

A shaft of blue moonlight spewed through the crack in the cave twenty-five feet up. The light showed thick stalagmites and stalactites that had formed columns around a pool of water on the other side of the cave. Bones littered the floor. Farther back, three figures huddled against the wall on the other side of the pool.

"Help us!" a woman's voice called out. She moved toward them, revealing the length of iron chain attached to the spike driven into the wall. A small boy cried helplessly, his arms wrapped around the woman. The third figure was a young man who'd picked up large rocks in both hands.

Sabyna noted the ragged clothing the three wore, as well as the obvious lack of nourishment, but she couldn't figure out what they were doing there. Sabyna didn't know if they could save themselves, much less free the prisoners. The crack in the roof, obviously created by the tremors, was the only way out of the cave.

"The columns," Glawinn said. "It's our only chance."

Sprinting across the room, Sabyna looked at the woman and the small child and asked, "Who are you?"

Glawinn and Azla slid into position behind two of the columns. The half-elf took up her bow again and put a shaft through the neck of the first pirate in the cave from less than fifteen paces. The man fell back, mortally wounded and drowning in his own blood. It gave the other pirates pause.

"Prisoners." The woman's face was grime-streaked, her hair knotted. Half-healed scratches covered her arms, neck, and shoulders. "A tribe of koalinth took our ship maybe a tenday ago. They brought us here." She glanced at the pile of bones by the pool. "There were nine of us once."

"How did they get you here?"

"An underground river," the woman replied. "It leads from the pool out to the sea. They brought us here so the sahuagin wouldn't take us away from them. Koalinth are able to breathe fresh water. This cave was a convenient place to keep their larder."

Azla loosed another arrow but missed her target as the pirates invaded the cave. They quickly fanned out and took cover behind boulders and other stalagmites. Vurgrom came in last, bawling orders at his men to attack. With Glawinn ready to face them, none of the pirates appeared too eager.

Iakhovas strode into the room with the elf woman behind him. One of his eyes blazed.

"I want them dead," he ordered. He pointed, spoke, and three of the columns near the pool shattered as if struck by a battering ram.

Sabyna dropped beside the woman and grabbed her chain in both hands. She pulled fiercely but the spike didn't budge.

"Don't leave us here," the woman begged. "Please."

"I won't," Sabyna promised. She slipped one of her daggers behind the spike's head and tried to lever it from the wall, putting all of her back into the effort.

"At them, you scurvy dogs!" Vurgrom ordered.

Glancing over her shoulder, Sabyna saw Glawinn whirl suddenly and engage a pirate. The paladin blocked the pirate's thrust with his soot-stained shield, then cleaved the man's head in twain. Glawinn kicked the dead man from his blade, sending the body sprawling in the middle of the open.

"Have at you, then," the paladin challenged. "By Lathander's swift justice, here you'll find a warrior tried and true."

Iakhovas raised a hand.

"No," a calm voice called through the shadows.

Recognizing the voice, not believing that she'd truly heard it, Sabyna looked up from pulling on the knife and spotted him standing in the opening leading to the last cave.

Jherek stood in the doorway, the cutlass level before him, the gaze in his eyes defiant. The cut Sabyna had seen on his face was really there, and the ship's mage knew that the times she'd felt he'd spoken her name hadn't been her imagination after all.

The young sailor wore breeches tucked into calf-high boots and a white shirt with belled sleeves. Blood streaked the shirt, proof that he'd come in through the cave's main entrance.

"You should have struck me from behind, boy," Iakhovas rasped, then he smiled. "But you couldn't do that, could you?"

Jherek threw himself forward, revealing the other men behind him. A lightning bolt shot from Iakhovas's finger and struck Jherek in the chest. The young sailor flew back out of the cave, slamming into two men behind him and disappearing over the ledge.

"No!" Sabyna yelled.

The knife blade snapped, and she fell, sliding across the rough stone floor toward the pool. As she started to push herself up, a face surfaced in the water. It was dark green and topped by coarse black hair. Pointed ears framed its head. The mouth was a broad, lipless slash filled with sharp fangs that gleamed in the moonlight.

The koalinth reached for Sabyna even as three other heads surfaced.

"You closed the Great Barrier around Myth Nantar?" Pacys was astounded at Qos's announcement.

The old bard sat on top of the coral in the courtyard south of the Maalirn College. Over the four days they'd talked, the storm giant seemed most comfortable there. Though he'd studied his host in detail, the old bard still hadn't managed to pierce the guise the Green Dukar wore, nor managed to find out why he wore it.

"I had no choice," Qos replied in his great, booming voice. "Myth Nantar represents the promise all Dukars made to each other and all of Serôs. When those we sought to protect and guide turned on each other during the Tenth Serôs War, I could stand it no longer. None of the Serôsian races deserved something as grand as this city and its promise."

"The Dukars have faced problems before," Pacys replied. His fingers idly strummed the saceddar, coaxing the tune he'd decided would best represent the storm giant.

"Yes," Qos said. The giant paced, looking at the tall, tiger-coral covered buildings in the Law Quarter. "For nearly eight thousand years, the Dukars held positions of influence. Within five hundred years of our alliance with the sea elves of Aryselmalyr and our triumph over the koalinth, nearly five thousand years of peace ensued." He closed his hand into a fist. "Can you imagine what those years must have been like?"

Pacys let his fingers roll over the saceddar, playing by instinct. "I can try."

"During that time we built Myth Nantar and we created the Dukarn Academy. We did not know it then, but the Aryselmalyr sea elves planned to exact a price for letting us build there.

"The Dukars were told to swear fealty to the elven empire and the Coronal at Coryselmal."

Qos clasped his hands behind his back and continued to pace. Being twenty-six feet tall, the giant's strides were impressive to the bard.

"The elves began fighting among themselves and began trying to expand their empires," Qos said. "The merfolk objected, and rightfully so. However, their first order of the day was to battle their way to Myth Nantar and claim it as theirs. The enmity between the elves of Coryselmal and Aryselmalyr escalated events. The Dukars stepped in, hoping to end it. Instead, the Dukars of Nantari who had sworn allegiance to Aryselmalyr warred against the other orders."

Pacys listened to the sad weariness in the storm giant's voice. Qos hadn't lived during those times but it was easy to see that he had taken the history to heart. The old bard made the giant's sadness and fatigue a part of the music, blending it so that it spoke eloquently.

"Never had anyone thought that Dukar hands would be raised against each other," Qos continued. "They lived to promote peace and harmony throughout Serôs and all races, believing that Serôs could only prosper."

"It was a grand dream," Pacys commented.

"It wasn't supposed to be a dream." Fire sounded in the storm giant's words. "That was the destiny of the Dukars, and why they founded their academies here in the City of Destinies. During that war, the merrow and the koalinth banded together to create the Horde of the Bloodtide, and mages aligned with Coronal Essyl created the Emerald Eye, which has been a bane in Serôs ever since. Also, our first new order among the Dukars, the Order of Nantari, was destroyed."

A school of fish swam in front of Pacys, creating a haze for a moment. He watched their gentle undulations, felt the miniature currents break against his body. His fingers moved a little more swiftly, adding in the motion that complemented the mood he sought to create.

"When the shalarin arrived after that and we allied with them, we made powerful friends," Qos said. "They easily took to the Dukar ways. Prosperity followed our orders again for a time, then a coronal was assassinated and the Dukars were blamed. The sea elves began striking out at the Dukar orders. In response, forty of the more aggressive of our order removed their normal colors and dressed in purple, calling themselves the Purple Order of Pamas, and began a limited war of their own."

"But things didn't end there," Pacys said.

"No. War continued to be a way of life here, and everywhere it went, the Dukars could be found in it. Finally, after the Ninth Serôs War, the Dukars helped draft the Laws of Battle, hoping it would stem the tide of violence that seemed unstoppable in this world. When that failed, when the Dukars could no longer believe, they left Myth Nantar."

"And without the Dukars to protect it, the City of Destinies fell to the sahuagin."

"Yes." Sadness almost quenched the angry, molten fires in Qos's emerald eyes. "After I joined the Dukars, I came to Myth Nantar." He gestured with one hand, taking in the expanse of the city. "I saw most of what you see here, and my heart could not bear it."

Pacys looked at the storm giant, seeing past the towering foe to the gentle spirit beneath. He coaxed that image with his song, building it note by note.

"So I chose to close Myth Nantar from those who'd deserted her."

Pacys knew the storm giant hadn't kept everyone who'd journeyed to the City of Destinies away. Dozens had slipped in past the Great Barrier over the years when Qos had deemed them worthy.

"Why did you let me in?" the old bard asked. It was a question he hadn't dared ask the first few days. Qos had obviously known he was coming but hadn't been too much in favor of his presence.

"If it had been my choice," the storm giant said, "I wouldn't have."

Pacys silently accepted that, his fingers never betraying the musical weave he worked on.

"The Great Whale Bard was my friend," Qos went on. "He chose you. I chose to honor both his request and his memory."

"What am I supposed to do?"

"What you normally do, bard. Tell the tale of what goes on around you." The storm giant gestured at the surrounding city. "This is history in the making. The legend of the Taker is true. If we don't remove him from Serôs, he will destroy everything."

"Everything?"

"The rebirth of Myth Nantar. A second beginning, one that will be of even more import to those below and above." Qos turned and pointed back to the Dukarn Academy off the Promenade of Kupav. "The weapon we need to accomplish that is there."

"What is it?" Pacys stopped playing for a moment and turned to look. It was the first anything had been said of a weapon.

"The Great Gate," Qos said. "Once it's activated, it will pull the Taker and his army through it and exile him from Serôs."

"Where will he go?"

"It won't matter. Anywhere but here." Qos locked his emerald eyes on the bard's and said, "Song That Brings Bright Waters believed that you were the Taleweaver, the one destined to touch the heart of the young hero who would slay the Ravager."

"How am I supposed to accomplish that?"

Qos shook his head. "These are legends, bard. As familiar with them as you are, you should know that legends never tell everything."

"My song will," Pacys declared. "When it's ready, and when I sing it, the listener will know all." He stretched, adjusting himself on the coral. "When will you open the Great Barrier?"

"As soon as Serôsian races can come to an alliance."

"I believe the sea elves would be interested," Pacys said. "As well as the shalarin, but the mermen remain adamant about staying apart."

"They won't," Qos said, "once Voalidru falls."

"I've overheard the sea elf warriors talking about that. The locathah keep information coming to us. The warriors believe the Taker has stretched his alliances too thin and that he doesn't have the power to challenge Eadraal at this point."

"The Taker is mustering his next army even as we speak."

A cold chill raced through the old bard. "How?"

Qos held up his right hand. Green coral suddenly emerged from his palm and flattened, covering his huge hand.

"The Taker has surrounded the Whamite Isles," Qos told him, "with an evil and ancient kelpie that sings its listeners to their deaths. He wracks the islands with massive earthquakes that will drive the people to the shore so they can hear the kelpie songs. Few, if any, will survive. When enough have died, the Taker will call the victims back as drowned ones in his service."

Horror filled Pacys, stilling his fingers. He gazed at Qos's palm where images formed. He saw the pallid figures hanging from kelpie beds in the black water, their arms and legs limp, their dead eyes red and blank, mouths hanging open. A few of them were drowning even as he watched, thrashing slightly as their lives left them.

"No," the old bard cried hoarsely. "We can't let this happen."

"It already has," Qos stated. "It must happen to make way for the only chance Serôs has at peace."

Unable to look away, Pacys watched as more people dropped into the black water, immediately tended to by the kelpie beds. No matter how great his skill nor the fact that Oghma himself had set his present course before him, he would never be able to capture the abomination being played out before his eyes.

Blasted by the lightning bolt that should have killed him, Jherek hit the ground hard, so hard that the breath was driven from his lungs and he almost blacked out. He clung to his senses, though, thinking of Sabyna, Glawinn, and Azla trapped like rats in the cave. Rolling over on his side, he felt blood trickle down the side of his face.

The journey that had taken only days before had extended to two restless months. A sahuagin attack had cost them their rudder. Replacing the rudder had taken tendays after *Steadfast* had finally made a friendly port. Despite the time, the pull in his chest had brought him to Sabyna without fail, never once wavering.

As he got to his feet, the young sailor noticed the lightning bolt fading in the high sheen of the bracer on his left arm. The bracer had somehow protected him from the magical assault.

Black spots whirled in his vision as he gazed around the main cavern. Two of Tarnar's sailors—the two he'd been thrown into—were down, alive but unconscious. Jherek looked for his cutlass but didn't see it. The sounds of battle and the screams of dying men continued above.

He started to take one of the sailors' cutlasses, but impulse drew his eyes to the chasm in the center of the cavern. Looking down over the edge, he spotted a man-made entrance cut in the left side six feet below him. Before he knew quite what he was doing, feeling pulled to get back to Sabyna's side, he hung over the ledge, staring down into a pit that looked fathoms deep. Thankfully, the chasm walls provided finger and toeholds.

When he looked into the opening, he saw the sword hanging on the wall at the other end of what looked like a man-sized pink pearl box. Glancing at the other side of the chasm, he noticed what appeared to be the other side to the pink pearl room. The sword's steel glistened with a lambent pink light.

Ignoring the reluctance that filled him, Jherek clambered into the room. It stood to reason that if a sword had been hidden as cleverly as this one, it had to be a powerful weapon. The question of whether the sword was good or evil only touched his mind fleetingly. As powerful as the mage in the other room was, Jherek needed a powerful weapon.

Wrapping his hand around the sword hilt, Jherek felt a small tingle run through his arm. He almost released the sword, but the tingle was gone before he did. He thrust the blade through his sash and climbed the chasm wall again, then he jumped up the ledge and ran back to the second cave.

Tarnar looked at him with a surprised smile and said, "I thought you were dead."

"Iridea's Tear saved me." Jherek drew the sword from his waist, surprised that the blade was a curved cutlass and not the long sword he'd thought it was. The blade still held the pink glow.

Two of *Steadfast*'s crew lay dead inside the second cavern.

Peering into the shadows, Jherek saw Sabyna and Glawinn battling koalinths rising from the pool. Vurgrom's men took advantage of the situation and rushed forward.

Azla stepped from behind a column, batted aside the pirate's clumsy attack, then slid her scimitar across the man's stomach, spilling his guts. Still on the move, the pirate queen engaged her next attacker. Steel gleamed as it moved, then she sank the dirk in her left hand between the man's ribs, stiffening him up at once.

Lifting his arm, Jherek willed the bracer into a shield, then stepped into the cavern. One of the pirates rushed at him. The young sailor stepped sideways at the last moment, letting the pirate's overhead swing go past him, then he slammed the shield into his attacker with all his weight behind it.

The pirate hit the wall and sagged, dazed by the impact. Before he recovered, Jherek knocked the man's blade from his hand.

Tarnar stepped up and grabbed the pirate by the shirt, yanking him into a stumbling run and passing him back to one of his men.

"I've got him," the captain growled.

"Don't kill him if you don't have to," Jherek said.

"In that, my friend," Tarnar said, "we are in agreement."

Vurgrom bellowed orders from hiding but didn't make a move to engage Jherek as the young sailor moved forward.

Iakhovas stood his ground, glancing at Jherek with real curiosity. "Who are you, boy?"

Jherek shook his head, peering over the shield and hoping it would hold against any further magic. "I'm no one," he said.

"What are you doing here?"

Jherek thought he detected suspicion in the dark mage's tattooed face and mismatched eyes. "Let my friends go," Jherek demanded.

"I don't know you, do I?" Iakhovas asked.

"I'm only going to ask you once."

The man's eyes narrowed and he said, "Boy, I've eaten creatures bigger than you."

Without warning, Jherek stepped forward. It bothered him that the mage didn't draw the sword at his side, but if he didn't have to kill the man he wouldn't. He swung the sword, surprised at how balanced it felt, like it was a weightless extension of his body.

Incredibly, Iakhovas grabbed the sword with his hand, stopping the swing, but from the pained expression on the mage's face, it was a surprise for both of them. He lifted his hand, gazing with ill-concealed astonishment at the blood that spilled from around his closed hand.

"Who *are* you?" the mage demanded.

Before Jherek had time to answer, Vurgrom bellowed and rushed from hiding. He barreled across the short distance and slammed into the young sailor with his considerable bulk.

Already sore from his earlier fall, Jherek couldn't keep his feet, but he did keep his grip on the cutlass. It felt as if his arm was being torn from its socket before the blade slid free of the mage's hand.

"Going to kill you now, boy!" Vurgrom roared as he came down on top of Jherek. "I remember you from Baldur's Gate. I should have killed you then."

Willing Iridea's Tear from shield to dagger, a handle forming in his hand, Jherek shoved it toward Vurgrom's face. The fat pirate captain's eyes rounded as he stared at the multi-colored blade. Taking advantage of the man's shifting weight, the young sailor levered his forearm under his opponent's jaw hard enough to make his teeth clack, then rolled out from under him.

Jherck willed the bracer into a hook, the handle fitting easily between his fingers. Vurgrom got to his feet at the same time as the young sailor, taking up his battle-axe in both hands. Iakhovas was still visible over the pirate captain's shoulder, his attention torn between his bleeding hand and Jherek.

Reversing the battle-axe so the hammer end of it was forward, Vurgrom swung at the young sailor. Jherek dodged, barely escaping the speeding weapon. The blunt head smashed against the wall, cracking rock loose and driving stone splinters into Jherek's face and left shoulder.

Lining up behind his blade, Jherek gave himself over to it, relishing the feel and movement. He whipped it forward, forcing Vurgrom into a defensive posture. The bigger man managed to block the sword strikes, but only just.

Another pirate stepped from hiding at Jherek's side, coming too quickly for the young sailor to bring the cutlass around. Jherek dropped, falling backward, watching the pirate's sword flash by only inches from his face. The young sailor kicked upward, rolling on his back and right shoulder to get the necessary height, aware that Vurgrom was renewing his attack.

Jherek's foot connected with the pirate's sword arm elbow hard enough to crack bone. He continued the roll to escape Vurgrom's battle-axe. More stone splinters sprayed against his back, then he was on his feet in a squatting position, ready to spring upward.

Vurgrom already had the battle-axe back and was swinging the blade at him, intending to cleave him between wind and water. Staying low, Jherek drove forward, firing off his bent legs and planting his left shoulder and neck at knee level.

Vurgrom squalled in surprise and toppled.

As the big man fell, Jherek rose to his knees and struck again, snaring the battle-axe's haft with the hook. He brought the cutlass down hard and sheared the head from the haft. A small blue light flared as the weapon came apart.

Vurgrom raised the haft in defense as Jherek stood and swung again. The cutlass blade sliced through the thick axe haft as if it were made of paper. With uncanny precision, somehow knowing he could trust the sword, the young sailor brought it to a stop less than two inches from Vurgrom's face.

"Surrender," Jherek told him, "and I'll not kill you."

"You broke my axe," Vurgrom said in disbelief. "That axe was enchanted. It's never been broken before—never failed me."

Jherek twisted the tip of the cutlass, emphasizing his point.

"Fight me hand-to-hand," Vurgrom roared. "Give me a true man's challenge."

Breathing hard, perspiration and blood covering him, Jherek replied, "If there were time, and if there were honor in it, I would, but there's no time, and the only honor at risk would be my own."

Jherek glanced at the mage, already willing the bracer into a shield again.

"Pray to your gods, whelp," Iakhovas said in a cold, hard voice, "that you never meet me again."

Jherek wasn't planning on it, but he didn't say anything. He also didn't break eye contact. If any of his friends had been hurt, it would have been a different matter.

Iakhovas turned, gestured, then walked into what appeared to be a solid wall, the elf woman at his heels.

When the mage had gone, Jherek left Vurgrom with one of Tarnar's men holding a sword to his throat. Tarnar's sailors flooded into the cave. Their captain cowed, the surviving members of Vurgrom's pirates surrendered easily enough.

Jherek sprinted to the pool where koalinth battled his friends, Tarnar at his heels. Two of the creatures lay dead, silent testimony to Glawinn's skill. The paladin was on the floor, his sword locked against a koalinth's spear and his shield holding the creature's savage jaws from his face.

Changing the shield back to a hook, Jherek hooked the koalinth's shoulder from behind and yanked the monster off the paladin. The young sailor kicked the sea hobgoblin in the face, driving it back into the pool. He offered the paladin a hand up.

"Hail and well met, young warrior," Glawinn greeted him in a strained voice.

"Hail and well met," Jherek replied.

"The helping hand was appreciated," the paladin said with a crooked smile, "but I'd just gotten him where I wanted him."

Glawinn's sword flashed, engaging another koalinth's trident. He shoved the tines aside, then slid back through and slashed across the creature's stomach, mortally wounding it.

Jherek shifted the hook back to a bracer and swung his arm out to slap aside another koalinth's spear. The young sailor chopped the cutlass into the koalinth's neck, nearly beheading it. He stepped around the falling corpse, moving toward Sabyna.

When he saw her, the copper tresses framing her face, Jherek felt as though he'd been hit in the heart with Vurgrom's great hammer. Eighty-three days they'd been apart, and not one of them had passed that he didn't think of her with both longing and trepidation.

Now she was there before him, bent over in a knife-fighter's stance, a blade in each hand, battling for her life against a koalinth. The creature struck with its spear but Sabyna turned it to one side and darted in to score a wound on her attacker's arm. The wound wasn't life threatening, but it bled heavily.

The koalinth howled in pain, then shoved its head open, the massive jaws aiming to bite her head.

Jherek thrust the cutlass forward, not willing to attack the creature from behind. The blade settled between the creature's jaws and it snapped its fangs on steel instead of flesh.

"Lady," Jherek said softly as the koalinth withdrew, "I am here."

Sabyna glanced at him and said, "You're alive."

"Aye."

Jherek stepped between her and the koalinth as another joined it. Despite the stench of wet leather, the closed-in stink of the cave, and the smell of blood, he caught the scent of the lilac fragrance she wore. Just one breath steeled his arm in spite of the beating he'd taken and the fatigue of racing across five miles of rugged terrain to reach the cave. He felt calm and centered.

"I thought you were dead," Sabyna said.

Jherek batted away a spear thrust, riposting and slicing the koalinth on the forehead so that blood ran down into its eyes.

"As I feared you might be before I returned," he told her.

"I wasn't sure you cared about that—even cared enough to come back from wherever you'd gone."

Her words hurt Jherck more grievously than any wound he'd received. He grabbed the next spear thrust in his free hand, held the haft, and stepped forward to pierce the koalinth's breast with the cutlass.

He yanked his blade free and turned to her, full of anger and pain. He kept his words as calm as he could, not understanding how she could doubt him.

"Please, lady," he said, "I have told you I would lay my life down for you. I would never desert you in troubled waters without seeing you home."

"You've told me that," Sabyna agreed, "but there's much you haven't told me."

Jherek gratefully turned back to face the koalinth he'd wounded.

"Perhaps we could talk about this another time," he said.

He parried a spear, knocking sparks from the weapon.

"Do you swear?" Sabyna pressed, stepping up beside him to engage another koalinth.

Her knives flashed as she blocked the spear thrust, then one of the blades flew from her hand, burying itself in her opponent's throat. Crimson sprayed over her and Jherek.

Jherek hesitated, blocking the spear twice more, then stepping in as he formed the bracer into a dagger and punched it through the wounded koalinth's heart. Even as the creature fell, another shouldered up to take its place.

"Promise me," Sabyna said.

"Lady, please."

Jherek tried to turn the koalinth's attack, but it was too savage, too fierce. It drove him back as he tried to find an opening.

"I will not be denied, Jherek," Sabyna said.

"Now," the young sailor said, thrusting and breaking his opponent's attack, "is not the time."

"Your secret, whatever it is," Sabyna said, "is holding both of us back. Neither of us can be happy until we know where we stand."

"Lady, I care deeply for you."

The conversation and the emotion that went with it distracted Jherek. He missed a parry and watched as the spear streaked toward his chest. He managed to turn at the last moment, letting the iron point graze his ribs. He willed the bracer into a hook and tore out the koalinth's throat before it was able to withdraw.

"Pretty words," Sabyna said. "Jherek, I wouldn't ask this if I knew you weren't confused, scared, and hurting, too."

He faced her, his chest heaving from emotion and exertion, and said, "Lady, I have never known any other way."

He was only dimly aware that the last of the koalinth were being beaten back by Glawinn, Azla, Tarnar, and the sailors from *Steadfast*. Skeins had claimed one of the koalinths, wrapping the creature and using it against the others.

"I have never known pain like this," Sabyna replied. "Never known confusion like this. My world was far simpler before I knew you."

Jherek was silent for a moment as the sounds of the battle died down. His voice was quiet, barely above a whisper when he said, "Lady, I'd never known my world was as small as it was before I knew you."

"If you feel that way," Sabyna asked in frustration, "then why have you put up all these walls?"

"Walls are a part of my life, lady."

"I won't have them in mine."

Sabyna gazed at him fiercely. The fact that he'd pushed her into such a position shamed Jherek. His heart ached and a lump that he could scarce swallow filled his throat.

"What is there to risk?" she demanded.

"The friendship that we have between us."

"But it could be more."

That she'd voiced the possibility of something more both embarrassed and terrified Jherek even more than getting hit with the lightning bolt only moments ago.

"Lady," he said, "I have treasured every moment of it, and if that friendship was all that would ever exist between us—ever could exist—I would be happy."

"Jherek," Sabyna's voice was thick with emotion, "it's been hard these last—what, nearly three months—never knowing if you were alive or dead. I truly don't know the depth of my emotions for you. I'm not sure if I'd know true love, but I do know that I've never felt this way about anyone before. Even as tense as things have been between us since we arrived in the Sea of Fallen Stars, I still remember the meals we shared aboard *Breezerunner*."

"Aye," he said.

"That was the reality that could exist for us, Jherek, but we'll never know unless whatever shuts the door on that possibility is revealed. If I could, I would tear it down with my own hands."

"You don't know what it is you ask."

Her eyes were sad. "Maybe you can live with what we have and never know anything more than that, but I can't. I can't limit myself the way you do. I'm not that strong."

"Lady, you're one of the strongest people I've ever met. Please don't think you're weak because of me."

"Then trust me, Jherek. Whatever it is you're hiding, trust me with it."

Tears welled in the young sailor's eyes and the pain in his throat and chest was almost unbearable. He tried to speak but couldn't.

Sabyna lowered her voice, and it was as if there were only the two of them in the world. "You believe in love, Jherek. I heard you say it, and I saw the strength of your conviction bind a spell that was very powerful. That wouldn't have happened if you didn't mean it. As you believe in love, believe in my love for you." Tears ran down her cheeks, tracking the blood and dirt on her face. "Tell me what holds us apart."

Jherek spoke the words he knew would doom him to unhappiness for the rest of his life. "As you wish."

23

"Are you going to tell her then, young warrior?"

Jherek gazed at his hands as he toweled himself off once more. He'd never seen them shake that way. Except, perhaps, for the night he'd chosen to leave his father's ship and leap into the sea, not knowing if he would live.

He glanced up at Glawinn and said, "I promised her."

The paladin nodded slowly. "There's a case to be made for the fact that she coerced you."

They were in the warrior's quarters aboard *Azure Dagger*. Returning to Azla's ship in the dark with Vurgrom and his pirates as prisoners—and with the weakened prisoners the koalinth had held as livestock—had taken hours.

During that time Sabyna had concerned herself with the prisoners they'd rescued from the koalinth and given Jherek time to think. Unfortunately, all he'd been able to think on was this moment. When they'd reached the ship, he'd begged off time to bathe and tend his wounds, hoping the words he needed would come to him.

He'd drawn a bucket of fresh water from the ship's stores instead of bathing in the salt, wanting to be at his best even though he felt everything was going to end at its worst. He'd washed with lye soap, then groomed himself as best as he could, borrowing Glawinn's shaving kit to scrape the sparse stubble from his chin like he was a man in danger of raising a beard. When he was finished with the task, with his hands shaking the way they were, he guessed that he'd drawn more blood than Vurgrom and the koalinth had.

"As much as I don't wish this," Jherek said, "I know she needs—and deserves—to know."

"And you? Could you love her from afar if it comes to that?"

Jherek looked at his friend and mentor. "Aye," he said, "without hesitation."

"Ah, but you've got Lathander's heart in you, young warrior." Glawinn's voice turned husky and his eyes shone brightly. "Then you will never lose her, no matter how this goes."

"And her?"

Glawinn shook his head. "I cannot speak for the lady, young warrior. The thing that crosses the two of you is strong. It's not just her, it's you, too. She'll look at you and think of her brother, but you'll look at her and think of your father."

"No."

"You will, and you need to face that."

"My father will not be a part of my life forever," Jherek objected.

"No," Glawinn responded. "I don't think he will, but for a while longer yet, he will be."

Jherek folded the towel and looked around for his clothes. They weren't on the bunk bed where he'd left them when he'd gone to bathe in the crew's head.

"I took the liberty of seeing to your breeches," Glawinn said, taking them from the built-in chest of drawers. "I washed them while you were tending yourself, then dried them in the ship's galley."

Jherek took the breeches, amazed at how clean they were. He'd never gotten real clothes while on *Black Champion* or *Azure Dagger*, and the things he'd traded for while on *Steadfast* remained aboard her on the other side of the Whamite Isles. Azla sailed *Azure Dagger* around to the south of the island, intending to stop briefly at Agenais to replenish the ship's stores before returning Tarnar and his crew to their ship.

"Thank you," Jherek said.

"I knew you'd want to look your best. Here are your socks."

Jherek took them and pulled the pants on, then his socks and boots.

"I'm afraid there was nothing that could be done about the shirt," Glawinn said, kneeling and taking his kit from under his bed. He opened the kit and pulled out a sky-blue shirt with white ruffles and belled sleeves. "I thought perhaps you could wear one of mine. The breadth of our shoulders are about the same."

"That's far too fine."

Jherek loved the look of the shirt but he couldn't imagine himself wearing something like that. Velen had been a simple sailors' town and he'd established early in his relationship with Madame Iitaar that he wouldn't accept charity. She'd accepted that, but she'd also cared for his clothing.

"Perhaps something else?" Jherek asked.

Glawinn didn't look in the kit. "There's nothing else." He held the shirt up and said, "Unless you're prepared to walk out there with your father's tattoo showing for all to see, I'd suggest accepting the loan."

Reluctantly, Jherek took the shirt. It felt incredibly smooth.

"Silk, young warrior, as smooth as a caress from Sune Firehair herself." Glawinn smiled. "That shirt has seen me through many a difficult situation."

"You wore this in battle?"

"In King Azoun's courts, where the pecking order is oft determined by dress. Put it on."

Jherek pulled the shirt on, amazed at the feel of it.

Glawinn took a mirror from his kit and hung it on a peg on the wall. "Let's have a look at you."

Feeling very self-conscious, the young sailor glanced at the mirror. The image he saw surprised him. His tanned face and pale gray eyes stood out against the sky-blue shirt. Sun streaks colored his light brown hair. The scar on his cheek lent him a roguish air. His gaze was direct, challenging. The past months had been hard, and they'd hardened him with it.

The look was all too familiar and disturbing. He turned from the mirror.

"What's wrong?" Glawinn asked.

"For the first time," Jherek said in a thick voice, "I see my father's face in mine."

Glawinn was silent for a moment, then he stepped behind the young sailor and held his shoulders. Gently but firmly, the warrior turned him back to the mirror and said, "Look deep."

Jherek did, captivated by the unacceptable resemblance he now noticed. It was something about the set of his eyes, the square of his jaw. Maybe more, but at least those things.

"Young warrior," Glawinn said, peering into the mirror over Jherek's shoulder and still clasping him tightly, "you may find your father's likeness in your features, but you'll never find your father's ways in your heart."

Jherek nodded as if he accepted that, but he knew he didn't.

"Thank you for the loan of the shirt," he said. "I should be going. We agreed to meet on the forecastle. This time of morning, it's the most private place on the ship."

He took his sash from his bed and wrapped it around his hips, then shoved the newly acquired cutlass through it. At first he'd felt guilty about taking the weapon, but it had come from the destruction of Lathander's disk, so he felt he owed it to the priests at Baldur's Gate to take it to them.

"There is one other thing." Glawinn took a small bottle from his kit. "Cologne. Hold out your hands." He pulled the cork stopper from the bottle and poured. "Rub your hands together and slap it onto your face."

Jherek did, finding that it stung the cut on his cheek, but it had a pleasant, if bold, fragrance. "You make me feel like I'm suiting up for a battle."

"All true affairs of the heart between two people who have the trials between them that you two have *are* battles, young warrior. Too often, in the right circumstances, a man's—and a woman's—dress is a weapon."

"I've got to go."

Glawinn put his hands on Jherek's shoulders again and said, "Wear your heart on your sleeve that she may know your mind truly. All the worries, all the fear, as well as all the love. When you are done, should you need me, I will be here in this room." He leaned forward and kissed Jherek lightly on the forehead. "Should I ever be blessed with a son, young warrior, nothing would please me greater than to see him turn out like you. May Lathander bless you."

The lump returned to Jherek's throat. It was all he could do to nod and walk through the door. He took the stairs from the nearly empty cargo hold that still stank of slavery and walked up on deck.

Morning tinted the eastern sky a rosy pink peering through wheat-colored clouds. Sabyna Truesail stood in the middle of it on the forecastle deck, peering east, in the direction *Azure Dagger* was headed.

Jherek gazed at her with longing. Though the rising sun behind her reduced her to a silhouette, he could picture every line and every rounded curve of her. No matter what happened from this moment on, he knew he'd never forget that sight.

He crossed the deck hurriedly and went up the steps to the forecastle.

"Lady, I'm sorry I kept you waiting."

She turned at his voice, and surprise lighted her eyes.

"So it would appear well worth the wait," she said. "Had I known, I'd have dressed accordingly."

She wore dark green breeches and a white shirt with her sleeves rolled to mid-forearm. She'd bathed and combed her hair, and the scent of lilacs was gentle around her. Jherek thought he'd never seen a lovelier woman in all his life.

"It's the shirt," he said lamely. "Glawinn loaned it to me."

"He has good taste."

"I'll tell him you thought so." Jherek paused, wondering how to continue. How did you tell someone you cared about that your father killed her brother?

"Jherek, about last night," Sabyna said, "I was perhaps out of line."

"Does that mean you've changed your mind about talking?" Instead of feeling relieved, Jherek was anxious, wanting to be done with the secret he kept. It was confusing.

"No, we're going to talk," she said adamantly. "I meant it when I said I can't go on like this, but I think perhaps I could have waited for a better time or spoken somewhat less harshly."

"You did what you had to do, lady. I claim no foul there."

"Good, because I'm not leaving here without knowing your heart."

Jherek took a deep breath and said, "You know my heart, lady. It's my past you're unaware of." He paused, uncertain of where to begin.

"You said you were wanted," Sabyna said. "For what?"

"For things I never did, lady. I'm innocent of any crime, but I had the misfortune to be born the son of a bad man."

"No man is responsible for the mistakes his father has made."

"You may not feel that way after you hear the whole story." With a trembling hand, Jherek unfastened his sleeve, his eyes on Sabyna. "When I was twelve, I ran away from my father, from all the things that he did."

"That was a very brave thing to do."

Jherek forced himself to roll the sleeve up. "But I found running away didn't rescue me from my father's heritage." Rolling over his arm, he showed her the tattoo of the flaming skull masked in chains.

Sabyna's face drained of color and her eyes filled with cold, hard tears. She wrapped her arms across her breasts and glared at him. "That's the mark of Bloody Falkane," she whispered.

Jherek nodded slowly and said, "Bloody Falkane—the man who killed your brother—is my father, lady."

Sabyna turned from him and walked woodenly to the prow railing.

Not knowing what else to do, Jherek followed after her. He stayed back, wishing he could comfort her. Why did it have to be her brother? But he knew that wasn't a fair question. There were a number of families who'd lost brothers and fathers, and other family to the notorious crew of *Bunyip* and Bloody Falkane. It was only his ill luck that numbered Sabyna's family among their victims.

He stood quietly waiting. He had no words. All he could do was try to figure out how a day that was starting so beautifully could be so bad already.

"Anything," Sabyna croaked hoarsely as she turned around to face him with a face wet with tears and wracked with pain. "I was prepared for anything but that."

Jherek nodded but couldn't get a word past the lump in his throat. He looked at the deck between his feet and tried to think. Even if he could speak, what would he say?

Sabyna's startled scream ripped through the morning.

Looking up, Jherek saw two pallid gray arms seize the pretty ship's mage from behind. They wrapped around Sabyna's body and yanked her from the deck. The young sailor caught a glimpse of the gray corpse that had climbed up the ship's prow as it fell back into the water. Two more corpses pulled themselves up the ship's prow as well, throwing their arms over the railing.

"*Boarders!*" Jherek yelled as loudly as he could.

He ripped the sword from his sash, knowing he was in danger of losing Sabyna. *Azure Dagger* had all sails out and was running with the wind. He sprinted toward the port railing and threw himself over.

The Sea of Fallen Stars sparkled blue-green for an instant, and he heard other sailors aboard *Azure Dagger* take up the warning cry.

"Boarders! Boarders!"

"Boarders my arse! Them are sea zombies straight from Umberlee's—"

Jherek hit the water cleanly, following the line of the cutlass. Foam churned white around him as he dived. Turning in the water, he floated, using his empty hand to turn himself around.

Dozens of bodies floated in the sea, all of them pallid gray and bloated from drowning. A hundred and more walked the sea floor, followed by schools of fish and crabs that feasted on their dead flesh.

An eerie, haunting melody suddenly filled the water. Jherek felt a tingle run through his whole body and a warm lassitude started to creep in on him. He pushed the music away, remembering that Sabyna was down there somewhere.

A heartbeat later, the young sailor spotted her, still pulled along by the drowned one that held her less than forty feet away. Jherek kicked his feet and took off after her. Even with the cutlass in one hand and wearing boots, he overtook the sea zombie in seconds. His muscles screamed silent protests after the beating they'd taken the night before.

Other sea zombies noticed the young sailor and swam for him. Two of them were male, but the third had been a little girl no more than ten.

Sabyna struggled against her captor who held her with its arm locked under her throat.

Jherek's optimism flagged. Zombies of any type could prove incredibly hard to kill. They had to be chopped literally to pieces or have the necromancer's spell that created them broken.

Sabyna's eyes widened when she saw him.

Fisting the drowned one's chin with his free hand from behind, Jherek twisted with all his strength. The drowned one's spine cracked as the head came fully halfway around. Still, the creature didn't release its hold on Sabyna.

The young sailor shoved the cutlass forward, preparing to cut the thing's water-rotted arm from it. As soon as the sword touched the drowned one, electricity sparked the length of the blade. The zombie convulsed, its limbs flaring out and the seaweed-tangled hair on its head standing straight up. Great boils erupted on the dead flesh, causing a sudden eruption of blue-purple cuttle worms three inches long and as thick as a man's finger.

Jherek waved the worms from his face, knowing he was safe because they didn't like live flesh. He glanced up, seeing Sabyna swimming for the surface. Before she made it, long vines from a kelp bed snaked out for her, curling around her and pulling her in.

For the first time Jherek realized the hypnotic melody came from the purple-leafed kelp beds. He swam toward her, watching as other zombies closed in on her.

What felt like iron bars wrapped around his ankles and dragged him down. He plummeted toward the ocean floor like he'd been tied to an anchor. Glancing down, he saw that a large man with eye sockets picked clean by a hermit crab still curled up inside one of them had grabbed him. The man's waterlogged weight was enough to drag them both to the bottom.

Jherek shoved his cutlass into the man's face, hoping whatever magic filled the blade hadn't exhausted itself. The zombie's limbs and hair popped straight out and the flesh boiled. Lungs near to bursting, the young sailor swam after Sabyna.

A pair of drowned ones reached her first, digging into the kelp bed with her. Sabyna fought against them, but their teeth dug into her right thigh and left side. Blood stained the water.

"No!" Jherek shouted, causing an eruption of air bubbles from his mouth.

He shoved the cutlass into the creature biting on Sabyna's thigh. Jherek watched as the magic in the blade destroyed the undead thing, then he attacked the one worrying at Sabyna's side, destroying it as well. Sabyna's movements showed definite weakness.

Jherek sawed at the vines holding her to the kelp, cutting her free. Her wounds bled freely. He hooked an arm around her waist and swam for the surface, knowing even if he made it there was no way they could reach *Azure Dagger* or out-swim the rest of the drowned ones.

Another zombie swam at them from above, giving Jherek no time to dodge away. With no warning, a rush of golden scales intercepted the drowned one, snatching it up in a huge mouth and crunching it to pieces.

Even with only that brief glance, Jherek knew it was the sea wyrm that he'd first seen when they'd salvaged *Black Champion*. The creature had followed *Steadfast* all the way to Aglarond and back, but he thought it had been left on the other side of the island with *Steadfast*. Somehow it had known where he was and made its way to him.

Jherek watched the sea wyrm constrict in the water, flipping its body around so that its fins caught the currents in such a way that it turned back around on itself like a corkscrew. The fins on its head flared out as it regarded Jherek. Then another zombie seized its attention less than ten feet away. The sea wyrm streaked there and bit the dead woman in half. Both halves remained active for a time, arms and legs moving desperately but without an ability to control their direction as they dropped slowly to the sea floor.

A moment later, Jherek brought Sabyna to the surface. She looked into his eyes, coughing and gasping. He glanced down at the wounds in her side and leg, knowing he had to put pressure on them to stop the bleeding. Furthermore, if there were any sharks in the water, the blood scent was sure to bring them.

"Go," she gasped hoarsely. "I'm getting cold, Jherek. I don't think I can swim."

"I'm not going to leave you," he said.

"By yourself you might have a chance."

"No, lady." The young sailor gazed down at the sea wyrm still darting through the water below. It struck like lightning, destroying zombie after zombie that swam toward Jherek and Sabyna. He locked eyes with the creature and said, "Help me."

The sea wyrm curled in on itself, then exploded into motion. It streaked through the water like an arrow, surfacing almost casually beside Jherek. Cautiously, it folded the fins down around its head and stretched its muzzle forward.

Not daring to believe, yet knowing it was somehow true, Jherek placed his hand on the sea wyrm's broad head. The scales felt slippery and solid and a buzzing filled his palm. After a moment, the sea wyrm wrapped its coils around Jherek and Sabyna. The young sailor moved quickly, aware of the sea zombie heads that broke the surface around them.

He pushed Sabyna onto the sea wyrm's neck behind its head where the dorsal fin was missing. He slid on behind her, wrapping his arms around her and his legs around the creature's thick torso.

The sea wyrm lifted its head clear of the ocean, gazing back at Jherek expectantly.

"The ship," the young sailor said, hoping he wasn't wrong.

The sea wyrm's body undulated and sent them speeding through the water. Jherek held Sabyna tightly. The creature easily avoided the bobbing zombie heads that gnashed their jaws in frustration and reached for them as they passed. The sea wyrm swam unerringly for *Azure Dagger*, overtaking it with ease.

As he got closer, Sabyna became dead weight in Jherek's arms. Spray from the sea wyrm staying so close to the surface blew back over them. It was cold and salty and stung his nose and eyes. The young sailor watched a vein throb slowly on the side of the ship's mage's neck and took heart in that. As long as she lived, there was hope.

Azure Dagger's crew pointed at the sea wyrm as it swam along the port side. Two men hung from the prow, cutting away the net the drowned ones had used to set their trap and catch the fast-moving caravel. Once it had caught onto the prow, they'd climbed it to attempt boarding the ship.

Glawinn and Azla stood at the port side railing. The pirate queen ordered a longboat put over the side. It was a dangerous move. If it got too low and hit the water, it could be pushed back to smash a hole in the hull. Glawinn and two other sailors manned the boat as it swayed unsteadily down from the cargo arm.

The sea wyrm swam for the longboat, getting alongside it as if it was an everyday thing. It lifted its neck from the water and put Jherek and Sabyna closer to the longboat. Holding Sabyna in his arms, Jherek passed her up to the paladin.

"I've got her, young warrior," the paladin said. "Climb on up."

Glawinn sat cautiously, holding Sabyna tenderly. He inspected her wounds.

Jherek caught hold of the longboat and pulled himself inside. He gazed back down at the sea wyrm, still not believing what had happened. The creature looked back up at him and flared its head fins again.

"Thank you," the young sailor said.

The sea wyrm gave a trumpeting call, then dived beneath the waves. Jherek turned his attention to Sabyna.

Pacys swam across the Dukar Quarter in Myth Nantar as fast as he could. His heart still pounded from the dream that had awakened him. He'd slept in the Dukar Academy room Qos had offered him. The seaweed bed had proven surprisingly comfortable and, despite his excitement, when he'd lain down, he'd had no problem sleeping. Until this morning.

He stopped at the coral in the courtyard near Maalirn's Walk where he and Qos usually met. The storm giant was already there, or perhaps the Green Dukar Paragon had never left.

Pacys tried to keep his voice calm. "Grand Savant Qos."

The storm giant looked up.

"I have to go," the old bard said.

"No—there are things not yet done."

Pacys felt frantic. "You've got to understand, this is about the boy, Jherek."

"The one you believe to be the hero of your song?" Qos nodded. "I know."

"The girl he loves—"

"—lies dying," Qos said. "Truly, Master Pacys, I do know these things. I keep watch over a lot of currents at this time. I also know a huge army of drowned ones marches on Eadraal."

"I must go to the boy. He's on the verge of giving up."

"Your place is here," the storm giant said, his voice holding a note of warning. "There are parts that have to be played yet, and you need to be ready to play yours. You could be called upon to open the Great Barrier. When that time comes, we'll have little time."

"You can open the Great Barrier."

Qos's emerald eyes blazed with angry impatience and he said, "If I could open the Great Barrier, you wouldn't be here."

The revelation stunned Pacys into silence for a moment.

"You can't open the Great Barrier?"

"No," the giant said.

"Why?"

"Because it was my decision to close it," Qos answered. "I can allow others in, but I can't return Myth Nantar to Serôs. The prophecies about the Taker creating a reunion of the peoples of Serôs must come to pass first. That's the price I paid for salvaging what was left of the City of Destinies. If events don't go as I hope, if you aren't able to open the Great Barrier, Myth Nantar may never rise again."

Pacys stood mute, feeling the pressure of the depths above him for the first time since he'd descended into Serôs.

"That's why the boy must wait," Qos said patiently. "Everything must come in its own time."

"He may break before I reach him," Pacys said. "He's that close to hopelessness."

"Master Pacys, we all are. We must each hold to our individual strengths just a little longer."

⇥————•————↤

"Is she going to be all right?" Jherek asked.

He stared at Sabyna's limp form lying on the bed in her private quarters aboard *Azure Dagger*. She looked so small and pale.

Sabyna's wounds had been cleaned and tended, but they were inflamed and leaked pus. Glawinn had attempted to cure them with his paladin's ability, and Arthoris had tried a healing potion. In both instances some of Sabyna's strength and color had returned for a short time only to dwindle away again. She hadn't regained consciousness.

"I don't know, young warrior," Glawinn said. Kneeling by the bed, he took a compress from a small water pitcher, folded it, and tenderly laid it over her head. "The bite of the undead can be toxic, carrying diseases even advanced healers know little of. Her fate is in stronger hands than we have aboard this ship."

"We'll find a priest when we put into Agenais," Jherek said. "Everything will be all right then, won't it?"

Glawinn hesitated, then said, "Mayhap." He took the compress from her head and wet it again. "The main thing is to keep her fever down, give her body a chance to heal itself. Even then, the battle she fights is a draining one."

Jherek felt so helpless and empty inside. "It's my fault," he said hoarsely. "If I had not loved her, she would not have been cursed by my ill luck."

"No," Glawinn said gruffly. "I'll have none of that kind of talk in here. The girl may not be in her right mind now, but I've seen people like this come back and know every word that was spoken around them. If you're going to stay here with her, you're going to speak positively. Do you understand me?"

Jherek met the older man's gaze and said, "Help me, Glawinn, I can't be this strong."

Glawinn put the compress back on Sabyna's head. "Yes you can, young warrior," he said. "You'll be as strong as you need to be, whether to hang on or let go. You'll see it done because that's how you are. It's the only way you can be."

Jherek clenched his hands into fists, hating the helpless feeling that filled him. "What do I need to do? Tell me and I swear it will be done."

"Believe."

"In what?"

"I can't tell you."

Jherek looked at the small, pale form on the bed and begged, "Give me something to believe in."

"I can't. You'll have to find it within yourself."

Jherek knelt there beside the bed and searched his heart. He reached out to Ilmater the Crying God, the god he'd rejected months ago. He prayed the way he used to, but there was no comfort.

Sabyna's breathing remained ragged.

"Everyone's dead," Azla announced, looking through the spyglass she held.

Jherek stood beside her, raking Agenais with a spyglass as well. The port city's streets remained empty. Even the ships in the harbor were untended.

"Now we know where the drowned ones came from," Tarnar said. "I have to worry about my ship."

"The kelpies seem to have attacked the civilized areas first," Azla said. "Since you weren't anchored near a port, maybe they've survived."

"If they didn't decide to come looking for me."

"By the end of the day," Azla said, "you'll know."

Resolutely, Jherek kept the spyglass trained on the shore. Azla had ordered the helmsman to keep *Azure Dagger* far enough away from the evil kelpie beds that the haunting melody they sang was barely audible. There was no hope in his heart, but he wasn't ready to go back to the small room where Sabyna lay just yet. He wasn't helpful there and the rasp of her strained breathing tortured him. At least here he could search for someone who could help her.

"Survivors!" the pirate in the crow's nest shouted. "Survivors starboard!"

Reflexively, Jherek swung his gaze around and spotted the small boatload of people a quarter of a mile or more out to sea.

Azla gave orders to pick them up and the crew hung the sails. Silently, Jherek hoped one of them would be a priest or a healer. Unfortunately, priests had proven extremely susceptible to the call of the kelpie beds.

24

Laaqueel swam above the army advancing northeast to Voalidru, lost in her own thoughts and fears. The two previous merman cities had fallen after a considerable amount of bloodshed.

The sea zombies Iakhovas had raised from the shallows around the Whamite Isles had proven to be the turning point of the sweep through Eadraal's holdings. Despite their fierceness and their familiarity with the terrain, even the strong-willed merman warriors had given ground. The once-dead were harder to kill the second time around.

The malenti priestess also knew that, as large as the army was, it was also extremely vulnerable—not from external forces, but from internal pressures. T'Kalah and the other sahuagin princes grew steadily more displeased with Iakhovas's decisions.

What had once been jealousy over the crown turned now to unrest with how the war progressed. That feeling was spreading through the sahuagin of both the inner and outer seas as they marched to the very eye of the storm between all the nations of Serôs. If they chose to unify, they could attack the sahuagin from three sides. Only the retreat back to the Xedran Reefs seemed secure.

Adding the legions of undead from the Whamite Isles had been strategically the best move to increase the army's strength, but the sahuagin didn't believe Sekolah had anything to do with the sudden appearance of the sea zombies. Scouts that had ventured too close to the kelpie beds had succumbed to the ancient magic as well, becoming undead themselves. Those were the hardest of all to bear, and Laaqueel had destroyed them as soon as she'd discovered them.

If it hadn't been for Laaqueel, the sahuagin wouldn't have been put back to take care of the flanks, away from the undead. The koalinth saw the sea zombies as flesh-and-blood battering rams that softened up the merman defenses so they could roll over them more easily.

She gazed down through the murky water, watching the drowned ones swim through the currents toward Voalidru as Iakhovas had commanded them. They looked like a school of scavenger fish hugging the sea floor along the shallows.

"Little malenti, you think too much. Your thoughts cause doubt instead of hope."

Startled, Laaqueel looked up in time to see Iakhovas glide into position beside her.

"There's much to think about," she said, then glanced back and saw *Tarjana* in the distance.

"On the contrary, the time for thinking is almost over. Voalidru will be mine within hours."

"Perhaps, but the merfolk will continue to fight to win it back."

"I'm not intending to hold it," Iakhovas said. "It will only be a staging area for the attack on Myth Nantar."

"Then what happens?" Laaqueel asked because she knew it was expected. She no longer really cared, but Iakhovas enjoyed taunting her.

"Then the High Mages save the world," Iakhovas replied, "just the way their legends say they will—but not before I get what I came for."

Laaqueel studied him, noting how confident he was of himself. His manner was so sahuagin it hurt, yet he talked casually of defeat while hinting that everything was going as he'd planned.

"How can you be so sure Myth Nantar won't prove your undoing?" she asked.

"Because I know how those people think. They care more for their precious City of Destinies than anything else. The whole idea of unity in Serôs is based around Myth Nantar."

"But it didn't work," Laaqueel protested. "I've read some of their histories. In the end, Myth Nantar failed because they fought over it as well."

"As it might fail again. But for now, they'll believe, and they'll attempt to save it and themselves. You'll see. Every step of this war has been carefully orchestrated. None have been born, little malenti, who will ever get the best of me."

Laaqueel was silent for a moment, knowing he wouldn't like what she next had to say. She didn't pause out of fear for herself; there was none of that left. She let the pause add weight to her words and glanced at Iakhovas to see his reaction.

"You hadn't planned on the boy in the cave, had you?"

With a mocking smile, his golden eye gleaming, Iakhovas gazed at her.

"No," he admitted, "I hadn't. He was a surprise engineered by someone else."

"Who?"

"I don't know, nor do I care. He is no threat to me. He is too lost in his own pain to look past that."

"His sword cut you when you thought it wouldn't."

"There's not much that can now," Iakhovas said. "I am almost whole."

"But he did."

"It's no matter. Don't irritate me, little malenti. I've got victories to arrange and a war to lose."

In the next instant he faded from the water.

Laaqueel assumed he'd teleported back to *Tarjana*. The fact that he no longer bothered to hide his magic bothered her as well. She reached up to touch the white shark symbol between her breasts and tried to feel the connection to the Shark God she'd once had.

It wasn't there. Still, the powers granted by her love and devotion to Sekolah worked. When a priestess truly lost her faith, those went away as well. How was it then, she wondered, that she could doubt so much yet still retain them?

She had no answers and nowhere to turn. So she swam, heading to Voalidru because there was nowhere else to go.

"Lady, I do hope that Glawinn was right and that you can hear me," Jherek whispered.

He took a fresh compress from the water pitcher by Sabyna's bed and placed it across her fevered brow. Even the paladin's daily attempts to heal her and Arthoris's attentions with his waning supply of healing potions didn't stave off the infections that wracked her body. She enjoyed a brief respite from the fevers, but the bite marks deepened, turning black around the edges, drawing in the flesh around them as they consumed her. Both of the wounds were the size of one of his hands now. It had been seven days and still she had not regained consciousness.

Azla had ordered *Azure Dagger* to sail north but they lingered still around the Whamite Isles. At present the nearby seas were filled with drowned ones, morkoth, koalinth, and sahuagin. Once they'd even been turned back by a merman patrol claiming the waters as something called "Eadraal's."

The young sailor ministered to Sabyna with care. Tears filled his eyes as he listened to her harsh breathing and his hands shook as he touched her hot flesh. Over the days he'd cared for her, he'd found he talked incessantly. He'd told her of his life aboard *Bunyip* and in Velen, of Madame Iitaar and Malorrie, and of the mysterious voice that had led him this far by speaking the cryptic, *Live, that you may serve.* And he'd talked of her; what she'd shown him, what she'd come to mean to him.

In the quiet moments of the long nights when he'd sat by her bed working to keep her fever down, he couldn't help recalling how her face had looked before the drowned one had grabbed her and dragged her into the sea. Had she been about to forgive him, or about to condemn him? He didn't know and the waiting was unbearable—only second to knowing whether she would ever awaken.

"I love you, lady," Jherek whispered.

He told her that several times a day, hoping that she might seize onto it and return to them. That was the declaration she'd challenged him for, but he felt it wasn't enough to truly turn her from the dark path she walked into the shadowlands. Still, he told her because she'd asked and because he did love her and wanted her to know even if she was taken from him.

A knock sounded at the door, then Glawinn's voice said, "Young warrior."

Jherek brushed his eyes free of tears and cleared his throat. "Aye."

"May I enter?"

"Aye."

Glawinn entered the room carrying a plate of food. He didn't ask if she'd awakened, and Jherek was grateful for that. If Sabyna opened her eyes, the young sailor didn't doubt that everyone on the ship would know.

"I brought you something to eat," the paladin said.

"I'm not hungry."

Glawinn put the plate on the chest of drawers against the wall and asked, "When was your last meal?"

"Not long ago," Jherek answered, applying a fresh compress to Sabyna's fevered forehead.

"Not long for a camel, perhaps," Glawinn replied. "I know you've not eaten in two days. It will do no good for you to get sick as well."

"I won't get sick. I haven't so far."

"When was the last time you slept?"

Jherek looked at the man's eyes and said, "I don't remember."

"This isn't healthy. Others can care for her."

"I know," the young sailor whispered, "but I would rather."

For a moment he was afraid Glawinn would argue with him, then the paladin got down beside the bed on his knees and prayed to Lathander, asking for the Morninglord's guidance and succor.

Jherek joined him on his knees but couldn't join in the prayer. No gods were interested in him. He was cursed by the fates, and now that curse had spread to Sabyna. He only wished that he might die soon after she did. He truly believed he wouldn't be able to live after that.

Before the battle was joined at Voalidru, Laaqueel sensed that Vhaemas the Bastard's loyalties would not stay with Iakhovas. She saw the pained look in the eyes of Thuridru's ruler as they marshaled the skirmish lines just south of the merman capital. His father hadn't abandoned the city as the regular citizens had, and stood proudly among the army he'd assembled.

Vhaemas the Bastard held Thuridru's forces to the west, awaiting Iakhovas's signal. The drowned ones marched in first, shoving the front line of the mermen back and opening holes that the koalinth rushed to fill. The killing went on in the lowlands for more than an hour before the merman line really began to cave. Still, the warriors didn't run, staying in and doing battle as the drowned ones and koalinth ground them down. Bodies floated in the water, drawing marine scavengers that weren't too afraid of the combatants.

Iakhovas rode *Tarjana*'s forecastle deck as the mudship bore down on King Vhaemas's waiting forces in the second wave of battle. Laaqueel stood beside him. They hadn't talked since earlier in the day, and she was comfortable with that.

Sahuagin packed the deck around them, armed with heavy crossbows.

King Vhaemas controlled his army from a rock shelf, relaying orders through his commanders. Even as *Tarjana* raced for him, the merman king held his ground, staring back at Iakhovas.

The line of attacking koalinth hammered into the mermen at the same time Iakhovas gave the order to fire the crossbows. The heavy quarrels took down rows of merman warriors.

Iakhovas leaped over the mudship's side and swam toward the merman king. The sahuagin followed him, advancing rapidly on the royal guard.

Having no heart for the battle, Laaqueel still followed and defended herself as she needed to.

Flanked by one of his daughters, Vhaemas swam to meet Iakhovas. The merman king had been in his share of battles while holding Eadraal together, and it showed in his ability as he engaged Iakhovas.

A merman wearing Voalidru's colors attacked Laaqueel. Distanced from the danger, the malenti priestess battled flawlessly, turning the other man's trident then using her finger talons to open his throat. Survival still took precedence over the absence of fear.

When she glanced back at Iakhovas, she wasn't surprised to see Vhaemas the Bastard had joined his father in battling Iakhovas. Merman king, son, and daughter all swarmed on Iakhovas, who barely held his own against their combined might.

The koalinth and merman warriors spread out, battling around the four of them.

Little malenti, to me.

Laaqueel felt the black quill next to her heart quiver demandingly. She gutted the latest merman warrior that had engaged her and swam toward Iakhovas.

The trident Iakhovas used was magical in nature. Through it, he'd been able to affect the outcome of past battles, affecting the luck that his army had. It had been one of the many items his searchers had found for him around the Sea of Fallen Stars.

Waiting for a chance to reach his side, Laaqueel darted in and engaged Vhaemas while his son and daughter sped toward Iakhovas. Vhaemas the Bastard caught Iakhovas's trident in his own even as his half-sister, Princess Jian, swam in with her sword.

Jian swung the sword as she passed, breaking the trident haft with a thundering crack that rolled over the hills. When the broken trident fell away, Vhaemas the Bastard pulled his own back and rammed it at Iakhovas.

"No!" Iakhovas shouted in rage.

His shape blurred, becoming the thing Laaqueel remembered from the cave near Coryselmal. Fins appeared on Iakhovas's head and face, arms and legs, back and chest. If she hadn't already seen the form before, the malenti priestess knew she would have thought it was a trick of the sediment and sand swirling around Iakhovas.

Before Vhaemas the Bastard could shove his trident tines through his opponent's head, Iakhovas grabbed it with superhuman speed and shoved the weapon to one side. He rammed the broken haft of his own trident through the bastard king's torso. Iakhovas continued to push until his talons reached Vhaemas's abdomen. He ripped out the merman's entrails and strung them through the water. Vhaemas the Bastard struggled only briefly before going limp.

Still in motion, Iakhovas pursued Jian, who turned to confront him. The mermaid warrior lashed out with her sword, scoring a slash across Iakhovas's chest. Iakhovas kept going, driving himself at the mermaid and receiving another wound to his arm.

Vhaemas redoubled his efforts against Laaqueel, driving her back so that he could disengage. He swam through the water, stopping only long enough to pick up the end of Iakhovas's broken trident. Still in motion, the merman king slammed the mystic trident into Iakhovas's back, burying the points deeply.

Roaring in pain and rage, Iakhovas batted Jian's sword aside and seized her head in an impossibly huge hand covered in sharp edges. Holding her head, he raked the long fin from his other arm across her midsection, ripping her into halves—one belonging to a beautiful girl and the other to a fish.

King Vhaemas tugged at the trident tines imbedded in Iakhovas's back, trying to free them. Iakhovas whirled, closing his massive fist and hammering the merman king on the head. Partially senseless, Vhaemas tried to retreat but couldn't move away fast enough. Iakhovas made a fist and brought it down on top of the king's crown.

Before the dazed merman king could move or defend himself, Iakhovas dived at him, grabbing him around the throat. Blood and sand misted the water around the two combatants, obscuring the view as the battle raged around them.

Laaqueel kicked out, flicking her toe claws out and gutting the merman warrior who swam at her. She whirled and brought up the barbed net hanging at her side, whipping it out to drape over another merman warrior she narrowly avoided. She gloried in the battle, embracing the thought of death because then there could be no more doubts. A smile twisted the corners of her mouth, and she felt more alive than she had in days.

Little malenti, you've come back into your own.

The malenti priestess didn't bother to reply. The exhilaration she felt was only temporary, and she knew it. As the merman warrior fought the net, the barbs buried themselves in his flesh. She choked up on the trident haft and raked the tine across another merman's face, taking out his eyes.

NO!

The female voice echoed in Laaqueel's head, driving her to her knees in the loose sand. The malenti priestess put her hands to her temples, willing away the pain and the vertigo.

This is not your path, Laaqueel. Not anymore.

"Stop!" the malenti priestess pleaded, gazing out at the battle before her. "This is what I was born and bred for. This is Sekolah's purpose for me."

Little malenti, are you hurt?

Laaqueel looked at Iakhovas. "I am all right."

"Then get up. There's a battle to be won here before we lose the war."

Iakhovas held the unconscious merman king by the throat. King Vhaemas's head bled profusely, bits of gold and bone glinting amid savaged flesh. Iakhovas's blow had driven the crown into the merman king's head.

Staving off the vertigo and uncertainty, Laaqueel picked up her trident, taking the fight to the merman warriors.

I will not allow you to take the lives of these people, the feminine voice stated.

"I am sahuagin." Laaqueel engaged the nearest merman, thrusting her trident at his face.

No.

Laaqueel's trident thrust stopped short. The merman warrior moved to take advantage of his luck. As he thrust, though, a wild current sprang up from below him and pulled him away.

Nor will I allow you to be harmed. Not unless you make me.

"Then strike me down if you can." Laaqueel gazed around the depths. "Come out of hiding. I will fight you. My life has not been my own, and I'll spend it gladly."

I come to give you your life, Laaqueel.

"How?" As the malenti priestess looked around, she noticed that none of the merman warriors even seemed to know she was there, as if she'd suddenly become invisible.

There is another path you must take that is better suited to your nature.

"I am sahuagin."

You do not have to be.

"It is all I have ever wanted to be."

Then you should raise your standards, Laaqueel.

"Sekolah gave me life and gave me the strength to kill in his name. It is enough."

And Sekolah let you be placed in the power of the Taker.

Laaqueel had no reply.

Yes, you know him for who he is, and you know the kind of destruction he's brought to this world. If he should return to the Sword Coast, it will only be the same. And Iakhovas no longer needs you. You know that.

"The Great Shark gives me power to serve his will."

Sekolah gives you power to kill in his name.

"Yes."

You could have more.

"I only want to be sahuagin."

You're not. You have never fit in with your people, Laaqueel, and you know you never will.

"I can."

No. You live a lie now, and you know it. As long as you remain in Iakhovas's grace you will be protected, but should you fall, you will be killed and rent. Meat is meat. I can give you more than that.

"Why should you?" Laaqueel shouted. "What am I to you?"

You are strong, Laaqueel. The times coming after the Twelfth Serôs War will not be easy. I have use for that strength.

"So I could serve you instead of Iakhovas?" Laaqueel shook her head. "No."

When the time comes, you will live or die as you choose, but if you kill any of those under my protection, you will know my wrath as you have known my benevolence.

"And should they attack me?"

They won't. You are under my protection, and they will know it. Iakhovas remains your only true enemy, but one is coming who has the power to deal with him.

"The boy in the cave?" Laaqueel couldn't believe it.

Though the human had put up a good fight against the koalinth in the cave, he couldn't challenge the savage deathbringer that was Iakhovas.

Yes.

"He's too weak."

Not once the Taleweaver brings him into his belief. Wait, Laaqueel, wait and see if I don't have more to offer than you've ever known.

Emotion ripped through Laaqueel as she felt the voice fade from her mind. Uncertainty and doubt plagued her, and her faith wasn't there to shore her up. She prayed to Sekolah, but she felt the words were only empty effort.

"I am *Iakhovas!*"

Turning, Laaqueel watched as Iakhovas swam into the midst of the battlefield. He looked every inch a proud sahuagin warrior-king. His voice boomed, gaining the attention of the warriors around him.

"Your king has fallen," Iakhovas roared in triumph, "and I have killed his children."

He threw the merman king down to the torn bodies of Princess Jian and Vhaemas the Bastard.

"I am death—unstoppable and merciless. Oppose me and die!"

As Laaqueel looked across the war-torn sea floor, she saw the wave of defeat sweep over the surviving warriors of Eadraal. The Thuridru mermen screamed in triumph. The malenti priestess felt the arrival of a thundering presence hammering against her lateral lines. She looked to the east, in the direction from which the shifting currents came.

Whales materialized out of the deep blue-green depths. Half a dozen four-hundred-foot-long humpbacked whales swam in the lead, trailed by dozens of smaller ones. They stampeded over the battlefield, scattering both armies.

Iakhovas hung in the sea, staring at them.

An auburn-haired mermaid swam with them, flashing between the two lead humpbacks.

"Arina."

Several of the mermen near Laaqueel spoke the name, and she assumed it belonged to the young woman with the whales.

The whales broke before Iakhovas, swimming under him, knocking the nearby warriors around in whirlwind currents that drew sand up from the ocean floor in massive clouds.

After the whales passed, Laaqueel noticed that King Vhaemas's body was gone, evidently taken up by one or more of the great creatures. The morale of the mermen disappeared with the merman king, and they began disengaging where they could and falling back.

Iakhovas evidently wasn't going to give them an easy retreat. He issued orders at once to begin the pursuit. It was going to be a bitter death march back to Voalidru.

Tu'uua'col swam through the clutch of rocks and settled gently on the ocean floor behind Prince Mirol as he prayed to Eadro.

Built lean and angular, Mirol didn't look like a warrior, or the newly named heir to the throne of Eadraal. King Vhaemas had awakened only once after the whales and Princess Arina had transported him to Naulys, the merman city west of Voalidru. During that time he named Mirol as his successor, then slipped back into the coma that held him still.

Tu'uua'col hadn't accompanied King Vhaemas during the Battle of Voalidru. The prejudices the merman warriors had against him because he was shalarin ran too deep. Still, he had not allowed himself to be put on the sidelines as the Taker's army closed on Naulys. His place, for the moment, was at the prince's side. Quietly, the Green Dukar put his hand on Mirol's shoulder.

Unhurried, Mirol finished his prayer to Eadro, asking for deliverance in this time of need. He flipped his tail and turned to face his advisor.

"Our scouts have spotted the Taker's advance guard," Tu'uua'col said.

"How soon will they be here?"

"Within minutes."

"And their numbers?"

"As at Voalidru," Tu'uua'col answered.

"Do you think we can hold them from Naulys?"

The Dukar hesitated. Mirol had remained very true to his calling as a priest until his father had handed him the reins of leadership. As a result, the boy didn't know much about the ways of war and warriors.

"No, my prince. Not without a miracle."

Mirol showed him a brave smile and said, "Exactly what I was praying for. Now let's see if Eadro can deliver."

He took up the trident that had been his father's and swam to the front of the line.

The land around Naulys was hilly, rife with coral reefs. They'd used those reefs to set up ballistae that had been salvaged from surface world ships. The Taker's army came on, the drowned ones at the lead.

Tu'uua'col watched as the first rows of warriors clashed. Priests of Eadro, summoned by Mirol, worked to turn the undead, chanting praises to Eadro. Many of the drowned ones were turned away, leaving the koalinth to bear the brunt of the first attack while their own ranks were broken by the zombies' retreat.

For a moment, confused by the retreating zombies, the koalinth gave ground in the face of the vengeful assault by the merman warriors of three conquered cities who'd managed to join Naulys's defenders. The sheer numbers of the koalinth turned the tide yet again. The merman warriors were slowly driven back.

Tu'uua'col watched, desperately seeking some way out of the situation though he knew there wasn't one. The Taker had planned too well, and the priests had not turned all of the drowned ones. He gazed at the Taker's flagship floating above and behind the koalinth, then noticed the fluttering movement that came in from the north.

The winged shapes sped through the water without warning, and they came by the thousands. They descended on the staggered line of koalinth without mercy.

"What is that?" Mirol asked. He peered into the deeper reaches of the sea.

"Ixitxachitl," Tu'uua'col answered, feeling somewhat better. "Apparently, they decided to join in and retaliate against the Taker."

"It's a miracle," Mirol said quietly.

Tu'uua'col didn't agree, thinking it was more like the demon rays taking advantage of the diversion the mermen provided. As he watched the ixitxachitls swoop in on the koalinth, the Dukar thought the real miracle would be if the demon rays didn't turn on them next.

The merman warriors pressed to the forefront, cutting down koalinth as chance presented itself.

"Col," Mirol asked, "do you think there's a chance to form an alliance at Myth Nantar to stand against the Taker?"

"Yes," the Dukar replied quickly.

Excitement flared within him. The merman cities held the largest population in the immediate area around Myth Nantar. If they took a step to form an alliance he was certain the other races would agree.

"I would like you to start on this immediately after this battle is finished," Mirol said. "Provided we both yet live. I will go with you."

"Of course, Prince Mirol."

Tu'uua'col turned to watch the battle as the koalinth continued to retreat before the savagery of the ixitxachitl. If Myth Nantar rose again, as was alluded to in some of the legends, the Dukars would also rise once more.

Nine days later, Pacys stood close to the Great Barrier. Senior High Mage Reefglamor and the other High Mages of Sylkiir stood there with the others who agreed to the Nantarn Alliance. After nearly a tenday of hammering out the details, the old bard knew them all. While they'd bickered and argued among themselves, he'd written, adding their songs to the epic that came so readily now to his lips.

The Taker's army had been turned at Naulys, leaving the city intact, though Voalidru was still heavily occupied at the moment. Scouts had also determined that Iakhovas was pulling together reserves from the sahuagin raiding parties and guiding even more of the drowned ones that continued the occupation of the Whamite Isles.

With arms as thick as oak trees crossed over his huge chest, Qos faced the Great Barrier beside the old bard. When he'd first put in his appearance there had been many who had known him.

"Know you this," Qos said in his booming voice, "as we begin this alliance. If any of you who represent your nations and people are not truthful, the Great Barrier will know and it will not open. Only the true interest of saving all of Serôs, of seeing Serôs once again healthy and whole, will allow the barrier to unlock the City of Destinies."

The faces on the other side of the Great Barrier regarded him solemnly.

"Myth Nantar holds her secrets jealously these days," Qos went on. "She has been betrayed, the ideals she was founded on corrupted. Blood of those who were to make this city their home has run in her streets and scarred the mythal that surrounds it. The Weave will have to be honored and respected for now and for always." He paused. "Else we may lose great Myth Nantar forever."

The rulers and representatives of the world below, the High Mages, and Khlinat all stared through the barrier.

"We will begin," Qos said. "Step forward, place your hand against the Great Barrier, and speak your name."

The crowd hesitated for a moment, then Reefglamor strode forward and pushed his hand to the invisible wall.

"I am Senior High Mage Taranath Reefglamor of Sylkiir, and I am here to see that the City of Destinies is reopened."

Pacys closed his eyes, listening to the vibration the sea elf's voice started within the Great Barrier. The other High Mages followed suit and Pacys listened intently to the changes in the vibration.

"Princess Arina of Eadraal."

"Prince Mirol of Eadraal."

"Tribune Akkys of Vuuvax."

The triton Akkys stood aloof, as all his kind did. He was slightly built compared to the mermen, but everyone in Serôs knew not to judge the tritons lightly. They were savage fighters. He wore his shoulder-length blue hair tied back and carried a tapal, the signature weapon of his race, which curved in the middle like a fishhook and seemed to be made of all sharp edges.

Pacys knew that the Vuuvax was of the avenging protectorate within the triton race. His people had undertaken the job of bringing the Great Whale Bard's killer to justice. The triton slapped the Great Barrier forcefully, changing the pitch of the vibration.

"Dukar Gayar," a thin voice said, "Grand Savant of the Third Order and Paragon of the Kupavi Order."

The morkoth had been a surprise but Qos had vouched for him. His touch was soft, hardly changing the vibration at all.

"Lashyrr Maerdrymm, Grand Savant of the First Order and Paragon of the Numosi Order."

Pacys recognized her as a baelnorn, a once-dead elf returned to life as a guardian for others. Her body had transformed into living pearl upon her acceptance of her destiny. She was pale blue and ivory, and could have been mistaken for an elegant statue. Her hand slapped flatly against the barrier, changing the vibration's pitch more than anyone.

"Keros the Wanderer, of . . . Serôs."

Though the young triton Keros showed hesitation, his voice was strong and clear. The young triton had come to Myth Nantar for reasons of his own and stayed away from the others of his kind.

"Roaoum, subchief of the Tiger Coral tribe."

The locathah's voice was soft and carefully measured. Over the last days he had a habit of not speaking unless he truly had something to say. He and Prince Mirol had been friends for a number of years.

"Khlinat Ironeater," the dwarf said, putting his callused palm against the Great Barrier as well. He stared through the barrier at Pacys. "By Marthammor Duin, I'll stand with ye long as me heart beats and I got me good leg under me."

The roll of names continued until there was only one to go.

"Dukar Peacekeeper Tu'uua'col of Eadraal. I swear my allegiance for I have dreamed of this day for many years."

The shalarin Dukar slapped his palm against the Great Barrier.

Pacys listened to the vibration running through the structure. His ear was trained by long years in his craft, gifted by the passion that existed within his heart and had never faltered, and guided by the need in him to be the best he could be.

He opened his mouth and sang, holding the one note at perfect pitch, feeling it resonate within his body as the Great Barrier reacted to it. He continued, lifting his arms at his side so that he could put all of himself into it.

Like a bubble bursting and vanishing within the space of a heartbeat, the Great Barrier shattered.

And the outside world rushed in over Myth Nantar once again, leaving it vulnerable to its greatest enemy.

25

"Are ye sure we'll find the swabbie here?" Khlinat Ironeater asked. He sat in the saddle of a seahorse they'd borrowed from the sea elves, and shaded his eyes against the morning sun with one hand. "That ship has surely seen some better days, I'm thinking."

Seated on a seahorse as well, Pacys nodded, feeling his heart race as he neared the boy he'd searched for. The hero's song played in his head, making his fingers itch for the yarting slung across his back in a waterproof bag.

"He's here," Pacys assured the dwarf.

A guard of twenty sea elf warriors rode with them as the seahorses cut across the ocean's surface. The ship's crew had already seen them and hurried across the decks to get into defensive positions.

"Well, and they're surely promising a heated welcoming if we're the wrong 'uns," Khlinat said.

"We're not."

Pacys guided his mount toward the ship, the seahorse straining only a little to catch up to it. When he drew abreast of the caravel, he found himself looking up at half a dozen bowmen with only tattered mercy and trust left in their souls.

"State your business and be quick about it," a woman dressed in black ordered from the railing.

"I'm here to see Jherek," Pacys called up.

"How do you know him?"

"I'm Pacys the Bard. I'm a friend."

The woman glanced at the sea elves. "We haven't seen too many friends lately," she said, "and damn few of them promise to come from under the sea."

"Lady—" Pacys began.

"Captain." The woman's voice was unrelenting.

"As you will, Captain. As Oghma is my patron, I'm only here in Jherek's best interest." Pacys kept his voice loud to be heard over the slap of the waves breaking against the ship's bow and the whip-crack of the canvas pulling tight in the rigging. "I know that he's wasting away, unable to control the darkness trying to consume his soul. I promise you, if you don't let me come aboard and speak to him, you're going to lose him. We'll all lose him."

A bearded warrior stepped forward and said, "Let him come aboard, Captain. He's speaking the truth."

The ship's captain hesitated.

"I'd know if he was lying," the warrior said.

The captain nodded to her crew. They put away their bows and dropped a cargo net over the side, leaving it caught up at the top.

"Climb on," the captain said. "We'll pull you up."

Jherek sat beside Sabyna's bed, his forearms resting heavily on his bent knees, his forehead pressed against them. He held her hand, not daring to let it go, afraid she might drift away from him in her sleep.

Glawinn continued using his power on her daily, but there were no healing potions left. Now, every day, the ship's mage lost ground. Her wounds festered, growing larger, taking her away from him a piece at a time.

The young sailor was ragged and unkempt. Not an hour passed that he didn't feel pain—hers as well as his. He ignored the knock on the door, not wanting to deal with Glawinn trying to get him to eat or leave. If he had kept his distance from Sabyna, she would have been fine, but he'd returned.

"Young warrior," Glawinn spoke softly, "someone has come to see you."

"No." Jherek knew he was being petulant, but he'd had enough of looking at other people.

"Jherek."

The musical voice captured the young sailor's attention, striking a chord deep within him. He found it immediately uncomfortable. "Go away."

"I can't. I've waited all my life to meet you."

Shamed by his own lack of manners, knowing Glawinn wouldn't think well of him either, Jherek pushed himself to his feet and opened the door. It took him a moment to recognize the two men standing beside Glawinn. He'd met both of them the night Iakhovas and the pirates attacked Baldur's Gate.

"Hail and well met," the old man said.

His clothes were wet, almost dripping, and he smelled of the sea. He offered his hand.

"You're the bard," Jherek said, his tired mind wandering through all the memories. He clasped the old man's arm.

The bard bowed and said, "Pacys."

The resonance continued in Jherek but he still didn't understand where it came from.

"Hail and well met, swabbie," the dwarf greeted him good-naturedly. "Khlinat."

Seeing the dwarf sailor standing there brought the beginnings of a smile to Jherek's lips. He took Khlinat's arm and felt the powerful grip.

"Hear tell ye've been betwixt some proper demons' brews since these old eyes last seen ye."

Jherek nodded quietly and glanced back at Sabyna. "It's been far harder than anything I could have imagined."

"This is the one who holds your heart?" the old bard asked.

Pacys glided into the room, in motion before Jherek even knew it. He stood by her bed and trailed his fingers across her feverish brow.

Jherek didn't know how to respond. Sabyna never had the chance to let him know her mind after he'd revealed who he was.

"The look in your eyes is all the answer I need," Pacys said softly. "The love you share is a powerful thing."

Tears clouded Jherek's vision but he didn't let them fall. He spoke through a too-tight throat. "As it turns out, I wasn't the man she thought I was."

"On the contrary, my boy," the old bard said, "it's you who aren't the man you think you are."

"Can you help her?" Jherek had put off the question because he'd been afraid of the answer.

Sadly, Pacys shook his head. "No. The young lady lies beyond any help I might give her."

Jherek tried to will himself into a state of numbness but couldn't. The resonance within him that the bard's presence elicited wound him up inside.

"You should go," Jherek said.

"I can't. I was sent here to find you and to help you."

Jherek shook his head. "The only way you can help me is to help her."

"You don't know all there is yet."

The old man took the waterproof bag from his shoulder and opened it. He sat on the floor of the small cabin.

"What are you doing?" Jherek demanded.

Pacys's practiced fingers brushed the strings lightly. He twisted the knobs at the end of the instrument, adjusting the string tension. When he brushed the strings again, creating a mellow note that seemed to fill the room with light and warmth, he smiled and said, "Blessed Oghma, after being under the sea for so long and not able to practice, I thought I might have lost the gift."

"You have to go," Jherek said sternly, unable to believe the audacity of the bard.

Pacys effortlessly played a tune. It was soft and quiet, melding the gentleness of a stream running over smooth rocks and the sight of the wind through winter's bare tree branches.

"Music is a balm," the old bard said. "Let me play to her that I might ease her mind for a while."

"You said you couldn't help her."

"I can't, but I can ease the pain she suffers from."

Pacys nodded toward the unconscious woman. His fingers whispered across the strings, coaxing soothing notes that filled the room. Turning, Jherek saw that Sabyna's face appeared more relaxed than it had in days.

"Will that be all right then?" Pacys asked.

"Aye."

Jherek returned to the bed and took a fresh compress from the pitcher, then gently wiped Sabyna's face. He sat, the resonance within his chest unfaltering.

"She's very pretty," the old bard said.

"Aye." Jherek slumped forward, trying to find a way to be comfortable.

"I'd like to hear how you met her."

"It's a long story."

The old bard smiled and said, "Actually, those are my favorite kind."

At first, Jherek wasn't going to speak, but there was something about the music that loosened his tongue. It changed subtly, though he couldn't point to exactly what the change was. So he began with how he met Sabyna on *Breezerunner*. Of course, that meant dredging up everything that happened at Velen. Pacys asked how Jherek happened to be there, which meant explaining about Bloody Falkane.

He also mentioned the voice that haunted him all his life and the cryptic message it gave him: Live, that you may serve. As the music played, he realized that there were only the three of them in the room. He couldn't remember when the others left. He didn't remember ever talking so much in his life.

Even when Jherek finished speaking, Pacys continued playing. The tune was different from when he started hours ago. Khlinat brought a plate of food, but the old bard turned it away, as did the young sailor. When Pacys finally stopped playing only the sound of Sabyna's ragged breathing filled the room. The weight of it almost broke Jherek.

"It seems," the old bard said, showing no signs of discomfort after sitting on the floor for hours, "that you have searched everywhere you might for help for the young lady except one."

"What?"

The old bard's hazel eyes flickered with reflections from the lantern hanging on the wall.

"All your life," the bard told him, "you've had a benefactor who has looked out for you."

"The voice?"

"Yes."

"I never knew who that was."

"Perhaps it's time to ask."

Jherek put another compress on Sabyna's fevered brow and said, "I did ask."

"When you were on *Black Champion,* following Vurgrom."

"Aye. I asked, and I got no answer."

"Perhaps that wasn't the time. Perhaps you were supposed to wait a while longer."

"Why?"

The old bard shrugged. "I don't know how these things work, my boy," he said. "Faith in the gods is like a good song. You must wait to have everything revealed. You can try to force it to happen, but a song, and that faith, has its own time and place."

"But I had a faith."

"You could have already been spoken for at the time you sought out the Crying God."

"Spoken for?" Jherek echoed incredulously. "By a god?"

"Priests are called to serve their gods," the old bard said softly. "That call is undeniable. I've had friends who were good bards and artists who worked with passion at their craft only to be called into service of one of the gods."

The young sailor changed the compress again, thinking hard. Everything he thought forced him to the same conclusion. "I'm no priest."

"No, I never thought you were." Pacys began playing again, and this time the tune was a little faster, more uplifting than calming. "Remember in Baldur's Gate when Khlinat lay wounded? It seemed as if the wound might even prove fatal. Yet, you laid your hands on him and he was healed."

"It was the necklace he wore."

"No," Pacys said. "I've handled magical things in my time. That necklace holds no magic."

"It could have been used up saving his life. He even believed it saved him."

"Khlinat doesn't believe that now," Pacys said softly.

The whole idea confused Jherek. "You think I somehow saved him?"

"Yes." Pacys found another chord, and the resonance within the young sailor's chest felt stronger, more sure. "Why did Malorrie teach you?"

"I don't know."

"You said that someone pointed him in your direction."

"Aye." Jherek felt as though the room was closing in on him.

"And Madame Iitaar, whom you respect and love, told you there was a destiny ahead of you."

Jherek sat quietly and still, wanting only to deny everything the old bard said.

"Look at your whole life, my boy. Have you ever raised a hand against another with malice in your heart?"

Jherek thought back to the bar fight in Athkatla. "Aye. Against Aysel from *Breezerunner*'s crew."

"The man who insulted Sabyna's honor?" Pacys smiled. "Why, Jherek, I could expect nothing less from such as you."

"Such as me? What do you think I am?"

Pacys shook his head. "It's not what I think," he said. "When you needed the astrolabe from the diviner at the Pirate Isles and you were asked what you believed in, what was your answer?"

"Love," Jherek whispered, looking at Sabyna and feeling like he was about to fall apart. He grew angry with the bard for speaking in such a circumspect way.

"How can you believe in love after the way you were brought up?"

"Because it was shown to me by Madame Iitaar and Malorrie, then by old Finaren, captain of *Butterfly*."

"A phantom with a geas laid on him?" Pacys asked. "A lonely widow woman who could use a strong back and a pair of hands around her house to fix it up? A ship's captain who let you go once it was discovered you were one of Bloody Falkane's claimed? What could these people know of love? How can you trust their motives?"

Jherek shook his head. "Say what you will, but they loved me when no one else did."

"And you gave them love back."

"Aye," the young sailor said, "all that I had. Only to be driven from them."

"For a reason," Pacys said softly. "There were things you had to learn." He glanced at Sabyna and said, "Perhaps a new love to be found."

"Only to have those taken from me because I was cursed the day I was born?"

"I've seen the love Glawinn has for you," Pacys said. "The man has laid his life on the line for you."

"He was only serving Lathander, who guided him to help save the disk I pridefully took in Baldur's Gate."

"You were meant to have that disk."

"I didn't have it, and it was used to kill all those people on the Whamite Isles."

"Perhaps they were forfeit anyway," Pacys said. "So the best was done that could be, and the disk saw you to that sword."

"It's not mine."

"Yet I've been told no hand may comfortably hold it but yours."

Jherek couldn't argue; it was true. Others in Azla's crew tried to hold the sword but none of them could do it, or even wanted to, for any length of time.

"The Great Whale Bard sought you out and gave you a gift."

Jherek looked at the old bard and said, "All these things you say are true, but I can't make any sense of them."

"They were a path, my boy," Pacys said softly. "A path that led you here, to this time and this place."

"To do what?"

"What you were born to do. Battle the Taker."

Jherek couldn't help it; he laughed. The sound was bitter and insane and rude, but he couldn't help himself. Fatigue and pain had broken down his self-discipline, made it impossible to keep all those feelings to himself.

"It is your fate," Pacys said. "Even the whales told you so."

"Don't you see?" Jherek asked. "It's a mistake. Another part of that ill luck that has followed me. It's just my misfortune, and yours, that you're here wasting your time when you should be with this hero you're looking for."

"You've already faced the Taker once," Pacys said, "in the caverns. You wounded him, survived his attempt to kill you with the buckler given to you by the Great Whale Bard. Iakhovas is the Taker."

"He was just a mage."

"No."

The firm denial shook Jherek, brought him back under control a little. He sobered and looked at the bard. "What you're saying is impossible," he insisted.

"What I'm saying," Pacys stated, "could be no other way. You are the champion that these times call for."

"I'm a sailor."

"And more."

Jherek shook his head.

"It's true," Pacys said. "Every step you took, every decision you made, has brought you to here and now."

"I've brought only bad luck to everyone I know," Jherek said. "Madame Iitaar probably lost business in Velen after it was found out that she was harboring one of Bloody Falkane's pirates. Finaren probably lost work as well."

"You don't know that," Pacys said. "Even if it's true, you could change all that by becoming what you're meant to be."

"And what is that?"

Pacys eyed him again and stopped playing. "Ask."

"I have asked."

"Not me."

"Then who?"

"The voice that has been with you all those years."

Jherek shook his head and felt empty inside. "I've not heard it in months."

"And you think it is gone?"

"Aye. Don't you see? Even if what you were saying was somehow true, I've already broken faith with the voice."

"Ask," Pacys said gently.

"How can you be so certain?"

"How can you be so *un*certain?"

Jherek looked at the bard incredulously. "Have you not listened to what I've told you?"

"Oh yes. Even better, it seems, than you have. Ask."

"I have asked."

"Ask now."

"If the voice cared whether Sabyna lived or died, it wouldn't have allowed her to be infected by the bite of the drowned ones."

"And you would never have had a reason to search so deeply within yourself these past few days. Ask, Jherek. The truth is the tonic you need."

Anger gripped the young sailor. The old bard dangled false hope like fat fruit hanging on the vine. "Fine," he said. "And after I do, I want you to leave."

Pacys ignored Jherek's anger, keeping his voice soft. "Ask, Jherek." The old bard put the yarting down, then rolled to his knees. "Ask properly, and with respect, as you would ask one of those you love."

Seeing the old bard's belief brought stinging tears to Jherek's eyes. How could anyone believe what the man said after everything he'd been told. Why did the bard's words have to ring so true? Angry with himself, so scared of the final denial he was about to experience, he rolled to his knees. He faced the bard and brought his hands together in supplication. The young sailor was surprised at how his hands shook. He looked around the room for some inspiration, not knowing where to begin. *Azure Dagger*'s gentle sway as she sailed rocked him.

"I don't know how to begin."

"Live," Pacys said, "that you may serve."

"I live," Jherek said, the words coming somehow naturally to his lips, "how may I serve?"

The great voice that answered filled the cabin. Even the lantern light seemed brighter.

I am here.

Jherek saw the old bard's eyes widen and knew he heard the words, too.

"You are back," the young sailor said.

My son, I have never left you. On every step of your journey, I have been with you. When your heart faltered, I gave you the strength to carry on.

"Why?"

Because I have chosen you.

"For what?"

To be my champion. To work in my name. To live by living and serve by serving.

"Why me?"

I have looked into your heart, my son, and found it to be one of the truest I have seen. You love with all the length and depth and breadth of your soul, never holding back any of yourself, never letting your fear that you might be hurt stand in your way.

"I would not listen to you."

Pride is not a bad thing when tempered properly, my son. You did not yet know me when you turned away.

"Why didn't you tell me more?"

You were not ready. You had enough things in your life that you still held to that you could not have accepted, could not have believed.

Jherek didn't understand that. "I had nothing," he maintained. "I'd been driven from my home, never had family. Nothing."

You had no belief. You would not have listened to me. Now, there is nothing else for you to cling to. Before you would have rejected the destiny that is yours.

"Now I have no choice?" Anger boiled up in Jherek. The shaking hands before him turned into fists. "You would try to enslave me?"

"Jherek," Pacys warned softly.

"No," Jherek said to the old bard in a harsh voice, "this is not your affair. I'll speak as I wish."

I would not enslave you, my son, the great voice said. *You could never live under those conditions, and I would never ask. Your doubts in yourself would have kept you from turning to me and allowing me to give you the gifts I have for you.*

Jherek trembled, sensing the truth behind the words. "I'm sorry. I should not have spoken in such an ill fashion."

The voice spoke, and Jherek felt he could hear the smile in the words. *My son, you are going to be one of the very best. I knew it was so when I saved your life as a boy.*

"Who are you?" Jherek whispered, not as afraid of the answer as he had been back in Velen when he'd first contemplated it.

I am the spring, dawn, birth, and renewal, my son. I am beginnings and hidden potential. I am conception, vitality, youth, and self-perfection. Know that I am Lathander, called the Morninglord. And you, my son, are one of my chosen champions.

"Glawinn," Jherek croaked, "does he know?"

He has suspicions, but he does not know. That has not been his to know until you tell him.

Jherek glanced at Sabyna, hardly daring to ask for what was on his mind. "What of Sabyna? She is my heart. I could not live knowing I had caused her life to be taken."

That was no fault of your own.

"She believed in me when I couldn't believe in myself."

She saw the goodness in you, and the potential.

"Must—" Jherek's voice broke and tears streamed down his face. "Must I lose her? I would ask you for her life, Lathander, and pledge mine in its place. Save her and do with me what you will."

No, my son. I would never bargain over a champion. You will serve me only if your heart wills it.

"But you could save her."

Yes. And you would look to me as though you forever owed her life to me. I will not have that.

"So I'm to watch her die?"

My son, you have the power to save her. As you saved Khlinat, and as you have saved yourself upon occasion in the past. Trust in yourself, Jherek. Trust in the love you have for her, and in your own ability to do what must be done.

Slowly, Jherek reached for Sabyna. He remembered how Glawinn came into her room and laid his hands upon the ship's mage, but it didn't seem right that he do so. "I don't know how," he said.

Love her, my son. That is your greatest gift. But you must give and receive it. You cannot lock yourself away from it.

Trembling, his face covered in tears, so afraid that he would be somehow found wanting, Jherek laid his hands on Sabyna's face. He willed her to be well, pictured her in his mind hale and whole, saw her with the smile on her lips that he knew so well.

Power coursed through his hands, filling them with heat. He knew it wasn't enough. Tenderly, he leaned forward, pressed his lips to hers, and kissed her. He remembered how she'd been in the rigging the day she kissed him. The love and the hunger crashed down over him, threatening to sweep him away.

Sabyna kissed back, her lips soft against his.

Jherek opened his eyes to find her staring back at him. He tried to back away, knowing the question of his birth still lay between them, embarrassed by what she must think of him to find him there, obviously taking advantage of her weakness.

"Lady," he said breathlessly, "I know this must appear unseemly, but I swear I only had—"

"Shut up," she ordered. She wrapped her arms around his neck and held him tightly, then covered his mouth with hers and kissed him deeply. "Hold me, Jherek, and don't let me go."

The young sailor wrapped his arms around her, pulling her to him fiercely. Somewhere in there, the old bard had the decency to leave.

"Are you sure you want to do that, young warrior?"

Glawinn's quiet words startled Jherek from his reverie. He stood on *Azure Dagger*'s stern castle, the wind blowing through his hair. Late morning tinged the eastern sky pink, but the rest of it was pure cerulean. Bright white doves winged overhead, and the young sailor chose to take that as an omen.

"Aye," Jherek replied. "I can see no other way of it."

"This thing you're undertaking," Glawinn said, "it's no easy thing."

"Would you talk me out of it?" Jherek asked.

Glawinn shook his head.

"I would see it done, then, if you're willing."

"Young warrior," Glawinn said in a voice that was suddenly hoarse with emotion as tears glittered in his eyes, "if you only knew the honor you show me."

Jherek reached for him, his own eyes tearing even as he smiled fiercely. The young sailor pulled the man to him in a bear hug that was returned full measure.

"I only show what you have shown me," Jherek told him.

Azure Dagger lay at anchor with only the small wind blowing over her, so the song from Pacys's yarting was audible from one end of the ship to the other.

Jherek gathered himself, standing on the stern castle in borrowed clothes, his sword thrust through the sash at his waist. He gazed at Sabyna, who stood with the small crowd around Pacys at the other end of the stern castle.

During the last two days, the ship's mage had made a complete recovery. No scars remained to mark the drowned ones' bites. She wore a dress that Azla loaned her. Even the old-timers among the pirate crew were surprised to learn the half-elf captain owned a dress, though they all had a care not to say anything of the kind in her presence. Khlinat stood beside her, his chest puffed up proudly. Captain Tarnar of *Steadfast* was there as well, unable to cross the dangerous seas yet. He wore vestments that bore Mystra's mark. The crews of both ships stood on their decks, *Steadfast* within easy hailing distance.

Jherek hadn't known so many would be interested, but Azla declared the proceeding as an official event and her pirates even cleaned up a bit for it. The young sailor glanced at the audience and felt self-conscious.

"I didn't know so many people would be here," he said to Glawinn.

"Young warrior, the word spread quickly last night when you asked for this. Those people out there, once they learned of it, they would have it no other way. This is not something that is often witnessed."

"It was only you and I," Jherek pointed out. "And I told only Sabyna."

Glawinn shrugged, grinning. "And I told only the bard because he needed to know for the tale he weaves. So, we have two suspects. Choose one."

Jherek couldn't keep the smile from his face. "No."

"Then, perhaps we should begin."

"Aye."

Excitement and anxiety hummed inside Jherek and he had second thoughts about his own worthiness. Quietly, he shoved those aside and gazed at Sabyna. He knew she was proof that Lathander had found him deserving, even if he couldn't yet see it himself.

"Kneel, Jherek of Velen," Glawinn ordered.

Quietly, Jherek knelt, placing his hands before him, palms pressed together. He bent his head forward in benediction.

"You have been blessed by Lathander," Glawinn said, "to be among those who would defend the Morninglord's name and His wishes. How say you?"

Jherek marshaled his courage, hoping to overcome his nervousness. Surprisingly, his voice sounded strong and clear over the gentle wind. "I, Jherek of Velen, do hereby pledge to honor the strictures of this sacred heritage and promise by my faith to be loyal to Lathander, maintaining my devotion against all persons without deception or forethought. Further, I vow to promote and uphold the principles of fealty, courtesy, honesty, valor, and honor, and to solemnly and faithfully follow the edicts of the Morninglord."

"May your heart be forever true to Lathander's cause to hold compassion for those who will need your help and to hold righteous anger for those who have been trespassed against," Glawinn said. "May your arm be forever strong in the Morninglord's service."

Jherek listened to the silence around him and felt more complete than he ever had. By Lathander's sacred covenant, this was where he should be. His heart swelled inside his chest as he awaited Glawinn's next words.

"For the Morninglord's glory and in my true and unwavering service to him, I name you Sir Jherek, paladin in the service of Lathander."

Jherek felt Glawinn's sword touch both his shoulders.

"Arise, Sir Jherek, and be whole of heart and spirit to show Lathander's great love for you."

The crowd aboard *Azure Dagger* clapped, and the pirates hooted and hollered their support. Rising on shaking legs, Jherek stood, looking up at the blue sky above.

"Thank you," he said to the sky," for finding me and freeing me."

My son, the deep voice said, *you were never lost, and you have freed yourself. Take your shirt off.*

Jherek hesitated for only a moment, then did as he was asked. As he stripped the shirt away, he noticed the clapping and hollering quieted, until the ship was silent once more. He was conscious of the tattoo—a flaming skull masked in chains—that showed so plainly on his arm.

No one, the deep voice boomed, startling the people on the ship and letting Jherek know he wasn't the only one who could hear the words now, *may mark one of my own.*

A pink incandescence flared to life in the middle of the flaming skull, burning brightly. Jherek watched, surprised there was no pain, only a tingling feeling. When the incandescence passed, only unmarked flesh remained behind.

Jherek held his arms out at his sides, staring at the clear skin through tear-blurred eyes that spilled over his cheeks.

The stain of your father's heritage is gone, my son. Live free of it.

26

"Why would Lathander be involved in any of this?" Qos asked.

Pacys swam beside Qos as the storm giant looked over the preparations being made to the Great Gate beside the Dukars' Academy.

"For several reasons," the bard answered.

Mermen, shalarin, sea elves, locathah, tritons, and even some of the men from *Azure Dagger* and *Steadfast*—both ships now at anchor above—labored to clear the great plaza. They chopped down coral reefs and carried them away. The humans used all manner of potions and magical devices to reach Myth Nantar, but once there, the mythal surrounding the City of Destinies allowed them to stay, breathing the water as if it were air.

"What reasons?" the giant asked.

"The Morninglord is the god of beginnings," the old bard said, letting his fingers stray across the gems inset in the saceddar. "There have been several beginnings involved in the legend of the Taker."

"Those legends have been around for thousands of years, as has this city. There are no beginnings there."

"Lathander is also the god of renewal. Just as you hoped to open Myth Nantar so that Serôs might again unite, the Morninglord wanted to see that happen. He has been working toward this end for a long time as well, else how would Jherek be here now?"

"The young paladin truly holds great promise," Qos said. "I've looked at many young men and women in my years at the academy, but the potential in him is strong."

"Jherek is another beginning," Pacys said. He'd talked to the young paladin himself after Sabyna's recovery, and Jherek told him some of what the Morninglord had revealed to him. "Not only does Lathander believe that Jherek will be one of the finest warriors to serve in his name, but Jherek will also be the first paladin to be based upon and in the seas of Toril."

"I have heard of 'seaguards,' " Qos said, "Paladins who ride upon ships and protect them for their lieges."

"Yes," Pacys agreed, "but none of them have understood the sea as Jherek will. You've only begun to see the promise in him."

"If the Taker doesn't destroy him."

Pacys studied Jherek among the crews seeking to clear the debris from the Great Gate. He didn't say anything.

"I'm sorry, Taleweaver," Qos said after a moment. "I know that is never far from your mind. Nor, probably, from the young man's."

"No."

"I'm still adjusting to the fact that Myth Nantar is once more open and no longer truly under my safekeeping."

"It will be all right."

"I hope." Qos let out a long breath. "And how goes it for you, Taleweaver? I have listened to your music, and it sounds good to these ears. I've even heard parts of your songs being sung in the Resonant Horn Inn. The song you wrote for the *alu Tel'Quessir* during their long trek seems popular."

Pacys smiled, letting his pride grow. "Give me time, my friend, all who have participated in these efforts will have their part of the song."

"But at the heart of it will be the story of Iakhovas and that young paladin."

"Yes. I'm still working on that. It is going to be the best thing I've ever written."

"Provided your young hero survives," Qos said.

"The merfolk lead us into a trap," Laaqueel said.

She stood beside Iakhovas on *Tarjana*'s deck, watching as the mermen battled sahuagin and the few remaining drowned ones. Only a few koalinth remained among them after the ixitxachitls' attack during the assault on Naulys.

"Of course they do," Iakhovas said. "They seek to slow us and let Myth Nantar prepare to meet us."

Laaqueel had seen that the city had been opened through the images in the crystal brain coral. Iakhovas peered through the crystal almost incessantly. She'd had no contact with the female voice that spoke with her at the Battle of Voalidru. She also hadn't had to fight for her life since then.

And since that battle, she hadn't once prayed to Sekolah.

"Then we're going to go into the trap?" Laaqueel asked.

Iakhovas smiled confidently. "I wouldn't miss it, little malenti."

"Are you afraid?" Sabyna asked.

Jherek cracked open a crab leg and dug out the tender meat inside. He sat with Sabyna on one of the benches on Maalirn's Walk near the Fire Fountain. The flames blazed up in spite of the water, and cooks used the heat to prepare meals for the humans who weren't used to eating uncooked seafood. They'd been in Myth Nantar now for five days.

"Aye," he told her without hesitation. "By all the stories I've been told of the Taker, by all the legends that Pacys has seen fit to tell me, he's a fearsome creature. I'd be a fool not to be afraid."

"You don't have to fight him."

Jherek was silent for a moment, then said, "Aye, but I do, lady. It's as Lathander would have me do, and there are those who believe I might be the only chance there is to end his menace for all time."

"You mean Pacys and Glawinn believe that."

"Aye."

"One wants to sing about you, Jherek, and the other believes in heroes."

"Do you find me so hard to believe in, lady?"

Sabyna shook her head, the anger in her features softening. "No," she admitted, "I believe in you, Jherek, but I'm afraid for you, too."

"It only shows you have good sense."

"How can you joke about this?"

"Lady, forgive me. I'm not joking. I just don't want to burden you—or myself."

"What if I asked you not to do this?" Sabyna asked. "What if I asked you not to stand and fight with these people?"

Jherek was silent for a moment, looking into her copper-colored eyes. "Would you?" he asked finally.

She looked away from him. "Selûne help a misguided fool," she said, "I should never have brought this up."

"Would you ask me?" Jherek asked quietly. "Now I need to know."

"If I was going to ask you, I already would have," she told him. "I know what your answer would be anyway. It just seems so unfair that we have this between us and we stand on the brink of losing it all."

Jherek took her hand in his, squeezing it lightly. "Lady, I prefer to think that we stand on the brink of having more than I'd ever dreamed."

Tears glittered in her eyes, and he could tell she searched for something to say. "I'm sorry I even thought about asking you this, Jherek. It's a streak of selfishness in me that I'm not proud of."

"It's good to know the things you want."

She smiled through her tears. "I know I want you."

"As I want you, lady." He lifted her fingers to his lips and kissed them softly. "Neither of us knows what the future may bring, and I've had enough of living in the past. I will take what I can get."

"I know."

"As for fighting the Taker, I won't be going into that battle alone. Glawinn will be there, as well as a host of warriors who have spent their lives in battle."

"I don't know why it has to be you."

"Nor do I, lady. I only know that I won't walk away from this. All my life I've looked for something to believe in. Lathander is teaching me to believe in myself. No one caused me to be the way I am. I walk the path I do because I chose to walk it. I stayed with the people I did because I wanted to, not because I had to. Looking back as Lathander has bade me, I realize now that I had more choice in those matters than I thought I did. I stepped away from my father in search of becoming what was in me, not because of what I wanted but because I couldn't accept what was there. If I walked away from this, I couldn't accept myself. I wouldn't feel as though I deserved you."

"I wouldn't judge you harshly for walking away from this."

Jherek nodded. "I know."

"I love you."

Her hand trailed gently across his face, briefly touching the water-softened scab that covered the slash on his cheek.

"As I love you." Jherek touched her face with the back of his hand, wiping away the tears he found there. "I could not love you so much did I not love honor, lady. It is all I know to be, and I would die before I betrayed that honor or my love for you."

"I know," she said hoarsely, holding his head between her hands. "I know. One does not come without the price of the other. For either of us."

She pulled him closer and wrapped her arms around his waist. Jherek put his arms over her shoulders and held her tightly.

"Die, huu-mannn!"

Jherek lifted the cutlass and blocked the sea devil's trident thrust. He willed Iridea's Tear into a hook, reaching out quickly and tearing the throat from his opponent. He pushed the dying sahuagin away, almost bowled over by the next sea devil pushing up from behind.

The young paladin stood with other defenders of Myth Nantar at Chamal Gate. The Taker's final attack came after the triton offensive of the fifth of Uktar—only a couple days before—had split his forces. According to the tritons who'd reported to Qos, fully half his remaining army of sahuagin had turned and swam back to the Alamber Sea.

The sound of steel against coral filled the area, ringing more stridently than Jherek was used to. Over it all he heard Pacys singing. The bard's song rang true within him, making him feel stronger and more confident. Iakhovas's army still outnumbered the Myth Nantarn defenders nearly two to one, even after the tritons' victory.

Fighting undersea wasn't like fighting on a ship's deck, Jherek discovered. Underwater, the sahuagin could come at him from above as well as ahead and behind—and they didn't have any sense of honor. Nor did they abide by the Laws of Battle he'd heard so many of the Serôsians lived and died by.

"Fall back and regroup!" Morgan Ildacer shouted, waving his troops back. The High Mages had named the sea elf captain to head up one of the defensive units.

The young paladin fell back with the rest of his group. He swam with the others, finding it easier to battle in the mythal that covered the city than he expected. His moves in the water came more naturally since he didn't have to hold his breath. Somehow his sense of balance seemed more sure as well.

A sahuagin thrust a spear at him from the right while another yanked its weapon from a mortally wounded sea elf.

Jherek swung the enchanted sword and chopped the trident head off, leaving the sahuagin with only the shaft in its hands. Once under water he'd found the sword swung as easily as if he stood on dry land, the blade not slowed at all.

The sahuagin seemed startled, then angrily threw the useless shaft away and spread the claws of both its hands. The second sahuagin approached in a flash, its fins pushing at the water.

Jherek willed the bracer into a two-foot shield and set himself as well as he could. He pulled the shield in against his body at the last minute. Like the sword, the bracer—in any shape he willed it into— had no water drag at all.

The trident slammed against the shield then deflected harmlessly over Jherek's shoulder. The sahuagin shoved a hand out with its finger webs spread to slow and turn. Jherek uncoiled his arm and lashed out with the shield. The razor-sharp edge, thinner and more solid than the finest steel, sliced through the sea devil's stomach, disemboweling it at once.

Still moving, Jherek swept the shield in, catching the water now because he willed it to, and lifted himself from the first sahuagin's path. He brought the sword down and nearly severed his opponent's neck.

Before he could recover, one of the few koalinth survivors caught him with a spear thrust in the chest. The silverweave mail shirt he wore prevented the blade from slicing through his chest, but the impact knocked him backward, slamming the breath from his lungs.

The young paladin went with the motion, flipping backward and reaching out to the water element of the mythal, letting it buoy him up. He'd discovered within the mythal that he could treat the city as if it were two-dimensional, like a city on dry land, or three-dimensional as if he were underwater.

Jherek kicked his feet and twisted as he willed the bracer into a hook. When the koalinth shot over him, the young paladin flicked the hook and caught the marine hobgoblin in the leg. He used the creature's momentum to pull him faster, angling his body so he came up behind the koalinth.

The young paladin reversed his sword as he swung toward the koalinth. Though the creature's back was toward him, he couldn't strike. He switched the bracer to a dagger and readied himself as the koalinth turned toward him, lashing out with its spear. Jherek blocked the spear with the dagger, then drove his sword through his opponent's heart.

Even as the koalinth died, Jherek changed the bracer back to a shield as a dozen sahuagin leveled their crossbows and fired. The short, heavy quarrels flashed across the distance and thudded against the shield. One of the sea elves a few feet away didn't fare so well and took a quarrel through the throat.

In the next moment a Dukar stepped forward and formed a fireball in one hand. He threw the swirling flames at the mass of sahuagin. They had only a moment to attempt escape before the fireball detonated with a thunderous crack that left only burned and torn bodies behind.

Blood filled the water around Jherek and created a salty taste to the water he breathed. It was like nothing he'd ever experienced.

The sea elves kept falling back, having no choice as their numbers dwindled. Jherek caught sight of the House of the Waves on his left, then it was lost to the sahuagin forces as well. He lifted his sword and kept fighting, knowing the battle was continuing on a number of fronts.

"Pull those damned sails!" Azla roared as she ran across the decks, keeping her quarry always in sight. "Bring her about!"

Sabyna stood beside Arthoris on *Azure Dagger*'s forecastle. Skeins floated at her side, riding the wind. Sabyna's attention was torn between helping Arthoris with his spells and with worrying about Jherek. She wished she could have stayed with him in the City of Destinies, but with the attack coming from the surface, they both knew she would be of more use there.

Twenty pirate vessels sailed the sea above Myth Nantar. The crews worked to dispose of Vurgrom's poisoned kegs. The pirate had told them about the kegs after being taken prisoner. He bargained for his own freedom by telling. Jherek, in turn, informed the Myth Nantarn defenders.

Mermen and locathah swam under the water with nets, trying to catch as many of the barrels as they could.

Azure Dagger and *Steadfast* harried the pirate ships. In the beginning they'd thought there would have been a chance to prevent some of the sabotage, but with twenty ships against them, it was only a matter of time until they were captured or sunk.

After Captain Tarnar of *Steadfast* found out about the poisoned kegs, he'd sent a patchwork crew under his first officer south to Ilighôn in the hopes of reaching Corymrean Freesails that might be using the port city as a staging point. So far none of the hoped-for reinforcements had arrived.

As Arthoris prepared his next spell, a pirate ship closed on *Azure Dagger*, running broadside to her. Ballista crews worked to crank their deadly devices around and take aim.

Sabyna invoked one of the new spells Arthoris had taught her, knowing that the ship's mage was vulnerable on the forecastle. She inscribed the mystic symbol in the air, and it glowed briefly before disappearing.

"Very good," Arthoris said as he pulled on a leather glove that looked like it was equipped with brass knuckles.

"If Selûne guided me well enough," Sabyna said.

Arthoris spoke a command word and held his glove-covered, clenched hand before him. A huge, disembodied hand appeared in the air before him. It measured five feet across at the knuckles.

"Deck crew—stand by to repel boarders!" Azla called, taking her place at the starboard railing. Pirates sprang to her side. "Ballista crews—fire at will!"

Under Arthoris's control, the disembodied fist flew across the water, ignoring the ship that paced them, and hammered the mainmast. Three hits later, the mast cracked and sheared off. Sinking the ships wasn't a good idea. The kegs would sink with them, and there were no guarantees the poison would drift far enough away not to hurt anyone. As soon as the mast crumpled, Arthoris moved the magic hand on to the next ship, attacking the rudder there.

Archers targeted the mage, who stood out against the rest of the crew as he gestured. Arrows sped from their bows, few of them getting anywhere close to Sabyna or Arthoris. Only a handful struck the invisible shield Sabyna had raised in front of them. They dropped to the deck, spent.

Grappling lines tossed from the pirate ship landed over *Azure Dagger*'s railing but were quickly cut away by the ship's crew. Her own ballistae fired, clearing the pirate decks.

The fore ballista on the pirate vessel cut loose. The huge shaft came straight at Arthoris and Sabyna, then splintered against the magic shield. The impact, however, was enough to send both mages to their knees. Arthoris lost control of the disembodied hand, and it faded away.

Less than thirty feet away, Vurgrom's pirate crew linked up.

"Stand ready," Azla yelled.

Her crew raised their shields and their weapons.

The other ship's crew all leaped together, using magic to span the distance to *Azure Dagger*.

"Haul!" Azla commanded. "Haul, damn you, if you would live!"

Men at either end of the caravel's main deck pulled ropes and ran up a cargo net that spanned the distance across the main deck. The enspelled pirates thudded into the cargo net, caught off guard. Before they could slash their way through the net, Azla's crew attacked them with swords, daggers, and bows. Up against the cargo net as they were, it was like stabbing fish in a barrel.

Sabyna helped Arthoris to his feet, peering out at the water. They hadn't stopped many of Vurgrom's pirates from dumping their deadly cargo, but she hoped they'd slowed them enough that the undersea rescue teams could gather most of the falling kegs before they descended to Myth Nantar.

"Now there's a welcome sight," Arthoris said.

Turning south, Sabyna looked out over the horizon and saw the sails from at least five tall ships running with the wind. All of them flew the colors of Cormyrean Freesails.

"Let's hope they're not too late," Sabyna said grimly.

Hurry, little malenti. There's not much time.

Laaqueel swam after Iakhovas high above Myth Nantar. She glanced at the gates leading into the city, realizing that few of the koalinth had actually penetrated the city itself, proof that the mythal that protected against such creatures still worked.

The maps Iakhovas had drawn of the area from stories they'd gathered were very accurate. She saw Chamal Avenue to the left, noting the fighting going on there, all of it garishly lit by the Fire Fountain.

Iakhovas swam boldly, using his claws against any Myth Nantarn defenders who made it through his defenses. Over a hundred sharks swam with him as a living wall of protection, all under the control of the headband he wore. The sharks acted like battering rams, barreling through would-be defenders or ripping arms and legs off in their cruel mouths as they passed.

The sea elf rangers and mages of the city tried battling the possessed creatures as well, but they were too tightly packed and controlled to be turned away. A shalarin Dukar slashed through them, arching his body and gliding gracefully toward Iakhovas while using the sharks themselves as cover.

Laaqueel spotted the shalarin and almost shouted a warning. Her first instinct was self-preservation, and she knew without Iakhovas she would never escape the city. *Tarjana* waited outside the city, hidden behind a reef and the magic spell woven by Iakhovas. Before she could get past her hesitation, the shalarin Dukar cut through the sharks and engaged Iakhovas.

The shalarin's hand glowed white and changed shapes, becoming trident tines that flashed out for Iakhovas. Reacting immediately, Iakhovas shifted his arm into the edged weapon Laaqueel had seen before as he engaged the Dukar. The sharks changed courses, swirling around their master to deflect other potential attackers.

The Dukar thrust the trident hand out but Iakhovas blocked it effortlessly and slashed the shalarin's arm off with his own altered limb. Before the shalarin recovered, Iakhovas slashed again and decapitated his opponent. A shark glided by and snatched the tumbling head from the water, swallowing it whole.

Iakhovas turned at once and streaked for the collapsed ruin surrounding a circle of green and blue marble with coral mosaics that created a picture of a beautiful mermaid. Her hair, arms, and tail flukes each pointed to the seven carved coral arches set around the circle. Beneath her tail was the word AMTOLA, which Laaqueel recognized from her studies. Translated, it meant "traveler."

The malenti priestess wasn't sure what the mosaic represented. The information Iakhovas gave her regarding Myth Nantar's history and geography was limited.

Shooting from the protection of the sharks, Iakhovas swam down to the ruins. He dropped to one of the coral arches as a squad of mermen raced for him from above. Iakhovas flung one hand out, blue fire shooting from his fingertips. A moment later a huge web uncoiled across the seven arches in front of the approaching mermen. Unable to stop, they slammed into the webbing. Sharks finned that way at once, attacking the easy prey.

Iakhovas moved to the nearest coral arch, a smile on his dark face. He hammered one side of the arch with his fist, breaking a section of it into pieces that floated through the water. He caught one of the coral chunks and crushed it in his hand, brushing the flakes away.

"See, little malenti?" Iakhovas showed her what was in his palm.

Laaqueel floated closer and saw the tiny jade gem carefully set into a dark red fire opal no bigger than her thumb. "What is it?" she asked.

"My eye, little malenti," Iakhovas laughed. "The eye that Umberlee took from me. The eye I made to make me more powerful than ever. Until the Great Barrier around this place was shattered, I could not reach it—but with it, little malenti, with it I shall be invincible!"

Currents swept against Laaqueel, pushed by the mermen trying to escape the web and the savaging sharks. She glanced up to see other mermen, sea elves, and locathah working desperately to free their comrades from the death trap.

"Stand ready, little malenti."

Iakhovas formed a fireball in his hand and threw it into the web. The strands caught fire, burning the trapped victims and those rescuers who were too close. Laaqueel dodged the falling bodies and the flaming web ropes.

"Now, little malenti!"

Iakhovas leaped up from the mosaic. Laaqueel followed, wanting to be free of all the enemies surrounding her. When she'd first entered Myth Nantar, even with an army twice the number of the defenders, she'd felt little chance of emerging from the battle alive. Now that Iakhovas possessed his prize, the slim hope that she might yet live entered her thoughts. Even so, she had no idea what she would do next.

She watched as a keg dropped on top of a nearby coral-encrusted building. A vaporous sediment billowed out from holes cut in the keg's sides, and the purplish hue looked immediately familiar. The sediment spread quickly, enveloping a group of sahuagin battling a clutch of tritons. Within seconds all of them were dying, gripped in the paroxysms of the sahuagin poison.

More kegs drifted down around the city with the same effect. The poison spread quickly so it didn't last long, and its killing radius extended no more than twenty feet. Glancing up, straining her eyes, Laaqueel saw huge nets manned by mermen and locathah already burdened with dozens more kegs. Their effort spared Myth Nantar a lot of damage.

Laaqueel halted for a moment, still stunned even after everything she'd seen that Iakhovas would so willingly sacrifice the sahuagin. She knew if the kegs were present that Vurgrom's pirates must be on the surface. She doubted that would prove an effective escape route, but she had no idea of any other he had in mind.

"Live or die, little malenti," Iakhovas called as he swam toward the surface.

She hesitated, not knowing which would be better.

Live, the feminine voice called out. *Live, that you may serve.*

Reluctantly, fearfully, Laaqueel swam.

Pacys stood atop the Colossus of Dukar. His fingers effortlessly found the sac=eddar's gemstones, and the notes rang out as pure as dwarven steel.

At ninety feet tall, the statue was the tallest structure in Myth Nantar. The old bard stood on its head and sang, pouring his heart into the ballad he'd written for the defenders of the City of Destinies. Carved from lucent coral, the statue glowed brightly, providing nearly a third of the light filling the city. The statue held a tapal high in its right hand and stood straddling the entrance to a most revered tomb.

From his vantage point, Pacys could view the battle clearly. Qos, the High Mages of Sylkiir, and the Dukars led by Tu'uua'col stood in a circle around the Great Gate west of the Dukars' Academy.

The mosaic plaza that held the Great Gate was almost two hundred feet across. The mages around the perimeter all glowed lambent blue-green from the ancient, eldritch forces they controlled. They continued their spell even though their defenders were swiftly falling to sahuagin tridents.

Drawn by the powers that connected him to the story that he told, blessed by Oghma, the old bard was able to see the main players in the battle as if he stood next to them. When he focused on them, he even heard their words.

His attention was drawn to Iakhovas as the Taker swam for the surface. Jherek remained low in the city, battling from building to building as the sahuagin and drowned ones continued pressing toward the center. Khlinat and a handful of sea elf guards stood watch over the old bard.

Pacys sang, giving voice to the words and the music that filled him. Never before had he felt the strength and confidence of a performance the way he did now. He knew his music affected the valiant men who battled below, adding strength to their flagging bodies and courage to their hearts in the face of a superior enemy.

" 'Ware now, friend Pacys!" Khlinat roared.

The bard ducked as the dwarf sailed overhead astride a sahuagin nearly three times his size. One hand axe was buried in the sea devil's neck and Khlinat held the other back, ready to strike. The sahuagin flailed with a handful of claws, narrowly missing the dwarf's face. Khlinat put the hand-axe blade through the sea devil's skull.

A burst of magic that suddenly flooded from the mythal staggered Pacys. With his senses fully open and receptive, he was overly attentive to such things. He turned back to the Great Gate plaza and watched as the sahuagin struck within the ranks of the High Mages and Dukars, driving their defenders back before them. The claws of the sea devils pierced the bodies of the magic-users.

At the same time, a yellow-green comet roared from the Great Gate mosaic and streaked for the surface. The comet's tail stretched from the comet's head to the mosaic, maintaining contact. The yellow-green glare washed over the City of Destinies, stripping away all other colors.

Qos roared and drew the huge two-handed sword he carried. Twice as tall as his attackers, he swept the blade through the sahuagin in a glittering arc, shearing them limb from limb. The Dukars that survived the initial attack summoned weapons from their bodies and battled desperately.

Even from as far away as he was, Pacys could see that Tanarath Reefglamor was among the fallen, a sahuagin's trident shoved through his heart. Still, the old bard's voice didn't falter, remaining steady and true.

The yellow-green comet struck the ocean's surface above and exploded into bright embers that whirled in the air. Several of them struck pirate ships, reducing them to rubble in heartbeats. The embers whirled faster, coming closer and closer together. The ocean's surface whirled in the opposite direction of the embers, creating a swirl of white-capped peaks that abruptly inverted and stabbed down deeply into the Sea of Fallen Stars.

Even though he wore one of the mystic gems that all the Myth Nantarn defenders wore to spare them from the effects of the Great Gate, Pacys felt the pull of the huge whirlpool that suddenly formed and reached from the Great Gate to the ocean's surface. The eldritch energies lighted the whirlpool from the inside, throwing out yellow-green light like it was a giant lamp. He watched as the swirling waterspout around the pirate vessels broadened to a thousand feet and more, sucking them down into the deep trough that opened.

The ships turned sideways and tumbled down into the waterspout. The vessels that went prow or stern first stayed level even though they followed the circular motion of the whirlpool, but the ships that went down sideways rolled over and shattered, filling the whirlpool with deadly debris that slammed into the other ships.

"Blessed Oghma," the old bard whispered, stunned.

From everything Qos, the Dukars, and the High Mages had talked about, he was certain no one expected this. The Great Gate had never been opened before, it was intended as a desperate, final effort against invaders.

The sahuagin, drowned ones, and koalinth barred from the city by the mythal were drawn into the whirlpool as well. The ships, whole and broken, smashed into them, killing dozens in a sweep. The mythal was all that prevented the city itself from being pulled into the whirlpool.

Pacys caught sight of *Azure Dagger* as the caravel was yanked into the whirlpool as well. No one thought to give the two ships any defense against the whirlpool. No one believed it would reach so far. Miraculously, *Azure Dagger* went into the whirlpool prow first, followed by *Steadfast*. Three Cormyrean Freesails followed next.

Though filled with horror and hurt, Pacys's pain was nowhere near that of another's.

———————

"No!" Jherek screamed in disbelief.

Azure Dagger seemed to sail straight into the whirlpool's jaws.

Within seconds, the first of the ships and the sahuagin reached the eye of the whirlpool at the Great Gate and disappeared, thrown half a world away—for all anyone knew. The only thing the High Mages and Qos agreed on was that the Great Gate took all in it far from Serôs.

Something shoved the young paladin from behind. Angry, he turned, only to find the golden sea wyrm floating there. It coiled and flexed, struggling against the whirlpool's pull. For the first time, he understood the creature's attraction to him; why it mysteriously followed him to Aglarond and back, and why it helped him rescue Sabyna from the drowned ones.

Azure Dagger plummeted toward the whirlpool's eye as Jherek reached for the sea wyrm and pulled himself up onto the creature's back. He slapped it on the neck gratefully and urged it forward. The sea wyrm darted forward like an arrow. Jherek ripped the necklace with the whirlpool gem from his neck and threw it away, feeling the pull of the gate at once.

"Jherek!"

Knowing the voice, the young paladin glanced ahead, spotting the bard atop the statue.

"I must know the end of the story," Pacys shouted.

Jherek hesitated for an instant as the sea wyrm closed the distance to the old bard. Doing what he planned was without question dangerous, but he knew Pacys was as driven by his part in the events as he was. He willed the bracer back into its resting form and reached for Pacys's hand.

Though the force of the contact must have almost ripped the bard's arm from his shoulder, Pacys didn't say a word. The old bard twisted himself expertly in the water until he sat behind Jherek.

The sea wyrm jerked suddenly.

Glancing back, Jherek saw that Khlinat had managed to grab the creature's tail. The dwarf held on fiercely.

"Leave him," the young paladin told the sea wyrm.

In response, the dragon-kin curled the dwarf protectively in its tail. Jherek watched *Azure Dagger* plunge toward the whirlpool's eye. Two masts hung in broken shards, wrapped in sailcloth. The sea wyrm reached the outer edge of the whirlpool and they were sucked inside.

byna gazed up in disbelief at the swirling wall of green-blue water that surrounded her. *Azure Dagger* stabbed straight down into the maelstrom. The roaring water made conversation impossible. The ship's mage thought she might be screaming, but she'd have never known.

She lost her footing on the deck as the caravel tilted forward even more. As she fell toward the prow, aware of the tangled rigging and the broken mast ahead, Sabyna angled her body and managed to seize the rigging with one hand. She swung under it and prayed that her fingers wouldn't be pulled off.

She was hit from behind, and when she spun to see what had happened, she found herself face to face with a pirate who'd been hanged in the rigging. The bloated face and protruding tongue let her know it was too late to cut him away.

The caravel hit the bottom of the whirlpool and the world went away.

Laying low along the sea wyrm's neck, the old bard's arms wrapped tight around his waist and with Khlinat in tow, Jherek guided his mount through the swirling wall of water into the center of the whirlpool. For a moment they hung motionless in the raging roar of the ocean, then they fell toward the bottom of the whirlpool. The sea wyrm convulsed, then poked its head down.

Jherek locked his legs around his mount and leaned back, forcing himself to stay on its back through sheer willpower. They hit the bottom of the whirlpool, followed immediately by a moment of blackness, then crashed through a tumbling seascape.

Pirate ships lay scattered along the ocean floor, smashed, broken, and driven into the mud and sand. Ships crashed into the reef, became buried in broken coral strands, and hopelessly tangled in each others' rigging.

The sea wyrm flared its fins and angled its head, bringing them up from the steep dive only a few feet short of the ocean floor. It turned its head and twisted its body, rolling neatly around the coral reef, then it angled toward the surface.

Away from Myth Nantar's mythal, Jherek suddenly found he couldn't breathe without drowning. Though Pacys wore some kind of bracelet that allowed him to move underwater with ease, Khlinat was in the same shape as Jherek. Somehow the dragon-kin knew that.

Ahead, *Azure Dagger* and four other ships that survived the wild ride rose toward the surface, buoyed by the air in their cargo holds.

Jherek knew the ships probably wouldn't last even if they reached the surface. Though there was still some air in their holds, the structures were weakened beyond repair and would be taking on water rapidly. Quick crews might man the bilge pumps and keep themselves afloat for a time, but that assumed any crew was left.

"There is the Taker," Pacys said, still able to talk thanks to the bracelet he wore.

Jherek spotted the big sahuagin ahead. Only the Taker didn't resemble a sahuagin any more. He looked human as he fumbled with an object in his hands. A pale female elf holding a trident swam close behind him.

In the next instant, the sea wyrm broke the surface and Jherek drew in a long breath. Glancing over his shoulder, he saw that the sea wyrm had raised Khlinat to the surface as well, holding the dwarf in its curled tail.

Turning, Jherek watched *Azure Dagger*'s stern clear the surface first, revealing the broken stern mast. Then the crow's nest bucked up, wavering with the sea's motion.

The young paladin headed for the caravel by tugging on the sea wyrm's forward fin. The creature raced across the ocean surface.

Frantically, Jherek searched *Azure Dagger*'s deck.

"Jherek, here!"

Drawn by her voice, the young paladin spotted Sabyna crawling down from the twisted remnants of the foremast rigging where a corpse hung. He guided the sea wyrm to the caravel.

Azla stood up, coughing and gagging in the stern, then took a deep breath and started bellowing orders to her crew. *Azure Dagger* listed heavily in the sea, nearly half of her below the waterline.

"Look," Pacys said softly. "The Taker."

Jherek turned in time to see Iakhovas pull up from the sea, grabbing hold of *Azure Dagger*'s stern. The helmsman turned on the man, swinging a cutlass.

Iakhovas blocked the blade with his bare arm and the steel broke with a sharp ping. The Taker shoved his arm against the man, thrusting a sharp-edged fin through the helmsman's chest in a spray of blood.

Striding to the railing, Iakhovas roared, "Get off my ship or die!"

Laaqueel tasted the salt in the water around her and knew she was home. She gazed through the deep blue-green sea and tried to sense in what direction the sahuagin kingdom of Alkyraan in the Claarteeros Sea lay.

And should you go back there, the female voice asked, *what do you think will be waiting for you?*

"Leave me alone," Laaqueel demanded.

A hero's homecoming? A grateful return for the Most Sacred One? And what happens when some of the sahuagin in these waters return there as well with stories of the way Iakhovas has betrayed them? What if Iakhovas himself returns there intending to control the kingdom he won while he plots war with the rest of Toril?

"No."

Those are his plans, Laaqueel. You cannot deny that.

The malenti priestess cowered in the water, wishing there was some way to be free.

You can be free.

"By giving myself to you?"

I will teach you to live free, Laaqueel. I will show you things you've longed for all your life and have never been able to name. You've changed too much now to go back to what you were.

"No."

Yes.

Laaqueel floated in the water, watching as sahuagin and pirate continued the war they'd begun in Serôs. Some of the sahuagin wore the bluer colors of the Inner Sea.

"Who are you?"

I am Eldath, called the Green Goddess and the Quiet One. The Twelfth Serôs War has destroyed much of the harmony my priests and priestesses have wrought over the last years. This is necessary, though, to promote the greater harmony we've striven for throughout the Inner Sea.

"Why have you come to me?"

During your association with the Taker, Laaqueel, you have changed and grown. I see much promise in you. Like you, Serôs will have to change and grow. There are noble malenti in Serôs who have no ties with the sahuagin. I would introduce you to them.

Laaqueel adjusted her air bladder and floated effortlessly, torn between what she hoped for and what she knew to be true. Home could never be home again unless Iakhovas was there to enforce her privileges. She would give up more than she would gain.

Little malenti, Iakhovas called, *to me. There is a ship I want, and we'll need a crew to get it to Skaug where we may begin planning anew.*

Skaug was the pirate capital of the Nelanther Isles, a place Iakhovas had taken Laaqueel before. She hesitated.

Little malenti!

The quill next to Laaqueel's heart twitched in warning. She started up to the surface, tracking the bond between her and Iakhovas.

Placing a hand on the sea wyrm's back, Jherek vaulted to *Azure Dagger*'s tilted deck. Azla ran up the stern castle steps toward Iakhovas, her scimitar in her fist. The Taker grinned cruelly at her and a ruby beam leaped out from his golden eye.

The beam touched Azla and blasted her in a shower of sparks. She flew back over the railing to the main deck, her blouse afire and the stench of ozone in the air.

Jherek broke stride, thinking to go to Azla's side.

"Go, young warrior," Glawinn thundered.

The paladin lurched across the broken deck, dragging his right leg heavily at his side. His left arm was curled up tightly by his chest, blood streaming from a wound marked by a wooden shard protruding from it.

Jherek ran up the stern castle stairs, watching as Iakhovas swung on him with the mystic eye. The young paladin leaped, taking advantage of the tilted deck, arching his body in mid-air and flipping to land on the stern castle only a few feet from Iakhovas.

Though he hadn't fought a mage before, he knew from stories that their power relied on being able to cast spells, and spells took time. He intended to give Iakhovas none. He willed Iridea's Tear into a two-foot shield and advanced on the Taker.

"You're the boy from the cave," Iakhovas said. He grinned and took a step back as he drew the sword at his side.

"I am Jherek, a paladin in the service of Lathander, the Morninglord. If you would surrender, I would allow it." The young paladin didn't expect the man would, but the opportunity had to be offered.

Cruel lights glinted in Iakhovas's real eye as well as the golden one that sat in the scarred socket. His runic tattoos made his face seem even darker. He laughed loudly.

"And you would kill me otherwise, boy?"

"Aye, and praise Lathander for giving me the strength."

The words still sounded strange to Jherek's ears, but in his heart they felt right and true.

Iakhovas drew himself up to his full height of nearly eight feet and drew the sword at his hip.

"I *invented* swordplay, boy. Edged steel . . . sharp as a shark's tooth . . . shaped like a fin. Who else but me could create that?"

The great sword came around much quicker than Jherek anticipated. The young paladin stepped back and ducked, letting the blade go harmlessly by. Even as he started to set himself, Iakhovas brought the blade back at Jherek's knees faster than any human could have done.

Leaping over the blade, Jherek flipped and came down on his feet. He lifted the shield just in time to keep the blade from cleaving his skull. He parried with his cutlass, scoring a deep cut on his opponent's arm.

Iakhovas scowled and took a step back. A violet ray shot at Jherek from the Taker's golden eye.

Reacting instantly, the young paladin raised his shield, which absorbed the ray and threw it back into Iakhovas's face, staggering him. The young paladin immediately went on the offensive again, driving Iakhovas back. He thrust and parried, then lunged and slashed, moving steadily into the bigger man. Blood from Iakhovas's wound dripped on the ship's deck and left burned stigmata.

"You cannot kill me, boy," Iakhovas shouted. "I will not allow myself to die. Even Umberlee tried to kill me and failed. Who are you to challenge me who would be a god?"

"I am a strong right arm of Lathander," Jherek replied, burying the cutlass in the railing then ripping it free and diving back. He blocked Iakhovas's return blow with his shield this time and slashed his opponent across the chest. "I am a beginning, chosen by the Morninglord."

"Chosen to die," Iakhovas taunted.

"No," Jherek said, "chosen to live."

Jherek thrust and swung and parried. His blade moved even faster, picking up the pace in spite of all the battles he'd been in this day.

Iakhovas's scowl deepened as he was forced back. Steel rang on steel, and for the first time Jherek realized some of the surviving sahuagin were attacking *Azure Dagger*. Her crew defended her, aided by the sea wyrm. Pacys fought on the deck, his staff whirling as he chopped into the sea devils that fought to board. Khlinat was at the old bard's side, his axes whirling madly.

Taking advantage of the young paladin's distraction, Iakhovas stepped forward suddenly and chanced a sidearm blow straight for Jherek's head. Jherek barely got his cutlass around to block the sword, but he was driven stumbling backward, off-balance.

Iakhovas came at him, snarling and with bloodlust in his eye. He raised the great sword two-handed and brought it down.

Jherek turned quickly, barely escaping the blow that shattered the navigator's table behind him. He rolled to his feet, willing the bracer into a hook as he ducked under Iakhovas's backhanded blow. He caught the blade in the hook, stopping it short and pulling the Taker off balance. Turning in, knowing the chance he was taking, the young paladin brought the cutlass crashing down on the trapped blade.

Harsh green light exploded on impact, and electricity filled the air. Steel shattered, falling in two pieces, leaving only an inch or two sticking out from the hilt.

Iakhovas stepped back in surprise, but a crafty smile lit his scarred and tattooed features.

"You haven't seen all there is to me, boy," Iakhovas said.

He turned and sprinted for the stern railing, leaping over it in a long, flat dive.

Jherek followed the movement, but stopped at the rail, amazed at what he saw.

By the time Iakhovas hit the water, he was no longer anything human. A manlike form went down, but a ninety-foot great white shark surfaced. Scars and tattooing showed around a golden eye. It sped out to sea and gradually went down, leaving only the triangular dorsal fin—as big as a house—sticking out of the water.

Sahuagin swarmed up the stern, and Jherek spent a few moments riposting their attacks and killing them. As he kicked the corpses back into the water, he noticed the triangular fin streaking for *Azure Dagger.*

"Hold on!" he roared in warning.

In the next instant, the huge shark slammed into the caravel. Timbers cracked and gave way as the predator hammered through the hull.

"Abandon ship, damn it!"

Jherek turned and saw Azla up and about. Wounds still covered her, but evidently Glawinn had healed the worst of it. She was mobile, but hurting greatly.

"Get the boats over the side and get into them!" she shouted. "We're taking on water like a sieve!"

Glancing back out to sea, Jherek watched the massive predator come around for another pass.

Laaqueel watched Iakhovas in awe as he transformed into the great shark.

Not a shark, Eldath corrected. *Iakhovas is a megalodon, a prehistoric creature and perhaps the first such of his kind.*

"But he once walked with gods," Laaqueel said, watching as Iakhovas sped toward the ship.

With Umberlee, yes, and possibly even with Sekolah.

"He was never one of Sekolah's chosen?"

No. He's an aberration, a thing whose time is well gone.

Iakhovas turned from attacking the ship and fixed her with his real eye. *Little malenti,* his voice sounded in her head, *you are slow to come when I command.*

You must make a choice, Eldath said, *here and now. Will you stay as an outcast with the sahuagin and keep Iakhovas as your master, or will you take what I offer?*

"Brace yourselves!" Jherek yelled as he grabbed the stern railing.

Iakhovas rammed *Azure Dagger* again, splitting the hull even more. As the huge predator pulled away this time, the young paladin felt the caravel listing, taking on water. He glanced over his shoulder as the vessel sank to its midsection. The crew routed the attacking sahuagin. The sea wyrm raised its golden finned head from the sea and returned Jherek's gaze.

"I need you," Jherek said.

The sea wyrm dived without hesitation and swam to the stern section. Out in the distance, Iakhovas came around for another pass. Jherek was certain this attack would leave the stricken vessel in tatters and the crew vulnerable to that great mouth filled with serrated teeth.

"Jherek!" Sabyna called from behind him.

"Lady," the young paladin said. "You need to get in one of the boats and row for shore." He pointed toward the low, green-forested hill that could be seen in the distance.

"What are you going to do?"

Jherek gave her a smile and answered, "All that I may, lady. I can do naught else."

Sabyna took her kerchief from her hair and quickly tied it around his arm. "I would not stop you from doing as Lathander has directed, but you heed my words well." Her voice cracked with emotion and a sheen was in her eyes. "You finish what you have been given to do, and you come back to me in one piece."

Jherek's heart soared, pushing aside even the fear and insecurity that thrummed inside him. He took her face in his hands and kissed her deeply.

"As you wish, lady," he said, then threw himself from the stern castle in a dive that took him straight at the approaching shark.

Curving up toward the surface, watching the huge predator bearing down on him and suddenly realizing how vulnerable he was when the shark could swallow him and the sea wyrm whole, Jherek grabbed hold of the dragon-kin's dorsal fin and pulled himself up on its back.

The bond between Jherek and the sea wyrm was strong. He guided it with his knees as he willed the bracer into a shield. He held his sword in his hand as they sped toward their foe.

Ninety feet of silent, sudden death sped at the young paladin. Jherek sat his mount, holding on tightly, gambling that the bracer's power would see him through. The sea wyrm didn't falter as it finned toward Iakhovas.

Holding on tightly to the grip inside the shield, Jherek narrowly avoided the black, cavernous mouth ringed by serrated teeth and smashed the shield into the huge predator's snout. The impact hurled him dozens of feet from the sea wyrm and almost knocked him out, but the shield absorbed the brunt of the blow.

Iakhovas, incredibly, seemed staggered.

"You'll die for that boy," he said as he turned in the water.

The sea wyrm swam to Jherek's side in a flash of golden light. Fighting the disorientation that gripped him, the young paladin tried to mount again.

Iakhovas's snout was bloodied. His golden eye gleamed.

Jherek tried to pull up onto the sea wyrm but missed. He concentrated, keeping his grip as the dragon-kin pulled him backward. The great predator bore down on him.

Laaqueel swam toward the young warrior trying to pull up onto the sea wyrm. When she reached him, she pushed him up onto his mount and turned to face Iakhovas.

Little malenti, what do you think you're doing?

Laaqueel made no reply. There was none to make. In the next few heartbeats, she'd live or die. She summoned her powers, intending to crush Iakhovas if she could.

Where she'd once felt all the gifts Sekolah had given her, there was only emptiness.

Your belief in the Shark God is gone, Eldath said. *As goes the belief, so goes the power. There is no other way.*

Helplessly, Laaqueel watched as Iakhovas rushed toward her.

Die, traitorous bitch!

Laaqueel felt the quill stir next to her heart, then it, too, was gone. Before she could move, though, Iakhovas was on her.

Transfixed with horror, Jherek watched as the huge shark overtook the elf woman and swallowed her in a single gulp. Jherek urged the sea wyrm up, feeling the need for air burn his lungs. They surfaced and Jherek grabbed a couple deep breaths before they plunged back beneath the waves. He heeled the sea wyrm around, going directly at Iakhovas again.

"I won't miss this time, boy."

Jherek tightened his grip on his shield as they sped toward their opponent. This time he directed the sea wyrm down, at the same time striking up with the shield. He held the shield edge on, slicing deeply into Iakhovas's side, feeling the hard muscle and rough skin slide along his forearm. The cut, nearly a foot deep and almost the length of the body, bled profusely.

Iakhovas screamed in pain.

Kneeing the sea wyrm, Jherek turned back around, intending to pursue Iakhovas if he fled. Instead, the Taker came at him again, the great slash along his body flaring wide. Behind Iakhovas came dozens of sharks, drawn by the blood spoor Iakhovas trailed.

The young paladin willed the bracer into a hook. The sea wyrm went high this time, turning at the last moment and going over the predator's head. Jherek leaned down and buried the hook in the muscle above the Taker's good eye. He held on and let himself be dragged from his mount. He straddled the great shark's head as best he could, then reversed his sword as Iakhovas dived deep.

"I'll take you down, landling," the Taker said. "So far down you'll never make the surface again before your lungs burst."

Fiercely, despite the fear that rattled inside him, certain he was doing Lathander's will and saving the life of the woman he loved, Jherek hung on. He knew if he turned loose and the sea wyrm couldn't get back to him in time, Iakhovas would eat him as well. He couldn't outswim the Taker.

Jherek leaned forward, using the hook to brace himself, and drove the sword into Iakhovas's good eye, plunging it deep.

Iakhovas screamed in pain, and the shrill squeal echoed through the sea. Blood streamed from the ruined eye, but the Taker still did not give up.

Noticing how the golden eye glowed more brightly and remembering how his sword seemed to surprise his foe when it cut him, Jherek pulled the sword free. He steadied himself, pushing the need to breathe from his mind. He rammed the sword down into Iakhovas's eye.

The resulting explosion blew Jherek from the huge predator's back. Dazed, he struck out at a shark that got too near him, turning the animal away from him. He looked down, seeing that the destruction of the magical eye had blown the Taker's head almost completely away. In Jherek's hand, though, the sword was miraculously still whole and unmarked.

Remembering the elf woman, Jherek dived after the sinking carcass, spots whirling madly in his vision as his lungs ached for air. The sea wyrm came up to him just as he reached Iakhovas's ruined head.

Jherek peered into the cavern of torn flesh and spotted the elf woman. He climbed into the Taker's ruined maw and cradled the woman in his arms, taking her up from the blood and gore that filled what was left of the creature, covered in it himself from his passage. For a moment, the young paladin believed the elf was dead. The great teeth had torn her body in several places.

The gills on the side of her neck feathered, and she opened her eyes and looked up at him.

Jherek's whole body ached. If they hadn't been in the water, he didn't think he'd have the strength to lift her. He turned and started toward the grievous wound where the Taker's head had been, but his legs failed him. His lungs were on the verge of bursting.

The sea wyrm batted furiously at the sharks that came for the fallen giant, keeping them free of the wound. Still, it wouldn't be long before the sharks overpowered even it.

Out of breath, spots swimming before his eyes, refusing to believe that he could fail now, Jherek sagged, struggling to keep his mouth closed, struggling to keep from taking a breath.

The woman in his arms took his face in her hands and pulled his mouth to hers. At first, he resisted, but even her weak strength was greater than what waned within him. She held her mouth on his and opened her lips. The gills on the side of her neck flexed and she blew air against his closed mouth. Bubbles raced for the surface.

Understanding, Jherek opened his mouth and received the breath of life she pushed into his lungs. He drank deeply from what she had to give, then stood again and pushed them out into the ocean.

He caught hold of the sea wyrm and pulled them onto it, holding the woman in his arms as she held onto his face. Gazing at the Taker's corpse, watching it settle slowly into the black depths of the sea, the young paladin saw the sharks feeding at the raw meat and knew in hours it would be gone.

EPILOGUE

"Jherek!"

The young paladin glanced up, hearing the sound distorted by the water.

Pacys swam down for him, protected by the magic bracelet. He stopped when he saw Jherek was on his way up, then swam alongside.

When they reached the surface, Jherek breathed deeply and shook the water from his eyes. He was facing east, toward the green lands he saw along the coast. Morning had only lately come, filling the sky with pinks, oranges, yellows, and reds.

"I saw the end," Pacys said excitedly. "I witnessed your battle with the Taker and your triumph. Blessed Oghma, I will have my song and my name will be known throughout Faerûn. There will not be a shore you ever touch, Jherek, that will not know your story."

"Aye," Jherek said, embarrassed, "but make sure you don't make my part too big, old bard. I played such a small part in everything, and I have never been a hero."

The woman in the young paladin's arms hacked and shifted weakly.

For the first time, Jherek noticed the shark's tooth embedded between her breasts near her heart. He sluiced water over her, washing away the clotted hunks of meat from the Taker's corpse.

The woman smiled weakly as she peered down at the tooth. "Even in death," she rasped, "he has managed to kill me."

"Her name is Laaqueel," Pacys said quietly. "The mermen learned of her at the Battle of Voalidru. She served the Taker."

"Not in the end," Jherek replied, washing the blood from his hands and slipping the cutlass through his sash. "In the end she stood for what was good and right."

757

"It's better this way," she whispered. "I am finished."

Her eyes glazed slightly.

"No," Jherek promised, drawing on the powers Lathander had seen fit to give him.

He prayed to his newfound god who watched over him for so many years, waiting until it was time to reap the harvest, and he asked for the Morninglord's blessing.

The young paladin put his hands on the woman's breast, cupping the embedded shark's tooth. As he continued to pray, golden light gleamed from his palms. The tooth shattered and fell away. Blood gushed from the wound, but he placed a hand over it and continued praying. When the golden gleam dimmed, he scooped water over her chest, washing the blood away, and revealed only whole, unblemished skin.

"No," Jherek repeated. "You'll not die this day, lady." He helped her sit, seeing the amazement on her features. "Lathander is a god of beginnings, not endings."

Laaqueel slipped from his grasp and slid into the water. She broke eye contact.

"Gratitude is not something I was brought up to believe in. My people have always taken what they wanted, and it was a weaker being's ill luck to have it taken from them." She glanced back at Jherek and added, "But I thank you for my life. There are new currents in it that I would follow."

"I wish you well in them," Jherek said, "and I thank you for saving my life."

Without another word, Laaqueel dropped under the ocean and out of sight.

"Jherek!"

Twisting, the young paladin spotted Sabyna standing on a ship's forecastle beside Glawinn. Jherek urged the sea wyrm forward and it cut across the ocean through the shattered remains of other ships, the longboats filled with pirate survivors, corpses, and the sharks that fed on them.

Khlinat threw a cargo net over the side and called, "Pipe aboard, swabbie. We done found us a ship that a gaggle of pirates didn't have the guts to keep once we decided we liked the look of 'er." The dwarf was splattered in blood, but not much of it looked like his. He offered a hand as Jherek climbed aboard. "Ye done for that bad 'un, yeah?"

Jherek nodded and glanced at the ship. The stern mast was broken, the rigging was in tangles, and most of the canvas was gone.

"Aye," Khlinat bellowed, "she ain't no pretty 'un, swabbie, I'll grant ye that, but she's tight as a duck's arse and she's got some promise."

"There's also a pretty impressive cargo below," Azla said. She stepped up from the hold, limping only a little. "No matter where we're at, we're not going to be broke. We'll find a port and get this ship fixed up."

"Then where, Captain?" Jherek asked. "Back to the Sea of Fallen Stars?"

Azla hesitated, then smiled a little. "I don't know," she said. "I'm beginning to think I've been around you and Glawinn too long. The life of a pirate doesn't hold quite the allure it once did."

"And maybe you've taken a better look at yourself," Glawinn said, cradling his injured arm as he approached. "Maybe you aren't as uncaring or disbelieving as you think you are."

"Back off, Sir Knight," Azla said with only a trace of humor. "I'm quite capable of finding my own way. Without your help."

Glawinn turned his gaze on Jherek and asked, "What about you, young warrior? Where are you bound?"

Jherek looked at Sabyna, then took her into his arms, enjoying the warm feel of her.

"Home," he said, looking into her eyes. "I want to see Madame Iitaar and Malorrie again, and make sure old Finaren and *Butterfly* are still hale and whole."

Glawinn softened his voice. "Not all of your troubles are over, young warrior. Your father and his crew still roam the waters along the Sword Coast."

Sabyna gazed into Jherek's eyes with her copper-colored ones. "Whatever his troubles may be," she promised, "great or small, he'll never have to face them alone."

"Lady," Jherek began, "you don't know the kind of trouble—"

The ship's mage placed her hand over his mouth. "No," she bade him, "no arguments. There's been enough of those. I mean what I say, Jherek, and I ask only that you love me in turn. Without restraint, without remorse. With all of your heart." Tears glittered in her eyes, but she was smiling.

Jherek held her to him tightly, smelling the lilacs in spite of the brine that clung to her. He grinned at the dawning sun in the eastern sky and said, "As you wish, lady."